WHERE THE RIVERS RUN NORTH

SAM MORTON

Notice: This book is a work of fiction. Names, characters, places, and incidents are either a product of the author's imagination or are used factitiously and any resemblance to actual events, locales, or persons, living or dead, is entirely coincidental.

Cover Credit: Montana Historical Society, Helena. "Hat X Outfit: Hot Noon Beside the Roundup Camp," July 19, 1904, L.A. Huffman, photographer.

Published by River Grove Books
Austin, TX
www.rivergrovebooks.com

10% of Author's proceeds from the sale of the book will be donated to the Salvation Army of Sheridan, Wyoming.

For ordering information or special discounts for bulk purchases, please contact River Grove Books at PO Box 91869, Austin, TX 78709, 512.891.6100.

Design and composition by Greenleaf Book Group
Cover design by Greenleaf Book Group

Publisher's Cataloging-In-Publication Data
(Prepared by The Donohue Group, Inc.)

Morton, Sam.
Where the rivers run north / Sam Morton.—1st [paperback] ed.
p. : maps ; cm.
Republication of 2007 hardcover edition.
Issued also as an ebook.
ISBN: 978-1-938416-70-5

1. Indians of North America—Montana—Fiction. 2. Indians of North America—Wyoming—Fiction. 3. Frontier and pioneer life—Montana—Fiction. 4. Frontier and pioneer life—Wyoming—Fiction. 5. Horses—Fiction. I. Title.

PS3613.O77868 W44 2014

813/.6 2014936279

First Edition

For Karl Lindholm

Foreword

OVER A HALF CENTURY AGO, A MOVEMENT AROSE AMONG the citizens of southeastern Montana and northeastern Wyoming to create a new state called "Absaraka." Half tongue-in-cheek and half serious, it reflected the dissatisfaction of the people of the region with the distant state capitals in Helena and Cheyenne, and the bonds they felt with each other and the land where they lived. Nothing came of the movement, but like many of the stories in *Where the Rivers Run North,* it shows a unique blend of independence and unity that makes the Western spirit what it is.

Both horse and man are transplants in the West. In the land between the Bighorns and the Black Hills, both have thrived for generations. I am what is known as "a native," yet my family history in the region only goes back to the 1920s. Yet I am part of this land, as are those whose roots go back to the 1600s, 1800s, or yesterday. You think you own the land and use it, when in reality, it takes you and remakes you into what it wants you to be. Sam Morton came to this land over forty years ago, and like the loving mother it is, the land took him and made him part of it.

I am not a horseman. My father, Deacon Reisch, cowboyed and homesteaded during the 1930s, riding the land and becoming one with it at a time when many old warriors, soldiers, cowboys, and pioneers from the 1880s were still alive. Through my father and by being nurtured by the land, I came to love the West as deeply as those who were part of it in centuries past.

Perhaps the ideal animal to live in this area would be the mythical centaur. Half man and half horse, this creature could roam the land freely like the horse and appreciate it with the feelings of man. In many ways, the horsemen and horsewomen in this book became such a being.

The land of the West and the great cities of the East—New York, Philadelphia, Boston—all nourished the people of this book. The tall buildings, plays, museums, and social life of the East helped shape them. But once they discovered the grass, open lands, and mountains they were soon as much—or more so—at home on the open lands of the West as they were on Washington Square. The amazing thing is how they moved seamlessly between these two worlds.

It was not only the rich and privileged who experienced this. Cowboys and Indians, as their life on the open range drew to an early ending, traveled with Buffalo Bill and the other Western ringmasters of the era to metropolitan venues—including Madison Square Garden—where they displayed everyday skills to audiences that were amazed by acts that happened hundreds of times every day on hundreds of ranches, homesteads, and reservations in the land where the rivers run north. Even after the open range was long gone, rodeos in the Big Apple brought many a young bronc rider or roper to the East.

Dude ranches in the early twentieth century often provided opportunities for the young of the East and West to meet, get to know each other, and often create bonds between these two worlds of our nation. The interaction and union of these different yet closely connected spheres still exists today, and will continue into the future.

Sam did massive research for this project, but he did not let the forest of facts block out the fun and legends that are the spirit of the people, animals, and the land itself. There is much to be learned in this book, but read it for the enjoyment as well as education.

Sonny Reisch
Curator Fort Phil Kearny
Story, Wyoming

Acknowledgments

THERE IS NO WAY TO DESCRIBE THE UNSELFISH ENTHUSIasm people have shown me in completing this book. Summerfield Johnston, a crony of Bob Tate's, might have picked any number of reputable authors to record the area's fast-fading history. To Mr. Johnston I am eternally grateful. It was your concern for history and generosity that made it possible that these stories were preserved before they faded away forever.

In Miles City, Montana, Esther Kornenman kept me in a steady stream of new materials with her knowledge of research and of the area. Bob Barthelmess, the guardian of the Range Riders Museum, and Amorette Allison of the Miles City Historical Society, provided me with some helpful leads.

Karen Woinoski, Jeanne Sanchez, and Andy Wenburg at the Sheridan County Fulmer Public Library Wyoming Room went above and beyond the scope of librarians helping me with my research. None of them, I might add, ever woke me when I fell asleep after lunch while pretending to read.

Thanks to Tom Buecker, superintendent at Fort Robinson, Nebraska, and Mary Diercks, the widow of Colonel Daniels, for assistance with the Remount. Dana Prater at the Sheridan County Museum and Cynde Georgen were also a great help. Laura MacCarty and Shannon Whittle provided artistic and technical help with the art and photographs. Teresa Mock provided information on the Cheyenne.

Sonny Reisch, curator of Fort Phil Kearny, was my sounding board throughout, which more than anything kept me inspired. Jean King at Kings Museum in Sheridan and her husband Bill at the Bozeman Trail Gallery shared a variety of material. George Dupont at the Museum of Polo was a great help as was

Hayne Hamilton with Johnston Southern. Danny Mears, Lauren Crowe, Jane Rubin, Robert Doyle, and my brother Geoff were ambitious enough to plow through my early drafts, and Annette Chaudet assisted during editing. Thanks to John Ingram for his help with publishers and to everyone at Greenleaf Book Group who was involved with this book. Alan Grimes and Jay Hodges were especially patient with all the material and personalities they had to deal with.

The Montana Historical Society and American Heritage Center in Laramie were amazing. John and Liz Gale were generous with their help in copying letters.

Bea Gallatin Beuf and the Tate family for their friendship and generosity, and Carolyn Walker and Mary Wallop for the trust they bestowed in me in this project. Irv Alderson and his entire family could not have been more encouraging or helpful. Audrey Long, Dee and Denny Dunning, Bob Gaskill, Tom Alderson, Chuck Larson, Jack Bailey, Don King, Kay Lohof, Immy Mitchell, Nancy Carrel, Lovida Irion, Karen Ferguson, Pete Thex, Bill Gardner, Joe Medicine Crow, Marvin Bookman, Wilson Moreland, Amanda Kaufman, and all the others whose family lived it, thank you.

Finally there is no amount of thanks I can give the people whose families lived these stories and the amount of trust and the wealth of material they so entrusted me with. It was their enthusiasm towards this project that kept me inspired. Horses, horsemen, and events in the most colorful and beautiful country in the world: God is great.

Preface

IN SOUTHERN MONTANA AND NORTHERN WYOMING, AN area called Absaraka is defined by rivers that run north from the Bighorn Mountains. Inside, the grasslands have produced several horse cultures. For over forty years the Shoshone, Crow, Cheyenne, Arapaho, and Lakota Sioux evolved into the most effective light cavalry in the world. Hundreds of inter-tribal battles were fought on horses culminating in the massacre of two entire U.S. Army commands.

When the Indian wars ended, wealthy sons of British nobility weathered range wars, killing winters, and outlaws to raise some of the finest horses on earth. They added spark to the wildest town in the West, where soldiers, cowboys, courtesans, politicians, and Indians congregated.

As the frontier settled, Ivy League horsemen built lavish estates in one of the most picturesque canyons in the world, drawing visitors from American presidents to the Queen of England. With the advent of dude ranches, thousands of wealthy families came West for the summer to ride horses and enjoy the country. Some bought ranches, some young men hired on as cowboys, and dozens of young women fell in love and married cowboys.

The common thread through the generations was the area's horses. As horses elevate the human spirit, there is no place on earth where the human spirit has burned brighter than in the warriors, cowboys, and horsemen from Absaraka. The warriors were fiercer, the cowboys wilder, and the wealthy horsemen had more spark. Epic battles were fought, fortunes were made, and fortunes were lost. Marriages and friendships that crossed socioeconomic barriers all tied together through a passion for one animal—the horse. From the earliest horse to the present day, the area and people have distinguished themselves through their relationship with horses.

The heart of it all is the grassland with its broken contour, bracing climates, and plenty of water. It is a haven for hoofed animals that has hosted millions of buffalo, deer, elk, antelope, and hundreds of thousands of horses. The horses raised here are tougher; they are fed from the land their ancestors grazed, and they are watered from the melted snow that flows from the mountains where the rivers run north.

Introduction

Otter Creek, 1840

IT HAD BEEN A VIOLENT CLASH OF TWO, THOUSAND POUND animals in their prime, fighting for the grassland and the mares. The yellow stallion challenged the sorrel, with flying hooves and ripping teeth, across the banks of Otter Creek. Immediately the sorrel stallion attacked, sending kicks to the yellow stallion's knee and jaw, but the yellow stallion found his opening and caught the sorrel with both back feet in the chest. When the sorrel reeled, the yellow stallion spun around and struck the sorrel with both front feet to the head. The sorrel lunged underneath the challenger and bit away a part of his flank.

For a full fifteen minutes the fight continued until the sorrel was reduced to fighting little more than a defensive struggle. He limped away covered in bite and kick wounds and a part of his neck torn away, leaving the mares, foals, and grasslands to the yellow stallion.

The yellow stallion took immediately to his new role as the herd leader like he was born to it. He learned the area, its escape routes, ravines, and forests. He brought the mares to the river to drink and led them to the high flats, which blew clean of snow in the winter, to graze. He sniffed the air for trouble, keeping a constant vigil for mountain lions, bears, wolf packs, and men on horses. Each spring and fall, he fought young stallions that challenged him for the mares.

The stallion's range on Otter Creek was located in the center of Absaraka (pronounced ab-SAR-ka), the best horse country in the world, where a sea of grass grows up from rich limestone deposits. The grassland grows strong-boned, hard-footed, and long-winded horses. The peaks of the Bighorn Mountains shine with snow year-round and feed the Tongue, Powder, and Bighorn rivers and the dozens of tributaries that run clear water to the Yellowstone. The area is lush, an oasis of water surrounded by sandhills, badlands, and dry basins.

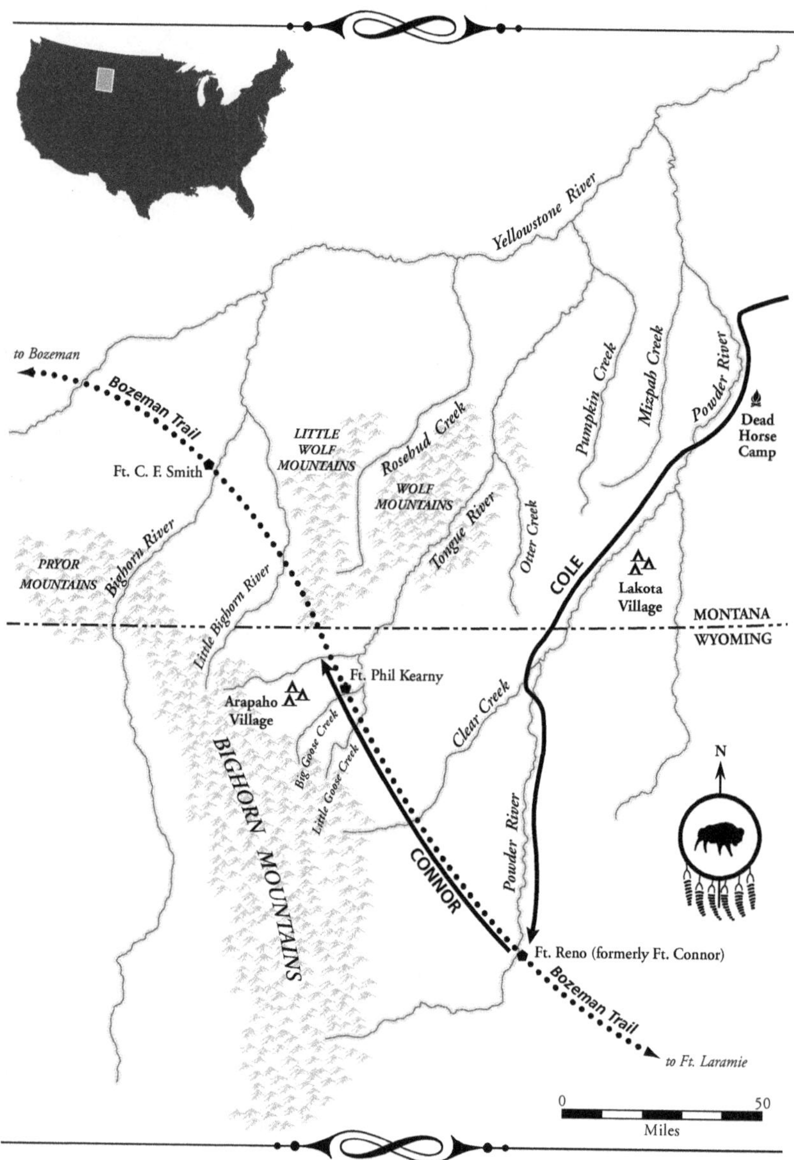

to Bozeman
Bozeman Trail
Ft. C. F. Smith
Yellowstone River
LITTLE WOLF MOUNTAINS
Rosebud Creek
WOLF MOUNTAINS
Pumpkin Creek
Mizpah Creek
Powder River
Dead Horse Camp
PRYOR MOUNTAINS
Bighorn River
Little Bighorn River
Tongue River
Otter Creek
COLE
Lakota Village
MONTANA
WYOMING
Ft. Phil Kearny
Arapaho Village
Clear Creek
Big Goose Creek
Little Goose Creek
BIGHORN MOUNTAINS
Powder River
N
CONNOR
Ft. Reno (formerly Ft. Connor)
Bozeman Trail
to Ft. Laramie
0
50
Miles

I

The High-Toned Sons of the Wild

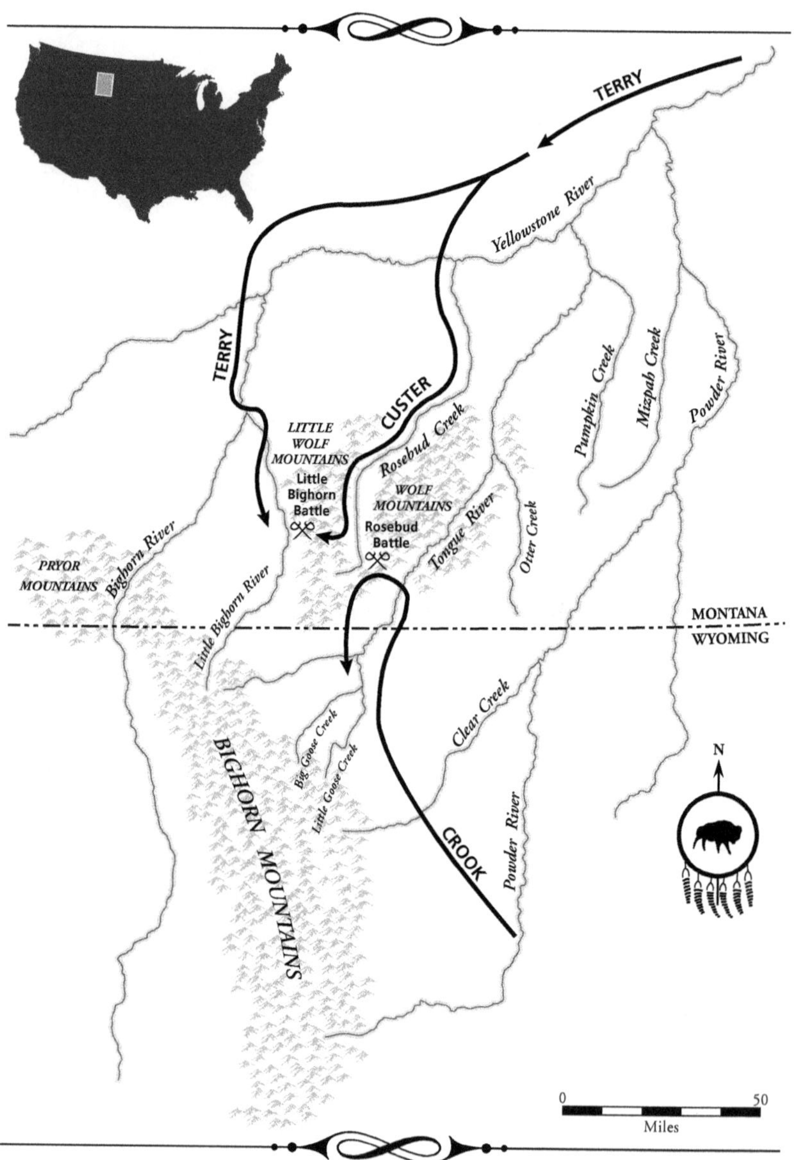
TERRY
Yellowstone River
TERRY
CUSTER
Rosebud Creek
Pumpkin Creek
Mizpah Creek
Powder River
LITTLE
WOLF
MOUNTAINS
Little
Bighorn
Battle
WOLF
MOUNTAINS
Rosebud
Battle
Tongue River
Otter Creek
PRYOR
MOUNTAINS
Bighorn River
Little Bighorn River
MONTANA
WYOMING
Big Goose Creek
Little Goose Creek
BIGHORN MOUNTAINS
Clear Creek
CROOK
Powder River
N
0
50
Miles

1

When they first got horses, the people did not know what they fed on. They would offer the animals pieces of dried meat or take a piece of back fat and rub their noses with it, to try to get them to eat it. Then the horses would turn away and put down their heads and begin to eat the grass of the prairie . . .

—Wolf Calf, Piegan (Blackfoot)[1]

Little Goose Canyon, 1844

IN THE GRAY CHILL OF AN AUTUMN MORNING, CRAZY Horse rode down from the timberline of the Bighorns, letting his horse pick its way over the wet gumbo soil. Fall was almost over. The brilliant colors of the aspens that lined the face of the mountains were laced with a thin layer of fresh snow.

Leading a packhorse loaded with a cow elk, Crazy Horse stopped to scan the horizon for enemies. He pulled his robe tighter around his shoulders, protecting himself against the wet cold. He had left the lodge before the sun rose that morning to get one last hunt in. The tedious task of moving the village would consume the rest of the morning. Horses had to be packed, meat loaded, and travois—the scaffolds dragged behind horses—hitched. Despite the fact that the Lakota Sioux and their major subtribes of Brulé, Oglala, Hunkpapa, and Miniconjou were the most powerful tribe on the plains, this was Crow country. It was best to move east after hunting rather than stay and risk an attack.

The Crow were the great horsemen of the northwest. They were expert horse thieves, often slipping into an enemy village in the dark or even in a blizzard to steal horses that were tethered to a peg inside the lodges. Crazy Horse's brother had recently been killed in a fight with the Crow. Besides the Crow, the Shoshone and a half dozen other deadly enemies were at war over the area. Tribes moved in, hunted for meat, and moved on.

Crazy Horse was an Oglala Sioux medicine man named after his father. He was a rare holy man who accompanied warriors into battle. It was joked among his clansmen that Crazy Horse "said his prayers and went to war." The hunting trip to the eastern face of the Bighorns was a pilgrimage to him. He had ridden to an ancient rock formation in the mountains called a medicine wheel.

As he rode out of the timber, Crazy Horse's thoughts drifted to his wife. Rattle Blanket Woman was a Miniconjou. They had married six winters prior and had two children: a girl, six, and Curly, a young, yellow-haired four-year-old boy. Rattle Blanket Woman was pleasant but prone to fits of depression. The winters were always hard on her; the long gray months and bitter cold of last winter had been especially crippling. Sometimes she would barely speak for days. Crazy Horse did what he could to comfort her, but his brother's recent death had sent Rattle Blanket Woman into the darkest depression of her life.

With his village in sight, Crazy Horse descended the last ridge, his horse slightly slipping on the slick ground. While riding through a stand of aspen trees, a strange feeling came over him, as if someone—or a spirit—was next to him and all around him at the same time. He pulled his horse to a stop and said a prayer, then listened and watched. A great lone heron flew overhead. Crazy Horse watched it glide away over the far ridge.

When he reached the village, Crazy Horse noticed that no smoke was coming from his family's lodge. As he approached, he found Curly outside.

"Where's Mother?"

The four-year-old merely shook his head; a feeling of panic washed over Crazy Horse.

"Where's your sister?" he asked. Curly pointed to a nearby lodge. Crazy Horse swung off his horse and took his son by the hand to the place where his daughter played with a friend.

"Watch your brother, keep him here," he told her.

He went to three lodges looking for his wife, but no one had seen her that morning. The concerned friends began to search, and within minutes a piercing scream broke the morning stillness. Warriors rushed out of lodges brandishing weapons, expecting an attack, but Crazy Horse knew what it meant.

In a small copse of trees, a woman had found Rattle Blanket Woman hanging from a cottonwood tree. Crazy Horse lowered her to the ground, then sat with her body and prayed. He knew that the spirit he had felt that morning had been his wife saying good-bye.

The women of the village sewed the body of Rattle Blanket Woman into a buffalo robe. Crazy Horse erected a platform in a large cottonwood tree that grew on the bank of a small creek. He laid his wife on the platform, then brought her mare to the base of the tree and prayed that the horse might carry his wife through the spirit world. He cut the mare's throat, said a final prayer, and turned back to the village to comfort his distraught children.

Meadowlark watched the light-haired son of Crazy Horse disappear into the woods alone, and her heart felt heavy. He did not play with the other children, nor did he accept her or her sister, Rain, as his new mothers. They were Brulé Sioux and had married Crazy Horse shortly after Rattle Blanket Woman committed suicide. They had taken to raising the children of Crazy Horse as their own. Rain had given Crazy Horse a second son, Little Hawk, but Meadowlark was unable to have a child. So she did her best to mother Curly.

The village was a tough place for a boy who was different. Being blonde, light skinned, and small for his age made Curly a target for bullies. After his mother's death, Curly had remained withdrawn, but he found comfort in nature. Curly took long rides on his pony away from the village. When he was lonely, he would remember the words his father told him when his mother died: "She always said you were special. She felt you were destined to become a great warrior." For a boy ostracized by his peers, a life in which a person is judged by his actions and not his physical appearance held promise. Curly studied the warriors from a distance, shadowing them through the village. When warriors gathered around fires to talk, he would linger nearby, careful not to disturb them, listening intently. He began to learn the nuances of a warrior's life. If warriors had their horses' tails tied up, they were going to war; if the tails were down, the warriors were hunting or returning from a raid. They earned feathers for acts of bravery, or coups. The greatest coup was to ride up and slap an armed enemy before killing him. And though the elders made the decisions for the tribe, it was the warriors who held the true power in the village. Their status was based on personal bravery and the ability to lead successful raids against the enemy, as well as charity toward the tribespeople. Curly longed for the warrior's life.

The late 1840s was an exciting time for a boy to grow up a Lakota Sioux. By sheer numbers it was the most powerful tribe on the plains, and it had recently formed an alliance with the Cheyenne. Sioux warriors frequently led raids against the Crow and Shoshone. Magnificent pageantry pervaded the war parties. The warriors prepared by painting their faces and horses. They wore feathered headdresses, hides, and horns from antelope and buffalo. The braver the warrior, the fancier his dress. Women shrilled when warriors paraded through the village on their way to a fight or on their way back after a successful raid. Warriors were sung about in the village and feasted when they returned. Dances were held in their honor, and women made fine clothes for them, decorated with colored beads and porcupine quills.

Curly practiced constantly with the small bow and arrows his father had given him, and it was with great pride that he brought his first rabbit to his stepmothers in the lodge. Meadowlark beamed and fussed over the boy when presented with the rabbit. "Look what Curly has brought!" she called to Crazy Horse. "Soon he will be bringing meat to everyone who doesn't have enough to eat."

It had never dawned on the eight-year-old that there were people in the village with little food. The notion pulled at his heart, and he immediately jumped on his pony and rode through the village crying out his message: "Come to my parents' lodge tonight and you will be fed; they have plenty." Much to Meadowlark's chagrin, a long line of hungry people appeared at the lodge that evening holding bowls and plates. Meadowlark and Rain cooked every scrap of food they had to feed the horde.

Hunting to feed Crazy Horse's family, now grown to six people, had become a chore. A medium deer might last only a week. With his other duties as medicine man, Crazy Horse had to rush his hunting trips, and now his son had given away what little food he had stockpiled. Crazy Horse would have to rise early to hunt in the morning.

When Crazy Horse saw Curly line up for a bowl of stew, he pulled the boy out of line and sent him to bed with no supper. After the children were asleep, Crazy Horse sat with his wives. "Our boy has a caring heart; he gave away our food because he felt for the hungry. He'll feel it more when he realizes what it feels like to be really hungry."

Later that evening Meadowlark slipped the piece of jerky she had saved for Curly under his buffalo robe.

Shortly after an accomplished Miniconjou warrior named High Back Bone came to Crazy Horse's village, he noticed a young, blonde boy shadowing him. The warrior noticed that the boy seemed to avoid other children. He also saw how the boy followed the older herders out to watch what they did with the horses, taking great care to not be spotted.

In the villages, young boys were often mentored by warriors outside their families, and Curly was coming of age. He had been honing his skills and already surpassed most of the older village boys as a woodsman, rider, and hunter. High Back Bone recognized both promise and sadness in Curly. After speaking to Crazy Horse, the warrior invited Curly and four older herders on a ten-day trip to catch a horse from the yellow stallion's band.

The first step was to locate the herd without disturbing it. High Back Bone, having harvested foals from the herd before, had an idea the stallion would be somewhere on the east bank of Otter Creek. Using his spyglass, he spied the herd a few miles away from where he stood. He kept his riders downwind and out of sight until he could show them the distant hills on which to position themselves. They would signal to each other with mirrors. It would take more than half a day for a rider to reach the farthest butte. Each herder rode one horse and led another to keep it fresh for the chase.

Curly accompanied High Back Bone to the spot where they had seen the herd. They used the hilly terrain to sneak as close as possible, then tethered their horses in a draw and crept up a knoll to have a look. "There's the stallion. There's a roan foal by itself with no mare. If we can catch that one, I'm going to give it to you. Can you see it?" High Back Bone handed the spyglass to Curly. The boy's heart leapt when he spotted the yellow stallion he had heard so much about.

"The stallion knows we are here. Look at him pacing," High Back Bone said. The stallion was indeed the most active animal in the herd, moving stragglers along with his ears pinned back. Curly watched as he brought a mare that had grazed away from the herd in closer. Since the riders were far off and did not appear to be stalking them, the stallion let the mares continue to graze.

High Back Bone watched the herd intently. "Horses are amazing animals. I have seen a wolf pack stalk a herd, looking to eat the foals, but horses will herd up like buffalo when wolves approach. The mares surround the foals with their tails out. If the wolves move in, they get their heads kicked in by the mares. Pretty soon those wolves lose their taste for horse meat. Some horses keep friends within the herd their entire lives, and others are fickle, just like us. They love the ranges where they were foaled and will travel long distances to get back to them. If you catch a horse that was born here and he runs away, chances are you'll find him back here."

Curly watched the mares water on Otter Creek. "Drink up, girls, it will slow you down on the chase."

High Back Bone smiled at Curly. "Look how they wait their turn for the good water. If they all were to walk in at once, the water would be muddied; they like a good clear drink like we do. This is the best horse range between the Bighorns and the Black Hills, and the yellow stallion keeps it for himself. If you get a foal by the yellow stallion, you'll be mounted as well as anyone in the tribe."

"Why don't we catch him and breed him with our horses?" Curly asked.

"Many have tried, with three times the riders we have, but he has the endurance of three horses and is as wary as a panther. He would die before he'd let himself be tamed." Before long, a series of flashes from the distant hills to the north let High Back Bone know the riders were in position.

"You had better get them started," he told Curly, who looked at him in disbelief. High Back Bone walked down the hill with Curly and handed him a blanket. "Ride in waving this, and follow the herd until you get to the next rider on that high butte. Then wait for me."

The boy fairly levitated with excitement as he launched himself onto his small horse. High Back Bone crept back up the hill and watched as the yellow stallion, ever vigilant and already alert to the riders, began to lead the mares away. There would be no danger to the boy; High Back Bone watched with great satisfaction as Curly rode off in pursuit of the horses.

From his vantage point, High Back Bone signaled the riders that the horses were moving. Curly immediately proved his skills as a rider and a hunter, running the herd without spooking the stallion into the high country. Less than half an hour into the chase along Otter Creek, the orphan roan foal fell back with some old horses and a lame mare. Curly and the herders moved in and took turns running the foal until it could be roped.

When High Back Bone caught up, he roped the lame mare around the neck, choking her down to the ground so he could tie her legs. He then inspected her hooves and found that the coronet band on her right front foot was embedded with porcupine quills and had become infected. He removed the quills and dressed the wound with a mud poultice covered with a strip of doeskin. The foal was fitted with a halter, and the party left the hills to return to the village with their new horses.

In the two days it took to get back to the camp, High Back Bone took his time with both horses. He demonstrated the patient give-and-take relationship necessary to tame a horse, working closely with Curly and the foal. "He's lost his mother like you."

While High Back Bone led the foal with a rawhide rope, Curly hazed the animal from behind with a whip. They did the same with the mare. Soon both animals were reluctantly but steadily traveling with the group.

When they arrived in the Oglala village, High Back Bone put the horses in a corral, tying them to gentle horses to keep them calm, and then went to the lodge of Crazy Horse. He explained his intention to give Curly the foal.

Crazy Horse lit a pipe, blew smoke to the four compass points, and said a prayer: "Thank you for sending this young warrior to my lodge. His heart is good. He has seen my first son is a lonely boy. He has not only brought him a horse but something to make him feel proud." He passed the pipe to the young Miniconjou. "You are a good man to take an interest in my son."

"I had a warrior do the same for me when I was growing up," High Back Bone replied.

Meadowlark left the lodge to check on Curly, who had dragged his buffalo robe out to the corral to sleep near the foal. She placed a hand on her son's light-colored hair. "You are a good boy."

High Back Bone spent many hours teaching Curly how to handle the foal. The mare was let out of the corral so Curly would be the only living thing the foal had contact with. Each morning, the foal waited in anticipation for the young boy who brought him cottonwood boughs, grass, and water. Curly sometimes spent all morning sitting in the middle of the corral with grass piled between his legs while the foal, hungry but not quite trusting, edged his way closer to his caregiver.

Soon, the roan began to trust the boy, and Curly trusted the roan. He led the foal out to graze, then he tied the foal to the neck of a gentle mare in the herd, and finally he turned the foal loose. The foal could have run, but chose to stay. The horse and the boy had become inseparable. Meadowlark and Rain twice scolded Curly for leading the animal inside their lodge. He painted his roan with a different design almost every week and braided a strand of his own hair into the tail hair of his horse, which was said to join the souls of the horse and the rider together.

The horse earned Curly new respect in the village. Warriors and Chief Man Whose Enemy Is Afraid of Even His Horses, whom most called Man Afraid, came to look at the yearling son of the famed yellow stallion. But High Back Bone was especially pleased by two particular visitors who came to watch Curly with his horse day after day: Lone Bear, a chubby, talkative boy; and He Dog, a serious boy who came from a prominent family. Soon the three were inseparable.

High Back Bone took the trio under his wing as part of his mentorship of Curly. He challenged them to bravery tests, took them on hunts, showed them how to dress an animal, and taught them to ride through the country undetected. He also began to teach them the ways of the warriors: how to choose the best horse for a raid, how to camouflage bodies and horses with colored clay, and how to shoot with a bow and arrows from horseback.

Curly, Lone Bear, and He Dog idolized High Back Bone and hung on his every word. They dreamed of the day they might ride out as warriors. They played war games and honed their skills as fighters and hunters. As their rides into the forests and grasslands around the village became longer and longer, the elders became more and more concerned. It was decided that, to keep the boys from spooking game away or wandering into enemy raiding parties, they would be assigned jobs as herders. One morning, as High Back Bone left on a raid against the Crow with other warriors, Crazy Horse decided to take his son on a hunt, for he was afraid the young boy might sneak off to follow the warriors. In the pale dark before dawn, Crazy Horse woke Curly, and they were soon mounted and riding out of the village.

As they rode, Crazy Horse felt great pride that his young son didn't complain of the bitter cold or of hunger. They spotted a group of deer grazing near a copse of trees. They secured the horses and quietly crawled up a ravine. Lifting their heads just over the edge, they watched the deer; again Crazy Horse felt proud that he did not have to tell Curly to remain quiet. When the deer were within twenty yards, Crazy Horse sank down, looked at his young son, and nodded. Curly hugged the ground and crawled forward slowly, hidden by the short grass. He rose slightly, eased his bow in front of his body, and notched an arrow in place, all the while watching the grazing deer. He pulled his arrow back and let fly before quickly dropping back to the ground. A swish followed by a thud broke the silence. Curly quickly notched another arrow, but his father's hand on his shoulder stopped him. The deer Curly had shot had an arrow sticking out of its side and was striking at the arrow with its hind foot.

Crazy Horse kept his eye on the wounded animal while he and Curly moved quietly down and around the small band of deer. The father then pulled an arrow back and hit a doe that was grazing at the front of the band. At the sound of the arrow's swoosh, the deer trotted off a few steps and turned to look for predators. By this time Curly's deer was down, and it was time for father and son to retrieve their kills.

By midmorning Crazy Horse had dressed and packed both animals on the spare horse. "We'll say a prayer of thanks for our good fortune. Sometimes you can hunt for days and find nothing," Crazy Horse said.

When they returned home, where the stepmothers fed and praised the hungry boy, Crazy Horse turned to his son to ask, "What do you want to do with your deer?" The boy paused to consider what he should do with his first real kill. "I want to give my mothers some meat and give the rest to the poor." The three adults smiled at the boy's generosity.

After he ate, Curly walked through the village to find Lone Bear and He Dog and show them his deer, but he was stopped by two older boys. "Look at the little dog face; he thinks he's something because he shot a deer." Curly tried to walk on, but they cut him off. It was beginning to get ugly when a girl from the Bad Face band of Oglala suddenly appeared and began to badger the older boys. "I don't see you two shooting any deer," she jeered. The boys were a bit intimidated by the girl and her temerity.

"Come on, let's leave the dog face and his girlfriend alone," the older boy said, leaving Curly alone with a girl he had never laid eyes on before.

"How did you know I killed a deer?" he asked, but before the girl could respond, He Dog and Lone Bear appeared.

"Who's she?" Lone Bear asked.

"Oh, look, it's stumpy and snotty," the girl said, summing up Curly's two friends. Lone Bear was stocky, and He Dog dressed better and carried himself in a more refined manner than most boys his age.

"You have a sharp tongue," He Dog said. The girl straightened, looked down her nose at He Dog, turned, and walked away. "That girl is crazy," He Dog said as they watched her walking away.

"Her name is Black Buffalo Woman. She's a niece to the warrior Red Cloud. I think she likes you," Lone Bear said to Curly. The next night, Black Buffalo Woman's grandmother found a small doe outside of her lodge. No one had seen who had put the animal there, but some herders claimed they had seen the light-haired boy with a deer over the front of his horse at dusk.

2

We do not want your land, horses, robes, nor anything you have; but we come to advise with you, and to make a treaty with you for your own good.

—Colonel D. D. Mitchell, opening speech to the Big Council of 1851[1]

Fort Laramie, 1851

JIM BRIDGER AND TOM FITZPATRICK STOOD TOGETHER outside Fort Laramie watching the growing throng of Indians filing in for the treaty council called by the U.S. government. The two mountain men had partnered together for the Rocky Mountain Fur Company since the 1820s. Despite all their dealings with Indians, they had never seen a gathering this large: fifteen thousand Indians from more than twelve tribes, including Crow, Cheyenne, Blackfeet, Sioux, Shoshone, and Arapaho, were there. The Comanche, Kiowa, and Pawnee had refused to attend, fearing an attack by their enemy, the Lakota Sioux.

Fitzpatrick filled Bridger in on the government's plans to make one man in each tribe its leader. Bridger was doubtful the plan could work. He had spent time with each of the groups within the Lakota Sioux and knew that the Great Sioux Nation was divided into more tribes, subtribes, and family clans than the whites could ever hope to follow. "Hell, the Oglala alone are split into so many factions that it's risky getting them all together, much less the Brulé, Miniconjou, and Hunkpapa."

Fitzpatrick had to agree, even though he was being paid well to help the government make peace with the Indians. "The government men think it will be easier to deal with one man per tribe. It will also make it easier to hand out annuities," Fitzpatrick said.

"What's an annuity?" Bridger asked.

"$50,000 a year in goods to stop killing travelers on the Oregon Trail," Fitzpatrick said. Bridger shook his head at the news.

"Well, that will put some traders out of business."

"The government also wants them to stop fighting each other and has drawn up boundaries for each tribe."

Bridger had a laugh at that one. "That'll last until they get those annuities, and then they'll start lifting each other's scalps again."

The land to the north in the Bighorn Valley had been a raging war zone for years. The area possessed an abundance of game and unparalleled beauty, but to wander in carelessly could mean getting attacked by any one of a dozen rival tribes. The Crow had pushed the Shoshone west of the Bighorns; the Lakota had pushed the Crow west and north; and the Kiowa had long been pushed south. The northern Cheyenne and Arapaho also had stakes in the area.

The Oregon Trail was rife with violence between migrants and Indians. Anxious travelers seeking their fortune in gold took potshots at friendly Indians, renegade Indians shot peaceful travelers, and white outlaws dressed as Indians robbed and murdered whites. The government, believing the Indians were entirely responsible for the violence, thought it could bribe the tribes with supplies of beef and a variety of trade goods to leave the travelers alone.

"Look at the fort loafers step aside when the real fighters show up," Bridger said, nodding toward a group of warriors from the north moving through a crowd of Indians known to spend most of their time hanging around the forts panhandling from the whites. The warriors, resplendent in their war clothes, paint, and headdresses, could barely contain their contempt for the fort loafers, who gave the warriors a wide berth.

Enemy tribes at the treaty council maintained an uneasy truce, for the whites had set a condition of no fighting or horse stealing during the council.

But as Bridger and Fitzpatrick looked on, a young Sioux on horseback, rifle in hand, charged at Chief Washakie, leading the Shoshone delegation. Washakie had killed the youth's father in battle. In the nick of time a French trader chased the boy down and pulled him from his horse, averting a potential intertribal battle.

Curly, He Dog, and Lone Bear, now eleven, were old enough to join the Lakota delegation as herders. They stared in astonishment at the people and activity around Fort Laramie. Traders, Indians, mountain men, soldiers, and the warriors from the north talked and traded. Horses, guns, and buffalo hides remained the prime currency. A plain riding horse might bring a gun and one hundred rounds of ammunition. A trained buffalo runner, the elite of the Plains Indians' horses, might bring one hundred rounds of ammunition and two rifles. A top racehorse might bring as many as ten guns. The personal warhorse of a warrior was almost never traded.

Whites had always lived among the tribes, whose people were drawn to such strange and wonderful goods as metal arrowheads, guns, ammunition, metal flints (for making fire), and spyglasses (for spotting game miles away). Curly and his friends had eaten the candy brought to their village by white traders, but they had never seen soldiers before. More than one hundred of them—all outfitted with new rifles, dark uniforms, and brass buttons—stood at attention around the fort.

A sea of horses grazed in four directions outside the immense camp. Each tribe's horse herd was kept separate and divided into warhorses and packhorses. The warhorses, with their great quickness, strength, and endurance, were the pick of the herds. Each warrior kept several, the best of which he kept outside his lodge at all times ready to be mounted at a moment's notice. The packhorses were predominantly mares or older males.

The Oglala horse herd rarely did any roaming during its evening grazing, so the three boys took the opportunity to laze in the tall grass. "Put my horse back, Curly," Lone Bear yelled when he realized both his horse and Curly were gone. "Curly, you're not fooling anybody; if you don't leave our horses alone, I'm going to stick you in an ant hill!" He Dog said.

Lone Bear soon found his horse in a nearby strand of trees. Curly sat smiling on his roan on the other side of the boys, trying to appear innocent. Lone Bear swung up on his horse and rode over and slapped He Dog with his whip.

"I count coup on a Crow dog." Lone Bear stuck out his chest and lifted his chin defiantly. In an instant, He Dog slapped Lone Bear back, who in turn slapped Curly, who slapped He Dog. The three circled around each other on their horses, jockeying for position.

"I count coup on you, and I take your horses. Hiiiye!" He Dog shouted. The boys immediately pulled their horses around for a mock battle.

"I am Man Afraid, the great chief of the Oglala," He Dog yelled. In an instant, He Dog and Lone Bear were galloping off at a dead run around the horse herd.

Curly pulled his roan up and hid in a thicket, waiting for his friends to gallop back around. Lone Bear was in the lead looking back when Curly rode out and yanked the bow from his hand and struck He Dog with it as he galloped by. As Lone Bear looked back, his horse veered at a washout, dumping the boy, and then galloped away. Curly stood on a small rise of grass above them.

"I am High Back Bone, the greatest warrior of them all," Curly said before he galloped off to catch Lone Bear's horse.

Unknown to the boys, Crazy Horse and the real High Back Bone had walked out of the encampment to discuss the treaty council and look at the various bands of horses.

"They won't catch that one," High Back Bone said, watching Curly galloping away on his roan.

"I don't think they'll hurt the other one either," Crazy Horse said, watching the pudgy Lone Bear tromp through the grass after his loose horse.

Just as Curly was about to suggest a game, he noticed Lone Bear frozen in terror. "Look there, that white man is putting a curse on us!" Curly looked over and saw it was true. On a small knoll, a white man in a black robe was making signs toward them with his hands.

He Dog laughed. "That is Black Robe. He's a Holy Man. He is blessing us, not putting a curse on us."

Father Pierre De Smet had lived for more than a decade among several of the Plains Indian tribes as a Jesuit missionary. He had ridden five hundred miles from Fort Union on the Missouri River to the council with a party of

Crow and Minnetari Indians. He had come to the knoll for a quiet place to pray and, seeing the boys at play, said a prayer over them. Later that afternoon, High Back Bone took the three boys on a long ride around the perimeter of the entire encampment to show them enemy tribes. As herders, they were the front line of defense if an enemy tribe tried to steal the Oglala horses.

Curly sat stiff as a board on his horse as they rode past the Shoshone herders, who eyed them suspiciously.

"Don't worry; there won't be any fighting until the whites break up the council," High Back Bone said. "These are Shoshone; they are the best fighters. The Crow, with their high pompadour hair, are the best horsemen of the north. They can steal a horse right from under a man's nose."

"When will I be able to go on a raid?" Curly asked.

"You have to learn how to fight first," High Back Bone replied, steering the boys to a clearing near the Miniconjou horse herd.

"Give me an arrow," he said. Curly handed High Back Bone one of his arrows. The warrior pulled out the arrowhead with a jerk, leaving a blunt tip.

"Now, you stand here and try to shoot me with this." High Back Bone rode one hundred yards away and then charged. Curly lifted the bow to take aim, but High Back Bone suddenly veered right. Curly swung his bow right just as High Back Bone veered left and began to yell, causing the boy's roan horse to dance. Before Curly could get a clear shot, High Back Bone was on him, spooking the roan with a wave of his shield. Curly nearly dropped his bow and just managed to hang on as the roan ducked underneath him. The Miniconjou rode up smiling.

"Good, you did not waste your shot. What did you learn?" High Back Bone asked.

"I must train my horse to stand still when I fight," Curly said. High Back Bone was pleased with his pupil's keen mind.

"This time I'll ride straight by; see if you can hit me." With that, High Back Bone made another run. Just as Curly took aim, however, the warrior rolled to the far side of his horse. He had slipped his arm through a braided loop in his horse's mane and had tucked his leg in a rope that ran behind his saddle. His shield covered his knee and thigh. The only parts of him that were visible as he tore by in a blur were his foot, his ankle, and part of his lower leg. Curly rode over to get a clear shot, but the Miniconjou turned his horse between them until he was out of range.

Finally, High Back Bone let Curly have a shot, which he deflected with his shield. The he rode in upon Curly and slapped him twice with a whip before the boy could react.

"Do you still want to go on a raid? Had I been a Shoshone, you would already be headed for the spirit world. Now, you charge me."

Curly turned the roan and charged from a hundred yards away. High Back Bone waited for the boy to draw his arrow back and then rolled off the far side of his horse that shielded him from the boy. As Curly galloped by, High Back Bone rushed out on foot from behind his horse and slapped Curly across the back.

"Always get off your horse when you shoot. Good warriors are good horse trainers first, and you must have a horse that will stand in a fight," he said. High Back Bone attached a long rope to the roan horse's jaw and tucked the spare coils in Curly's belt. "Now, call your friends over and practice jumping off and firing at them when they charge. Remember, the best time for a clear shot is when you spook their horse. They'll be too busy hanging on to shoot back or shield themselves."

For the rest of the day the three boys played war games with blunt arrows. Curly would jump off his horse and give a sharp tug on the long rope, which caused his horse to stand still as Lone Bear and He Dog charged in mock battle. Soon Curly's horse stood as still as night when Curly jumped off and fired his weapon.

Curly decided to take a ride over to the Bad Face camp to visit the sharp-tongued girl he had met earlier. Her teasing wasn't mean-spirited like the others. He fixed himself up the best he could and painted a sun design on his horse. He skirted the village lest he draw the wrath of older boys. When he arrived, Black Buffalo Woman was playing with some of her friends.

"Look, it's the great fawn hunter," she said, seeing Curly ride up. Curly tried to look relaxed but barely managed to choke out his words.

"I thought you and your friends might want to go riding sometime; I can get you horses," he offered; the words came out in spurts as his shyness around the girls practically paralyzed him.

"Well, what are you waiting for?" she said.

Curly had to think of something fast. He hadn't meant right then; he had thought the girls would come and ride the next time he was herding. Curly found He Dog and asked him to help get some pack mares. The two rode into the herd deliberately and caught three gentle pack mares, fixing halters with rope and long lead lines. The herders on duty figured someone sent them for horses.

"Where are we going?" He Dog asked as they led the mares away.

"You'll see," Curly said, and soon the boys found themselves on a ride with the cream of the Bad Face girls their age. The girls had no sooner gotten on their horses than Black Buffalo Woman turned to Curly. "I want to ride your horse."

To He Dog's astonishment, Curly slid off his roan and let the girl crawl up. Curly took the packhorse. As Curly had been the only one to ride the roan, He Dog was sure the roan would launch the girl into the bushes, but the roan was as well mannered as an old packhorse. They rode to a branch of the Platte and found a pool to swim the horses in, holding the animals' tails as they glided through the water being pulled along. In an adolescent manner of affection, one of Black Buffalo Woman's friends rode next to Curly and whispered, "She likes you," as she nodded toward Black Buffalo Woman. Curly's light hair barely hid his ears that were red with embarrassment. Inside, he was beaming.

The first stumbling block to the Treaty of 1851 was, appropriately, horses. Thirty thousand hungry Indian horses had shown up at Fort Laramie with their owners. No one, white or Indian, had seen such a herd before. Since the land around Fort Laramie had been overgrazed by travelers' stock, the treaty site had to be moved from the fort to a site on Horse Creek where the Kiowa had held massive horse fairs and the grazing was better. Since the whites' supplies were late in arriving, thousands of dogs were dumped into the cooking pots of the assembled tribes. Horse races and trading went on during the idle hours.

Jim Bridger's prediction soon proved true. When cattle and wagon trains loaded with kettles, knives, rolls of canvas, and other provisions rolled in for the treaty, the bickering broke out almost immediately among the tribes. Agent David Mitchell, whom the government had put in charge of the affair, spent two days settling a near riot over which tribe should sit where at the council. Despite the trouble, the whites named Conquering Bear, a Brulé chief of the Lakota, as head of the entire Lakota nation. Conquering Bear grudgingly accepted the post, knowing it would probably be a death sentence from jealous rivals.

At the time of the treaty, the Indians controlled half of the present-day United States; before 1896, they would control less than five percent. Few of the assembled tribal leaders signed the agreement in 1851. Plenty of Indians present did, however, leaving the whites with the false sense that they had an agreement and a central leader in each tribe with whom to deal on matters concerning the Indians.

One hundred thousand travelers had crossed the Oregon Trail during the gold rush of 1849. Even the most backwoods warrior understood what that meant: disease, death, and conflict with the whites. As a result of the Treaty of 1851, some Indians were convinced that the country to the north—called Absaraka—might be a better option for a home range. At the very least, it held the promise of less trouble from the whites. The danger from other tribes was another matter.

On De Smet's trip through Absaraka to the council, the Crow who accompanied him named a lake in his honor. Lake De Smet was located in the heart of a region that was about to erupt in battles involving over a half-dozen separate armies fighting from horses. Father De Smet wrote in a prophetic vision, "*The silence of death reigns in this vast wild.*"

I do not expect to be compelled to fire a single gun, but I hope to God we have a fight.

—Lieutenant John Grattan

Oregon Trail, 1854

CHIEF CONQUERING BEAR WAS PULLED OUT OF CAMP ON a travois, dying from a fatal wound. His dying words had been a plea for his tribe not to escalate the conflict with the whites.

The battle, if it could be called a battle, began when a Mormon's cow wandered off the Oregon Trail and into a large Lakota village camped near Fort Laramie awaiting its yearly annuities. When the cow couldn't find her way out of the village, she panicked and began to run wildly, crashing into cooking pots and scattering groups of playing children. Straight Foretop, a Miniconjou warrior, saw the likelihood of the cow causing a serious accident and dropped the cow with his rifle. Already indignant from having been harassed by panhandling fort loafers for two hundred miles along the Oregon Trail, the Mormon complained to the authorities at the fort.

Conquering Bear offered the Mormon the pick of his horse herd as compensation, but Lieutenant Fleming, the ranking officer at the fort, wanted to punish the man who shot the cow. Fleming sent a hot-blooded Irishman named Grattan to arrest Straight Foretop the next day. Accompanied by a force of just over thirty soldiers and two cannons, Grattan marched into the village of four thousand Indians and demanded to take Straight Foretop.

The Indians expected trouble, and they had prepared for the worst. Seeing the soldiers approach the village, Crazy Horse yelled to Curly and Lone Bear, who were target shooting: "Get the horses in now." The adolescents galloped hard toward the herd, then slowed as they approached it so as not to scatter the animals. He Dog and other herders soon joined them as they eased the horses toward the village. The warriors rushed out to catch their horses and disappeared quietly around the side of the village.

Meadowlark and Rain frantically pulled stakes up around their lodge. Crazy Horse tied two packhorses to a nearby tree for the women to load up in case a quick departure was necessary. Suddenly, two explosions shook the ground and spooked the horses. The soldiers had fired the thunder guns in warning.

Following the cannon shots, Grattan had his men fire a volley into the peaceful camp. The assault might have scattered a large group of fort loafers, but this village was made up of the High-Toned Sons of the Wild, which a reporter named Chambers had written about at the Big Council two years prior.

It was over before it started: Lieutenant Grattan and all his soldiers lay dead and hacked to pieces in the village, and Conquering Bear lay mortally wounded in front of his lodge. His dying words had been to pacify the tribes and dissuade them from going to war against the whites.

Crazy Horse and the rest of the elders also tried to calm the warriors and forbid them from taking further action on Fort Laramie, even though at the time fewer than twenty soldiers remained behind to defend it. There was not a chief among them who doubted that the whites would soon retaliate for the killing of the soldiers.

The relationship between Indians and whites was now a confusing and dangerous mess. The result was a migration of the wilder, more ambitious Lakota to Absaraka, where they would renew their fight with the Crow and Shoshone.

It was not long after the attack on the village that Curly, eager to become a man, asked if he might spend a year in the Brulé village of Meadowlark's brother, Spotted Tail. Crazy Horse and his stepmothers assented, knowing that life in a new village would bring the boy out of his shell.

Meadowlark began to cry as Curly mounted his roan. "If anything happens, stay close to Spotted Tail," she said and squeezed his hand.

The gangly boy carried a bow, a war club, and a knife which he had tied around his waist. Curly smiled. "I'll bring you a buffalo robe," he said and turned to ride south. As he passed the horse herd, he waved good-bye to Lone Bear and He Dog.

"Bring us a Pawnee scalp," Lone Bear yelled. The boys then sat in silence as they watched their friend ride away.

After the Grattan massacre, General W. S. Harney was called back from Paris to punish the Indians responsible. Harney was a gruff veteran of the Mexican War and a successful Indian fighter against the Creek and Seminole tribes. Unfortunately for Curly, Spotted Tail's village—camped just off the Oregon Trail—was the first village Harney found.

The general struck with six hundred infantry and mounted dragoons. He used an old trick on the Sioux that he had used in the Seminole wars in Florida. He called a parley with Spotted Tail and Little Thunder under a flag of truce while his mounted dragoons quietly circled to the back of the village. Suddenly, Harney ordered the infantry to attack the village from the front. Spotted Tail and Little Thunder made a run to escape capture, but Little Thunder was killed. Spotted Tail was shot four times and received a saber wound, but he escaped on a captured cavalry horse.

As the women and children attempted to escape out the back of the village, the mounted dragoons met them with gunfire. When the scene was over, women and children, ripped apart by bullets, lay crying and moaning. The Grattan massacre had been nothing compared to this: eighty Indians had been killed, and seventy, including Spotted Tail's wife and children, were captured. After searching the village and seeing the survivors to safety, Spotted Tail, in a brave act of leadership, turned himself in to be with his family.

When a rider galloped into the Oglala village with the news, Meadowlark felt as if a dagger had been driven into her heart. The rider had no news of Curly, only that eighty had been killed and more than seventy, including her brother Spotted Tail, were prisoners.

In intertribal battles, three or four deaths were usually considered tragic. This was catastrophic. Meadowlark and her sister packed food for Crazy Horse, who had taken only a moment to catch his horse and prepare for a ride south. "I'll bring him back," he said solemnly. Crazy Horse had ridden less than a mile when two riders galloped up from behind him; it was Lone Bear and He Dog.

"We're going with you," Lone Bear said. Crazy Horse merely nodded, and the three riders kicked their horses into a slow lope to the south to see what had become of Curly.

The fact that Curly was one of the best hunters in the Brulé village might have saved his life. He was away for two nights on a hunt exactly when the village was attacked. Young men were usually forbidden to hunt buffalo, lest they spook the herds away, but by his fifteenth winter Curly was one of the few his age who was trusted to hunt alone. His roan horse had risen to the elite rank of a top buffalo runner.

For a horse to be a good buffalo hunter, it had to be reasonably fast, for a slow horse will not catch a fast buffalo. The horse must be steady, allowing the rider to drop the reins over its neck at a gallop while maintaining its course just next to and slightly behind a running buffalo. If a horse were to gallop too close to the buffalo's head, the buffalo was liable to turn in to the horse and kill both horse and rider. When a rider picks a buffalo out, a good horse will stay with that animal without cues from its rider.

Once a well-placed arrow was shot behind the last rib of a buffalo, the wounded animal would stop and stand still, and the hunter could go on to shoot another prey, returning later to finish off the wounded. A poorly placed shot could result in an animal running for miles, sometimes escaping the hunter entirely. The key to the hunt was a well-trained, athletic horse that seemed to enjoy the hunt as much as its rider.

On the second morning out, Curly had given chase to and shot a young buffalo cow. Once he zeroed in on the animal, his roan took over and Curly dropped the reins and drew an arrow in his bow. When the buffalo veered left, the roan stayed with him, and in an instant Curly had two arrows in the animal. Curly retrieved his packhorse, and by the time he returned, the buffalo was dead. He skinned the hide, cut up the meat, and loaded it on the packhorse. As he was tying the load down with rawhide straps, he noticed the smoke from the burning village.

When he reached his new home, he stripped his packhorse, checked his weapons, and rode through in silence. The carnage of the Grattan massacre had been nothing compared to this. The village was destroyed. Burned lodges and dead bodies lay everywhere. Unsure of what to do next, Curly followed some tracks north and eventually found the survivors.

When Crazy Horse, Lone Bear, and He Dog found him, Curly was relieved to see his father. Crazy Horse decided right then that he would take his family to the fringes of Absaraka to the north, far from the whites' wagons and forts that dotted the Oregon Trail to the south. Absaraka was bordered by a mountain chain to the west and barren badlands to the north, east, and south.

The problem, however, was that at least six tribes would be contending for the lush hunting ground there. The relocation of many Lakota into the Bighorn Valley intensified the war with the Crow, Shoshone, and several other tribes that migrated in to hunt. Thousands of stolen horses would crisscross the area and become members of a new village, only to be restolen by a third tribe within a year.

The yellow stallion climbed to the crest of the butte and watched the column of mounted soldiers moving in the distance. He looked back at his mares, grazing peacefully, and proceeded cautiously down a mile-long ravine. When he climbed to the top of the hill again, he saw the mare with the mules.

The horse was a bell mare, a gentle female the army horsemen used to herd grazing mules. The mules would stay near the sound of the bell around the mare's neck. When the teamsters wanted to catch the mules, they would catch the mare and the lovesick mules would follow.

When the soldiers stopped to camp, the yellow stallion watched as the horses were turned out to graze. He cautiously approached and began to call the mare. Immediately the long ears of all the mules went up in his direction. In his life on the plains, the yellow stallion had encountered bears, mountain lions, and wolf packs, but at the sight of the long ears, he snorted and retreated a few steps before turning and facing the odd horde.

He continued to call, and eventually the mare began to call back. In a few moments she trotted over, her neck arched and her tail in the air. The stallion was halfway to breeding the mare when—to his dismay—the mules trotted up and began to belt out the most horrid sound the stallion had heard in his life. Infuriated, the stallion charged into the mules, but the clumsy-looking animals were extremely nimble and, for the most part, avoided his kicks and bites.

The stallion saw the soldier galloping toward him in the distance; quickly he spun and tried to haze the mare away. In a moment the two horses were down a low depression out of sight of the herder.

The soldier rode to a high ridge and listened; he could see for fifty miles, yet the mare was not in sight. The mules were behind him and were beginning to drift toward the direction the mare had gone. If he let the mules go, they would lead him to the mare, but they would also lead him away from the command. They were deep in Indian country; there was a chance he could lose both his hair and his mules. With the help of another soldier, the mules were trailed into camp and tied to a picket line. The bell mare branded US now belonged to the yellow stallion's band of mares on Otter Creek.

4

His first big fight was against the Arapaho.

—He Dog

West of the Bighorns, 1857

WITH THE MIGRATION OF SEVERAL TRIBES INTO ONE area, combined with the mobility of their horses, Absaraka would produce the greatest generation of warriors in the history of Plains Indian warfare. From the Shoshone west of the Bighorns, to the Pawnee east of the Black Hills, no one was safe from enemy tribes. Young men living in Absaraka would hone their skills in battle from the back of a horse against a variety of enemies. For Curly, Lone Bear, and He Dog, their first raid was all too glorious—even though they were only along to hold the spare horses.

Each warrior took two horses with him on a raid. He rode his spare and led his prized warhorse so it would be fresh for the battle. A few packhorses were also brought along, but for the most part, because the country they were entering was so full of game, little in the way of food would be needed. When the warriors camped at night, they drank large quantities of water before lying down to rest so they would awaken to answer nature's call and therefore get an early start. A primitive, but reliable, alarm clock.

The raid would take the warriors over the Bighorn Mountains, whose snow-covered peaks were visible from better than one hundred miles distant. When a scout returned with the news of an Arapaho village ahead, the Lakota warriors painted their faces with colored clay and switched to their warhorses, which had been painted with each warrior's personal symbols. A few warriors painted stripes on their horses' flanks to signify their previous coups counted in battle. One warrior attached a scalp to his horse's bridle to show that his horse had run an enemy down in battle.

All the warhorses were galloped in short sprints so they would get their second wind during the upcoming battle, and some were fed an herb that was supposed to enhance their stamina. Feathered and horned war bonnets, lance bows, and a few guns stood in the forefront of the party once they were mounted in formation.

Arapaho scouts had detected the Lakota and sent warriors galloping out to meet the threat. Soon two mounted lines of fewer than thirty warriors each were drawn, three hundred yards apart. Each side sized the other up for strengths and weaknesses. Curly, Lone Bear, and He Dog craned their necks for a glimpse of the enemy. As a taunt, High Back Bone galloped out toward the Arapaho lines and made a brave run across their front line two hundred yards away. Arrows and a few gunshots were fired, but he emerged unscathed and turned his horse again toward the Arapaho, daring them to ride forward. Thereafter, an Arapaho warrior made a similar run in front of the Lakota lines.

As war cries and insults were being traded by both sides, another rider dashed out from the Lakota lines.

"Where's he going?" He Dog and Lone Bear asked, horrified as they watched Curly gallop toward the enemy.

As Curly and his roan galloped within 150 yards of his enemy, he saw Arapaho warriors taking aim. He veered the roan across the front of their line, making himself a more difficult target. The country went by in a blur as he heard bullets and arrows whiz by.

The Lakota warriors cheered. Two Arapaho realized Curly was a boy and galloped out to intercept him. Instead of running, Curly pulled his roan horse up and rolled off to the ground, keeping his horse between himself and the enemy. His long rope uncoiled from his belt, and he gave it a sharp pull to let the roan know he was caught. The two Arapaho galloped past, waving a blanket to spook the roan away, but other than sidestepping and throwing his head, he stayed at Curly's side.

With an arrow strung in his bow, Curly kept the Arapaho at a distance, but then they turned and ran at him from opposite sides. He rolled underneath his horse for cover, his bow at the ready as the two warriors galloped in. Fueled with the quickness of youth and a rush of adrenalin, Curly recognized that the warrior on the left did not sit on his horse as well as the one on the right. If he had to fight one or the other, it would be the one on the left. Curly ducked a war club swung from the warrior on the left as the one on the right galloped past and tried for a shot at him with his bow.

Some Lakota charged in to cover Curly, which turned the two Arapaho back toward him. As one of the Arapaho approached him, Curly jumped from behind his horse and shot an arrow dead center in the man's chest. The Arapaho straightened for three strides, then fell from his galloping horse. Curly swung up on his roan and galloped over to the wounded warrior. In an instant Curly disabled him with two hard blows to the head with his stone war club. He hurriedly cut a circle around the top of the Arapaho's head and gave a jerk. With a tear and a dull popping sound, the scalp came free.

When Curly turned to remount his roan, he saw that the entire ground around him had erupted in battle. The Arapaho line had charged, and the Lakota had countercharged, leaving Curly in the middle. He tried to remount his horse, but his knees buckled. He was shaking all over. The exhilaration that moved him to make a brave run had changed into a panicked fear.

Lone Bear and He Dog could see the predicament Curly was in. "Hold these," Lone Bear said and tossed his lead ropes to He Dog.

"Go!" He Dog yelled, trying to hold six horses that were dancing nervously on the end of their ropes.

The battlefield had changed into a surreal vision of men galloping toward and dodging away from each other. The roan pricked his ears forward, causing Curly to look in that direction. An Arapaho with a lance was galloping toward him from fewer than twenty yards off. Curly vaulted onto his horse, but it was too late; the man was on him.

Curly ducked off the far side of his roan, which ran three strides, leapt in the air, and fell with a crash to the ground. Curly rolled to his feet and saw the lance sticking from the roan's neck. The animal struggled to rise and fell again, striking at the spear with his hind foot as it lay with blood pumping from the wound. Curly pulled his knife and cut the rope that tied him to the roan. He grabbed his bow and ran across the battlefield in a panic; he was going to die. He begged the Great Spirit for help and thought of his father as bullets and arrows flew and mounted warriors fought all around him.

He caught sight of a long rope dragging from a loose Arapaho horse. Curly grabbed the rope and swung up on the frightened animal. The horse bolted directly into the enemy line, and in an instant Curly found himself on top of an Arapaho who was attempting to load his gun behind some rocks. Curly jumped off and drew an arrow as the Arapaho pointed the gun at him. Before the man could shoot, Curly fired his arrow through the man's midsection. He then pulled his knife and cut the man's scalp, which he tucked in his belt next to the first.

He was now well behind Arapaho lines, but he was determined to live. The fear that had possessed him had given way to a fight for survival. He tried to mount, but the panicked horse pulled back. He cursed the horse, grabbed the mane, and slapped the animal with his bow. A sudden shock of pain in his leg caused him to release his grasp and fall. He saw an arrow sticking from his calf but was up and off, hopping on one leg toward his own lines.

"Hoka Hey!" he heard High Back Bone yell as the warrior swept down and grabbed him by the arm. Curly was up in one bound behind the warrior. The Lakota were retreating as more Arapaho warriors poured onto the battlefield from the village.

High Back Bone stopped near the horse holders to cut the arrow shaft from Curly's leg. "Can you ride?" he asked. Curly nodded, and High Back Bone tossed him up onto a spare horse. Then Curly watched High Back Bone turn and charge the Arapaho to give the Lakota time to retreat.

After a few miles, the Lakota stopped to rest their horses. Scouts were posted to look for any Arapaho who may have followed.

As one warrior inspected Curly's leg, another began to yell at Lone Bear: "Who told you to leave the horses?"

"No one," Lone Bear hung his head.

"I told him he could go," He Dog said.

"What! Who are you to make such a decision? We might have lost our horses, then we would be in a hard place," the warrior scolded.

He Dog said nothing.

The warrior now turned and yelled at Curly.

"Who said you could leave the horses?"

"No one," Curly said.

"I told him he could go," Lone Bear offered. The warrior became so frustrated he acted like he was going to quirt the boys until High Back Bone intervened and pointed at He Dog.

"This boy watched the horses by himself so this other one could go and help their friend. An Arapaho ran him down and hit him with a war club, but he kept on drawing fire from the light-haired boy, who was in a hard place." The men all looked at Lone Bear, who shrugged.

Another warrior asked Lone Bear if he was injured. Lone Bear held up an arm that had a lump the size of a goose egg on it, and he also had a growing welt on his back below the shoulder blade.

"He may have a broken rib," a warrior said, inspecting his back. When High Back Bone joined the others, he carefully cut the steel arrowhead from Curly's leg as Lone Bear and He Dog looked on. "The fighting herders," quipped High Back Bone as his face broke into a smile. But Curly sat despondent while High Back Bone washed the wound with water and wrapped it tightly.

"Fix him up good, and when we get to the village he will have to dance. Two scalps! You did good, Brother," Lone Bear said. The adrenalin from the fight still ran in the young men, but Curly looked on the verge of tears.

"Maybe Black Buffalo Woman will notice you now," He Dog joked, but Curly ignored him. After his leg was wrapped, he limped away from the group and sat alone. He had just killed two men, but the pain he felt came from having left his roan horse wounded on the battlefield. In his mind he saw the animal on the ground, kicking in pain. Curly folded his arms across his knees, put his head down, and began to cry. It seemed his life had only begun when he accepted the yellow stallion's foal that High Back Bone had given him.

Over near the horses, the warriors began to recount the battle. Two Arapaho had been killed, and coups were counted. The Lakota had lost two horses but had captured two. The one thing everyone had seen was the young light-haired boy who had galloped out and fended off a charge by two warriors.

"His roan horse stood watching next to him as he fought," a warrior said, and then all the men realized that the good roan horse had been killed.

As He Dog and Lone Bear stood together in the dark, watching Curly suffer, they developed a plan. "Go now if you are going to go, but be careful. Our scouts are to the west about a mile. Go north and then veer west. Walk up hills to save your horse if you can and watch out for Arapaho," He Dog said as Lone Bear snuck away with his horse undetected.

When daylight came, He Dog walked out to unhobble the grazing horses and saw Lone Bear leading an exhausted horse back. Relieved, He Dog approached his friend.

"Did you make it?" he asked. Lone Bear held up his hand, showing a braid of tail hair around his wrist. The braid contained some of Curly's hair he had woven into the tail.

"His roan is dead," Lone Bear answered glumly.

Lone Bear was dead on his feet but managed to mount another horse and leave with the war party for the four-day ride to their camp on Powder River. As the three boys fell in together, Lone Bear rode alongside Curly, who looked haggard and in pain. Curly glanced over his shoulder twice as they left the camp.

"He's not suffering," Lone Bear said.

"You don't know that," Curly said.

"He knows," He Dog said. Lone Bear reached over and handed the braid of the roan's tail hair to Curly.

"You went back?" Curly asked, putting a hand on Lone Bear's shoulder. No one had to tell Curly that Lone Bear had twice risked his life for him: once on the battlefield and once to check on his roan. "If you weren't so ugly, I'd hug you," he said gratefully. The boys then began to unwind and talk about their first battle as they rode across the grassy plains at the foot of the Bighorn Mountains. Curly took a long look up Little Goose Canyon and remembered his mother, who was buried there.

"They say the Little People live in that canyon," Lone Bear said.

"That's Crow superstition," He Dog said.

"No, my uncle was married to a woman whose brother saw one," Lone Bear said.

Riding along the shore of Lake De Smet, He Dog told Curly how Lone Bear had galloped into the Arapaho broadside as he was throwing his spear at Curly, forcing the spear to miss Curly and hit the roan. Both Lone Bear's horse and the Arapaho horse had gone down in a cloud of dust.

"What happened then?" Curly asked.

"You were gone, so I jumped on and ran like a rabbit back for the horses. That's when I saw He Dog lobbing arrows from a distance while trying to hold all the spare horses," Lone Bear said.

"I think I hit an Arapaho, but he didn't go down," He Dog said.

"I think you hit Curly," Lone Bear laughed.

"Be quiet!" He Dog said and went to give Lone Bear a slap with a whip but thought better of it. Lone Bear had battle wounds and had ridden a long way.

When they stopped to rest, Curly limped over to take Lone Bear's horse for him so the boy could lie down. Within minutes, Lone Bear was fast asleep. Curly sat by him so no warrior might catch him sleeping. A bond of trust that would last their entire lives had been forged in the three boys. It would span the great conflict that was coming and end only in death.

When the boys returned to their village, Crazy Horse and his two wives tended to Curly's wounds and brought him hot meals and water. His half-brother, Little Hawk, now ten, was ecstatic with the news of his brother's deeds and ran through camp announcing that Curly had taken two scalps from Arapaho warriors.

Later that night, when High Back Bone stopped by, he found Curly solemn.

"It wasn't what you thought it would be, was it?" High Back Bone asked.

"No, I threw up when it was over," Curly said. High Back Bone tried not to smile; he had felt the same way when he had first killed.

"If you didn't feel that way, you would have a small heart," he said. "You'll be asked to go on many raids now. Choose carefully. Some warriors have no honor in fighting. They kill when it is unnecessary. The true honor in a fight is not whom you kill but whom you don't kill," he said. Curly looked at his mentor and swallowed hard.

"I will tell you the truth; I never intended to fight. I only wanted to make a brave run and draw them out for the warriors. I had an easy shot. When he fell, I hit him with my war club and began to scalp him, but halfway through I got sick. Another Arapaho charged, and . . ." The boy's voice cracked. Curly looked down, and his eyes welled with tears. "I left my horse. I never even got my bridle." It was a tradition to remove your bridle if your horse was killed in battle. It was a sign of bravery, and he had not done it.

High Back Bone had seen the roan horse drop and could not have been more proud; not only had Curly proven himself as a fighter, but also he was extremely modest about it. He had even given the scalps away the night after the battle.

"The roan's bloodline grazes the breaks on Tongue River near the Panther Mountains.[1] We'll catch another when your leg heals," High Back Bone promised.

"There's something you need to know about fighting. When you are on a raid, the cowards are separated from the brave hearts, but back at the village it is not easy to tell. The cowards will try to discredit the deeds of the brave because they are jealous. Pick your own men to raid with: men you can count on, who are out for the good of the tribe and not themselves. You already have two good friends. The stocky boy is loyal, and the son of Black Rock is a good start."

Curly had brought Crazy Horse's family honor among the Oglala. When he returned home that night, Crazy Horse called Curly to a private talk. "I am going to have a feast in your honor," Crazy Horse said.

Curly winced. "I don't want a feast, Father, please," Curly protested.

"Your mothers are extremely proud of you. It would hurt both of them if you decline this." Curly finally assented. Throughout the celebration, he remained withdrawn. Only Lone Bear, He Dog, and High Back Bone pulled any conversation from him.

After the meal, some of the elders began to funnel into the lodge of Crazy Horse. High Back Bone motioned Curly inside.

"Come on, Curly, your father is waiting."

Crazy Horse sat on a buffalo robe smoking with some elders of the tribe. "Many here have known Curly since he was young. He played alone, but High Back Bone showed him the ways of the horse. It gave my son purpose, and for this High Back Bone is a great man." Crazy Horse handed the pipe to High Back Bone as the elders acknowledged the Miniconjou with a chorus of "Hou, Hou."

"My son has grown into a warrior. He has shown kindness by gifts of meat to many people's parents sitting here tonight." Crazy Horse looked to Curly, who sat staring at his moccasins. "Some of you here knew my father Makes the Song. He gave me his name of Crazy Horse when I became a man. He would be proud of his grandson if he were here, just as I am proud as his father.

"I will now pass my name Crazy Horse to my son Curly. I will take the name Worm so that from this time on my oldest son will be known as Crazy Horse."

"Crazy Horse!" yelled Little Hawk, who had snuck into the proceedings.

"Crazy Horse," the men repeated.

Just then Curly, now Crazy Horse, caught sight of his stepmothers shuffling in and out of the lodge, tending to the men. A wave of emotion swept over him, and despite the ceremony, he jumped up and followed Meadowlark and Rain outside.

"Mothers, I have not always said the things that are in my heart, but I have never looked on you as anything except my real mothers," he said. Both women flushed; he had acknowledged them at his celebration. They had both loved him as their own, and now he had brought their lodge recognition. For the first time in his life, he stepped up and embraced them both.

After the ceremony, High Back Bone stopped Crazy Horse outside. "It's time you started to use one of these," he said, handing the young man a prairie rifle and one hundred rounds of ammunition. "Tomorrow we shoot, Crazy Horse."

"One more thing," High Back Bone whispered, taking Crazy Horse aside. "Your father is an important and respected man in this tribe. It would mean a lot to him if you let him know that. He is a medicine man, and yet you never sought his blessing before you went off on a raid."

When things settled down, Crazy Horse dropped by the lodge of Black Buffalo Woman. Her mother was careful to watch her daughter's suitors, but Crazy Horse and Black Buffalo Woman had been friends for so long, her mother saw no harm in a visit. Besides, she liked the soft-spoken boy; he was always courteous to her daughter and her. When Crazy Horse appeared at her lodge, Black Buffalo Woman was genuinely excited, but she remained somewhat reserved. Soon they were bantering and joking as before.

"I feel privileged to have such a great warrior of the Oglala in my presence," Black Buffalo Woman said. "Am I supposed to call you Crazy Horse now, or can I call you Curly?"

"You can call me what you like, if you don't mind me calling you mosquito."

"Mosquito! You . . ." She flushed red. Crazy Horse had a laugh, which loosened up the two.

"There's going to be a council and dance tonight," she said.

"I may go hunt instead."

"You should come. Why won't you ever participate? I'll be there. You hunt too much. My grandmother appreciates the meat you left; she told me about it." Black Buffalo Woman's tone changed; it was softer and kinder.

She rose and served Crazy Horse a bowl of stew. As she turned, the young man's eyes fixed on her shape. He looked at her face until her eyes met his and then he took the bowl. He could barely stand the anxiousness of being close to her. Though the two had been friends for a while, they had just started to notice one another's bodies. It took great effort for Crazy Horse to focus his wandering eyes on Black Buffalo Woman's face. To him, the girl's beauty set her apart from the other girls in the village. Black Buffalo Woman saw her mother approach and knew their visit was about to end. In a hurried fluster, she sent a desperate plea to her suitor. "No more scalps! Next time you go on a raid, keep the horses instead!" she said quickly.

"What?" Crazy Horse asked, but before she could clarify her request, her mother appeared.

"Black Buffalo Woman, you have chores to do!" The mother interrupted, approaching the two. "Hello, Crazy Horse. I guess we won't be calling you Curly anymore. It is a fine honor to take the name of your father," she said.

When Crazy Horse returned to his father's lodge late that night, Worm was sitting by the fire. After a few minutes of silence, the son said: "I'm sorry I didn't confer with you more or ask your blessing before the raid. When I thought I was going to die, I wished you were there to help me. I have seen that many warriors' fathers accompany them in battle to help with weapons and the horses; now I know why. I will never again feel good about going into battle without you being with me."

Worm took out a pipe and lit the bowl before passing it to his son. A long period of silence passed before he spoke. "I did the same thing to your grandfather on my first raid. And, like you, I realized after the first battle how much I needed him near when I fought. "

The yellow stallion awoke to the sound of a mare squealing. Immediately he ran toward the sound. He found the bell mare spinning and kicking, trying to shake off a mountain lion that clung to her back. In an instant, the stallion sunk his teeth in the back of the cat and flung it into the brush.

The bell mare had been a constant worry to the stallion since he had hazed her away from the army mules. She had almost died her first winter out in the plains. He had to bring her to a windbreak and show her where to graze when the ground was covered with a hard crust of snow. Now she had lost her foal; the colt lay, its eyes open, gasping its dying breath. The mare, terrified and confused, made an effort to nudge her offspring, but the stallion hazed her away to where the rest of the mares stood.

The yellow stallion was beginning to feel his age. For over a decade, he had protected his mares from predators, challenges from young stallions, and traps set by horsemen. The stallion then took the herd to a high flat knoll half a mile away. The bell mare made several attempts to circle back to her foal, but the stallion managed to keep her with the herd. By the time they were out of hearing distance, the lion had emerged from the brush and dragged the foal's lifeless body to a place where he could eat in peace.

Five war drums beat at what may have been the greatest gathering of Plains Indians since the Treaty of 1851. The Cheyenne, Arapaho, and Lakota were gathered in one immense camp that stretched from the forks of Goose Creek[2] all the way to the Tongue River.

For a decade, the Crow had been besieged by raids from four directions: the Blackfeet to the north; the Flatheads and Shoshone to the west; and the Lakota, Arapaho, and Cheyenne to the south and east. The Bighorn Valley had been home to the Crow, and now three other tribes were united to defeat them.

The raid had been a year in the planning. At a final council on Goose Creek, the Arapaho chief, Night Horse, who was Crow by birth, declared that to exterminate an entire race of people was unjust. He left the camp with his two sons, whom he sent north to warn the Crow.

The chief's boys found a small Crow camp a half-day's ride on Pass Creek. The Crow village moved northwest to Pryor Creek until it found another group of Crow and made a stand. Being horribly outnumbered, counting coup was abandoned in favor of killing the enemy in this battle. Breastworks were erected, made from lodge poles and hides. After a series of charges and countercharges, a Crow chief rode out to warn the Lakota that they had reinforcements coming and were ready to fight to the death. It was a bluff. As luck would have it, a herd of buffalo stirred up by the battle began to stampede in the distance, which the Lakota mistook for riders. That, combined with some brave charges made by Crow warriors, turned the Lakota back.

After the Pryor Creek battle, Crazy Horse led a small band of warriors on a horse-stealing raid against the Crow. Worm went along to serve as a holy man, and Little Hawk went to hold the horses.

The Lakota found the Crow where the Bighorn River joins the Little Bighorn. In excess of two hundred lodges were pitched in the encampment, a sign the Crow were coming together for a war party.

When they neared the village, Worm took some dirt from a gopher hole and sprinkled it on Crazy Horse and his horse to keep both invisible, like the gopher when it disappears in the ground.

In the dark of night, Crazy Horse and Lone Bear rode to the outskirts of the village and left their horses in some brush with Little Hawk. He Dog approached alone from the opposite end of the village while the other warriors waited outside the village to run off the Crow herd and cover the trio's retreat. If the alarm were sounded, Crazy Horse, Lone Bear, and He Dog would be stranded in the enemy camp.

Crazy Horse crawled through the grass until he found a pinto horse grazing outside a lodge. The rope around the pinto's neck ran to a stake inside the dark lodge.

Crazy Horse studied the pinto as he grazed. It was crucial he not spook the horse but let the animal see his presence and become comfortable with him before he cut the rope around its neck. The clouds had parted, and moonlight shone across the landscape. Crazy Horse crawled into the shadow of the pinto and watched inside the lodge. For all he knew, the horse's owner was sitting inside watching him with a bow drawn or a gun pointed at him. Just as he rose out of the grass to cut the rope, someone stirred inside the lodge. Crazy Horse's heart began to pound as he sank back under the pinto. He knew he must move quickly; the other Lakota would soon make a move on the Crow herd, and the alarm in the Crow camp would be sounded.

Swallowing hard, for he had heard movements within the lodge, he rose on the far side of the pinto, running his hand along the animal's shoulder to reassure it he meant no harm. Crazy Horse held his breath as he backed the animal slightly toward the lodge to let the rope slacken. He took his knife and cut the rope. Keeping the horse between him and the lodge, Crazy Horse led the animal over to another lodge, staying below the animal's withers and keeping his legs next to the horse's. He noticed a nice bay horse tied to the back of the lodge. Just as he was cutting the rope around its neck, shots cracked and the shouts of Crow warriors pierced the night air. In an instant Crazy Horse swung up on the pinto, leading the bay toward the spot where Little Hawk held their horses, but his younger brother was gone.

Crazy Horse swung off and untied the horses in the brush and waited. He could hear pandemonium in the village. Soon Lone Bear galloped in on a stolen brown horse.

"Little Hawk is gone," Crazy Horse said. "I think he has gone into the village." In the distance, war cries told that the Lakota had started off with the Crow herd.

"Take the horses. I'll go back," Crazy Horse said.

"No, we'll both go. We'll tie the horses up here." The moon had broken through the clouds, illuminating the area that exposed the Crow warriors galloping out of the village above and below them. "He'll be there; that's where we went in," Crazy Horse said, pointing to the dark area that was still open to the village. He turned and saw Lone Bear pointing a drawn arrow right at him. Instinctively he ducked just as Lone Bear sent an arrow into a Crow who had crept up behind Crazy Horse. Crazy Horse turned and hit the man with his stone war club and pulled his scalp.

"We've got to move. I'll go in and get Little Hawk." Just then two Lakota rode up with more than fifty horses from the Crow herd. Crow were boiling out of the village as Crazy Horse handed the horses to the men, keeping the bay to ride. He turned and was off toward the village, leaving Lone Bear and the two Lakota to gallop off with the stolen horses. Lone Bear and the two warriors were at a high gallop when He Dog rode up alongside, leading a stolen horse.

"Give your horse to them. Little Hawk went into the village. Crazy Horse went after him; he said he'll come out here." Both He Dog and Lone Bear threw the lead ropes of the stolen horses to the warriors and veered off to the small draw in the dark. The two men ducked down on their horses' necks as a dozen Crow galloped by.

Crazy Horse rode at a trot, calling for his brother above the noise as he searched every dark clump of grass and brush for Little Hawk.

"Brother." A voice called out. Crazy Horse galloped over, and in an instant Little Hawk was up behind him. Their only chance was to ride through part of the village and duck out through some low draws to the west. Crazy Horse lashed the bay into a dead run. Little Hawk was fumbling with his bow while trying to hold on.

"Use your club!" Crazy Horse yelled to Little Hawk. The two tore through the village, which was in chaos. A Crow warrior saw them coming and drew an arrow, but Crazy Horse ran close and struck the man's bow as they flew past, spoiling his shot. He veered the bay back out of the village and toward the escape path of the fleeing Lakota warriors.

Lone Bear and He Dog strained their eyes toward the village. "There!" He Dog said, pointing toward the silhouette of two riders together on a galloping horse, a half dozen Crow warriors behind them. He Dog and Lone Bear swung off their horses and screamed Lakota war cries, hoping to slow the pursuing Crow. They shot their arrows as fast as they could at the dark forms that followed Crazy Horse and Little Hawk.

They took off across the plains with one hundred warriors in pursuit. Lone Bear began to fall back. He Dog slowed and rode next to his friend and saw the arrow sticking from Lone Bear's back.

"Can you make it to the timber?" Lone Bear did not reply but managed to gallop on. When the boys reached the timber, High Back Bone spread out the Lakota warriors in the trees and opened fire on the oncoming Crow.

Upon reaching the village, Lone Bear, pale and weak, was laid in the lodge of his parents. His condition had worsened. Worm cut out the arrowhead, which he feared had been poisoned. Rattlesnakes were sometimes held over deer livers, their fangs milked into the meat. The meat was then dried and pounded into powder. Wet arrowheads were dipped into the powder to make poison arrows.

He Dog, Crazy Horse, and Little Hawk sat with their friend. Little Hawk was mortified, for Lone Bear had mentored him much as High Back Bone had mentored Crazy Horse.

"It's all my fault," Little Hawk said as Worm tended Lone Bear. "Father, please don't let him die."

"He needs to rest," Worm said, motioning his sons and He Dog outside.

Crazy Horse caught his new bay and two packhorses and left the camp. He had come to detest village life. The Lakota could be jealous, scheming people when they hung around the village too long. Only under the leadership of level-headed chiefs like Man Afraid was bloodshed sometimes avoided.

Crazy Horse crossed Buffalo Creek (Piney Creek) and skirted around a large ridge that protruded eastward from Little Goose Canyon. He rode up the ridge, pausing often to let the horses catch their breath. They snaked their way through the mountain pines to the top where he was exposed to the country in all its glory. Just below him to the east, Lake De Smet sparkled beneath the hills. With his spyglass he could spot the Powder River. To the north Little Goose Creek wound its way into Big Goose Creek, which emptied into the Tongue River as it rolled through part of the Wolf Mountains and into the Yellowstone River.

Crazy Horse paused to say a prayer for Lone Bear and then a prayer of thanks for the country before him. Even the Black Hills where he was born could not compare to the eastern face of the Bighorns.

5

Red Cloud led a raid and sent his nephew back with a bad tooth. When the war party returned, the nephew had married Black Buffalo Woman.

—He Dog

Powder River, 1860

BLACK BUFFALO WOMAN'S FAMILY ANNOUNCED A COMING-out party for her while Crazy Horse was off raiding the Crow. The news took Crazy Horse off guard. His friendship with Black Buffalo Woman had begun to change when she arranged places where they could meet alone. Other young Lakota men had started to take an interest in her too, which stirred strange emotions in Crazy Horse and lay heavy on his mind. The thought crossed his mind that one of them might show her some attention, even pledge himself in marriage.

Now it would be impossible for Crazy Horse to see her unless he went through the formal ritual of the established courtship. And it was well known that he tended to avoid tribal ceremonies. As he sat on the eastern ridge of the Bighorn Mountains thinking about Black Buffalo Woman, he decided he would have to give in just this once.

Armed with a restless passion, he decided to start his courtship by giving Black Buffalo Woman a pair of prized elk teeth. This ivory that grew from the animal's lower jaw was considered the pearl of the plains. Elk teeth were sewn on women's shirts for decoration.

Riding down the north side of the ridge, Crazy Horse spotted a herd of close to a hundred elk grazing the high flats on the face of the mountain. He tied his horses in some brush in a low draw, and carrying the prairie rifle that High Back Bone had given him, he began to crawl up the flat, where two bulls were grazing.

The bulls had not detected him; he backed away, cocked his gun, and shot the closest one, which was standing broadside to him. Crazy Horse then scanned the horizon for enemies. He would be vulnerable with three horses, two of which he hoped to load with meat.

The elk was down in a moment, and as Crazy Horse snuck over the hill he noticed a presence. A flock of birds flew out of a draw to the north, and now he spotted three deer in that direction that were looking back at something. He hurriedly pulled the guts from the elk, saving the liver for Lone Bear. His sick friend had been on his mind since he left the village.

Crazy Horse then returned to the draw and brought one of the packhorses. He blindfolded the animal as he lifted half the butchered carcass onto the horse's back, securing the load with a rawhide strap. He removed the blindfold, and other than making a few nervous sidesteps, the horse settled. Crazy Horse brought the second packhorse and was tying the final load on its back when the horse's ears shot up toward the north. Crazy Horse's first instinct was to grab his gun and flee, but he knew his enemies would be more likely to expose themselves if he pretended to be ignorant of their presence.

On foot, Crazy Horse led the two packhorses down into a draw, then he quickly mounted his horse. Keeping out of sight, he crossed a tributary of Little Goose Creek and started up a second draw to reach the shelter of the timber.

He snuck up on a knoll and looked down to the grassy flats where he had killed the elk. With his spyglass he could see three wolves move in for scraps, but soon the wolves moved away. Lowering the glass he scanned the entire country, seeing no movement. As he raised his glass again, however, a chill ran up his spine. The forms of two small men appeared on the flat and they were looking right at him.

Though Crazy Horse had taken great caution to hide his path of retreat, these men knew exactly where he was. At once he recognized them as the "Little People" of the legends he'd heard. It was said there lived in the Bighorns and the Pryor Mountains a tribe of dwarf Indians. In Crow lore, these people were a type of demon or god, depending on who told the story. They were vicious fighters, with great strength in their long arms. Stories circulated that the Little People slipped into camps and cut the bellies of the warriors' horses and then the throats of the men while they lay sleeping.

Crazy Horse thought it best to ride into the mountains and give these people a wide berth on his way home. Once in the high country of the Bighorns, Crazy Horse still remained alert: the pine forest that concealed him could also conceal his enemies. He ate only some dried buffalo rather than making a fire and cooking meat. As he lay on his buffalo robe that night and watched the stars, he thought of Black Buffalo Woman: her laugh, her pretty face, and her figure.

The next morning, in a distant clearing, Crazy Horse spotted a band of bighorn sheep. He tied his horses in the brush and soon had a ram packed upon his horse along with the elk meat. After descending the mountains and following Clear Creek, he came across a small herd of buffalo just five miles from his camp. Soon he had the meat of a young cow to load onto the Crow warhorse he rode. The walk to the village would be a small sacrifice to pay for the meat he had for his people.

Crazy Horse said a prayer of gratitude for his good fortune on the hunt. The Great Spirit had blessed the country along the Bighorns with ample game and breathtaking beauty. Even in lean years, when the buffalo migrated elsewhere, game could be found, as well as chokecherries, raspberries, wild strawberries, and serviceberries. But the Blackfoot, Crow, and Shoshone would never hand this territory over to the Lakota. To linger in this paradise meant a certain fight, and to linger long enough meant death.

In a rare show of bravado, Crazy Horse walked into the village leading his horses, tied head to tail, loaded down with meat and crowned with the heads of an elk, a bighorn sheep, and a buffalo. He paraded his horses past the lodge of Black Buffalo Woman, who stood outside watching with her mother.

"You are a great hunter, Crazy Horse," the mother called, waving, but Black Buffalo Woman showed no such respect.

"You forgot the antelope," she called as Crazy Horse passed. Crazy Horse smiled slightly and kept walking to the lodge of Man Afraid, who was known for his charitable ways. When the chief of the Oglala saw the heavy-laden horses, he nodded his approval.

"I thought you would know better than I where this meat is most needed," Crazy Horse said. The old man motioned to his son and wives to unload the meat.

"Come and smoke with me," Man Afraid said. "You have worked hard to feed the poor of the tribe."

"It is what my father and High Back Bone have taught me to do," Crazy Horse replied.

Man Afraid smiled. "They are both good men, and you have done them proud, both as a warrior and as a man."

Crazy Horse visited Lone Bear and was relieved to find out his friend's health was improving. Lone Bear was making a meal of the liver Crazy Horse brought him. "For a skinny boy you are not a bad hunter." Meadowlark lingered with the boys. She and Black Buffalo Woman's mother had been conspiring on Crazy Horse's behalf, but the young woman's father and her uncle, Red Cloud, had been pushing her to marry a boy named No Water, whose older brother, Black Twin, was becoming the most revered and respected chief among the Lakota.

Meadowlark returned the prime cut of meat Crazy Horse had given her. "You need to have a talk with Black Buffalo Woman's mother. Take this meat as a gift," she said.

At the lodge of Black Buffalo Woman, her mother sent the girl off to do chores, then turned to speak with Crazy Horse. She served him a bowl of stew and counseled him while he ate. "There are men now who seek the affections of Black Buffalo Woman. What you do by giving everything you have away to the less fortunate is admirable, but you need to start saving something for yourself."

"I have everything I need," the boy said.

"What about horses?" she asked.

"I have given away more horses than most people own. I have a horse, and if I need another, there are many I can borrow from those I have given horses to," Crazy Horse said as he finished the stew.

The mother took a deep breath; Crazy Horse, in his youthful innocence, had no idea that forces were working against him to keep him from Black Buffalo Woman.

"There are many whose families are connected with my husband who seek her affection, sons of powerful men. She is partial to you, you know that, but you must offer enough horses to Black Buffalo Woman's father to appease him," she concluded.

That night, as the feast and celebration continued, young men came to Black Buffalo Woman. Each one in his turn put his blanket over them in a ritual that allowed young suitors to talk in private yet remain under the watchful eye of the girl's mother. It was obvious by the way Black Buffalo Woman turned away from the young men after short conversations that she was waiting for another. Soon Crazy Horse stepped up from the shadows. He stood in front of Black Buffalo Woman as drum beats and singers' voices pierced the night from around the large council fire.

"You've been busy," Crazy Horses said and smiled, watching No Water walk away.

"Stop it!" she protested and in a bold move grabbed his blanket and put it around the two of them. She touched his thin face. He took her hands, and she felt smooth elk ivory pass into her palms.

"Thank you, they are beautiful," she said.

"We'll run off tonight. Are you ready?" Crazy Horse asked, putting his hands around her waist.

"You know I can't do that to my parents. Why didn't you capture horses instead of taking scalps?" she pleaded.

"I did. I gave them to a cousin who needed them . . ." She cut him off and put his lips to her neck. She felt his hands slip between the soft doeskin dress and her skin. Just then Black Buffalo Woman's mother called, "Is that Crazy Horse? Come and show yourself. There are many here who want to see the famous warrior. Your parents are here; come, make them happy." The woman took Crazy Horse by the hand and led him to the council fire, where hundreds sat and sang and watched the dancers.

"Look there," He Dog said, standing with Lone Bear and pointing to Crazy Horse across the crowd.

In the light of the big fire they watched the mother take the daughter away, leaving Crazy Horse by himself in the crowd. In a moment his friends were at his side.

"How'd it go?" Lone Bear asked. They knew their friend's position, probably more than he did.

"They kept mentioning why I took scalps and not horses. I don't understand."

"Brother! Either your father or High Back Bone forgot to explain something to you or you don't see the big picture," He Dog said.

"What?" Crazy Horse asked.

"That's what you get for spending too much time alone," Lone Bear said.

"It's the horses! You have to give a lot of horses to her father before she will marry you. Not just any horses, but good fat slick buffalo horses and warhorses; especially for Black Buffalo Woman. I can't believe you don't know this! Do you want someone else to marry her?" He Dog asked.

"She won't marry anyone else," Crazy Horse offered.

"It's not her choice, Brother. Her father makes the call, and her father likes horses," Lone Bear said.

"Her father is sitting with Black Twin now," He Dog said.

Crazy Horse looked across the fire at Black Buffalo Woman's father, who was seated next to Black Twin. "Maybe I'll cut No Water's throat and take Black Buffalo Woman."

"No! It's not your choice. You cannot split the tribe apart over a woman. This is between her father and you," He Dog warned.

Crazy Horse had had enough. He walked off alone, into the dark, to contemplate his friends' advice. It hurt his head to think that another man might marry Black Buffalo Woman.

After Crazy Horse left, He Dog watched as Black Buffalo Woman gravitated toward No Water; she was playing both sides. Black Buffalo Woman was in this for herself, and the final choice would likely be hers and hers only.

A wave of panic swept over Crazy Horse, and before he knew what he was doing, he had walked out in the corral to saddle his horse. He stopped; where was he going? He was being foolish; if it were horses her father wanted, then horses he would get.

Red Cloud and Black Buffalo Woman's father knew of her attachment to Crazy Horse, and they conspired to lure Crazy Horse away from the village. Though the son of Worm was but a young warrior, he nonetheless commanded a small but loyal band of fighters. If an intertribal conflict should erupt, it would be disastrous. At the end of the celebration, Red Cloud announced that he would lead a raid on the Crow and requested that both Crazy Horse and No Water come along.

The next morning the village lined up to watch the parade of warriors leave.

"Take care of your younger brother," Meadowlark told Crazy Horse as the raid went out. Little Hawk rode next to Lone Bear, who gave the boy a poke with the bow.

"Having Little Hawk with us will be like having three Crows against us," Lone Bear said.

"You wait!" Little Hawk said.

Red Cloud rode a new horse from No Water's family. He kept the burly, coarse-looking young man next to him. He Dog, Lone Bear, Crazy Horse, and Little Hawk rode together about a hundred yards to the rear. Even at his young age, Crazy Horse surpassed the other warriors. He was the best rider, the best shot, the quickest, and the bravest of any of them. A keen strategist, he always carefully formulated a plan before going into a fight.

As they passed the lodge of Black Buffalo Woman, No Water kicked his horse up so it would prance. He lifted his chin and stuck out his chest as he rode next to Red Cloud.

Black Buffalo Woman was in tears; her father said she had no choice but to marry No Water. "Come, come send off your uncle and husband-to-be," her father ordered.

Black Buffalo Woman slumped on a buffalo robe but remained seated next to her mother, who did her best to put on a brave face for her daughter.

"Get her up and outside now!" The man ordered his wife. The woman glared at her husband but submitted.

"Come," she said, gently taking her daughter by the hand. Black Buffalo Woman could barely raise her eyes when No Water passed, and when Crazy Horse approached with his younger brother and friends, her heart felt it would break. She knew Crazy Horse had no idea what was going on. Black Buffalo

Woman's father turned her toward their lodge, but she broke away and quickly walked through the passing horses to Crazy Horse.

"Don't get hurt stealing horses, it doesn't matter anymore," she blurted out to the surprise of the young warriors. The look she gave Crazy Horse confused him. Her father was behind her immediately and yanked her away by the arm, which caused Crazy Horse to turn his horse and grab for his war club. Lone Bear, loyal to his friend, followed, but He Dog quickly rode between them.

"Leave him," He Dog said.

As he watched Black Buffalo Woman's father drag her into their lodge, Crazy Horse decided that when he returned he would either make the man an offer or run off with the girl. What he didn't know was that Black Buffalo Woman's mother had already suggested to her daughter that she run off with Crazy Horse. The girl had balked, and her mother was at once surprised and disappointed. Her daughter was choosing a life mate based on prestige, not love.

That night Worm paid a visit to the father of Black Buffalo Woman. When Worm entered the lodge, the father ordered the women out. In a slight of etiquette, Worm was offered neither food nor a pipe.

"I have come to make an offer of horses," Worm said.

"I didn't know you had horses to spare," said his host.

"I have five to give."

"Five is all you have. What will your family ride?"

"It doesn't matter; my sons can get us more."

Black Buffalo Woman's father was amused. This medicine man, though he was poor, was willing to give everything he had for the happiness of his son. He motioned for the man to sit.

"I have twelve good horses given to me by No Water's family in the herd now. More important, I will now have a seat at the councils of Black Twin. The matter between my daughter and No Water is settled, but I want to make a gift of a horse to your family. You can take the blue roan in my herd."

Worm bristled; the man was trying to appease him through the gift of an old horse. Worm rose and glared down at the man.

"I have no need for your horse. I have taught my son since birth to keep nothing for himself but to give to the needy of the tribe. Remember the meat he gave to your own mother, or the horse he gave to your cousin who needed another to move her lodge? My son does not need to sing his own praises at the councils; his deeds do it for him," Worm said, referring to Red Cloud's arrogance. Before Black Buffalo Woman's father could tell Worm to get out, the medicine man left.

On the second night out, No Water left the raiding party. Red Cloud explained that he had sent him home with a toothache because it was bad medicine to have him along. No Water's absence troubled Crazy Horse, for it would be two weeks before the warriors would return home.

The raid on the Crow netted Crazy Horse eight fine horses. He had stolen four, and He Dog and Lone Bear had gotten two apiece. He intended to take them directly to Black Buffalo Woman's father when they got to the village, but when the warriors were a day out from their village on Powder River, an Indian rode out to them to drop the axe. No Water had married Black Buffalo Woman the week before.

Lone Bear seethed: "It was Red Cloud; he knew it. The whole thing was a setup. I'd like to kill that sneaking dog!"

"Hold on! Black Buffalo Woman may have been pushed, but she could have run off if she had wanted to," He Dog replied.

"Besides, I think it may take both of us to kill Red Cloud," He Dog said. The thought of doing battle with Red Cloud was not appealing. Lone Bear rode along angry. They had hurt his best friend and insulted his family.

Crazy Horse took the news with little interest, but inside, his world had collapsed. Lone Bear watched his friend ride apart from everyone back to camp. When they arrived at the village, Crazy Horse gave his horses to Man Afraid to distribute to the tribe. Instead of attending the celebration that night, Crazy Horse lay in his parents' lodge and tried to sleep. But with Black Buffalo Woman's marriage heavy on his mind, he could not. He left in the middle of the night and rode alone toward the Bighorn Mountains.

Lone Bear and He Dog saw that their friend's horse was gone from the herd the next morning. "It's not right, Brother. They'll see. He's twice the man as No Water," Lone Bear said.

Since the death of her first foal, the bell mare had raised two nice colts: a white-faced bay that was nearly two, and a yellow yearling. She was learning to cope with the elements and had readily acclimated to herd life, so when she first heard the sound of an unknown stallion approaching, she immediately herded her foal toward the other mares.

It would be the last fight for the yellow stallion. The high-headed brown stallion had smelled the mares and come to make his challenge. Dodging the brunt of the yellow stallion's attacks, the brown stallion came in and pounded him mercilessly with hooves and teeth. The fight came down to the endurance of the younger stallion. Had he given up, the older horse might have lived. A desperate counterattack ended with a fractured leg. The brown stallion hazed the mares away, leaving the yellow stallion, now past twenty winters, to limp along calling out for the brown stallion to return and fight.

"Hou!" High Back Bone gasped as his eyes focused on something distant through his spyglass.

"What is it?" Little Hawk asked, straining his eyes to see. There were wolves below them on a grassy flat, feasting on a carcass. The two riders rode straight for the pack, which dispersed before them. It was summer, so the pelts of the wolves would not be worth taking.

"The yellow stallion," High Back Bone replied. He reached down and reverently touched the mane that no man had laid a hand on. He went to a bag on his saddle and took out a long pipe that signified his status as a warrior chief. He lit a bowl and smoked, saying a prayer and singing of the stallion's life and of his roan foal that had been killed from under Crazy Horse.

High Back Bone showed Little Hawk the stallion's old scars and fractured leg. "He died fighting. I think we might capture the herd now, but it will take a lot of planning and work."

Having sung about Crazy Horse's roan made High Back Bone think of the pain the young warrior must be in. Looking off to the distant white peaks of the Bighorns, High Back Bone knew Crazy Horse was up there somewhere. The young man was quiet and reclusive as it was; having his only love marry another man would pull him deeper into his shell. He would be hurt and alone, but if any man was at home in the wild, it was his young apprentice. Crazy Horse had become a man of the earth.

6

The nights in Absaraka were peculiarly beautiful when cloudless . . . in the glory of the full moon the snow-clad mountains shone as silver.

—Margaret Irvin Carrington

CRAZY HORSE WATCHED THE COUNTRY BELOW HIM FROM the easternmost point of the Bighorn Mountains. Here, with hundreds of miles laid out majestically below him, he would pray and fast for three days.

He knew he must stay awake as long as he could to have a vision. Watching the sunset fade on the high grassy flats on either side of Little Goose Canyon, he prayed for guidance. He burned an offering of sage and then smoked a pipe. He wanted the Great Spirit to show him in a vision or a dream the way to live his life. He listened to meadowlarks and doves and watched an elk herd walk out of the pines down to the grassy flats.

During the night, Crazy Horse watched the stars revolve around the heavens. The only sounds were a few wolves howling and the soft sound of his horse tearing at the grass. He began to doze but fought sleep by walking to the bay horse he had stolen from the Crow. He put his cheek on his horse's neck and let the warmth of the animal's neck channel the hurt from his heart. No matter how much he prayed, his thoughts kept creeping back to Black Buffalo Woman.

The horse lifted his head, and Crazy Horse felt his warm breath as the animal turned to smell him before returning to grazing. In the moonlight he sat and watched the eye of his horse.

He was a student of horses. Some were kind, some jealous. They became homesick like people. Some had night vision, while others didn't. Some were born with a strong heart, sure feet, or an alert manner. It paid to know these things, for in a country full of enemies, it could mean the difference between life and death.

At dawn's first light he prayed and watched the sun appear over the Powder River to the east.

He rode down from the ridge and onto the shores of Lake De Smet. He sat at the old ruins of Portuguese traders and watched the reflection of the sunset in the water.

At dark, he wearily mounted his horse and rode to some timber nearby and sat staring out onto the lake. He fought sleep for the second night but began to doze in the early morning hours of the third day. He awoke as the sun sent a blinding light off the lake. A warrior was riding toward him. The warrior's body was painted with white hailstones, and his horse's tail flowed freely instead of being tied up for war. It began to thunder, and Crazy Horse saw hundreds of threatening Indians surrounding him. Then he saw Black Buffalo Woman holding him in a lodge. There was shouting as he lay with his face in the dirt. Then he was back facing the warrior. Crazy Horse asked him why his horse's tail was not tied, since he was painted for war. The rider told Crazy Horse that horses need their tail for balance and to swat flies. He heard the sound of the whites' bugle. Then Crazy Horse watched as a long knife was thrust into him, and he saw He Dog standing over him.

At dusk Crazy Horse jerked awake. He looked out onto the lake and realized he had been dreaming. Weak from the fast and depressed about Black Buffalo Woman's marriage, he rode to his village. His stepmothers fed him, and then he collapsed on a pile of buffalo robes.

Worm let Crazy Horse sleep. He knew his son had been on a vision quest. When Crazy Horse awoke, he and Worm sat alone in the lodge, and Crazy Horse told his father about his dream. Worm explained that the man in his vision was Crazy Horse. Like the man in his dream, he should dress plainly, and like the man in his dream, he should ride at the front of his people. Worm then pulled out a pipe and handed it to his son, and the two had a smoke.

As soon as Crazy Horse regained his strength, he gathered his weapons and left on a raid. He Dog and Lone Bear worried that he might have a death wish, which wasn't uncommon among young heartbroken warriors. With Little Hawk in tow, Crazy Horse soon began joining every raid within a thirty-thousand-square-mile area. He was wary as a wolf once out of the village; he constantly scanned the country around him, smelled the air, and looked for signs in animals. Birds flying over a horizon or a deer trotting out of a draw could mean trouble. His skills as both hunter and warrior fed off one another.

Crazy Horse had begun to fight with an elite band of Cheyenne called the Elk Horn Scrapers, and his status as a great fighter soon rose. In a raid against the Shoshone on the west side of the mountains, the fight had turned desperate as the Lakota were fleeing for their lives. Crazy Horse, in a suicidal attempt to cover his comrades' retreat, charged the Shoshone. While the Shoshone warriors galloped all around him, his bay gave out. Crazy Horse jumped off and turned his horse loose to make a stand on foot with his rifle. In a moment, Little Hawk fought his way back and turned his own horse loose to fight alongside his brother. Theirs was a last-ditch effort to stay alive by distracting the Shoshone, who would try to capture the warhorses as a prize.

"Take care of yourself. I'll get us out," Crazy Horse said and then acted as though he were fleeing on foot, which immediately drew two Shoshone toward him. When they were almost on him, Crazy Horse turned his rifle around and shot the closest at point-blank range. In an instant he cut the man's dragline that ran from his waist to the horse's neck and was up and off, charging the second Shoshone, who had dismounted to shoot.

Crazy Horse killed the Shoshone with his pistol and quickly cut the drag rope. He led the spare horse to Little Hawk, who mounted it. Miraculously, they fought their way back to the fleeing Lakota. A single warrior who had seen their bravery turned back to cover them. He was on foot firing arrows into the Shoshone pursuers. "Take him behind," Crazy Horse ordered Little Hawk, who rode to the warrior and offered his hand. The warrior swung up on the horse as Crazy Horse swung off his and shot the closest Shoshone with his pistol. In a flash, Crazy Horse was again galloping off on his captured horse, following the retreat.

When the Lakota stopped for a rest, Crazy Horse inquired about the young man and found out he was the youngest son of an Oglala man he knew.

"My name is Good Weasel, and I have chosen to follow your warrior society," he said. Crazy Horse had no formal society, but it was plain to see this man was serious, so he simply nodded.

Good Weasel looked at Crazy Horse admiringly and continued. "They say you are the greatest fighter among the Oglala, even greater than Red Cloud. I believe it now. I only turned back today because you and your brother were protecting all of us. What do you call your society?" he asked.

Crazy Horse stared into the fire for a moment and thought. "It is the society of the youngest child. The society is a chance for the youngest of the family to prove himself in battle." Crazy Horse smiled at his own quick thinking; he and Little Hawk were the youngest boys of their own mothers. Lone Bear, who was home with his wife, was also the youngest male in his family. Only He Dog had a younger brother, a fact they could all keep from Good Weasel for a while. "You are welcome in our lodge," Crazy Horse said and handed him a pipe. It was a friendship tested in battle, the strongest kind.

At a coming together of many bands of the Lakota, Crazy Horse found himself drifting toward the lodge of No Water. Black Buffalo Woman, now heavy with a second child, watched the lean form of the light-haired Oglala and walked over to him as he approached. "I have heard you fight well," Black Buffalo Woman said. Crazy Horse reached out his hand, holding something for her to take. As she extended her open hand, he lowered his fist until he felt her soft hand, and for a moment they both froze. It was the first time they had touched since she married No Water. He let the elk teeth he was carrying drop into her palm.

"You should give these to another girl," she offered.

"I had a girl; she left me," he said.

"It wasn't my fault—"

"You don't want the elk teeth?" he interrupted.

"No, they're beautiful. I just thought that you must have a girl to give these to.

"I'll sew these onto a shirt with the others you gave me."

"Then you'll have the nicest shirt in the village," he said.

"It's nice already; why don't you come tonight and see it? No Water is in the councils; shouldn't you be there?" she asked.

"I don't like councils; too many speeches. I tell them to let me know what they decide and we'll do the fighting for them."

"No one asks No Water, but he still goes," Black Buffalo Woman quipped. It was meant as a joke, but Crazy Horse didn't laugh. Instead he lingered, staring into her face, neither speaking nor getting off his horse. A pull he had not felt in over a year tugged at his heart. Their eyes locked on each other, and in an awkward attempt to explain something that she had no real explanation for, a rush of words poured from her.

"I have never forgotten you; it was my father's fault. I wanted you to bring horses . . ." Crazy Horse cut her off.

"It wasn't about horses; his family was thought better of than mine," he said. Black Buffalo Woman began to cry. She had hurt a good man, and the sight of him in front of her heightened her sense of regret. The irony was that she had left him for a socially connected man, but now it was Crazy Horse who was becoming the most celebrated warrior in the Lakota nation.

Little Hawk had been exhilarated during the capture of the yellow stallion's herd. The high-headed brown stallion that had taken over had neither the endurance nor the clever wariness that the yellow stallion had possessed. High Back Bone had set a trap on the breaks of the Powder River by tying a mare to a tree inside a corral. With Lone Bear and Little Hawk, High Back Bone had studied the herd's habit and built the corral where the stallion brought the herd to water. When the stallion entered the corral with a few mares and their foals, High Back Bone pulled the gate shut with a long, braided horsehair rope.

High Back Bone then caught the stallion by the front foot by sliding a snare through the fence when the horse ran by. The three warriors soon had the stallion thrown and castrated. High Back Bone walked over to the gentle mare with the bell around her neck branded US. She was easily cut out from the others and roped. He pulled his knife and cut the bell off. "We'll keep her for a pack mare," he said.

Little Hawk wanted some of the yellow stallion's bloodline, but High Back Bone stopped him. "We'll trap you a young male that this stallion has run off. They'll be lured in like the others." Within a day, three young stallions made their appearance and were similarly trapped. One, a blaze-faced three-year-old, was roped and tied down. "Here is your horse from the yellow stallion," High Back Bone said to Little Hawk. On the first day of dragging and hazing the blaze-faced stallion back to the village, High Back Bone occasionally stopped to search the country with his spyglass. He watched a young horse approach the corral cautiously. The animal backtracked and walked to a ridge and smelled the air. He approached the outside of the corral, then suddenly bolted. High Back Bone smiled and gave the spyglass to Lone Bear. He judged the young colt to be a yearling stallion, and there was no mistake about the yellow color. "He's wary like his father. If it's not too bad a winter, he may grow enough to get his own herd someday."

7

They must be hunted like wolves. You will not receive overtures of peace or submission from Indians, but will attack and kill every male Indian over twelve years of age.

—General Patrick Connor

THE PEACE BETWEEN THE TRIBES OF ABSARAKA AND THE U.S. government lasted almost ten years after the Harney massacre of Spotted Tail's village. It ended with the slaughter of a peaceful village of Cheyenne by a drunken army colonel in Colorado. Unlike Harney, Colonel John Chivington took no prisoners. Women, children, and infants were mutilated. Chief Black Kettle's wife was shot nine times but somehow survived. In one instance, three soldiers used a toddler for target practice. Members of the Colorado militia paraded through the streets of Denver with Cheyenne body parts pinned to their clothes.

Cheyenne Dog Soldiers rode north to the Bighorn Valley and asked for help from the Lakota to wage a full-scale war on the whites. War councils formed almost immediately.

The following January, one thousand Cheyenne and Lakota warriors rode south and rained down on the Oregon Trail. Around Julesburg, fifteen soldiers were killed in one incident, and dozens of ranchers, travelers, and stage station operators lost their lives to the warriors. A second raid followed, and a third—the largest attack of its kind—was being planned for the spring. The

Oregon Trail, lined with telegraph wire and stagecoach stations, was now bleeding red. Crazy Horse fought with the same skill he had used against the Shoshone and Crow. He and Lone Bear, He Dog, Good Weasel, and Little Hawk trapped bands of soldiers and stole dozens of horses. Compared to the mountain men and whites living in the villages, some of the soldiers and travelers on the Oregon Trail were poor fighters—but they were well armed.

In May, when the Moon of Shedding Ponies shone, the largest village since the raid on the Crow had been erected on the forks of Goose Creek. Pipes of war were passed among clans that gathered in a thousand lodges. All tribal animosities were put aside as Oglala, Miniconjou, northern and southern Cheyenne, northern Arapaho, Brulé, and Sans Arc placed their lodges in vast adjoining circles. It was probably the last time that a gathering this size would set out for battle with all the traditional formalities and ceremonies.

The Lakota held their sun dance, and the Cheyenne their medicine lodge ceremonies. Mounted on their finest warhorses, warriors wearing headdresses paraded through the village, adorned with eagle feathers and painted by medicine men with designs to protect their horses in the impending fight. Ribbons were braided in tails and manes, or tails were wrapped in cloth and tied up for war. Breast collars and bridles, decorated with beads and porcupine quills, were braided in various colors, and saddles were adorned with ornamentation. The lodges would soon move from Goose Creek to Powder River to Crazy Woman Creek, where the warriors would start their ride to fight the whites at Platte River Bridge.[1]

Worm had insisted that Crazy Horse sit in some of the councils that were held to discuss the whites. "There are people who look to you as a war leader," Worm told his son. Reluctantly, Crazy Horse took his place around the council fire. Some of the Oglala men craned their necks for a look at the brave who was rarely seen except on raids. Among the great leaders assembled there were Man Afraid, Black Twin, and High Back Bone. The climbers—Red Cloud, and No Water—were there too. In the middle of the council meeting, He Dog noticed Crazy Horse slip away.

The elders decided the point of attack would be a small outpost of soldiers on the Oregon Trail where it crossed the Platte River. If the fort could be overrun and the bridge there burned, perhaps the whites would stop using the Oregon Trail. The lodges would soon be moved from Goose Creek to Powder

River to Crazy Woman Creek, where the warriors would start their ride to fight the whites.

What the leaders of the Lakota did not take into consideration was how far reaching the impact of their earlier raids had been. Washington was bombarded with demands for retribution, and it was materializing in the form of a military invasion into the Lakota and Cheyenne strongholds in Absaraka.

The U.S. Army sent General Patrick Connor and three thousand men, equipped with seven-shot repeating rifles, six cannons that fired artillery rounds, and more than six thousand horses and mules, into the Bighorn Valley at roughly the same time the Indians were preparing for war. If Connor's soldiers found the villages while the warriors were down on the Oregon Trail, it would be the Harney massacre all over again.

In July, fifteen hundred warriors left the Bighorn Valley to attack the Platte River Bridge to the south. The only strategy the Indians used at the time was the decoy, but they were so adept at it, even the most seasoned enemy fell for it. The small band of elite warriors could lure a larger enemy force into a trap of waiting warriors. Better than a thousand warriors were hidden over the hills near the Platte River Bridge, but the decoy was ruined when impatient warriors rode out too early. The small band of soldiers who had been lured out of the fort was able to hightail it back across the bridge, covered by the fort's artillery fire.

As luck would have it, an incoming wagon train the next day forced a group of soldiers to leave the fort. A courageous young lieutenant named Caspar Collins led the handful of soldiers. Collins was the son of the former commander of the district and one of the few officers who had camped and hunted with the Oglala and made an effort to learn their sign language.

Unfortunately, most of his experience had been among the fort loafers to the south. Not a year before, Collins wrote a letter home commenting on Indian horses: "The company now is nearly all mounted on Indian horses, which are the laziest things on earth unless it is their Indian masters. They have two good traits: one is being able to live on sage brush, almost the only product of the soil of this country, and the other that they can travel on a slow lope for almost incredible distances."

Ironically, the last anyone saw of Collins, he was stampeding on an out-of-control cavalry horse through a group of Cheyenne with an arrow sticking out of his forehead. The men who survived were saved in part by the hard fighting of a small group of Confederate prisoners called Galvanized Yankees who had been released to fight Indians on the plains.

The wagon train was likewise overrun by the Cheyenne as the soldiers watched helplessly from the fort's rooftops. One of the teamsters had unhooked his mules before the attack, and in the heat of the battle, a Cheyenne caught the bell mare. Amid the war cries and gunfire, the warrior leading the mare was delighted to see several teams of mules obediently following their leader. The attack on the wagons also netted the Cheyenne horses, guns, and supplies, but the bridge and the fort held.

Crazy Horse remained south to raid white travelers, ranchers, and telegraph stations. He gathered both ranchers' and soldiers' horses and counted numerous coups. Scalps were relatively easy to come by compared to ones he had gotten in the war zone around the Bighorns. It was while on these raids that Crazy Horse began to have strange dreams. Something to the north was wrong, but he could not explain it. Maybe the Crow were staging a large war party; he could not tell. He prayed for the Great Spirit to guide him but to no avail. One night, when he awoke from a dream in a sweat, he shook Little Hawk and whispered, "Wake up, we're going home."

The source of Crazy Horse's apprehension materialized on the second day, when he crossed the tracks of hundreds of soldier horses heading north toward the villages on the Powder River. With them were the ruts of one hundred–plus wagons and tracks of cattle.

Crazy Horse knew the camps would be defenseless with the warriors off raiding. He thought of Meadowlark and Rain, but he also felt the old tug at his heart for Black Buffalo Woman.

"We're going to cover some country; just do what I do and keep up," he told Little Hawk. Crazy Horse and Little Hawk made the four-day ride in a day and a half. To preserve his horse and make as much time as possible, Crazy Horse jumped off and wrapped the horse's tail around his wrist when they approached steep hills. He then ran behind his horse, slapping the animal with a strap all the way up. Only at the top of the hill would he mount the horse again and be gone at a lope.

8

It was insufferably hot, no cool breeze fanned the brows of the sunburnt warriors, who faced death in many hard contests in Dixie, and would sooner do it again, than suffer so intensely from thirst in this inhospitable country. The Gentleman who sits in his room and drinks his brandy and ice water . . . does not dream of the suffering of the soldiers on the Indian frontier, and probably grumbles because his beer isn't cold or fresh enough; let them come out here and they will pay $5.00 for a drink of not only warm but actually hot pool water with tadpoles, lizards, and snakes in it.

—Lieutenant Charles Springer

They could go with their ponies where it was difficult for our men to go on foot.

—Colonel Samuel Walker

The cavalry is the only arm that can be used effectively in pursuing Indians. Unfortunately, nothing can be accomplished for a number of reasons; the super abundance of recruits who are not horsemen and are only awkward children in points of horsemanship when compared to the Redskins . . . The character of the horses . . . are almost as inferior as the men for this type of service on the plains. Many of the new soldiers, thoroughly frightened by ridiculous reports and absurd commentaries on the Indians, have become accustomed to considering them so dangerous that they think more of avoiding them than fighting them.

—Colonel Phillipe Regis de Trobriand, Governor of the Dakotas

Dead Horse Campaign, Powder River, 1865

GENERAL PATRICK CONNOR'S INVASION OF THE VILLAGES in the Bighorn Valley started poorly because of a lack of horses. More than a million and a half horses and mules were killed during the Civil War, so it was with some difficulty that Connor could mount all his men. In any event, procuring horses delayed his departure until July first.

The plan was to march three separate groups into the Cheyenne and Lakota strongholds to the north. The first column of fourteen hundred men, under Colonel Nelson Cole, was sent on the longest and most difficult ride in U.S. history. The expedition was doomed from the start; the length of the trip and number of animals made it impossible to haul enough feed. It took 10 to 12 pounds of corn daily to feed each of the three thousand animals. To reach Powder River in sixty days from their base at Omaha, Nebraska, close to 2 million pounds of corn would have to be loaded onto 130 wagons, each pulled by six mules. After loading bedrolls, modest food rations, ammunition, shoeing tools, and a mowing machine, there was little room for any feed at all. The result would be exhausted and starved men and horses.

It was hoped that grazing along the thousand-mile route could supplement the horses and mules' meager diet, but it was a drought year, and the migrating buffalo had already grazed the area bare. Colonel Cole's men may have been heading to the best horse country in the world, but they had to cross some of the worst to get to it.

The barren mazes of ravines and washouts of the sand hills of Nebraska and the badlands of Dakota were brutal on horses. Their guides were unfamiliar with the territory, and the mules were too young to pull the loads placed on them. Wagons sank to their hubs in deep sand or had to be lowered with ropes down steep canyons, straining men and livestock alike.

> *July 12, 1865*
> *Some fool set fire to the prairie as we came to rather a big creek . . . my horse got mired, . . . my left foot got [stuck] fast in the stirrup. The horse jumped up, got scared, and ran at top speed dragging me along with my carbine slung to me and loaded. I thought "Goodbye Springer" but luckily the grass was long and thick . . . no bones broken.*

I had been dragged about fifty yards. The horse had run to the top of the hill, looked around, snorted, and come back to where I was lying; after a little while, I recovered and we effected a crossing a little farther up the creek, on a beaver dam, leading the horses alongside in the mud and mire up to the belly . . .

The second column, led by General Connor, would ride north from the Oregon Trail with just under a thousand men and establish a fort—to be named Fort Connor—on the Powder River. Mountain man Jim Bridger would serve as Connor's personal guide. Connor also had a force of Pawnee scouts, enemies of the Sioux and Cheyenne, led by Captain Luther North. Connor's command had its own problems: disgruntled Civil War veterans, whose enlistments would expire before the expedition was over, had to be forced to march west by aiming cannons at them.

A second horse culture in the form of U.S. Army warhorses was now entering Absaraka. Grain fed and shod, they were not acclimated to foraging for themselves or having to deal with the severe weather conditions they were to encounter. But the biggest threat to these animals, as far as the army was concerned, was their being stolen.

Wanting to avoid the fiasco that befell a colonel on the Oregon Trail who recently had eighty horses stolen from him, General Connor issued General Order #1:

No galloping of horses on the march will be allowed, and officers will see that the utmost care is taken of the animals.

Horses will not be saddled in the morning until Boots and Saddles is sounded from these headquarters.

Horses will be brought inside the lines at sundown or when stable call is sounded, and securely hobbled and tied.

On the march, when a halt is made, officers will see that the girths of the saddles are loosened, bridles are taken off, and the horses are allowed to graze.

In case of night attack, the troops will surround their horses, and if the enemy is not close up to the horses and cannot be seen, the men will lie or kneel down so as not to make a mark for the enemy.

The third column, six hundred men under Colonel Samuel Walker, rode north from Fort Laramie to rendezvous with Colonel Cole near the Black Hills. The plan was for General Connor to meet and resupply Cole and Walker on the Tongue River near the Wolf Mountains around the first of September.

At roughly the same time, close to one hundred men, under James Sawyer, were to be conducting a road-building survey through the middle of it all. It would be a busy summer in Absaraka.

When Crazy Horse and Little Hawk caught up to General Connor on Powder River, they saw that the soldiers had stopped to build a fort. Crazy Horse picketed his horse in some tall grass down a depression and sat on the ground to pray. After a couple hours, Little Hawk walked over. "Shouldn't we get going?" he asked.

"The soldiers have stopped. We should pay our gratitude; they might have gone into the villages; besides, our horses need to rest," Crazy Horse said. Little Hawk was puzzled: why not ride home to the village and let the horses rest a week? He wanted to see his parents, and it would be good to rest in the lodge with his mothers' cooking. It had been a hard month keeping up with his brother.

"If you want to go, then go. I'll be along," Crazy Horse said. Crazy Horse needed time to think. In the last several months he had seen death like he had never seen before. He smoked and prayed, but he also studied the soldier camp. They had tremendous firepower: almost all of them had repeating rifles as well as a pistol and plenty of ammunition. In addition, there was more than one cannon. As for the Lakota, fewer than one in a hundred even had a gun, and most of those were old prairie rifles. During Crazy Horse's raiding on the Oregon Trail, he noticed some of the white travelers were helpless as fighters; there had been little honor in killing them. Some he had spared; it was what High Back Bone had told him: being a great warrior gave you the power to let live as well as kill. It was not always the case with other warriors; the Cheyenne in particular were merciless in their revenge for Colonel Chivington's massacre of Black Kettle's village. Ironically, it would be the Cheyenne who would pay the dearest from Connor's invasion.

Twenty-seven Cheyenne warriors, riding home from the Platte Bridge fight, were ambushed by ninety Pawnee scouts, under Captain North, on the high banks of the Powder River. In a brutal fight, all the Cheyenne were killed. One Cheyenne, who had been wounded at the Platte Bridge fight and was laid out on a travois, threw himself off the cliffs along the Powder River rather than be captured by the Pawnee. But one of the Pawnee backtracked down to the river, found the Cheyenne, and ran him through with a saber.

Shortly after the fight, Captain North and his Pawnee found a huge trail leading down to Powder River made by thousands of Indians; a village that size could wipe out Connor's entire force. Fearing for the safety of his scouts, Captain North returned to the camp of General Connor, making no mention of the huge Lakota village. Jim Bridger, having noticed signs of the huge camp's trail north, also made no mention of the village.

When Crazy Horse returned to his village after the raid, Little Hawk returned to the lodge of his parents while Crazy Horse rode his horse behind the lodge of Black Buffalo Woman and waited. He let his gelding loose to graze along the creek.

"Tasunka witko!" the small boy pulled at his mother's buckskin frock and pointed at the light-haired warrior across the creek. Crazy Horse gave a small smile at the terrified boy, but the youth clung to his mother. Black Buffalo Woman took her frightened son's hands and held them. "He heard you live in a cave and eat your enemies." She said and smiled.

"Don't be afraid," she told her son, "he is a friend to our people. Look, you see, he is not here to hurt us, he protects us from the Washita (white men)." The boy had heard too many stories, however, of the light-haired warrior who had killed more Crow, soldiers, and Shoshone than all the other Lakota combined.

"Go and get your older brother, he won't be afraid." Her young son ran down the path for the lodge. Black Buffalo Woman walked down where the stream narrowed, skipped over, and sat next to Crazy Horse. She looked at his drawn face. He looked tired.

Soon three young boys appeared down the path and sheepishly gawked at Crazy Horse. The youngest son of Black Buffalo Woman appeared in the distance but stayed back in the winter shoots of the willows around the creek. Crazy Horse retrieved a deerskin sack from a saddlebag on his horse, and motioned to the small boy to come forward. Still frightened, the boy grudgingly moved ahead to see what the warrior offered.

Crazy Horse dipped his hand in the stream and then into the sack. Gently and deliberately, he painted solid white circles on the young boy's face, and when finished, repeated the procedure for the other boys, to their delight.

"Now," he said, "you will grow up to be great warriors. You will hunt together and fight together and take care of the old and helpless. Go and tell the herders Tasunka Witko said to give you each a horse to ride. You can help guard the herd this afternoon."

The four tore off like a shot, leaving Crazy Horse and Black Buffalo Woman on the banks of the stream. After a long visit, she took his hand.

"I missed you; I was worried. No Water says there are soldiers moving from the south."

"I saw them. They're building a fort for now," Crazy Horse nodded. Then he touched her cheek before walking to his horse and mounting. He looked back and saw she was still looking at him. "When I heard the soldiers were coming, I rode north . . ." He didn't need to finish; he saw her eyes welling with tears. He thought with time he would move on, but his feelings for her were stronger than ever. After a long glance, Crazy Horse rode out and checked on the four boys; they sat proudly on horses, watching the herd. It brought him back to his youth with Lone Bear and He Dog and the lessons he had learned from High Back Bone. For an hour, Crazy Horse rode along with the boys, explaining the various aspects of herding and telling stories.

That night he returned to the lodge of his parents, where Worm and his stepmothers fed and visited with him. Meadowlark was thrilled to have her boy back. She presented him with a buckskin shirt decorated with scalp hair and beads. Instead of relaxing, Crazy Horse went out for a hunt the next morning.

When he returned to his parents' lodge, Lone Bear and He Dog reported that a rider from the Hunkpapa had discovered another group of soldiers moving toward the Powder River a day's ride to the north. If this were true, the village would soon be between Connor and Cole. Conflicting stories of soldiers on the Tongue, the Powder, and to the west in the Black Hills had been circulating for a week. Captured army horses, brought in from the four corners, seemed to confirm those stories.

General Connor took off to the west with three hundred men looking for Colonel Cole, who was lost in the wilderness. Cole, who was short on food, was going in the wrong direction. While General Connor was looking for Colonel Cole, he passed Lake De Smet and the mouth of Little Goose Canyon, where they saw Absaraka in all her beauty.

> *The country is perfectly charming, the hills all covered with a fine growth of grass, and in every valley there is either a rushing stream or some quiet, babbling brook of pure, clear snow water, filled with trout, the banks lined with trees, wild cherries, quaking aspens, some birch, willow, and cottonwood. No country in America is more picturesque than the eastern slope of the Bighorn Mountains.*
> *—Captain H. E. Palmer, 11th Kansas Cavalry, Connor's command*

No sooner had General Connor reached the Tongue River than Captain North and his Pawnee scouts spotted a small Arapaho village upstream.[1] The soldiers were brought up through the cottonwoods along the river to conceal their movements.

As General Connor's men lined up for the charge on the village, hundreds of Indian horses grazing on the flat began to whinny, became spooked, and ran toward the village, setting off the camp dogs in a chorus of barking. Captain H. E. Palmer, who had finagled his way from the supply train to the cavalry charge on the village, recorded:

> *I felt for a moment that my place was with the train, that really I was a consummate fool for urging the General to allow me to accompany him. I was reminded that I had lost no Indians, and that scalping was unmanly, besides being brutal, and for my part I did not want any dirty scalps; yet I had no time to halt; I could not do it—my horse carried me*

forward against my will, and in those few moments—less than the time it takes to tell the story—I was in the village in the midst of a hand-to-hand fight with warriors and their squaws.

Not a man realized that to charge into the Indian village without a moment's hesitancy was our only salvation. We already saw that we were greatly outnumbered, and that only desperate fighting would save our scalps. Many of the female portions of this band did as brave a fighting as their savage lords. Unfortunately for the women and children, our men had no time to direct their aim; bullets from both sides and murderous arrows filled the air; squaws and children, as well as warriors, fell among the dead and wounded.

General Connor charged in too fast and found himself positioned between the two sides. One of his aides was shot in the mouth with an arrow and another hit with a bullet that ran up his backbone. The Pawnee scouts corralled eleven hundred of the Arapaho horses, which the soldiers attempted to ride because their own horses were played out. The cavalrymen were flung ass-over-teakettle throughout the village. The Arapaho horses were as terrified of the whites as the cavalry horses were of the Arapaho.

The Arapaho retreated up Wolf Creek toward the Bighorn Mountains with Connor and fourteen of his men in hot pursuit. Soon, however, Connor was galloping back for his life, for once the Arapaho had taken their women and children to safety, they led a fierce counterattack on the soldiers.

Connor was soundly beaten back to his base of supplies after losing half of the stolen Arapaho horses in the fight. Ten soldiers were dead, and the general had no idea where Nelson Cole and Samuel Walker were. Neither did they. Their starving men and horses were wandering lost in the wilderness, dangerously close to a huge Lakota and Cheyenne village three times the size of the Arapaho village on the Tongue.

Not a drop of water to be found, things began to look awful serious, our animals began to give out. More than twenty horses and the same number of mules fell down dead, on we marched. At twelve o' clock from the

top of a hill we saw in a distance the Powder River . . . and a shout of joy rose into the blue sky. That was a terrible march, God preserve us from another. The bed of the river is covered with a kind of blue clay, which sticks to the feet and mires both horses and men. We are in camp where the headquarters of the Sioux Indians were last winter. As the signs show, there have been no less than two thousand lodges there.
—Lieutenant Charles Springer, Cole's command

Colonel Cole's weak, thirsty horses smelled the Powder River and stumbled forward as fast as they could. During the day, the temperature had risen to 106 degrees, so at the sight of the Powder, the men cheered; it was the most water they had seen in a week. The celebration was short-lived, however, as teepee rings, horse tracks, and fire rings indicated a village of thousands of Indians. A small detachment, mounted on the best horses, was sent west to find General Connor, but they returned the next day having found no sign of him.

Cole had no idea that Connor was to the south. After seeing smoke to the north, he marched off in that direction. He and his starving soldiers and horses were strung out in a three-mile column when Hunkpapa warriors from Sitting Bull's camp discovered them.

About 50 Sioux Indians had dashed in among our picked-out horses . . . the 2nd Missouri Artillery dropped their guns and ran; only two or three showed fight . . . the thieves had gathered about twenty horses and fled . . . five of our men were killed by arrow shots from the Indians; two were wounded.

Officer call was sounded, and a council of war was held. Col Cole informed the officers for the first time of his orders. His orders were to proceed with his command to the Powder River; there he would find General Connor's command and draw fresh supplies and get further orders . . . General Connor was not there . . . We marched down the river and took our dead soldiers with us.
—Lieutenant Charles Springer

A small band of cavalry under Lieutenant Springer was decoyed away from the command while one hundred Lakota disguised in U.S. Army uniforms rode in from behind, appearing to rescue them. Before the cavalrymen realized their mistake, the warriors rode through them shooting arrows and striking them with war clubs.

> *The Indians were growing stronger and tried to cut us off from the hill... their number increased every moment. They appeared to grow out of the ground.*
> *—Lieutenant Charles Springer*

That night, Colonel Cole decided to turn what remained of his party around and ride to Fort Laramie, which inadvertently headed his column right into the Lakota village that was camped between him and General Connor.

As if starvation, exhaustion, and Indian attacks were not enough, the weather turned horrid. After a sweltering hot day in excess of 100 degrees, a "blue norther" blew in, dropping the temperature to almost freezing that night. The following morning, stiff soldiers awoke to find 225 horses and mules dead of exhaustion and exposure on the picket line. That was only the start.

An ice storm hit Cole's men, who had camped out in the open for protection. Despite their own suffering, cavalrymen committed numerous acts of compassion on behalf of the dying horses. With freezing fingers and toes, they led shaking horses into the timber and lit fires around them to try to save them. Cottonwood boughs were cut and fed to them by men who had neither raincoats nor adequate shoes. A few men each spread his spare blanket over his animal's back and put brush underneath for insulation. For the soldiers, their horses had been their companions and friends for more than two months in a lonely, hard country. Horses and mules, already exhausted, turned their tails to the north and put their feet almost together before spreading them in an effort to stay upright. Finally the weak animals tottered and fell dead out of hunger and exhaustion.

As daylight broke, Cole's men in camp faced the horrible sight of dead horses on the ground and mules that had died in the harness. Exhausted from battle, hunger, and fatigue, the men broke down at the sight and sound of their faithful horses' suffering. Soon the dreaded order came to shoot the animals that were down. Friends unable to perform their duty shot one another's horses, saving the rider from the morbid task. Three to five hundred horses died there—along with those killed during the days of fighting between the Indians and soldiers. The spot would be forever known as Dead Horse Camp.

As the soldiers moved away from the dead horses, the spirit of the men died with them. They had been trained as cavalrymen to care for their horses. Through their long and arduous journey, the cavalrymen had risen each morning an hour before sunrise to give their companions a thorough brushing and feeding followed by a saddling. A bond between troopers and their horses formed where the animals whinnied at their masters each morning in expectation of getting fed. With the death of their companions, the demoralized soldiers, lost in a hostile wilderness, fought to hang on. Many of the men were now barefoot. In a cheerless, cold camp, voices called out to the soldiers in the night.

"Hey, white bastards! You thought you could kill us; now you sons of bitches can walk. We'll kill you all before you get home."

> *There is no fun among the boys; they all look down in the mouth; no joking, no laughing going on, everyone busy with his own thoughts. Should the old saying of the Sioux nation prove to be true for us? That the white man who enters the Powder River valley would never take his scalp back home to tell the story? Everything is looking like it.*
> *—Lieutenant Charles Springer, Nelson Cole's command*

Crazy Horse was surprised at the soldiers' condition. "They are trying to leave. Look at them; they are starved."

He Dog rode over. "We need to keep them from hunting, and then they will go home."

The following day a thousand warriors massed against Cole and Walker. Artillery was hurried up to shell out the woods in front. An explosion hit the cottonwoods above Crazy Horse and Lone Bear. Crazy Horse was blown from his horse and lay stunned on the ground. He felt a strong hand take him by the arm and pull him up. He saw Lone Bear's face but could hear nothing but a loud ringing. Regaining his senses, Crazy Horse pulled away from his friend and walked back to his horse. A ball had ripped through the horse's kidney. Crazy Horse sat on the ground next to the animal's head, wiped dirt from its face, and watched the life leave the animal. He smoked and prayed next to the bay. Little Hawk brought Crazy Horse up another horse, and soon Crazy Horse's hearing came back.

In a desperate effort to find food, eighty soldiers waded across Powder River to hunt, but while they were gone, a party of Cheyenne stole their horses, saddles, packs, and ammunition.

Up along Powder River, a soldier from General Connor's command strained to hear. "There it is again," a soldier said, listening to the low boom of cannons in the distance.

"That's got to be Cole's men," another trooper said.

"They must be in the thick of it," Jim Bridger said. His son was a cannoneer with Colonel Cole. Then an eerie silence followed as if death were awaiting them just downriver. General Connor sent Captain North and his Pawnee scouts to try to find Cole's men. The scouts were horrified as they came to Dead Horse Camp. It looked as if there had been a spectacular battle and the soldiers had killed their horses for breastworks.

September 5, 1865

Colonel Cole's men watched a few Indians make a bold taunting charge through what cavalry was left. Crazy Horse rode though the soldiers at the front of his small force of decoys.

"Wait until Crazy Horse brings them past!" High Back Bone yelled at the young warriors, who were hidden in a deep depression on their fleet buffalo horses. It was no use, however; they broke again just like they had twice at Platte River Bridge. High Back Bone, wearing a black buffalo cap and his war shirt, galloped in on his warhorse to direct them.

The men with Cole, starved though they were, by no means were through fighting.

> *We had a good deal of fun with the Indians, or as the men called them, the Idaho Militia; how they dodged when they saw the smoke of the artillery muzzle of the piece, and what excellent horsemanship they displayed.*
> *—Lieutenant Charles Springer*

"Dirty rotten son of a bitch!" Corporal Rivers yelled. His company had been ordered to turn their horses over to the men of Company H and walk the remaining two hundred miles to Fort Laramie. The burly Irishman appealed to Lieutenant Springer.

"It ain't right, Lieutenant; we kept our horses alive because we took care of them, and now we got to turn them over to those horse-killin' sons of bitches in H Company and walk?" The corporal threw his tin cup on the ground. His own sorrel gelding was growing weaker by the day. He was a beautiful animal: reddish brown, with a white spot at the base of his tail. He was branded US 12 B for 12th Cavalry, B Company. "I may as well shoot him myself as turn him over to Company H," Corporal Rivers grumbled as he stormed off to the picket line.

He looked in his sorrel gelding's eye and ran his hand along the animal's neck. The corporal would be damned if he would not make an effort to save his companion, even if it meant being arrested by the army or shot by the Indians. Quietly the corporal mounted the sorrel and rode across the Powder. He looked back across the river toward camp; no one had seen him leave. He ran his hands over his loyal friend for the last time as the sorrel buried his head in the stand of tall grass next to the river.

"I'll not let them ride you to death," the corporal promised, eyeing the trees for warriors. He took the bridle off but then reconsidered; it would be better if whoever found him used the bit he was used to. He led the sorrel into the trees until they were at the edge of a clearing. He then took off the bridle, loosened the curb chain, and tied the bridle to the saddle.

"Good-bye, old friend. I ain't seen an Indian ride a horse to death yet." He stepped away and raised his pistol.

The sound of gunfire from across the river caused the troopers to spring into action. Lieutenant Springer led his company to the banks of the Powder River to see Corporal Rivers wading across, firing his pistol behind him. The men waited but saw nothing.

"I saw an elk and went in to kill it and was jumped by some Indians; they got my horse," the corporal told Springer.

"To your horses!" the lieutenant yelled, but before the order could be carried out the corporal interceded.

"Sir, my horse is long gone; I saw them leading it over a far ridge. It will only wear out horses and men, and it may be a trap," the corporal said in somewhat of a pleading tone, well aware that he would be in serious trouble if the truth was known. Lieutenant Springer agreed; this expedition into Indian country had been reduced to staying alive and fending off attacks rather than an offensive maneuver.

> *About ten o'clock we came in sight of some big mountains (Bighorns) whose summits were covered with eternal snow. The sun shone on them, and they looked like pure silver. Everybody looked pleased as we came in sight of them . . . Men are actually starving or on the point of starvation, killing mules and horses and eating them as our only food, but a horrible scene I have seen today. A dead horse was lying by the roadside, and men around it thicker than buzzards cutting the meat off quarreling about the liver. The horse belonged to the 16th Kansas cavalry and had been dead about three hours before; consequently, it began stinking. We managed to fare tolerably well by killing mules that are in good order yet, and mule meat is better than horse meat.*
> *—Lieutenant Charles Springer*

Less desperate men cooked their mule meat, which took to jumping like frog legs when cooked. After eighty-eight days, thirty men had died of starvation, and more than two thousand mules and horses were dead or stolen. The surviving horses and soldiers were emaciated skeletons. Soldiers dropped their rifles on the trail, too weak to carry them. Saddles, wagons, and supplies were dumped or burned for lack of animals to pull them. A cannon was left in the middle of the Powder River. It had been one of the worst abuses of U.S troops in history.

Colonel Cole claimed his men had killed between two and five hundred Indians, but Colonel Walker, who was with him, stated, "I cannot say we killed a one."

> *I did not see anyone throw his hat in the air, but I did hear the language used at the mention of General Connor's name, and the language used by Nelson Cole would not be printable.*
> *—William Devine, teamster, Cole's command*

"Hey, Brother, look at this horse," called Lone Bear as he led a poor sorrel gelding and a mule. Crazy Horse looked over at the sorrel that was branded US 12 B. He had a bridle with US stamped on the bit, and like the other stolen horses was extremely thin.

"You got a nice one," Crazy Horse said.

"He's weak now, but he'll fill up on green grass in the spring and be a good buffalo horse," Lone Bear said.

"What are you going to do with the mule?" Crazy Horse asked.

"I'll give it to the old Red Water Woman. She needs something to pack her lodge. I got her a horse too," Lone Bear replied.

"You're a good man, Lone Bear. A rich man has many horses, but a great man gives away many horses."

"Little Hawk has turned into the best horse trainer in the tribe; have you seen what he has taught his blaze-faced horse?" Lone Bear said; he was proud of his young apprentice and wanted his friend to know it. Crazy Horse agreed; Little Hawk had a passion for horses, and it showed in his training. The blaze-faced gelding was a half brother to the roan Crazy Horse had trained as a boy.

"Lone Bear, we have to teach the warriors to fight differently. Counting coups is a brave thing, but it kills too many of our men," Crazy Horse said to his friend.

Lone Bear was curious. None in the Oglala was braver or had counted more coups than his friend. Now Crazy Horse was questioning the most revered part of a warrior's life, however. What Lone Bear didn't realize was that Crazy Horse was doing what few military leaders are blessed with—the ability to adapt to their enemy.

Crazy Horse had had enough experience fighting the soldiers that he had begun to change his style of fighting. The business of killing was replacing the tradition of counting coups. The old method of shielding yourself with your horse from the soldiers was ineffective; an Indian would not deliberately shoot a horse, but a soldier would shoot the horse and then draw a bead on the limping Indian. Crazy Horse saw that most soldiers were somewhat harmless on a horse, but the foot soldiers and their long rifles had to be respected. The main problem in fighting the whites was their firepower.

In two moons your men will not have hoof left.

—Man Afraid to Colonel Henry Carrington

Fort Laramie, 1866

EIGHT MONTHS AFTER GENERAL PATRICK CONNOR'S three thousand men limped out of Absaraka without their horses, the U.S. Army sent back just eight hundred more soldiers armed merely with muzzle-loading weapons, who were to guard a trail that would take travelers' wagons right through the heart of that area in the Bighorn Valley. The Bozeman Trail ran from the Oregon Trail to the gold mines in Virginia City, Montana.

At a treaty council at Fort Laramie, Colonel Henry Carrington informed a roomful of Lakota, before an official agreement had been made, that he was going north to build forts along the Bozeman Trail. Even the daftest of the Indians knew what this meant: the last area that was free to hunt without the white tide moving through would now have disease, no game, and the whites would be there.

Red Cloud, whom the whites were enabling to become the Lakota leader, stood up and complained about the conniving. The leadership he had so desperately sought over his own people was now bestowed on him by the whites.

Ironically, he would become the U.S. government's greatest protagonist in conquering the last of the Plains Indians.

Red Cloud's protest took Colonel Carrington by surprise. General William T. Sherman had not only misled Carrington to believe the Indians would readily grant him permission to build the forts, but he had also told him it was safe to take women and children along.

With the grumblings of the Indians present, the treaty proceedings had to be called off immediately lest a fight break out. Red Cloud watched Colonel Carrington walk from the platform over to an orderly who was holding his dapple-gray gelding. Red Cloud considered killing Carrington right there. *Let it begin now*, he thought.

By October, Colonel Carrington had designed and built one of the premiere frontier stockades on the continent. Fort Phil Kearny was an architectural wonder, constructed with more than twelve thousand logs. The walls enclosed seventeen acres on which thirty quarters would ultimately be built. The church had stained glass windows, and the sutler's store was stocked with everything from champagne and oysters to whiskey and flour. A 124-foot flagpole stood in the parade ground.

The Bighorn Mountains rose up to the west within a mile of Fort Phil Kearny. Piney Creek ran through the southwest corner of the fort, and another branch of the river ran about a half mile to the east. Lake De Smet was but three miles away.

During the dedication ceremony in October, a dress parade, picnics, and horse races were held. The regimental band played throughout the celebration, which was short-lived: at nine o'clock that night two civilian contractors were shot by Indians who had snuck inside the picket line. All men were called to arms when Indians could be seen dancing around fires atop Sullivant Hills, just a half mile away. Their screams carried across the parade ground, taunting the soldiers to come out and fight.

Colonel Carrington ordered the howitzers brought up and had the three cannons placed in position to fire on the hill. Spectators inside the fort watched the flight of the artillery shells: two out of three exploded directly above the

Indians. Shrapnel tore through the warriors as they tramped out the fires and ceased their dancing. Unbeknownst to Carrington, the Indians had been planning a general siege of the fort, but the cannon blast changed their plans.

Colonel Carrington had little experience as a fighter, but he was a smart man, He realized he would have neither the men nor the equipment to launch an offensive campaign against the Indians—even after building a second fort in the area. That was not likely to change because officials in Washington, D.C., were largely ignoring his requests for arms, supplies, and more men. Ironically, however, as word of the casualties on the Bozeman Trail reached the nation's capital, pressure was put on Carrington to engage the hostiles. Unless he received reinforcements, Carrington was, in essence, to follow a suicide order.

Carrington had sent numerous pleas for the seven-shot Spencer carbines that had kept Connor's and Cole's men alive the year before. Unfortunately, one of the supply masters down at Fort Laramie was the same demented preacher who had slaughtered the Cheyenne at the Sand Creek massacre. John Chivington was also a thief who sold supplies intended for the soldiers. Not only had Chivington stirred up the Indians two years prior, he was now starving the soldiers who had to fight them.

The soldiers had no sooner arrived than they became the prey of native guerrilla warfare. Woodcutting and hay crews that had to travel up to five miles from the fort were constantly attacked, and even sentries on the fort's parapets were killed.

As for the young warriors of the Lakota, Cheyenne, and Arapaho tribes, they were given the green light to attack wagon trains and to view the forts as an all-you-can-steal horse market. Once the immediate area surrounding the fort became overgrazed, herders were forced to move livestock out of direct sight of Fort Phil Kearny. Within five months of Carrington's arrival in Absaraka, more than 150 horses, 300 mules, and 300 head of cattle had been stolen.

Cutting his already thin force almost in half, Carrington sent another detachment of soldiers north to the Bighorn River to build a third fort, named C. F. Smith. Luckily, this fort was on the border of lands of the Crow, whose warriors had allied themselves with the whites to secure protection from the Lakota.

The officers at the new fort quizzed the Crow on the meaning of their horses' decoration. A knotted rope hanging from his horse's neck told of the cutting of an enemy's picketed mount. The number of horses captured by a warrior could be read from the stripes of white clay painted under his horse's eyes or on its flanks. From a white clay hand on those flanks, one learned that the owner had ridden down an enemy. A group of Crow horsemen under chief Iron Bull were in Fort C. F. Smith trading when seventy-five Lakota appeared on the flat by the fort. Iron Bull joined Captain Kinney to view his enemy through a looking-glass. The chief then gathered his warriors, who mounted their warhorses and rode out to hurl insults at the Lakota. The soldiers, eager to see such a fight, lined the walls, their guns at the ready. The two tribes galloped around in large circles; at the one spot where those circles came together, both sides began to shoot arrows or rifles at one another from underneath the horses' necks.

After twenty minutes of fighting, Iron Bull roped the Lakota chief off his horse and dragged him by the neck toward the fort, ending the battle as the Lakota withdrew to the east.

At the time, there were approximately eighty thousand Indian horses between the Powder and Bighorn rivers. In addition, another twenty to forty thousand ran in the wild. It took up to six horses to move a large council lodge that was made of up to twenty-five buffalo skins that were sewn together and kept in two sections to pack. The poles for a lodge this size were twenty-five feet long and five inches in diameter.

It took between six and twelve horses for a small family to operate on a hunting trip. Mares were used predominantly for pack animals and for women to ride. Teepee poles were bundled with rawhide straps and tied to each side of the horses with the back dragging on the ground. The two bundles of poles were connected behind the horse by a wide rawhide flap that might serve as a carrier for more equipment or supplies.

Crazy Horse rode up with Lone Bear and a dozen warriors as He Dog sat on the far hillside studying Fort Phil Kearny below. He noted the tall stakes that the soldiers had placed along the perimeter of the fort to mark the cannons' ranges. He Dog smiled, knowing Little Hawk and some other young warriors had slipped in at night to move the stakes so that the cannoneers' aim would be handicapped.

"What do you think we Lakota should do now?" He Dog turned to ask his friend.

"Too many will die if we attack the fort. We need guns. There's not a gun for every ten warriors, and then no two are the same," Crazy Horse replied.

In the background, the Indians could hear the forty-piece regimental band inside the fort play as the sun began to fall behind the mountains. "I could not stand to live with such songs in my ears every night," Lone Bear said. He Dog looked to Crazy Horse. "We have to find a way, then, to lure them out of the fort," countered He Dog. "If this road turns out like the Holy Road, we are done as a people. There will soon be more whites here than there are blades of grass."

"These soldiers are hard to decoy, but maybe we'll catch one who is not so smart," Crazy Horse said. His wish was about to come true.

Captain William Fetterman hadn't been at the fort one day before he openly criticized Colonel Carrington for not launching an assault against the Indians. As Lieutenant John Grattan and General Patrick Connor had likewise thought, Fetterman gave the Lakota and the Cheyenne little credit as fighters.

"I never heard of an Indian that would stand and fight; a full regiment could whip all the hostiles from the Black Hills to the Bighorns. With eighty men, I could ride through the Sioux nation," Fetterman boasted to a small crowd gathered at the sutler's store. Jim Bridger, who knew Indian fighting and Indians better than all but a few in the entire West, laughed out loud.

"These Indians don't fight the way you West Pointers fought the Rebs," Bridger warned Fetterman. "No offense to your former adversaries," Bridger added, nodding politely at a couple of Southerners in the room. "You put a soldier and an Indian side by side on horseback, and the soldier is in trouble every time," Bridger continued. Fetterman merely scoffed.

"After Sand Creek, I wouldn't want to get captured by any Cheyenne. The best you can do is save the last bullet for yourself," Bridger warned. His point was lost on Captain Fetterman, however, who turned on his heels and stomped out. A fighting man, he was determined to take a fight to the Indians—one way or another.

Within two weeks of his arrival at the fort, Captain Fetterman approached Colonel Carrington and demanded that he be allowed to set an ambush for the hostiles using hobbled mules as bait. Carrington reluctantly agreed. Fetterman spent the night hiding outside the fort with a party of soldiers while Indians ran off a herd of cattle less than a mile away. Two days later, Fetterman rode out with Captain Ten Eyck to a woodcutter camp, where they were ambushed. Miraculously, no one was hit. When a relief column arrived, no signs of Indians were found. The next day, Fetterman resumed his discontent at Judge Kinney's store. "We were ambushed yesterday by twenty Indians, and not one of them could hit us at close range. Captain Ten Eyck was there; tell them, Captain." Fetterman appealed to the captain, who sat in the corner nursing a drink and listening to the ranting. The last thing Ten Eyck wanted to do was get into this kind of debate. To his way of thinking, they were alive by the grace of God; he was content to let the warm glow of alcohol wash away the unnerving experiences of the day before.

Tenodore Ten Eyck was a veteran of the Army of the Cumberland. His health had been weakened from a stay in a Confederate prison, which also left him addicted to laudanum and alcohol. After his first wife died giving birth to his son, something inside the man died. The one passion that brought him happiness was his private string of well-bred horses. Turk, his racehorse, had won him $30 at the races during the fort's dedication. A young foal was born to his bay mare on the trip west, and it had become a pet around the fort. There were so few horses left in the fort, however, that Colonel Carrington had requisitioned all the private stock for army use.

Like Cole's men who had lost all their horses the year before, Ten Eyck seemed to lose hope with the loss of his horses. Colonel Carrington had hoped to turn the responsibilities of running the fort over to the captain, but when Ten Eyck showed up drunk at a review, the commanding officer was forced to arrest him. Unfortunately, Ten Eyck was one of the few competent and loyal officers Carrington had; the remaining officers at Fort Phil Kearny were beginning to gang up on the colonel, labeling him a coward for not taking the fight to the Lakota. Leading the detractors was Captain Fetterman.

Ironically, it was Carrington who came to Fetterman's rescue when the captain rode into a decoy. Fetterman had led some men out of sight of the fort and had been caught in an ambush in which several men were killed. True to form, however, Fetterman criticized Carrington's tactics instead of expressing his gratitude. The Indians who had witnessed Fetterman's ineptness realized that an opportunity lay in a mass decoy if enough warriors could be assembled.

It would be the largest gathering of warriors since the Platte River Bridge raid. Riders went out to the camps of the Cheyenne, Arapaho, and Lakota to organize councils. Too many chiefs, too much bickering, and too many egos to pacify, however, made it almost impossible to organize a combined trap. The elders knew it would take a man with exceptional integrity and combat experience to lead the three tribes in an assault. After much deliberation it was decided that High Back Bone would lead the attack.

Immediately High Back Bone placed Crazy Horse in charge of the decoys.

It would take two weeks for the tribes' warriors to organize themselves, but by the twentieth of December, close to two thousand warriors had assembled over Lodge Trail Ridge on Prairie Dog Creek. The night before the attack, close to three thousand horses were put into motion up Prairie Dog Creek toward Fort Phil Kearny. High Back Bone found Crazy Horse, He Dog, and Lone Bear preparing for battle and pled his case.

"We have to keep the warriors from breaking from the ambush early. I will bring the soldiers, but you must keep the warriors hidden until the signal," he said. All the warriors knew the raids on Julesburg and Platte Bridge had been ruined by younger warriors who had rushed out early, alerting the soldiers to the trap.

"He's sounding more and more like Red Cloud," Lone Bear joked, but He Dog had to agree.

"He's right. Our job will be more restraining the young warriors than fighting," He Dog said. Lone Bear reached across the small lodge for a leather strap and slapped it against his own thigh.

"I guess we fight with horse whips," he said and made the over and under motion of a man whipping his horses. "I'll keep their heads down, or I'll take some ears off." Lone Bear smiled, waving the strap over his head. Crazy Horse smiled; he could count on Lone Bear. There was no braver or loyal man in the Oglala. It was good to know he would be at the battle tomorrow.

Little Hawk, riding his prized blaze-faced horse and leading another, found his brother. The blaze-faced son of the yellow stallion had grown into a top warhorse with Little Hawk's training. Crazy Horse took his brother, who could be brave but reckless, aside. "Little Hawk, tomorrow we have to keep the warriors from breaking. Do you understand what I am saying?" Crazy Horse looked at his brother. "Help Lone Bear contain the warriors. I'm counting on you," he said. Little Hawk nodded and rose to leave but stopped his brother first.

"Take my horse tomorrow," he said. Crazy Horse smiled at Little Hawk and hooked the horse's lead rope over the anchor stake in the lodge.

"Hey . . ." Crazy Horse looked at his brother, who was fiddling with his carbine.

"Don't forget your bullets tomorrow," Crazy Horse said and broke into a broad smile. The hard fact was, most of the Indians would be fighting with bows and arrows. The following day, an elite force of Lakota, Cheyenne, and Arapaho warriors, painted for war and riding the best horseflesh of the northern plains, hid behind the eastern slopes of Lodge Trail Ridge. An elite decoy, representing each of the major tribes, waited outside Fort Phil Kearny. Crazy Horse, He Dog, Black Shield, and Black Leg of the Lakota; Little Wolf, Left Hand, and Big Nose of the Cheyenne; and Eagle Elk and Black Coal of the Arapaho waited in the timber along Piney Creek and watched the fort.

The plan was for an Indian party to attack the daily wood train on Sullivant Hills. Crazy Horse and the decoys would intercept the soldiers who rode out to the rescue, leading them over the ridge to the waiting warriors.

Colonel Carrington looked out on the country surrounding the fort. It was a bright crisp day, but a winter storm was approaching from the north. The wood train had just been sent out, and soon thereafter Indians were seen moving within a few hundred yards of the fort.

"Come out and fight, you sons of bitches!" yelled a voice from the woods. Colonel Carrington ordered one of the howitzers to shell along Piney Creek.

As the loud boom of the cannonade echoed over the ridge, the blood began to rush in a thousand hidden warriors. Grips tightened on bows as the young warriors burned to have a look and began to creep over the ridge. Lone Bear galloped right into the midst of some young warriors to keep them back. His sorrel gelding slipped and fell on the hard, frozen ground and slid into the young warriors, who scattered backwards down the ridge. Without hesitation, Lone Bear got to his feet and drew his bow.

"Let the soldiers pass, or I will kill the coward who breaks," he shouted. Despite his outward rage, Lone Bear smiled. He was surprised someone had not shot an arrow in him yet. He stopped his yelling for a moment and nodded a recognition to a patient older warrior along the Lakota lines. The warrior nodded in support. He recognized Lone Bear's bravery, and he would tell of it after the battle.

Within moments, the sentry on Pilot Hill signaled an attack on the wood train. Colonel Carrington stood on the ramparts with a looking-glass, scanning in the direction of the attack. A general alarm had sounded in the fort, and Carrington called for Captain Powell to lead a relief force out to the woodcutters.

While Captain James Powell was preparing to leave, Captain Fetterman stormed over to the colonel. "Colonel, I am the ranking officer here and request permission to lead the relief force," the captain barked as the bugle's call of "Boots and Saddles" pierced through every tent and building inside the fort. The frozen parade ground was brought to life as teamsters, civilians, and wives walked out of their shelters to watch. Fetterman was the ranking officer, but Powell was Carrington's choice.

The cold wind howled around Sullivant Hills from the north and carried the sound of gunfire from the besieged wagons. Colonel Carrington wavered, then made the biggest mistake of his military career.

"All right, captain, but you are to relieve the wood train and report back to me, and under no circumstances are you to pursue the Indians past Lodge Trail Ridge."

What was working for the Indians was the weather. A cold front was blowing in from the north, dropping the temperature by the minute; the younger warriors were hunkered down shivering in their blankets and showed no sign of breaking the trap early.

Four miles away, Crazy Horse rode into the clearing with Big Nose and watched the soldiers under Captain Fetterman leave the fort. He saw no cannons, a good sign, but half the soldiers were walking, which was a bad sign. The soldiers on horses would ride off and leave the walking soldiers, making it hard to ambush them all.

Captain Fetterman cut over toward Piney Creek to cut off the Indians' retreat. Crazy Horse and Big Nose stood a hundred yards apart and taunted Fetterman's advancing men. Almost simultaneously, the two warriors charged both flanks of Fetterman's column. Soldiers fumbled to dismount and fire their rifles as the infantrymen caught up.

Crazy Horse watched the soldiers aim their rifles and veered his blaze-faced horse—on loan from Little Hawk for the event—to the left; instantly, bullets kicked up chunks of frozen ground in front of him. Big Nose veered in the opposite direction. The soldiers in the middle looked back and forth at the two Indians who sat on their horses, just out of rifle range, taunting them.

"Look at those two bastards," Lieutenant George Grummond said, waiting for the infantry to close up with the mounted soldiers.

James Wheatley, a civilian scout for the fort, rode up for a closer look. "That's about as good a horseflesh as I've seen since I got here." He was half-admiring the Indians' horses and half-looking for his own horse, which had been stolen outside the fort that winter. Wheatley drew a bead on Big Nose with his new Henry rifle, but by the time he was ready to shoot, the Indian had made it over to a grove of trees. While the soldiers were paused, Crazy Horse and Big Nose, in a silent challenge of bravery, started back toward one another across the front of the troops.

The sporadic firing aimed at the two continued until Captain Fetterman ordered the eighty men forward. Had any of the large-caliber bullets struck Crazy Horse, they would have shattered a bone or torn an arm or a leg off. In a casual but defiant act, Crazy Horse dismounted and turned his back on the soldiers who shot around him. He picked up his horse's foot as if it were lame. The blaze-faced horse stood as still as night next to Crazy Horse as bullets whizzed by him. Then Crazy Horse remounted, galloped up the hill, slid to a sudden stop, swung off, and sat on the ground five yards away from his horse.

"Someone shoot that arrogant son of a bitch!" Grummond yelled, and immediately three or four men opened fire on Crazy Horse. Crazy Horse wrapped the horse's tail around his wrist and clucked to the young stallion, which began to pull him slowly up the hill as if the Lakota warrior were wounded.

"There's my scalp to take home," Captain Fredrick Brown said as he spurred Calico, the pony he had borrowed from Carrington's son.

On the other side of Lodge Trail Ridge, a thousand hearts began to race in the gray cold as Big Nose crested the hill.

"Stay down! Wait! This is for all the people; think of your families, not glory or coups. Stay down!" Lone Bear commanded.

The cavalry were the first over the top, led by Lieutenant Grummond, for they had left the infantry behind to struggle up the frozen hill with Captain Fetterman. A cold north wind stung the soldiers' eyes and faces as they topped out Lodge Trail Ridge. Had they taken a good look around, they would have seen activity on the edges of all the distant ridges, but they were concentrating on the decoys.

Lieutenant Grummond heard an eerie sound, like that of dozens of hidden voices, giving orders beneath the cries and taunts of the decoys. He strained his ears, but the wind picked up, drowning out the voices. The decoys stopped halfway down the other side of the ridge and continued their taunt of the soldiers. Worm hurried forward with a spare for Crazy Horse, who quickly mounted and rode on; an aide to Big Nose did the same. Lieutenant Brown charged after Crazy Horse with the cavalrymen as hundreds of hidden warriors lay down on their horses' necks and pinched the muzzles to keep them from whinnying at the soldiers' horses. Brown had boasted that he would take the scalp of Red Cloud before he was transferred to Fort Laramie. It was brave talk for a bald man. When Captain Fetterman reached the top of the ridge with the foot soldiers, the cavalry were a mile down the hill. The captain looked along the top of the ridge and saw that his men were too spread out.

Although impetuous, Fetterman was nevertheless an able commander. He ordered the recall of the cavalry, but that required him to bring the infantry down the slope to support the soldiers on horseback. As the infantry disappeared over the ridge, the hidden warriors behind him galloped into position to close off his retreat.

From his rooftop inside the fort, Colonel Carrington watched the last of Fetterman's infantry disappear toward Lodge Trail Ridge. Colonel Carrington swung his field glasses around and saw the large groups of mounted Indians moving into the tree line behind Fetterman. "Damn it!" He knew the groups were but a fraction of what awaited Fetterman on the other side of the ridge.

"Captain Ten Eyck, take thirty men and an ammunition wagon and go to the relief of Captain Fetterman," Carrington ordered, though it meant there would be fewer soldiers to defend the fort.

Ten Eyck had no doubt of what lay ahead. If there were as many Indians as he thought, his thirty men would not make a difference. After Ten Eyck left the fort, Colonel Carrington ordered the fort's howitzers to be loaded with grapeshot, preparing the fort for a general siege.

If George Grummond could have heard beyond the wind, he would have noticed Fetterman's bugler blowing recall. If he could have seen Pilot Knob, he would have read the signalman's message that the enemy was moving in. As it was, he now realized he had ridden into a huge trap. Lieutenant Grummond rode after Captain Brown, who was oblivious to everything except obtaining an Indian scalp. When Brown and the trailing cavalry closed to within one hundred yards of the decoys, the decoys rode away from each other, then turned suddenly and rode across each other's path. It was the signal the hiding warriors had waited for.

"Up up, for your families!" Lone Bear yelled. Lakota, Cheyenne, and Arapaho war cries erupted. High Back Bone stood on a high spot opposite Lodge

Trail Ridge and waved his robe, which sent hundreds more warriors thundering up the low draws below the soldiers. The sound of hundreds of drumming hooves mixed with the war cries to create a deafening roar.

As Captain Brown reached the bottom of the hill, twenty Indians rose up from the brush and fired arrows directly at him. Calico leapt in the air, striking with his hooves at the arrows stuck in his chest and side. The pony fell to his knees, dumping Brown, who scrambled to his feet and was immediately hit with an arrow. "Leave the horses; kill the soldiers!" High Back Bone shouted as he rode among the warriors. Crazy Horse galloped full speed back up the hill. He swung off his horse, scrambled up a side hill, and fired a round from his Spencer point-blank into the first foot soldier coming down to support the cavalry.

With the help of three soldiers, Grummond threw the wounded Captain Brown on a horse and sent him up the hill. Miraculously, Brown made it through the confusion to Captain Fetterman. Meanwhile, Grummond dismounted his men and fired a volley into the Indians to his front. Cavalry tactics, which dictated that every fourth man stand and hold four horses, were taking their toll on the small force of soldiers. So many arrows were fired from all sides that they began to stick in the animals' backs, causing them to bolt and pull away from the holders. Some arrows missing their mark hit Indian allies on both sides of the ridge. Gunfire from the cavalry below and the infantry above covered the ridge with a layer of thick blue smoke.

"Brave hearts to the front! Come on, now's the time for coups and scalps," He Dog yelled at some young warriors paused on the outskirts firing arrows at the soldiers from a distance.

From a knoll, High Back Bone saw his opportunity to split the infantry and cavalry and galloped toward the fray. He did not have to rush, for Crazy Horse, Lone Bear, and He Dog had seen the same thing. Lone Bear was the first in. He turned the sorrel and charged over a soldier who was leading his horse up the hill. As the soldier rolled over to his hands and knees, a Cheyenne ran up and shot an arrow in him from point-blank range. The sight of such bravery moved the young warriors to follow him into the fray.

Captain William Fetterman, standing on a ridge with fifty men, found himself surrounded by over a thousand warriors. To his front, hundreds of horses were galloping out of hiding on the frozen ground, and he was now taking fire from the Indians who had closed in from the rear. Fetterman led his men to a small knoll toward the top of the ridge and made a stand.

"Form a skirmish line. Keep your spacing!" he yelled from a cluster of rocks on the knoll. His command was now hopelessly split. His only help would come from the fort, and he knew if it did arrive, it would probably come too late. Warriors were pouring in from the four corners. Soldiers were fumbling with paper cartridges and ramrods, frantically loading their Springfield rifles.

"Keep your spacing; load your gun, soldier!" Fetterman shouted at a terrified soldier who crouched, clutching his gun. The remaining soldiers began to huddle together as the mass of warriors crept closer.

American Horse galloped into the group, knocking Fetterman with a war club. Before the captain could rise, the Oglala clubbed him again and cut his throat.

With Fetterman dead, all military protocol collapsed. The wounded Captain Brown watched as warriors rushed in and overran the last group of soldiers. The officer who had been so eager to procure an Indian scalp put his pistol to his head and fired his last round. Within minutes, Fetterman's entire command was dead.

"We killed them all!" Little Hawk yelled, walking through the corpses of Fetterman's men, from which warriors were cutting rings and stripping uniforms. "You have done well with your blaze-faced horse, Little Hawk," Crazy Horse said.

"We got them all; you brought them to us. They'll sing for you at the village. I killed one with my club. There's more on the hill. We can get behind them and cut them off from the fort," Little Hawk shouted and let out a war cry.

Crazy Horse and High Back Bone looked up the hill at Ten Eyck's soldiers, who waited for reinforcements. The cold wind howled over the ridge, taking their breath away.

Captain Ten Eyck, with thirty well-spaced men, crested over the top of Lodge Trail Ridge and looked down. There were wounded and horses all over the field.

"My God," Ten Eyck said to himself. He stood with his men, looking at close to two thousand warriors a half mile down the ridge.

"Sir, have you seen Captain Fetterman?" an orderly asked, looking down into the valley.

"Private, I want you to ride to Colonel Carrington and tell him I need all the available men he can spare, and a howitzer," Ten Eyck ordered.

High Back Bone looked again at the ammunition wagon and the soldiers on the ridge. From where he stood, the wagon looked like a cannon. On the field lay more than fifty dead or wounded Indians.

"Enough for today; there is a storm coming, and we have wounded to tend to. You fought well today," High Back Bone said, looking at Little Hawk. The young warrior replied, "You should have seen Lone Bear; he rode through the soldiers twice, telling us he would kill us if we spoiled the ambush. He kept them back for you, Brother."

Crazy Horse froze and looked at He Dog and High Back Bone; they should have seen Lone Bear by now. Crazy Horse turned his horse and rode back through the crowd of frenzied Indians, looking for his friend. His mind began to race; maybe Lone Bear had gone to scout the soldiers on the hill or was helping with the wounded.

After a search down the eastern slope, he spotted Lone Bear's sorrel horse with the cavalry brand. The animal stood quivering, shot through the neck and flank, blood running from his mouth. Crazy Horse paused, looking at his friend's markings painted on the horse. In a quick motion he drew his knife and cut the throat of the suffering animal, which fell as he walked away.

On the other side of the battle ridge, Crazy Horse spotted two warriors kneeling by a third. He rushed to them, realizing before he reached them that Lone Bear was the wounded one. His friend had but a few short breaths left in him.

"Tell Little Hawk to bring our father," Crazy Horse ordered one of the braves, but before Worm could be found or a travois could be brought, Lone Bear died. Crazy Horse took his blanket off and put it around his friend. High Back Bone walked over with He Dog; no one spoke. Little Hawk broke the silence when he threw himself on the body of his mentor and cried.

As the Indians pulled out in the face of the incoming storm, Captain Ten Eyck descended the far side of Lodge Trail Ridge with his thirty men and began the morbid task of loading the frozen body parts onto the one wagon. The next day Colonel Carrington rode out to bring back what was left. He privately left word that if the fort should fall while he was gone, they were to blow up the powder magazine with the women and children inside to spare them falling into the hands of the warriors. The carnage that greeted Carrington over Lodge Trail Ridge was described in his official report.

> *Eyes torn out and laid on the rocks; noses cut off; ears cut off; chins cut off; teeth chopped out; joints of fingers; brains taken out and placed on rocks with other members of the body; entrails taken out and exposed; hands cut off; feet cut off; arms taken out from the sockets; private parts severed and indecently placed on the person; eyes, ears, mouth, and arms penetrated with spear heads, sticks, and arrows; ribs slashed to separation with knives; skulls severed in every form from chin to crown; muscles of calves, thighs, stomach, back, breast, arms, and cheek taken out; punctures upon every sensitive part of the body even to the soles of the feet and palms of the hands.*[1]

For the next hundred years, the site of the battle would be known as Massacre Hill. As if to cleanse the area of the violence, heavy wet snow fell the night after the battle, followed by plummeting temperatures.

Crazy Horse returned to the high lookout point on the southeast wall of Little Goose Canyon. He had seen the snow owls from the north before the battle—a sure sign that a bad winter was coming. Soon the wind and cold forced Crazy Horse, with the horses and travois that carried Lone Bear, into the shelter of thick pines. He would bury his friend in the same canyon Rattle Blanket Woman was laid to rest in. In his mind he saw Lone Bear smiling at him. He had once told Crazy Horse they would come back here and raise their families.

He sat on the high ridge in the dark night wrapped in a buffalo robe alone in his thoughts. If there was a man who could survive a storm like this, it was Crazy Horse. He could hunt in the side canyons that would hold game seeking shelter from the storm. He could stay here all winter hunting and watch the spring bloom in Little Goose Canyon, but he knew the old in the villages might suffer. There were men who were content to sit in their lodges while the poor among the tribe bordered on starvation. He wouldn't, nor would He Dog, Lone Bear, or Little Hawk. He would bury the best man he had ever known and start back for the village on the Powder and bring in some meat.

When Captain George Dandy received the news of the Fetterman massacre at Fort Laramie, he saddled his horse and rode the frigid 237 miles alone to Fort Reno. From there he traveled on to Fort Phil Kearny with a small escort. Six companies of infantry and two of cavalry followed Captain Dandy north, but the storm stopped them. After ten days, their supplies gave out. The men chopped holes in the ice to water the horses; the mules ate each other's manes and tails.

Arriving at the fort, Captain Dandy found sick, demoralized survivors and starving animals. A third of the soldiers were hospitalized for scurvy, and many other officers and enlisted men were being treated for frostbite. The starved horses and mules were eating their harnesses and the wooden wagon tongues. Dandy ordered the horses back to Fort Laramie, where there was feed, but they never made it: 150 horses either froze or starved to death on the trail.

Colonel Henry Carrington was relieved of command and left the fort with his wife and two young sons and a small escort party as temperatures dropped to forty below zero. When they reached Fort Reno, Surgeon Hines had two frostbitten fingers and several men required amputations of either feet or hands because of frostbite.

By the time he arrived at Platte River Bridge (which had been renamed Fort Caspar), Carrington had managed to accidentally shoot himself in the leg. As if that weren't enough, his horse, Gray Eagle, which had been given to him by the people of Indianapolis during the Civil War, was dying of colic. East Coast newspapers spread the news of the Fetterman massacre, blaming the entire incident on Carrington.

Crazy Horse waited until No Water was in council before visiting Black Buffalo Woman. The two went behind the lodge like they always did, but their visits were not unnoticed in the village. She brought out a blanket and motioned for him to sit, but he remained standing. Crazy Horse wanted this woman more than anything in his life, but he knew unless she left her husband he had no right. Seeing that he would not sit with her, she stood and took his hand.

"People have been worried about you; no one has seen you since the battle with the whites," she said.

"He should have been a chief," he said. She knew he was speaking of Lone Bear, but it was custom not to speak the name of a dead person. She saw his pain, and it pulled her heart that he would come to her. His horse grazed along behind them, pawing through the snow to uncover the tall grass underneath. Finally he sat and let her place her hand on his shoulder, but when her young ones began to call, he took his leave, looking back twice as he returned to the lodge of his parents.

Half of us pulled our shoes off after the fight had started, tied the laces together, one loop to go over our right foot and the shoulder loop to fit on the trigger of the rifle so that if the Indians ever got inside the corral we were going to stand up, and putting the small loop on the trigger, we would place the muzzle of the rifle underneath our chins and blow our heads off before we would be captured by Red Cloud's cut-throat Indians.
—Private Sam Gibson

The following summer a second large Lakota assault on woodcutters outside Fort Phil Kearny ended badly. Once again, impatient warriors broke out and let the soldiers entrench themselves behind wagon boxes[2] stacked in a circle. The soldiers held out against several hundred warriors until a howitzer was brought up from the fort. Crazy Horse managed to route a group of woodcutters from their camp, but the warriors who followed him stopped to loot the camp and left Crazy Horse to chase the fleeing soldiers alone.

Despite that debacle, less than a year later the government called for the abandonment of forts Reno, Phil Kearny, and C. F. Smith, as well as the entire Bozeman Trail. In the brief time the army had moved in to protect the travelers on that trail, five officers, ninety-one enlisted men, and fifty-eight civilians had lost their lives. The army signed a peace treaty with the Lakota, but this success was overshadowed by news that the Oregon Trail had been replaced by a railroad line.

Little Wolf of the Cheyenne had been given Fort Phil Kearny after the military pulled out. Upon reflection, however, he saw the danger in it. Brave Cheyenne warriors—Strong Wind Blowing, Big Nose, and Sun's Road—had died fighting against the fort. So Little Wolf took a torch and went from building to building, setting everything on fire. From a ridge along Piney Creek, he watched the fort go up in flames.

The smoke could be seen as far away as the Wolf Mountains, the Powder River, and the villages on the Tongue. The ashes blowing over to Lake De Smet carried the ghosts of the warriors, soldiers, contractors, and miners.

Once the bell mare had been brought into the Indian herd, she was used to pull a travois. Despite the fact that she had been raised as a domestic horse by the whites, she was homesick for her old range and herd on Otter Creek. She had been guarded with the Oglala herders, but during the brutal winter storm, the herd had been left to their own devices. The first day the herders failed to appear, the bell mare saw her chance. By midday she had traveled well beyond the village despite the deep drifts and frigid temperatures. The herd was hunkered down on Bear Creek, a small tributary to Otter Creek, which ran into Tongue River. The mare survived by sticking to creek bottoms and chewing on tree bark as the snow piled up. It was too deep to paw through and find grass, but by sticking to draws and working her way around drifts, taking frequent rests out of the wind, she found the herd after almost a week. The yellow stallion was dead, and the brown stallion was now a gelding inside the village herd on Tongue River. The remainder of the mares had stayed together on Otter

Creek, being herded by a dominant mare. Her yellow colt had come back to the herd after the brown stallion had been captured. For the rest of the winter, the herd backed up to the winter and tried to survive.

More than three thousand army horses and mules were stolen by the Indians between August 1865 and August 1867. Many of these died in their first winter, but the strong survivors added to the thousands of Indian horses already living in the area. Countless warhorses of both Indians and soldiers had been killed in battles on the Powder River, the Tongue River, and Lodge Trail Ridge. Tales of their heroism would fade over time. The wolves and coyotes would scatter their remains, which would fertilize the buffalo grass and feed generations to come.

10

The ladies clustered in Mrs. Wands's cabin as night drew on, all speechless from absolute stagnation and terror. Then the crunching wagon wheels startled us to our feet. The gates opened. Wagons were slowly driven within, bearing their dead but precious harvest from the field of blood and carrying forty-nine lifeless bodies to the hospital with the heartrendering news, almost tenderly whispered by the soldiers themselves, that "No more were to come in" and that "probably not a man of Fetterman's command survived."

—Frances Grummond

Absaraka, 1870

AS WARRIORS, CRAZY HORSE AND HE DOG WERE GIVEN AS high an honor as existed among the Lakota Sioux. Each was presented with a three-hundred-year-old ceremonial lance, and both were made shirt wearers. He Dog had become a shirt wearer in Red Cloud's band; Crazy Horse was chosen in Man Afraid's band. Whether he liked it or not, Crazy Horse was now one of the top political leaders of his tribe. Man Afraid told Crazy Horse that he was now expected to protect the weak, settle tribal disputes, and put the interest of the tribe before himself. He was to lead by example: if one of his close kin was killed in battle, he must not stop to look, lest he feel the need to retaliate. He must never lose his temper or react to jealous words among fellow tribesmen. He was to feed all who visited his lodge and offer them tobacco.

Man Afraid searched the face of the young man. Crazy Horse was no diplomat; he had never shown an interest in tribal matters or councils, but he had been the most charitable among the Oglala. He had led raids past the Black Hills against the Pawnee, past the Bighorns against the Shoshone, and down on the Oregon Trail against the whites.

During the ceremony, Crazy Horse saw Black Buffalo Woman in the crowd. She had pushed her way to the front, and in a bold move, she approached Crazy Horse with a pair of beaded moccasins.

"These are a gift from the women whose families you have protected," she announced. This caused some mumbling among the Oglala women; they knew only one woman had worked on those moccasins, and she had a husband and children at home.

By 1870, the relationship between whites and Indians was confusing. Whites had lived among the Indians since before Columbus discovered America. White traders had lived among the Oglala long before Lakota moved into Absaraka. John Twiss, for example, an honors graduate of West Point, became an Indian agent, married an Oglala woman, and eventually moved in with the tribe. Bob North had married an Arapaho and fought with the tribes around Fort Phil Kearny.

Frank Grouard was the son of a Mormon missionary and a Polynesian princess. He had run away from home in California and ended up in Montana with the dangerous job of carrying mail on a route that took him through Lakota and Blackfoot territory. Some Lakota, led by Sitting Bull, ambushed the young Grouard during a snowstorm. Sitting Bull mistook Grouard for a Lakota who might have been captured by whites as a boy and gave him the nickname "Grabber," because he had wrestled with a warrior when he was captured.

As a pretend Lakota, Grouard used his knowledge of the mail routes to raid with Sitting Bull's band. He could also read stolen documents and translate them for the Indians. After visiting with some soldiers at an outpost, Grouard led soldiers to arms dealers who were selling guns to the Indians. When Sitting Bull found out, he threatened to kill Grouard, who took safe harbor with Crazy Horse's band of Oglala.

Grouard had gained the respect of Crazy Horse because he was a good shot with a rifle and had provided meat to the village when the buffalo migrated out of the country and the Oglala were hard-pressed for food. Both men appreciated quality horses and possessed the ability to train them.

As payback for allowing him to stay in the Oglala village, Grouard made Crazy Horse a deal on a mare that had descended from the yellow stallion.

11

I have just killed Crazy Horse!

—No Water

Little Goose Canyon, 1870

FOR BLACK BUFFALO WOMAN, THE BEAUTY OF THE SEASON was lost to the passion of her conviction to leave her husband and be with Crazy Horse. She told herself that her father had forced her into a marriage with No Water five years before. In truth, No Water had been a bigger man socially than Crazy Horse when she married him, but now Crazy Horse was one of the most revered warriors in the Lakota nation.

Lakota tradition makes it acceptable for a woman to leave her husband at any time by placing his belongings outside their lodge. It is also acceptable for a man to make an offer for another man's wife with a gift of horses or other property. Black Buffalo Woman and Crazy Horse did neither; they simply left. Arranging for her children to stay with relatives, Black Buffalo Woman accompanied Crazy Horse on a raid against the Crow while No Water was off on a hunt.

Enjoying freedom with the woman he loved for the first time, Crazy Horse was happier than he had ever been. The ride from Goose Creek to Clear Creek below the snowcapped Bighorn Mountains sped by. The couple spent the night on buffalo robes under the bright stars of the north, basking in each other's company.

He had spent years thinking of her and what her body would look and feel like, and now she was there.

"I never wanted to marry No Water, I swear . . ." Black Buffalo Woman tried to explain, but Crazy Horse put a finger to her lips.

"It doesn't matter now; you're here," he said.

"I'll never leave you again, I swear."

Crazy Horse let her brush his long sandy brown hair, and he then took her and held her. He had assumed Black Buffalo Woman had taken care of all the details of her marriage, but the fact was he didn't care as long as she was there with him. As it was, No Water returned home and found his wife and children gone. He went from lodge to lodge, saddled a captured army mule and, with a small band of warriors, rode in pursuit of Crazy Horse and Black Buffalo Woman.

Crazy Horse awakened with Black Buffalo Woman at his side, and the two lingered into the morning before resuming their ride. He would take her to another Oglala camp on Powder River and lead a raid.

On Powder River, Crazy Horse found the Oglala camp of Little Big Man. Unaware that No Water had just arrived at the village, the couple was basking in the glow of the fire in the lodge of a friend when No Water entered the lodge brandishing a pistol. "My friend, I have come," he said.

When Crazy Horse saw No Water, he pulled his knife, but Little Big Man grabbed him to prevent bloodshed in his lodge. While Little Big Man had hold of Crazy Horse, No Water shot Crazy Horse in the face with a pistol at point-blank range. The blast drove Crazy Horse to the ground. Before he lost consciousness, he watched the puddle of blood form around his face and heard Black Buffalo Woman's scream. No Water fled into the night with his warriors. "I have just killed Crazy Horse!" he yelled.

There was mass pandemonium in the camp. Black Buffalo Woman crawled out the back of the lodge, leaving Crazy Horse to lie where he fell. The warriors with Crazy Horse searched for No Water, but they found only his mule, which they killed. No Water fled to the camp of his brother, Black Twin, who made it known that if there were any trouble, he would fight with his brother. Black Buffalo Woman went to relatives and begged for protection.

A general civil war inside the Oglala tribe was ready to break out before elder tribesmen met to prevent further bloodshed. He Dog, a relative of No Water's and a lifelong friend to Crazy Horse, sat in endless council with the elders on behalf of his friend.

The bullet that struck Crazy Horse had entered just below one side of his nose and exited from the base of his skull. Crazy Horse's parents traveled to the Powder River village to help with his convalescence.

As he regained consciousness, his emotional wound far outweighed his physical one. For the second time in his life he had lost the only woman he ever loved, and this time he knew it must be for good. Beyond that, he knew that he had dishonored his position as a shirt wearer.

The elders arranged for No Water to give his three best horses to Crazy Horse to atone for the shooting. It was decided that Black Buffalo Woman would be taken to the lodge of a third party and returned to No Water. Because of Crazy Horse's adultery, he could no longer be a shirt wearer or a lance bearer. His ceremonial shirt, pipe, and lance were taken back, stripping him of his status as war chief.

As part of the agreement, Crazy Horse insisted that Black Buffalo Woman not be punished. None of it mattered now; a light had gone out in his heart. While Crazy Horse was convalescing, High Back Bone visited, bearing tragic news.

"Little Hawk has been killed on the other side of the mountains. He was leading a raid on the Shoshone."

Meadowlark and Rain began to wail. Crazy Horse, still weak from his wound, stood up on wobbly legs, wrapped a robe around himself, and slowly made his way to the edge of the camp. He knew Little Hawk's propensity to be reckless, but he felt responsible. If he had not run off with Black Buffalo Woman, he would have been with his brother in battle.

Crazy Horse avoided looking at his face for several weeks after the shooting. Once, while passing along the shore of Lake De Smet, he gazed at the water's surface, and his heart sank. The left side of his upper lip and mouth had healed in an ugly scar, giving his face a drawn, puckered look.

In the fall, High Back Bone and Crazy Horse led a raid on the Shoshone over the Bighorns to avenge the death of Little Hawk. The two Lakota spotted a group of thirty enemy warriors, but Crazy Horse was apprehensive. He and High Back Bone and their small raiding party were greatly outnumbered, and almost all the Shoshone had guns. The Lakota had less than a half dozen.

A heavy rain had fallen all morning long, turning the soil to a mushy gumbo that was almost impossible to traverse on horses. Crazy Horse called Good Weasel over. "Go to High Back Bone and tell him the ground is bad for fighting. We need to call this off," he said.

High Back Bone came galloping over in a tirade. "This is the second time you have called off a raid here. Think of our reputations with the warriors who follow us," he said.

"Look at our men," argued Crazy Horse. "We have four guns among our twelve warriors. The Shoshone have thirty men, all with rifles. If we fight over this ground, our horses will break down and they'll finish us off to the man."

"Do what you like; I'm fighting," High Back Bone said and rode back to the warriors. Crazy Horse resented being goaded into fighting a one-sided battle, but despite his reservations, he lined his men up for the charge.

The plan was to split up into two groups—one under High Back Bone and one under Crazy Horse—and charge from different directions. In less than five minutes, it became a rout. The Lakota horses sunk into the thick mud over their ankles. High Back Bone rode his lathered horse over to Crazy Horse. "We're up against it now," he said.

"We were up against it from the beginning," Crazy Horse said, noticing that High Back Bone's horse had bullet wounds. The two men reloaded their guns, split up, and charged again to cover their warriors' retreat. It was futile; the Shoshone now directed their fire on the two men, who were forced to turn toward the small party of retreating Lakota. Across the field, Crazy Horse saw High Back Bone's horse falter and drop. More than ten enemy warriors were shooting at Crazy Horse, and when he looked back, he saw a dozen Shoshone on High Back Bone, hacking him to pieces. At that moment a bullet tore away part of Crazy Horse's arm.

"Come on!" Good Weasel said. Crazy Horse swung off his horse, knelt, and shot a Shoshone who was leading a charge toward them. There was no time to reload; he swung back up on his horse and galloped for his warriors, who were in full flight to the east. They barely had time to switch to fresh horses before the Shoshone were on them. The chase lasted for better than fifteen miles.

When the Lakota made camp, Crazy Horse took the first watch to the west. He wanted to be alone. High Back Bone had given Crazy Horse his first horse and was as much a father to him as Worm. He was one of the great Lakota war leaders of all time, and yet he had let the young warriors shame him into a fight he knew he could not win. Crazy Horse wondered how he would die; his dream that he was killed by a long knife was still in his mind.

His face was scarred. He had lost his best friend, his brother, and his mentor. The only woman he had ever loved had left him—twice. It was on a buffalo hunt north of the Yellowstone River that Crazy Horse finally let his frustrations out. Several bands of Lakota had come together for a tribal hunt. He had not seen No Water since the man had shot him in the face. When Crazy Horse spotted him in the distance, a rage rose up in him. Once No Water spotted Crazy Horse, he took flight on a horse toward the Yellowstone, with Crazy Horse in hot pursuit. In desperation, No Water jumped his horse into the Yellowstone and swam to the other side. Crazy Horse, cooling somewhat, pulled up and watched him swim away.

There was much deliberation by the elders of what to do about Crazy Horse after the trouble with Black Buffalo Woman and No Water. It was feared that Crazy Horse might go to war over Black Buffalo Woman. Someone mentioned that if they arranged a marriage with another Oglala woman, it might settle him down. Black Shawl, like Crazy Horse, had never married despite being almost thirty winters. The tribal elders approached both Black Shawl and Crazy Horse about a marriage arrangement—or at least cohabitation in one lodge.

Crazy Horse was well aware of the damage he had done in the tribe and agreed to go along with the arrangement. Black Shawl also accepted the arrangement as a matter of convenience. Crazy Horse was known to be one of the better hunters of the tribe; her lodge would never want for meat. They soon shared both a companionship and a compassion for one another. Less than a year after their marriage, Black Shawl gave birth to a baby girl whom they named They Are Afraid of Her. For the first time in his life, Crazy Horse experienced domestic contentment. He began to stay around the lodge and hunted more than he raided so he could be with his wife and daughter. He held his daughter, played with her, and took her for long rides around the village.

In 1870, a delegation of chiefs representing close to thirty groups within the Lakota tribe had accepted an invitation to see the Great Father in Washington. During their visit they were given the specifics of the Treaty of 1868, which (unbeknownst to them) had called for the tribe to relocate to the east. Trade was banned with the Indians near Fort Laramie. Military demonstrations near Washington were staged for the chiefs to intimidate them. One chief was so despondent that he tried to kill himself in his hotel room rather than return west and tell his people what was being done.

Red Cloud and Spotted Tail were in such a row over who was to act as the main chief of the Lakota Sioux, they had to be locked in a room by their interpreters lest they make a mockery of the entire delegation. Spotted Tail gave in and was rewarded with a gift of horses to his delegation from the whites. Red Cloud found himself in the humiliating position of riding around in a carriage.

In Absaraka, the whites were again probing. In 1872, the government sent Major E. M. Baker with four hundred soldiers to survey the Yellowstone River for a new railroad. The Northern Pacific, if completed, would finish off the wilderness to the north. A group of Oglala, Miniconjou, and Cheyenne attacked the soldiers northeast of where the Tongue River runs into the Yellowstone. Crazy Horse tried to organize a decoy, but there was too much dissention among the various tribal leaders, and the warriors were out to steal horses for themselves. To show his bravery, Sitting Bull walked out onto the prairie just inside the soldiers' rifle range. There he sat down and smoked a pipe, challenging any warriors to do the same. White Bull and a few Cheyenne joined him but did some fast smoking as bullets whizzed by.

Crazy Horse, sitting on his pinto, saw this as a bravery challenge between himself and Sitting Bull. He challenged White Bull to make a run in front of the soldiers in an effort to draw them out from their lines. As the gathered warriors watched, Crazy Horse and White Bull galloped around the entire front line. Most of the soldiers took a shot at the two, but neither was hit. Crazy Horse's warhorse, however, was dropped at the end of the ride. Crazy Horse rolled to his feet, walked over to his horse, and casually removed his war bridle as bullets whizzed by. He Dog rode out and pulled him up behind him.

"It's good you weren't riding your good bay mare," He Dog said.

"They wouldn't have been able to hit her," Crazy Horse said.

The following summer, Colonel David Stanley led a second railroad survey expedition. Colonel George Custer and fourteen hundred men accompanied Stanley. Custer had made a name for himself fighting under General Phil Sheridan in the Civil War. Custer's success came under competent commanders: Gregg at Gettysburg, Torbert at Cedarville, Merritt at Winchester, Sheridan at Yellow Tavern, and Crook at Sayers Creek. Custer had learned the art of flamboyance as an aide to both Phil Kearny and George McClellan. Custer wore his blonde hair down to his shoulders, and he had dark velvet suits sewn with broad yellow stitching, giving him the appearance of Little Boy Blue.

After he achieved the brevet rank of general in his early twenties, the press fell in love with this boy general and the boy ate it up. In an army whose generals were full of mostly dull Midwesterners by the end of the war, Custer gave journalists something to write about. To say the least, his appearance and behavior did not endear him to many of his contemporaries.

Custer was a bold fighter, but he had few other leadership qualities. He had come along at a time in the war when casualties were irrelevant to the Union, which masked his shortcomings as a commander. When turned loose on his own, Custer had proven inept. At Trevillian Station, he almost lost his entire command because he failed to reconnoiter the Confederates' force. At the Washita River, Custer charged a village of Cheyenne, but he was forced to retreat when Indian reinforcements beat him back. With eighteen of his men still trapped in the village, Custer fled, leaving them to fight to the death. He was court-martialed and suspended from service for abandoning his troops in the field.

At his worst, Custer was an idiot. He had on three occasions accidentally shot his own horse dead while hunting. One such incident in Indian country left him alone and on foot, away from his men. On a hunting excursion, Custer barely missed shooting General Sheridan because he failed to watch where he was going while chasing a buffalo. In a grand review of the Army of the Potomac, Custer had the poor judgment to ride a horse too hot for him to handle and got run away with in front of his men and the president, losing his hat in the stampede.

> *The Indian pony has no harnessing to load him down. If he is too tired, his master will jump on a fresh (mount) chosen from among those that usually accompany the war parties and will let him continue the trip unburdened. If one of our horses is exhausted, we have an unmounted horseman. In brief, the movement of Indian horsemen is lighter, swifter, and longer range than that of our cavalry, which means that they always get away from us. Certainly General Custer is a good Cavalry officer, brave, energetic, intelligent. What has he done against the Indians? Nothing. Vainly he exhausted men and horses, pursuing the Indians without making contact with them, and his best reports amount to four or five men killed to one of the enemy.*
> *—Phillipe Regis de Trobriand*

One thing Custer did have was a good understanding of horseflesh. He rode several thoroughbreds; his favorite, Vic, won seven races in Saratoga Springs, New York. Vic was unused to the harsh weather of the plains, however, and on occasion, Custer had to bring the shivering animal into his tent to warm him.

As an Indian fighter, he had no more success than any of the other men on the plains at the time. This did not stop him from writing a book on his favorite subject: himself. One thing he did have experience in was chasing Indians. He had chased Indians all over Kansas and Texas—and had very rarely caught one.

Like his predecessors Lieutenant John Grattan and Captain William Fetterman, Custer had a poor understanding of the difference between fort loafers and the wild Indians who lived to the north. Not far from where Major E. M. Baker had fought the year before, Crazy Horse lured Custer into a decoy on the banks of the Yellowstone. Unable to withstand the temptation, Custer made a dash for the decoying warrior with his pistol drawn.

Despite Vic's speed, Custer found he was not closing ground; the thoroughbred was no match for Crazy Horse's bay mare. In an instant, Custer recognized the trap. Turning back toward his men, Custer spurred Vic just ahead of the hundred warriors in pursuit. Crazy Horse turned to see the warriors had sprung the trap early. Custer and his small force were saved by Colonel Stanley, who shelled the warriors with artillery fire.

In a series of skirmishes up the Yellowstone River, the warriors delayed the soldiers long enough to allow the Lakota to move their village to the south side of the river. It was imperative to find a good crossing site because bogs and quicksand could cause horses to become mired and injure themselves. Lodges were bundled tight with clothes and other articles so they floated when placed in the water. The children and elderly were helped onto these makeshift rafts that the horses pulled while swimming across to the opposite shore. Lodge poles were also floated across in this manner.

With the soldiers pressing, Crazy Horse rode back to help Worm and his stepmothers cross the river. Black Shawl already had their lodge packed tight, and Frank Grouard, who lived with Crazy Horse's band, was helping on the riverbank.

When They Are Afraid of Her caught sight of Crazy Horse, she began to pull at her mother. "Papa!" she yelled and held out her arms for him to take her up on his horse.

Crazy Horse smiled and lifted her up on his horse and rode down into the Yellowstone until they were swimming to the other bank.

"Cool water, baby," he said, cradling his daughter in his arms, holding on to his horse's mane as he swam.

"Coo wauta," They Are Afraid of Her tried to repeat, as they glided across the Yellowstone. On the opposite bank he handed They Are Afraid of Her to Black Shawl. As he went to ride off, They Are Afraid of Her began to cry.

She yelled after her father, who pulled up and turned his horse back. With over twenty anxious warriors waiting next to him and hundreds waiting to engage the whites on the far bank, he reached down and pulled his daughter up and gave her a kiss.

"I'll be back, I promise," he said and put her back down before galloping away, his daughter's cry ringing in his ears. Crazy Horse now turned and led an attack on the soldiers' right flank, but lacking guns and ammunition, the warriors gave way to a withering fire. But Custer's men could not figure out how to cross the Yellowstone, whereas the Indians had crossed their horses with ease.

On the bank of the Yellowstone where he stood, Frank Grouard strained his ears to listen; he heard music. He was pinned down behind a tree as bullets from Custer's soldiers chipped away at the bark. The military band with Custer was playing "Garry Owen." The song brought Grouard back to the time he had lived among the whites.

Soon thereafter word came to Custer that the Northern Pacific survey had been called off. Relaxing for the first time in weeks, the soldiers bathed under Pompey's Pillar in the Yellowstone River. Crazy Horse's warriors couldn't resist taking potshots at the naked soldiers in a parting note of farewell.

12

They . . . had Spencer and Winchester and other breech-loaders, but probably the majority of them had muzzle-loading rifles and many revolvers. Many of them had bows and arrows in addition to their firearms. Most of them were well mounted—much better than we were.

—Addison Quivey

Bozeman, 1874

FEWER THAN SIX MONTHS AFTER COLONEL DAVID STANLEY left the area, another deadly force of white fighters was organizing in Bozeman, Montana. Although the lands of Absaraka were off-limits to whites under the terms of the Treaty of 1868, 150 frontiersmen nevertheless left Bozeman in February headed for the Wolf Mountains. It seems that a group of entrepreneurs spread lies about a gold strike in order to start a war with the Indians. The gold prospectors had no misgivings: they were headed into a war zone and so were armed to the teeth with two cannons and the best rifles money could buy. Pieces of cut-up mule shoes were soldered inside oyster cans for "grapeshot" to use in an old Napoleon cannon, and 150 artillery shells were stored for use in a howitzer "borrowed" from Fort Ellis. Forty thousand rounds of ammunition were loaded into one of the twenty-two wagons.

Sprinkled among the men were veterans who had fought at Fort Phil Kearny and along the Bozeman Trail. Their first order of business was to protect the 250-plus horses and mules used by the expedition. The men sent off fifty of their party to try to stampede their own horses in a type of war game before getting too deep into Indian country. This trained the horses at the first sound of gunfire or sign of trouble to run for the corralled wagons. The second thing the group did was to camp on large mesas that could be defended against attack. By the time the expedition was into Lakota and Cheyenne country, the men and horses could quickly assume a defensive position.

The first confrontation came on Rosebud Creek, where some Lakota lured Henry Bostwick, who was herding the horses, over for a talk. Jack Bean, who was guarding a second horse herd, heard gunshots. He galloped over to see Bostwick riding for his life, with Indians galloping alongside, swinging war clubs at him. Bean jumped from his horse, aimed his .44/90/500 Sharps rifle with a scope, and fired at the Indian next to Bostwick. The slug practically tore the arm off the Indian, and as a result, the warriors pulled back. Bean turned and with another picket brought the horses safely to the corral. The men braced themselves for the attack they knew was coming. They made camp on a shelf above the Rosebud and dug foxholes. The cannons were brought up and readied, and logs were placed on dirt mounds in front of the rifle pits. The best horses were placed inside the corral, while the reserves were tied to the outside of the wagons.

Just after midnight, numerous Indians were spotted far in the distance, moving toward the wagons. Soon the booming voice of an Indian broke the silence as he gave a lengthy speech in Lakota. The speech ended, and silence fell once again, followed by the tinkle of a bell. At that signal, the Indians stood and fired. A deafening explosion of guns in the night sent fire and lead from the Lakota guns toward the men in their rifle pits. A loud chorus of howling war cries from hundreds of Indians followed. The miners were under strict orders not to engage or return fire.

After several successive volleys, with no return fire, the Lakota Sioux became careless in exposing themselves. The Napoleon cannon double-loaded with grapeshot was leveled and aimed where the Indian firing had been heaviest. Another speech was given, but when the Lakota rang the bell for the warriors to stand to fire, the miners cut loose with the cannon. The percussion of the blast rocked the earth as chunks of metal ripped through the surprised warriors. Within seconds another blast ripped through a nearby coulee where Indian snipers had preyed on the miners' horses.

Almost immediately twenty-five miners charged over the ridge, surprising some warriors in a close hand-to-hand fight. Nine Indians were killed, and eight guns and twenty-three horses were captured. As the warriors withdrew to a hill almost a mile away, twenty miners—Indian scalps tied to the ends of their rifles—mounted the captured horses, let out their own war cries, and motioned to the Indians to come down and fight. It was an attempt to "out Indian" the warriors.

Later that day the miners moved out, leaving behind strychnine-laced biscuits and pemmican in their abandoned camps to poison the Indians. In addition, the men cut up pieces of dynamite and placed them in rifle shells, which would explode in the warriors' faces if they tried to use them. A grave was booby-trapped with an artillery shell that would detonate should the warriors dig it up.

High Bear was the first to find the grave the next day. When he began to dig, he found a wire. He jerked it and was thrown thirty feet by the explosion, along with Red Hawk and others. Flying pieces of metal left dead, dazed, and wounded scattered around the grave.

The next raid occurred at Lodge Grass Creek, where the 150 frontiersmen faced an estimated fourteen hundred Lakota and Cheyenne. The battle raged on for five hours: the miners did not lose a single man, but they had fired their last shell from the howitzer. The only ammunition left were a few dozen "mule shoe" rounds for the Napoleon cannon. Even the most optimistic of the adventuresome young miners knew their time was limited if they did not get out.

The miners decided to abandon their plan to mine the Wolf Mountains, but not without a parting shot. Jack Bean, one of the best riflemen in the outfit, drew a bead on a warrior with his Sharps rifle and dropped him from a mile away. It was a grim reminder of the whites' killing power. If any of the Indians in Absaraka had been peaceful, the miners cured them of that.

The miners' invasion had been the third in three years by whites into Absaraka, which was guaranteed to the Indians in the Treaty of 1868.

Crazy Horse now gave his elk teeth to Black Shawl, who cooked him good meals and accepted his family as her own. The love of his family slowly healed the loss of High Back Bone, Little Hawk, Black Buffalo Woman, and Lone Bear. Crazy Horse took rides with They Are Afraid of Her riding in front of him and showed her different animals of the grasslands and imitated the songs of the various birds. He was concerned, however, when They Are Afraid of Her developed a cough, as had Black Shawl, and her energy began to wane.

It was with some trepidation that he left on a raid against the Crow. He instructed Good Weasel to move the village on the Little Bighorn River back east to the Powder River the next day, where they would be safer from Crow retaliation. Although Crazy Horse was uneasy about the upcoming raid, he kept it to himself. He took great caution when they came upon a Crow village across the Bighorn River, but the fight was a success, yielding both scalps and horses. On the ride back to Powder River, he began to relax.

The third night on the journey back, Crazy Horse had a dream in which he saw Meadowlark crying. He woke and went to his father, who had accompanied him on the raid. "Father, I am going ahead to the village on Powder River. I feel something bad has happened. If there is trouble, I will send for help."

As Crazy Horse approached his village, he saw one of the herders gallop toward the lodges. It was the custom of a war party to announce its return after a successful raid, and the village would turn out and cheer the victors. Crazy Horse said a prayer of thanks, but before he could ride off to hunt, he saw He Dog gallop out to meet him. Crazy Horse brightened, but his friend's face told him something was wrong. He kicked his horse up to meet him. "Is it Meadowlark?" he asked, but He Dog shook his head no.

"It is your daughter. She became sick not long after you left. She died between the Little Bighorn and the Rosebud." Crazy Horse immediately turned and started to lope off to the west, but He Dog stopped him. "Wait! You'll need fresh horses and someone to show you where she is. I was not there . . . And you need to look in on Black Shawl. She has the cough, but it was the other sickness that took your daughter."[1]

Crazy Horse turned his horses out with the village herd and walked the last hundred yards to the village. Meadowlark met him with tears in her eyes. "We did all we could." She composed herself enough to point to a friend's teepee. "She is there." When Crazy Horse entered the lodge, the women tending Black Shawl left the couple. Black Shawl had cut her arms in mourning and was in a daze of grief and sorrow. Crazy Horse held her until Meadowlark and her sister arrived with food in the morning.

When the war party arrived, there was no wild whooping that usually accompanied a successful raid. Out of respect for Crazy Horse, the only sounds were wails of sorrow. The next evening Crazy Horse went and found Frank Grouard, who had been in the village when They Are Afraid of Her died. "Can you lead me to where my daughter is buried?" he asked Grouard. Although Crazy Horse was asking him to ride back across Crow country, Grouard did not hesitate to say yes to the man who had once saved his life.

The two men rode into enemy country, and on the second day, Grouard pulled his horse up and pointed to a scaffold that held the toys and trinkets of Crazy Horse's daughter.

"Find yourself a camping spot. I'll be along," Crazy Horse said, giving his horse to Grouard. Then the grief-stricken father climbed up on the scaffold and fasted for three days. Early on the fourth morning he awoke Grouard, and together they rode back to the village on the Powder River in silence.

The Indians living in or around the Bighorn Valley saw that their world was coming to an end. The land that the Comanche, Kiowa, Shoshone, and Crow had been pushed out of by the Lakota and Cheyenne was now about to be taken over by the whites.

By 1875, the Oregon Trail had been replaced by the Union Pacific railroad, which thousands of whites traveled along. Trains bearing sportsmen looking to shoot buffalo would stop at the sight of a herd, and its occupants would blast away from inside the cars. Almost fifty years prior, Sir St. George Gore, equipped with a private chef, gun bearers, and Jim Bridger as a guide, killed over four thousand buffalo, five hundred bear, fifteen hundred elk, and two thousand deer. Gore slept late, drank expensive wine, and rode through Absaraka like the Irish ass that he was. His trip was officially terminated when a band of Lakota captured his party, took his horses, and forced him to walk naked off the American Plains forever.

Wasteful slaughter was not limited to whites, however; fur traders had used tribes whenever possible to procure buffalo robes for them. As far back as 1832, Indians slaughtered buffalo for their tongues, which were salted and shipped down the Missouri in barrels. The hunters only received whiskey for their trouble.

Other industrious Indians used a natural buffalo herding method in order to harvest robes. When Lieutenant G. K. Warren led an expedition west of the Black Hills years before, he was stopped by a band of Lakota led by Bear's Rib. The chief told the officer they were holding buffalo between the Black Hills and the Bighorn Mountains until the cold weather turned the buffalo fur into a soft thick texture, making the hide from the animal a more valuable commodity called a robe. If Warren's soldiers went on, it might spook the herd. As a matter of courtesy, the lieutenant backtracked and circled northeast of the Black Hills so as not to disturb the Lakota's food and clothing supply. It was an act of respect between the U.S. Army and the Indians rarely expounded on by the press.

By 1875 the buffalo herds were numbered. Buffalo, unlike cattle, reproduced only every other year, so the herds that normally migrated into the Bighorn Valley were becoming spotty. The Union Pacific had split the great mass of Plains buffalo into northern and southern herds, and encroachment by the whites was shrinking the habitat of both the buffalo and the Plains Indians.

California was now a state, and Idaho and Montana sported large towns. Cheyenne on the rail line to the south were growing by the day, and plans were being formulated to take the Black Hills, even though that land and the Bighorn Valley had been deeded to the Indians. This time the government needed another way to get an Indian war started without sending troops out, so Colonel George Custer went into the Black Hills with more than a thousand men and newspaper reporters to survey the country for minerals. Custer wrote exaggerated reports of gold and wonderful farmland in the territory the white men were not allowed to trespass. Such reports had the desired effect: civilians flocked to the area, and the government made mock attempts to stop them. Spotted Tail and Red Cloud traveled to Washington to complain, but President Grant told them there was no way to keep the civilians out. He advised the chiefs to sell the Black Hills for as much as they could get.

The elders, still resisting life on an agency, elected Crazy Horse and Sitting Bull as dual war chiefs of all the Lakota Sioux. The whites had recently hazed Sitting Bull's band south of the Yellowstone. As a result, Frank Grouard moved to Red Cloud's agency to take a job as emissary between the whites and the Lakota living in the wild. He knew it would be but a matter of time before Sitting Bull or one of his Hunkpapa killed him if he remained with the Lakota.

One of Grouard's first jobs was to travel into the Bighorn Valley with one hundred agency Indians to convince the wild Indians to come and discuss a treaty for selling the Black Hills. Grouard found a large village of Sitting Bull's Hunkpapa and Crazy Horse's Oglala located on Tongue River.[2] Sitting Bull said he would fight the whites to the death rather than come into the agency, and any Indians interested in selling the Black Hills were robbing their children. Crazy Horse sent his uncle as his emissary to say that Crazy Horse would not talk to the whites. If any in his band wanted to listen to the discussions, however, he could go.

Sitting Bull planned to respond to the whites' request by killing Grouard and the agency Indians with him. When rumor of the trap spread around the camp, Crazy Horse came to Grouard's defense. "When a man walks into our camp, friend or enemy, we hear him, feed him, and smoke with him. Any man fighting them will have to fight me," he said. It was the second time Crazy Horse had saved Grouard. To play it safe, he and the agency Indians broke camp a day early with their scalps intact.

A thousand Indians—with their forty thousand horses standing by—were present near Red Cloud Agency. As with the Treaty of 1851, there was much dissention among the tribes.

General Alfred Terry, a Yale law school graduate, was a commissioner at the council. With him was a small guard of soldiers. Young Man Afraid was there with a contingency of agency warriors to protect the commissioners.

In the middle of the proceedings, seven thousand hostile warriors galloped in and surrounded the assembly. Little Big Man rode in dressed for war, and he waved a Winchester at the commissioners, saying he was there to kill the white men who were trying to take his land. Although Young Man Afraid wrestled the gun from Little Big Man's hand, the warriors surrounding the council nevertheless started to run their horses in short sprints—a sign they were preparing for battle. Captain James Egan pushed his way toward General Terry to let him know they were totally surrounded. Louis Richard, an interpreter, told Terry they were all dead if the shooting started.

The site of seven thousand armed mounted warriors appearing out of nowhere in a coordinated move must have made a sobering impression on General Terry.

Terry knew it would take more than three thousand well-armed men with cannons to confront a force like the one he was facing. The Cheyenne and Lakota warriors in the area were the best horse soldiers in the world; they would not give up until they were whipped, and whipped good. If pushed, these men would die hard; and the United States government was about to initiate a huge push.

More than half of the Lakota were now living, at least part-time, on the reservations, but a considerable force of Indians still lived in the wild in Absaraka. There was no sign that they intended to relocated to the agencies. The cost over the previous seven years to contain the Indians had reached $13 million. Grant's advisers, some of whom were his old lieutenants from the Civil War, felt it was time once again to exercise military force. As late as November 1875, the government gave the remaining Lakota in the wild sixty days to go into the agencies, or the army would forcibly take them in.

13

I hope that good results may be obtained by the troops in the field but am not at all sanguine . . . We might as well settle the Sioux question now; it will be better for all concerned.

—General Phil Sheridan in a telegram to General William T. Sherman, May 29, 1876

THE FINAL MILITARY EXPEDITION INTO ABSARAKA WOULD end the first horse culture of the last free-roaming horsemen. In less than six months' time, more than five thousand soldiers would comb the area. General Alfred Terry and General George Crook would send close to three thousand men to move the remaining tribes to the agencies. Close to five thousand army horses and mules accompanied the expedition.

While Terry and Crook were experienced Civil War veterans, they were leading the most inexperienced soldiers ever to enter the country. Most were raw recruits and bad riders who had never seen an Indian before. The skeletons of dead horses all along the old Bozeman Trail reminded them it was a deadly country. Names like Sitting Bull and Crazy Horse had become legendary around the soldiers' campfires. Though Sitting Bull was known around the frontier forts, few whites had ever seen Crazy Horse.

His image was built on the soldiers' frightened imagination. Sitting Bull, on the other hand, had for years frequented the forts on the upper Missouri.

He is not much worried by the commissioners sent by the government to make peace. His business, he says, is to kill whites, and he will kill them as long as he and his band last. He boasts that war is more profitable to him than peace; that it brings him arms, ammunition, clothing, and especially great numbers of horses and mules.
—General Phillipe Regis de Trobriand

March 3, 1876

General Crook planned to launch a winter campaign from Fort Fetterman, which had been built not far from the rail line on the old Oregon Trail. His guides were Frank Grouard, Baptiste "Big Bat" Pourier, and Louis Reshaw.

As Frank Grouard led General Crook's men out of Fort Fetterman in a cold spring blizzard, he had mixed feelings. He had friends in the villages, but he felt if he weren't leading the soldiers, it would be someone else. By the time Crook got to the burned remains of Fort Reno on Powder River, a picket had already been killed and two-thirds of the command's cattle were stolen.

With temperatures dropping to forty below zero, the soldiers walked for ten days and led their horses to keep their feet from freezing. On Hanging Woman Creek, Grouard hit an Indian trail headed for Powder River. The command marched all night as Grouard crept forward, following the tracks of Indian horses in the snow.

He Dog was welcomed by his old friend and given a meal. After supper, Crazy Horse took a pipe, loaded it with tobacco, and tamped the mixture exactly twelve times before he lit the bowl and offered it to his friend. He Dog took the pipe and smoked. "The soldiers are coming back," he said.

"I heard." Crazy Horse's eyes lit up. "They don't do so well in this country."

He Dog did not return his friend's smile. "Too many have died," he offered, pausing to choose the right words. "I am thinking of taking my family into an agency." There was no need for He Dog to get approval from Crazy Horse, but he had come out of respect for his friend.

He Dog wanted to stay and fight, but he did not want to expose his family to attacks by soldiers. Before he could think of any more to say, Crazy Horse put his hand on his friend's shoulder. "I can use a good man I trust at the agency. Teach that boy of yours to be as good a warrior as his father, then send him to me. We'll run the Crow, the Shoshone, and the whites out for good," Crazy Horse said and smiled.

He Dog only nodded as he stood to leave; words were stuck in his throat. Crazy Horse followed and unhooked his spotted warhorse from the lodge anchor peg. "You may run into trouble; take my horse." He handed He Dog the lead rope. He Dog shook his head no and turned, but Crazy Horse again pushed the rope toward him. "Go on; I have the bay mare," he said. He Dog rode away, torn between loyalty for his friend and protecting his family.

Of the 15,000 Indians living in the Powder River Region, a third lived on the agencies, among them Red Cloud and Spotted Tail, both of whom had been on an agency for over five winters. A third of the Indians lived on the agencies in the winter and in the wild in the summer, and the final third were wild, the "high-toned sons of the wild."

From the bluffs above Powder River, Frank Grouard could hear the bells tied around the horses' necks. The Indian village below was covered in a fog that rose from the river in the pale light before sunrise. He immediately sent a rider back for the soldiers. When a nervous Colonel Reynolds arrived, he sought Grouard's counsel but was indecisive; he suspected Grouard was a spy for the Indians, and he feared an ambush.

"There's your Indians, Colonel. Crazy Horse is down there. I saw his spotted horse in the village," Grouard whispered, looking down through the haze. Grouard watched as Captain Egan's cavalrymen lined up for a charge through the sleeping village. Grouard felt a pang of guilt: Crazy Horse had saved his life twice; the least he could do was give the man a fair chance to defend himself. In a moment of calm before the charge, Grouard called out to the sleeping village.

"Tasunka Witko! You wanted to fight the soldiers; come on out, there's plenty out here." He paused and then raised his voice. "Go for the rocks to the north; it's your only chance!"

He Dog stirred in his buffalo robes as Egan's cavalry thundered into the village. A Cheyenne boy herding horses found himself directly between the soldiers and the village. Despite his predicament, the young herder screamed a warning to the village.

He Dog jumped up and grabbed his gun. Running out in the bitter cold, he shot a soldier galloping by, and then took a quick survey of the ground. He spotted the young herder and ordered him to ride downstream and tell Crazy Horse. He then directed his wife and son and the other women and children toward an undefended gap up the bluffs. He and the Cheyenne warriors covered their retreat.

Colonel Reynolds had positioned his men poorly. Through the haze, soldiers on the bluffs fired into Captain Egan's cavalrymen, thinking they were Indians. With the women and children safe, He Dog led a furious counterattack on the soldiers. Frightened soldiers fled for their lives in a disorderly retreat, leaving wounded and dead soldiers in the smoking village.

Meadowlark saw the rider before she heard him. The snow was deep and muffled the sound. Crazy Horse sat with Black Shawl in their lodge as the Cheyenne boy galloped into camp. "Soldiers have hit the Cheyenne village upstream; He Dog sent me!" In a moment, Worm had the bay mare saddled for his son, and Black Shawl and Meadowlark had his weapons and a bag packed as Crazy Horse prepared his medicine and said his prayers. Black Shawl doubled over in a fit of coughing. Crazy Horse stepped off and put a hand on his wife. "Are you all right?" Black Shawl motioned him to get back on his horse. "Go, I'm fine."

In less than ten minutes, Crazy Horse had gathered his warriors to attack Reynolds, who was soon in the fight of his life. His soldiers, who had not slept in over twenty-four hours and were starving and freezing to death, retreated up the Powder River as fast as they could.

During the night, Crazy Horse and thirty warriors recaptured the seven hundred horses the soldiers had stolen, but the young herders assigned to trail them back ran into General Crook, who recaptured most of the horses. Crazy Horse harassed the command until Crook had the remaining Indian horses corralled and killed.

It was a morbid scene: the Indian horses were hit in the head with axes or had their throats cut. The trumpeting of the dying horses through severed windpipes echoed into the frozen night, demoralizing the exhausted soldiers who huddled before small fires, eating the captured Indian ponies for nourishment.

Crook's shot-up command returned to Fort Fetterman, where Dr. Munn performed twenty-three amputations on the frostbitten and wounded soldiers. It was a bad start of a bloody year for both the Indians and the U.S. Army, which had attacked and burned a village of Indians on its way to surrender at the agency.

With General Terry planning his invasion of Absaraka from the north, General Crook would try again from the south. He would be totally out of contact with Terry, who would be marching in from the north. As John F. Finnerty of the *Chicago Times* rode out of Fort Fetterman with Crook, Colonel Reynolds said good-bye to the reporter and offered some parting advice: "*Never stray from the main column, and never trust a horse or an Indian.*" On the ride north, Crook had picked up a group of gold miners who threw in with the column. One woman, Martha Jane Canary, aka Calamity Jane, was discovered posing as a teamster. It was too dangerous to send her back, so for now she was put under wagon arrest.

General Crook was counting on a regiment-sized force of Crow warriors to meet him at the charred remains of Fort Reno, but they had not shown up. The General called on Frank Grouard to ride north with Louis Richard and Big Bat Pourier to find the Crow. "I'll be back in fourteen days if I live," Grouard said to the general as the two shook hands. "We'll meet you back at the forks of Goose Creek," Crook said as his scouts rode out to find the Crow.

Grouard would have to sneak through the Lakota to reach the Crow. On the east bank of the swollen Bighorn River, Grouard and Big Bat were building a raft when they saw the large band of Lakota warriors charge from the east. The two scouts called for Richard to bring the horses, but before they could mount, another band of warriors plunged their horses into the river from the west. Realizing they were surrounded, and with no time to saddle up, the men jumped on their horses and rode off bareback.

At the sight of the Indians charging across the Bighorn from the west, the warriors charging from the east turned aside. As the Indians swam their horses close, Big Bat recognized the tribe as Crow. By crossing the river, the Crow had spooked off the group of Lakota. The relieved scouts were greeted and taken to the Crow camp. It took two days of cajoling, but with the promise of unlimited arms and cartridges, Grouard and Big Bat got an elite force of just under two hundred Crow warriors to agree to join Crook to fight their enemy.

Without his guides, who were off to find the Crow, Crook lost his way to the rendezvous spot. The battle site on Massacre Hill and the charred remains of Fort Phil Kearny must have distracted Crook because he missed the Bozeman Trail and turned down Prairie Dog Creek and ended up on Tongue River instead of Little Goose Creek.

After realizing his mistake, Crook and his men began to entertain themselves with horse races.

Captain Andy Burt nominated his gray gelding for a half-mile race between various companies. Over three hundred men crowded the finish line as the gray edged Lieutenant Robertson's bay. The little gelding won H Company bragging rights to having the fastest horse in the command. Andy Burt held the can of corn; his winnings for the race, and led his horse off to cool him down. Being a true horseman, he unsaddled his horse rather than hand it to an orderly. He rubbed the gray down and even massaged his legs before retiring with the men for supper.

As the soldiers were cooking their evening meal, shots rang out from the high bluff overlooking the camp. Bullets ripped through tents, wounding two men. General Crook walked from his tent and saw the pickets galloping toward camp. Crook sent Andy Burt's infantry to drive off the attackers. In addition, Captain Mills, with three companies of cavalry, splashed across Tongue River and charged up the bluffs.

Upon reaching the crest, Mills's cavalry dismounted, with every eighth man holding the horses, and pursued the retreating Cheyenne to the next ridge. A handful of Cheyenne charged the rear of the camp to steal the horses, but fortunately for the soldiers, the animals had just been brought in for grooming. It was over within twenty minutes. It had been a small party of Cheyenne hunters. Crook knew the element of surprise would now be gone.

In the aftermath, Captain Burt was called over by an orderly. "It's your gelding, Captain," the herder said.

"Is he tying up from the race?" He figured it to be a stomach problem after being overheated. "No, sir, he was hit during the attack. Bad luck, sir, with all these horses and mules, only one mule and your gelding were hit," the soldier said. Captain Burt was covering two yards per stride heading for the tie line. The gray gelding that had served him faithfully on the attack on the Powder River was wounded.

"It's bad, sir," the orderly said. "We didn't want him to suffer so I came for you right away. We thought you would . . . or if you want, I could . . ." Both men slowed as they caught sight of the little gray gelding, whose bloody leg had been shattered by a bullet. Captain Burt turned and thanked the man, who respectfully turned away, as did the other onlookers who had gathered there looking at the horse. The captain pulled back the tarp on a wagon, grabbed a handful of corn from an open sack, and approached his horse.

"Whoa, fella," he said in a soft tone. The horse recognized the captain's voice and let out a low nicker. Burt reached out with the corn, which the gray took in a hurried nip, confused by the pain. The captain ran an affectionate hand along the gray's neck and waited patiently until the gray took another mouthful, emptying his hand. Burt stroked his horse's neck as the animal crunched on the corn. As the gelding was still eating, the captain went to get another handful, but he knew that soon the pain would be too great for the horse to eat. He pulled the pistol from his holster and fired. Andy Burt's gray had started with the Lakota and died with the cavalry at the mouth of Prairie Dog Creek, much as Lone Bear's sorrel that had started with Connor's soldiers and died with a Lakota on Lodge Trail Ridge.

Crook led his men back to the forks of Goose Creek.[3] The green meadows rolled up to the snowcapped Bighorn Mountains. There was abundant firewood along the banks of the river, which ran melted snow teeming with trout. Men brought in sacks of fresh strawberries and elk, antelope, deer, buffalo, and various species of bear. Even Crook indulged in procuring rare specimens of butterflies along the Bighorns.

Frank Grouard was a week late, but soon almost two hundred Crow warriors appeared on the bluffs above Crook's camp. The Indian horses whinnied at their cavalry brethren. Within the hour, two vastly different mounted armies, fully dressed and armed, stood in review of one another. The soldiers in blue coats, buttoned with brass, sat on horses separated by color: black, gray, sorrel, and bay. Their boots and tack were polished to a shine. Bits, swords, and rifle barrels gleamed in the sun.

The Crow wore feathered headdresses and war paint and galloped down firing their rifles into the air. Warriors swung off their horses at a gallop, then jumped back up to show off. The horses, too, were painted and decorated with braided tack and silver bits. The Crow horses pranced and side passed in front of Crook, who sat on his horse saluting his allies. Young Crow herders followed with the spare horses driven in a herd.

No sooner had the Crows gone into camp than eighty-six Shoshone warriors made their appearance with ex-Confederate cavalryman Tom Cosgrove. Where the Crows were wild in their entrance, the Shoshone were eloquent. They performed a right front maneuver that would have impressed the most rigid West Pointer.

The Crow and Shoshone warriors turned their horses in with the soldiers', swelling the herd to just under three thousand horses and mules.

One hundred miles to the north, on Rosebud Creek, Sitting Bull was at the end of his fast and the religious torture of the sun dance. He had cut strips of flesh from his arms and chest and had not eaten, drunk, or slept while he danced in a daze to receive a vision for his people. After the attack on the village on Powder River, Sitting Bull sent runners out to all Sioux, Cheyenne, and Arapaho both on and off the reservation to come together on Rosebud Creek. "We must stand together or they will kill us separately" was his message.

When Sitting Bull collapsed, he told his vision to Black Moon, who announced it to the leaders of the village. Sitting Bull had seen the image of many soldiers falling upside down into camp. It was a sign that a fight was coming and that the Indians would be victorious. He went on to say that when these soldiers came, they must be killed but not stripped or plundered, or it would curse the people.

Once he recovered, Sitting Bull walked to the medicine rocks that had been struck by lightning and drew his vision. Crazy Horse rode his mare over to the rocks and inspected all the drawings from people long ago. There were drawings of the Little People tribe and various religious symbols. He tied his mare to a bush and began to carve a prophecy of his own death, a warrior with a long knife stuck through him.

Crook knew the key to his command's success was speed. And he knew his walking infantrymen would only slow the column down. So he decided to mount these men on the mules that usually pulled the wagons.

Foot soldiers were not good riders, and the mules had never been saddled to ride. The mules exploded in a furry of kicking hooves and squealing bucking fits, leaping in the air and ending with a dull thump to the ground. Indian allies, packers, miners, and cavalrymen on the bluffs cheered and shed tears of laughter as the flat next to the forks of Goose Creek turned to chaos. Saddles were broken and holders run over and dragged. Soldiers were vaulted into the air and slammed to the ground, only to be run over by another bucking mule, whose rider clung to its neck by a thread.

"Yee-haw! Ride 'em, soldier boy!" Calamity Jane cheered and spit tobacco as a mule sun-fished by her with a terrified soldier hanging on to the saddle. A young Shoshone boy who had befriended the soldiers caught a stray mule that had bucked soldiers off and swung up to show the "walks a heaps" how it was done. He galloped back and forth along the lines of the spectators to a rousing ovation; in three days he would lie dead and scalped on the Rosebud.

By noon, most of the mules were saddled and had riders on their backs. That night, the green soldiers lay in their tents and wondered what kind of army awaited them. Spears were sharpened and loads were checked; if these Crow and Shoshone warriors were any indication, the whites may be in for a hard fight.

Plenty Coups and nine Crow scouts rode north under the stars to scout the Lakota. They had gone less than a mile when they heard the howling of wolves, which they knew were Lakota scouts signaling one another.

The following day close to thirteen hundred soldiers and Indian allies moved north to find the enemy. Supplies were packed on mules, which were divided into five groups of eighty, each having a bell mare that the cook rode. A packer was assigned for every five mules, with each mule packed with a load of between 250 and 325 pounds. The horses and mules were well rested, having spent almost two weeks on the spring meadow grass.

Despite Crook's order for silence on the trip north, Shoshone scouts charged into a buffalo herd, killing about a hundred. It had been awhile since the Shoshone could ride so boldly and hunt in the area, and they would take advantage of it. Four young Cheyenne roasting a buffalo heard gunshots. The Cheyenne boys thought they saw some of their Lakota allies riding in the distance. One of the boys decided to play a joke on them and pretend to attack. He galloped up a ridge while the others saddled their horses to follow. The Cheyenne swung off his horse and crept over the top to see where the Lakota were, but to his horror, he beheld hundreds of mounted soldiers, close enough to throw a rock at. The boys raced into the brush along Rosebud Creek and galloped north to warn the villages.

As news of the whites' advance spread in the Oglala village, hurried councils of war were called. Riders were sent off galloping along the tributaries of the Little Bighorn and the Rosebud to alert the villages and let them know all war parties should hold up at a spot below the big bend of Rosebud.

Crazy Horse had been waiting for this. He was making his medicine when his lieutenants rode in, painted for war. Among them were Good Weasel, Little Big Man, He Dog, and Red Feather.

"Tell the young warriors to concentrate on killing the soldiers. They should not be greedy for scalps and horses. Everyone must get off his horse to shoot. Wait for the good shot; do not waste ammunition."

Before he left, Crazy Horse checked on Black Shawl and his parents. Worm saddled up and went with his son. Young boys herding the horses tried not to look scared. The entire village was in motion: women were taking lodges down, for they would move west to the Little Bighorn while the warriors rode south to meet the soldiers. Crazy Horse rode a gray gelding, and a young herder led his bay mare. Worm led his spotted horse. The greatest cavalry battle ever fought on American soil was about to begin.

When the soldiers rode into camp for the night, the cavalry formed a three-sided square, leaving one side open for the bruised, mule-riding infantrymen who were last to arrive at camp. Major Alexander Chambers attempted to form the infantrymen and mules into some sort of line, but before he could give the command, a lonely mule, looking for his wagon mate, began to bray. That set off 175 mules in a chorus of braying that filled the valley. The cavalrymen, who were sitting around watching, burst into hysterics as the foot soldiers sawed their mounts into position amid the deafening noise. Major Chambers, exasperated, threw his sword to the ground and walked away in a huff.

The soldiers slept within the large square, placing the horses in the middle. Men used their saddles for pillows and kept their guns at their side. As Plenty Coups lay in his robes, he could hear the enemy howling like wolves through the night. He was sure the Sioux would attack before morning.

June 17, 1876

Nine hundred Cheyenne and Lakota warriors gathered at the rendezvous point. Crazy Horse watched the young ones; they were restless and some were afraid, which they tried to mask from the others. Horses pranced in place, picking up on the nervousness of the riders. Crazy Horse's presence instilled bravery in the men; he was their greatest fighter. He sat on his horse in perfect confidence. Unlike his reticent persona in the village, here he was open, talkative, and even joking. A battlefield was where he made his name and where he was most at home. Crazy Horse rode over to calm the young ones.

"The soldiers don't ride very well; the time to charge them is when they are getting on or off their horses. I have seen them drop their guns and fall to the ground like this." Crazy Horse knew well the difference between fighting soldiers and fighting other Indians; there was a lot more lead flying around fighting soldiers, but they panicked more easily than warriors. "I remember when I was young, High Back Bone sent me to scout a Shoshone village. I was so nervous that I almost rode into their camp," Crazy Horse laughed and watched the young warriors relax.

The plan for this battle was to be the same as always: once the soldiers were located, he would find favorable ground and lead them into a decoy and kill them all. In the meantime, he would help hold the gathered warriors back. A group of young Lakota and Cheyenne scouts were sent ahead to scout the soldiers' exact location.

As luck would have it, the scouts sent out from both sides stumbled onto one another. The larger band of Crow gave chase to the Lakota and Cheyenne scouts, who galloped back toward their warriors waiting over a ridge. When the Lakota and Cheyenne warriors caught sight of the Crow, they broke ranks, giving chase. The *ackita*, or tribal police, tried to stop the rush. "Wait! Stop! You'll ruin the ambush." It was no use. Crazy Horse galloped forward; he knew there would be no way to recall the warriors, so he would lead from the front.

Captain Alexander Sutorius of the 3rd Cavalry heard faint shots over the high bluffs to the north. *The Crow must be shooting buffalo over there,* he thought. Captain Anson Mills mounted his horse and galloped up the north bluffs for a clear look. On the far horizon he saw silhouettes of a huge flock of birds moving together over the landscape. As his eyes adjusted, he realized the birds were hundreds of enemy warriors heading right for them.

Below, the soldiers were lounging on the ground taking advantage of the break. Some made coffee, and some napped. General Crook was playing cards with some officers. Mills galloped back down to his cavalrymen, who were stretched out for a quarter mile along Rosebud Creek. "Saddle up, men; quickly, saddle up there!" Mills said as calmly as he could.

14

The scouts came back as fast as their ponies could carry them, followed closely by the hostiles, both yelling at the tops of their lungs, giving the war hoop that caused the hair to raise on end.

—General George Crook

June 17, 1876

IF A DOZEN RUNNING HORSES SOUND LIKE THUNDER, then several hundred sound and feel like an earthquake. Soldiers scrambled for their weapons and saddles on the open creek bottom below. Were it not for the fast action of the Indian scouts, Crook's command would have been overrun. Two hundred Shoshone and Crow warriors immediately countercharged into the Lakota and Cheyenne.

Bull Snake, a Crow warrior, had his horse shot from under him and made a stand next to his dead horse and was shot above the knee, shattering his upper leg. He dragged himself to a tree and propped himself up.

"Shoot them! Today we take back our land," he yelled above the battle, screaming his war cry. Within moments, another Crow warrior, Fox-Just-Coming-Over-the-Hill, was shot from his horse. The boom of large-caliber rifles, combined with the screams of four battling Indian tribes, turned the entire valley into a spectacle of sound. For a full twenty minutes, a ferocious hand-to-hand close-range Indian fight raged. The scouts momentarily broke the Lakota and Cheyenne line, but the hostiles turned their flank and fell on the soldiers.

Crazy Horse turned to the young herder and called for his bay mare, painted for war. He made a quick switch, handing his winded horse to the herder. "Keep the spare horses back there," he ordered, pointing to a thicket of pine trees. He galloped off and watched the hill opposite; somewhere in the group working its way up the north ridge was the soldier chief.

"Keep your fire on that hill!" Crazy Horse yelled at the warriors as he galloped past.

General Crook quickly mounted his black gelding and rode up the north ridge to get a view of what was happening. In an instant, his horse was shot out from under him. The general rolled to his feet, picked up his field glasses, and continued to study the landscape around him. The battle was raging over the hills and valleys of a mile-long front.

Andy Burt's infantrymen were the first soldiers to aid the Crow and Shoshone scouts; no one was laughing at the mule riders now. The soldiers dared not fire into the fray for fear of hitting one of their Indian allies. Unfortunately, some of them did, and the Crow and Shoshone were forced to draw off toward the soldiers. Burt organized some Shoshone scouts to lead a decoy in the bluffs next to a buffalo jump. Comes-In-Sight, a Cheyenne chief, made a charge with some warriors through the gap between Burt's infantrymen and the Crow and Shoshone warriors. In the pine thicket, the young herder holding Crazy Horse's spare threw his lead rope to his older brother in order to follow Comes-In-Sight. To his brother's horror, the boy veered into some Crow and Shoshone scouts, who shot him off his horse. For the first twenty minutes of the battle, soldiers kept getting ridden over by Indians from different directions and Indians rode into soldiers that they did not know were there.

When Comes-In-Sight made a second run through the gap, the soldiers killed his horse, leaving the chief stranded in front of the enemy. As the bullets cut blades of grass all around him, Comes-In-Sight, showing contempt for his enemies, casually walked over to his dead horse and removed the war bridle. On the bluffs overlooking the gap, Comes-In-Sight's sister, Buffalo Road Calf Woman, saw her brother's predicament and galloped through the shooting gallery and slid to a stop beside the chief, who jumped up behind her. Together they rode back to the cheering Lakota and Cheyenne. For the Cheyenne, the battle would forever be known as *The Battle Where the Sister Saved Her Brother*.

Jack Red Cloud, the son of the famous Lakota warrior, was being chased by Crow warriors when he had his horse shot from under him. He ran, panicked, across the battlefield. The Crow yanked the war bonnet off him and took his Winchester, slapping the boy with coup sticks. "Go back to the agency where you belong; you are not worth killing," they yelled.

Captain Mills, leading two hundred cavalrymen, finally engaged the enemy. On their charge east of the gap, however, their horses—unused to the rough country—stumbled out from under cavalrymen who crashed to the ground and scrambled to remount. Lakota and Cheyenne charged through Mills's cavalrymen, knocking them from their horses with war clubs and lances. To his horror, Captain Mills saw a soldier hit the ground, where some Cheyenne fell upon him and cut his arms off at the elbows. The army horses became uncontrollable at the sight of the warriors, so Mills had his men dismount and the horses led behind some rocks. Every fourth man held the horses as the other three fought. The Lakota and Cheyenne zeroed in on these holders, trying to kill or spook their animals, which pulled the holders in four directions. Horses were now dropping on all parts of the field.

Elmer Snow, a bugler with the 3rd Cavalry, was shot through both wrists just as he mounted his terrified horse. Unable to stop or turn, Snow stampeded through the soldiers toward the Lakota and Cheyenne lines. Frank Grouard galloped in to save him but couldn't reach the reins.

"Jump off!" Grouard yelled. The wounded Snow threw himself off the stampeding horse, struggled to his feet, and retreated to the soldiers under heavy fire.

Crazy Horse now began to decoy parts of the command with Good Weasel, Bad Heart Bull, Black Deer, and Kicking Bear. Crook fell for the ruse and sent Captain William Royall, with more than two hundred men, to clear off a high hill to the west that the Lakota occupied. Spreading his command even further, Crook sent Captian Mills with Grouard and another two hundred calvarymen north to find the Indian village.

With Royall and the cavalry gone, Crazy Horse and He Dog turned and directed all the warriors they could against Crook in the center and Royall on the flank. The general was now in a fight for his life; to the west, Royall became surrounded by five hundred warriors. Royall was desperately trying to get back to Crook, but he was cut off.

Captain Guy Henry galloped in—leading reinforcements to save Royall from being overrun—until a bullet caught him in the right cheek, knocking him to the ground. The frightened soldiers broke and left Henry on the ground, but a countercharge by the Crow and Shoshone scouts into the Lakota and Cheyenne saved the fallen captain. A scout named Ute John galloped in, turned his horse loose, and fought his way to Captain Henry. He put Captain Henry on his back and carried him over to his battalion while other Crow and Shoshone scouts held the Lakota back.

In these desperate moments, courage was brought out in the soldiers. John Henry Shingle, a horse holder stranded across the ravine, galloped into the fray and rallied the soldiers. Another horse holder, John Robinson, left his position of safety to lead the horses to the besieged men.

In the center, Andy Burt passed General Crook as bullets and arrows flew around them.

"General, they say that those who have experienced heavy fighting like this get used to it. I was wondering if you feel like I do right now," Burt asked.

"How do you feel, Captain?"

"Like if you weren't here watching me, I'd be running like hell," Burt said and smiled.

"Well, Captain, I feel the same way," Crook said. In a desperate attempt to unite his fractured force, the general sent an aide galloping off to bring Grouard and Mills's cavalry back. With the fight in its fourth hour, the valley was littered with dead horses and men.

The Indian horses began to falter from exhaustion. Crazy Horse galloped back to the pine grove and gave Worm his mare. He had asked a lot of the mare, two complete circles around the battlefield, three miles each at a gallop. He made numerous dashes in the fighting, but the mare had held up like no other horse he had ever ridden. Running a quick hand down her sweaty shoulder, he turned and swung up on his spare.

"Where's the boy?" he asked, looking for the young herder.

"Shot on a brave run," Worm said. Crazy Horse turned and galloped back into the fight.

Five miles away, Frank Grouard was riding down the Rosebud with Captain Mills, looking for the Indian village. Grouard did not like the canyon they were riding through; it was eerily quiet after being in the battle, and a perfect spot for a trap. If the enemy galloped down on them from either side, they would be easy prey. There was a commotion in the ranks as a dust-covered Captain Azor Nickerson rode up on a lathered horse. "Mills, Royall is hard pressed and must be relieved. Henry is badly wounded, and Vroom's troop is all cut up. The general wants you back."

The cavalrymen led their horses out of the canyon and mounted. They headed cross country for Crook at a trot. It was the first stroke of luck for the soldiers, as the maneuver put the cavalry behind the Lakota's lines, who were massed for a charge on Crook. Mills took the initiative and sounded a charge.

Worm saw the cavalrymen approaching and sent a rider to tell the warriors. He quickly moved the horses toward the warriors, who mounted and scattered in front of Mills's charge. Thirteen dead warriors, scalped by soldiers, were left behind. The Indians pulled back down Rosebud Creek for a decoy. Crook began to follow, but Grouard recognized the trick and advised him against it. Grouard also argued that ammunition was running low; after a count, it was found there were only ten rounds left per man.

The Lakota and Cheyenne withdrew from the field, tired and low on ammunition and horses. They had lost so many horses that some had to walk off the battlefield. Over one hundred and fifty Indian horses lay dead alongside the soldiers' horses across the battlefield.

Crazy Horse and He Dog rode back to look at the soldiers and heard the wailing of a Lakota boy crying over the dead body of his twelve-year-old brother. He looked up and saw the two warrior chiefs, their faces still painted and black from gunsmoke.

"They killed my brother. I will fight these whites until I die," he said. The two men frowned. It was a suicide vow. Crazy Horse had felt the same way when Lone Bear and Little Hawk had been killed and again when They Are Afraid of Her had died.

"No," he sighed, putting his hand on the boy's shoulder, "they will die tomorrow." But it was not to be. Crook was gone; the greatest cavalry battle fought on American soil was over, but another to the north was taking shape.

After the Rosebud battle, the large Indian camp moved from lower Rosebud to the Little Bighorn River. While scouts kept a sharp watch for both General Crook and Gibbon, they failed to notice General Alfred Terry, who had slipped in with a thousand troops. Colonel Custer was chomping at the bit. Custer was accompanied by his younger brothers Tom and Boston, his nephew, and his brother-in-law. Custer had recently been arrested again and was anxious to clear his name by engaging the enemy.

Despite his predicament, Custer could not help himself on the ride west with Terry. He barely escaped sounding a general false alarm on a scout when Custer and Tom snuck ahead and began shooting around Boston to scare him. Boston, a civilian, rode in a mad panic back for Terry's soldiers to sound the Indian alarm. Tom and Custer raced back to catch Boston before he got them court-martialed.

At the confluence of the Tongue and Yellowstone rivers, the Custer brothers and their nephew, Autie Reed, joined some other men desecrating Indian graves. Some of the men rode around with these items as though they were trophies of valor. Unfortunately for the Custer brothers, they were about to collect more arrows than they could possibly carry home.

> *Armstrong, Tom, and I pulled down an Indian grave the other day. Autie Reed got the bow with six arrows and a nice pair of moccasins which he intends on taking home.*
> *— Boston Custer*

At the mouth of the Rosebud, Terry made the same mistake his Yale brother Colonel Henry Carrington had made ten years prior. He sent an irresponsible officer to lead an insufficient number of soldiers. With just over six hundred men, Colonel Custer rode up the Rosebud in search of the hostile enemy camp, using a small force of Arikara and Crow scouts.

General Terry took the rest of the force, some four hundred soldiers, with a cannon to circle west and then south up the Bighorn to the Little Bighorn, where he would rendezvous with Custer.

At the site of Custer's third camp on the Rosebud, there was an outcropping of sixty-foot rocks that had a blue line running down the length from a lightning strike. The Crow scouts inspected the rocks and found drawings of the Little People, prehistoric animals, and more recently Sitting Bull's drawing of soldiers falling into camp; for the Crow scouts, it was a bad omen. Running along the Rosebud was a trail big enough for a blind man to follow, made by hundreds of travois and thousands of horses.

On the fourth night, on some broken hills of the Wolf Mountains, Private Peter Thompson awoke from a nightmare where an Indian was bearing down on him with an axe. Unable to sleep, he strolled through the horses and noticed how poor and gaunt they were becoming. The army horses had been traveling for five weeks. In addition to carrying troops the three hundred miles from Fort Abraham Lincoln, many of the horses had accompanied Major Marcus Reno on his grueling 250-mile scouting expedition. The only horses with any flesh on them were those of the Crow and Ree scouts.

Bobtail, a Ree scout, had a large paint horse that stayed near his owner even as he slept. The Ree had a special whistle he used to call the horse.

On the evening of the fifth day of the journey, Custer broke camp after only a few hours, giving his men and horses little time to eat and rest. Riding his thoroughbred Vic at the head of his troops, Custer pushed the campaign-weary horses and men on. To his credit, Custer, with just over six hundred soldiers, had successfully snuck up on one of the largest Indian villages ever assembled. It was the last credible act of Custer's life.

Hidden in the cottonwoods along the Little Bighorn, a sea of teepees from the Oglala, Miniconjou, Hunkpapa, Blackfeet, Sans Arc, and Cheyenne had come together in a huge village that stretched out for four miles. Several thousand Indians had gathered there in the wake of General Crook's invasion. Had the soldiers hit the village a couple of days earlier or later, they would not have encountered nearly the volume of Indians amassed against them. And had the Indians spotted the soldiers as little as an hour earlier, some would have successfully fled to the hills with their families. But the speed with which Custer snuck up on the village never gave them a chance.

What the warriors in this huge village lacked in weapons they more than made up for with experienced war leaders. Crazy Horse, He Dog, Gall, Black

Moon, Tall Bull, Big Road, and dozens of other veteran warriors were capable leaders by themselves; together they would be deadly.

The day Custer's soldiers rode in, the Indian women were out on the flats next to the river digging turnips. Young boys tended the individual herds, which stretched for miles. Buffalo Road Calf Woman, who had saved her brother at the Rosebud battle, was with her husband in the Cheyenne camp. The young Lakota herder whose young brother had died at the Rosebud had acquired a pistol and was attempting to load his own ammunition. He had one shell finished. He had vowed to fight the whites over the death of his brother. He was about to get his chance.

More than twenty thousand horses grazed outside the massive village on the east bank of the Little Bighorn. Warriors met and discussed the state of things at the agencies, but for the most part, the people napped in the shade. After the Rosebud battle with Crook, at least fifteen lodges had lost a husband, son, or father, and countless others were tending the wounded. The medicine men and women were kept busy caring and transporting the casualties.

Crazy Horse and Black Shawl had their lodge next to his parents'. There was much counseling on what course to take. The previous night had been alive with ceremony, and people visited back and forth. Boys courted, men and women traded, and there was a general aura of festivity despite the mourning for those lost at the Rosebud.

Just before the attack, Black Elk's father took his thirteen-year-old son to the horse herd. "Leave a long rope on one horse so you can catch him, then you'll be able to catch the rest. If anything happens, bring the horses in as fast as you can, and keep your eyes on the camp." The father was well aware that two columns of soldiers were within striking distance.

By midday, Black Elk and three young herders left the horses with his cousin and went for a swim in the river. The cousin soon became bored and drove the horses into the water so he could go join his friends. From the water, Black Elk heard a rider yelling in the village. "The soldiers are coming! They are charging from the Hunkpapa camp!" Since his cousin had brought the horses into the river for a swim, Black Elk was among the first to mount his horse and spring into action.

Divide and conquer was a lesson Custer must have slept through at West Point. Without actually seeing the village, he split his men in four separate commands, each one out of visual contact with all the others. Custer ordered Major Reno to take just under two hundred men across the river to attack the southern end of the village; he and his men would circle along the high bluffs to attack the northern end. Custer sent Captain Frederick Benteen to scout the southwestern perimeter of the village to make sure the Indians were not escaping there. The pack train with the spare ammunition brought up the rear.

As Major Reno's tired and thirsty horses approached the Little Bighorn River, they broke and ran for the water while the soldiers sawed on the reins. Jumping off high-cut banks with their riders, the horses took long drinks while crossing the Little Bighorn. Reno drew 175 men in lines of battle and charged the village. Twenty-five Ree scouts with Reno were ordered to run off the Lakota horse herd during the attack. The Hunkpapa village was in pandemonium as the guns of the cavalrymen boomed. A southerly wind carried a rolling wave of dust from the soldiers' horses into the village, turning it dark. The Hunkpapa women and children scattered north, toward the trees, in front of the charging soldiers. Warriors grabbed their weapons, and the young herders brought their horses at a gallop into the fight.

15

It looked like thousands of dogs might look if all of them were mixed together in a fight.

—Wooden Leg (Northern Cheyenne)

He [Crazy Horse] was the first man to cross the river. I saw he had business well in hand. They rode up the draw, and there was too much dust. I could not see anymore.

—Short Bull

We felt terribly alone on that dangerous hilltop. We were a million miles from nowhere, and death was all around us.

—Private Charles Windolf

CRAZY HORSE BARELY HEARD MAGPIE'S SHOUTS OVER THE rumble of the galloping horses.

"Get away as fast as you can," cried the Lakota woman. "Don't wait for anything; the soldiers are charging!" she yelled as the distant sound of Major Reno's guns filled the camp.

Crazy Horse figured Crook had come back to fight. If that were so, he had picked the wrong village to attack; no soldiers would stand a chance with a village this size. Waiting for the herders to bring in the Oglala horse herd, he prepared his medicine. Good Weasel and a dozen others gathered around Crazy Horse, impatient to fight but dutifully waiting until Crazy Horse had prayed and painted himself and his horse to invoke spiritual powers. He had weathered too many fights not to heed his medicine. When finished, he saddled his horse and rode, Winchester in hand, toward the sound of guns four miles away.

In the Hunkpapa camp, the first wave of defenders retreated into the timber. Gall, a Hunkpapa war chief who lost his wife and daughters to the Ree in this first charge, galloped up and rallied them. "Turn and fight!" he ordered the fleeing warriors. Gradually, a growing number of them moved against the soldiers.

Scanning the area, Major Reno saw the tops of hundreds of teepees and realized his force would be swallowed up if he proceeded. He quickly sent off two privates to find Custer and relay a message for help.

Reno then dismounted his men and formed a skirmish line on an open flat. There they would wait for Custer's detachment to support them. As Reno halted the command, some of the soldiers' horses ran off into the Indian camp, taking their helpless riders with them. With every fourth man holding a horse in the timber by the river, Reno actually had fewer than eighty men in a position to fight. In less than half an hour, nine hundred warriors were massing toward his position. The charging warriors turned his left flank, Indians were at his rear, and the horse holders were under attack in the timber. The major's Ree scouts had retreated from the village.

The Lakota and Cheyenne were now on top of Reno's men. The major knew that whatever he did, he needed to do it fast. Looking to the high ground across the river, he ordered his men to fall back to the timber and mount their horses. When the soldiers turned their backs to get on their horses, the warriors charged. With only a few brave officers covering the retreat, it turned into an every-man-for-himself flight up the hill.

Having galloped up the hill, privates William Morris, Dave Gordon, and Bill Meyer paused and looked down. "That was pretty hot down there," Morris said. In the next instant he was shot in the left breast, Gordon through the windpipe, and Meyer in the eye. All three of their horses were also hit. On top of the hill, soldiers lay behind dead horses for breastworks and dug rifle pits or indentations in the hard ground using both their rifle butts and their fingers. Nine hundred warriors commanded the elevated peaks around Reno. Fifty percent of Reno's force was now killed, missing, or wounded. What he needed was help from Custer.

Just before Reno called his retreat, Custer, three miles away, was looking for a suitable place to cross the river. Suddenly, he realized his mistake: hundreds of lodges were poking through the trees as far as he could see. It would have been a good time to change battle plans, but the colonel continued to distance himself from the rest of his command, trying to get to the rear of a village that was still over a mile away.

Custer galloped Vic back to his men and summoned Sergeant Kanipe. "Tell Captain McDougall to bring the pack train across the high ground. If the packs get loose, don't stop to fix them; cut them off. Tell him to come quick, there's a big Indian camp."

Custer then called for Lieutenant Cooke. "Get Captain Benteen here now! Tell him to bring the packs." Lieutenant Cooke scrawled a quick message and handed it to bugler John Martini: "Benteen. Come on. Big village. Be quick. PS: Bring packs. W. W. Cooke."

Riding through groups of scattered warriors who fired on him, Martini managed to get through. When he handed Benteen the note, the captain saw that Martini's horse had a number of bullet wounds.

Custer then received an urgent message from Major Reno requesting help. Custer's decisions kept getting worse as he split his forces once again, sending his brother-in-law, Captain Calhoun, and Captain Miles Keogh up on a ridge above the river crossing, and taking the rest of his men with him between the ridge and the river, which required them to climb and descend steep ridges. It was horrible ground from which to fight: the six- to eight-foot-high sagebrush growing all around would allow the warriors to get almost on top of the soldiers before being seen.

Black Bird of the Cheyenne caught sight of Custer's soldiers riding up and down the steep ridges along the river. He and five other Cheyenne warriors—Mad Wolf, Bob Tail Horse, Calf, Roan Bear, and another—turned their horses across the river to intercept the soldiers; it was six against two hundred. A half dozen Lakota rode in front of Custer's men, trying to draw them away from the village.

The six Cheyenne dismounted behind a ridge and, together with the six Lakota, opened fire on Custer's front line. In the village, old men grabbed bows and arrows and headed up the hill to meet Custer; they were not just old men, they were old warriors. Buffalo Road Calf Woman, the heroine of the Rosebud battle, fought in this attack along with the men. The dust and smoke cut visibility, so arrows were as effective as the longer-range rifles of the troopers.

The actions of these few gave runners just enough time to gallop to the warriors surrounding Reno and tell them to come back. Grabbing ammo and guns off the dead soldiers and horses, the warriors tore back for the village.

The ground around captains Calhoun and Keogh began to vibrate with the pounding hooves of four hundred Indians' horses. The Indians attacked the soldiers' left flank. Within minutes, four hundred more Indians galloped across the river and fell on Custer. The colonel retreated through the high sage to the high ground and realized he was doomed. Half his men were down, and the rest were fighting desperately in small pockets, surrounded by charging warriors. Visibility was so bad that two Lakota accidentally killed the Cheyenne chief Lame White Man, thinking he was a Ree scout. Crazy Horse led two charges on his bay mare between Calhoun and Custer, sealing the gap between the two forever.

By now, some surviving soldiers saw their cause as lost and began to shoot themselves rather than be captured alive. Another group of soldiers broke and ran from a charge over the hill and were hacked to pieces by He Dog and some warriors who intercepted them in a deep ravine.

If there was help to be had for Custer and his men, it would have to come in the form of a lightning strike: Major Reno was four miles away, and before he was cut to pieces, he had ordered Captain Benteen to remain with him.

The pack train was lagging back. General Terry was on the Bighorn River, and General Crook was fishing in Little Goose Canyon.

A few soldiers from Keogh and Calhoun made a last dash along the ridge to reach Colonel Custer, but Crazy Horse led a mounted charge through these men and it was over.

Armed with guns and ammunition from Custer's men, the Indians attacked Reno and Benteen with a fury. After a miserable night, Reno's entrenched men were hit by furious charges of the warriors. At one point, the Lakota and Cheyenne pressed close enough for a warrior to hit a trooper with a coup stick.

Around 7 o'clock that evening, through the billowing smoke, Reno's besieged soldiers caught sight of Indians riding south with their dead and wounded loaded on horses and travois. From the hill, they probably gave no thought to the fact that they were witnessing the exodus of the "High-Toned Sons of the Wild" and their warhorses, who had just fought their last big battle. It had been their finest, and no one would ever forget it. There would be no more warhorses or buffalo runners trained; the era of the Plains Indian horses was over.

16

I regard Custer's massacre as a sacrifice of troops brought on by Custer himself that was wholly unnecessary.

—President U. S. Grant

GENERAL TERRY AND COLONEL GIBBON, WITH FOUR hundred soldiers, arrived at the abandoned village. They thought, at first, that either Custer or Crook must have won a victory. They found two teepees, surrounded by sacrificial horses, with a total of eight dead warriors inside. Despite the orders against it, the soldiers had stripped the bodies for souvenirs.

Their elation was short-lived, however, as a search upstream, led by Lieutenant Bradley, produced a buckskin shirt with a bullet hole through it and the label "Porter" inside. Next discovered were a single glove with "Yates, 7th Cavalry" written on it and bloody underwear labeled "Lieutenant Sturgis." Dead cavalry horses lay in the village; four severed heads had been placed on the ground facing each other. Lieutenant Bradley galloped back to General Terry and dropped the axe.

"General Terry, I counted the bodies of 190 dead cavalrymen across the river. They are stripped and cut up." After two days in the hot sun, the bloated bodies of the dead men and horses emitted an unbearable odor.

Next, two scouts from Reno Hill appeared and escorted Terry upstream to Reno's survivors. A cheer rose up from the filthy, battle-fatigued men when they saw General Terry. The celebration ceased once they learned the fate of Colonel Custer.

The remains of Custer and his men had just enough dirt thrown on them to keep the flies and smell down. Like the Rosebud battle eight days earlier, dead horses were everywhere. On the hilltop where the last of Custer's men died, dead army horses ringed the hill where they had been killed and used for breastworks.

Comanche, a large bay gelding that Captain Miles Keogh had ridden, was found on the field with several bullet wounds in his body. When the order came down to shoot the wounded horses, Comanche let out a whinny at the trooper that approached. The trooper did not have the heart to shoot the animal and was permitted to care for the horse, which was escorted back with the command.

Lieutenant Edward Godfrey found a gray warhorse tied in some brush. The horse had had his mouth tied shut and grass tied to the bit to keep him from whinnying. Godfrey led him to the river, where the famished animal plunged himself in up to his eyeballs. The horse proved to be an excellent buffalo hunter and remained Godfrey's personal horse until it was killed a year later at the Battle of the Bear Paw against the Nez Percé.

The big paint horse of Bobtail Bull was turned in with the pack string of Reno's and then taken back to the Ree reservation where the horse's deeds were sung about in Arikara villages for the next hundred years.

After the Custer fight, Crazy Horse had become a celebrity in a world he knew nothing of. His name was in every newspaper in the nation and across the Atlantic. From London to San Francisco, people had now heard his name. The most famous saloon in Paris would bear his name, yet outside of a handful of traders and scouts, few white men had ever laid eyes on him.

While Custer was being slaughtered, Crook fished for almost six weeks in Little Goose Canyon, waiting for supplies and reinforcements. Terry likewise stayed on the Yellowstone. Neither officer knew the location of the other. From the top of Little Goose Canyon, Crook searched the surrounding country for signs of General Terry. From his vantage point on the first crest above the canyon, Crook could see north for a hundred miles. As the magpies, wolves, eagles, and coyotes began to uncover Custer and his soldiers on the Little Bighorn, fishing fever swept through the ranks of Crook's bored soldiers like wildfire. Captain Mills and two soldiers caught 126 fish in a few hours, once they abandoned their homemade flies in favor of native grasshoppers. Irish packer O'Shannessey, who was an avid salmon fisherman, had to admit he had never seen anything like it; it was a sportsman's paradise.

In August, Colonel Wesley Merritt, with the men of the 5th Cavalry, joined Crook and his men, and after a brief march, they met up with General Terry, swelling the command to four thousand men and seven thousand animals. Joining that force were 250 Indian allies. William F. "Buffalo Bill" Cody, in response to Custer's death, took himself out of the theater and into the Bighorn Valley to reenlist as an army scout. With Colonel Merritt, the scout came upon a group of Cheyenne leaving the reservation and shot one of their chiefs, whom he scalped, proclaiming the deed "the first scalp for Custer." Cody was not so brave when he was dropped off on the Yellowstone from a steamer and told to scout south. When the steamboat returned for the scout, the boat captain remarked it appeared Cody had sat in the bushes until it was time for the steamship to reappear.

Crazy Horse sat on his bay mare and looked at the expanse of white tents that lined both sides of Little Goose Creek. The canyon was the heart of the country he had fought for his entire life. Absaraka in the Bighorn Valley had at one time been Kiowa and Comanche country, Shoshone and Crow country, but during his lifetime it had always been Lakota country. Now the whites had taken the area and allied themselves with Lakota enemies—the Crow, the Shoshone, and the Pawnee. The large Indian camp on the Little Bighorn had splintered into a dozen factions, while the number of soldiers in the country was growing by the day. There was nothing left to do but ride out to set fire to the grass, as they did every fall to bring new grass in the spring, and continue on to the east.

Like Colonel Cole's death march eleven years prior, General Crook was about to engage in his own starvation march. Crook marched four hundred miles over burned-out land, exhausting both horses and men. The commissary had the morbid task of picking out which horses and mules were to be shot and butchered for the men to eat.

Frank Grouard found an Indian horse herd and a small Lakota village at Slim Buttes. The Indians were initially routed, but warriors under Crazy Horse rode in and turned the tide. When Crook's two thousand exhausted men straggled into the village, they found themselves in a defensive fight against two hundred Indians.

The strategy proposed by generals Phil Sheridan and William T. Sherman was that by keeping the hostiles on the move, they would soon be starved into capitulation. It worked; warriors began to defect and turn coat in droves. Two Cheyenne warriors surrendered in Crook's camp under a flag of truce, and they informed the general of a Cheyenne village located on the headwaters of the Powder. The Cheyenne were about to suffer the most heartbreaking attack on their people since Sand Creek.

On a cold November dawn, 350 combined Lakota, Cheyenne, Shoshone, Pawnee, Bannock, and Arapaho scouts, now fighting for the soldiers, led the charge into Chief Dull Knife's Cheyenne village hidden in a canyon of the red fork of the Powder River. Backed by U.S. cavalry, the battle was a rout. Women grabbed their babies and herded children away from the attack toward the high ground as warriors covered their retreat. Bill Rowland, using a Cheyenne scout as an interpreter for the army, opened negotiations with Chief Dull Knife from a distance. Dull Knife responded by yelling to the Cheyenne scouts who had opposed him, "Go home. You have no business here. We can whip the white soldiers alone, but we cannot whip you too."

That night, the Cheyenne survivors fled over the mountains in thirty-below- zero temperatures, some without as much as a blanket or shoes. Babies froze to death in their mothers' arms; the few horses they escaped with were butchered and eaten. The Cheyenne used the warm entrails of the animals to temporarily warm their frozen feet. Warriors lit fires on the trail so that trailing bands with no protection against the cold could warm themselves. Without food or shelter, they struggled north to find the village of Crazy Horse.

December 8, 1876

Just as had happened after the Fetterman massacre, the bloody year of 1876 was followed by a killing winter. The snow had frozen hard, making it difficult for the animals to paw through to the grass.

Crazy Horse had taken his people back to the burned-out area on the Tongue River to elude the soldiers. He hunted clear to the head of Hanging Woman Creek but saw very little in the way of game. In the course of three days, Crazy Horse killed only two deer, which he left in the crowded lodges of women whose warriors had died in battle. He kept a small cut for Black Shawl and his parents but none for himself. Now there was no game, and the horse herds were growing weaker by the day.

Worm entered the lodge of his son and saw his drawn look as he sat next to Black Shawl. "Hunting's not good," Crazy Horse said, loading a pipe for his father. Worm dropped the news on his son: "Some Cheyenne have been attacked by soldiers on the Powder. They are on their way here." Both knew what this meant. Their village was bordering on starvation as it was; with the addition of the Cheyenne, the situation would be even worse. "How far south are they?" Crazy Horse asked.

"Three days, maybe two. A runner from Dull Knife's village came in this morning."

He Dog, followed by Meadowlark, entered the lodge. His stepmother carried a bowl of weak soup for Crazy Horse that she had made by boiling the leg bone of a deer. A weary Crazy Horse pointed for her to give it to Black Shawl, then motioned for He Dog to sit. Black Shawl rose and put some more wood on the fire, triggering her cough.

"You heard?" He Dog asked, looking at his friend. Crazy Horse nodded. "You can't be gone for so long. People here are counting on you." He Dog looked around and saw the lodge had a small piece of fresh meat, barely enough for a meal for one person. "Little Hawk is here," Crazy Horse said, referring to his uncle, who was the true leader of the village. "It's not like that now; they look to you, especially the young warriors. Some stole horses from the Miles's village downriver while you were gone. There are others who wanted to talk to Miles to see if we could trade some robes for supplies . . . and to see what he has to say," He Dog added.

Colonel Nelson Miles had made a camp where the Tongue River runs into the Yellowstone and was making peace overtures to the Lakota to surrender. His strategy worked; many Lakota warriors had begun to defect.

Crazy Horse took this news calmly. He knew some wanted to go to the agencies. A way of life was ending, and he knew it. What truly bothered Crazy Horse, however, was how eager so many Indians were to scout against their own people. The only good news about the incoming Cheyenne was that it gave them more warriors to fight the whites.

"We need to go out and meet the Cheyenne now." Crazy Horse rose, not having eaten since he had taken a bite from a deer liver the day before. Black Shawl, embarrassed for not having food for the visitors, stopped her husband.

"Let me cook you the meat," she said. Crazy Horse looked at his wife; Black Shawl was a good woman. She had gone without also, and now she had come down with a coughing sickness.

"We'll have visitors here soon. We can give them our lodge and move in with my parents," he said and left in the cold. "Eat what I brought; it will make you feel better. We may have some hard times ahead."

Worm walked along with his son as he went out to catch a fresh horse from the herd. Crazy Horse turned his warhorse out to fend for herself along the cottonwoods. Crazy Horse looked at the horse herd, some he had known for years, good warhorses. Now their hips stuck out and their rumps were drawn. Some of the younger horses were as good as starved. Horses captured from the soldiers at the Little Bighorn were dying so fast that hardly any were left.

Outside of Captain Miles's camp, five Lakota chiefs rode with white flags tied to the end of long spears. They had come in to talk to Colonel Miles about terms of surrender. A group of Miles's Crow scouts rode out to the Lakota, offering their hands in peace, but in an instant they ambushed the chiefs and killed them in cold blood.

Hearing the commotion out by the woodpile, the soldiers went out to investigate and found the bodies of the slain Lakota chiefs. Colonel Miles was furious; he immediately commandeered the Crows' horses and sent them to the Lakota to atone for the murders. It was too late. The enraged Lakota led a series of attacks on Miles until the colonel led his soldiers up the Tongue.

During a blizzard the next day, in thirty-below weather, armed with a Napoleon cannon and a three-inch Rodman gun, 650 soldiers engaged Lakota and

Cheyenne on the Tongue River in an all-day battle. The place would soon be called Battle Butte, or the Battle of Wolf Mountain. Miles was saved by artillery fire; he retreated to his base of supplies and called the fight a victory.

In the cold snowy recesses of the Little Powder River, He Dog found Crazy Horse hunting in the cold. He had not eaten, nor would he eat, while his people starved.

"Spotted Tail is in the village," He Dog said. For a moment, the thought of his uncle Spotted Tail wading through the snow amused Crazy Horse, but he realized that Meadowlark's brother had ridden two hundred miles and brought needed supplies to the starving village.

Spotted Tail had left word that if Crazy Horse brought his people in, he would be given his own agency wherever he wanted it. As the snow swirled around the two friends, He Dog produced a pipe with tobacco. "A gift from the whites," he said, and the two had a smoke. "They sent packhorses loaded with food also."

Crazy Horse was no statesman, but he knew if he brought his people in, they would have food and maybe the whites' medicine could help Black Shawl's sickness. He had lived for almost thirty-seven winters and was the Lakota's greatest warrior; now he must make the transition to becoming their greatest leader. "It is time to go in to see what the whites have to say. I have been thinking I would like a reservation in the canyon where my mother is buried," he said.

17

When we started in, I thought we were coming to visit and to see whether we would receive an annuity, not to surrender. I thought we would be allowed to go back home afterwards. But when we got near Fort Robinson, I found we were coming to surrender.

—He Dog

What fools we were not to incorporate these nomads—the finest light cavalry in the world—into our permanent military force. With five thousand such men, and our aboriginal population would readily furnish that number, we could harass and annoy any troops that might have the audacity to land on our coasts, and worry them to death.

—Lieutenant John Bourke

HE DOG AND CRAZY HORSE RODE SIDE BY SIDE AS THEY approached the Red Cloud agency. Crazy Horse was unaware that his entering the agency was no less significant than Lee's surrender at Appomattox Courthouse. It ended the era of free-roaming horsemen.

Lieutenant William Philo Clarke and Red Cloud rode out to meet the two veteran warriors who rode at the head of their people. Crazy Horse was surprised to see Red Cloud, who had come out to get in on the surrender. Crazy Horse dismounted with He Dog, spread his blanket on the ground, and sat with Red Cloud and the lieutenant to smoke a pipe of peace.

His first night at Red Cloud agency, Crazy Horse had one visitor he was genuinely pleased to see: Frank Grouard. "Grabber, I'm surprised Sitting Bull has not killed you yet." Crazy Horse got up and shook his old friend's hand.

"He won't kill me as long as you're around to protect me," Grouard said and smiled. Crazy Horse lit a pipe and offered it to Grouard.

"How is it here?" Crazy Horse asked.

"Do yourself a favor; don't go to Washington until they agree to give you your own piece of land; otherwise you might not get one," Grouard said.

"I was thinking about the land where Goose Creek runs into the mountains."

"That's a long way off; I think you'd have a better chance picking some land closer to the Black Hills. Any chance of you trading me your bay mare?" Grouard asked.

Crazy Horse shook his head. "She has been trying to run off since we got here. I've had to keep her hobbled when someone is not watching her since I got her. She wants to go back to the range on Otter Creek," Crazy Horse said.

Once Crazy Horse learned the ropes of the agency, he was appalled at the backbiting and scheming, but it did not surprise him. Crazy Horse's main concerns were to get help for Black Shawl's sickness, and to obtain a reservation for his people. Dr. Valentine McGillycuddy, a Fort Robinson post doctor, was tireless in his efforts to help Black Shawl, but the matter of the reservation was not as easy.

Crazy Horse was doing everything he could to accommodate the whites so he could get his own agency and get away from the bad blood around the Red Cloud agency. When General Crook asked for a meeting, he was met by a grand review of mounted Indians. Crazy Horse sat next to Lieutenant Clark and was the first to dismount and shake Crook's hand.

At the coucil that night, He Dog had told Crazy Horse that if he were ever going to speak in council it had to be now. The whites considered him a leader, and they would not understand his reluctance to speak in council as other Oglala had. When the council started, it was decided to let Crazy Horse speak first, a fact that made Red Cloud seethe.

"General, you sent tobacco and provisions to our camp when we were hungry. From the time we received those gifts, I kept coming in toward the post. All the time since I have been here, I have been happy. While coming this way, I picked out a place and put a stick in the ground for a place to live hereafter, where there is plenty of game. We can raise our children there. All of my relations who are here were with me when I picked out that place. I would like to have them go back with me and stay there with me. This is all I have to say."

Crazy Horse sat and watched the others talk. Young Man Afraid spoke of wanting a reservation in the Bear Butte area of the Black Hills, and Red Cloud asked for schools and wagons. Then Crazy Horse's old nemesis, No Water, rose to speak. He took partial credit for bringing Crazy Horse into the agency and reiterated what Red Cloud had said. It seemed to Crazy Horse that No Water was trying to impress the whites as being an important leader. Iron Hawk spoke, as did High Bear. Red Cloud, in an effort to show his prominence, spoke a second time, but it was Spotted Tail who spoke last, who cut through the smoke laid down by the others.

He told Crook that the Indians had not been given the provisions promised and that whites were now crowding the land the Lakota had been promised. He wanted the land the government had given them to be surveyed. They received little for their trade goods, and their only store on the agency charged them double. Their children needed decent teachers. He wanted the whites out of the Black Hills. He listed broken promises made as far back as the Treaty of 1851. He said he had gotten Crazy Horse to come in so the soldiers would not go after him. Spotted Tail concluded by saying he wanted to go back and meet with the Great Father in Washington to discuss these things.

Spotted Tail's talk discouraged Crazy Horse. If Spotted Tail had such complaints, there must be problems. Crazy Horse attended a meeting concerning a lawless element of white men and Indian renegades who were stealing horses off the reservation. Crazy Horse was seated next to Lieutenant Clarke at the meeting, which caused jealousy among the other chiefs. Then, when the army officers proposed having a feast at the lodge of Crazy Horse in honor of his status as war chief, Red Cloud stormed out of the meeting. He felt all the feasts should be at his lodge. Clarke buckled and canceled the feast altogether.

Four months passed at the Red Cloud agency, and it became clear that Crazy Horse would probably not get his own agency as promised. The Cheyenne were being moved away to the Nations in Oklahoma. He made a concession and opted for an agency on Beaver Creek, which was not as far as his beloved Little Goose Canyon, but it would at least be far enough away to distance himself from the bad blood at the Red Cloud agency.

Crazy Horse was forced to listen to more talk than he had heard in his life. What bothered him the most was the steady stream of visitors he and Black Shawl received at their lodge: the whites came all day, and the Lakota came all night. They got less than a few hours' sleep a day.

Jealous Indians schemed to create a rift between Lieutenant Clarke and Crazy Horse, and they did the same between General Crook and Frank Grouard. They filled the officers' heads with rumors that Crazy Horse was plotting an uprising with his warriors. Billy Garnett, a scout jealous of the friendship between Frank Grouard and Crazy Horse, began to drive a wedge between those two, saying Grouard had deliberately misinterpreted Crazy Horse to the army officers. American Horse and Little Big Man, who had both fought alongside Crazy Horse, were also part of the plot.

Crazy Horse gathered his old warriors to see Grouard and Clarke. Nothing came of either incident except Grouard and Clarke became afraid for their lives, and a general aura of panic swept the area. General Crook was called back to the Red Cloud agency, and he and the other officers there called a council meeting.

All the Indians at the Red Cloud agency were told to move their camp across the creek for the council. Some of the agency Indians, jealous of Crazy Horse's status with the whites, told him there would be a plot to kill him there, hoping to keep him away.

He Dog visited Crazy Horse in a last-ditch effort to convince him to attend the council and found out that Crazy Horse refused to move his lodge near those of the Indians who were plotting against him. A group of his loyal followers were also remaining with him. "If I move across the creek, does it mean you will be my enemy?" he asked. For the first time in a long while, Crazy Horse broke out in a heartfelt laugh.

"I am no white man. They are the only people who make rules for other people that say, 'If you stay on this side of the line it is peace, but if you go on the other side I will kill you all.' There is plenty of room; camp where you please."

In an effort to assure the soldiers that he wasn't threatening them by his absence, Crazy Horse sent a note to Lieutenant Clarke: "Tell my friend [General Crook] that I thank him and I am grateful, but some people over there have said too much. I don't want to talk to them anymore. No good would come of it."

Woman's Dress approached General Crook, who was on his way to the council, and told him that Crazy Horse had devised a plot to pull a knife and stab the general during the council. Crook initially discredited this, but then the demons began to work on him, and he turned back and ordered the arrest of Crazy Horse. It was a decision the general would regret the rest of his life.

Eight companies of soldiers and four hundred Indians armed to the teeth surrounded Crazy Horse's camp the next morning to have him arrested. Lieutenant Clarke had secretly offered No Water $200 and a good sorrel horse to kill Crazy Horse.

It might have been a routine arrest except that the man they came to arrest had survived his entire life on his wits, honed with battle savvy. When the mob of traitors showed up to arrest him, all they found was an abandoned village.

September 4, 1877

At a gallop, Shell Boy and Kicking Bear jumped over the ravine, holding their rifles up so they wouldn't accidentally discharge when the horses landed on the other side. They would need what little ammunition they had.

The two warriors rode with Crazy Horse and Black Shawl in their escape to the Spotted Tail agency. Crazy Horse galloped his mare down the steep hills and walked them up, sometimes holding the horse's tail or a long lariat tied to the horse to pull him along. Using this technique to save the horses' strength, he began to gain ground and his pursuers began to fall back. Crazy Horse looked back, and his heart lifted. He was in danger, but it felt good to be off the agency and riding free again. He could tell his bay mare enjoyed being out also. She had enough endurance to lose them, but Black Shawl and the others did not have such good horses.

He was chased by fifty-five riders, themselves trailed by almost four hundred more mounted on the best horses and carrying the best guns on the agency, whipping their sleek ponies to white foam. No Water rode three horses to death on the chase.

After traveling more than forty miles to the east, Crazy Horse and Black Shawl finally arrived at his uncle's agency for safe harbor. He took her to her own relatives' lodge and turned to say good-bye.

"I'll come back when this is over." She tried to smile, but they both knew there was only a slim chance they would see each other again. There were too many people against him. His own people had poisoned the whites against him, yet he had to try. Before long, Spotted Tail stormed up to his nephew.

"This is my agency. I am in charge here. If you want to live here, you will live by my rules, do you understand?"

Crazy Horse nodded.

"They are trying to kill me back at Red Cloud, and he is part of it." Spotted Tail softened; he knew firsthand what an instigator Red Cloud could be. That was the whole reason he had his own separate agency forty miles away.

Crazy Horse went to see the white agent Jesse Lee at Spotted Tail Agency. He informed Crazy Horse that he would have to return to the Red Cloud agency, for soldiers had just ridden in with those orders. When the lynching party galloped in, they found themselves surrounded by warriors sympathetic to Crazy Horse. Both Jesse Lee and Spotted Tail decided to make the trip back to the Red Cloud agency with Crazy Horse so no harm would come to him. It was decided that the party would leave early the next morning. Crazy Horse sat and smoked in the lodge of an old warrior friend, Touch the Clouds, that night.

After dark, Crazy Horse rode the bay mare to the western end of the village. He knew the bay mare would be good to have on the ride back the next day, but he also knew that his time of needing a good warhorse had passed. He dismounted, sat on the ground, and lit a pipe. "Keep this mare safe on her journey home," he prayed. The same heart that carried him along in battle had never stopped its longing for her home range between Powder River and Otter Creek. *Perhaps she misses a stallion*, he thought.

"You have wanted to go home since I first got you. Go return to your home. I wish I could go with you." He took off the halter with the long strap and let his hand brush along her top line as she turned to the west. He saw the bullet wound, now healed, from the fight at the Little Bighorn. As the mare turned and bolted west, it lifted Crazy Horse's spirit to watch her run.

In less than three days, she would cross the Powder and turn north, follow Bear Creek, and then be home. There would still be good grass, and the grazing on the high flats east of Otter Creek would blow clean of snow in the winter. The herd would be there on a ten-mile stretch, but a new stallion would have taken over the herd.

When Crazy Horse and the arrest party returned to Fort Robinson, they passed the lodge of He Dog. He Dog had been livid with Crazy Horse for running off. His friend had stirred up an entire agency. His anger melted away to concern when he saw the mob of armed Indians surrounding his friend. He Dog grabbed his war bonnet, swung up on his horse, and galloped through the crowd to Crazy Horse.

"Be careful. You are going to a dangerous place," He Dog warned.

Crazy Horse looked confused. He had not slept well in a month and had ridden eighty miles in two days. He knew if a fight broke out he was cut off. His only weapon was a knife, which was concealed under a blanket.

As he was led to the soldiers' headquarters, Red Cloud and his men stood on one side of the office, and American Horse and his men stood on the other. Spotted Tail followed his nephew. After a brief stay inside, Little Big Man led Crazy Horse through the hundreds of Indians to another building. Through the mob of people, it was hard for Crazy Horse to see where he was going. They entered a door guarded by a soldier, and Crazy Horse saw Indians in shackles and smelled the stench of human waste. It was the jail. Crazy Horse whirled and bolted toward the door, pulling his knife. Little Big Man immediately jumped onto his back, pinning Crazy Horse's arms. In an instant Crazy Horse threw Little Big Man off as he fled outdoors toward the parade ground. The Indians standing around began to yell, "Shoot him! Kill the son of a bitch!"

Before Crazy Horse could turn, a soldier poked him from behind with a bayonet, piercing his kidney, which sent him to the ground. In that long moment, the only sound was of guns cocking and rounds being chambered. A potential bloodbath was about to erupt between rival Indian factions and the soldiers, until the cavalry surrounded the mob. Spotted Tail, Red Cloud, and Lieutenant William Philo Clarke were separately surrounded and protected by their men. It was as if the man lying on the parade ground of Fort Robinson was now an afterthought to the potential bloodbath that was threatening.

He Dog pushed his way through the crowd to Lieutenant Clarke and asked if he could approach his friend. Crazy Horse was taken inside an adjutant's office, where Doctor McGillycuddy tended to his wound and administered morphine. Crazy Horse's father and Touch the Clouds had also been allowed in, and they waited with the doctor.

He Dog left to keep order among his people lest a massacre break out. There were women and children to think about. In the middle of the night, the greatest cavalryman ever to ride the American West died in an office at Fort Robinson, Nebraska, betrayed by two races of people. He was a horse herder, horse trainer, and as a man, had excelled in fighting from horses. Crazy Horse had probably spent more time with horses than he had with people. His life spanned the high-water mark of the Plains Indians horse culture fighting over a 30,000-mile area on the back of a horse. He had been instrumental in the Fetterman massacre, the Rosebud battle, the Little Bighorn fight, and dozens more. As a cavalryman he had bested Miles, Crook, and Custer. The night of Crazy Horse's death, a lunar eclipse marked his passing. On a large group of rocks overlooking Rosebud Creek, a vision of his own death had been carved into stone.

> *That night I heard mourning somewhere, and then there was more and more mourning until it was all over camp . . . He never wanted anything more than to save his people. I cried all night, and so did my father.*
> *—Black Elk*[1]

When Worm entered his lodge the night Crazy Horse died, he found Meadowlark dead on a blanket. The sorrow of losing her son had proved too much for a mother's heart. She was laid to rest on a scaffold next to Crazy Horse at the Red Cloud agency. Worm was disgusted at his own people's role in the death of his son, so he left the Red Cloud Agency to live at the Spotted Tail Agency. On the trip to relocate the tribes to the east, in the chaos surrounding the death of his son, he had secretly taken the remains of Crazy Horse, which he buried at an undisclosed location en route east. Worm trusted neither Indians nor whites.

He Dog and the rest of the surviving horsemen settled into a sedentary life on the reservation. The hardships brought by war with the whites were not worth fighting for, so they did what was best for their families and tried to keep peace between the young warriors and the whites.

Crazy Horse's bay mare was on her way back to Otter Creek. She had never really acclimated to the Indian herds and had on numerous occasions tried to escape to her homeland, where she had spent the first three years of her life. Her mother, the old bell mare, died in the winter after Custer's stand at Little Bighorn. She had raised several foals, and one, a yellow stallion, had taken over the Otter Creek herd.

The bay mare stopped only sporadically to graze and rest. The same stout heart that made her a great warhorse drove her onward to reach her former range. It was uncommon that a horse would keep its longing for home for such a long time, but she was a unique mare. With two hundred miles of broken country and several streams to cross, the mare was on her way.

On her way back to Otter Creek, she would find no Indians. The tribal camping spots along the Powder, Tongue, Rosebud, Bighorn, and all their tributaries were now void of tribes. The famed warhorses and buffalo runners of Absaraka had either been sold off to telegraph crews and homesteaders, or kept by U.S. Army officers. The last of the great buffalo herds of the plains were still present in Absaraka, but their days were numbered. They had all but vanished from Colorado, Oklahoma, Kansas, and Texas. Wealthy easterners were already taking advantage of the open grasslands by trailing in herds of cattle under the reins of a new type of horse and horseman—the cow pony and cowboy. Unfortunately, if men were to raise cattle in the area, the buffalo had to go.

Fatigued from her journey, the bay mare's judgment was impaired as she rushed to cross Powder River and became bogged. Thrashing and struggling, she sank to past her belly; the heavy sand pulling her energy and body lower into the swirling water that ran north toward the Yellowstone.

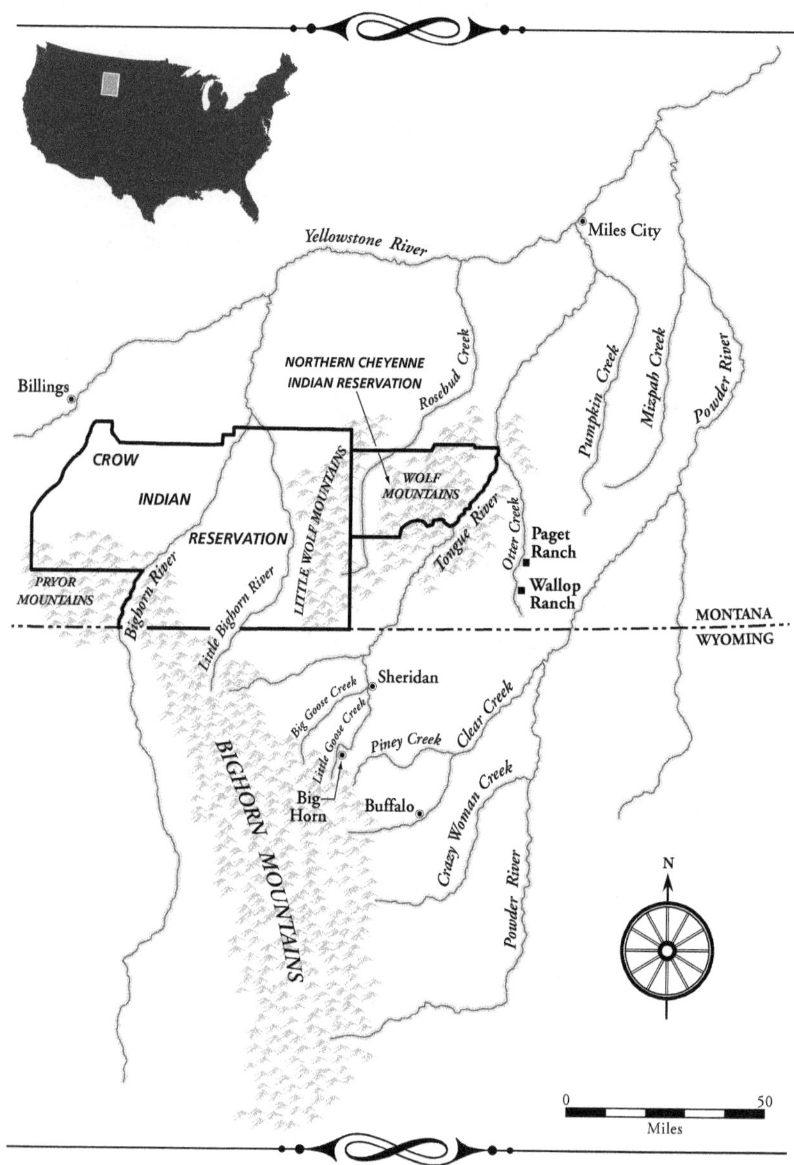

Yellowstone River
Miles City
Billings
NORTHERN CHEYENNE
INDIAN RESERVATION
Rosebud Creek
Pumpkin Creek
Mizpah Creek
Powder River
CROW
INDIAN
RESERVATION
LITTLE WOLF MOUNTAINS
WOLF
MOUNTAINS
Tongue River
Otter Creek
Paget
Ranch
Wallop
Ranch
PRYOR
MOUNTAINS
Bighorn River
Little Bighorn River
MONTANA
WYOMING
Sheridan
Big Goose Creek
Little Goose Creek
Piney Creek
Clear Creek
Big
Horn
Buffalo
Crazy Woman Creek
BIGHORN MOUNTAINS
Powder River
N
0
50
Miles

II

The Wild Sons of the Queen, the White Sons of the Wild, and the Royal Bloodlines from the East

18

It is a most fertile valley with room for 200,000 horses. A small investment can reap up to $90,000 a year in raising horses here.

—General James Brisbin

WITH THE SURRENDER OF THE FIGHTING NATIVE HORSEmen of the area, the last frontier in America was now open for settlement. A new horse culture of cow ponies, workhorses, and imported thoroughbreds was quickly replacing the warhorses and buffalo runners of the Plains Indians.

The first town in Absaraka was born from alcohol. At Fort Keogh, located at the confluence of the Yellowstone and Tongue rivers, whiskey gave Colonel Nelson Miles more problems than the fight against the Indians. The guardhouse was full of drunken soldiers. At least one had died from drinking moonshine, which resulted in Miles banishing the whiskey trader from his camp. The trader packed his kegs on the back of a mule and moved a few miles east, starting a community that first became known as Milesburge, then Milestown, and later Miles City.

Buffalo hunters, whiskey peddlers, prostitutes, horse thieves, bullwhackers, gamblers, and cowboys mixed with British nobility and wealthy, educated ranchers in the wide-open frontier town. Steamers chugged chandeliers and pianos up the Yellowstone and buffalo robes and wolf pelts back down to Saint Louis. Milesburge would, appropriately, grow into one of the wildest towns in the nation and—on the strength of the surrounding grassland—into one of the largest and most colorful horse-trading centers in the world.

With the protection of Fort Keogh next door, Miles City became a gathering place for ambitious men bent on raising livestock.

General James "Grasshopper" Brisbin, who arrived at the Little Bighorn battlefield in time to kick dirt on the bodies of Custer and his men, claimed in his book, *The Beef Bonanza: How to Get Rich on the Plains*, that there was room for two hundred thousand horses in Absaraka. He estimated that two hundred stallions and a thousand mares might produce a herd of ten thousand horses—all of which could be run in the area like cattle. The grass was free, so all one had to do was throw his livestock out and let them eat. The climate was right and no shelter or feed would be needed year-round.

Brisbin speculated that an investment of $48,000 could start to yield $90,000 a year after the first four years. Before the ink was dry on Brisbin's book, industrious men were already trailing livestock northward.

> *When a man walked in front of them or reached his hand to touch their head, it was just as natural for those horses to strike as it was for them to eat or drink because a man had never been near them except to brand them or hurt them in some way . . . We would start to show him that we did not want to hurt him, and that was hard to learn for some of them. This was the wildest trip I ever made up the trail . . . These horses stampeded night and day . . . the rumble of the heaviest freight train would be quiet in comparison to the terrible noise they made. Finally after two months we got those horses to Wyoming. We were not sorry when we could turn those horses over to their new owners.*
> *—Bob Fudge, Texas cowboy*

The horses were usually from four to seven years old, and some weighed close to eleven hundred pounds. The riders would hold the horses on the edge of a barricade while a lone roper would calmly ride toward the herd and rope the bronc by the neck and pull it away from the rest of the herd with a stout rope horse. Another roper would then rope the hind legs, pulling the horse down. From here the rope around the head was switched, and the horse's feet were tied while a cowboy sat on the animal's neck and held its head back so it could not rise. Another cowboy would unsaddle his horse and saddle the horse that was tied down. The cowboy practiced mounting with the horse's back foot tied up. Once the cowboy was able to mount it, the horse was set free with the cowboy astride. It was man against beast, loose on the prairie; the cowboy's only salvation was his friends hazing him along with their saddle horses.

September 1877

Charlie, a seventeen-year-old cowboy, and his friend Ed trailed sixteen hundred cows north from West Texas, and then rode west after drawing wages at Spearfish, South Dakota, to try their luck as buffalo hunters. Charlie rode a gelding that he was given for breaking ten others down in Texas. He carried an old cap-and-ball pistol in a holster and a Winchester tied in a scabbard on the side of his horse. With saddlebags and bedrolls tied behind their saddles, Charlie and Ed rode into the wilderness cautiously, as there were small bands of hostile Indians still at large. When the two cowboys reached the hills overlooking the Powder River, they spotted an animal mired in the quicksand in the distance. "I hope it's a buffalo," Ed said, but when the two rode closer, the animal proved to be a horse.

When the two cowboys approached, the mare began to thrash on the banks with her front hooves, causing her to sink further. Without hesitation Charlie dismounted and walked toward the mare cautiously with his rope in his hand. "Whoa, there, we're not going to hurt you, we're just going to pull you out." Charlie tested the soft sand with the toe of his boot. He stopped fifteen feet away and tried for a head catch. He caught on the second try, and then handed the other end of the rope to Ed, who still sat on his horse.

"Give me your rope." Ed handed his rope to Charlie, who placed it around his waist.

"Why don't you let me just pull her out by the head?" Ed asked.

"It might kill her; she's weak already. I'm gonna try to tie a halter on that won't choke her."

I think she's a broom tail.[1] Don't get killed over her," Ed replied. Charlie sat on the ground and took his boots and socks off and eased his way into the wet sand until he began to sink. Following the rope that ran to the mare, he reached out, but when he touched the loop around her neck she exploded in a panic. She tried to lunge for the bank, using Charlie as footing. The mare got both front feet over the rope that was tied around Charlie, and sinking back into the quicksand after a second lunge, the mare's weight pulled him under.

Ed watched from astride his horse, unsure of how he could help aside from pitching slack to the ropes and hoping for the best. The mare pawed her way over the top of Charlie to the solid bank. Just as Ed began to think his friend would not resurface, Charlie appeared, covered in the wet sand. Breathing heavily, Charlie twisted the mare's right ear to steady her with one hand while threading the rope into a halter with his other hand. Soon Ed had them pulled out to dry ground.

"Don't let her go; I worked too hard for her," Charlie gasped, after catching his breath. He approached the mare on her right, and she pulled back. Ed sat on his horse holding his dally while his horse, trained to lean against a rope, held his footing against the pressure. "Looks like you'll have to break this one," he said. "Whoa, girl, I know I smell funny to you, but I'm not gonna hurt you. She's an Indian mare. She's just not used to people approaching her from the left." Charlie ran his hand gently across her neck and shoulder, scraping handfuls of wet sand off her. Soon she began to relax and work her mouth.

The two found a solid crossing downstream and led the mare across. As soon as they hit the bank, she began to fidget on the end of the rope. "Look at how this mare acts. She was going somewhere when we found her." Charlie had noticed that the mare looked and pulled toward the west. "I bet she was hunting home. She ain't all mustang either; they're all short bodied, husky, and big bellied. This mare is more refined."

Charlie spread out his wet clothes on branches, and then led the mare to a patch of tall grass, where his hand grazed her. "She's put together good, ain't she?" He looked her over and found a scar on the left side of her rump. "Looks like a bullet wound." Charlie gently swung up on her right side. "Look here, she's plumb broke!"

Ed found a new respect for his young partner. Charlie was only seventeen, but he was horse savvy. Ed's attention was suddenly drawn toward something white scattered along the banks of the Powder. He rode over and saw it was thousands of old bleached horse bones. He called to Charlie, who rode the mare over bareback. "What do you suppose killed these horses?" Charlie asked his friend, as the two stood among the bones, noticing some horseshoes lying among them.

"I'd say a bullet killed this one," Charlie replied. Ed walked over, and sure enough, there was a .50-caliber bullet lodged in the horse's skull. Having just ridden past the eerie remains of burned wagons and saddles—remnants of Colonel Nelson Cole's death march twelve years earlier—neither cowboy wanted to think about or even mention Indians.

That night, sitting by the campfire, Charlie tamped extra powder in the cylinders of his pistol. Sitting Bull and Gall were still out there somewhere, although everyone said he was heading to Canada. And the boys had heard that Custer had ridden to his death while being chased by ten thousand warriors on the Little Bighorn, which was not far from where they camped. To spook the young cowboys even further, there was a lunar eclipse. Unknown to either boy, the eclipse marked the death of a warrior whose warhorse Charlie had tied to a nearby cottonwood tree.

A loud snap in the middle of the night jerked both cowboys from their sleep. They awoke to the sounds of drumming hoofbeats. Charlie pulled his pistol, and his partner grabbed his rifle. "The horses!" Charlie whispered, and in a moment they were at the tie line. Charlie examined the broken rope that had held the mare. Both their saddle horses were still there, which ruled out a horse thief.

"Let's go back to sleep; we'll find her in the morning," Ed said. Charlie shook his head. "She was headed somewhere when we found her, and she's headed somewhere now." The next morning it was obvious the mare had put too much distance between them to follow, so they let her go.

From the start, the two cowboys had hell as buffalo hunters. Their first hunt dissolved when a small herd outran them before they could get into rifle range.

"Dang, I wonder how the Indians did it," Charlie said, as the two pulled up their exhausted horses and watched the buffalo gallop away. "I never knew buffalo could run so fast. I guess the Indians' horses were faster than ours."

The thought suddenly struck both cowboys that if attacked, they wouldn't be outrunning any Indians either. "Our rifles ain't worth shit; we need bigger guns," Charlie said.

"I say we go back to being cowboys," Ed said.

"Sounds good to me, but this would be good cow country; look at the damn grass." The two had already come upon some cattle branded TV that had been turned out on the free grass of the area.

The cowboys had heard of an old settler named Bradshaw who had homesteaded off Otter Creek. When they came across his place, they rode in for a visit. Bradshaw invited the boys in for a meal and to spend the night.

"You boys have reached the land of the grasshopper. I've seen it so bad, there wasn't a blade of grass between here and the Bighorn Mountains," Bradshaw said to the boys.

"How come you ain't been killed by the Indians?" Charlie asked.

"They don't bother you as long as you don't stir them up," Bradshaw replied. "There's been whites living with Indians forever."

The cowboys weren't so sure.

Charlie and Ed planned to head back the next day on the telegraph road between Fort Meade, in the Black Hills, and Fort Keogh. Their host sent them on their way with this warning: "You boys be careful. There's worse than Indians on the roads these days." Bradshaw had seen that the teenage cowboys, though good-natured, were neither experienced nor prepared for the dangerous element that had moved into the area since the Indians had moved out. His concern would prove well-grounded.

On the road back to the Black Hills, the two cowboys stopped at Telegraph Station[2] between Fort Meade, South Dakota, and Fort Keogh. Soldiers, gamblers, hide hunters, and thieves stopped there to rest, drink, and play cards. Ed was lured into a three-day game of cards by a professional gambler. Charlie stood by his friend as an interested spectator, but he stayed clear of the game. On the third day, a frustrated loser, full of whiskey, accused Ed of cheating.

"You didn't mind my dealing when you won. But it seems nobody but you wins when you deal, so I'd just settle down and play cards," Ed replied.

"I don't have to take shit off no ignorant cowboy," the man said, and before anyone could react, a gun went off under the table. Ed doubled over and fell on the floor.

When he realized his friend was dead, Charlie flew into a blind rage. The card players had fled outside, and Charlie rushed after them to find Ed's murderer. He quickly spotted the man, pulled his pistol, and shot the killer five times at point-blank range with the hot "Indian" loads. The man lay on the ground with five smoldering holes in him.

"Son of a bitch kilt my friend," Charlie said to the card players, who had just witnessed two killings in less than three minutes.

"I think you killed him on the first shot," the bartender said, looking at the smoking corpse.

"He had that coming," another frightened man said in a calm voice.

Charlie felt he was in a dream. Moments earlier he had been at peace watching a card game, and now his friend was dead and he had committed a murder. Feeling this could escalate, the bartender intervened. "Son, we'll take care of your friend. That man had it coming, but it might be better if you git. We'll tell the soldiers it wasn't your fault."

Within minutes, Charlie was galloping off for the Black Hills, leading Ed's horse with all their gear packed on top. In every face he encountered on the road, he imagined it was a lawman coming to hang him for the shooting. In Deadwood, he tried his hand at gold mining, but the town seemed a more dangerous place than Telegraph Station. Wild Bill Hickok had just been murdered, and a lawless element was everywhere.

While buying supplies in a Deadwood store, a clerk approached Charlie. "Hear about the big killing?" His words nearly stopped the boy's heart. He was sure word of his shooting had made it to Deadwood. Charlie looked at the floor and shook his head no. "They killed Crazy Horse down at Fort Robinson. A soldier bayoneted him. This country will open up to settlers now."

Charlie pulled his hat down and decided he had better get to Texas before he was hanged. He rode south for the Indian territory, staying clear of the cattle herds moving north. He shot antelope and grouse for food and filled his canteens whenever he hit fresh water. When he got to Texas, he traded both his horses for ten cows, which he threw in with the first herd he found work with. Charlie watched cattlemen and cowboys flocking north to build large herds on the free grassland he had just left. He knew that was where the opportunity lay, but he wasn't going back anytime soon and get hanged.

Back in Texas, Charlie worked on cattle drives between Texas and Arizona. He never gave his last name and signed his name with an X. Fellow cowboys began to call him Charlie the "X," which soon merged into the alias Charlie Thex. By the time he would return to Absaraka, English horse breeders had moved in and were raising thousands of horses from the world's great bloodlines.

19

He is an Englishman—the son of a Lord, and the most harum-scarum man I ever saw. He talks with a slight English accent in a continuous stream. Harry says he seems to be able to talk right on telling his own story and answer your questions at the same time. [He] is the most happy-go-lucky, good-natured soul that ever lived. He will do anything for you while he is with you but will forget anything and everything while he is away. He is quite a gentleman and is well read.

—Waldo Emerson Forbes

Summer 1883

OLIVER HENRY WALLOP, OR "NOLL" TO HIS FRIENDS, HAD grown up riding to the hounds, playing polo, and shooting pheasants on his father's thirty-thousand-acre estate in North Devonshire, England. Noll was somewhat of an embarrassment to his family because he spoke with a slight stutter and, in some situations, was completely absentminded, but he always seemed to have a pleasant anecdote to share and had no problem laughing at himself. Underneath it all he was a brilliant thinker. Also, he could speak Latin and quote from the Bible or the classics, both of which he knew inside and out. After graduating Oxford, he applied for a position in the British Navy but was turned down because of a respiratory ailment.

Noll's father, Lord Isaac Newton Wallop, the fifth Earl of Portsmouth, gave Noll a hunting trip to the American West as a college graduation present. After bagging grizzly bear, elk, and deer in British Columbia, Noll Wallop got off the train in Miles City, Montana, with his shotgun and rifle. Despite his formal education, Wallop had indulged in dime-store novels portraying the romantic image of the American West. Crazy Horse, mountain man and guide Jim Bridger, and Buffalo Bill were already household names in England.

After Sitting Bull surrendered to Colonel Miles, the country was officially open. By 1881 Miles City, with a population of a thousand settlers, boasted more than forty-two saloons. In an average day, a thousand bottles of beer and four hundred gallons of whiskey were consumed. At the half-dozen brothels and opera houses, for a price you could watch a show from a private box that could be entirely closed off with curtains should the box holder desire. The soiled doves of the plains worked the boxes during and after the show, and rooms were also available in the back. On one occasion, a drunken patron leaned over his railing in an attempt to watch the doings in the box below and got his throat cut in the bargain.

For all its wild times, there were comparatively few murders, as Fort Keogh housed a thousand soldiers just across the Tongue River. Wealthy businessmen stood shoulder to shoulder in the saloons with buffalo hunters, old army scouts, and Texas cowboys.

In Miles City, cowboys wore guns and rode broncs in the streets, which were abuzz with talk of how fortunes could be made throwing livestock out on the free grasslands. Homesteads, tracts of 160 acres, were free to anyone who could put a house on the land.

Noll Wallop felt Miles City was where he belonged. The clean, thin air and wide-open spaces of the Great Plains were like a tonic to him, and his health began to improve. On the frontier he could hunt bear, elk, deer, antelope, and grouse, as well as fish for trout.

According to the English law of primogeniture, the first son in a noble family inherited the father's estate; subsequent sons generally took up careers in the armed services or the clergy, or they emigrated abroad—aided only by a small allowance called a remittance. Unfortunately for Noll Wallop, he had two older brothers; fortunately, however, he had to look no farther than Miles City to find other such remittance men. So it was that during his sojourn there Noll made it a point to pay Lord Alfred Paget's son Sydney a visit.

Noll Wallop was in a Miles City saddlery inspecting a saddle decorated with a naked lady carved on the skirt when a tag labeled "Paget" caught his eye.

"Excuse m-m-me. The tag on this saddle says P-Paget. Could you tell me if that might be Sydney Paget?" The clerk in the saddle shop looked at Wallop suspiciously.

"That's his saddle all right. You a friend of his?"

"We've shot pheasant together, and I p-played p-polo with him in school. Could you tell me where I might find him?"

"Sam Pepper's Saloon, most likely, there or the 44," he said.

"Would you be k-kind enough to direct me to the saloons? If I remember ol' Syd c-correctly, it's about the right time of day to find him enjoying a gin."

"The 44's not a bar, although you can get a drink there. It's what you English call a . . . what is it Paget calls it?"

"A gentlemen's club?" Wallop offered.

"That's it," the clerk said. "Anyway, Sam Pepper's is two streets east, then turn right. You can't miss it."

"Sp-splendid," Wallop said.

Sydney Paget loved to chase women, bet on racehorses, and hunt buffalo. He fit right into the Miles City social scene. Paget's grandfather, Field Marshal Sir Henry William Paget, had been the hero of Waterloo, directing Wellington's cavalry against the French. Sir Henry was a brilliant and gallant cavalry officer, but as a man he was neither wise nor virtuous. He had fought a duel over his involvement with a married woman in a scandalous affair that broke up two marriages.

His son, Lord Alfred Paget, had traveled to America with Lord Waterbury and hunted buffalo with Colonel George Custer in Kansas before Custer's demise at the Little Bighorn. Lord Paget was concerned that Sydney's undisciplined amours could damage the family name in England, so he bankrolled his son in a cattle operation in Montana.

In Miles City, Sydney ran up bills all over town, and after a few months, his father would send money from England and everyone would get paid. Sir Sydney had already started a relationship with a courtesan called the Queen of Miles City. Connie Hoffman was a striking brunette with large brown eyes and a figure built for speed. One of the most beautiful women in Miles City, she was one of its most notorious characters too. Had she been located in

Washington, D.C. or New York, Connie Hoffman might well have been the hostess to the social scene there. With an abundance of intelligence and common sense, she had an engaging personality that opened doors for her wherever she went. After her arrival in Miles City from Deadwood, Connie became the sweetheart of all the wealthy ranchers in the area.

Connie left Deadwood when Miles City became a booming town filled with rich businessmen from the East and remittance men from Britain. She took up residence at the 44 house as a high-priced courtesan. She soon made acquaintance with Sir Sydney Paget, which began with a romp of elaborate meals and champagne nights and soon blossomed into a genuine relationship.

In a scandalous and flamboyant fashion statement, Connie made national news:

> *The Yellowstone Daily Journal*
> *December 16, 1882*
>
> *The following item is at present enjoying the run of the eastern press:*
>
> *One of the Deadwood "girls" is having a dress made and embroidered with the cattle brands of the various cattlemen whom she counts among her admirers . . . under contract for two hundred dollars. Some of the investors will no doubt be heartily ashamed of their fool investment before they die if not sooner. The brands and initials of her favorites cover the side of her neck and bosom, and the brands of those occupying an indifferent corner of her affections are attached to the bottom of the skirt, and some are located so as to be frequently sat down upon. After reading this explanation, her admirers will be enabled to discover at a glance their standing in the girl's sinful love whenever she appears in the novel frock.*

When Wallop entered Sam Pepper's Saloon, he found Sydney Paget holding court with two other Englishmen and a brunette beauty wearing a silk crimson dress.

"Noll Wallop!" Paget sprang to his feet when he saw the young man approach. "Here is the best shot in all of England!" Paget announced to the bar.

"It's good to see you, S-Sydney," Wallop said.

"Noll, may I introduce the Queen of Miles City, Her Royal Majesty, Connie Hoffman."

Noll bowed politely. "It's an honor, your m-majesty, and m-may I say that you are wearing a lovely dress."

Connie stood up, revealing her figure, and reached for Noll's hand. "Please, it's just Connie. The pleasure is all mine." Noll immediately blushed, which caused the men around the table to chuckle.

"What do you think, Noll?" Syd asked.

"I have on occasions seen Victoria in all her glory, and m-may I say never have I seen a dress more fit for r-royalty."

"This calls for a celebration," Paget said. Over drinks the conversation turned to ranching. "This is horse country. Four years ago, I trailed two thousand head of cattle from Texas with my foreman and a crew of cowboys. A hard winter hit, and we lost all but two hundred. The horses, however, wintered fine, so I decided to go into the horse business. The one thing everyone needs in this country is horses. Roads, homes, and businesses are being built, and they all need horses. Homesteaders and the cattlemen all need horses. It takes almost ten horses per cowboy to ride herd on cattle so they don't get lost or stolen."

"What keeps horses from running off?" Noll asked.

"They tend to drift until they find a range of about ten miles that they will locate in and remain there. Good lord, old boy, the buffalo grass here will feed tens of thousands and it's all free! The best part is the buffalo grass grows strong horses, and the thin air and cold climate give them endurance beyond compare. I am building a half-mile track on my Otter Creek ranch, ninety miles from here. I can time the fastest of the Indian ponies and cross them with thoroughbreds, and when I acquire one with real speed, I'll be off to England to show them what kind of horses we raise in Montana."

"What about farm land?" Wallop asked, causing Paget to laugh.

"It's grazing land, old boy. There are farmers here now, but they won't last. They try to plow the ground and fence their crops, but the topsoil is too thin and the climate too dry. They tend to fence up the spots on the river where everyone's cattle on the open range go to water."

Connie Hoffman studied Wallop. Her livelihood, and at times her life, had depended on her ability to judge men. He seemed different from the other men. He was a gentleman who seemed to relish company, yet he had a restless side to him. Unlike almost every man she came in contact with, Noll hadn't yet given her a lingering look, nor had he shown any carnal interest in the working girls sitting around the saloon. Her observations proved correct; within an hour Noll announced, "I thought I might rent a horse and ride to the Missouri River." You could have heard a pin drop.

"You just got here, old boy. Why not stay and enjoy a bit of Western society? That's one hundred miles, over dry country. There's a rough element up on the Missouri breaks, and there are gangs of horse thieves up there. If you want to explore, go south to the Bighorns. That's where you'll find the good grass and water. I'll show you my ranch on the ride down," Paget offered.

"Ever since I was a lad, I've w-wanted to retrace part of Lewis and Clark's travels. I'll be b-back in a few days; now, if you might direct me to the livery stable, I'd be much appreciative."

"Charlie Brown, one of our founding citizens, runs our livery stable. He's German and serves as our town veterinarian, justice of the peace, auctioneer, and owner of the Cottage Saloon. He's also been a strongman in the circus.

"He brought his family by steamship up the Yellowstone before the railroad arrived. His children had three buffalo and a bear they raised from a two-week-old cub for pets. The bear stood six feet on his haunches, wandered Main Street, and slept behind the saloon until it was shot for taking a baby out of its mother's arms.

"Charlie's heart is as big as the plains. He keeps a tin pot of Mulligan stew in the back room of his saloon for bums or cowboys who are down on their luck. Local elections are held in his saloon—the votes are tallied on the gambling machines. The best part for us is that his auction yard is turning into quite the center for buying and selling horses. The railroad is even starting to issue free passes to ranchers' livestock to promote land sales here."

The table went silent, something Wallop noted, as if there was more that was unspoken. While walking to work that spring, Charlie heard shouts coming from a prominent family's home. He investigated and found two drunken men verbally and physically abusing a woman and her daughter. Charlie Brown grabbed a pick handle and brained the ringleader, causing the second intruder to flee. The fallen man was taken to the jail, where he died from the blow.

Some townspeople who worried Charlie might face a manslaughter charge took the dead man out and hanged him.

Noll bought a round of drinks for the table, tipped his hat, and excused himself.

"That might be the last you'll see of your friend," one of the men at the table said. Syd shook his head. "He's a good bit tougher than he appears," Sydney said. Connie watched him leave and looked at Sydney. "He's lonely, Syd."

Noll Wallop and Charlie Brown hit it off immediately. Noll recognized the man by Paget's description and greeted him in German. Soon Wallop mounted a sorrel bronc Charlie let him use for the ride. Charlie supplied him with a bedroll, a scabbard for Noll's rifle, and a bottle of rye for his saddlebags.

"You vatch out. Der bad men on da Missouri. Horse tieves. I vork mit one in army. Big red-headed man named Harvey Gleason from Roat Island. Vas teamster mit General Crook. Call himself Teton Jackson now. You come back und do like Paget. Start horse ranch. Everybody need horses."

Noll smiled at Brown. "If I could find a woman as lovely as M-Miss Hoffman, I m-might take up sweeping the floors in the gentlemen's club.

"Connie gut girl, but new vimmen don't like it zo vell, her valking around mit Paget. People change here. Not zo friendly as early days. Don't lose your horse; be a long vay mit no vater." Noll smiled and waved good-bye, the act of which spooked the sorrel, who dropped his head and began to buck. Noll was thrown every way but off and somehow clung to the horse until he settled with eyes bugged out and nostrils flared. Charlie walked over and handed Noll his rifle, which had shot out of its scabbard during the bucking. "Here, I tie dis for you."

Noll had eased the horse down only two blocks of Main Street before a woman spooked the sorrel when she walked out of a store. This time the horse bucked across the street into a woodpile, which fell over. The sorrel was balling in a fit of anger as Wallop grabbed for mane, saddle, and anything he could get his hands on. After bouncing off the corner of the store, the bronc made his way across a side street onto a sidewalk and scattered several pedestrians.

There was no expertise in Noll's riding. Instead it looked as if only the hand of God kept him aboard the sorrel. When Noll gathered his wits after weathering a second storm, he looked around at the townspeople who had stopped to watch. "T-terribly sorry; is everyone a-alright?" He gathered his reins and began to ride away but was hailed by a young boy: "Hey, mister, you forgot your hat." Noll turned back but was at wits' end as to how he might reach out for his hat without sending the sorrel into another fit of bucking. He decided to dismount and walk slowly over to the boy. "There's a bottle of whiskey!" the boy said, pointing to a bottle lying in the dirt. Noll checked his saddlebags and, sure enough, the horse had bucked the bottle out. Noll took the bottle and remounted, which sent the horse into another bucking fit, though by this point he was wearing down.

"Thhhhhank you," Noll managed to blurt out to the boy as he rode east out of town on the hopping horse.

The ferry across the Yellowstone was operated by James McNaney, who had come to the area with his brother three years earlier to hunt buffalo, and stayed. The brothers also had a business providing meat for the 5th Infantry, which was stationed at Fort Keogh.

McNaney was now watching the odd form of a horse and rider sidetracking to the right and then the left as they approached. "I hope we can get that one on the ferry," McNaney said, as he watched Wallop frantically kicking the sorrel that had balked thirty feet away from the ramp to the ferry. "Mr. B-Brown kindly let me use this horse if I was willing to give him a ride."

McNaney smiled as he watched Noll Wallop approach the ferry—an adventure his sorrel gelding appeared reluctant to try. Once Wallop was finally close enough to dismount, James led the horse on board, his brother hazing it from behind.

Once they got the horse settled, the three men began to talk about guns, hunting, and buffalo. "When I first got here, buffalo steers and cows used to drift onto Main Street during snowstorms," said James. "We had seventy-five thousand cross the river above here this spring. That had every buffalo hunter in town running for his Sharps. I doubt many will make it back on their migration next time around. They say the herds to the south are about gone."

Wallop pulled the bottle from his saddlebags and handed it to McNaney. The young man smiled and took a drink, and then Wallop did the same.

"Two hundred thousand buffalo were killed along the Yellowstone during the winter of 1879," James continued. "Used to be that the hills outside Miles City were black with buffalo. Cattle and horse ranchers would stake buffalo hunters with whatever they needed because cattle and horses tended to get swept up with the buffalo and leave the country. All that's about over, which is why I run this ferry now."

When Wallop mentioned Sydney Paget to James McNaney, the young buffalo hunter had a laugh. "When you get back to town, ask Paget about his first buffalo hunt. About ten miles from his homestead, Syd spotted a large buffalo cow and got off his horse to shoot it. His first shot missed and spooked his horse, which ran back to the ranch, leaving Sir Sydney to walk home.

"The next day he returned on a thoroughbred racer, intending to gallop in on the herd Indian style. He was flying over clumps of sagebrush and rocks while he white-knuckled his rifle and attempted to point it in the direction of the rumbling herd. His first shot landed who-knows-where, but Sydney managed to chamber another. Before he could fire again, his horse stumbled, which caused him to squeeze the trigger. The bullet killed his horse in midstride. Sir Sydney was vaulted to the ground and had to walk home again.

"Paget finally rode a quiet old ranch horse and killed the largest bull recorded in the area. He loaded the buffalo on a wagon and drove into town and got drunk. He had the buffalo's head stuffed and mounted above his bed in his cabin. As if he hadn't suffered enough during his buffalo hunting, the head fell off the wall in the middle of the night and crushed him in his sleep."

The men continued to visit after disembarking. From where they sat, they could see two dark-skinned men riding along the opposite bank. "What do the Indians do around here?" Noll asked.

"They're trying to make farmers out of them. I guess that's what they did before they got horses, but their hearts ain't in it any more than a cowboy's would be. They say the Cheyenne did the fighting, the Sioux got the glory, and the Crow got the land. They shipped the Cheyenne to Oklahoma a few years ago, and they fought their way back. Dull Knife made it to Fort Robinson, and Little Wolf made it here. Colonel Nelson Miles finally gave them a reservation across the Tongue. I've seen Dull Knife and Little Wolf around the fort several times.

"The army still uses Cheyenne as scouts here, but for the rest of the tribe, they mainly sit and wait for the government to send them their beef. They still slip off and kill buffalo so they don't starve. The government is cutting their beef something terrible; when the buffalo are gone, they'll really suffer.

"The Crow, Cheyenne, Blackfeet, and Sioux still raid each other even though they're not supposed to. It's their culture. No big battles, just small skirmishes and horse-stealing raids that they try to hide from the army. They know if they stir up any real trouble or if a rancher gets killed, the army will come down on them hard. There are still survivors of the Sand Creek massacre around and those that lived through the Indian wars. They don't want any trouble."

The two men exchanged another pull on the rye bottle before Noll mounted up. McNaney watched Noll circle his horse to the north, but then Noll stopped, turned, and rode back. "I thought you might l-like another drink," Noll said. McNaney laughed and eased over and took the bottle from the saddlebags while the sorrel stood quivering, ready to explode. "You'd better get going, Stay off the Fort Union Road. The way I told you is the quickest." McNaney took a drink and gently slipped the bottle back into the saddlebag so as not to spook the horse. "You'll have this son-of-a-bitch broke by the time you get back."

"It's been a pleasure, M-Mr. McNaney," Noll said, tipping his hat. Just before stopping to camp that evening, Wallop spotted something on the horizon and rode over to investigate. The sun's red light reflected off the large skeletons lying on the sparse Montana grass. Upon inspection, Wallop realized these buffalo had been killed for their hides, leaving the meat to rot on the bones. Raised a sportsman, the Englishman had a lot of respect for his prey; what he saw moved him to gallop away from the spot, but the farther north he rode, the more dead animal bones he saw.

He had well intended to kill something for his supper, but his appetite was content with the biscuits and dried meat Charlie Brown had packed him. He slept in a fireless camp and was soon in a deep sleep. When he awoke, he found his sorrel fidgeting on the picket rope he had tied. Noll had been following a rough game trail north but had made his camp down a draw from the trail. After saddling his horse, he rode up to a ridge, and on the far horizon he spotted several riders trailing horses north at a fast pace. By midday, just after crossing Dry Creek, he caught sight of Smoky Butte in the distance. He shot a young antelope and cut off several steaks, which he roasted over a fire. When he hit the Missouri that evening, he sat and read from a Bible while the great river rolled past. The next day he explored the south bank until the evening, when trouble in the form of several riders shadowing the horizon hit.

On his second day along the great river, Noll noticed two riders about a half-mile off; they sat still upon their horses, neither approaching nor riding away. The country was broken with ravines and side hills. Instinctively, Noll rode toward the men, but they vanished down a draw. Riding up on a hill for a look, he saw two more riders to the west; as had the other two men, these vanished as soon as he appeared.

Wallop had no doubt he was being stalked and that these were some of the men he had been warned about. *No use running*, he thought. His only chance was to face his assailants. He reached for his looking-glass in his saddlebags, but just then something spooked the sorrel. Noll lost his seat and crashed to the ground. He clung to the reins, but the sorrel began to run backward, dragging him and causing Noll to release his grip.

"Hold up right there," a voice yelled out. Noll rolled to his feet and saw two men riding toward him.

"I seem to have lost my horse. Would one of you men be kind enough to ride over and catch him?"

One man had a rifle in his hand, and both men wore two pistols. They sat on their horses thirty feet away and stared, but neither spoke again.

"I b-borrowed that horse from Charles Brown in Miles City, and I would hate to lose him. He's a b-bucker but travels nicely. Can I offer you men a drink?" Since neither man responded or moved, Noll started walking after his horse, which had disappeared over a hill to the south.

"I said hold up, you stuttering limey prick," one of the horsemen said and pointed his gun at Noll, who stopped but continued to converse as if he had been in a conversation. In a moment three men appeared, leading the sorrel. "Thank you, gentlemen; M-Mr. Brown will be most appreciative." Just then a man with red hair and beady dark eyes rode forward, blocking Noll from his horse.

"Charlie Brown, you say, from Miles City?" the man asked.

"Yes, he was k-kind enough to loan it to me. I'm looking for a man named Gleason. I m-may be a distant relative of his. You see, I had a great uncle who settled in Rhode Island as a b-boy. He sailed over with the Pilgrims, and his family followed soon thereafter, but my great-uncle was never found. We think he p-perished with Sir Walter Raleigh in the Carolinas. My point is, I traced members of my family to Rhode Island, which led me west to meet more relatives here. Can I offer you a drink?"

"You're ain't got no more to drink, you ignorant limey."

A cowboy had ridden down the sorrel and caught the reins. He reached over to pull Noll's rifle from the scabbard. The sorrel spooked, causing another man to rope him and choke him down. "There, see what he's got in his saddlebags." The sorrel stood with his legs spread, gasping for air while the men pilfered Noll's possessions.

"That's Charlie's brand, alright," confirmed the redheaded man, Teton Jackson.

"Sir, might you be Gleason? I see we both have red hair. Perhaps we are cousins, although I see by your size you might be one of the larger Wallops. My father, the Earl of P-Portsmouth, while portly, is no giant. You, sir, look like a cavalryman. We Wallops have a history in the navy . . .," he bantered, until the redheaded man told him to shut up.

"Teton, let's kill him and make it look like Indians," one of the gunman said just as the sorrel fell over from lack of air.

"Ahh, so you're the famous T-Teton Jackson, aka Harvey Gleason. Splendid! We can compare family notes," Noll lifted his hat to expose his red hair. "You men see any r-resemblance?" He looked toward the men. Most of them looked amused, but one seemed ready to kill.

The man holding the dally on the sorrel let the rope slacken to give the animal air. The sorrel lay motionless for a moment and then drew a great breath and struggled to his feet. "Well, that should take the b-buck out of him, I have to admit that animal . . ."

"Will you shut your stuttering?" one of the gunman yelled.

"Can you shoot?" Teton Jackson asked as he looked at one of his men, who was already examining Noll's rifle.

"I've had some experience, yes," Noll answered.

"Good. I'm leaving you one bullet to shoot something on your way back to Miles City. Now git!" Jackson commanded. The man holding Noll's rifle looked appalled, but a hard look from Jackson checked his defiance. Jackson led the sorrel to Noll, who mounted and tipped his hat.

"I am eternally grateful, Mr. Gleason. If you're ever in Farley Wallop, England, you have a friend there," Wallop called over his shoulder as he trotted off.

"Why the hell did you let him go?" one of the outlaws asked Jackson.

"Are you forgetting that the last person who stole one of Charlie Brown's horses got trailed to Denver from Miles City and put in jail?"

"I ain't afraid of that fat bastard."

"Maybe not, but if we steal one of his horses, he won't stop till he finds us. If we kill him, chances are, everyone in Miles City with a hard-on will follow us, maybe even the soldiers from Fort Keogh. All for an English gun and a bronc."

Teton Jackson watched Noll Wallop ride away to the grumbling of his men. The last thing he needed was a band of soldiers riding out to avenge the death of the son of an English earl's son. The large redheaded man commanded over fifty men in different stages of a horse-stealing operation that stretched from Idaho to the Black Hills. His plans now revolved around a larger prize: the kidnapping of President Chester Arthur on his upcoming visit to Yellowstone Park.

Noll Wallop had no reservations about his close call. He pondered how he could have avoided being trapped as he had. He considered his future as he roasted the meat of a young doe he had killed with his one bullet. "*Fortuna de luna primus,*" he said as he looked into the roaring fire.

"Dat sound like Jackson. Lucky he don shoot you." Charlie Brown stood looking at the sorrel after Noll Wallop arrived back in Miles City. "Good vork. Da sorrel he like a new horse," Brown said.

"I'm afraid your outlaw friend t-took the rye you gave me, but if you'll allow me, I'd like to buy you a drink," Noll said.

"Vee go find Paget, he vaiting for you to kum baak. Yaa, he'll be glat you don get kilt."

Noll was relieved to have lived to return the sorrel to Charlie Brown. The two men had a drink in three different saloons before they found Paget drinking with a band of Englishmen at the MacQueen House by the railroad depot.

"My older brother had given General Custer a pair of Wembly .44-caliber pistols as a gift for taking him buffalo hunting in Kansas. I imagine there's a chance Custer might have had them on him when he was killed. With any luck they may surface with the Cheyenne across the Tongue. In any event they may make a nice gift for my father in England; keep the finances coming, so to speak."

Paget looked up and saw Wallop and Charlie Brown walk in the door. "Look here, Noll is back and has our founding mayor with him. Take a seat, old boy, and tell us of your travels."

"Found Teton Jackson, he did," Brown said.

"Glad you lived through it, old boy, we'll have to celebrate, but first we have to let Walsh know of your arrival. Noll, did you know Bob Walsh was here?" he asked.

"I had n-no idea."

"Come on, old boy, I'll show you the most profitable business in Miles City."

Paget soon had Noll through the streets of Miles City and into the parlor of the 44. Crimson curtains hung from the walls, and the sound of piano music came from the lobby. Wallop smiled at the sight of young Bob Walsh playing the piano. The boy had been a stall boy at the racetracks in England. "Noll!" Walsh exclaimed and pounded out the opening lines to *God Save the Queen* on the piano. A portly woman in a blue dress entered the room and approached the men. Walsh rose and made introductions. "May I introduce our host: Miss Burns, this is Oliver Henry Wallop."

Noll pulled off his hat and took her hand. "I'm honored, M-miss Burns. P-please call me Noll."

"Call me Mag, sweetie. Welcome to Miles City. Why don't we take a stroll in the back room and meet the girls?" With that Mag took Noll by the arm and had him in the back room, where six girls sat around in various stages of dress ranging from evening gowns to petticoats.

"L-lovely, Miss Burns," Noll stammered.

"Honey, if you turned any redder we'd pronounce it a rash. C'mon, I'll buy you a drink." Mag took Noll out to the bar, where Sydney and Bob Walsh were trying not to make light of Noll's embarrassment. Both knew Noll was no whoremonger. Paget, on the other hand had run up such a debt in the house when it was first built that only the large checks sent by his father kept him from being banished. Bob Walsh pretty much squandered most of his check on favors from the girls. He was given the title of professor of the 44.

"This establishment has produced the largest deposit in a Miles City Bank to date: $50,000," Paget remarked to Noll, whose color was beginning to return.

The next day Paget and Wallop loaded supplies up on a buckboard wagon and made for Sydney's ranch eighty miles south on Otter Creek. They passed a Cheyenne camp, where Paget conversed in limited sign language with some of the men. Wallop looked over a grassy flat, and sure enough, there was a crew of men building rails and another leveling a dirt track with a team and skid.

"What are you b-building, Sydney?" Noll asked.

"It's my racetrack, complete with quarter poles, rails, and a dirt surface. It'll be five-eighths of a mile when it's done. I can train and time them here, and if I get something that will run, I'll be off to Chicago or New York. The ones that don't make, I'll ship them off as coach or saddle horses," he said.

Beyond the track lay an extensive set of corrals, a barn, a cabin, and a bunkhouse. "With my father's compliments," he said. What interested Noll more than anything were the horses. Paget's herd had grown to more than fifteen hundred thoroughbreds. The foundation to his breeding operation was Empire Regent, a stallion he had bought from Marcus Daly, the copper magnate out of Bitter Root Valley, Montana. There were also a few imported thoroughbreds from England.

"With ranchers and homesteaders filling the area, horses are at a premium; I've sold one saddle horse for $150 already. I suggest you go back to England, put together some investors, and start a ranch," Paget said. Noll spotted the large buffalo head mounted over the main room of the cabin. He made no mention of the story McNaney told him, but he did notice a hole in the wall over Paget's bed where the head must have hung before it fell. "Why don't you stay here until the snow flies, and then we'll return to England together in a few months. You can become better acquainted with the land and sell your father on backing you on a ranch." It all seemed perfect to Noll: horses hunting and wide-open spaces had always been passions of his.

Since arriving at Paget's ranch, Noll had risen every morning before breakfast and accompanied Gus Birdsell to check on livestock. Birdsell had been with Paget for three years as foreman after coming north with a herd of Texas cattle. After ten days Paget became restless for town and Connie Hoffman. "Shall we journey back for town, Noll?" Paget asked as the two were having drinks around the stove one evening.

"I'll b-be along. I thought I might ride to the Bighorns and have a look."

"Good lord, old boy, haven't you had enough adventure for one trip?" Paget asked.

"*Casus fero spiritus*," (adventure brings life), Noll winked at Paget.

"I have a black mare that needs riding. I'll have Gus wrangle her in the morning."

Noll left at first light. The ninety-mile trip to the Bighorns sealed his love for the area. He followed Tongue River to the forks of Goose Creek, to the newly formed town of Sheridan, and then on to the community of Bighorn. He met homesteaders, cowboys, and merchants in both settlements. In every case he left feeling he had made a friend.

Noll Wallop was a unique blend of good-naturedness and grit. He never complained and seemed to have an inexhaustible supply of energy, which won him points with the cowboys. He also may have been the best shot with a rifle or a shotgun in the territory.

With the eclectic mix that entered Absaraka after the Indian wars, people didn't judge you for a bad past, nor did they judge you for a good one as long as you held up your end, and Wallop did exactly that. He had plenty of try and took the elements and long hours like everyone else, although at times he took them in his own unique way.

He genuinely liked all kinds of people, and they liked him. He was a unique individual who was at ease talking horses with a Cheyenne, a cowboy, or a trapper, as well as conversing about politics with members of the royal family.

When Noll Wallop returned to Miles City, he found Sydney Paget, and the two got gloriously drunk for three days in Sam Pepper's Saloon, the Cottage, and the MacQueen House.

"I've decided to make a go of it here," Noll announced. "I have w-written Father to see if he m-might sponsor me in a horse ranch." Paget and Connie Hoffman let out a whoop of pleasure.

What Noll needed right off was a job, as his money was playing out. His first employment was working as a horse breaker on local ranches. As a joke, cowboys sometimes put him on the meanest, most dangerous animals in the corral, yet when Wallop climbed aboard, the horses rarely bucked—to the dismay of the pranksters. It was his unique approach to the animals: he was quiet and gentle, took his time, and sat relaxed on the outlaws, who were used to having spurs dug into them when ridden. The irony was that Noll would sometimes fall off horses that had done nothing more than prop or balk.

In November, Wallop returned home to England with Sydney and Connie. At a function at the London Club, Paget was explaining to his father how he had seen a cowboy, who was chasing a steer on Powder River, inadvertently gallop off a sixty-foot cut bank. The horse and steer were both killed, but the cowboy somehow survived unscathed.

"Young man, is it not enough you drain my finances? Now you bring these trumped up American tales home and expect me to believe them!"

Overhearing the conversation, Lord Bennett approached Lord Paget. "Begging your pardon, Lord Paget, but I believe your son's story has some merit. My brother has a ranch on the Powder River, and I happened to be at the roundup your son described. The cowboy and his horse were concentrating on the steer, and the steer was trying to flee his pursuers. Just at the moment the cowboy's loop caught the horns, all three disappeared over the edge. Your son speaks the truth. I saw with my own eyes the cowboy walk away from the wreckage."

Lord Paget just shook his head at his son. "Now I suppose you'll try and convince me that your Queen of Miles City is having tea with Victoria this afternoon."

What had totally surprised the lord were the horses Sydney had shipped back and sold at a profit. One horse, Wolf Catcher, set the roof on polo prospects. Syd had used the horse to chase down wolves in the snow on Otter Creek.

Meanwhile, Noll spoke in practical terms with his father, who not only agreed to finance his son but also gifted Noll with two thoroughbred stallions, Sailor and Columbus, to start his own herd. Each horse could be traced to English Derby winners. Noll then convinced his brother-in-law, Vernon Watney, to invest in the ranch.

Upon returning to Miles City, Wallop borrowed $30,000 from a bank there and began the construction of his ranch next to Paget's on Otter Creek. He had consigned old man Bradshaw, the original Otter Creek rancher, to haul logs in for the buildings and corrals. Noll hired Bob Walsh as his foreman, and soon the two were on a horse-buying trip to the Crow and Cheyenne reservations. Both tribes had large herds of horses containing everything from top racers to native range horses, or cayuses. Wallop saw that despite the culls, these Indians had bred up some tough, long-winded bloodline of their own.

Noll and Walsh had their saddlebags loaded with gold coins, as the Indians refused to accept paper money. Both men realized they would in no way feel as secure in a white settlement with as much gold, but the Indians were both respectful and honest to the men.

Wallop's ranch was located on a wilderness thoroughfare between the community of Sheridan and Miles City. It was also between the South Dakota agencies of the Sioux and of the Crow on the Bighorn River and the Cheyenne on the Tongue. Older men, trusted by the government agents, were issued passes to visit Indians on other agencies, but young men, eager to gain respect in the tribe the old way, would slip off and either steal horses from enemy tribesmen or, in isolated instances hidden from the whites, engage in raids.

In his first summer on his new ranch, Noll was inside his house writing a letter to his sister Lill when he heard a whooping outside. From the door of his cabin, he saw three riders who looked to be galloping around in some sort of sport, until he realized that two of them were pursuing the third with war clubs. They were three hundred yards away, but it became obvious the two had the one run down on a tired horse. Finally, a gunshot rang out, and the third man fell off his horse. In an instant one of the others got off and scalped him while the other caught the bedraggled horse. As they were tying the body on the weary horse, one of the Indians noticed Wallop in his doorway. Noll had his rifle behind the door of his cabin but decided not to show it yet.

After they had the body loaded, they led the horse toward Wallop and in sign language tried to communicate with Noll.

"G-greetings, I hope you men have resolved your differences," Noll said as the men sat on their horses thirty feet away. "Good Indian," one of the men on the horses motioned to himself and his friend. He then turned and motioned toward the dead man straddling the horse. "Son-of-a-bitch," he said. The one rode up to Wallop and held out the scalp. "You friend." Wallop accepted the bloody tuft of hair and the two men rode away in silence.

"*Finis terminus aequitas*" (frontier justice), Wallop said as the Indians rode away.

Captain Calvin Howes pondered what Noll had told him. "The dead man was probably Crow and the other two probably Blackfeet or Sioux. They either figured you weren't home, or they got caught up in the chase and didn't care," Howes said while running the thread through the back of Noll Wallop's pants. Wallop was a dinner guest at the Howes' Circle Bar Ranch, but much to his dismay when he rode up to the house, he discovered his pants had split and he stayed outside until Captain Howes rescued him with needle and thread.

"The d-dead Indian on the horse had a floral beadwork on his moccasins, leading me to believe he was indeed a Crow," Noll said.

Howes looked concerned. "I don't think they will bother you, but I've seen so few buffalo this spring, I fear they have been hunted out. Now the Indians will be hard-pressed to steal cattle just to live." Both men knew that riding upon an Indian in the act of butchering a steer would put a white man in jeopardy.

Captain Howes was a retired sea captain from Cape Cod who had brought his wife and three sons to Miles City in the early 1880s. Along with George Brewster, Howes was one of the early ranchers on the Tongue River. Brewster had come west from Massachusetts to hunt buffalo for the railroad crews before settling on his own ranch, called the Quarter Circle U. Captain Howes had bought a herd of Indian mares from the government and crossed them with thoroughbred stallions. Some of those Indian horses had bullet wounds from the Custer fight.

The Circle Bar cowboys were frustrated with the Indian horses, as the Indians mounted their horses from the right side while cowboys mount from the left. Finally the cowboys changed to the Indian method and got along fine.

Once his trousers were mended, Wallop entered the ranch house, presenting Mrs. Howes with two bottles of champagne. "Compliments of the Honorable Charlie B-Brown."

By 1883 Absaraka was beginning to fill up with ranchers and livestock. The Powder, Tongue, Rosebud, and their tributaries seemed to sprout cabins and corrals overnight. Noll Wallop's ranch was no exception.

Before long he had built up seventeen stud barns for his thoroughbred stallions, which now included two more British imports—Cross Keys and De Beauvoir, both of which had been imported from England. Sailor, his first stallion, was not only prolific in his breeding, but also passed on athleticism and a good disposition to his colts.

Besides having his pick of Indian mares, Noll also had the chance to buy thoroughbred mares and stallions from Senator McAllister in Oregon. The trip cost Wallop a great deal of time and money, but the investment was worth it. The senator sent his nephew, Tom, to trail the horses to Wallop's ranch from the railhead, and Noll later hired the young man to break horses. In Tom McAllister, Noll Wallop recognized someone who not only knew horses but, more importantly, also how to run them in the wild.

I have got together a good lot of horses, about 260 head, some 180 head of she stock and 85 colts running with their dams, and if I take out two cayuse mares and show my she stock only, I don't fear comparison but with one band (Sydney Paget's) in Custer County if I can get them through all right. Please remember me to the boys.
—Oliver H. Wallop, in a letter during his trip to Oregon

When first I had occasion to stop at Mr. Wallop's ranch at Otter Creek (ninety miles southwest of Miles City), he was superintending the building of extensive and well-planned horse corrals. He seemed quite enthused over a shipment of thoroughbred stallions imported from England to put with his Oregon mares, and as we sat atop the corral fence talking, one of

> *his riders came through a whirlwind of dust with a bunch of mares which were hell-bent on getting back to their native haunts in Oregon. The rider found them well off their range, and he was determined they should forget Oregon and learn the good qualities of Montana bunch grass, so he chugged them into a corral, sweat lather dust and all, to think it over for a few hours.*
>
> *—Luke Sweetman*

Wallop's breeding operation was growing to three thousand horses, some of which drifted as far south as the Bighorn Mountains ninety miles away. A tireless rider, Wallop covered the range and could tell one of his cowboys just what drainage or draw to find a certain animal in when breeding season or a horse buyer came along.

By 1884 all types of horses were imported into Absaraka: thoroughbreds, draft horses, German coach horses, and even ponies. No less than thirty-five horse outfits followed Sir Sydney Paget in the 1880s, raising horses. From the Tongue to the Powder, there were close to eight thousand thoroughbred mares running loose on the buffalo grass on Otter Creek, not to mention the non-blooded animals. Workhorses, equally well bred from Shire and Clydesdale bloodlines, ran in the thousands.

20

Cowboys are smaller and less muscular than the wielders of axe and pick, but they are as hardy and self-reliant as any man who ever breathed—with bronzed set faces and keen eyes, they look all the world straight in the face without flinching as they flash out from under their broad-brimmed hats . . . . They do not walk well, partly because they rarely do any work out of the saddle . . . But their picture is striking for all that, and picturesque too, with their jingling spurs, the big revolvers stuck in their belts, and big silk handkerchiefs knotted loosely around their necks.

When drunk on the villainous whiskey of the frontier towns, they cite mad antics, riding their horses into saloons, firing their pistols right and left, from lightheartedness rather than from any viciousness. They indulge too often in deadly shooting affrays, brought on either by accidental contact of the moment or on account of some longstanding grudge, or perhaps because of bad blood between two ranches or localities.

Yet, except while on such sprees they are quiet, rather self-contained men, perfectly frank and simple. On their own ground, they treat a stranger with the most wholehearted hospitality, doing all in their power for him and scorning to take any reward in return.

—Teddy Roosevelt

Spring 1883

PROBABLY NO OTHER MEN IN AMERICA WERE AS COLORful as the cowboys who came north with the Texas trail herds. Most of them threw caution to the wind and spent their money on wine, women, and fancy clothes. When they went to town they could drink, eat, and dress like the men they worked for. They usually returned to the ranches flat-broke, but at the ranches and on the roundups they were fed and given at least a tent over their heads in bad weather. Though there was no room for advancement, they worked endless hours with little sleep and were hardworking, proud, and content to live the free life.

Although most cowboys were let go in the winter, one of the great advantages for the cattlemen was the loyalty the cowboys gave them; they were fiercely protective of their boss's livestock and range.

Cowboys also seemed possessed of a unique sense of humor. Malcolm Moncreiffe, the son of Lord Moncreiffe in Scotland, was accompanying his cowboys on a Powder River roundup and found that the long daylight hours from 4:30 a.m. to 10:00 p.m. made for a grueling day in the saddle. With his head hung at the chuck wagon, Malcolm watched a cowboy he had ridden with all day saddle a fresh horse to ride out as a night herder. "My God, when do you sleep?" he asked.

"In the winter," the cowboy cheerfully responded.

Despite their loyalty to their employers, these early cowboys were no man's patsy. When Lord Bennett's son came looking for Moncreiffe, he asked one of the ranch cowboys, "Can you tell me where your master is?"

The cowboy looked the Englishman over and replied, "The son-of-a-bitch ain't been born yet."

We had been told at Fort Laramie that from the Cheyenne to the Powder River, there was likely to be no water, which we surely found out. The worst suffering I have ever seen in my seventy years with cattle was on this drive from the Cheyenne to the Powder River. This suffering cannot be told in words. The weather was terribly hot, and at the end of the second day these cattle commenced to grind their teeth in their suffering, and when they were lying down their groans were something to make a wooden Indian's hair raise . . . We lost between one and two hundred from thirst. Every one of those cattle that died, died with their head pointed toward Texas.

We got to the Powder River on the third night . . . That river was a paradise after what we had been through. After leaving the Powder River, we came in sight of the Bighorn Mountains. We went near where Sheridan, Wyoming, now stands. This country had more water than any place we had gone through from Texas to the end of our trail.

After our herd and our horses were counted, our work was done. Matt Murphy had brought all the horses, our wagon, and everything but our saddles. There was regret in every cowboy's heart when Matt Murphy started us in a mountain wagon to Miles City. We had loved those cattle and those horses and the life with them. We didn't have anything else to love, I guess.

—Bob Fudge

The young cowboys in the area were hard-pressed to meet any women out on the frontier, so falling in love with a working girl from the saloons was a common occurrence. It also gave the young women a way out of a life of prostitution. More often than not these women made good wives and mothers.

It was the newer women of proprietary backgrounds in Miles City that frowned on the former girls of the evening. At a social at the Miles City Park, a former prostitute who was trying to start her new life as a wife was ostracized by a churchgoing hypocrite. The woman gathered up all the other women and told them not to converse with the young newlywed. Every attempt the young woman made to approach the group was met with turned backs and silence. Finally the young wife approached the ringleader.

"Excuse me . . ."

"I don't converse with prostitutes," the woman snapped, causing an awkward silence on the lawn among the group of ladies.

In a pleasant, cheerful voice the former courtesan continued.

"I was just wondering if your husband ever had that mole removed from his back."

Thus ended any verbal attack by wives whose husbands all spent time in Miles City for meetings or supplies.

In the time immediately following the Indian wars, the buffalo runners and warhorses in Absaraka were replaced by cow horses, workhorses, and imported thoroughbreds. In one early roundup on the OW Ranch, two hundred cowboys, representing every large ranch from the Powder to the Bighorn rivers, rode two thousand horses to sort the cattle.

Like the cowboys that rode them, cow horses were trained professionals. They studied the herd right along with the cowboy, waiting for a command. Once a cowboy made a slight signal—the touch of a rein on the side of the neck or the squeeze of the cowboy's leg—the horse was off at a fast, smooth walk. A good horse knew the game and moved easy yet quickly, so as not to scatter the cattle. Like the cowboy, the horse's mind was wide awake, yet they moved with a quiet grace. Rider and horse were one in separating an animal from the herd. Once the cow was cut out and the cowboy shook out a loop, his horse kept him right on the animal's tail.

If the horse felt a struggle on the end of the rope while heeling calves, it would instinctively quicken its pace, which pulled the calf at such a speed that it would quit struggling.

As cowboys almost always rode alone checking livestock, rider and horse had to work together to doctor steers that weighed up to nine hundred pounds. A two-hundred-pound calf that needed doctoring was one thing to get off your horse and throw if his back legs were caught, but a nine-hundred-pound steer was something else altogether. Steers had to be roped and tripped, which called for poise, speed, and power in the cowboy's horse. With one end of his rope tied to his saddle, the cowboy and his horse gave chase to a steer that was then roped around the horns while running. Next, the cowboy rode alongside the running steer and threw the slack of his rope over and around the back of its legs, and turned off. When the rope tightened, the sudden jerk tripped the steer in midair, enabling the cowboy to dismount and tie its legs while it was down.

These animals, like the buffalo runners and warhorses that grazed Absaraka before them, emerged out of hundreds of horses; it was the same with cowboys. On a large ranch, each cowboy was usually given six to ten horses for his sole use while he worked there. Out of his string of horses, he might have one top cow horse—if he were lucky.

A good roping horse never let the rope slacken, and could about turn on a dime. A cow critter is mighty quick on the turn when they want to be, and it takes a good horse to keep a tight rope and dodge this way and that like a flea. There was lots of tricks for a cowboy to learn, and lots of them for his horses to learn. A night horse had to have good eyesight, and the rider had to find out whether he had it or not before he bothered to spend time on his training. Some horses seemed to see as well in the night as in the day, while others would get lost after dark came down on a cloudy night and walk right away from the herd instead of walking around it, or maybe even blunder right into it. Such a horse was never used again . . . for it could cause a stampede.
—Texas Andy Jones[2]

It had been several years since Charlie Thex had shot the man at Telegraph Station and fled south. He had worked trailing cattle herds from Texas to Arizona until border skirmishes broke out with the Apaches and Mexicans; that's when Charlie joined the Texas Rangers. Not long afterward, witnessing a gunfight between two Rangers convinced him to head north, and he got a job accompanying a herd of cattle from Texas to Ogallala, Nebraska. With a $20 gold piece in his pocket, a saddle horse, and a longing to see the knee-deep grass country in Montana, he rode west.

After arriving at Miles City, he found work breaking teams at Noll Wallop's ranch. In Wallop, Charlie found a business mentor. Despite his eccentricities, Noll was a brilliant businessman and was genuinely interested in helping the cowboys advance in life. Most ranches wouldn't let cowboys run their own stock, but Wallop encouraged it. This displayed a trust Wallop put in the men, who in turn showed him both loyalty and respect.

From day one Noll gave Charlie his first business lesson. "I'll give you one horse for every five you b-break. But I don't want you to sell this horse. I want you to break five more and teach your two horses to drive as a team. A team is worth more than two saddle horses. Then I'll take your team with me to Chicago and trade it for ten yearling heifers. We'll bring your cattle back to Otter Creek and turn them out on the open range."

"What about bulls?" Thex asked.

"There are p-plenty of bulls on the open range already, Mr. Thex," Noll responded with a wink.

While Charlie Thex traded for cattle, another Wallop cowboy, young Tom McAllister, also took Wallop's advice, except he kept his horses and ran his own herd on the open range. Wallop wisely knew that giving honest workingmen their start in the livestock business would also protect his own stock from theft. Whenever one of his horses was stolen, Wallop posted a $300 reward in the *Stock Growers Journal* for information leading to the arrest of the thief. Several other ranchers did the same.

> *It is a funny world here—men that are the right sort are willing to do anything to "pull a man out of the hole," and having done so, to show their satisfaction by chaffing him for having got there. I think I have the best lot of boys working for me I ever had—they are all equally reckless and equally kindhearted—that makes a good cowpuncher. I never had men work so well to my interests before. They have more than they can do, but it makes no difference. The eight-hour system has no adherent here yet.*
> *—Oliver Henry Wallop*

With livestock valued at $35 million running over seventy-five thousand square miles of uninhabited country, stealing horses or cattle was a common occurrence. For a lone cowboy to stumble on a gang of armed thieves twenty miles from the ranch was risky business. Whereas Tom McAllister, Charlie Decker, and Bob Walsh were no fighters, the same could not be said for Charlie Thex. Charlie claimed he had been a Texas Ranger, others claimed he was wanted by the Texas Rangers; either way, he might be the kind of man to have on your side if a band of armed thieves moved in. Many men carried guns, and no one doubted that he would use his if he had to.

For the second annual Stock Growers meeting, Miles City was dressed up with colorful bunting across Main Street, and parties and horse races were held for all the ranchers who would be in town. Noll Wallop rode in from his ranch with Sydney Paget in a wagon with two of Paget's racers tied to the back. As the two drove their team to Brown's livery stable, Sydney looked toward the MacQueen House. "I'll catch up shortly; I'm going to look in on Miss Hoffman," Sydney said. "I'll see to the horses with Mr. Brown."

Wallop looked over Brown's horses and discussed the market in general. "Mit the railroad vee can bring buyers to da horses. Vee send vord to Chicago and udder towns. Make big party in town like now." Charlie Brown's auction yard was now promoting horse sales several times a year that had recently boasted over three hundred horses sold. The prices ranged from $3 for a range foal to $150 for a broke saddle horse. Teams went for as high as $250 a pair. Every sheep man, cattleman, horse rancher, and cowboy within a hundred-mile radius was there. Teddy Roosevelt, a Dakota rancher from New York, the Marquis De Mores from France, and Moreton Frewen from England were all in attendance. The prostitutes, saloons, and gambling houses were in full swing. Charlie Brown organized a horse sale and theatrical productions were advertised. The MacQueen House was renting beds out, one bed for every two men. There would be three days of festivities in town during the meetings.

Granville Stuart, a Montana rancher, presided over a meeting of four hundred cattlemen in which the issue of cattle and horse thieves was addressed. From Buffalo, Wyoming, to Miles City, Montana, and from the Black Hills to Oregon, armed men stole horses and relayed them to gangs who trailed the animals north to the rough, broken country of the Missouri breaks. The thieves frequented the saloons and the stores, mingling with the trail cowboys. Gangs like Teton Jackson's were stealing stock at an alarming rate.

The ranchers began to call for the stock growers to raise a vigilante army. Stuart opposed such a move, claiming that cowboys wouldn't be a match for the thieves, who were armed to the teeth and expert marksmen. An armed bunch of cowboys riding out to meet the rustlers would accomplish little aside from getting a bunch of cowboys shot up or killed. In Alzada, a sheriff and two cowboys were killed when members of the Axelby gang tried to free a captured member of their ring.

Stuart also knew that the eyes and ears of the rustlers were among them at the meeting, so making a public decision would only alert the thieves. The cattlemen voted down the notion of armed vigilantes, but a decision was made to hire private detectives to watch the activities of suspected thieves.

While Stuart was away from his ranch at a spring roundup, horse thieves boldly came to his ranch and stole a stallion and a few other horses. After the roundup, three gangs of vigilantes were formed, resulting in the hanging of fifty-seven men in Montana territory. The cleanup was seen as murder by some and tarnished the image of the large ranchers forever; the term "robber baron" had spread to the north.

The good news was that the horse thieves who lived quit the business or left the country. For the time being, the area was somewhat tranquil and businessmen began to exploit the area.

Nonstop trail herds now poured into the country from Texas. With over seventy roundups in Wyoming, the countryside was filling up. Private herds drifted into one another on the open range and were separated every spring and fall by crews of cowboys assembled from the various ranches. The Cheyenne River roundup in the eastern part of the state, for instance, gathered four hundred thousand head of cattle at a time.

21

> I was trying to perfect myself in the cowboy game, learning how to work a herd quickly, efficiently, without disturbing the cattle, and above all to be fast. Fast about getting out to relieve the herders after supper, fast about going on guard, and quick to see and do any extra work that is always coming up in working cattle. My model was Gus Birdsell, the fastest hand I have ever seen on a roundup. For real professional skill in the cowboy game, I think the Otter Creek in those days had something on any other section of the country. Grant and Luther Dunning, Ed and Dan Kelty, out of Nevada in the eighties and rawhide men to the end, Charlie Mosger, another rawhide man, Gus Birdsell, old Levi Howes himself . . . they were real cowmen.
>
> —Albert Gallatin Brown

AT A ROUNDUP ON POWDER RIVER, SOME OF THE AREA cowboys got their first taste of Noll Wallop's eccentricities. "Look what's coming," Gus Birdsell said, looking off at the small speck a mile away that was approaching the roundup wagon. The cowboys, sitting on the ground eating their dinner, looked up at the rider who was skirting the herd. The man didn't sit quite right on his horse.

"Who the hell is that?" one of the cowboys asked, looking up from his tin plate of beef, beans, and bread. In a large open country, a man could be identified by the way he sat on a horse long before his features were distinguishable.

"That'd be Wallop," Birdsell said. The cowboys now turned to watch the approach of Oliver Henry Wallop riding on a high-strung bay thoroughbred. Noll rode up to the cook's wagon and seemed to study the group of cowboys. To everyone's shock, he leaned over his horse's neck to look under the tarp that was roped to the back of the cook wagon and asked the cook to remove his hat.

No one, not even the roundup foreman, fooled with this cook. Like most roundup cooks, he was known to be a testy man. Down in Casper, Wyoming, a chuck wagon cook had shot a man for taunting him by not scraping his plate. The cook was tried and let off on the grounds that the shooting was justifiable homicide.

The cook seemed taken off guard and, to the astonishment of everyone, reached up and lifted his hat. Wallop, satisfied, now began to stammer apologies. Over twenty silent cowboys sat on the ground with their mouths agape, expecting the cook to produce a pistol or at least knock the man from his horse, but he did neither; instead, he invited the man to supper.

Wallop was still apologizing as he dismounted, and to the further shock of the cowboys, tied his horse to the end of the tarp that was propped up by a pole.

"I'm t-terribly sorry, but I wasn't sure if this was my roundup wagon. My cook had been scalped by the Indians years ago, and I couldn't tell if you were him except you had your hat on. Forgive me; I've only met the man twice."

The younger cowboys began to laugh, which drew a hard look from Gus Birdsell, who stood and greeted Wallop. Birdsell was the only older man there except for the cook. He was repping for Sydney Paget and his own livestock at the roundup. Five or six of the older cowboys were still out looking at the cattle.

"Hello, Noll," Gus said.

"Mr. B-Birdsell, thank heavens, it seems I've lost my roundup wagon," Wallop said, oblivious to the fact that his horse was impatiently pawing the ground where it was tied to the tent post, which had begun to rock the tarp the cowboys ate under. Wallop eventually noticed the tent's rocking and walked over and calmed the horse. Wallop had a vest on, out from under which hung two long shirttails down the back of his pants. This also took the cowboys aback, for as a group they prided themselves on their neat dress. The Englishman who stood before them looked like an unmade bed.

"I've c-come over from Lyon Creek and wanted to see Captain Howes about some horses, and when I got back here I thought my wagon would be in the vicinity. Have you seen or heard of its whereabouts?"

The cowboys were surprised. This man was not much older than they were, and he had his own roundup wagon. In addition, he claimed to have started out from Lyon Creek, which ran into the Otter over the divide and north. This man had put in a long ride.

The cook had no sooner produced a plate for Wallop than his horse, in a frustrated design to free himself, pulled back and took the entire tarp with him. The wreck was now on; before anyone could react, the bay thoroughbred was fifty yards away at a gallop, dragging a thirty-foot tarp across the prairie. Gus Birdsell was on his horse in a flash, shaking down a loop as he galloped after Wallop's horse.

"Get after him, Gus!" a cowboy yelled.

"A dollar says Gus catches him before he crosses the ridge," another yelled. The cowboys sprang to life watching the race across the plains.

"Get him, Gus!" another yelled. Gus was already a hundred yards away and closing.

"He won't catch that one, not even on that horse." Wagers were made on everything from how many throws Gus would take to catch him, to whether he would catch him at all. He was the top hand among the cowboys, most of whom were all fairly green, though none would admit it. The far ridge was just over a mile away. In between was the rolling slope of the grasslands on the west bank of the Powder River.

Gus Birdsell bore down on the racing bay. He knew he would need a break to catch him, as the bay had no rider and was thoroughly spooked. Grabbing his saddle up, Grant Dunning, a "rep" for the Circle Bar Ranch, headed for the horses in the rope corral; the sight of a crazed horse dragging a tarp would probably start a stampede.

"I hope them boys on evening herd are awake. C'mon, boys, I suspect we'll have some sorting to do."

But before the cowboys could bring in their horses to saddle, Gus Birdsell appeared over the far ridge, leading Wallop's thoroughbred. He had the tarp neatly folded and tied across the saddle.

A young cowboy rode out from the cook tent toward Birdsell.

"Gus, that man ain't right, is he?" the cowboy asked, referring to Wallop.

Gus smiled. "Don't let the stuttering fool you. He graduated from one of the best schools in the world. That's probably the smartest man you've ever met. He just borrowed $30,000 from the bank in Miles City to raise horses with on Otter Creek," Birdsell told the young cowboy.

"I hope he's got better horses than Paget. He ain't won a race in Miles City yet." The young cowboy was not sold on the competence of the British horse breeders. Birdsell sighed. He was Paget's foreman, but he knew the cowboy was not smart enough to realize the comment might have gotten him slapped or worse from another man. He doubted half the cowboys at the wagons had an idea of what a magnificent animal that Wallop had ridden up on.

"Paget don't win those races for the same reason Wallop won't when he sends horses to town. They're sportsmen. If Sydney sent his top three horses to town, there wouldn't be a cow horse in the country that would get close enough to get dusty," Birdsell said.

"Paget sends his culls to town for the fun of it. He ain't out to show up a bunch of cowboys; he's out to win the world. That man loves this country, but horse racing is what drives him. You wait till he gets one that can really run; he'll be off to New York or England."

"I don't see it," the cowboy protested. Birdsell seemed disgusted with the cowboy's ignorance.

"Take a good look at the horse I'm leading and the one you're riding; you can't be dumb enough not to notice the difference." As Birdsell was losing his temper, the boy decided to shut up and listen.

"You have any idea how far Wallop has ridden today to get here? He's come over thirty miles. Does this horse look tired to you? Hell, no, he ain't, and he just took off with a thirty-foot tarp and barely stepped on it. These ain't cold blooded cow ponies; these horses go back to world champions. Someday I expect you'll get on one, and you'll find out. I hope you got enough sense not to cowboy 'em, either. These horses won't take a lot of that. Most cowboys don't have the horse sense not to. You have to be patient with them, and when they do make, you're *horseback*.

"Paget and Wallop are probably the best horsemen in this country, although Noll don't ride so well," Birdsell said.

To the young cowboy's surprise when they returned, Wallop was at the anvil, surrounded by a small captive audience to whom he was explaining corrective shoeing. The best horseshoer among them was genuinely impressed that the Englishman knew some useful innovations to help horses with bad hoof problems.

As the evening settled, the entire crew had gathered around Wallop, who captivated the cowboys with stories covering everything from grizzly bear hunting to excerpts from *The Odyssey*. His stories were laced with poetry, Latin phrases, and historical references dating hundreds of years back.

"One of my ancestors was an admiral of the British Navy. He defeated the French more than fourteen times in naval battles, and thereafter the word 'Wallop' was used to denote a sound thrashing," Noll explained to the cowboys in the firelight.

By the time some of the men turned in for the evening, Noll Wallop had won over everyone's respect in the outfit, not the least of which was the skeptical cowboy who had belittled his horses. The cowboy sat off alone and decided to study the two thoroughbreds that Birdsell and Wallop rode. They had been turned out to graze not far from the wagons. Compared to the rest of the horses, they were taller and leggier, their necks not as thick, and their bones and conformation were sleeker and more refined. The thing that impressed the cowboy most was their eyes. They seemed more alert, maybe smarter than the others. It bothered the cowboy that he had never noticed this before, but he crawled in his bedroll happy with the discovery. It lit a spark of interest, which was the first step in his becoming a horseman.

Over at the campfire Noll held court with the remaining cowboys.

"How come you like thoroughbreds so much?" one of the cowboys asked.

"The thoroughbred is the 'mostest horse that ever was,'" Wallop said with a twinkle in his eye. "Thoroughbreds are the fastest horses on earth, b-but they have a quality greater than speed; they have heart, hence the saying 'thoroughbreds don't cry.'"

"A p-paleontologist named Marsh, I believe he was a Yale man, found the remains of Eohippus, the oldest horse on earth, in Nebraska not far from here. The horse he discovered was the three-toed animal that thrived on these grasslands before spreading through the Americas. According to Professor Marsh, horses migrated across the land bridge into Asia before the Ice Age killed them here. They were extinct in America for ten thousand years before the Spanish brought them back to Mexico. The C-Comanche brought them north, and your Crow brought them back to the land of their ancestors: around the world in ten thousand years," he laughed.

"M-Marsh eventually became the champion of your chief Red Cloud after he retired to the reservation. A professional c-courtesy for letting him keep his scalp while digging b-bones in Lakota land."

When Wallop had not shown up at his roundup wagon, Charlie Thex decided to backtrack from the ranch, checking the roundups that were in the vicinity between Rosebud and Otter Creek. Thex knew his boss's penchant for wandering and visiting, a trait that might get a man in trouble riding alone in this country, but Wallop, for all his absentmindedness, possessed a knack for navigating strange country and surviving the elements when most of his English countrymen would have perished. At midmorning, with branding in full swing, a cowboy holding a calf down on the ground nodded toward an approaching rider.

"That's Thex," he said to his partner. "That man's a killer. They say he's killed men in Arizona and Texas, and all the way up to Alzada."

Gus Birdsell rode out to meet Charlie, and soon all the younger cowboys were craning their heads for a look. They all noticed that he wore a gun on his hip and had a Winchester in a scabbard on the side of his saddle.

An older man running a branding iron shook his head at the two young cowboys. "You've been reading too many dime novels. Charlie breaks horses and works the teams for Wallop. He ain't no killer. If he killed somebody, it's because they deserved it."

22

He was the last of the Range horsemen.

—Colonel Bill Rand

WHILE THERE WERE MANY COMPETENT HORSEMEN IN Absaraka, none were more competent with range horses than Tom McAllister. McAllister was a gentle man who, in the summer, spent as much time sleeping on the ground as he did in bed. With a packhorse and bedroll, he would sometimes be gone for longer than a week, checking on livestock and studying bands of wild horses. The cowboys who ran across him said he was part horse. He was a unique individual who learned to ride among wild horses without disturbing the herd.

Coming back to Wallop's ranch, Tom found a battered stallion standing outside the gate of the corral. He had a flap of skin the size of a fist hanging from his shin that exposed the cannon bone. His neck, rump, and chest were full of kick marks, and there was a bloody gash on his ribs. The wounds were obviously the work of another stallion. The wounded horse was imported from an Oregon racetrack and had been raised in a stall his entire life, so it was natural that after being hurt he should come back to the ranch for help.

"Whoa, son," Tom said and slipped a rope halter gently over his ears. He led the stallion into the barn and sprinkled the small wounds with lime. The wound on the leg, however, would take some doctoring and a bandage.

The stallion had recently been turned out with a small band of mares on a small tributary of Otter Creek called Lyon Creek when he was attacked. After doctoring the stallion and putting him in a small pen, Tom saddled a gelding, loaded a packhorse, and rode out ten miles to Lyon Creek to find the band of mares.

When he went to find the mares that had been herded by the wounded stallion, he found two were missing. After a quick scan he saw an Indian mare and a bay thoroughbred were missing. He left the herd and rode a large circle around the area until he came on the tracks leading south. He knew this was probably a group of wild horses. He followed the tracks for five miles until he stopped on a ridgetop and did a survey of the country. In the distance he spotted a small herd of horses. He got his binoculars from his saddlebags and saw the two missing mares in a band led by a yellow stallion. "I'll be darned," he said and smiled. He had seen one of these stallions just east of the Bighorn River, but this was definitely another stallion. "Must be his brother," he said to his gelding, which was now looking at the distant herd and pawing at the ground. "No, I don't think you want any part of that stallion, but I think it's time Sailor got a taste of the wild and the wild got a taste of Sailor."

"Preposterous!" Bob Walsh protested at the cookhouse of Noll Wallop's ranch. Walsh, Tom McAllister, Charlie Thex, and Noll Wallop were sitting around after supper discussing turning out Wallop's prized imported stallion on the range to pasture-breed. McAllister's thought was that Sailor had been nothing but a fighter since he had been brought to Montana and it might be time to let him out with the mares now that the weather was right. The stallion had routinely jumped the corral poles in his pen to start fights with other stallions in their separate pens.

"He's going to have to go out sometime anyway. Besides, I don't think the yellow stallion would take any of Sailor's mares," Tom explained, but Bob Walsh interrupted.

"I believe he's right, Noll. I think Sailor will send that yellow stallion or any other back to their range," Charlie Thex agreed.

"I don't think you two have any idea what a stallion like this is worth," Walsh said.

"You have a big opinion on horses, don't you?" Charlie Thex considered Walsh's comment somewhat pretentious, as the man had been playing a piano in a whorehouse before Noll had shown up and given him a job.

"I think T-Tom has a legitimate point. I think we can try it as long as we keep an eye on him," Noll said, which sent Walsh out to the bunkhouse in a huff. When it came to horses, Wallop trusted Tom McAllister completely. McAllister spent as much time out with the separate herds as he did at the ranch. He could trail a skittish bunch of horses by himself that four cowboys would have trouble moving.

Wallop also knew it would only be a matter of time before McAllister and Thex left him and moved out on their own. McAllister had close to fifty horses of his own and was about to purchase another six mares from his uncle in Oregon. Thex had over one hundred head of mother cows.

What Noll didn't know was both men remained with him because of their loyalty. They liked him, and neither was particularly convinced that Bob Walsh had Noll's best interests at heart. Thex gave McAllister a wink when Bob Walsh stormed out. "I'd like to be there when one of those wild studs makes a run at old Sailor."

"I'll camp with the herd for the first week. Even if he meets a better fighter, I imagine he'll be too quick to let any stud do too much damage," Tom said.

The next day Tom and Noll led Sailor out to the range where the mares were. When they closed to two hundred yards, Tom reached over and took the halter off Sailor, who immediately bolted for the mares.

"OK, boy, show them how much horse is under that well-groomed hide," Tom said and smiled at the stallion as he ran down and ducked three successive kicks from different mares. Within an hour Sailor had asserted his dominance of the herd and had bred one mare. Despite his experience, the sight of a horse kept in captivity his entire life going back to his natural state in the wild moved the horsemen. "I h-had a feeling you were right," Noll said. "We'll bring him up in the fall; he'll be a little gaunt, but there's no better feed than right here."

A few months later, when Tom was gathering Sailor and his band of mares, he noticed an additional mare. Not only had Sailor not lost any of his mares, but he had taken one from the wild band. She was a bay mare with a yellow foal by her side. When the mares were run in the corral at Wallop's ranch, Charlie Thex took a long look at her. "I think that's the mare that I fished out of Powder River almost ten years ago."

Charlie walked over and inspected an old scar on her rump.

"That's her all right; I suppose she found her range. Now she's quit her band for Sailor."

Before long, Noll was at the corral inspecting the mares and noticed he had an extra. "Looks like you were right, Tom. Other than a few m-minor scrapes, he's kept his mares and stolen another," Noll said and smiled at McAllister.

"Shall we cut the colt while we have her in the corral?" Thex asked. Wallop walked over for a look at the horse colt.

"It appears that this one may be related to the famous yellow stallion that my Crow friend Yellow Foot spoke of. Let's wait a year and see what we have."

"I'm with you; we can always cut him," McAllister said.

Bob Walsh walked over at the tail end of the conversation and could not believe his ears. "You can't mean to tell me you're serious. The last thing we need is a mustang bloodline."

"I'll give you $10 for him," McAllister said.

"Twenty," Thex countered. Wallop shook his head no and smiled with Tom and Charlie as Bob Walsh stomped off, cursing.

"I d-don't think Walsh has our appreciation of native horse flesh."

23

Our little dirt roof shack didn't matter because our other house was a building . . . there was a glamour to it while it lasted. Raising cattle was never like working on a farm. It was always uncertain and exciting—you had plenty of money or you were broke—and then to work on horseback, while dangerous and often very hard, wasn't drudgery. There was more freedom to it. Even we women felt it, even though the freedom wasn't ours.

—Nannie Alderson[1]

TOM MCALLISTER WAS IN THE COTTAGE SALOON VISITING with some cowboys when he saw the form of a small woman lugging a heavy baby down the dirt streets of Miles City. "That's Walt Alderson's wife," one of the cowboys said.

Nannie Alderson was a petite, refined southern girl who had met her future husband during a visit with relatives in Kansas. She fell in love with the cowboy and agreed to marry him. Walt traveled two thousand miles to wed his sweetheart and then brought her west to the frontier.

Most of the cowboys at the cottage had heard of Walt Alderson's wife, who had accompanied her husband to their ranch that was nothing more than a camp down on the Rosebud. Charlie Brown had set her husband, Walt, up in the cattle business with his son-in-law 100 miles south of Miles City.

Nannie and Walt's first home was an old logging cabin in which musty buffalo, wolf, coyote, and fox pelts were used as throw rugs across an old wagon sheet that served as a floor. The roof was made of dirt; there was one door and one window. Over the doorway, a human skull was stuck on a pair of elk antlers.

She became as tough as she had to be, battling rattlesnakes in the summer and unexpected visitors from the wilderness at all times of the year. Cheyenne would silently appear outside her window, asking to be fed. They were a long way from help, and the thought that these were the same Indians that had killed Custer seven years prior made her skin crawl. Her fear was that they would all be murdered and scalped, but her husband had no such reservations.

Despite the inconveniences and her fears, however, Nannie obliged the Indians and met some of their famous warriors. Young Man Afraid of the Oglala, a fellow tribesman of Crazy Horse, let Nannie have a lock of his hair. Little Wolf watched Nannie's children when they played to keep them away from rattlesnakes. Mabel Alderson grew up speaking fluent Cheyenne, thanks to a Cheyenne woman who helped Nannie with laundry.

On a sunny summer afternoon buggy ride to the Little Bighorn River, Nannie visited the battlefield where Custer had led his men to their deaths thirteen years earlier. The ground around the battlefield was strewn with horse bones mixed with a few human ones. Nannie picked up a link of vertebra and a finger bone as souvenirs.

When she traveled into Miles City for the birth of her daughter, Nannie was befriended by Connie Hoffman. The two shared female companionship and took long walks together in Miles City with Mabel.

Eventually, jealous wives whose husbands often stayed at the MacQueen House while in Miles City forced the proprietor to evict Connie when it was found out she was kept by Sydney Paget.

After Connie Hoffman was banished from the MacQueen House, Nannie's long walks with Mabel became laborious. After one cowboy leaving a saloon caught sight of the tiny woman lugging a large baby down the street, word got around, and soon Nannie was called downstairs to the MacQueen House parlor and found a group of cowboys, hats in hand, standing around a brand-new baby carriage; Nannie was moved to tears. There was heart in the wild town, and it beat the loudest in the chests of the cowboys.

The relationship between whites and Indians in and around the Cheyenne agency became strained, however, when younger men on the reservations, who had not experienced the horrors of war, became restless. One such incident involved ranch hand Bob Ferguson. He had ridden over a hill looking for some lost horses when he inadvertently came upon some Indians butchering a stolen steer. The Indians murdered him and hid the body. Walt Alderson rode with a group of ranchers to search for Ferguson along the side drainages of the Rosebud. Walt spied a saddle horn protruding from a mound of loose dirt and discovered Ferguson's body underneath. From that point on, Nannie was beside herself with worry for her husband, who was constantly out riding in the big, open country surrounding the Rosebud. It wasn't long before tragedy indeed would strike.

While Walt and Nannie and their children were away in Miles City, a ranch cowboy shot the hat off a sleeping Indian as a prank but "creased" his head by accident. The man, a minor chief among the Cheyenne, returned to the agency convinced the cowboy had tried to kill him. That night young Cheyenne warriors rode to the Alderson cabin and burned it to the ground. They also killed the family dog while the cowboys fled for their lives. The sheriff investigated the incident and had four men jailed. One died in captivity, and two others died shortly after being released.

Frank Grouard was one of the few men living in the area who had experience with both the fleet buffalo runners of the Indian tribes and the cow horses now moving north with the whites. Riding along the eastern face of the Bighorns, Grouard instinctively searched the signal hills for Indian signs—either a plume of smoke or a flash of light from a mirror—but he saw none. He looked up Little Goose Canyon and remembered General Crook's camp, a city of tents sprawled along the banks of Little Goose Creek. Though it had been only ten years since his life with the Lakota, it seemed like a lifetime. Crazy Horse was dead, and Sitting Bull had joined a touring circus-like attraction called Buffalo Bill's Wild West Show.

Riding across a small tributary of Otter Creek, Frank Grouard took out a looking-glass and studied a herd of horses. On the edge he spotted a black stallion with some mares. All of the horses were branded Quarter Circle Bar Quarter Circle.

In the herd of mares, he saw what he thought was the bay mare he had traded to Crazy Horse. How she got all the way to Otter Creek from Fort Robinson was a mystery. The sight of her piqued his curiosity and made Frank nostalgic for the past.

He was now a lawman, tracking down horse thieves and road agents, men who robbed travelers. Big Nose George, Teton Jackson, and a slew of other bandits were preying on settlers, ranchers and herds, and mail carriers who traveled along the old Bozeman Trail or the roads over the Bighorn Mountains.

As a sideline, Grouard had taken up raising horses in a partnership with some Crow horsemen living on the agency. In a small community called Bighorn, located on Little Goose Creek at the base of the Bighorn Mountains, Frank rode his horse along the banks of Little Goose Creek toward the Johnson County fair. To the delight of the Big Horn crowd, Grouard rode in the half-mile open race. A group of Crow entered a shaggy, broken-down-looking horse in a match race and cleaned everyone out, including the local newspaper, as the homely beast turned out to be a speedster. While the Cheyenne and Crow were done as mounted warriors and hunters, they were by no means finished as horsemen.

It wasn't long after that race that Grouard and the Crow noticed the appearance of the white owls of the north. Both parties recognized them as a precursor to a bad winter. True to form, the winter of 1885 brought temperatures of fifty-two degrees below zero. In Miles City, the cattle from the surrounding plains wandered Main Street looking for shelter and food. More than one hundred Blackfeet Indians to the north had frozen to death. Noll Wallop moved his stallions up Tongue River and over to Sheridan, Wyoming, where they might have better feed. After the frozen scare the previous winter, a few ranchers put up what little hay they could raise, but it was a dry summer, too dry.

In the spring of 1886, Captain Joseph Brown, a former Confederate cavalryman, drove a cattle herd from Texas to his Three Circle Ranch on the Tongue River. Calves were born on the trail, which Brown gave to settlers lest the newborns perish on the drive. This bad timing might actually have saved Captain Brown in the cattle business. Without sucking calves draining them, the cows were stronger going into the frozen hell that was coming.

A flood of foreign investors entered the Western cattle market to get rich quick. Modern technology in the form of refrigerated boxcars and shipping compartments made it possible to ship beef abroad, so everyone and his brother speculated and threw cattle out on the open range. Cattle drives into Montana were unending. Fights began to spring up among neighbors over cattle spilling into each other's ranges. There were too many cattle on the range competing for the quickly depleting grass.

The lure of free land brought a few farmers into the area to settle on the free homesteads with the misconception that lush grazing land would work for farming. These small outfits would settle on water holes blocking cattle herds, which had formerly watered there for years. Disputes broke out not only between homesteaders and ranchers, but also between sheepmen and cattlemen because the sheep tended to bed down along the riverbanks near water and keep cattle away from drinking. Between 1880 and 1890, the production of barbed wire in the United States tripled; much of it was unrolled in Montana. Before matters could come to a head over grass, God was about to settle the issue of open range in Montana forever.

24

God settled the question of the open range forever.

—W. D. Knight

October 16, 1886

"I THINK HELL HAS FROZEN OVER," CHARLIE DECKER SAID to Tom McAllister as the two Wallop cowboys pushed their horses into the cold, biting wind. They had ridden over to the Circle Bar to deliver a team for Noll Wallop and had decided to get back to the ranch rather than stay the night at the Circle Bar as planned. The blizzard moved like a curtain across the landscape, whose hills and draws disappeared from view under the storm; the entire skyline to the northwest was as dark as night. It was going to be an early winter.

"We'd better get moving," Decker said. The two men trotted down a side draw toward Otter Creek. Both knew the dangers of getting caught in a blizzard. Men had frozen to death wandering aimlessly in whiteouts; some died only a few feet from shelter. By the time the men reached the barns at Wallop's, they were engulfed in a blinding cover of swirling snow. Tongue River rancher George Brewster had spent the night out in a winter storm four years earlier while hunting buffalo for the railroad. He had wrapped up in a green buffalo hide to stay warm. It protected him, but he had to cut his way out the next morning because the hide had frozen stiff around him during the storm.

Charlie Thex and Noll Wallop had backed a team and wagon up to a haystack next to the barn. They were forking hay on as fast as they could while the snow blew by them with a fury. After they had a load, they drove the team into the barn, where Decker and McAllister helped them pitch the hay into the loft. All four men knew that if winter started this early in the fall, there would be neither grass nor hay to sustain the livestock through the winter.

November 1, 1886

At the first break in the weather, the men drew straws to see who would take a wagon into Miles City for supplies. Noll pulled the short straw and hitched up a team, carrying a list of supplies that might have to last the winter through.

Upon arriving in town, Wallop was greeted with the news that a huge formal party was going on at the MacQueen House that night and that he was invited. Leaving his team at Charlie Brown's livery stable, Wallop set out to find something to wear other than his bib overalls.

Improvisation being born of necessity, he made a trip to the undertaker and borrowed a black formal cutaway from a deceased gentleman who was to be buried later in the week. The young Englishman secured a silk flower for his lapel by ducking into the 44 bordello, which put the finishing touch on an outfit that made him look every bit the son of an English lord that he was.

Sydney Paget was there with the Queen of Miles City. The party ran to a three-day affair, which was attended by cattlemen from the Black Hills to the Bighorn River. There were meetings, dinners, teas, brunches, and lunches, discussing horse and cattle thieves, Indians, wolves, grasshoppers, prairie fires, and drought. Despite these setbacks the area ranchers enjoyed free grass, an excellent climate, reasonable taxes, and freedom from government regulations.

When it was over, Noll loaded his wagon with supplies and headed for the ranch. It had already started to snow again, and a brutal north wind was blowing in. Driving his team and wagon down Tongue River to Otter Creek, Wallop was overtaken from behind by a cowboy galloping hard on an urgent mission.

"Mr. Wallop, the undertaker sent me to catch you. That corpse won't keep much longer; I think he needs his suit back." Pulling on the lines and stopping the team, Wallop, who'd forgotten that he was still in the borrowed cutaway, stripped to his underwear next to the wagon and handed the clothes over to the embarrassed cowboy.

"Please express my g-gratitude for the use of the clothes to the owner. My mind was totally on the ranch, and I forgot I had them on," Wallop said. Oblivious to the harsh weather, Noll climbed up on the wagon in his underclothes and produced a pair of brogans and bib overalls from under the canvas tarp. He dressed in the snow flurry; apologizing again to the cowboy, he gave the young man a drink of whiskey from the back of the wagon.

When Noll returned to the ranch, another blizzard was raging. Drifts of ice shards piled up, cutting the legs of the cattle and horses that blundered into them. A quick thaw melted the top layer of snow, which quickly refroze, making a rock-hard ice shield over any feed hidden below.

While Wallop and his crew braved the elements at the ranch, Sir Sydney Paget stayed in Miles City. He refused to let the winter storm break his spirit and organized a sleigh race on the trotting track near the Miles City stockyards. Spectators bundled up in buffalo coats and rode out in rented sleighs from Charlie Brown's livery to watch the race. Connie Hoffman sat in her sleigh alongside the track, bundled in beautifully tanned wolf, otter, and mink furs that would have been the envy of any woman in Europe.

Paget's horse, Yakima, won the first race by two lengths. In the second race, Yakima was pitted against Dan McMillan's horse for $40 a side; Yakima won.

What reprieve the citizens gave themselves from the winters' bleak hand was quickly ended. The arctic owls Frank Grouard had seen the year before appeared, as they had after the Fetterman fight and the Little Bighorn battle. In both cases the following winters had killed men and animals alike. The difference now was that the area was full of short-haired cattle instead of woolly buffalo. Before December was over, two more blizzards descended on the plains.

Early in January it snowed an inch an hour for 16 hours, with temperatures at twenty-two below zero or colder.

Like a bad drawn-out joke, the punch line is "And then the BIG blizzard hit." Starting January 28, the storm continued until February 3 with only a brief break. At times the snow was so heavy a rider could not be seen at 50 feet. Some ranches recorded temperatures of 63 below zero.[1]

Cattle were frozen in piles; some were found in groups standing up. Noses of cattle were seen poking out of the snowdrifts, where they had frozen gasping their last breaths. The animals that drifted down draws to get out of the frozen wind were suffocated under the snow. Some simply starved to death. Horses and cattle alike piled into corners of barbed-wire fences, hidden by drifts, and were cut or trampled to death.

Gingerbread, an imported English thoroughbred stallion, was lost, as he had been allowed to run out with the mares. One of his foals had grown to be one of the top polo horses in England for Lord Drybrough.

Deer and antelope died along with the ranch stock. More than seventeen hundred frozen sheep were found in one pile. The N Bar Ranch had lost all but seventeen hundred of its seven thousand cattle. Men like Captain Howes at the Circle Bar, George Brewster at the Quarter Circle U, and Captain Brown at the Three Circle did better than most. Walt Alderson had put up hay for winter feed the previous summer and had also weaned his calves off the cows in the fall. The animals went through the winter without the impediment of a sucking calf and had gathered strength before the first blizzard hit.

March 1887

In Miles City there had been no word from the outlying ranches for almost three months. Walt and Nannie Alderson had gone to West Virginia to have their third child when the storms first hit in the fall of 1886. Hearing bad reports of the storm in the west, the Aldersons left West Virginia and boarded a train for Montana. Even so, it took two engines and a snowplow to push through the massive snowdrifts of Dakota; the Aldersons crept toward home. The only sign of towns along the way was the rooftops that poked through the snowdrifts.

Upon reaching Miles City, Walt learned from Charlie Brown that there had been no traffic from upriver since the January storm hit. "Dere's no sense in trying to make da trip before the vedder breaks," Charlie advised, but Walt decided to move while the stream crossings were still frozen. When the melt off came, rivers and creeks would flood the banks.

"If I don't get there now, I may not get there till the end of June," Walt said. Charlie helped him procure a large, sturdy sleigh and a strong team for the hundred-mile trip down the Tongue River. Walt shod the team with leather snowshoes, and Charlie Brown filled the sled with sweet grass and supplies.

Walt loaded Nannie, baby Fay, and three-year-old Mabel on the sleigh with a hired man and headed up the Tongue. Bundled-up spectators watched them pull away as a north wind cut the air and a dark gray sky approached from the north. The strong team pulled in tandem across the snowy expanse.

"I hope they make it," one of the spectators said.

"They'll make it," Charlie Brown answered, noticing the large, somber group watching the Aldersons pull out. Many had friends and relations who had been stranded on the ranches since December. People would be ruined. Charlie turned and addressed the crowd: "Dat is the sure sign that this vinter is over. Come on, everyone, the drinks are on me, and there's Mulligan stew in the back of the saloon. Let's celebrate." He ushered everyone to his saloon, but when no one was watching, he snuck a worried look at the northern skyline; there was a chance this thing wasn't over yet.

For five days, Nannie sat in the sleigh on buffalo robes with her children as Walt and hired man Johnny Logan shoveled through the snowdrifts. Dead cattle were piled up in frozen heaps along the route. To make matters worse, it began to snow again. Walt cut willows from the creek bottoms and made half-loops to put over the sleigh as a frame for a canvas shelter.

Foreign investors were ruined; the "Big Die Up" had killed cowboys as well as livestock. The overcrowded ranges were now full of rotting carcasses and broken spirits. Wolves, mountain lions, coyotes, magpies, and eagles gorged on the remains of thousands of animals left dead by the killing winter. The freedom of running livestock lost its luster. Teddy Roosevelt left the open country to return to New York. Granville Stuart said he never again wanted to own an animal he could not feed. Some Texas cowboys, ill equipped for such weather, headed south—never to return.

But while some men were ruined, others prospered. Ambitious small operators like Charlie Thex and John Kendrick were able to add to their own private herds by offering the large cattle owners 25¢ on the dollar on what was left of their herds.

The men who were the least affected were the horsemen. Most of their animals not only survived the bitter winter, but they also came back fat in the spring.

25

We have already remarked that everything is characterized by change. How often have we seen this truth verified by personal observation in this country. First the Indian and the buffalo; then the cowboy and the herd; and finally the settler and civilization. The cowboy—how shall I pay proper tribute to his fortitude and kindness? He has defied the torrid heats of summer and the frigid blasts of winter without shelter and at times without food and clothing. He has braved fury of savage beasts and still more savage men. He has turned his back on the comforts of home and the love of kindred to sweep across the trackless desert in the face of dangers seen and unseen, to pave the way for advanced civilization. He has endured every hardship, scorned every danger, and surmounted every obstacle that rude and untamed nature could throw in his pathway. Civilization owes him a debt of gratitude greater than is conceivable and one that will never be either fully realized or repaid.

—H. H. Campbell[1]

THE STORM THAT KILLED THE CATTLE BOOM UNFORTUnately killed one of the more colorful characters in American history—the cowboy. As open ranges were fenced in and hay production increased, the free-roaming horsemen were turned into part-time farm workers. Cowboys spent less time riding and more time working in the hay fields and building fences.

The killing winter also brought a resurgence of horse and cattle thieves. The *Stock Growers Journal* printed more than a dozen ads from ranchers who were offering rewards ranging from $10 to $300 for information about anyone interfering with horse stock in barns or on the range. Charlie Thex had asserted himself as the range regulator: he rode the land along Otter Creek, checking the livestock for Wallop, Brewster, Howes, and several other area ranchers. The cattle and horse thieves from Miles City to Buffalo, Wyoming, knew if they got caught stealing on Otter Creek, Charlie Thex would kill them if he got a chance.

Teton Jackson's gang was beginning to become active in the area again. As Jackson was a Mormon, he enjoyed protection from the law from many of the families to the west. When three deputies came to arrest him for violating civil laws, Jackson simply killed them. A second group of men were thus deputized to ride across three mountain ranges into the Jackson Hole area to find him.

The U.S. marshal—accompanied by three deputies—found Noll Wallop at his cabin on Otter Creek. "You O. H. Wallop?" the marshal asked.

"To what do I owe the p-pleasure of a visit from the magistrate?" Wallop replied.

Wallop's cook, saw the armed men approach through a window and loaded his shotgun. The cook had survived being scalped by Indians and had lived through the early years on the frontier when men were killed and hanged for no more than being in the wrong place at the wrong time. Since Wallop's ranch was located not far off the Otter Creek road, there were frequent travelers who stopped in for a meal or to spend the night. It was an unwritten code of the frontier that all travelers that were often a half-day's ride between destinations were offered hospitality.

When Bob Walsh walked by the cookhouse, he was hailed before he rounded the corner to the yard. "Where's Thex?"

"Out doctoring stock, why?"

The cook grabbed Walsh, pulled him in the cookhouse, and shoved an old cap-and-ball revolver in his hand.

"Here, take this and wait."

"Good God, man! Are you daft?" Walsh asked.

"I don't like the looks of them men, and I ain't takin' no chances. They may be here to arrest the boss," the cook said.

Walsh thrust the pistol on the stand near the washbasins and walked out into the yard. The marshall was sitting on his horse speaking with Noll.

"We understand you have made the acquaintance of Teton Jackson."

"I think I m-met him and a few of his men on the Missouri five years ago. Large man with red hair and black eyes, as I remember."

"He's killed three sheriff's deputies over in Jackson Hole. We're here to deputize you. I hear you know the country fairly well. Can you get us to Jackson Hole?"

"I imagine I c-could find it again. The shortest way would be over the Bighorns on the old Shoshone trail."

Much to his cook's dismay, Noll invited the men in for dinner, and the next morning the five men rode out. Their trip was for naught, however; Jackson had already left to seek refuge with a Mormon family in Idaho.

Wallop kept his job as deputy, and in three months' time it took him from the foot of the Bighorn Mountains to the Yellowstone River and from the Bighorn River to Rosebud Creek. Leading a packhorse and riding another, Noll showed an endurance and physical toughness that won him respect from both whites and Indians in the area. In his travels he had taken a pack string clear over the high country of the Bighorn Mountains and had hunted from Cody to Casper. His experience convinced him that some of his missing horses were probably not lost but stolen.

The issue proved a more complex problem than anyone could have imagined. Many of the thieves were ex-cowboys who stole merely a few horses from each of the wealthy ranchers' herds. With the size of the sparsely populated land, there was little chance to catch the wily thieves. And it was still risky business to attempt to go up against a professional band of armed thieves. Teton Jackson had twelve men, for instance, who had collected better than a thousand horses, changed their brands, and trailed them to the Black Hills. There was even a type of Robin Hood atmosphere surrounding many of the thieves. Several would anonymously leave skinned stolen beef hanging outside poor ranchers' homes to prevent them from starving.

> *A man who was supposed to be a cattle rustler was tried by some men who were going to hang him for it. They put him on a horse and put the rope around his neck and tied the rope around a limb on a tree, and they asked him if there was anything he wanted to say before they pulled the horse out from under him. He said, "Yeah, I want the man in this crowd that never stole a cow or calf to lead this horse out from under me." They all got to looking at one another, and finally a man went up and took the rope off his neck and turned him loose.*
> *—Charlie Florey*

Noll Wallop's position as deputy sheriff also took him to the Crow reservation to inspect brands for stolen stock. At a tribal ceremony, he sat next to a Crow acquaintance named Yellow Foot. "*Laus Deo, post equitem sedet atra cura*" (praise be to God, behind the horseman sits dark care), Noll said.

"That's not white man talk," Yellow Foot said, listening to the Latin mumbo jumbo that Noll recited.

"I'tchic! You are a very smart man indeed," Wallop said in the Crow tongue. "It is the language of the angels," he explained, continuing his banter, much to the amusement of the Crow.

> *Two branches of my education my mother used to grieve over [were] my sporting and my classical disciplines. And yet seeing the life I have, although so widely apart in their natures, both these tastes have given me infinite pleasure. Am I saying too much if I say that one has sustained my manhood, the other to preserve my gentlemanhood?*
> *—Oliver Henry Wallop*

It was obvious to Noll that neither the Cheyenne nor the Crow were stealing horses—at least not from the whites. Some Indians did continue to raid each other's livestock in the age-old test of bravery. Despite being located on distant reservations, for instance, in 1889 a group of Blackfeet stole close to forty horses from a Crow camp. The raiders were apprehended by soldiers who had been mobilized from three different forts between Hardin, Montana, and the Canadian border. Technology had robbed the area of some of its color; the Blackfeet might outrun the Crow, but they couldn't outride the telegraph lines. Unfortunately, ranchers like George Brewster were losing cattle to the Cheyenne—not because they were stealing for profit, but because the Cheyenne as a people were starving. The government had fed the agency Indians well during the Indian wars, but in the 1880s and '90s the government cut the number of cattle they had promised them for not fighting.

Charlie Thex studied the horse tracks and his blood began to boil. The horse thieves had always given the range on Otter Creek a wide berth, but now they were getting greedy or, in Thex's opinion, stupid. It was too small a country; the men who did this had to know both him and Wallop. There was no doubt in Charlie's mind where his horse was. Nor had he any doubt where a few of Noll Wallop's, George Brewster's, or Captain Howes's were. The thieves had gotten so bold as to steal two horses out of Captain Howes's barn at the Circle Bar while no one was around.

Thex had already claimed a homestead next to the Circle Bar Ranch and was prospering as a rancher. In an area where a man was judged by his actions, Charlie had proved a hardworking and enterprising cowboy. One thing Charlie Thex continued to do long after others had quit was to carry a gun.

Charlie knew the area where the thieves congregated, and he wanted to catch whoever had stolen his horse before they reached their headquarters. The thieves worked the cattle drives and had friends in the area. If he did not act quickly he might be up against a small party of armed men. He rode out alone on one of Wallop's thoroughbreds, leading a packhorse across the Yellowstone River toward the Missouri breaks.

Thex had not ridden sixty miles before he came upon a trail of horses being driven north, and he knew right away it might well be the thieves. Staying out of sight in the low depressions, he galloped on until he came upon two men trailing a small band of horses. Charlie waited for the two to gather horses in a rope corral for the night and to start a fire for their supper. Charlie recognized one man as a thief who spent time in Miles City lurking around, collecting information on herds and ranches. The other man looked to be in his late teens. Once the men were seated, Charlie shot the older man where he sat. Before the younger man knew what happened, Charlie was on him.

"That's my horse you're trailing, and three of the others belong to my neighbors," he said, looking down his gun barrel at the terrified teenager. The young man began to beg for his life. Charlie reached in his pocket and produced a piece of paper with several brands drawn on it: the Circle Bar, Quarter Circle U, OW, Quarter Circle Bar Quarter Circle, SP, and his own, THEX.

"Take this note north and give it to the people you're delivering horses to. Tell them if a horse with one of those brands ever turns up missing, I'm coming north with a hundred men and will kill every thief to the Canadian border." Thex cocked his pistol and stuck it to the young man's head. "If I ever see you again as long as I live, I'll kill you. You're lucky I need someone to deliver this note."

He let the teen ride off bareback, with a rope halter and no boots. Then he put the thieves' saddles on two of the loose horses and turned to herd all of the stolen property back to Wallop's ranch. The brands he recognized, he returned to their owners for the reward. The spare horses no one claimed, he traded for cattle.

As long as Charlie Thex lived, the thieves gave a wide berth to the Otter Creek livestock.

26

The Montana horse leads America! The victory of Spokane, the Montana horse is not only a reason why Montana should point with pride to him as a single animal that has vanquished the best horse in Kentucky.

—*The (Miles City) Stock Growers Journal,* May 18, 1889

APPRECIATION OF A GOOD HORSE WAS ONE THING THAT united area Indians, cowboys, and wealthy horse ranchers. While buffalo runners and cow horses differed somewhat in their respective trades, one thing everyone understood was a good racehorse. More than a dozen British remittance men were now raising livestock in or around Absaraka, the cream of which were raising horses. Some of them now sat in Sam Pepper's Saloon to visit and discuss business, but mainly to get updates via telegraph from Lexington, where a Montana horse was running as a long shot. While Paget and Wallop were raising some of the world's great bloodlines in southern Montana, Noah Armstrong, stabled out of Twin Bridges, had entered a Montana-bred colt in the Kentucky Derby.

Sydney Paget sat with Connie Hoffman, Noll Wallop, Bob Walsh, and James H. Price. Although Price usually sported a monocle and bow tie, he could appear as "western" as any of the locals. Price was an interesting study among the characters who lived near Miles City. He had once served as a witness at a trial in Miles City when a local lawyer, who should have known better, tried to discredit his testimony.

"Mr. Price," said the lawyer, "I have heard you were a college professor. Is that true?"

"Yes, that is true," Price replied.

"Well now, just *where* were *you* a college professor?"

"Oh, a little institution called Oxford University."

The lawyer wanted to shrink in his shoes. James H. Price had taught Cecil Rhodes, founder of the Rhodes scholarships, during his stint as a teacher there. The connection between Price the horse raiser and Rhodes the South African diamond magnate would soon benefit all the horsemen in the area.

All totaled, there were close to seven thousand horses owned by the men sitting at the table. Throw in the Knowlton bunch, and there were over twelve thousand at least half-blooded horses in the area from English breeders. By now there were over forty horse breeders of imported stock between the Tongue and Powder rivers.

The English horsemen were making a killing selling their best horses in England as racers, foxhunters, and polo ponies. They were doing equally well stateside: two high-end Miles City horses had recently sold for $10,000 in the East. Horsemen who had been breaking horses to ride or pull a wagon now found themselves taking horses through their paces on the racetrack or polo field, or over a jump course.

Major Dowson and Captain E. P. Elmhurst had joined Walter Lindsay at the Cross S Ranch on Mizpah Creek. Lindsay had bred more than five thousand horses from such champion stallions as French Grand Prix, English Darby, and Ascot Gold Cup: fancy bloodlines for a country that had been covered with buffalo five years before.

It was a sellers' market, and there was no bigger sales center in the world than Miles City. Thousands of horses were shipped out of Miles City by train to cities all over the United States, where they were used for construction and transportation. By the mid-1880s, one hundred thousand horses across America pulled streetcars.

Wallop picked up a copy of the *Times* Sydney had shipped in and started reading an article that described this year's Kentucky Derby as the "greatest field of three-year-olds ever assembled." Proctor's Knot, Once Again, Come-to-Taw, and Hindoocraft led the eight-horse field as favorites. Proctor's Knot, the thoroughbred of the season, had won the Belmont futurity as a two-year-old and was the odds-on favorite to win the Derby.

"I'll bet $20 on Spokane," Connie Hoffman said to the table, which drew chuckles from the men.

"What do you base your wager on, Miss Hoffman?" Price asked.

"Montana lungs breathing eastern air will be an advantage down the stretch. The air is thinner out here, and it's a long race. Spokane's lungs developed when he was a yearling before he was shipped east a year ago."

"Well, Syd, it looks like you've got yourself a handicapper," Bob Walsh said.

"You gentlemen have no idea what a quick study this woman is. I don't think she ever lost money on our entire tour of tracks in New York or England," Paget said, filling Connie's glass with champagne.

A young messenger burst into the saloon with an update: "Proctor's Knot is the favorite. Heavy track. Ten-to-one odds on the Montana horse!" Paget gave the boy a generous tip.

"Proctor's Knot is the favorite? Evidently the bookmakers haven't consulted Miss Hoffman," Price laughed.

These men lived a long way apart, and their visits were cherished events. As the afternoon passed, there was much talk of horse prices in the East and the state of things abroad. The meeting was interrupted a second time by the joyous cry of the messenger bursting into the saloon.

"He won! He won! Spokane won the Derby; ten-to-one odds!" he shouted, waving the telegram.

Connie Hoffman let out a yell and there were smiles all around. The boy from the telegraph station approached Paget.

"Mr. Paget, 'er, Lord Sid, I mean Sir Sydney, I suppose you'll be the next one from Montana to win the Derby," the boy stammered. Paget read the telegram sent by his brother aloud: "Congratulations to Montana, stop. Four-horse race, stop. Spokane by a nose, stop."

It was not just an upset; Spokane had set a world record for three-year-olds at a mile-and-a-half. The four leaders again ran only a length apart. The racing world considered it a fluke, and a rematch was staged just five days later in the Clarke Handicap. It was grueling to ask a three-year-old to run that distance again so soon, but the owner's pride overruled their judgment. Sore from the

Derby, the pack ran on something no trainer can instill, but when they find it in an animal, they do everything they can to protect it: try, heart, and courage. Spokane defended his upset in the Derby and won the Clarke Handicap. Proctor's Knot's owner called for yet another rematch in Chicago, which Spokane again won.

None of the fabled field from the Kentucky Derby would ever run well again. It had been too much to ask of them in too short of time. The demise of Spokane, Proctor's Knot, and the rest of the fabled field had been the size of their heart, which pushed their bodies beyond their limits but the win in the Kentucky Derby had brought worldwide attention to the area and set the Kentucky bluebloods on their ear.

Spokane was crippled for good when a groom accidentally stuck a pitchfork in him while the horse slept. Spokane rose too quickly and tore ligaments and muscles, which hindered him for the rest of his life. His legend would live forever, though, as would the credibility he gave to Montana horses.

The repercussion of the Derby win was not lost on the British horse breeders, who lost no time in promoting their own bloodlines in the East and in England.

During the winter Sydney Paget, Noll Wallop, Walter Lindsay, and Bob Walsh returned to England like conquering heroes with a load of Montana-raised thoroughbreds. Wallop, Lindsay, and Paget had consigned Bob Walsh to sell their horses, a step up from his former job as piano player in a Miles City bordello. Wallop brought a bearskin rug to his brother, the Earl of Portsmouth, and Paget showed up with the stuffed buffalo head he had killed years earlier. Noll also touted the Crow scalp that the Sioux had given him on his homestead.

The English horsemen looked at these returning cowboys with a combination of admiration and curiosity. The English peerage, on the other hand, weren't quite sure how to take these sons of earls. The bottom line was that Wallop and Paget had made something of themselves and had money in their pocket, which was more than could be said for three-quarters of the other remittance men, who were financed by wealthy fathers.

While Walsh worked prospective horse buyers, Noll Wallop took time to remember his friends in Miles City with a letter to the local newspaper.

> *I got here all right after the smoothest passage I ever had the luck to cross over in. Here they have had the hardest winter they have ever had since 1813. The Thames has been frozen over, and the other deviltries of Jack Frost are common.*
>
> *Our Hampshire place has just been burnt down, and my people are very much downhearted at it. However, it was insured for nearly five hundred thousand dollars, so that is at least some little compensation, but most of the old books and paintings of bygone Wallops went up in smoke.*
>
> *Have shipped over twelve head of cayuses. I don't know how they will sell, but they are almost sure to commit some deviltry before the natural term of their lives is ended. Probably they will shorten the term of life of diverse Englishmen, but then this country is overpopulated.*

Sir Sydney Paget showed up with Connie Hoffman on his arm. Connie had charmed everyone from members of the royal family to English jockeys. Much to his family's dismay, Sydney had not only failed to marry into money; he hadn't married at all. Two of his brothers had traveled to America and found wealthy wives.

27

As a young boy, Luther followed the troops back from the Wounded Knee massacre.

—Lee Dunning

GRANT DUNNING SAT ON HIS HORSE ON OTTER CREEK and read the letter from home that told him that his mother in Rapid City had passed away. Dunning ran the Circle Bar Ranch's horse operation for Captain Howes. He was one of the top cowboys on Otter Creek and, next to Tom McAllister, maybe its best horseman.

Grant had little time to mourn his mother, because the end of the letter stated that his younger brother Luther had taken a horse and run off to find Grant. Luther couldn't have chosen a worse time to head off across country alone. The army had been called in to investigate a ghost dance on the Pine Ridge reservation, which culminated in a slaughter of almost an entire camp of Indian civilians. Over three hundred were killed. It was a dark time for the former Plains horsemen. Around this same time, Sitting Bull had been killed by Indian police and Spotted Tail was murdered by a jealous Indian rival.

After the Wounded Knee massacre, the troops passed through Rapid City, where young Luther Dunning fell in and followed the command to Suggs, Wyoming.[1] Luther, heartsick and lonely, and against the warnings of the troops, decided to make the thirty-mile ride to Otter Creek alone. It was a big, lawless country; there was apt to be trouble with the Cheyenne after the Wounded Knee battle. In addition, the range wars were coming to a head and horse thieves rode rampant across the country; for a boy to stumble on a group of outlaws stealing stock could mean death.

"Why not write your brother and have him come get you, or at least wait for somebody else to come by who's headed that way?" one of the soldiers asked.

"Naw, I guess I'll go on, it shouldn't be but two easy days," Luther said.

"That's if you don't get lost," the soldier said.

Luther didn't give it a second thought. But once out and alone, he became frightened. He had heard the soldiers' stories of Indian fighting; they had told him not to expose himself on the skyline. He thought about kicking up to a gallop but knew better than to use up his horse riding across unknown country.

When the sun began to set, Luther picketed his horse in the bottom of a draw. In a fireless camp, he ate some of the hard tack and dried beef the soldiers had given him. As the day faded into twilight, a heartbroken loneliness set in. For the first time since he left home, it sank in that his mother was dead. He spread his bedroll on the ground, lay back, and began to cry.

When he was out, he looked up at the stars and said a prayer to both God and his parents. Luther figured his mother was with his father now and liked to think they could both see him, alone on the plains. He thought they might be pleased he was going to find Grant.

In the first light of morning, he was awakened by a sharp jerk of the rope he had tied around his waist. Something had spooked his horse, which was prancing and looking to the north. Luther sprang to his feet but saw nothing; the hills around him were empty. In a flash he was saddled and off at a lope around the side of a hill that would give him a view to the north. He slowed to a walk, trying to see what had upset his horse. He saw horse tracks close to his camp, and then saw the horses off in the distance.

Luther was watching a couple of yellow horses in the herd when his horse turned to look at something behind him. Two Indian horsemen were riding right for him. Luther thought of trying to outrun them, but they seemed neither hostile nor friendly. On closer inspection, he saw they looked poor and hungry. They rode up to Luther, who was at a loss what to do, so he raised his hand and said, "Hey."

The two men looked at Luther's gelding and began to speak in Cheyenne. They circled the boy as if inspecting his horse.

"Do you know Grant Dunning?" Luther asked. The two men looked at one another and then back at the boy. "I'm his brother," he continued.

The Indians made eating gestures and pointed to Luther's saddlebag. Luther immediately produced his hard tack and dried beef, which the Indians devoured. They gestured to the boy for more, and he gave them a small bag of dried apples and seven pieces of candy. He ate some of the dried apple and a piece of candy with the men before he was entirely cleaned out. The two Cheyenne then made a sign that they were looking for tobacco, but Luther shook his head no. Both men nodded a grunt of approval and rode away up a ridge. Luther sat dejected as he watched them go; he was lost, and now he was cleaned out of food.

"Dunning," one of the Cheyenne turned and called for him. Luther rode up to the top of the ridge beside him and looked toward where the man pointed. "Dunning!" the man repeated and pointed to a large herd of horses on the horizon. The Cheyenne made a circle with his finger and put a line through it and pointed again at the horses. Luther was puzzled until the man did it again.

"Circle Bar!" Luther said. It was Captain Howe's brand, where his brother worked. The Cheyenne nodded and gestured a little to the south, where the ranch was situated.

After Luther had ridden five miles, it seemed like the entire country was full of horses. He had passed three bands of young stallions that had been ostracized from their herds by the lead stallion. Two young stallions made a run at Luther's gelding, but a sharp slap from Luther's rope backed them off. From a high ridge he saw the timber-lined ridges and the expanse of lush grassland below. Without having seen the area before, young Luther Dunning knew he was home.

Crossing the divide facing Otter Creek, his attention was fixed on something black moving across the grasslands. From a mile away he concluded it was a covered buggy, pulled by one horse that was ambling along at a walk. He rode down to intercept the buggy and ask directions to the Circle Bar Ranch. He loped down about two hundred yards in front of the buggy that was down a depression, but as it pulled up within view Luther was horrified to see that the man and woman appeared to be naked with the woman sitting in the man's lap. Young Luther sat paralyzed in embarrassment. There was not a rise or a clump of brush to hide behind for a quarter-mile. If he ran, they would see him, and if he stayed where he was, they would see him. He opted to rein his horse away and ride down the road with his back to the rolling lovefest. There was nothing but grasslands and rolling hills for several miles, and yet he had managed to stumble on the most embarrassing situation of his life. Soon, he heard voices, and after a few minutes, he heard the carriage approach. He did not dare turn around, but to his dismay the carriage pulled up alongside him. To his relief, a well-dressed couple sat and hailed him.

Next to the driver sat the fanciest dressed and most beautiful woman Luther had ever seen. Luther removed his hat and introduced himself.

"Uh, sir, ma'am, my name is Luther Dunning, and I was wondering if you could tell me where I can find the Circle Bar Ranch."

Sir Sydney Paget got out of the buggy and shook his hand. "Greetings, young Dunning, we have been expecting you. My name is Sydney Paget, and this is the Queen of Miles City, Connie Hoffman."

"Hello, ma'am." Luther flushed red and clenched his hat, but Connie Hoffman knew how to handle shy cowboys.

"That is a fine horse you are riding, Luther, did you raise him or did you buy him?" she asked.

"Uh he was my mother's; she died."

"Grant is thrilled that you are coming to see him. We just saw him yesterday," Connie said.

Syd looked the boy over; he was all freckles. "Grant tells me that you're quite the horsemen. I am in dire need of someone to ride for me. I was hoping you might be interested."

"Yes, sir," Luther said.

"Don't you want to know what you'll be paid?" Luther asked.

"No, sir, I guess you'll pay me what's fair."

As the young Englishman shook the hand of the young cowboy, it began a career that ran through tens of thousands of horses, several armies, and every equestrian discipline from racing to rodeo.

"Tie your horse to the back of the buggy, and we'll talk on the way to my ranch. I'll send word to Grant to come for dinner tomorrow. First I want to show you our stallion that I just bought from Marcus Daly. He is imported from England. His name is Empire Regent."

Almost immediately Paget took Luther under his wing like the son he never had. In the next three months, Syd taught Luther about raising horses, and Grant taught him how to keep horses alive in the country where winter could be deadly to livestock. Luther soaked it up like a sponge, and as a rider, he was a born natural.

One afternoon Grant took Luther on a ride to find some Circle Bar horses that had drifted off their range. Grant had told him how to track horses that had strayed.

"Once you determine which way a track is heading, ride quickly to an open area in that direction and try to pick up the tracks, instead of staying with the tracks, which will take too long. By hitting an open area, a man might overtake the horses he was trailing."

"Range horses like the open country and tend to brush up or back up to a windbreak only in the winter. They'll climb out of the timber to the high flats that blow clean of snow and eat, whereas a cow will hang in the brush and starve.

"Once they are turned out, they will separate into small bunches. Saddle horses on a roundup will bunch in groups of two to five. In the wild herds they'll sometimes form bands of twenty to fifty, but that is decided by the studs. Horses will walk into or away from a storm but never across one. They like their water clear if they can get it; I've seen horses watering at a stream play a form of hopscotch where they constantly move upstream of one another to get a clear drink."

Luther soon met Noll Wallop, who gave the boy some additional work breaking horses. Noll gave Luther the same business lessons he had given Tom McAllister and Charlie Thex, both of whom were now successful livestock men.

When Charlie Thex met Luther, he gave the boy some valuable advice: "The horse always comes first, no matter what. You don't eat till your horse is fed. Don't go in the house and warm up in the winter unless you know your horses have got a place to get out of the weather or at least a windbreak they can back up to. Make sure they have plenty of grass in the winter. You gotta acquire an eye for horses when they begin to fall off their weight; if you wait till horses get skinny, it's too late.

"A high trot will get you way farther than a slow lope. If you got a tired horse on a cattle drive, switch horses or quit the cattle. Don't ever break a horse down because the cattle are turning back. If your horse is tired, go get another one."

Maybe the best advice Charlie Thex gave the young Dunning was about crossing streams on horseback: "Loosen your cinch and take the bit out of your horse's mouth. Not all horses swim the same. These streams can come up faster than you can get across them. There's been a lot of cowboys die from pulling their horse over on them crossing rivers.

"Horses have a better sense of direction than we do, so if you're lost in a blizzard, give your horse his head, and do the same at night when you've lost the trail." Soon Luther was constantly in the saddle, finding the bands of Wallop and Paget horses that had drifted off across the broken grasslands between Powder River and Rosebud Creek.

The art of running thoroughbreds on the range was in stark contrast to the lavish equestrian estates of the east. With huge corrals and unlimited grazing, the stallions lived in stalls in the winter and were sometimes turned out with the mares in the summer.

Luther would sometimes ride the stallion out to tease the mares to see if they were in heat. If they showed signs, he would drive them into the corral and breed them with a foot tied up so as not to injure the stallion. By now, Wallop and Sydney Paget owned thirty-five top-bred stallions between them.

> *Stallions were turned out with the mares during the summer, which he guards with jealous care. The bunch will soon become "located;" which means they adhere to an area about ten miles in diameter, watering at the same place every day. Mares that have been foaled on a run will not leave the ground, even if there is no stallion to guard them.*
>
> *A stallion can generally keep this country to himself but is occasionally beaten off by another stallion and sometimes even a gelding, which is called a "herder." Should this occur, the stallion would return crestfallen to the ranch.*
>
> *Stallions are supposed to be taken up and stabled during the winter but are occasionally lost all together.*

> *About mid-May, the mares are rounded up for the purpose of castrating colts of the previous year; they are again turned out in selected bunches, to each of which a stallion is assigned. In the late fall—October—the mares are again rounded up to brand the foals in the spring of the year. The best bunch of horses are called "tops" and the worst the "culls." During the six months they are in use, horses for cattle work are not shod and subsist entirely on bunch grass, which they prefer to oats, especially when it first grows.*
> *—Lord T. B. Drybrough, British polo player*

While Captain Howes's son, Robert, was home from law school to visit the ranch, he sat with his father and watched Luther Dunning float along on a horse that everyone else had trouble with.

"Father, why can't I ride like the Dunning boy?" the young lawyer asked.

"I guess you just don't have it in your briefs," the captain laughed.

28

A man's past was not questioned, nor a woman's either; the present was what counted. A man could be wanted by the law elsewhere, yet this was not held against him here so long as he showed a willingness to walk the straight path. Half the charm of the country for me was its broadmindedness. I loved it from the first . . . However, I was struck by the number of people who thought it necessary to apologize for being in the west . . . they would tell you who they were and how rich and important and aristocratic their connections were back east.

—Nannie Alderson[1]

THE VIBRANT OLD FRONTIER SPIRIT OF MILES CITY WAS fading into a dull aura of propriety. The old-timers of Miles City were not only forgotten, they were getting run down. Calamity Jane had been part of Absaraka during the Indian wars as a teamster, but now she and other survivors of the wild times were shunned in public. Old warriors were nothing more than old "bucks" to some of the newcomers. Churchgoers sat and worshipped on benches that Charlie Brown had donated the lumber for, but some were too stuffy to speak with him because he owned a saloon. Connie Hoffman caught the worst of it. She was called a whore in public and all but ostracized in the town she had once been the toast of. An old rancher friend had further insulted her by asking her to remove his brand from her famous dress; he was afraid of what his new wife might think.

One of the new implants to Miles City spotted Noll Wallop on one of his trips to town from his ranch. Wallop's shirttail hung half out, and he wore a worn-out hat.

"Mr. Wallop, what would your family say if they saw you dressed so? You should work on making yourself more presentable."

"Madam, that is the r-reason I escaped to this wonderful country; men are judged by their actions and not their dress," he said.

While in Miles City for a series of horse races, Noll Wallop accepted an invitation to attend church. As the congregation exited after the service, they heard a ruckus coming from half a block away. Sheriff Bill Hawkins cringed as he watched the spectacle in front of the churchgoers. In among the scrambling deputies, Hawkins, a former Texas Ranger, recognized the voice of Calamity Jane. Jane Canary had briefly become a minor celebrity of sorts. She had accompanied General Crook's men when they moved into the country to fight the Lakota and Cheyenne. Jane claimed to have married Wild Bill Hickok, which was a lie, but the two had been friends.

"Turn me loose, you bastard sons of bitches!" A coarse, heavy-set woman squirmed, twisted, and slipped through the grip of her captors, tumbling to the dusty street. She managed to rise from the dust and kick one of the deputies in the groin, dropping the man. Another ducked a roundhouse to his head, while a third deputy finally blindsided her, pinning her to the ground.

Noll Wallop smiled at the sight. He had had a pleasant conversation with the woman once while riding through Red Lodge, Montana. "It looks as if Miss C-Canary is in fine form this morning," Noll said. The woman next to Wallop was less than amused. "That woman is disgusting."

As Sheriff Hawkins approached the brawl, Jane called out to him: "Billy! Billy, tell these sons of bitches to let me go! I'll go to hell with you, Billy, but I ain't going to jail with these sons of bitches!"

Bill Hawkins waved his deputies off. He picked up Jane and dusted her off.

"Jane, it's Sunday morning. C'mon, I'll give you a private cell and get you some coffee."

"Coffee? I came to Miles City to drink whiskey!" The two laughed and walked to the jail, where Hawkins poured her a drink. After a few brief stories, she was fast asleep on a pallet.

Down in Kaycee, Wyoming, a skirmish between small and large ranchers started when Nate Champion was killed while holding off a band of hired gunmen who were bent on taking over the town of Buffalo. The gunmen had been hired by large ranchers to break up a small rival cattlemen's association and to hang suspected cattle thieves. The cavalry from Fort McKinney intervened to prevent further bloodshed, but loyalties would be split in the area for a century.

The rest of the summer, Sydney Paget worked tirelessly on a steeplechase track in Miles City. Once it was finished, he took Charlie Brown on a tour of the track. "It may be a little strong for the English," Syd told Charlie, "but it should suit the Irish."

> *Jump No. 1 is a plain brush fence, four feet high; No. 2 is a six feet ditch, guard rail in front. No. 3 is a water jump, fifteen feet wide, where the jocks will have a chance to wet their jackets if they don't put their horseflesh in it the right way . . . No. 6 is a new and stiff one, being the Irish bank fence, consisting of two ditches with a high bank fence in the center. This kind of jump requires special training, as the horse jumps over the first ditch onto the top, changes feet, and jumps off clearing the second ditch. The ditches are about twelve feet wide each; the base of the bank fence covers so that the horses have to make two jumps of fifteen to twenty feet in quick succession . . .*[2]

The day of the Miles City race was the biggest social event of the year. Over a four-day period, trotters, flat racers, steeplechasers, and Indian racers competed in front of a thousand spectators. Every woman in the country was turned out in her finest. The ladies of the town staged a tea in the infield, and outriders in pink foxhunting coats rode herd on the festivities. Connie Hoffman wore a custom blouse embroidered in Paget's racing colors of scarlet and cream. She sat in her carriage along the path the racers took to the starting line.

Every good cowboy and rancher in the country was watching. Luther Dunning, astride Sailor Jr., would ride in one of the steeplechase races. As he passed Connie on his way to the track, she called out, "Good luck!"

> *... professional and businessmen, amateur and professional sportsmen, cattlemen, farmers, deadbeats, and tramps. The hurdle race, in which they take such a deep delight, brought out the ladies in full force and finest feathers. The red contingent from the government side of Tongue River was more than usually large.*
>
> *The sensation of the day was the hurdle race, at least for the fairer portion of the spectators. Sailor Jr. was the leading horse coming home, much against his rider's wish, for Sailor Jr. will not jump unless he has someone to show him the way, and his rider wishes to keep him back until after the last hurdle and then make his race, but Sailor Jr. would not be held back. He came first to the last hurdle, and as he generally does under such circumstances, balked at it, his rider was dismounted, and one of his hands injured, leaving the race to Monte.*[3]

Sydney Paget vaulted over the rails toward his downed jockey. It was a hard fall. By the time Syd reached the boy, Luther was up, holding his wrist.

"I'm sorry, I couldn't hold him, Syd," he said.

"There's not a jockey in the world that could have held him, Luther. You did just fine. I think Sailor Jr. had best remain on the flat track from here on out," Sir Sydney said. He found himself visibly shaken at the sight of his injured young protégé. He insisted the boy go immediately to the doctor even after being told the boy was fine.

It was plain to everyone in the country that Sir Sydney was grooming Luther Dunning to take over his ranch. Syd had a father's affection for Dunning. The boy was patient, conscientious, and modest, yet there was a spark to him.

When Connie Hoffman jumped from her buggy to try to help Luther, she was cut off by a local woman. "Leave him alone, you're not his mother! You're a cheap tramp, and if you cared anything for that boy you'd stay away from him, and that goes for Sydney Paget too."

Connie ignored the statement and pushed by the woman, but the comment stuck. The luster of her crown was now dulled by a new set of people who were taking over the area.

It was at the Buffalo, Wyoming, racetrack that Sir Sydney Paget saw his ticket to big-time racing. A stallion named Black Diamond won two races, and when the colt came to Miles City, he won again. A Sheridan breeder named Vess Hardee, who had already sent one horse to the Kentucky Derby, owned the stallion. Paget bought the colt for $1,500 and ran him twice in one day in Butte, Montana, and won both races.

That fall, Paget took Black Diamond to Chicago and set the world record in the half-mile. The next stop was England, but the stallion developed a split hoof and was brought back to Miles City. Riding on the success of Black Diamond, Paget was now ready to enter racing on an international scale.

Paget began to sell off a large portion of his horses to finance keeping only the better ones in racing. It was good timing, because within the month the era of the large horse ranchers of Absaraka was about to come to an end. No one realized that the last big race meet in Miles City was the end of an era.

29

The time was when the common low-priced horses found ready market in street railway service, but those times are past. The electric power has displaced the cheap horsepower.

—*Stock Growers Journal*

Three years ago I owed $30,000 to a bank at Miles City . . . How did I spend it? Not in playing the fool, but on improvement of horses, believing that one day I will be getting high prices for my horses. And that it will all eventually come back with a rush. Well, I was mistaken; horses have gone to an unknown value. Those that I would sell in the old days for $150 are now not worth over $50, and there is but scarce sale for them.

—Oliver Henry Wallop

THE GREAT HORSE RANCHES OF ABSARAKA WOULD DIE A sudden death. Overnight, with every town in America running electric streetcars, the demand for cheap horses plummeted. The number of horses sold dropped by 75 percent. Never in the history of the country had the value of an animal dropped so severely. The financial panic of 1893 put the final stake in the heart of the horse breeders. Horse ranchers all across the country were wiped out.

J. R. McKay out of Miles City had advertised his entire herd—imported stallions, mares, foals, and the rest—for 50¢ on the dollar. It is doubtful if he got close to that. Captain Howes sold more than three thousand horses the next year. Owners stopped gathering and managing their horses because the animals had become worthless; thousands of stray horses ran loose south of the Yellowstone. The big horse outfits ended as quickly as the buffalo runners and warhorses before them.

Paget, Wallop, and James H. Price began promoting the area's horses as best they could. They expounded the value of Montana-raised horses in magazines and by word of mouth in their trips to England.

> *Montana horses are nearly all natural water-jumpers, which is doubtless caused by practice over washouts in their native badlands . . .*
>
> *The hunt were stuck up by a swollen stream, and Lord Cowley, Mr. John Fuller, and Mr. Lindsay rode at it abreast. Lord Cowley's horse broke his neck, and Mr. John Fuller's horse jumped short, but the Montana horse flew it with perfect ease and without hesitation.*
>
> *—Captain E. S. Cameron*

Plans were made to promote a huge horse sale featuring races, rodeos, and parties. They all realized the key to bringing the horse market back was getting the buyers to come to Miles City. With men like Charlie Brown handling the local logistics, and Paget and Wallop handling promotion in their travels, the birth of one of the greatest horse markets came to pass.

> *We produce horses which are classed all the way from the cayuse to the Derby winner, Hackney to the trotter, and in all cases where the Montana horses have come into contact with other horses, either in show ring or in trials of speed and strength, there have been no curtains drawn to screen our horses.*
>
> —Stock Growers Journal

> *Miles City can within a few years rival the annual horse sales at Lexington.*
>
> —Stock Growers Journal

In the spring of 1893, Sydney Paget found out Connie Hoffman was seeing Henry Ware, a cattle rancher on the Cheyenne River. She had hoped that by making herself unavailable to Paget, he might come around and propose, but he was too immersed in horse racing to be distracted. In ten years Connie had never turned him down or greeted him with anything other than a sunny disposition. Now she had not only turned him down, but her demeanor turned solemn.

Connie had refused to move to Paget's ranch with him years before, because she knew better than to cohabitate with a man without a marriage proposal. Sydney took the snub as her opposition to domestic life. Connie had also turned down offers of marriage by several wealthy ranchers, which Sydney took to mean she was not interested in marriage at all. Since then, their relationship had been a standoff of romantic misunderstanding.

"Connie, you've had other men the entire time we have been together. Why should now be different?" he asked.

"It's different now, Syd," she said and walked away. The Englishman had no idea what he had done. Syd walked to Charlie Brown's stable to load his wagon, but within fifteen minutes Connie reappeared.

"Bring Luther to town once in a while; it's not good for a boy to stay out on a ranch for so long. He's too dedicated to leave the ranch when you're gone," she said. The boy had been as much a son to Connie as he had been to Sydney. Syd turned; she was in tears. The Englishman started toward her, but she stopped him with a stiff, outstretched hand. Having no choice, Sydney hitched up his team and started for the long drive to his ranch. Though he didn't understand it, he knew their relationship was somehow in trouble.

While at the ranch, Sir Sydney Paget decided in the romantic English tradition of chivalry that he could win Connie Hoffman back at the Miles City races. With his new red and blue racing colors, he entered himself in six steeplechases over the course of two days in the Miles City fall race meet.

On the eve of the race meet, Sydney Paget was having drinks in the MacQueen House with some other horsemen who were there for the races. Paget had kept Miss Hoffman in the corner of his eye since she had entered the room with another man. He felt Connie was playing some kind of game; at least that's what he assumed until she stormed up to the table and lit into him.

"Sydney, you're not going to let Luther ride that idiotic steeplechase course you built, are you?" she asked.

"Hello, Miss Hoffman, how are you this evening?" he said, standing at her approach.

"Answer me, Syd! You'll get poor Luther killed if you put him out there."

"I can assure you that Luther won't be riding any more steeplechases; I intend to ride my own horses. Would you join us?" Sydney said, pulling a chair out from the table.

Connie immediately cooled. It was not in her nature to lose her composure; in fact, most of the men at the table, including Syd, had never seen her angry. Her face softened, controlling the hurt that was boiling inside. The color in her cheeks betrayed her, but the blush radiated such beauty that the men at the table had already forgotten the outburst. For a woman in her mid-thirties, Connie Hoffman was still a beauty, but few referred to her as the Queen of Miles City anymore. Her independence had come at a price. There were other wealthy ranchers who would probably keep her, but Connie Hoffman didn't want to be kept; she wanted to marry Sydney Paget. He was fun, extremely generous, and treated her with respect. It had been a passionate, fast-paced romance that had lasted a decade and took her to New York, Chicago, London, and Paris.

Composing herself, Connie addressed Sydney. "I was just worried for the boy. It looks to be a dangerous course. Thank you for the invitation, but Mr. Ware is here," she said quietly.

"Have Mr. Ware join us. Shall I go and ask him?" Sydney offered.

"No, Syd, please!"

"Very well, Connie, I hope to see you at the races," Sydney said cheerfully.

"I don't know . . ." She backed away from the table of standing men. A man at the table watched her leave.

"Sydney, what happened between you two? You were together for a long time."

"Over ten years," Sydney said, in almost a whisper. For the first time in anyone's memory, Sir Sydney Paget looked depressed. Walter Lindsay, seeing Syd's discomfort, changed the subject.

"Well, Syd, looks like you and I have a big day tomorrow." Both men were riding over the grueling course the next day.

September 8, 1893

The final day of the race meet proved no less exciting than the first. Billy Mann from England won the first steeplechase, but in the third he was dumped when his horse flew over the rail and landed on its knees. His horse regained its feet and ran into Miles City without his rider. Walt Alderson entered a horse in the one-mile Gentleman's Driving Race with Charlie Brown. In the last race of the meet, Paget brought his horse, Chief, home for the win. He was presented with a blanket covered with flowers that was draped over the neck of his horse. After the race, a weary but exhilarated Sir Sydney searched the crowd but couldn't find Connie Hoffman. Sydney dismounted and led Chief over to the stable, where to his relief, he found Connie sitting in her buggy talking to Luther Dunning. Sydney, all smiles, presented her with a flower that had been pinned to the winner's blanket.

"I'm glad you're here, Connie," he said.

"I only stopped by to say good-bye to Luther." She smiled politely and turned her buggy toward town and left.

"What did she say?" Paget asked his young trainer.

"She said for me to take care of you," Luther answered.

"I suppose she's probably leaving," Syd said. For the first time since Luther Dunning had known him, Sydney Paget seemed deflated. He stood with his horse like he didn't know whether to stay there or put his horse away. Chief, still hot from the race, pushed Sydney with his nose, snapping him from his thoughts.

"I'll take him," Luther said, taking Chief from Sydney.

Luther was confused as to why Miss Hoffman would ask him to take care of Sydney.

"Am I going to go back east with you?" Luther asked.

"Do you want to go east with me, Luther?" Syd was amused at the boy's question. He had never met anyone who was happier in his work. In the three short years since his arrival, Luther Dunning had become a horseman on the level of his older brother Grant, who was considered one of the best.

"I want to stay here with the horses," Luther said. Syd smiled, but his heart was focused on the only woman he had ever loved, who was driving away.

Connie Hoffman took a long drive past Fort Keogh; she wanted to watch a Montana sunset alone. To the west, the Yellowstone snaked its way along the naked prairie toward the Rocky Mountains; to the east, it emptied into the Missouri River. She pulled her horse to a stop and had a good cry.

She would always love Sydney. She had to leave Miles City before Sydney went east; she didn't want to watch him leave again. The 44 had burned to the ground, leaving her not much of a way of making a living. The demise of the horse market had left Miles City in a depressed state.

Henry Ware was throwing money at her, and if pushed, he would marry Connie, but her heart would never be in it. If she was going to have to go back to being a prostitute, she would do it where no one would know her. Within the week, the Queen of Miles City left on the night train for the Dakotas. She didn't tell a soul except Charlie Brown, who promised to sell her horses and carriage and send her the money. The kind old German walked her to the train. As he watched the train pull away in the dark, he was moved to tears; Connie Hoffman had been one of the early ones. With her departure, a bright light went out in old Milestown.

Charlie Brown sat with Walt Alderson at a horse auction and watched good horses run through the sale for less than $10. The large German was beside himself at the dwindling prices.

"Look at zis, Valt, a fine sorrel horse and only a five-dollar bid on him," Charlie Brown said.

"I'll give you $7!" Walt shouted from his seat on the top of the corral pole. Walt brought "Seven Dollars" home to Nannie, who was none too thrilled; money was scarce, and they had lost their ranch and were now living in town.

The next day a man came running into the saloon, looking for Charlie Brown. "Walt Alderson has been kicked in the head."

For six agonizing days, Nannie and Charlie Brown kept a constant bedside vigil beside Walt until he faded away, leaving Nannie a widow with four small children. Pressured by her family in West Virginia to leave the country they saw as barbaric and move home, Nannie declined. Her friends were there, in Miles City. She would roll up her sleeves and go on.

Charlie Brown, however, had had enough of the propriety and left for Alaska to mine gold, and Sydney Paget took his top horses and boarded a train to the East. Noll Wallop was the next to leave. Women did not understand him, and few of the newcomers appreciated him. His stuttering commentaries on various subjects spanning everything from Plato to cattle prices, often in the same breath, were taken by some of the newcomers around Miles City as bizarre. In his travels he had found a canyon in the Bighorn Mountains near the town of Big Horn, Wyoming, where he had decided to move.

30

NOLL HAD TRAVELED THE WORLD, AND HE RECOGNIZED beauty when he saw it. While delivering a load of horses to a ranch at the foot of the Bighorn Mountains, Wallop had found the spot to set up roots. Little Goose Creek spilled out of the mountains and wound its way through the lush green meadows. Trout swam in abundance, and pheasant, quail, grouse, prairie chickens, and ducks populated the area along with elk, deer, mountain lions, bears, and wolves. It was a sportsman's paradise.

At the mouth of the canyon, on the banks of Little Goose Creek, stood the small frontier town of Big Horn. The town had sprung up to accommodate travelers moving along the old Bozeman Trail. A small cabin, which had served as a blacksmith shop for wagon trains and cattle drives, still stood at the end of the town's main street. The canyon itself had been a hideout for various outlaws during the frontier years.

Noll bought land from Bear Davis, whose family was one of the first to settle Little Goose Canyon after the Indian wars. A veteran of Fort C. F. Smith, Davis had become a local legend for shooting more than sixty bears in and around the canyon.

Once Wallop moved to the canyon, he became friends with neighboring Englishman Mike Evans. Noll and Mike became running partners in everything from mining gold and setting up a work camp for the young sons of wealthy Englishmen, to polo games and stirring up the nightlife in the town of Sheridan, ten miles down Little Goose Creek.

Their hangout in Sheridan was the Sheridan Inn, which claimed to be the best hotel between Chicago and San Francisco. The Inn was built across from the railroad depot, which had recently been built through Sheridan. The Inn was an expansive wooden building with a huge veranda that wrapped around the front and sides, a restaurant, a bar, and luxurious accommodations to serve the growing cowtown of sixteen hundred citizens.

William F. "Buffalo Bill" Cody had gone partners on the hotel in its early stages and would occasionally drop in to audition cowboys for his Wild West Show or just kick up his heels in a town that had not yet become as socially restrictive as Miles City had. Like the old MacQueen House, the Sheridan Inn became the meeting place for affluent travelers.

The guests of the Inn were treated to an amusing contest of speed between a couple amateur sprinters last Saturday evening. Among the occupants of the Inn carryall on its second trip to supper were O. H. Wallop and Mike Evans, well-known ranchers on the Little Goose, who, true to characteristics of their nationality, are ready at all times for a bout of athletics or healthful sports of almost any description. In the course of the somewhat hilarious conversation, and when the idea advanced by one was combated by the other, a barter was instantly offered and as promptly accepted to run one hundred yards without further preparation than the removal of their spurs.

The distance was paced, the sprinters were required to toe the mark, and at the word "go" they were off at a pace which indicated that their early experience at college had not been entirely forgotten, nor their attention since to healthful sports without its beneficial results.

"Dead Heat" was the verdict of the judges at the outcome, and the only recourse to settle the amiable dispute was to try it over again, which they did in a few minutes, Mr. Evans winning this time by a foot or two. The writer who witnessed the pleasing event averred, without prejudice,

however, that Mr. Wallop won the first heat by about six inches, and that the decision in that instance was unfair to him and rendered purely with a view to having the sport continued for the edification of the large crowd of spectators which had been attracted to the scene.
—Sheridan Post, *1894*

Aside from Evans, Noll had plenty of Englishmen around Sheridan with whom he could visit. Captain F. D. Grissell of the 9th Lancers raised horses on his IXL Ranch in Dayton, Wyoming. Grissell had played in England's inaugural polo game when it was brought into the United Kingdom from India.

George Beck operated a flour mill west of Sheridan, which he named Beckton after himself. Beck ran unsuccessfully for various political offices ranging from the senate to the governor of Wyoming. Beck made up for his failures at politics with his ability to throw wild parties. He introduced a drink at the Sheridan Inn called the "Wyoming Slug"—a mixture of whiskey and champagne.

The Stockwell brothers had given up a commission in the British Army to find the "lost cabin gold mine" that was purported to exist somewhere in the Bighorns. The Stockwells were totally enamored with the Wild West and, like George Beck, threw their money away on lavish parties.

At the 1893 Sheridan Fair, Beck, the Stockwells, and Evans took on a team of cowboys from Sheridan in the game of polo. Frank Grouard, who was in town trading horses, was asked to umpire the game. The event, while insignificant to local standards, may have marked the beginning of the next horse culture in the area.

Seventeen years earlier, Grouard had witnessed the great mounted charge of four Indian tribes on Rosebud Creek, but somehow the polo game seemed more chaotic. The forty-five-minute melee both amused and confused the gathered spectators.

Grouard sat on his horse, wondering at how quickly everything had changed. Many of General Crook's and Colonel Carrington's veterans had come back and settled in the area for its beauty and its pioneer spirit, but like Grouard, they were soon left behind by civilization. Despite his competency as a frontiersman and horseman, Grouard had outlived his time. He was no businessman, and the slumping horse market had put him in a state of near poverty.

Grouard had become somewhat of a local celebrity. Joe DeBarthe, the editor of the Sheridan and Buffalo newspapers, had just published a book about Frank, but the book was a great embarrassment to the scout, as DeBarthe had embellished some of his stories to fit the times. The fame Grouard achieved served only to cause jealousy among his former colleagues. Billy Garnett, a scout living at Fort Robinson, blamed Grouard for the death of Crazy Horse. Another scout accused him of being an illegitimate son of a former slave. The same jealousy that killed Crazy Horse, Spotted Tail, and Sitting Bull was now directed at Grouard. The scout wandered from job to job, carrying mail, training horses, and guiding hunters.

While Noll Wallop liked a party as well as the next man, his heart lay in hunting and fishing in the mountains. The Bighorn Mountains that the Indians had fought so hard to keep were his new playground. With a rifle or a fishing rod, he was privy to a kind of hunting and fishing that existed in only a few select spots in the world. He loved people, but he loved to ride out in the country with a fishing pole or a rifle. Sometimes he would ride across the entire Bighorn Mountains to eat dinner or attend a party at Shell, Wyoming, and then hunt birds or deer on the ride back the next day. With cattle and horses running from Big Horn to Otter Creek eighty miles north, Wallop was constantly in the saddle.

On a ride from Sheridan to his ranch in Big Horn, Noll stopped for a visit at George Beck's, where a mint julep party was in full swing. At the party Noll met Frank Grouard who, like Wallop, was growing weary of the noisy proceedings.

"Mr. Grouard, I n-noticed some beaver on Big Goose Creek on my ride over. I might see if I might get a shot at one. Would you like to j-join me?"

"Sounds good, I've about had enough of this crowd," Grouard said.

The two men saddled their horses and went off to hunt. They never found any beaver, but for several hours, they shared stories of the frontier, horses, and the Indian wars.

"They say you were an a-acquaintance of Sitting Bull and Crazy Horse," Wallop said.

"Crazy Horse saved my life not far from where Captain Grissell lives. I was sent out by the government to get the wild tribes to come in to a treaty to sell the Black Hills. Sitting Bull wanted to kill all of us to send a message to the whites, but Crazy Horse stopped him. He was the bravest man I ever met, white, black, or red."

Grouard would have been surprised if he had looked over Wallop's horses and spotted the old mare he had traded to Crazy Horse. She was almost gone; there was gray hair on her face, and she had begun to drop weight. Noll had raised several horses out of her, one of which was one of his personal favorites, a gray gelding named Blue.

It wasn't long before the people of Sheridan began to accept Noll's eccentricities. His absentmindedness became a source of local amusement. Often at the end of a day of shopping, Noll would arrive at the Sheridan Inn only to realize he had left his packages at various stops he had made that day, but he had no idea where. Someone at the inn would go find his packages for him. When Noll left on long journeys by train, patrons of the Sheridan Inn would wager on how many times Noll would return to get something he had forgotten or to thank the hostess, the chef, or the bellman. Usually whoever bet that Noll would return five or six times before the train left won the pot.

For all his hijinks, Noll wasn't much of a bachelor. His loneliness kept him in constant motion, but benevolent neighbors from Miles City to Buffalo were always considerate enough to take him in for a meal. Perhaps the funniest story was the time he arrived at his neighbor's, the Hilmans', for Thanksgiving dinner and had to be pulled from the saddle. It seems his freshly washed but not yet dry pants had frozen to him in the five-below-zero temperatures.

The high flats on the eastern face of the Bighorn Mountains received more rainfall than the Otter Creek property, making the grazing better. Wallop's horse herd now exceeded three thousand, but its value had dropped out of sight. Not one to give up, he loaded horses on boxcars and shipped them to Chicago, Memphis, and Saint Louis. His plan was to trade each horse for up to six yearling steers. Noll would then ship the cattle home, graze them for a year, and triple his money. The railroads were issuing passes to promote its business, so Wallop had little shipping overhead.

It was on one such trip to Chicago that Noll met the love of his life. When Wallop first disembarked from the train, he asked a yard worker where the prestigious Chicago Club was. The yard worker, sizing up Wallop for a bum, directed him to a cheaper hotel on the other side of town, but despite his occasional shabbiness, Wallop could also present himself as a dapper gentleman of blue blood. At either end of the spectrum, he never lost his class. He showed yard workers the same good manners that he showed heads of state.

Noll was sought out by Chicago's social crowd as an entertaining and rather amusing social mixer. He could quote poetry and speak a few phrases in Crow or Cheyenne. At a social function in Chicago, Noll met Miss Marguerite Walker, the granddaughter of Governor Charles Morehead of Kentucky and niece of the wealthy financial wizard Joe Lieter.

Marguerite Walker was an eccentric and somewhat quiet woman. She had traveled the world and found in Wallop an adventurous, enterprising Englishman who showered her with genuine affection. She shared Noll's love of classical literature and became interested in his business, offering suggestions when she could. Ironically, she had been to the Wallop estate in England as a girl and had dreamed of one day being Lady Portsmouth. Miss Walker's shy manner hid a shrewd businesswoman who complemented Noll's wit and charm. The couple was engaged almost immediately after their meeting, but the date of the nuptials was kept open until Noll could build a ranch presentable for Marguerite.

While leaving Chicago to return to the ranch, Wallop sent his intended a farewell note:

In east elm street
Miss Marguerite.
When you kindly bid we dine
Though I know my wishful mind
Yet I must perforce decline
When my luck its
Offering duckets

Then I feel I must go
Where the larger breezes blow
Calling, Calling Westward Ho!
No fun the lack
'Ere I come back
With the merry cowboy crew
But I hate to say adieu
Sadly, Sadly, thanking you.
O. H. W.

Fueled with a passion for his newfound love, and armed with an energy and ambition few men possessed, Noll took to building Marguerite an estate tucked back into Little Goose Canyon that would rival any in the American West. He transplanted fruit trees and native flowering shrubs and designed a three-story log mansion complete with grass tennis courts, gardens, and lawns at the base of the mountains where, only thirty years before, Crow and Cheyenne warriors had battled each other.

All Wallop needed was a way to get back on his feet financially. He leveraged his Otter Creek holding to finance his new ranch to the south.

While in Wyoming, Noll was in a flurry of literary correspondence, sending as many as three letters a day to his beloved.

I just got back from the range after a 75-mile ride today in order that you might not be without a letter longer than I could help.

Yesterday I picked you out three horses, two very pretty mares that you can either ride or drive and one pretty little horse. I felt like "busting" them myself, only I believe I was under agreement to ride no more colts. Oh! My love, I wish you were here with me today. A lovely balmy spring morning, soft and sweet, and we could either stroll down to the stream and I could catch our first dish of trout, or we could ride along the edge of the thickets above and see if the old brown bear that dwells in a cave in the rocks above had sauntered out yet. Good-bye, dear love, may God keep you safe and sound till we meet. And then, dear Madge, you shall greet me as you said good-bye. Yours ever,
—Oliver Henry Wallop

Marguerite Walker not only cared for Noll, but she also seemed to understand him. In some ways they were much alike: both were overshadowed by more prodigious siblings. Wallop stuttered and tended to embarrass his family with his absentmindedness. Miss Walker was painfully shy and somewhat withdrawn, her sister Amy being the more outgoing of the two.

As Marguerite and Amy traveled to Rome and Paris, and from Chicago to Kentucky, Noll's letters followed them.

> *The day we marry, all I have will be yours, and I only wish it were more, for had I all that I could ask, it would not be worthy of you. Give me enough for ammunition, flies, garden seeds, a microscope, and books, and on the ranch at least you will not find me hard to manage, for my tastes out here are very simple and I have only one great extravagance and that is longing to have you with me. A longing that surges over me in waves, making me want to stretch out my arms and take with them the void, thinking in fantasy to grasp your dear self.*
> *—Oliver Henry Wallop*

The letters gave Marguerite a taste of local western life as well as a look into the heart of a sportsman.

> *I was rather amused at your wasted compassion for the magpie. He is the most cunning robber bandit of the air. He murders young birds, he steals eggs, and whenever he finds some sore backed horse he will literally eat him alive. If I let them exist, they will ruin every quail and prairie chicken's nest 'round here.*
>
> *Don't think that because I am daily gun-in-hand that I love shooting for killing's sake. Often I have crept up on deer when I have had my rifle and lain and watched them carefully till I was satisfied, and then left them undisturbed. The study of natural history has far too many charms for me to allow me to think that the taxidermist's lifeless mockery is except in rare instances any atonement for wanton slaughter. Can you supply those lines from ancient Mariner in which Coleridge says that "he loveth but, who loves all things both great and small?"*
> *—Oliver Henry Wallop*

With the help of Marguerite's connections in Chicago, Noll wrote a captain in the U.S. Army's cavalry division inquiring if the army needed any horses, and then proceeded to sell his horses one at a time to help finance the ranch. While on a horse-selling trip to Chicago, Saint Louis, and Memphis to trade for southern cattle, he met an interesting cross section of Americana.

West Plains, Missouri
My host at the hotel was a fiery little "Dutchman" who had a dispute with the sheriff over a bill and blacked his eye before I could get a hold of him. I was afraid the sheriff might shoot. I never saw a man so frantic with fury. He was simply crying mad; his family was also crying. I was very disappointed that in the ecstasies of their grief they did not cry on my neck while I was restraining them, as the two daughters were very pretty and kissable.

Tomorrow I am expecting another man, a very good [horse] trader and a great character. Moreover scrupulously honest, horse-dealing excepted. He is a deacon in the church, and offering up a prayer there, is perfectly conscienceless and delighted to cheat a preacher out of his horse.

I know so many horsemen who are so disgusted with their business and want to get out of it that I think I can do very well with them at no risk to my own pocket and also get them out of the hole.

—O. H. Wallop

By the mid-1880s William F. "Buffalo Bill" Cody was the most famous man in the world. As a boy, Cody had served as a pony express rider and a buffalo hunter for the railroad, and he had once killed an Indian who had attacked a group of men trailing cattle. He had served as a hunting guide to wealthy foreign noblemen and high-level army officials. Dressing in fancy buckskins to impress the hunters, Cody cut an impressive figure on a horse, which more than anything created the legend. Soon he was acting in melodramas portraying himself, which is what he was doing when Crazy Horse fought against Custer at the Little Bighorn. Cody was the hero of hundreds of dime novels that featured him as a Western icon. In a bizarre contrast of myth and reality, Buffalo Bill left the stage to join Colonel Wesley Merritt and the 5th Cavalry to hunt down the remaining hostile tribes and ended up killing and scalping a Cheyenne chief.

In 1883, Cody joined forces with a team of promoters that put on a traveling Wild West Show that featured him as central character. In 1889, Buffalo Bill's Wild West Show lured two and a half million spectators during its six months' tour in Europe. The show included a herd of buffalo, elk, bear, deer, and a pet moose that pulled a cart. The strong suit of the show was the horsemen. Russian Cossacks, gauchos, Mexican vaqueros, cowboys, Arabs, and ninety-seven American Indians were participants. In the middle was Buffalo Bill, who shot his guns alongside Annie Oakley, galloped his gray horse around the arena, and generally became a figurehead for the world's fascination with the American West. Even Queen Victoria, who had been reclusive for a quarter-century, attended. In London, five European kings were lured into the dilapidated Deadwood stage, which had more than once stampeded out of control over ten years of touring. By the time Noll Wallop moved to Sheridan, Cody had bought into the Sheridan Inn and served as honorary proprietor. Cody was generous to a fault, often bankrolling old buffalo hunters and Indians, or giving orphans a place in his Wild West Shows.

Cody was also a drinker, and there was no better place for him to hide out and let his hair down than Sheridan in the early nineties. While he had built a hotel named for his daughter in Cody, Wyoming, his involvement in Sheridan was more a recreational one. One citizen, who happened to be in Sheridan after-hours, spied Colonel Cody at the reins of a two-horse team and wagon wearing only his long johns and a pair of young prostitutes sitting next to him.

When Noll Wallop first saw Cody, he was holding auditions for bronc riders on the lawn of the Sheridan Inn to accompany him to Europe for his Wild West Shows. Noll's letter to Marguerite captured the scene.

> *Buffalo Bill was the honored guest of the place [Sheridan Inn], and all the cowboys were assembled to do honor to their little tin god. Two or three ambitious young bronco busters were assembled to show their prowess while we old and worn-out veterans sat and criticized then severely. Very poor bucking and very poor riding was our verdict.*

> *Just after the riding, we all adjourned to the hotel and, seeing my great friend Whitney the banker telling a yarn about broncos, I stepped over to him to hear it. Whitney was narrating how he had seen a cowboy ride a colt in Miles City in the great and glorious early days and how the colt had jumped through and over a pile of cord wood over six feet high. Not being able to see where he was going as his head . . . was stuck somewhere back between his hind legs.*
>
> *I turned to [Whitney] and said, "That was in May '85, wasn't it?"*
>
> *"Yes," he replied.*
>
> *"Roan horse in front of McQuick's stable?"*
>
> *"Yes!"*
>
> *"You were standing on the corner of the street?"*
>
> *"Yes, did you see it?"*
>
> *"I suppose I ought to have, [it was me on the horse]," I answered, to his great surprise.*
>
> *. . . Buffalo Bill comes up [to the ranch] tomorrow, and great is the excitement among my cowboys. They are going to make him buy my horses anyhow.*
>
> *—Oliver Henry Wallop*

Noll's and Cody's affection for good horseflesh and whiskey made the two fast friends. Buffalo Bill's visit to Wallop's ranch sent all Noll's cowboys running for their guns. Everyone wanted to display his shooting skills against the great Western showman. At Wallop's ranch in Bighorn, several marksmanship contests were staged. Buffalo Bill was beaten with a pistol by one of Wallop's cowboys and by Noll himself with a rifle.

On another visit to the Inn, Noll met Frank Grouard.

> *I had an interesting half-hour today chatting or rather listening with a stray question to Buffalo Bill and Frank Grouard, another old Army scout. As great a contrast lay the entire lives of both as between the appearance of both men. Buffalo Bill is an exceedingly good-looking man with splendid carriage and physique, with a kind of weak face but over it all a self-satisfied advertised air. He was well dressed, a little too well dressed, for the size of his pins and rings were not in accordance with*

the canvas of good taste, and beside him sat Frank Grouard, rough and dirty, still a scout and at his old trade, just in off an apparently impossible trip over the mountains with a single saddle horse and packhorse, heavyset and evidently possessed of tremendous physical strength, with the utmost courage and coolness apparent in his face marred by the stamp of the most repulsive cruelty. A man to whom tenacity of purpose was matched by his tenacity of counsel. Buffalo Bill had this much in common with Grouard, that he had been a scout, while he owed his future to his address, physique, and constant self-assertion. Grouard's life had been a kaleidoscope of dark romance. Originally a Kanaka, he lost his uncle in an attack on an immigrant train returning from California over the plains and was spared by the Indians on account of his color. He was "raised" by Sitting Bull. As he grew up, he became a minor chief among the Sioux until, seeing the natural outcome of the war between the races, he turned traitor to his adopted people and, joining the whites, he became their most hostile foe. But ever since he joined his new friends, has anyone questioned his loyalty courage or honesty? So they sat there, he and Cody, the latter doing nearly all the talking, the former watching through half-closed eyes with a contemptuous sneer just showing on his evil face. I don't think I have ever enjoyed a half-hour so much for a long time as I did these two men. Good night, my darling. God bless you.
Yours ever, OHW, 1894

While Buffalo Bill reveled in the limelight and played up to it, Grouard shrank from it. Grouard did not particularly like Cody. Wallop's good nature and a mutual passion for good horses encouraged a friendship with both men, probably something he alone could claim.

I would have been home last night, but I was not feeling very fit, and having to pass George Beck's ranch on the way back, I dropped in and was welcomed by a very cheery crowd assembled around a large bucket of Kentucky mint juleps. Among them was Frank Grouard, the scout of whom I told you once before, and tiring of the noisy crowd, I suggested to him to take a rifle and wait for beaver by some beaver dams by the river. No beaver appeared, but I had a very interesting hour's chat with a man

whose life must have been wild-chequered beyond fancy. I took a further fancy to him for the cool and modest way in which he told his tales and I think he must have rather liked me, for he wants me to go with him on a hunt in the fall for moose . . .
—Oliver Henry Wallop

Moncreiffe was one of sixteen children of Sir Thomas and Lady Louisa Hay Moncreiffe. Lady Louisa bore Lord Thomas Moncreiffe seven girls, then William, then a girl, then seven boys. A game sportswoman, Lady Louisa rode horses right up to the time she gave birth to her children. On one such excursion, her groom rode alongside and begged her not to jump while pregnant.

"My lady, think of the ones at home and the little one still inside!" he protested, trailing Lady Moncreiffe as she sailed over another jump riding sidesaddle.

When William first saw Little Goose Canyon, he consigned local pioneer woman Lydia Hilman to find him a ranch, which she did right next to Wallop on Little Goose Creek. Moncreiffe bought Lydia a dress made in Chicago for her trouble.

On a tour of his new ranch, Lydia showed William Moncreiffe the remains of an Indian buried in a tree along Little Goose Creek. Lydia's father Bear Davis had showed it to her with instructions never to disturb it.

Oliver Henry Wallop and Marguerite Walker were married in a huge wedding that was the social event of the year in Chicago. When the couple arrived in Sheridan, a three-day party followed at the Sheridan Inn. Cowboys, merchants, local politicians, and cattle ranchers from Miles City to Buffalo were present.

Noll had bought a new black carriage in which to transport his bride to Big Horn. A team of black horses was groomed for the sixteen-mile trip to the ranch. Lost in his thoughts of ranching, the slumping market, and a dozen other things, Noll got his team and headed for his ranch in Little Goose Canyon. The drive along Little Goose Creek was enchanting, lined with cottonwoods, aspens, and wild chokecherries. In the background, the Bighorn

Mountains rose out in an expansive blue-green wall. A crew of cowboys, gardeners, and cooks gathered on the manicured lawn to greet the newlyweds.

"Where's Mrs. Wallop?" one of the servants asked. Noll looked at the vacant seat beside him.

"Oh, my, I've got to go back!" Wallop quickly switched to a fresh team and drove back to the Sheridan Inn, where he found Marguerite waiting patiently.

Marguerite's first order of business was to throw out the Crow scalp that the Sioux had given Noll when he first moved to Otter Creek. Along with home decorating, she also took an active role in running the ranch and, through family connections, meeting with horse and cattle buyers and military men in Chicago, where she lived part of the year.

Noll Wallop's hospitality and wide collection of friends from England to Oregon began to draw others to the area. On a visit to Wallop's ranch in Little Goose Canyon, Scotsman William Moncreiffe fell in love with the area and soon built an expansive house on land he bought right next to Wallop on Little Goose Creek.

Moncreiffe, like Wallop, was extremely generous to the cowboys who worked for him. He gave them a way to progress financially, often cutting out calves at brandings for the men to build their own herds.

William's brother Malcolm moved a short while later to the canyon from Powder River. Malcolm got into breeding polo horses in a big way. His plan was to raise and train his horses in Wyoming, and then ship the best to England, where the money was.

Malcolm hired sixteen-year-old Johnny Cover from Noll Wallop to take care of his polo horses. Cover took to polo like he had played it all his life, and to the dismay of both Bob Walsh and Malcolm Moncreiffe, the American teenager was soon outplaying both men. Needing eight players to field a game, Moncreiffe soon recruited local Bighorn residents Floyd Bard, the Skinners, and the Hilmans to play matches.

In addition to shipping polo ponies to England, Malcolm Moncreiffe trained a mule to jump and shipped it to England, where it turned some heads in the foxhunting field.

Riding over his stock in Bighorn, Wallop noticed his calves were turning up dead and some of his cows had their tails pulled off. Riding to the edge of the timber at the base of the mountain pasture, Noll found the large tracks of a wolf. At dawn and just before dark, Noll waited with rifle in hand, but the wolf proved the hardest of all game he had encountered. Preferring to hunt alone for stealth, he left his hounds Punch and Judy in the kennels. After a week, Noll ran into Johnny Cover, who was trailing a cow that a wolf had chewed the tail off.

"Johnny, I think tonight I shall turn Punch and Judy loose and see if they might catch the wolf. If they come back without their tails, we'll know we have a serious problem," Wallop said.

With the financial panic and the depressed horse market, some horse ranchers gave up and turned their horses loose on the open range, where they mixed with the wild herds. This resulted in unmanaged horses running loose all over the area. With foal crops multiplying, these herds grew by a third annually.

When Noll moved south from Otter Creek, both Charlie Thex and Tom McAllister went off on independent ventures. Thex went to work for Captain Howes and continued to steadily build a cattle herd of his own. McAllister worked for himself, gathering the best of the free, abandoned horses off the range and branding them with his Lazy 6 brand.

On Meade Creek, near Big Horn, Wyoming, Tom Horn, a stock detective in Wyoming, rode into Charles Bard's ranch on an exhausted horse.

"I could sure use a fresh horse. Could I leave mine here and borrow one till I get back?" Horn asked. "Take the gray out in the pasture," Bard said. Tom Horn got the horse and left his own and was gone for three weeks. When Horn showed back up on the Bard's gray horse, he acted impressed.

"Well, Mr. Bard, this is the toughest horse I've ever ridden," Horn said to Bard.

"Oh, yeah, why is that?" Bard asked.

"I rode him clear into Canada before I unsaddled him," Horn said.

While the horses from Absaraka were making a name for themselves locally and in a few instances abroad, there was little in the way of a national market for them until W. B. Jordan of Miles City bought two hundred head for the U.S. government. This broke the eastern monopoly in supplying the U.S. Army with horses. If the government could be lured west to purchase horses, quite a few ranches might be saved.

From Sheridan, Dr. William Bruett, a special commissioner of the Bureau of Animal Industry, sent Will and Bert Gabriel on a twenty-four-hundred-mile ride to prove the sturdiness and endurance of the area's range horses. The cowboys rode two broncs that had never tasted grain or been shod. With no feed other than grazing along the way, the horses arrived in Galena, Illinois, after riding hard for ninety-one days. The promotion succeeded; the army's demand for Western horses in Chicago rose from fifteen hundred in 1893 to fifteen thousand in 1897.

Once again, the West was becoming the world's marketplace for horses. Suddenly Noll's old stomping ground of Miles City was booming again as a horse market. With army buyers taking the place of the streetcar market, new horse operations began to spring up. The FUF Ranch out of Forsythe, Montana, ran several thousand horses, the best of which went to the army and the rest sold for meat.

Army buyers arrived in Sheridan and Miles City looking for cavalry mounts and artillery horses as the United States prepared for war with Spain. Grant Dunning was in charge of riding the horses for inspection and getting them ready to ship out for the Philippines and Cuba. Some Cheyenne horsemen on the reservation had raised a herd of good horses that were also bought for the war.

Sydney Paget had no sooner arrived in New York than he got the break in racing he had been waiting for. His brother had married William C. Whitney's daughter. Whitney was a former secretary of the Navy and also one of the top racehorse owners in the world. Impressed with Sydney's knowledge of racing, Whitney gave him the job of managing his racing stables. In 1899 Paget's horse, Jean Bereaud, won the Belmont Stakes, but his success was short-lived, as the war in South Africa had become a nightmare to the British: one hundred British casualties, with twenty-two thousand of these buried on African soil. Sydney Paget, following his grandfather's lead as a military man, volunteered.

He was soon appointed captain of a machine-gun unit of the 12th Imperial Yeomanry.

The number of horses purchased for the Spanish-American War was a drop in the bucket compared to the number requested in South Africa. Horse breeders from Miles City to Buffalo were presented with the opportunity of a lifetime. The price of a decent saddle horse in Absaraka had been between $20 and $40, but now the British Army was scanning the globe for horses and offering $120 and $165 per animal.

31

IN 1884, A DIFFERENT KIND OF WAR WAS BREWING ON Otter Creek. Indians had murdered a sheepherder, and rumors of an Indian uprising on the Tongue River and Otter Creek had the ranchers up in arms. The women and children were sent to Miles City. The sheriff was called in from Miles City, and an army of cowboys was assembled on Captain Howes' Circle Bar Ranch. A stone fort was built on a knoll to hold off an Indian attack.

Hoping to resolve the tensions peacefully, Levi Howes, Charlie Thex, the sheriff, and eleven deputies rode onto the Cheyenne agency. The group soon found themselves confronted by five hundred Indians armed and ready for war. The ranchers wanted the man responsible for the murder of the sheepherder turned over to the authorities. Howes, with Thex at his side, approached the Cheyenne chiefs with their message: "This depredation has gone far enough; we ain't going to stand for any more. The only alternative is you've got to have this man punished or it's war."

The ranchers turned and went back to their stone fortress, called Fort Howes, where they saddled their horses but locked them in the corral. The Indians held a dance that night to see if they would fight or not.

In the end, the Cheyenne brought the guilty man into Miles City and a range war was averted. He was a Sioux named Badger who had attended Carlisle school in Pennsylvania. After a much-postponed trial, Badger was set free on lack of evidence.

Within a year, Badger and Levi Howes met again, this time on the Tongue River where Howes, his wife, and his sister were attempting to cross the river. Badger checked a swollen river crossing so they could get their buggy safely across.

Ranchers like George Brewster, Captain Joseph Brown, and Captain Calvin Howes had lost thousands of dollars' worth of cattle butchered by the Cheyenne. The ranchers appealed to the government for compensation. They could not blame the Cheyenne; the tribe had not received the beef the government had promised them. It's one thing if someone steals your stock for money, and it is something entirely different when they steal it to feed their family. The last big fight on the plains would not involve Indians and whites; it would be between the large cattlemen and the sheepherders over the free grass.

October 1900

Bob Selway was one of the largest sheepherders in the United States, running tens of thousands of sheep in various bands in the area. Historically, Selway usually had the sheep graze the range on Pumpkin Creek, but the summer of 1900 had been dry, and there was little grass. That year Selway decided to send John Daut over the divide to Otter Creek with eight thousand sheep divided into four separate bands, for which Daut would receive a percentage of the flock.

Daut filed a homestead site on a tributary of Otter Creek and brought Selway's sheep with him. As he was having his homestead surveyed, Levi Howes rode up.

"We got no problem with you filing a homestead on this side and running your own animals, but Selway's sheep aren't welcome here," Howes said.

"You mean I can't run my own sheep?"

"There are seventeen of us that say you can't run Selway's sheep on this range, and Daut, you had better keep out of it." With that, Howes rode off.

John Daut knew that what the men who ran livestock were trying to enforce was illegal, but these cattlemen weren't the kind to be pushed around.

Men like George Brewster, John Kendrick, and Charlie Thex had carved out a living and sizeable ranches through sheer hard work. They had weathered bad winters, droughts, and growing numbers of homesteaders, and they weren't going to let a large sheepman push them off grass they had used for their stock. George Brewster had hunted buffalo for the railroad, and John Kendrick and Charlie Thex had come up with Texas trail herds. While Kendrick and Thex had less than sixth-grade educations, both were shrewd businessmen. Kendrick had accumulated land and cattle much as Charlie Thex had, except Kendrick had married a wealthy woman.

The problem was that sheep and cattle did not mix. Cattle would head to the high flats where the good grass was and then return to water for a drink. The sheep would bed down next to the watering holes, which spooked the skittish cattle away, causing them to drift out of the area to look for a new water source.

In November, some cowboys purposefully denied several hundred horses water for three days and then turned them loose when Selway's sheep were bedded down next to Otter Creek. The crazed, thirsty horses trampled the sheep on their way to water, killing some and scattering the rest. John Daut had Dan Squires and three other herders all running two thousand sheep, each in different locations. Just before Christmas, Squires found a note pinned to his sheep wagon:

> *Move these sheep as far east as Bradshaw Creek or every damn one will be killed. By order of the settlers' committee. If this don't move out these sheep, we will kill the parties who brought them in.*

December 28, 1900

Dan Squires was in his sheep wagon cooking breakfast when the masked riders appeared at dawn carrying heavy clubs. Before Squires could get his rifle, a rider with a cloth sack over his head pulled a pistol from behind him and stuck it to the sheepherder's head.

"I'd like a cup of coffee, please," the rider said. Squires poured the gunman a tin cup full of coffee.

"I'll take some cream if you got it," he said, pulling the hammer of his pistol back as he handed the cup back to the sheepherder.

"Please," he added, causing the other riders to look at each other.

Damn it, Charlie, quit screwing around, one of the riders thought. They needed to get this over with.

On a deserted stretch of Bear Creek, which fed Otter Creek, the men clubbed two thousand sheep to death. The first band were put in a corral and clubbed, but the second band, refusing to be driven in over the dead sheep, were driven to a bend in the river and killed there.

"You'd better stay close to this wagon, and don't be following us unless you want to get shot," one of the riders warned before the group rode off.

The yellow stallion saw the group of riders approaching from the south and moved the mares away down a draw. Traveling up a ridge, he looked back and saw the riders were following. He hurried the mare ahead, and then down a draw and up over the divide toward the pines overlooking Otter Creek.

The riders were deliberately mixing their tracks with the tracks of the wild horses across the snow-covered hills. By midafternoon the men split up in different groups and put the country behind them. That evening at the Gilbertson Ranch on Tongue River, a crowded dance was in progress when six men entered the room, got a drink, and sat down. At John Kendrick's OW Ranch on Hanging Woman Creek, another dance was in session. Six more men rode in and joined the festivities. At each dance the men made it a point to mix and dance to secure an alibi; Charlie Thex even played the fiddle. Outside, tired horses were unsaddled and fed by cowboys while the riders, miles apart, lent their presence to the two "alibi" dances.

While the men were en route to the dances, Dan Squires rode into Captain Brown's Three Circle Ranch on Tongue River with the news. His entire band of two thousand sheep had been killed by eleven masked men. He said one sounded like Charlie Thex and thought the rest to be John Kendrick, George Brewster, William Boal, Booker Lacy, Shorty Caddell, Walt Snyder, Bill Munson, Tug Wilson, Frank McKinney, and Barney Hall.

After making his report, Dan Squires rode to Miles City, emptied an account with his name on it, and left the country for good. The next day John Kendrick rode over to John Daut to demand he get the rest of his sheep off

Selway's range. Daut asked Kendrick if he could wait and let him move his sheep the following October, lest he take a horrible loss. Kendrick agreed. Daut sent word to the Cheyenne reservation about the supply of free meat on Bear Creek. The next day the Cheyenne appeared with wagons, skinned the sheep for Daut, and hauled off the meat to the reservation.

When Bob Selway heard the news of his slaughtered sheep, he was livid. He visited the ranch of Charlie Thex and offered him $50,000 to turn state's evidence against the men who killed his sheep.

"Mr. Selway," replied Thex, "I am in no immediate need of any money at all, but if I were I wouldn't take up your proposition, as I've never handled any sheep, I am not familiar with their diseases, and I wouldn't know anything about the cause of their death. But if I did know about it, you or your whole sheep association couldn't dig up enough money to hire me to tell it." Selway then attempted to strong-arm Thex but got the barrel of his gun bent in the bargain.

The man Selway was really after was John Kendrick. Kendrick's OW Ranch had been a springboard for the business-savvy cowboy from Texas. Kendrick had married a rich man's daughter and, besides running one of the largest cattle ranches in Absaraka, had speculated in real estate in Sheridan, bought the First National Bank, and started to dabble in politics. Kendrick was inside his bank when Bob Selway tried to serve papers on him. Kendrick grabbed him by the collar and threw him in the street, thus ending that confrontation.

Money had been placed in a bank account to compensate Selway for the lost sheep, but he wouldn't touch the money. He wanted to bring down Kendrick. The case never came to a trial and was finally dismissed. What Selway had not counted on was the loyalty that existed among the men who had first settled the area.

32

My men would rather face Boer machine gun-fire than get on any more of those Montana broncs.

—British Lieutenant in South Africa, to his commander in London

CAPTAIN HEYGATE LOOKED SUSPICIOUSLY AT THE THREE men sitting before him. "You're telling me you can supply the English government with fifty thousand horses that will pass inspection?" he asked the trio.

"Fifty thousand fairly quickly, more if we have time to gather them," Malcolm Moncreiffe said. Malcolm sat with his brother William and Noll Wallop, hoping to secure a contract with the British. The three ranchers knew there weren't more than fifteen hundred horses in the area from Miles City down to Big Horn that would pass inspection. There were, however, thousands of range horses that, given a few days of being ridden by savvy cowboys, could be tame enough to be snuck through the inspections and pass. Malcolm was hoping that Noll, in his well-meaning honesty, would not kill the deal.

"They'll be fairly e-expensive if we have to buy only gentle horses for the cavalry. I suggest we buy some of the greener horses and let your men top them off so as to save the queen's money. But of course that decision should be yours," Noll said.

Heygate studied Wallop, who continued. "Another option is for us to hire c-cowboys to top off some of the greener inexpensive horses for a month before we ship. That's if you think your men could handle them; we breed the heartiest horses in the world, you know."

Heygate raised an eyebrow. "I think the British cavalrymen can handle horses without the help of Montana cowboys, don't you?" he chuckled. "If they're tame enough for a cowboy to ride, one of Her Majesty's soldiers should have little problem, or are you suggesting a British cavalryman is inferior to a Montana cowboy?"

Wallop and the two Moncreiffes just shrugged. They knew men like the Dunning brothers could ride horses most cavalryman would not have a prayer on. There was an awkward silence before Noll took the negotiations one step further. "You have no idea what our Montana horses could achieve if we had proper cavalrymen instead of cowboys to ride our horses," he said with a twinkle in his eye.

Captain Heygate looked across the table at the men. He knew that Montana horses had made their way to racetracks, polo fields, and foxhunts in England, thanks to the promotional efforts by Paget and Wallop. Both men were well known in England because of their connection to brothers serving in the House of Lords.

Captain Heygate had already received a letter from Cecil Rhodes recommending the Montana thoroughbreds. Rhodes, the British diamond magnate in South Africa, was aware that his former professor at Oxford University, James H. Price, raised thousands of thoroughbreds east of Miles City.

Heygate finally conceded. "I'm going to award you gentlemen a contract for twenty thousand horses. They must be between five and nine years old and above fifteen hands in height. You'll need to have a crew of cowboys ride them the length of a polo field at inspection. Our men will take them from there," he said.

Brilliant, Moncreiffe thought, suppressing a smile. Wallop had just talked the British captain into buying greener range-broken horses and made it appear to be Heygate's idea. Malcolm had underestimated his old friend.

Heygate stood and shook hands. "You will need holding pastures, feed, and someone to manage the train cars that will haul the horses to New Orleans, where they will board a ship for South Africa."

Walking out of the meeting, the three men increased the pace just thinking of what lay ahead: train schedules, feed, holding pastures, and inspection points. The logistics of filling the contract were mind-boggling, as were the fortunes to be made.

"We'll be busy for a while," William Moncreiffe said, walking from the meeting.

"So will the b-bronc busters," Noll said and smiled.

On Otter Creek, Leota Dunning looked with curiosity at the envelope addressed to her and Luther. Leota Kimes had come to Miles City as a young girl on a steamer before the railroad had come through. She had met Luther Dunning at a dance in town, and the two were married shortly thereafter. They had moved to Sydney Paget's horse ranch on Otter Creek to manage it in his absence.

That morning it had clouded up and turned cold. The wind whipped along the hills that bordered the ranch. Leota decided not to open the letter until Luther came in that evening; she had a feeling it was bad news. Right away she recognized the handwriting on the envelope as Sydney Paget's but not the postmark, and it worried her. She laid the letter on the kitchen table and waited, going about her normal chores. When Luther rode in, she took the letter to him, choosing not to wait until he came into the house.

After unsaddling his horse, he noticed Leota had fed the stallions for him already.

"This must be an important letter," he said and smiled at his wife, and the two went into the house together.

"It's from Sydney," she said. It took Leota a full ten minutes to read the six-page letter, which she summarized in places for Luther. "He's gone off to South Africa to fight with the British. Says the war isn't going so well, but the good news is they will need lots of horses. He says we can sell all the horses over fifteen hands tall that we can get broke. Wallop will need you to go with him. Mr. Moncreiffe has already sent notice to Grant to see if the Circle Bar will let him go help. He says we should stand to make enough money to buy our own ranch.

"He's left his racehorses with Whitney's man in New York. Mr. Whitney is sending us a new stud for the ranch; his name is Gold Seeker. He cost $12,000 as a two-year-old."

Leota was trying to digest the varied information that had just been presented to them. She looked at her husband.

"Will he be all right, Luther? Why would he go off to a war halfway around the world?" Luther had a clue it had something to do with Connie Hoffman.

Within the week, Noll Wallop and the Moncreiffe brothers had formed a "company" made up of every top hand among the horsemen from Miles City, Montana, to Buffalo, Wyoming. Wallop's in-laws in Chicago and Moncreiffe's family in Scotland financed the company. Wallop and the Moncreiffs bought horses for $20 to $40, and resold them to the British government. Cavalry horses brought $125, larger light-artillery horses sold for $150, and heavy-artillery horses brought $165.

Advertisements were taken out in every newspaper from Scots Bluff, Nebraska, to Ontario, Oregon, southward into Colorado. Noll Wallop hit the rails with a crew of cowboys and Luther Dunning as his right hand.

Deadwood, South Dakota, 1901

ENGLISH ARMY HORSES
AN AGENT IS BUYING THEM IN THE HILLS
ENGLISH ARE NOT VERY PARTICULAR

Oliver H. Wallop, who is here from Sheridan, is representing Moncreiffe Brothers in the securing of horses for the English Army—takes mares and geldings that are smooth and broken to saddle.

Oliver H. Wallop, who has been in Deadwood for several days, is purchasing horses for the British Army for use in South Africa. He is accompanied by two men, Mr. Benefeil and Mr. Dunning, and since their arrival in Deadwood Monday night have been scouring the country in this vicinity in quest of animals that would be serviceable to the English Army . . . they are taking some of the animals that are being rejected for the United States Army at Fort Meade, as the requirements in the British

> *Army are not as rigid as in the American . . . The English Army does not require as large horses as the American.*
>
> *Mr. Wallop will take animals from 14 hands up, mares or geldings. They must be broken to the saddle, and mares must not be with foals. Mr. Wallop has had a great number of relatives and friends killed in the fighting in South Africa . . .*

Wallop paid Luther Dunning $5 for every horse he brought that passed inspection. Bob Walsh was also hired as a buyer, as was Grant Dunning, who tried out the horses that were brought to sell in Sheridan. Wallop's buyers could earn up to $700 in a good month.

If the horses passed inspection in Sheridan, they were trailed twelve miles into Big Horn, where the British inspectors either passed or failed them. From his polo ranch, Malcolm Moncreiffe ran the inspection operations in Big Horn, handling the logistics of feeding, riding, and shipping such a large number of horses. His foreman, Johnny Cover, ran the Big Horn corral, where a team of cowboy riders rode their horses for the British.

The area was in constant motion, with horses arriving from the four corners and every horseshoer, cowboy, merchant, saloonkeeper, and prostitute was reaping the benefits of the increased activity. Mortgages were paid off, and ranches were bought with the earnings made off the sales. The high, lush flats in Little Goose Canyon, known as the starvation pasture, were kept for horses that arrived in poor condition. Other ranchers likewise leased their pastures for the huge volume of horses that required feeding while they awaited inspection.

> Sheridan Post, *June 27, 1901*
>
> *It does not appear that the English are ready to withdraw from South Africa. British agents are in this country asking bids on 20,000,000 bags of feeding oats, 20,000,000 bags of seed oats, 20,000,000 bales of alfalfa hay, and 20,000,000 bags of bran. It is understood that these supplies are for the troops in South Africa.*

The conflict that had started out as a police action had evolved into a full-scale war that began to be felt in British homes; Noll Wallop lost two relatives during the first months of the Boer War.

Horses were being killed as fast as they could land at Cape Town. The Boers had proved adept at fighting the outdated knee-to-knee mounted cavalry movements of the British, which resulted in thousands of equestrian casualties. Horses that weren't killed in combat died of exhaustion and disease. One of the worst enemies was the tsetse fly, which planted parasites in the horse's bloodstream, to which the animals had no resistance. Were it not for a few veteran horsemen, the British might have lost them all.

Veterinarian Joseph Grimes left New Orleans with a ship loaded with 1,040 horses. He dealt with terrible heat, lack of water and food, and struggles with pneumonia, abortions, and hepatitis. Dr. Grimes was up with the horses night after night. It was amazing that he lost only 35 head on the voyage.

"Here're your Montana horses, Captain," a soldier called to Paget, who was watching a shipload of horses unload at Cape Town's harbor. Captain Sydney Paget had not expected the flood of emotion he felt seeing the familiar brands on the horses as they walked past him.

Al Irion's 77 brand from Powder River, Tom McAllister's Lazy 6 brand, the Crown W brand of James H. Price, and Noll Wallop's Quarter Circle Bar Quarter Circle. One of the horses belonged to Frank Archdale, who had ridden in a steeplechase with Paget in the early 1890s, and there was even a horse with Charlie Thex's brand on it.

A sudden homesickness for Absaraka and its people pulled at Paget's heart as he stood and watched the horses of his friends come ashore halfway around the world. Paget looked back at the ship in hopes that a cowboy from old Miles City would walk off, but there were only cockney ship workers. Sydney ran his hand over a horse's shoulder. He smiled at the irony that he was almost as far away as he could get from Montana, yet here was a piece of Montana and something he was running from, the memory of Connie Hoffman.

In the middle of the horse boom, a final stake was driven into the heart of the old-timers around Miles City. Charlie Brown, the man with the biggest heart in Miles City, had died of heart failure in Alaska. More than one hundred people stood at the train station waiting to receive the body. The day he was buried, businesses were shut down and the schools were closed. The funeral was the last gathering of old-timers from Miles City. Elderly soldiers, hunters, Englishmen, Cheyenne, cowboys, and ranchers paid their respects. Few of the early residents of early Miles City had not benefited from his kindness. He had staked buffalo hunters, fed and housed cowboys, defended women, and was always present to lend a hand to its citizens.

Nannie Alderson stood with her four growing children as they lowered the casket in the ground. Charlie had brought her champagne when Mabel was born and had kept a constant vigil when Walt had died. It was almost too much for Nannie to bear; it stirred up loneliness for Walt. Charlie had been Walt's best friend and had shown her innumerable acts of kindness.

Walking away from the funeral, one man turned to another beside him to comment, "It's too bad he didn't live to see the horses come back; he always said they would."

From Omaha, Nebraska, to Ontario, Oregon, and into Nevada, Noll Wallop held inspections while Luther Dunning galloped out into the countryside looking for horses that would pass British inspection. Each town had its own set of characters and trials. In one town, for instance, a man who was sympathetic to the Boers accosted Wallop, and in another, he was attacked by a man because Noll had rejected his horses. Fisticuffs ensued, and the crooked horse trader found out that the well-mannered Brit could also handle himself in a fight. After getting his ears boxed by Noll, the man fetched the sheriff, who informed him he had got what he had coming.

In the first four months, Noll bought more than one thousand horses in a half-dozen towns. He no sooner filled an order than he was sent out by William Moncreiffe to go and find more. The pace was grueling; for over two years Noll was constantly on the road.

He was dedicated to providing the best horses while giving the lowest prices possible. He was up at five every morning but still found time to socialize in the evening and in between helping out the ranch hands, but his body couldn't match his inner drive. He tried to hide his failing health from Marguerite.

Noll bought the best horses for the best prices. He felt it was his duty to his former country. Unfortunately not everyone felt that way. At some railroad corrals at Orrin Junction, Wyoming, Luther Dunning approached Noll as some horses were unloaded from a train car.

"Those look like the horses we turned back in Idaho." Wallop walked over and saw red. "I just received a telegram from Malcolm that Walsh bought twenty-four head of horses in Idaho for $40 each!"

"Looks to me that these are the ones we turned down in Boise for $20."

"He's making deals on the side to line his pockets, Irish treachery!" Noll stomped off and wrote a note to the Moncreiffes, but to his dismay, nothing was done. Worse yet, Walsh had commandeered Luther Dunning as a horse buyer but paid him only wages instead of the normal commission.

While he was on one of his many horse-buying trips, Marguerite gave birth to Gerard Wallop, whom Noll rarely got to see in the infant's first months. While on the road, Noll bought a pony for Gerard, who was mounted before he could walk.

Hotel Bridger
Bridger, Montana

My darling,
I bought you a bay pony today that I think will suit you—he "lopes" very readily and will rack and is perfectly quiet. I will trade the buckskin for him at inspection. I find that he shies in riding him down the road. Next I have bought for Gerard a little brown pony about as big as a Newfoundland dog for $10—so gentle that when I bought him; I insisted on the owner turning his saddle upside down and leading him round like that. I hoped he would kick it to pieces, but he did not. Bill Daily, poor fellow, went to the reservation and only got 6 head. I have bought good, good horses this time . . .

Au revoir, my dearest wife. God grant health to you both till we meet.
O. H. W.
April 2, 1901

In the roaring town of Deadwood, Wallop waited as Luther Dunning and Jim Benefeil rode into the countryside asking where there were suitable horses for sale.

THE BULLOCK . . .
Deadwood, South Dakota, April 26, 1901

My darling,
I shall be glad to get to work, for it is very dull here and there is nothing to see except to stroll out in the evening to the saloon, cafés, and then early to bed. Besides, this town is Sodom and Gomorrah in one and I do not want to get salted.

After a trainload of horses was collected, they were shipped back to Sheridan. At the train yards, Luther Dunning who was looking after the hungry and thirsty animals, got into a scrape of his own.

The Sheridan Inn
My darling,
Back once more and so strange not to find you here to welcome me. We [I and Bill] got back here with one [train] carload.

Bill was nearly arrested last night on a charge of beating the yard master, but it proved to be Luther Dunning, who got mad at the horses not being unloaded immediately and seized a club and endeavored to slay the nearest official of the Burlington [railroad]. I of course could prove an alibi for Bill and peace regained, but I think Luther has fled to parts unknown. We are getting to be a pretty scrappy horse-buying outfit . . .
Yours ever,
O. H. W.

Sheridan, Wyoming, was alive with men on bucking horses and bunches of horses being driven twelve miles into Big Horn. At Malcolm Moncreiffe's polo ranch in Big Horn, some of the world's best bronc fighters were employed to bring some of the outlaws past the British. Men like George Gardiner, Tode

Bard, and Jim Carpenter entertained local crowds who came out from Sheridan to watch the cowboys ride the rough stock. Everyone who had a horse or could catch one from the wild herds got it ready to sell. Ranchers went partners with cowboys who would ride the horses in front of the British for inspection. With the huge volume of horses passing by the inspectors, it was possible now and then for a cowboy to sneak an unsubmissive bronc past them.

> *Just a few feet out from the corral gate there were two big posts set in the ground about fifteen feet apart, with a two-inch rope cable stretched tight from post to post. In the corral there were men roping and bridling horses with snaffle-bit bridles. The horses were led to the outside, where the reins of the bridles were wrapped two or three times around the cable. About forty yards from there was a little frame shed. Captain Heygate and Dr. Wall his vet were near this shed. When the riding started, Grant Dunning and I came out mounted. We trotted our horses out by the captain to a distance of a hundred yards, then we came back at a fast gallop right up to the small shed. Here the captain looked over the horses for blemishes, listening to their breathing. The horse's age was supposed to be from five to nine years of age. Height was from fourteen two on up.*
>
> *As soon as we rode out one horse, there was another one waiting. It didn't take long to change the saddle from one horse to another, just like a relay race.*
>
> *—Floyd Bard*

When one of Bard's horses began to buck, Heygate was unfazed. "That one shows some spirit, Bard, we like that," remarked the captain. But there were also some stallions that had been captured from the wild horse herds less than a week before. The corrals in Big Horn became a drawing point for local spectators to see man against beast at its best. These horses could fling cowboys out of the corrals. Of the dozens of riders, some decided that while the money was good, it wasn't that good.

When Marguerite Wallop's sister, Amy, came to visit her newborn nephew Gerard, Marguerite played the role of matchmaker by introducing her to Malcolm Moncreiffe, a bachelor living with his brother William. Before long, Malcolm Moncreiffe and Amy Walker were married.

July 25, 1901

My darling Noll,
I was so glad to get your letters on my way out here . . . Malcolm has gone to Dutch Creek, the first time he has left Amy. He says he hates it, but he feels he must do his share of the work.

Dear little Gerard is beside me and sends his love and a kiss to his dear father.

God bless you, darling, and may he bring you back to me soon, safe and well.

Yours ever,
MMW

After looking over thousands of horses for the British, Wallop and Moncreiffe were personally acquiring two of the best strings of horses east of the Bighorns. Wallop and Moncreiffe were not the only buyers keeping some of the better horses; Captain Heygate kept some of the better horses for his own personal use and had them sidetracked to England.

Sheridan Post, *May 2, 1901*
Huguenot, the chestnut gelding by Demagogue and bred in Wyoming by Captain F. D. Grissell and sold by him last fall to Captain Heygate, purchasing agent for the British government in South Africa, ran at Herefordshire Hunt Steeplechase meeting in England, April 8th, and won the North Herefordshire Hunt steeplechase of three miles carrying 175 pounds, beating several thoroughbred horses of good class.

The above speaks well for Wyoming as a place to breed horses, for it shows that along with a perfect body, excellent lung power is developed. Captain Grissell has reared many fine colts that have created much surprise in England.

The British Army purchased more than twenty thousand horses on Moncreiffe's polo field, which were then shipped to South Africa. If you added the horses purchased in Miles City, the number probably doubled. Close to forty thousand failed inspection once, but some passed six months later when buyers came back. Sydney Paget, Oliver Henry Wallop, and the Moncreiffe brothers' business sense had pulled the area out of an economic depression. Ranchers from the Powder River to the Crow and Cheyenne reservations profited.

March 4, 1902

My darling wife,
I did not get many horses today, but I can get 500 myself in this country. Herford showed me a letter from Lowther in which he said he had seen General Numan in London and that he had told him that the American horses had been found very satisfactory in South Africa.
God bless you ever, my darlings,
Yours ever,
O. H. Wallop

By the end of the Boer War, more than half a million horses and mules had landed in Cape Town, an average of six hundred animals per day for the whole period. The majority—109,000 horses and 90,000 mules—were shipped in from the United States. Austria, Great Britain, South America, Australia, and Canada, and India also sold horses to the British for use in the conflict.

In the closing days of the horse-buying trips, Noll's health began to break down. He was in Nevada riding the outlying country, a job Luther Dunning had been doing before Bob Walsh took him. In addition, he did his own job of riding, inspecting, and now feeding the animals. Both the Moncreiffes and Bob Walsh knew they had pushed him too hard. Finally his body gave out. He was bedridden with pneumonia and taken from his hotel in Nevada to a hospital.

When Marguerite arrived at the hospital, Luther Dunning was already there. As soon as he heard the news, he took a night train with a saddle horse to Nevada. Everyone felt guilty. Noll could outlast any three men, but for three years, he had been everywhere and done everything concerning the Boer War horse-buying trips.

Wallop's collapse came at a time when he and the Moncreiffes were due to travel to England to collect the money for the twenty-five thousand horses they had sold to the British Army. William, Malcolm, and Noll stood to receive about three-quarters of a million dollars each.

Ever the optimist, Noll thought a vacation might do him some good. With Amy and Malcolm Moncreiffe and Marguerite, Noll traveled by train to New York and then by ship to England. When they reached England, his breathing worsened and he developed a severe fever. Not long afterward he lost the ability to walk. The family doctors put him in an isolation ward and forbade all visitors.

While they prayed for the best, Malcolm Moncreiffe escorted Amy and Marguerite through London and Paris to keep their spirits up. Marguerite was smitten with the estates and lifestyle of her in-laws, Lord and Lady Portsmouth, and their home at Farley Wallop. Though the Walker sisters had experienced privileged lives as members of one of Chicago's affluent families, it was small potatoes to the standing their husbands' families held as members of British peerage.

When Noll awoke from one of his long sleeps in the hospital, he saw the blurred form of Sydney Paget standing over his bed. "*In angustis amici boni apparent*" (good friends appear in difficulties), Wallop muttered, opening his eyes. The nurse looked over to Syd and frowned.

"Poor thing has lost his mind. He babbles on like that every time he wakes." Syd could only smile at the woman's misperception. "I can't speak for his body, but I can assure you that his mind is as sharp and complex as ever," Syd said.

He sat and waited, and soon Noll opened his eyes. "Sydney, g . . . glad to see you well," Noll said and drifted back to sleep. His doctors kept him sedated for at least half the day, knowing he would try an escape otherwise.

On Otter Creek, Montana, Charlie Thex had ridden over thirty miles without seeing another person. On a divide Charlie recognized the form of Tom McAllister from a mile away by the way he sat on a horse. Tom also recognized Charlie from a distance and rode over. "Any word from Noll?"

"I just had a letter from him. He's in bed, but he's improving. He wanted his nurses to carry him out in a chair so he could hunt pheasants."

My darling,
The doctors and my mother have just left, and Sir Thomas [Moncreiffe] said that he did not believe that I could have done as well as I have done. I walked up and down the room 4 times alone and then stood up with my eyes shut.

Stay on as long as you can and enjoy yourself, my beloved wife. My darling, you are very most dear to me. God bless you.
Yours ever,
O. H. W.

My beloved Noll,
A few lines to tell you how I love and how I miss you. It seems ages since I left you and I will be oh! so happy, darling, to be with you again. I am going to drive tonight with Amy and Malcolm and go to the theatre.

Please give my dearest love to your dear mother. God bless you and watch over you, dear one.
Yours ever, MW

The doctors had judged Noll Wallop's condition according to how the illness would affect the average man. They had no idea that the man who lay before them had a fortitude few men possess. Not since Crazy Horse had a man ridden the length and breadth of Absaraka with such frequency. Noll's health steadily improved, and with the visit of Sydney Paget, he regained a little of his old spark in the hospital.

Sydney Paget had emerged from the war intact and, with a single-minded passion, resumed his racing career. On race days, Paget carried a red handkerchief tucked in his breast pocket for luck. It had been a gift from Connie Hoffman before Black Diamond had set the world record for the half-mile.

He carried it through the Boer War and onto the tracks in England and the East Coast. He made one last trip to Miles City to find Connie, but no one knew where she had gone.

The bright spot of Sydney's trip to Montana was his time at the ranch. He could not have been more proud of the way Luther Dunning ran his horse operation. The horses looked great, and the foal's of Mr. Whitney's stallion Gold Seeker had turned out better than expected. After a brief stay at the ranch, Paget returned to the East and racing. Luther sent the promising horses east to Whitney's stable. In 1905, Paget won the Preakness Stakes with Cairngorm, a grade-one race at Belmont Park with Ormonde's Right, and the futurity in Saratoga Springs, New York. In time Paget married a wealthy girl from Philadelphia, but he never forgot the Queen of Miles City.

While Wallop and the Moncreiffes had brought the world's horse buyers to the area, a controversial character named A. B. Clarke would keep it going. Clarke had been part of the Johnson County war ten years prior, providing the invaders with horses. Ironically, the first casualty was an overweight man who got bucked off, causing him to accidentally shoot himself in the leg, which resulted in his bleeding to death.

Clarke promoted horse sales in Miles City, Sheridan, and Gillette. Buyers came from all over the world to buy everything from racehorses to canners. During the summer of 1901, two such sales sold three thousand horses each. Miles City became known as the world's largest horse market. In July of 1902 Clarke promoted *The Greatest Horse Sale Ever Made West of the Missouri River* over six days in August in Sheridan, Wyoming. By the time Noll made it back to the canyon ranch, horses were once again at a premium.

33

We moved into the old Sheridan Inn and shortly became enamored with the area. The air was high, dry, and perfect for the curative purposes we sought. It was beautiful, fertile, and there was the sort of community we wanted for neighbors. There was good shooting and fishing within reach, the Bighorn Mountains with their rugged slopes and canyons for scenery, and their parks, forests, lakes, and rivers and mountain pastures were simply wonderful for a playground, or for a mountain adjunct to the ranch.

—Cameron Forbes

WITH THE MONEY THEY HAD EARNED SELLING HORSES to the British, Noll Wallop and the Moncreiffes tirelessly beautified their estates in Little Goose Canyon. Their wives had traveled the world extensively, so it was testimony to Little Goose Canyon's beauty that both clans built their dream homes there. William Moncreiffe had already built a beautiful English-style mansion surrounded by lawns that were lined with flowers. His wife, Edith, lined her driveway with a wall built from river rocks, cottonwood trees, and pansies.

Malcolm and Amy Moncrieffe built an impressive estate called the Polo Ranch, where guests were served tea on the grass tennis court after the polo matches. Malcolm also expanded his horse operation. He and Bob Walsh had bought the English stallion Golden Dawn from the famous California breeder

J. B. Haggin. Golden Dawn had already sired three horses that had sold for over $435,000.

Noll and Marguerite Wallop's canyon ranch outdid them all. Flowers and shrubberies circled the house and lined the lawns. The house was a mansion, with its eight bedrooms upstairs and a huge twenty-two-foot screened piazza, which faced the rock mountain walls that bordered the mountain pastures on both sides of the house. The setting was almost magical; one outcropping of rocks on the canyon rim resembled the head of a great lion. Little Goose Creek rushed off the mountain past the house in the spring and trickled past in the fall.

Helen Platte visited the estate and later wrote of the experience and the hospitality extended to her by Noll and Marguerite.

> *Upstairs the wood fire was burning brightly, the bed was opened, and best of all there was a hot water bottle inside. Once the lights were out and the casements opened, the great stone walls of the mountain seemed so close in the moonlight that one could touch them.*
>
> *Breakfast and luncheon were served English fashion. The oatmeal and bacon and kidneys were placed on a side table, and the men strolled over there and served themselves and incidentally Mrs. Wallop and me.*
>
> *Later Mr. Wallop told me about the pictures on the walls. They were of scenes in Devonshire, where his English home is. In the drawing room were two handsome engravings, one of his father surrounded by his dogs and one of his mother.*

The Wallops and Moncreiffes played host to everyone from Buffalo Bill Cody and Teddy Roosevelt to the old-time cowboys from Otter Creek. They threw lavish parties, dressing for dinner and serving a variety of meals from English platters.

Little Goose Canyon was formed to the east by a long ridge that runs a mile away from the Bighorns. The eastern tip had been used during the Indian wars by Crow, Arapaho, Cheyenne, Lakota, and Shoshone to detect movement along the Bozeman Trail. On a clear day it is possible to see in three directions for one hundred miles. Lake De Smet lies to the south like an emerald in the grassland, while the Wolf Mountains rise up between the Rosebud and

Tongue rivers off to the north. After the Fetterman massacre, this spot became known as Red Cloud's lookout. The chief, old and now blind, was still alive on his reservation in South Dakota. With the Indian wars now a distant memory, the eastern ridge of the canyon became known locally as Moncreiffe Ridge, after William Moncreiffe.

The relationship between the Wallops and the Moncreiffes went deeper than the closeness of the sisters. Noll and Malcolm, though polar opposites, formed a bond of friendship that would last their entire lives. Marguerite and Noll named their second son Oliver Malcolm in honor of their friendship.

Just to the north of Little Goose Canyon in Beckton, on Big Goose Creek, another prominent family settled the area. Cameron Forbes, known as Governor Forbes to the locals, had been one of the better polo players in the world at the turn of the twentieth century. In 1900 he was serving as governor of the Philippine Islands after the Spanish American War. A grandson of Ralph Waldo Emerson and John Murray Forbes, Cameron had come from one of Boston's finest families.

Forbes's father, William, was a horseman and former Union cavalry officer during the Civil War. A world traveler and head of the Bell Telephone Company, he raced yachts and horses, hunted, played polo, and established one of the premiere horse-breeding farms in the world. At an auction in the early 1890s, William took Cameron to Europe after his son's graduation from Harvard. In England, bidding against the Russian government, William bought Meddler, a thoroughbred stallion, for $75,000—the highest price ever paid at such an event. Meddler was shipped back to the States in a sling, and Cameron had a barn built especially for the horse. Meddler became one of the epoch-making sires of American turf history.

Shortly after graduating Harvard, Cameron coached the football team to its first victory over Yale in twenty-two years, winning the praise of then governor of New York, Theodore Roosevelt. Touring the West in a private railroad car owned by the family, Cameron stopped at Sheridan in 1898. He was looking for a healthy climate for his brother, Waldo, who suffered from respiratory problems.

Waldo's doctor had recommended to Mrs. Forbes either western Massachusetts or Wyoming as better locations for improving Waldo's health. After falling in love with the mountains around Sheridan, Cameron pleaded with the doctor to convince his parents that only Wyoming could save his brother.

The Forbes family bought a ranch that had been lost to the bank. Waldo took over running the ranch while Cameron was engaged in business in the East. They began to import purebred Clydesdale horses to the ranch along with some well-bred saddle horses.

When Cameron was on a visit to the ranch around 1900, the Forbes family was challenged to a polo game over at Moncreiffe field. Cameron, Waldo, Edward, and Gerrit Forbes all went over to play the Moncreiffe brothers and a couple of cowboys. Cameron was one of the few players in the world to hold a five-goal handicap. After taking an early lead in the game, Cameron was knocked unconscious when his pony fell on the hard Wyoming soil. He was carried off the field on a blanket, and when he awoke, Forbes had little memory of the game.

Malcolm Moncreiffe had put together a motley polo team that began to beat teams all over the West. With Englishmen Bob Walsh and Lee Bullington, Moncreiffe teamed with his cowboy foreman Johnny Cover to upset Denver, Colorado Springs, and an army team before losing to Kansas City in a nail-biter. It was neither Moncreiffe, the Scotsman, nor the two Englishmen who impressed the crowd in Denver; it was the tall, stout cowboy who played in a stock saddle and could hit the ball half the distance of the field. Johnny Cover, a Big Horn cowboy, had become one of the biggest hitters in the game. Cover drew the attention of Foxhall Keene, himself a ten-goal player, who inquired whether Cover might be interested in coming east to play with the American team in a series of matches against the English team.

"Thank you for the invitation, but I've got cattle to tend to," was Cover's reply.

Despite the colorful characters around their home, Gerard Wallop grew up lonely in Big Horn. Marguerite chose to school him at home, which kept him from other children. The boy had the run of Little Goose Canyon, and with his dog, Kinky, and his horse, Blue, which Noll had given him, he traveled the nooks and crannies of the canyon exploring beaver dams and bear tracks and fishing for trout.

While Blue often bucked cowboys off, he took care of young Gerard as a protector and friend.

> *Blue always allowed me to take any liberty, even to swarming up his tail by way of mounting . . . He took me everywhere and always kept me out of trouble. There was never any need to tie him up, for often I would go off for the day and with a book and a sandwich in my pocket, and maybe I would fall asleep under a tree. But I always awoke to find Blue close at hand. As a cowpony he was unequaled. All one had to do was to point out a calf to him in the middle of a herd, drop the reins on the pony's shoulder, and hang on while he sorted the calf from both the mother and the herd.*
>
> —A Knot of Roots *Gerard Wallop*

Much to Marguerite Wallop's dismay, Blue would follow Gerard up the front steps to the house and stand on the front porch while Gerard was inside. Kinky would wait in the evenings for the mother to tuck her son into bed and then after she left, jump in bed with her master. When Kinky was banned from the house, she would find Blue and lay beside him in the pasture.

The ranch cowboys used to tease Gerard about keeping an eye out for eagles, which they claimed were strong enough to carry him off. Lydia Hilman, a neighboring rancher, showed Gerard the site of General George Crook's camp after the battle of Rosebud Creek. The soldiers had dumped a lot of their garbage behind, which was a treasure to a young boy with a vivid imagination. Gerard also learned that the early settler women canned fruit with the hundreds of beer and champagne bottles that had been left behind.

Once when Gerard was accompanying his father on a winter ride, Blue fell through the ice, dumping Gerard into the frozen waters of Little Goose. Noll first pulled his son to safety and then pulled his rifle from his saddle horse and shot a deer. In his casual manner, he cut out the deer's liver and threw it to his son.

"Here, eat this, you l-look cold," he said. It was a trick Noll had learned from the Indians. Gerard ate the raw liver, which immediately warmed him for the ride home.

Gerard enjoyed the loving attention of Malcolm and Amy Moncreiffe and William and Edith Moncreiffe; both couples were childless. Malcolm and Amy took Gerard on a trip to Cody, where the boy met a pipe-smoking Calamity Jane.

"I know your daddy, he's a fine man; bought me a drink in Miles City one time. Where's he live now?"

Before Gerard could respond, his uncle Malcolm answered for him. "He's moved to the other side of the mountain but is mainly in England these days," Malcolm replied and whisked Gerard off before they were stuck with a permanent houseguest.

Once, when his mother was gone, Gerard met Buffalo Bill when he visited Noll at the canyon ranch. A three-day whiskey-drinking, storytelling marathon ensued between Cody and Wallop that ended in a test of marksmanship. Much to Gerard's amusement, they shot playing cards out of one another's hands and tin cans off each other's heads. Finally the only turkey on the ranch was wagered in a contest to shoot a silver dollar out of the air. First Noll threw, and Cody nailed the coin on the second shot, but Noll hit the coin on his first try, thus saving their soon-to-be holiday dinner.

For several years Noll had endeavored to raise pigs on his ranch, many of which had escaped and reverted to the wild in the canyon. One of these had managed to die in the spring that provided the house with water. The result was severe intestinal disorders in the Wallop household for several days until Noll and Gerard investigated and found the dead pig.

"Let's not tell your mother about this," Noll told Gerard after fishing the pig out of the spring.

After a few years the brush in and around Little Goose Canyon was full of third-generation wild pigs. The crowning fiasco of the canyon came one time when Marguerite was visiting her family in Chicago. During a drinking spree George Beck, Noll, Mike Evans, Buffalo Bill, and an assortment of Englishmen decided to relive the ancient British tradition of spearing pigs from horseback. In the absence of spears, Wallop recruited the help of his neighbor

Fred Hilman in borrowing the pitchforks of neighboring farmers and ranchers as a substitute.

By the time Hilman returned with the pitchforks, the sons of the queen of England were thoroughly illuminated. Some were so drunk they had to be helped onto their horses. What followed was an every man for himself, helter-skelter chase up the canyon. In the end, all the pitchforks were lost, all the pigs had escaped, and a few of the "lancers" were found passed out in the brush. Hilman decided to shoot one of the pigs so the hunters might have something to roast.

It was an odd mixture around Big Horn. Men like Malcolm Moncreiffe felt they were keeping the locals alive by providing them with work, but frontier residents like Bear Davis, the Hilmans, the Sacketts, and the Skinners knew damn well they were keeping the British alive.

Unfortunately, there was no one to protect Wallop and Moncreiffe from their old friend George Beck. They should have known better; George Beck had already taken their friends the Stockwells for plenty. After a failed ranching venture outside Sheridan, Beck had moved to Cody and talked Noll and the Moncreiffe brothers into investing in a lumber mill and hardware store there. The plan was to fell trees between Cody and Yellowstone Park and float the logs down the river to the mill, where they would be cut into lumber.

Beck, however, had gotten involved in an alternate plan, which was to promote a dam above Cody. When the dam was completed, the Wallops' and the Moncreiffes' lumber mill was ruined. To top it all off, their warehouse in Cody burned to the ground.

The Wallops were forced to roll up their sleeves and start over. The servants were let go and young Oliver, Gerard's little brother, was sent to town to peddle butter and eggs. Despite the family's financial setbacks, Oliver was sent off to the best schools America had to offer.

Gerard was plucked from Little Goose Canyon and sent to England to apprentice for Noll's childless brother, who was then Lord Portsmouth. When it came time for Gerard to inherit the title as the eighth Earl of Portsmouth, he would inherit the family's thirty-thousand-acre estate in England, which generated $15,000 per year, a considerable amount at the time.

Noll was less affected by their financial downfall than Marguerite. As far as Noll was concerned, he would regain his fortune; he felt he was in the greatest country in the world, where opportunity was available for those who would roll up their sleeves and work for it. He was broke when he got to America, made a fortune in horses, lost it when the market went bad, and got it back again when he got the Boer War horse contract.

34

His brand was the Lazy 6 and ran from the Missouri to the Platte.

—Al Irions

WITHIN A 150-MILE RADIUS OF MILES CITY, MORE THAN forty thousand horses were running loose on the open range. Though the market for high-priced horses had died with the end of the Boer War, the area had established itself as a center for range horses. A few men like Tom McAllister found a way to make a living from these wild horses. Tom rode the big, empty grasslands on both sides of the Yellowstone River and north as far as Canada, putting his Lazy 6 brand on foals and gathering strays from the wild herds. With the business sense that Noll Wallop had taught him and his inborn ability with horses, he culled out the wild stallions and injected domesticated thoroughbred and draft stallions into the herd. The money that McAllister made on the Boer War sales he put almost exclusively into stallions to breed to his horse herds and pay roundup crews. At the height of his operation, McAllister controlled close to ten thousand horses.

Every May McAllister ran a roundup wagon for horses that was made up of twenty cowboys, including a cook, a wagon boss, day herders for the cowboys' saddle horses, and cowboys. These range horsemen acted like gentlemen around women, wore fancy hats and boots, and spent their last dime on wild binges in town. When it was time to work, however, they were professionals.

If there was ever a job that required the skill of a real cowboy, it was running range horses. The cowboys who worked the range horse roundup wagons at the turn of the century were bronc fighters to the man, knew horses inside and out, and were masters with the rope. Their job was dangerous, but there was a freedom to it, which created a type of Western character as colorful as the original cowboys of the 1880s.

Corrals were built around water holes, and each day the cowboys went out and gathered as many as five hundred range horses in one bunch. These corrals were built with a large natural wing made up of sagebrush or cedar sticks so as not to alarm the wild horses to a trap. The trick was to ease the horses to the corral and not stir them up too much, as frightened, confined horses might trample each other in a mad stampede or impale or knock themselves out trying to run through the corral.

The riders might also use natural land breaks, such as the cliffs surrounding the Powder River, in which to corner and hold these horses. It took a savvy roper to slip in and catch an animal without stirring up the herd. Yearlings were roped and branded, and the two- and three-year-old colts were castrated. Lime was sprinkled on the wound, or creosote was put in water to use as an antiseptic. The tails were bobbed on castrated colts so the cowboys could identify the horses the next year and save themselves a wrestling match.

Five- and six-year-old colts were cut out of the herd to be sold. Horses younger than five were left unbroken because they would not hold up to a day's work. The old and crippled were cut out and added to the day herd, which could swell to as many as three hundred head. With up to twenty cowboys working, each man might have up to ten head in his string. Cowboys took turns guarding the horses in two-hour shifts from eight p.m. until midnight; the graveyard shift went from twelve until four a.m.; and the first shift came on until the day herders took over.

A bachelor, McAllister often lived out with his horses. He was a quiet, gentle man, who had a soft spot for animals and children. Tom would usually winter with poor ranching families and on more than a few occasions, his benevolence fed, clothed, and paid for school for ranch children. One such boy was eleven-year-old Sid Vollen, who sought out McAllister after his father had died in Belle Fourche, South Dakota. Vollen's father had spoken often to his son about how McAllister was a real Montana cowboy. The orphaned boy rode west to find his father's friend and become a cowboy. Riding bareback on one horse and leading another, Sid was fed at friendly ranches along the route. Vollen found McAllister who, true to form, took the boy under his wing.

On a trip to Chicago to buy a train-car load of thoroughbred stallions, McAllister and his young apprentice were walking by a store in Chicago when someone called out, "Hello there."

Tom and Sid turned, but no one was there. Before they walked on, the voice came back.

"Look, it's two rubes from the country." To their amusement, the cowboys spotted a talking parrot in a store window.

Tom, a man of few words, followed the creed "Talk if you have something to say, otherwise listen!"

McAllister winked at young Vollen. "Well, Pistol, when the screech owls know us, it's time to head home."

Young Vollen had grown into a top hand around livestock, but his quick progression caused the boy to grow somewhat cocky. On their way back from Chicago, Tom gave the boy a lesson in humility.

"Pistol, do you think you can drive a load of horses to the ranch from the train stop for me?" McAllister asked.

"I can do that blindfolded," Vollen boasted.

McAllister just smiled and left Sid in the pens at the railroad yard. Vollen mounted his big saddle horse and opened the gate to herd the horses south. After the first couple of miles, the stallions began to drift apart, sending Sid back and forth on his saddle horse to try and haze them back into some kind of herd. Before long the young cowboy was off at a gallop, cussing the stallions that had scattered to the four winds. The best he could do after the all-day chase was get one stallion roped and trained to lead.

As Sid rode to the ranch where Tom was waiting, he stomped in, infuriated by the unmanageable animals.

"How'd you make out, Pistol?" McAllister asked.

"Those damned studs are scattered from here to the Yellowstone," the frustrated cowboy said.

"Good, that's just where I wanted them." Tom laughed, knowing the stallions would find the mares on their own.

For these high-bred stallions that had lived in a stall most of their lives, it was survival of the fittest. It was sometimes ten miles between water and good grass. The survivors of the brutal winters proved to be exceptional horses. Almost every wild herd among the hundreds scattered along Absaraka contained the bloodline of some well-bred draft or thoroughbred horses.

Though the range horse cowboys had worked nearly every wild herd in Absaraka, there was a yellow stallion that had kept his small band of mares from capture. It was said by Crow and Cheyenne horsemen that his bloodline went back to a yellow stallion that had produced top buffalo runners and warhorses from the days of Crazy Horse.

It had taken vigilance and knowledge of the country to escape the cowboys with the roundup wagons. Part of the stallion's success was his abandonment of the range on Otter Creek that was home to several generations of his bloodline. He had taken his mares across the Tongue River and relocated them on a tributary of the Little Bighorn River called Rotten Grass Creek. There, on Crow land, the horses were left unmolested.

35

He was the wildest man ever to sit on a hurricane deck.

—*Sheridan Post*

THE BEST HORSE COUNTRY IN THE WORLD COULD ALSO produce the worst outlaws. With the advent of thoroughbreds being bred to range horses, the athleticism of these outlaws sent all but the top riders into the sagebrush. Neither Indians nor cowboys would keep a rank horse, but with the arrival of businessman ranchers, who weren't about to give up on a horse as long as someone else would do the riding for them, came the birth of the bronc fighter.

The bronc fighter had the respect of every man on the roundups, for the animals they rode were dangerous, having usually hurt at least one cowboy before earning the bronc title. Trying to determine whose outfit had the best roper and best bronc fighter made for good conversation among the spring gatherings. Before long, there was a competition and the sport named rodeo was born.

At a Billings, Montana, rodeo, Grover Brennan, touted as Sheridan's finest bronc rider, was matched against Billings's top rider George Williams. Both men rode three broncs to a standstill. Brennan was declared the winner since he used neither stirrups nor spurs, thus making his ride more difficult. If that were not enough, the event spilled over to bull riding as reported by the *Billings Gazette*:

> *After they had ridden three horses each, Brennan and Williams were matched to ride two bulls. Brennan experienced little trouble mounting his infuriated beast, but the bull picked out for Williams balked, doing a lively stunt. The enraged animal gored two horses, tipped a carriage over, and rushed into the crowd. People scattered in all directions, but no one was hurt.*
>
> *As a bronco buster, Brennan gave one of the most daring exhibitions ever seen in Yellowstone County.*

William Moncreiffe was left with some of the meanest animals known to man: the wild range horses that had flunked the British Army inspections because they were not rideable. In his typical generosity he kept the worst buckers around to let game young men try to ride. These horses soon became the stars of the early bucking contests.

Local Sheridan men like Grover Brennan, George Gardiner, and Tode Bard had secured jobs as bronc riders in Buffalo Bill Cody's Wild West Show that toured the world. Cody held auditions on the lawn of the Sheridan Inn for young cowboys who were more than eager to get out and see the world.

The early local rodeos were loosely organized affairs held on vacant lots, local fairgrounds, or out in the open. The men who staged the events made up the rules. There was no time limit for the cowboys, who rode the outlaw horses until they stopped. On any given weekend during the summer, someone wanting to see man versus horse in an exhibition of bucking and riding could witness the spectacle in more than a dozen locations, from Powder River to the far reaches of the Crow and Cheyenne reservations, where many of the Indians had become top cowboys in and out of the rodeo arena.

A typical rodeo might feature one hundred unregimented cowboys and twice as many unpredictable animals in the field. From Miles City, Montana, to Buffalo, Wyoming, rodeos and county fairs offered wonderfully wild, unpredictable feats of equestrian skill. Win, lose, or draw, the cowboys had a happy-go-lucky style that made light of all yesterdays and denied the existence of any tomorrows. The rodeo was their holiday, and like the Indians who came before them, they dressed the part: the brighter the shirts and handkerchiefs, the better. Shining bits and breast collars decorated with conchas adorned their horses, whose manes and tails were always combed out for rodeos. Leather boots were tooled with designs ranging from naked women to steer heads.

While Grover Brennan was thrilling audiences around the world with his daring rides, his brother Harry emerged as a local hero. He had honed his skill in the Boer War outlaw pens and was soon working for the government riding horses that were bucking soldiers at Fort Mackenzie in Sheridan. Entering rodeo competitions, he eventually became world champion after winning the Denver rodeo in 1902. The Sheridan native originated the method of raking a horse from neck to cantle with his spurs.

Despite his title of world champion, Harry always insisted that Grover was the better rider. Unfortunately, a gas leak in a New York hotel room caused Grover to fall ill while touring with Buffalo Bill. Grover was just able to return to Sheridan to die at the home of his brother Harry.

Harry rode some of the toughest rodeo horses of the day to a standstill; Pin Ears and Innocent Babe were "busted" in Denver, and the world-famous Steamboat was ridden in Cheyenne. In typical cowboy generosity and spirit, Harry once gave half his $200 prize money and cut a championship belt in two for bronc rider Tom Minor, who Brennan thought matched his ride.

Men who were handy with a rope were also making a name for themselves. Jim Carpenter, a Crow Indian, won the first steer-roping event at Sheridan, and he went on to become one of the best bronc riders in the world. In 1903 an Indian named Big Bear topped all ropers in Sheridan.

Just after the turn of the century, Indian agents wanting to promote farming on the reservations allowed a type of agricultural fair to be held on the Crow reservation. The purpose was to display certain farm products and give prizes for best squash, melon, and so forth. It didn't take the Crow long to turn the event into an Indian rodeo in which the two favorite events were horse racing and bronc riding. Much to the dismay of the Indian agent, the event soon turned into a multi-tribal gathering revolving around horses. The Cheyenne and Lakota soon had their own rodeos and set of competing stars.

In addition to being one of the top horsemen of the area, twenty-six-year-old Luther Dunning won the 1902 steer-roping contest in Sheridan. Dunning also competed in the Pony Express race in which the rider raced around the half-mile track, switched his saddle to a fresh horse, swung up and raced around the track again, and repeated twice more. Dunning rode Sydney Paget's string of horses while Johnny Cover of Big Horn raced Malcolm Moncreiffe's thoroughbreds.

In Miles City, Indians rode bucking buffalo in an exhibition during their rodeo. The Sheridan rodeo, known as the Stampede, expanded to offer a chuck wagon race, rep race, dude races, bull riding, steer wrestling, squaw race, indian races, bronc and bareback riding, roping, and the most daring of all, the women's trick-riding exhibition.

Later the Sheridan County Fair featured harness races, a polo pony class, an Indian race for Indian horses, and a ladies' and cowboys' relay race. There were squaw races, in which Indian women loaded and hitched a wagon and raced around the track with one lady driving and one riding in the back. There was even a fat ladies' race and a baby contest. The newspaper published the rules for the latter, which stated that "any baby caught smoking or talking during the judging would be disqualified."

> *. . . there were two accidents on Friday, one of them being in the cowboy relay race. The first was in the half-mile free-for-all, when Little Jim, ridden by Frank Stalcup, a lad of ten years, bolted, ran into the fence, and dislocated his neck. His rider was thrown heavily and severely bruised, but sustained no serious injury . . . Perry Aber, alighting from the first horse in the relay race, was run down by another horse and his knee and ankle badly sprained. He was unable to stand and mount his next horse and was compelled to quit the race.*
>
> *. . . the one serious accident on Sunday happened to Mr. Gentry in the stake race. At the turn another horse ran into Mr. Gentry's, throwing horse and rider to the ground. Another horse jumped upon the prostrate man, planting both feet in Mr. Gentry's back, inflicting severe bruises although no bones were broken . . . In the ladies' relay race . . . Miss Loman was unable to stop her horse when she reached the wire but threw herself from the saddle while traveling at high speed. Just as her*

feet hit the ground, another horse ran up alongside and she was wedged between the two animals while they traveled several yards. She clung desperately to the saddle horn, keeping herself upright, and in that way pluckily saved herself from being trampled and injured.
—Sheridan Enterprise

Besides rodeos, there was great demand for the area's re-creation of itself. Already the reenactments of the Wild West–like Buffalo Bill shows captivated audiences around the world. Parades, featuring Indian survivors from the Little Bighorn and Rosebud Creek battles, preceded fairs and race meets.

In 1902, the Midsummer Carnival in Sheridan offered rough riders, races, polo, war dances, and daily parades featuring a thousand Indians in native costumes. On the Fourth of July, there was even a reenactment of Custer's battle at Little Bighorn, with government and state troops and scouts and war chiefs who were near the scenery.

Both sides were given blanks to fire from their guns. When the Indians had finally killed all of "Custer's men," the "dead" soldier holding the American flag refused to release the flag to the Indian actor, which started a tug of war. Finally another "dead" soldier stuck his pistol up the Indian's loincloth and pulled the trigger. The shot lifted the powder-burned Indian off the ground and everyone sprang up and started fighting again.

The day before, a reenactment of a stagecoach attack was put on for tourists. The four horses that were pulling the coach became frightened and took off across an irrigation ditch. As a result, the stagecoach turned over, injuring the passengers. The team of horses, harnessed together and dragging the front wheels of the stagecoach, broke for the crowd of tourists. Within seconds, two cowboys shook down a loop, galloped in, and roped the team. The crowd was thrilled, thinking the wreck had been put on for their behalf.

Ironically, while men were starring in rodeos and re-creating the Indian wars for tourists, a major player in Absaraka's Indian wars arrived on the train in

Sheridan. Colonel Henry Carrington returned to the area, after four decades of trying to clear the tarnish on his military career. He was in Sheridan to dedicate a monument at the site of the Fetterman fight. A horde of old soldiers and spectators crowded the train depot to welcome the colonel back to Absaraka. Among the retired military were men from the 18th infantry and the 2nd, 12th, and 5th cavalries who had made their homes in Sheridan. Bear Davis had served at Fort C. F. Smith, and William Devine had served as a teamster for Colonel Nelson Cole during the Dead Horse March of the Powder River campaign. Curly, a Crow scout for Custer, was living on the Little Bighorn River, and several Cheyenne warriors who fought in the area were living on Rosebud Creek. As the town grew and the ranchers took center stage, the old soldiers and warriors of the Indian wars had been all but forgotten.

It must have been with melancholy that Carrington gazed at the site of the former fort that had been one of the last great stockade frontier outposts in the country. All that was left was some charcoal in the grass where the walls had been. Forty-two years before, Colonel Carrington had loaded the frozen, mutilated remains of Captain Fetterman and his soldiers onto wagons after they had been led into a trap by Crazy Horse. Now tourists came to see reenactments of the old battles between the whites and the Indians.

Red Cloud's lookout at the eastern point of Little Goose Canyon loomed over the site in the distance. The old chief himself was living on a South Dakota reservation where he and his people had been moved.

36

Many eastern people who have recently come to the city are taking up horseback riding, and being used to the light English saddles used in the East, express surprise at the weight and size of the cowboy saddle used here, but after riding them a few times will use no other. Both the women and men use the big cowboy saddles for riding, the women using divided skirts.

Although horseback riding is an older fad in the West than automobiling, westerners still cling to it, and to a great many easterners it is a novelty and consequently popular also.

—*Billing Gazette,* July 2, 1907

URBAN HORSE LOVERS FROM AROUND THE WORLD enamored with the American West began to flock to Absaraka. Entrepreneurs like Mike Evans at the top of Little Goose Canyon and the Eaton brothers on Wolf Creek built cabins and kept horses to accommodate these tourists, whom they called "dudes." The word "dude" was used to describe any city dweller unskilled in riding and ranch life.

Noll Wallop and Mike Evans had devised a plan for a type of summer camp where the sons of the wealthy British could learn to work on a ranch. The way Noll and Evans figured it, they could get free work out of the boys and the Brits would pay plenty to keep their sons out of trouble.

In any event, both Teepee Lodge, which Evans built, and Eaton's ranch, which the Eaton brothers started, became booming dude ranches. The Dome Lake Club was established in the Bighorn Mountains and catered to railroad officials and vacationers, and the HF Bar Ranch had operated near Buffalo. People were in love with horseback riding, and the western states appeared to be a safe place for vacationers to freely ride trails.

Most of the guests were wealthy easterners who would spend the entire summer out west. They brought their families, galloped over the mountain trails, took pack trips into the mountains, and lived in cabins. They traded their suits for cowboy garb and decked themselves out in ten-gallon hats, boots, and spurs. They fell in love with the land at the foot of the Bighorns the same way Wallop, the Moncreiffs, and the Forbeses had.

On its menu the Dome Lake Club offered elk steaks, fresh-baked bread and rolls, fresh strawberries, and a variety of imported foods that were shipped via the railroad that owned the resort. Before he was married, Noll Wallop had contracted to hunt fresh game for the guests of the Dome Lake Club and to supply the ranch with butter and produce.

Alden, Howard, and William Eaton had the earliest dude ranch in America in the Dakotas before moving to Absaraka. The brothers had come west during the frontier years. As a young man, Howard Eaton once roped a rare cream-colored buffalo, but the rope snapped like twine. Eaton then pulled his pistol and dropped the animal; when he ran his skinning knife up the back leg of the animal, the buffalo suddenly jumped to its feet. Eaton jumped on the stunned buffalo's back to get a laugh out of his partner but to his surprise, the animal took off galloping across the prairie. Eaton hung on until the buffalo stepped in a badger hole and crashed to the ground, sending Eaton into a bed of prickly pear cactus.

The three Eaton brothers had bought five hundred head of gentle horses and began to serve as tour guides to wealthy eastern travelers who were looking to experience the West. Of the three, only Alden and his wife produced any children. Young Bill Eaton grew up to be six-foot-two, two hundred pounds and, like his father and uncles, became an all-around cowboy who was an expert with a rope. As he entered high school, Bill began to date Nannie Alderson's daughter Patty, who was working her mother's ranch north of Sheridan. Patty sometimes rode to Eaton's ranch, and Bill sometimes rode to the Alderson's ranch during holidays.

On one such visit, Patty's younger brother Bud recruited Bill to ride a bad bronc he had: "Hey, Bill, I got a bad bronc with your name on it," Bud called, motioning to the horse in the corral. Bill pulled his saddle off his horse and carried it into the corral where the bronc was. In a flick of a wrist, he had the colt roped and saddled. He let the colt buck around the corral twice before climbing on.

With Eaton aboard, the colt blew up, bucking and bawling while Patty and Bud sat on the top rail of the corral watching the show. Two neighbor boys rode over from prairie chicken hunting and laid their shotguns on the fence. They watched as Bud took a turn on the horse after Bill finished. Bill joined Patty on the top rail of the fence, and for the first time the two could visit.

"Did you ride all the way from the ranch?" Patty asked Bill, who nodded.

"I'll get us something to eat," Patty said and went to the house.

When Bud got off his bronc, the exhausted horse walked over to the side of the corral and pawed the fence where one of the shotguns rested. The shock caused the gun to discharge, which blew Bill Eaton off the top rail of the fence. Patty heard the shotgun blast and a scream from the house. When Patty looked out, she saw Bill writhing in a pool of blood.

Bud and a friend were trying to hold down Bill, who was struggling to get up. Half of Bill's face and the inside of his thigh were torn away by the shotgun blast; blood flowed through Bill's hands from the right side of his head, which was blood and bone. Patty looked around at the paralyzed boys.

"Bud, ride to the coal mines at Monarch and get the doctor, hurry!" she yelled, sending Bud off at a run. Despite his injury, Bill managed to get to his feet. Bleeding profusely, he was taken into the house and laid on the couch.

"Get to the creek and bring me some water! Get it where it runs cold, not where the pools are!" Patty told one of the boys. She took cold wet towels and pressed them against Bill's face and thigh to try to check the bleeding.

Bud Alderson galloped across the broken sagebrush country for the coal mines at a dead run, while his sister Patty began to pray. She had been four when her father had been killed in Miles City; now the man she loved was bleeding to death in front of her.

Bud arrived at the Monarch coal mines but found the doctor had gone to another mine in Kearneyville. He galloped on and found the doctor, but he killed his horse getting there. Bud called Eaton's parents, who were having dinner at the Western Hotel in Sheridan. That night Patty held a lantern as the doctor picked buckshot out of Bill Eaton's face.

Bill Eaton lost the sight in his right eye, and the right side of his face was disfigured for life. He did, however, become the foremost figure in both rodeo and dude ranches in an area that was on its way to leading the Northwest in both categories.

The Eaton brothers' ranch gave the pent-up easterners more than just a chance to ride around and look at the scenery. In 1910, the Eatons started an annual event called Frontier Days, which was open to the entire area. Frontier Days' rodeo had events like the Pickup Race, in which the rider gallops at top speed and tries to grab three handkerchiefs placed on the ground in close proximity to one another. There were also the boys and girls' button race, foot race, girls' midnight race, potato race, greased pig, and a wrestling match from horseback. These events, along with traditional events like bareback and bronc riding, were for the entertainment of everyone, with Bill Eaton serving as master of ceremonies.

The dudes who didn't compete in the rodeo took part in a bizarre parade that snaked its way through the spectators and into the arena where the rodeo was performed. According to an article in the *Sheridan Post* dated July 13, 1915:

> *The results were fearful and wonderful to behold. All nations, peoples, and classes of the earth were represented. There was the Ku Klux Klan, Mexicans, Gypsies, convicts, circus riders, pirates, bathing men and bathing girls, Indians, a scarecrow, South Sea Islanders, suffragettes, Spanish dancers, mammies, dwarfs, dancers, cowboys, sleepwalkers, and Turks . . . In the costume contest, the chain gang: four desperate convicts in stripes linked together in leg chains, armed with picks and sentenced to seven weeks at Eaton's, were the winners . . . The Ku Klux Klan, nine riders in white, bearing fiery crosses, were second.*

In another parade, novelist Mary Roberts Rinehart, who had dressed as a rainbow, won first prize. Four pallbearers dressed in black and wearing tall black hats and white gloves mournfully carried John Barleycorn—a huge bottle—on a stretcher. Then came "Wine, Women, and Song," portrayed by three characters dressed in odd regalia.

Adventuresome easterners galloped across the landscape between the Powder and the Bighorn Mountains without a care in the world, wearing some of the gaudiest outfits known to man. If they had the gumption, they could not only play cowboy, they could also live it. Over the years, many of these dudes proved to have quite a little grit, and in a few instances they outperformed the cowboys in the rodeo stunts.

It was with great pride that Oliver Henry Wallop placed one hand on the Bible and took the oath of allegiance to the United States of America. He had been a solid citizen of the country from Miles City, Montana, to Big Horn, Wyoming, and now his constituency had elected him to the Wyoming state legislature in Cheyenne. By now, several of Wallop's neighbors from the old Otter Creek country had also entered the political arena. John Kendrick had won a bid for state senate, and George Brewster served three terms in the Montana legislature; Joseph Brown had served one.

Noll decided that he would concentrate his efforts in politics to one arena: game laws. Since he had come to the plains with his rifle twenty-five years earlier, he had seen the buffalo and elk disappear entirely on Otter Creek. Now elk were nonexistent in the area, and Bighorn sheep were all but gone. With the help of his local political friends and also Bill Eaton, Wallop put all his energy into writing game laws to manage hunting and protect the area's game. As a result of Wallop's tenure as legislator, wild elk were shipped in from Jackson Hole and released on Eaton's land and above Little Goose Canyon.

In Cheyenne, Noll ran into George Beck.

> *I met George Beck, who was "full," and he asked me to take a drink, so we went into a very nice saloon here where there was an electric slot machine. George got a really sharp shock from it—with a yell he said, "Damn the thing. I have spent $100 getting drunk, and 5 cents has sobered me. It is an outrage!"*
> *—O Henry Wallop, 1910*

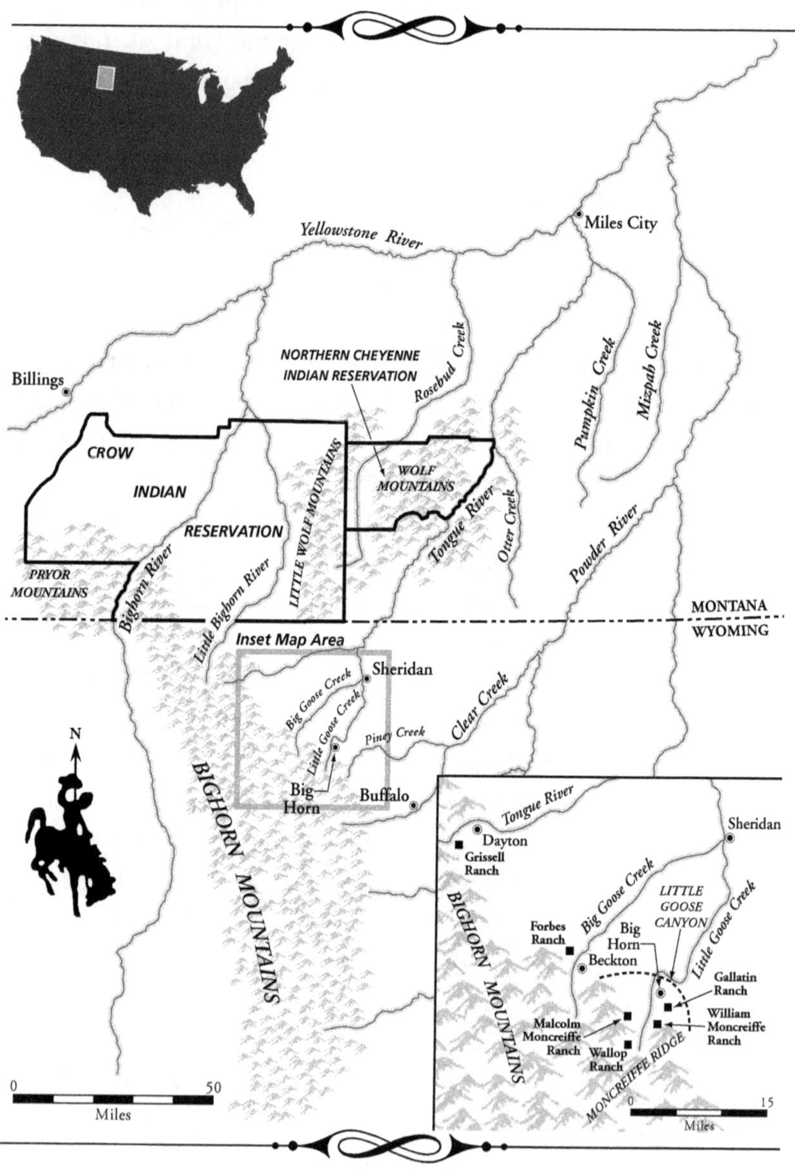

Miles City
Yellowstone River
Billings
NORTHERN CHEYENNE
INDIAN RESERVATION
Rosebud Creek
Pumpkin Creek
Mizpah Creek
CROW
INDIAN
RESERVATION
LITTLE WOLF MOUNTAINS
WOLF
MOUNTAINS
Tongue River
Otter Creek
Powder River
PRYOR
MOUNTAINS
Bighorn River
Little Bighorn River
MONTANA
WYOMING
Inset Map Area
Sheridan
Big Goose Creek
Little Goose Creek
Piney Creek
Clear Creek
N
BIGHORN MOUNTAINS
Big
Horn
Buffalo
0
50
Miles
Tongue River
Dayton
Grissell
Ranch
Sheridan
Big Goose Creek
LITTLE
GOOSE
CANYON
Little Goose Creek
Forbes
Ranch
Big
Horn
Beckton
BIGHORN MOUNTAINS
Gallatin
Ranch
William
Moncreiffe
Ranch
Malcolm
Moncreiffe
Ranch
Wallop
Ranch
MONCREIFFE RIDGE
0
15
Miles

III

In the Shadows of the Bighorns

37

The Gallatins were more local than some of the locals.

—Gerard Wallop

DURING NOLL WALLOP'S TERM AS A WYOMING SENATOR, William Moncreiffe and Mike Evans met an adventurous young couple at Evans's Santa Barbara resort. Goelet and Edith Gallatin had traveled the world hunting big game, sport fishing, foxhunting, and playing polo. Each had an ancestor who had signed the Declaration of Independence. They were the closest thing to a royal couple that America had.

Edith's grandfather, General Regis Phillipe de Trobriand, was an artist and author in New York before enlisting in the Union Army. He had been a hero at Gettysburg and was later appointed governor of the Dakotas. He served as commander of various frontier posts in what are now Montana, Wyoming, and North Dakota. In a strange contrast of cultures, his art was hung in the Louvre at roughly the same time he was being harassed on the frontier by Sitting Bull.

When Edith Post married Goelet Gallatin, a young New York attorney, it united two old, famous Washington Square families that were connected to some of the more powerful political figures of the day.

Edith Post grew up as an adventuresome, top-rate horsewoman. She could hitch a team as well as train problem horses. She rode through Central Park, foxhunted in the country, and became a crack shot with both a rifle and a shotgun. As a young lady, Edith served as first lady of Puerto Rico while her bachelor brother, Charles Post, served as governor. Her crowning glory as a person was neither her pedigree nor her ability as a horsewoman: she possessed a vivacious, energetic personality, and she gave compassion and love to everyone she came in contact with.

Goelet had recently graduated from Columbia University and was a member of New York City's Squadron "A" rough-riding team that met to play polo, trick-ride, and provide mounted escorts for VIPs in the city. He was the great-grandson of Albert Gallatin, who was secretary of the treasury under President Thomas Jefferson and President James Madison. Albert married Hannah Nicholson, whose father, James, had co-commanded the Continental Navy with John Paul Jones.

Albert Gallatin had arranged the money for the Louisiana Purchase from Napoleon and personally tutored Meriwether Lewis for his expedition with William Clark. In appreciation, Lewis named one of the three forks of the Missouri River after Gallatin (in present-day western Montana).

Over the years, the Gallatins married into the prominent New York Goelet and Almy families. Goelet's father, Fredrick Gallatin, was a wealthy adventurer who once converted his yacht, the *Almy*, into a gunboat and accompanied General H. H. Kitchener down the Nile River in the famous attempt to rescue General James Gordon, who was killed defending the city of Khartoum.

In the winter of 1910, Goelet moved his family to California because his daughter, Bea, had developed whooping cough and her doctor decided the climate might improve Bea's health. When the two met William Moncreiffe in Santa Barbara, he invited them to his Wyoming ranch in Little Goose Canyon. They fell in love with the area. During their visit, they purchased half of Moncreiffe's ranch on Little Goose Creek and another thirty thousand acres east of Sheridan in addition to a permit for summer grazing in the Bighorn Mountains.

Pioneering spirits, the Gallatins camped in tents along Little Goose Creek their first summer, waiting for their barns and house—a thirty-five-room log cabin—to be built. Edith also desgined an elaborate moon garden behind the house, modeled after one she had seen on a tour of China. It started with a ten-foot-high, ninety-foot-long rock wall. In the middle of the wall was an eight-foot circular opening through which to view the mountains just behind the house. Imported and indigenous flowers grew in the immense garden. Pools of water cascaded along channels next to the wall. On a flat area next to the house, Edith grew several acres of strawberries. The swimming pool in the front of the house served as a skating pond in the winter. Around the entrance to the ranch, Edith planted poppies whose large red blooms grew wild in the grass along the fence line.

Inside the entranceway to the house hung a magnificent painting of Paris in the early 1850s by General Phillipe Regis de Trobriand. A Mathew Brady photograph of the general manning a parrot gun during the Civil War hung nearby. In the living room, a massive fireplace was decorated with a large royal bull-elk head, next to which hung two Indian coup sticks. Buffalo robes and Indian blankets were draped over leather furniture. The living room was decorated with Indian artifacts, western paintings, and western furnishings.

The Gallatins entertained a variety of guests at the ranch, including western artist Ed Borein. In gratitude for their hospitality, Borein painted an elaborate frieze in the house depicting the history of the area from the Indians and the pioneers to the cowboys and ranchers. He also fashioned a bucking horse weather vane for the Gallatins' barn.

The Gallatin Ranch, known as the E4, became the best in the country. The family's hunting guide, Roy Snyder, became their foreman and put together a crew of top cowboys. Goelet Gallatin gradually built a herd of the finest purebred cattle and, with him and his wife being accomplished horsemen, stocked the ranch with some of the best horse flesh in the country.

The Gallatins' first horse-buying trip took them ninety miles north on a rough dirt road to the Otter Creek ranch of Luther and Leota Dunning. There they viewed the one hundred head of weaned thoroughbred colts the Dunnings had bred. The Gallatins had heard of the breeding operation that included bloodlines from Wallop's famous stallions Sailor and Columbus, Marcus Daly's Empire Regent, and William C. Whitney's Gold Seeker.

The Gallatins had traveled in circles with some of the finest breeders in the world, but the honesty and competency they saw in Luther Dunning and his operation both impressed and benefited them.

Within a few years, the cowboys working at the Gallatins' were mounted on the best horses in the country, and in a country full of top horses, that was saying a lot.

Two New York horsemen followed the Gallatins and began horse-raising operations of their own in Little Goose Canyon. Milt McCoy, a polo player, bought land in Little Goose Canyon and played on the Moncreiffe field; Ridgely Nicholas, a racehorse and show-horse breeder, did the same. Edith's cousin Fred Post, the largest horse dealer on the East Coast, often came out to visit the area and bought thousands of horses for the U.S. Army and polo buyers each year.

Within a few years of the Gallatins' arrival, few in Big Horn had not been privileged to their generosity. They gave a chemistry department to the school, had the church rebuilt, and donated land for a women's club and a city park. They had the old Bozeman Trail blacksmith shop rebuilt and had trees planted in the cemetery in Sheridan. In each case, the gifts were anonymous.

As people, the Gallatins extended a caring hand on numerous fronts. At Christmas they threw a huge community dance, and together with children and friends, the Gallatins loaded either a sleigh or a hay wagon and went caroling among their Big Horn neighbors. Each resident of the town received a present from the Gallatins, and in the weeks before Christmas, ranch cowboys were put to the monumental task of loading and delivering large boxes of food staples to the underprivileged in Ranchester, Dayton, Lodge Grass, Buffalo, Sheridan, Story, and all the way to Otter Creek, Montana.

While the cowboys were rarely invited to tea at the Moncreiffes', they were always welcome in the Gallatins' home. After a trip to the Crow Fair, Edith invited the old head chiefs to camp on the ranch to feast on Gallatin beef and to tell their stories. The Cheyenne and the Crow had become somewhat outcast in the area, but Edith showed them the same consideration and generosity that she did everyone else. When they camped on the

Gallatins' ranch, the Crow and Cheyenne pitched their teepees on Little Goose Creek and dressed in their native costumes. Some of the older men had fought intertribal battles on the ground that encompassed the ranch. Others had hunted buffalo in Little Goose Canyon. For many of the Crow and Cheyenne, it was a joyous homecoming.

Edith took note of everyone in the community and often sent the ranch cowboys to a neighbor's who needed help or would go herself. When someone in the community got sick, she nursed them. If it were a sick woman, Edith had one of the women who worked in her house to take food and to help with the household chores. It was also not uncommon for Edith to babysit the children of her workers.

Mary Rice, a shy Big Horn girl whose mother was employed by the Gallatins, was summoned to the huge large cabin before her first prom so Edith could admire her new dress. When Mary entered the Gallatins' home, she was petrified; she tried not to gawk, but there was so much to look at. The logs were enormous, and once the door closed, it fitted flush with the wall, making it disappear. The windows faced Little Goose Canyon and Moncreiffe Ridge.

"Mary, you look beautiful," Edith said and took the girl by the hand into the study, where Mr. Gallatin was working on the ranch books. "Goelet, look at how beautiful Mary is," Edith said to her husband. Mary stood before Mr. Gallatin, who terrified her. Goelet rose from his seat and smiled.

"Well, Mary, don't you look lovely," he said. Mary swallowed hard. She was a country girl; she had certainly never been called lovely by anyone, much less Mr. Gallatin, who was probably one of the smartest man in the state, she figured. Goelet possessed a reserved demeanor, which intimidated some. He was a straight shooter who did things by the book, yet he was extremely giving. His heart was exposed in the thousands of photographs he took of the ranch and the area. All Mary could do was stand there blushing until Edith spoke up.

"Your mother made that dress, didn't she, Mary?" Edith asked.

"Yes, ma'am," Mary replied, looking down at her feet.

"Well, it is spectacular, but I have something that will fit it perfectly. Come with me." Edith took Mary back to her bedroom. Reaching into a wooden box on her dresser, she produced the most beautiful necklace the girl had ever seen.

"Here, this completes it," Edith said, placing the necklace around the young girl's neck.

"Mrs. Gallatin, I couldn't . . .," Mary protested.

"It's something I will never wear, and I knew it would be perfect on you. It brings out your beautiful eyes," Edith said to the stunned ranch girl as she turned her toward the mirror.

"It's my gift to you."

For the Gallatin children, the Wyoming ranch was a wonderland. William Moncreiffe showed fourteen-year-old Bea and six-year-old Tom the rock that several tribes sent smoke signals from. While at a function at the Sheridan Inn, the children watched Buffalo Bill Cody jump his horse onto the porch and ride through the lobby to the saloon. Bea followed him as though he were the Pied Piper until Goelet caught her just short of the bar.

At the Crow Fair, Goelet and Edith took their children to watch the dancers and the rodeo. At night they were taken with the pageant of the event. The Indian children danced in resplendent costumes of elk teeth, feathers, and moccasins. The riders and dancers from all over the country competed as clans. They paraded in the fairgrounds on painted horses, exhibiting themselves as the great horsemen of Absaraka.

Edith bought Bea a small gray pony from the Crow tribe, which the little girl named Birdie. The pony turned out to be as mean as a snake, but under the watchful eye of the ranch cowboys, Bea became a strong rider despite the pony's stubborn tendency to stop and roll in the mud. After struggling with Birdie, Roy Snyder gave Bea an eight-year-old sorrel horse named Billy. The horse had appeared one day after a roundup on the Gallatins' Dutch Creek ranch. After an exhaustive search for the owners, it became clear why the horse had been turned out to run wild. He had a habit of tucking his head to his chest and running off with the cowboys.

Knowing that some outlaws will make good horses for children, Snyder let Bea try Billy on a lead line and then on her own. The result was a perfect match. Billy and Bea became inseparable from the beginning. Though she was too young to saddle Billy, Bea would walk to the pasture in the mornings and, in a comical routine, would straddle Billy's neck while he had his head down eating. Billy would lift his head, and Bea would slide onto his back. With no bridle or saddle, the two would get around the saddle horses and trail them to the corral. For his part, Billy maintained an even gait and never bolted or tried to run off with the girl.

The cowboys who worked for the Gallatins were clean and respectful, behaved well around women, and had a soft spot for children. They were following the same code that the cowboys of the 1880s adhered to. Bea adored the ranch cowboys and longed for their approval. On the far expanses of the E4 Ranch, Bea and Billie followed the cowboys. Floyd Bard, who had been a horse wrangler during the Johnson County war, taught Bea the art of riding through the country undetected, using the brush and the low country to conceal her movements just as the Crow, Cheyenne, and Sioux warriors had ridden on their horse-stealing raids.

During hay season, Bea asked the ranch foreman if she could help with the work teams in the field. She was allowed to lead a stacker team that was hooked to the cable that pulled a huge rake full of hay up to the men who stood atop the stack with pitchforks. Bea did fine on her first couple of runs, but she let the team pull too far when the giant rake was in the air, causing the entire apparatus to come crashing down.

"Powder River, let 'er buck," a cowboy yelled as the sound of fifteen-foot rake hitting the ground scattered the horses in the harness. Two teeth were broken on the rake, and the men scrambled to fix the wreck. Bea stood horrified and embarrassed with shame. To top it off, her parents were just riding over.

"What's happened, Roy?" Goelet Gallatin asked his foreman as his daughter stood by, mortified.

"The rake tipped over; we should be up and running shortly," Roy said.

"Is Bea in the way here?" Gallatin asked.

"No, sir, she's fine," Snyder said, not mentioning Bea's mishap.

After her parents rode off, Bea approached Roy with tears in her eyes.

"Thank you, Roy."

"Don't worry, Bea. We needed a break up here. Besides, I've turned over the rake a few times myself," one of the cowboys yelled down from on top of the haystack. Roy handed the girl a handkerchief and gave her a wink.

"Hey, Bea, if you're as quick on the dance floor as you were when that rake hit the ground, I want you as a partner at the next barn dance," another cowboy yelled, which brought a smile to the young girl's face.

During roundups and busy times at the ranch, Edith Gallatin worked alongside the cowboys, sharing the same hours and workload as the men, contributing a cheerful disposition in rain, cold, and heat. Her upbringing had taught her not to seek privilege while working, so Edith, much to the amazement of the men, took the graveyard shift on the cattle drives.

Even though eastern families had begun to settle the area, the west was still wild, and there were plenty of characters to prove it. On April 12, 1912, Sheridan cowgirl Alberta Claire rode her horse Bud into Buffalo, New York, to conclude a ten-thousand-mile trip that had taken her more than a year and a half. Staging a western act in the cities where she stopped, she was greeted by hundreds of spectators, who ate up the cowgirl who expounded on the attributes of western life. In a newspaper interview, she stated her views simply: "I never lose an opportunity to brag on Wyoming women. It never enters my head to be afraid or tired. My mother said to fear nothing but evil, and the great out-of-doors has been more of a companion to me than any human being."

In Cleveland, Ohio, Alberta rode into town simultaneously with Sylvia Pankhurst, the women's suffrage leader. "It's a good thing we did not meet, for I have no use for English window-breaking methods. She said she was almost tired to death from her terrible trip. Miss Pankhurst had traveled twelve hours in a Pullman, and the day I was interviewed I had ridden forty-two miles on horseback, but I had not begun to think about being tired."

In 1907, the U.S. government abandoned Fort Keogh, which was next to Miles City, but it returned in 1910 to use the post as a remount station for buying and training horses for the U.S. Army. By 1916 Fort Keogh had prepared 1,773 for the army. One hundred civilian cowboys with their spurs, chaps, hats, and boots whipped some of the wildest broncs on earth into shape in short order. The fort's corrals became a gathering place for the citizens of Miles City, who were always up to see a cowboy ride the broncs in their daily shows.

At the Sheridan Inn, Noll Wallop and Buffalo Bill sat at the bar and ruminated over the old times. Frank Grouard had long since died in a home in Missouri, and Cody's Wild West Show was failing to such an extent that he had hocked all of his personal belongings, including his horse, to pay bills. Wallop admired the pair of six guns Cody wore.

"Expecting t-trouble, Colonel?" Wallop asked when he noticed that the pistols were loaded.

"Naw, just use them for props anymore."

Several men approached Cody that evening wanting a handshake or a visit with a celebrity. During a lull Cody handed Noll one of the pistols.

"Shall we?" Cody asked with a twinkle in his eyes. The boom of the guns shook the room, and plaster rained down into the drinks, which drew a stern rebuttal from the manager. "Knock that off, or I'll send the two of you out of here!"

Cody and Wallop both apologized and fished in their pockets for the damages. Cody shook his head: "I used to own this place."

Noll had a laugh out of that one: "*Bonis a divitibus nihil timendum*" (good men ought to fear nothing from the rich).

38

Two Men Lost in a Blizzard

—*Sheridan Post,* 1917

IN AUGUST 1914, GERMANY, AUSTRIA, THE BALKANS, ENGland, France, and Russia were gearing up for war. Two million men and 860,000 horses were transported on eleven thousand trains to areas of troop mobilization in Europe. By the end of that month, three hundred thousand French soldiers, riding horses and wearing breastplates from the Napoleonic wars, charged into German machine-gun fire to predictable results. In a horrific turn of events, the world was at war in the bloodiest conflict known to man.

Once again there was a worldwide demand for horses to mount several armies. From the onset, the United States had taken an isolationist role, but astute horsemen from Absaraka were quick to realize what the demand would mean to local horsemen.

Malcolm Moncreiffe, Bob Walsh, and Goelet Gallatin staged Sheridan's first formal horse show for the purpose of promoting the area's horses to the French and English governments. In a shrewd move, the organizers got Captain de Juge of France and C. F. McNeil of England to judge the event along with A. L. Brock of Buffalo, New York.

As the Sheridan band played for the spectators, classes were held for polo ponies, saddle horses, children's pony class, U.S. cavalry class, heavy, lightweight hunter, and ladies' saddle class. There were also halter classes for horses of all ages, from foals to stallions.

Malcolm Moncreiffe set the state high-jump record on his horse with a five-foot-two-inch leap. Goelet Gallatin won the light polo pony class, and his daughter Bea, now nine, competed in the ladies' saddle class. Bill Eaton, Frank Horton, Luther Dunning, and his son Sydney Paget Dunning also competed in various events.

The promotion was a success: soon Italian, French, English, U.S. Army, and—in the early stages—German buyers rolled into Miles City, Billings, and Sheridan to buy warhorses.

> *Sheridan is at present a concentration point for the horses being gathered up for the British Army. Buyers are scouring nine northwestern states for suitable animals, and all are being shipped here, unloaded, rested, inspected, and reshipped to eastern points. The volume of business is greater than expected, and even where the purchases are made elsewhere, it naturally releases money in Sheridan County.*
> —Sheridan Post

Noll Wallop once again assembled his old crew of Boer War cowboys to scan the country for horses, but his heart was not in it. His mind was on his son, Gerard, now a lieutenant in the British Army. In the first year of the war, most of the British Army had been killed or wounded, and a million French had lost their lives. After two years the Russians had lost nine million men. By 1916, with the advent of mustard gas and flamethrowers, the death toll would turn even worse. At Verdun, the French Army was bled white, with six hundred thousand casualties in one battle.

A cloak of self-imposed guilt and shame cloaked Marguerite Wallop. She had pushed Gerard extremely hard in manners, education, and motivation. She had insisted he travel to England and become a protégé of his uncle, the Earl of Portsmouth, so he could succeed him in that title. Now Gerard's life was in danger, and Marguerite regretted sending him away.

The only word Noll and Marguerite received was a standard postcard from the front on which a soldier would sign his name and check a box that would let his parents know he was alive.

Finally a tattered letter, already opened twice by censors, appeared at Big Horn. A local cowboy rode out to the ranch to deliver the letter.

Aug 27th

Here I am again, father . . . After four days of the most uncomfortable form of war in the open, on captured German ground, the day before yesterday or rather the night preceding it, we assembled with quiet stealth to a bank which we're jumping off, and at 3:15 we did what was known as "Hopping the parapet, or over the top." I am too weary to write a long letter . . . Your very tired and nervous but rather happy son.
Yours ever,
Gerard

Once again, Sheridan and Miles City and Big Horn became central locations for military horse inspections.

Inspecting War Horses
Four hundred purchased at polo ranch.

Government Stamp
Placed on the animals that pass muster and are bought for service.

The center of the horse-loving population of northern Wyoming, the first two days of this week, was the polo ranch near Big Horn where Messrs. McNeil and Boze, official horse inspectors and buyers for the British government, were purchasing mounts operating in Europe.

Not only were many horse owners and sellers present, but several score of interested spectators watched the proceedings from start to finish.

> *The first requirement was that the animal be sound in every particular; the second that he be of the correct height, that is, fifteen hands or better; the third that he be between the ages of five and nine; the fourth that he be of dark color, not easily distinguishable by the enemy, and a good, free, natural-gaited traveler.*
>
> *Those [horses] which failed to meet the requirements were turned in the opposite direction and galloped away with as many manifestations of joy as if they realized what they had escaped. They were loaded into [train] cars in Sheridan and shipped to Canada, where they will be thrown with other bunches.*
>
> *All horses were supposed to be broken, but there were some that barely came within that definition. Practically all the horses offered belonged to the Moncreiffe brothers, Wallop, and Walsh and had been purchased by them or their agents in all parts of northern Wyoming.*

Some of the horses that failed the U.S. Army inspections because of their size were sold to the British. Most of the horses the British turned down were sold to the French. Finally, some of the horses the French turned down were sold to the Italians. Not surprisingly, the Sheridan newspaper reported that the Italians were complaining about the quality of the horses they had bought, not realizing the horses were the fourth or fifth pick. To pass inspection, the horses did not need to be trained, only rideable, and with the best bronc riders in the world riding the horses during the inspection, it was buyer beware.

Like the Boer War, the inspections for the Great War in Europe drew quite a crowd from town. Some brought box lunches so as not to miss any of the battles that went on, especially when the light, artillery horses were mounted for the first time. Some of the meanest, nastiest horses known to man presented themselves at Malcolm Moncreiffe's polo field, where the inspections were held. Bea Gallatin rode Billy over each day to watch her heroes take on the outlaw broncs.

Across the United States, more than one million horses were gathered and shipped to foreign armies, which generated $225 million for ranchers and farmers in America. In one shipment, forty thousand horses died before they reached Europe. A British commission was sent to investigate; they determined that the deaths were either the result of corrupt agents selling sick or old horses, or the handiwork of German spies who poisoned the animals.

Anyone with any horse sense at all could make money selling horses. Ed Love in Miles City received a contract for five thousand horses from Edith Gallatin's cousin Fred Post. He bought the horses for $50 to $60 per head, and resold them for $180 apiece. After Love filled the contract, he secured another on his own for ten thousand horses.

In May 1915, eight hundred French Army horses arrived by train in Sheridan to be shoed before they were shipped on. As most of the horseshoes in Europe came from America, the French officials figured they may as well let the horses haul them over rather than ship them over in bulk. The Sheridan paper reported the event: "All day yesterday and today the anvil chorus has kept a merry tune. It has been joyous music for the mighty smithies of Sheridan too, for every clang that resounded on the anvils was a stroke on a big iron dollar to line their pockets."

While war raged across Europe, a war with Pancho Villa on the Mexican border resulted in General John J. Pershing ordering fifty-five thousand horses for his troops. The range horses from the Northern Plains were more and more appreciated because of their steady improvement in type, breeding, and appearance.

At the Gallatins' ranch a brand-new tennis court had been completed at the outset of the war, but the court saw no play because Edith had it closed. She felt it was wrong for people to play tennis while the world was at war. Polo, however, went on as strong as ever. The young American phenomenon Tommy Hitchcock, whose parents were old New York friends of the Gallatins, played in a game at Moncreiffe field. Another of the top polo players in the world, Dev Milburn, also from New York, came out to play. Both easterners were impressed with the tall cowboy Johnny Cover's ability to effortlessly and consistently send back shots over one hundred yards.

Narragansett Pier, R.I.
August 11, 1916

Dear Mrs. Wallop,
We retain such a pleasant memory of our summer at Big Horn and all the kindness which you and Mr. Wallop showed us. We have been here in Narragansett for the polo season, and little Tom has played in some good matches, and the teams he has played on have been quite successful. Monday he starts as a sailor boy for the Maine *battleship. It was his own idea, and I think it will be a very good thing for him. He will not get back till the 10th of September, and I naturally hate losing him for much of his holiday.*

Tom and the children join me in love and very kind remembrances to you and Mr. Wallop and Gerard. Frankie sends his love to Oliver.
Affectionately yours,
Lulie Hitchcock

On one of his first missions, the young polo phenom was shot down in a dogfight in Europe and was captured and held prisoner.

Marguerite Wallop, like hundreds of thousands of other mothers with a son in the war, lived with the apprehension that hers would be killed. Her second son, Oliver, was attending Taft in Connecticut, so Marguerite was suddenly stuck in an empty nest after eighteen years of raising children.

"Noll, I want to go to Europe and help if I can," she said. Noll had been having similar thoughts. Both of them had suffered the loss of dozens of friends and relatives who were killed in action. Despite the fact that he was now fifty-six, Noll volunteered to fight, but he was turned down because of his age.

"I imagine Malcolm can watch the ranch for us," Noll said, and within the month, the two were on a ship bound for Europe. Marguerite's ship was bombed by German planes crossing the English Channel, but she made it to France to work for the Red Cross in makeshift hospitals. Noll was stationed in France, where he grew vegetables to feed the troops.

On his Otter Creek ranch, Luther Dunning rode into the yard and tied his horse to the side of the corral. He headed straight for the house, neither unsaddling nor watering his horse, which alarmed Leota, who watched from the door. In a polite but urgent manner, he handed his wife a letter from England.

"It's not from Sydney, it's from his lawyers," she said, looking at the handwriting while opening the envelope. Leota put her hand to her mouth and looked at Luther but did not speak. She wanted to cry, but Luther needed to hear what the letter said, so she pulled herself together.

"Is he dead?" Luther asked. Leota could only nod her head yes. Luther put his arm around her and took the letter. Sydney Paget had taught him about good horses, started him in the horse business, and was one of the best horsemen he had known. Leota and Luther had named their only son after the distinguished British rancher. Luther went outside to unsaddle his horse. When he finished, he walked out and looked at the remains of the racetrack he had learned to race on. A smile crossed his face when he thought of the first time he had seen Sydney. He had been a scared, lost fourteen-year-old, and he had wandered onto Sydney Paget and Connie Hoffman stark naked riding up Otter Creek in a buggy.

There had been no mention of Montana at all in the article; nothing about Paget coming up the trail with a herd of cattle, or raising some of the best horses in the world on Otter Creek. Nothing of buffalo hunting or the race meets he organized in Miles City. Nothing of the spark he had brought to the area or the bloodlines he had developed in the area.

"What's wrong with Dad?" Syd Dunning asked as he came into the house.

"Sydney Paget just passed away in England," Leota answered her son. Syd had never met the man, but he had heard stories. Leota sat, and then let the tears flow. Sydney Paget was a good, kind man who had shown both Luther and Leota generosity and respect.

With the war raging in Europe, some of their neighbors had already shipped out to fight. Major Dowson, James H. Price, Walter Lindsay, and Noll Wallop had all gone off to England and France. Jim Hereford, a Montana rancher, had joined the Canadian forces. After she composed herself, she went outside to talk to Luther. "I think maybe it's time our country joined the fight." Luther nodded. "If they are anything like Noll Wallop and Sydney Paget."

At a New York social function, Edith Gallatin was stressing the importance of drafting women into military service, to former President Theodore Roosevelt. "Mr. President, if we are to eventually draft men, don't you think there are plenty of jobs that American women can do if drafted? I think there are plenty of women that could be of use to the war effort."

Roosevelt was exasperated at President Wilson's slowness to enter the war. "President Wilson is like a school boy who fears a thrashing so he fortifies the back of his pants," Roosevelt said, referring to President Woodrow Wilson's cautious policy about entering the war.

Roy Snyder rose early to meet Floyd Bard, the Moncreiffes' foreman, and a young man who was to accompany them on a deer hunt. Snyder's wife, Pearl, stirred in the bed as she felt her husband leave in the dark. She would lie in for another hour, as Mrs. Gallatin had warned Pearl about getting enough rest during her pregnancy.

A few inches of snow covered the ground, so the men rode into the chinook belt along the face of the mountain, where it was warm enough to allow them to remove their coats and tie them behind their saddles.

Crossing Little Goose Creek, Roy halted the three, motioning to a rocky outcropping a thousand feet above them.

"Look over there across the creek, at the top of that knob. Do you see the big buck deer standing there? Two of us had better circle that knob and meet in back of it," he said.

They dismounted and tied their horses in a stand of small pine trees. The sun was out, and it was warm for late October, so the men left their coats with the horses. An hour later, a light flurry of snow began to fall as a cloud cover settled over the canyon. Within an hour it was a whiteout.

Bea Gallatin watched the blizzard from her window, and when she heard her mother in the front hallway, she knew something was wrong. Edith had phoned the Moncreiffes to check on the hunters' return, but no one had heard from them yet. The temperatures had plummeted, and when Floyd Bard finally showed up riding behind two horses with empty saddles, Edith's fears were realized. "I lit a signal fire on some driftwood on Little Goose, but Roy and the kid never showed up," Floyd said.

At once every cowboy in the Gallatins' bunkhouse fell out to organize an emergency search party. Edith sent every man with a small package of matches. In a short while, an army had materialized from second-generation homesteaders: the Hilmans, Custises, Skinners, Sacketts, and E. C. Bowman all moved out into the mountains they grew up in. A Swede trapper and forestry service representatives led the search, and the men took turns at the laborious task of breaking through the drifts. Bobsleds were loaded with beds and provisions. The Gallatins and Moncreiffes brought all their saddle and workhorses in for the volunteers. In Sheridan, a bakery sent out all its bread to feed the search party.

LOST IN A BLIZZARD

Roy Snyder and Melvin Sutton Caught in Storm on Mountains and Perish

Many Men Scour the Country

Snyder's body found on creek bank, Sutton's body still in Piney Creek

The details of the tragedy are strange and almost unbelievable. That two men, though both strong and rugged, should succumb to the rigors of the storm is not strange, but that one of them should be Roy Snyder, a man inured to hardship, bred in the Rockies and one of the best hunters and guides in the country, is a fact hard to grasp. Generally it is believed that he gave his life trying to save his companion, who had fallen in the river, and unhampered might have won his way to shelter. Fifty men from the Bighorn country and half as many men from the vicinity of Banner turned out, and every foot of the country in the mountains above Little Goose Canyon was combed. Finally tracks were found. The storm had filled the footprints, but with infinite care they were hunted out and followed. It was a job that took nerve as well as skill, as it is a wild and rugged country

> *and the snow was deep. Y. Z. David of the forestry service and L. N. Larson, with skill that rivaled an Apache, led in the hunt.*
>
> *. . . it seems that the men started for Piney intending to seek shelter in Dr. Whedon's cabin. They made the journey safely, and Snyder's sense of direction was not much at fault, for the trail shows that they missed the corner of the fence at the Whedon cabin by not more than four feet.*
>
> *The trail led down the Piney, and two miles below, David and Larson found the dead body of Snyder. He was lying on the ice near a pool, and a broken place on the ice shows where Sutton went in. Snyder apparently tried to save him, but becoming exhausted, lay down on the ice and was overcome by the cold.*
>
> —Sheridan Enterprise, *October 30, 1917*

The Gallatins gave Pearl Snyder a self-sufficient ranch and hired Roy's brother to run it. When her son was born, she named him Goelet. For the next eighty years, curious deer hunters and cowboys riding cattle on the mountain would find the silver plaque Edith Gallatin nailed to a tree near where Roy died. It read: *In loving memory of a brave man and a perfect friend, Roy H. Snyder, E4 Ranch.*

39

It's hell or burst, we're the 91st, the Boys from Powder River

—World War I poem

PRESIDENT WOODROW WILSON AND CONGRESS HAD passed a bill calling up approximately 10 million men for service in Europe. At Fort Lewis, Washington, a "Wild West Division" of thirty thousand cowboys, loggers, farmers, and Native Americans was assembled as the U.S. Army's 91st Division. They came from Wyoming, Montana, Nevada, Utah, Oregon, California, and Washington.

On the Cheyenne and Crow reservations, young warriors prepared for battle in the old way: the survivors of the Indian wars gave feasts and held ceremonies for the Indian soldiers to send them into battle. In this way a young man would prove himself. A crack team of Indian scouts was already fighting for General John J. Pershing in the border war with Mexico.

Though they were not U.S. citizens, Native Americans had the highest enlistment rate of any American minority. Thirteen thousand signed up to serve in the same army that some of their fathers had fought against.

Goelet Gallatin, who had graduated from the Presidio in California with the rank of captain, and his neighbors Ridgely Nicholas and Milt McCoy had all shipped out. Bill Eaton and Tom McAllister's adopted son Sid Vollen were also on their way. Gerard Wallop had suffered from mustard gas but was back at the front again.

In Sheridan, the town band played a variety of patriotic songs as parents said good-bye to their sons. In Miles City, the Red Cross served lunch to soldiers who yelled "Powder River" to the assembled crowd as the train pulled out. The ranchers, farmers, homesteaders, sheep ranchers, cattlemen, and merchants stood shoulder to shoulder to catch one last glimpse of their young sons.

On the banks of Powder River, a few citizens gathered the steel rims from the burned wagons of Colonel Nelson Cole's Dead Horse Camp as scrap metal for the war effort.

George Ostrum rode into Sheridan on his four-year-old gelding, Red Wing, to ship out for the war. The colt was a beauty: a dark red color with two white socks and a silver mane and tail. George had bought Red Wing as a foal from the Crow during the 1913 county fair in Sheridan. While the mare was entered in the one-and-a-half-mile race for Indian horses, the Crow held Red Wing on the infield. During the race he broke loose, jumped the rail, and to the delight of the spectators, finished side by side with the mare for the win, to the cheering of thousands.

Since the Crow were running the mare again in another race, they decided to hog-tie Red Wing to prevent him from getting on the track again. Ostrum walked up in the middle of the struggle and offered to buy the colt for $10, which the Indians accepted. Over the fall, Ostrum taught Red Wing to lead and gentled him into a pet.

After joining the army to fight on the Mexican border, George Ostrum returned to Sheridan to find Red Wing grown into a fine young horse and broke him to ride. Ostrum had planned to send Red Wing to his family's ranch with a neighbor, but seeing army horses loaded on the train, it occurred to him he might take his horse with him.

He approached the officer in charge and offered his horse for sale. The officer inspected Red Wing and found that he was too young by a year; his baby teeth were still on the corners of his incisors.

"I suppose we could pull those baby teeth out, and then he might pass inspection," the officer offered.

"Nothing doing!" Ostrum countered.

Ostrum was put in charge of a baggage car that was only partially full. Having already been to Mexico, Ostrum knew what he might get away with concerning the army. Before the train pulled out of Sheridan, Ostrum built a stall for Red Wing in the baggage car and smuggled his horse to Cheyenne, where the troops were being trained. In his innocence, Ostrum had no idea that by smuggling his horse on the train, he was putting Red Wing that much closer to a war in which more horses had been killed than in the Civil War.

Because Red Wing was the flashiest horse in the unit, Major Louabaugh, who was stationed at Cheyenne, chose him to ride for himself. During a review of the regiment's mounted troops, the soldiers sat stirrup to stirrup as the major passed in front on Red Wing. The Cheyenne post had two pet bear cubs that normally stayed down by a pond in the cool shade during the day and wandered up to the kitchen for scraps during the evening. On the day of the review, however, the bears broke routine and headed to the kitchen across the parade ground. Most of the horses at the post were accustomed to the bears, but having just arrived in Cheyenne, Red Wing had no such familiarity.

At first sight of the bears, Red Wing took off bucking with the major as the soldiers sat amused on their horses. It was a sight Ostrum would not forget.

When Ostrum's regiment shipped out to North Carolina, Ostrum again smuggled Red Wing onto a train full of horses. Sometimes at the feed stops there was nothing for the starving horses, so they began to eat the wooden slats inside the rail cars.

While going through the Great Smoky Mountains in Erwin, Tennessee, Ostrum took matters into his own hands. He stopped the train next to a farmer's field without proper permission, but it saved the horses' lives. The soldiers built an off-ramp for the cars and unloaded the horses, which immediately began to devour the grass.

The townspeople and farmers near Erwin turned out to welcome and feed the soldiers and their horses during a three-day stay. After a few days of R&R, the soldiers put on a Wild West Show for the citizens in return for their kindness. Ostrum gave the farmers government vouchers for the use of their pasture. Meanwhile, the U.S. Army was sending urgent telegrams to find out where the troops were.

Eventually, Red Wing followed the troops to North Carolina and then to Virginia, where the regiment was shipped out to France. In Virginia, Ostrum found fellow Sheridan cowboy Chet Cotton, who was in charge of shipping horses overseas, and got Red Wing on the roster that went to France. The colt had yet to formerly join the army and still belonged to Ostrum. At Tours, the men and horses were separated; Ostrum was shipped to the front, and he asked Major Louabaugh to watch out for Red Wing in his absence.

The preposterousness of the request during a war was not lost on the major, but reflecting on the young Wyoming cowboy's innocence and his own affection for the animal, the major agreed. It would save Red Wing's life.

In Europe, cowboys from Absaraka were making their mark in several ways. Casey Barthelmess from Miles City was assigned to his father's old unit, the 6th Cavalry. His father had been a lieutenant at Fort Keogh during the Indian wars. It was there in 1906 that Barthelmess died in an accident in a well cave. His three oldest children quit school to support the family by working at various ranch jobs around the territory. Casey Barthelmess broke horses for a living and competed in various rodeos. He had ridden Skyrocket, a famous bucking horse, at Miles City, a feat only a handful of men could claim.

In France, Corporal Barthelmess found himself sitting on an army horse in parade formation with two thousand mounted soldiers being reviewed by his commanding officer. Unfortunately, the officer was late, causing some of the more impatient horses to mill. When the commanding officer rode up, one horse broke ranks, bucking his rider off. There was no fence around the base, so the horse had a free run all the way to the Mediterranean Sea. Casey Barthelmess, acting on instinct, galloped out in pursuit.

"Where the hell are you going, Wild Bill Hickok?" the captain yelled. Casey galloped over and caught the loose horse, returning it to the rider. The captain then stood in his stirrups and leaned forward to scream in Barthelmess's face.

"Corporal, do you understand what keeping rank means? You have jeopardized your entire unit. I don't give a rat's ass how they do it in Montana, son; you are in the U.S. Army now, and you will obey orders! This kind of harebrained behavior can get the whole unit killed. Do I make myself clear?"

"Yes, sir," Barthelmess replied.

"Get your ass back in line, and if I see you break ranks again, I'll have you put in the guardhouse," he screamed.

Casey reined his horse back into the line of green soldiers, but the captain was still screaming.

"Cowboys! The last thing I need is a bunch of undisciplined cowboys who think they know how to ride. If any of you men think you know how to ride, you can forget it. You are going to ride the army way, or you are going to find yourself in deeper shit than you have ever dreamed of."

That night Barthelmess was ordered to the captain's office. The officer was sitting at his desk when Barthelmess was shown in.

"Barthelmess, you were the only man in two thousand who knew what to do today," he said. "You showed initiative today, and that's a good quality in a soldier. I had to make a point to the men, though; I can't have these green troops breaking ranks. They'll be under fire soon, and they need to maintain discipline, because it may save their lives."

Casey Barthelmess breathed a sigh of relief. He was but one of a large group of men from Absaraka who were about to distinguish themselves in Europe.

Paddy Ryan was a small Irish cowboy who was stationed in France to break horses. He grew up in the small town of Ismay, Montana. After a group of wounded American soldiers began to return from the front, Ryan got word that a buddy of his was in the infirmary, so he went to visit him. It was a sobering sight to see the suffering and hopeless cases. Ryan's friend was not expected to live through the night. When Ryan asked if he could do anything for him, the wounded friend stated that he would sure like a taste of French wine. Ryan snuck off the base and got the wine, but when he tried to return, the guards at the gate stopped him. Ryan tried to plead his case, but the guards stood firm.

"I'll go to jail with you if you just let me take this to a wounded soldier in the infirmary," Paddy said.

"You'll go to jail now, and I'll just keep the wine," the policeman said, but before he could detain Ryan, he found himself decked by the fiery Irish cowboy. Paddy made it to the hospital, where he gave the bottle to his dying friend. He was then put in a jail cell, sobered by the thought of his friend and the rest of the wounded soldiers suffering in the hospital. For the rest of his life, there was very little that would scare this cowboy after learning what those soldiers in France had endured.

Marguerite Wallop stood over the bleeding soldier and held pressure on the wound. The young man had received a shrapnel wound, which injured his hip bone and cut an artery. While he was convalescing, he remained cheerful—though he could walk only with the use of crutches—and quickly became a favorite among the nurses and other patients.

One day he took a funny step and the injured bone in his hip snapped, severing the artery again. The doctor said there was not enough of the artery to mend and it was in a position that made amputation out of the question. Marguerite held pressure while the doctor worked. There were hundreds of desperate cases fresh from the battlefield that needed immediate attention. Marguerite knew from the look the doctor gave her that there was no hope.

The boy somehow knew and asked Marguerite to write his parents. "I'll stay here and hold this for as long as you want." She was trying to keep stoic, but in the background of the hospital moans and cries of "Don't let me die; I want to go home . . . I want to go home . . ." spilled across the room from other wounded boys. The boy whose life she held in her hands neither cried nor complained. Instead, he accepted his fate and in a quiet tone looked up at Marguerite.

"Merci, Mademoiselle, you can let go now."

Marguerite watched the life drain from the young man as she had several others and said a prayer over his body. When Marguerite walked out, she passed a delirious soldier who cried out to her from his bed. "Mother, make them bring me my arm, they have taken my arm." She saw the bloody bandaged stump and noticed the boy resembled her youngest son, Oliver, who was back in the States.

By 1918 England, France, Russia, and Germany had all lost a generation of men. The French were demoralized, and the English, Russians, and Italians were down to their last lines of men. The American doughboys had injected new life into the Allies.

After a brief training period, the 91st "Wild West" Division was rushed directly to the front, where at Flanders field and the Argonne, they issued a final push against the Germans. Men huddled in filthy trenches in the dark war-torn landscape of the Argonne and waited for the signal. They were all scared, but the 91st had brought a unique frontier spirit with them from home.

"Powder River!" the cry echoed in the night.

"Let 'er buck!" someone answered in the dark. The phrase "Powder River, let 'er buck" spread across the battlefields of Europe until the Powder River had become the most famous river in France.

When the phrase reached Gerard Wallop along the Allied lines, it lifted his spirits. It brought him back to the cowboys, his horse Blue, and his dog Kinky and their rides into Little Goose Canyon.

After only a week in France, George Ostrum found himself in the thick of the fighting in the chateau defensive. While on the front, an officer offered any soldier a weekend pass who could draw the best symbol for the 148th field artillery regiment. Every unit but theirs had a patch with an insignia, but the Wyoming unit had only a number.

Ostrum jumped at the chance, conjuring the image of Red Wing bucking with Major Louabaugh on his back in Cheyenne country. The symbol was adopted, and soon the bucking horse symbol was on the unit's shoulder patches, road signs, helmets, and ordinances. Before long, all of Germany was adorned with the bucking horse symbol that appeared on everything from beer mugs to jewelry.

Four and a half million horses were now in use by the warring armies. The equine losses were significant: on the Western Front alone, an average of forty-seven thousand horses died per month. In no other theater was the loss of horse more tragic than among the workhorses. The horses used to pull cannons to the front were unhitched and slaughtered when they reached the line, as there was no way to feed or care for them.

The war had been the most horrible known to man: eight million soldiers lost their lives, an average of five thousand a day for each day of the four-year war. By the end of the war, there were three thousand American casualties. Six thousand soldiers of the 91st Division had either been killed or wounded in the fighting in France and Belgium. Five would receive the Medal of Honor.

In a tribute to the western men of the 91st Division who gave their lives to World War 1, the old poem "Powder River, Let 'er Buck" was rewritten.

"Powder River, let 'er buck!" The foe began to shiver
When the cry swept o'er the front: "Hurrah for Powder River!"
Thirty thousand buckaroos on Flanders field so bloody,
Side by side they crept and died and each one for his buddy.

Shrapnel burst the Ninety-First with all that hell to blind 'em
Thundered through the Argonne 'til they left the flags behind 'em!
Where the golden poppies grow and glorious they quiver,
Each one represents a soul who hailed from Powder River.

When we landed in New York, they crowded all around us;
Everyone seems to wonder where and how they found us!
From the mountains and the plains and the hills and the valleys,
Thirty thousand heroes left their ranches and their Sallys.

On they come through Belgium, a-whoopin' and a howlin',
"We're from the wild and woolly West, that's where we do our prowlin'!"
Everywhere the Allies stare and hand out their decision:
There's the cowboy regiment of the Ninety-First Division!

Hear 'em yell as wild as hell, with victory to vision:
"Powder River, here we come, the Ninety-First Division!
Let 'er buck, we're full of luck! We're woolly, wild, and airy!
She's one mile wide and one inch deep from hell to Tipperary!

We're full of fleas from overseas, and none of 'em can match us!
Up in France we made 'em dance: it took all hell to catch us!
When we get riled, our teeth get riled; we're 'pisen' to the liver!
It's hell or burst, we're the Ninety-First, the boys from Powder River!"

Before shipping out for home, George Ostrum located Major Louabaugh in Bordeaux and found out that Red Wing was in a French riding school in Tours. Since the U.S. Army wasn't shipping many horses back to the United States, and it would cost Ostrum $1,500 to do so, he sold Red Wing to his good owners for $165 and returned home with the troops.

Red Wing, the Crow foal that had crossed the finish line alongside his mare, had survived a war few horses had. It was fitting that a Crow horse would share the emblem that represented a western battle unit. Fewer than fifty years before, the Crow Indians had been the great horsemen of the Northwest and the first tribe to bring the animal east of the Bighorns. Years later, Ostrum's image of Major Louabaugh and Red Wing would end up on Wyoming license plates.

At New York harbor, Edith Gallatin stood with Bea and her son Tommy in their best outfits. Edith had received a telegram informing her that her husband would accompany a shipload of the infamous Powder River Division. Citizens crowded every dock, waiting for the troop ships that were carrying their loved ones home.

"Come on, let's be the first to welcome your father's ship home," she said, leading her children to the end of the dock. As the troop ship passed by, Edith waved a large straw hat over her head at the homesick survivors crowding the rail. In the largest voice she could manage, Edith yelled, "Powder River!"

A cheer broke out, and the bullhorn on board responded.

"Let 'er buck!" it boomed.

"How big is it?" she yelled back, still waving her hat.

"An inch deep and a mile wide!" the bullhorn responded, and every western boy on that ship knew he was home.

Goelet Gallatin, Noll Wallop, Bill Eaton, and dozens of Crow and Cheyenne returned to Absaraka with hundreds of others. Edith had a plaque put in the blacksmith shop in Big Horn to honor the men who served in both the Spanish-American War and World War I.

40

SCARLET FEVER WAS KILLING TENS OF THOUSANDS OF children in the United States. The epidemic penetrated the most remote regions. The Crow and Cheyenne tribes were hit especially hard, as were Billings, Miles City, Sheridan, and Buffalo. Local rodeos barred admission to children for fear the disease might spread even farther.

Noll and Marguerite Wallop had nearly lost one son in the Great War in Europe, and now their second son was in danger of being exposed to the plague that was sweeping the East Coast.

Taft School
Watertown, Connecticut

Dearest Pa,
I can write only a few words, as I have a great deal of studying for Tuesday's classes.

You couldn't imagine if I wrote a book to you what a joy it was to get the telegram and sweet letter that came this week from you . . .

As you know, another case of scarlet fever has broken out, and they are holding more boys over at this infirmary as suspects. Rumors have started around school that school will close in a very short time on this account. It would be awful for us fellows who live so far from home if the "darned old school" should close now.
Your devoted son,
Oliver

After a long, hot morning of gathering cattle, Edith Gallatin and twelve-year-old Bea rode down the dusty road toward the Verona corrals.

"Come on, Bea, I know the family that lives in this ranch house. We can water our horses and get a drink here." As Bea rode up to the house, she watched a sad-looking woman approach them and invite them to get down and have a drink. Edith and Bea led the horses to a trough in the backyard. Bea drank from a ladle that hung from a post next to the tank. When Edith noticed the yard was bare of the toys that were usually strewn about in front of the house, she asked, "Where are the children?"

"They're up there." The woman pointed toward a hill behind the house. Bea froze and put down the ladle when she spotted the three crosses on the hill. Edith took the woman in her arms and held her. Her children had taken sick and died in less time than it took her husband to drive a team into Sheridan to get supplies. He had left on a Monday, and when he returned on Saturday, his children had taken sick, died, and been buried.

Later that winter, Edith and Bea drove their car over snowy roads in the countryside to the cabin of a homesteader woman who was at death's door with scarlet fever. With no regard for her own health, Edith remained to nurse the woman while Bea, barely tall enough to reach the pedals, was sent to fetch the doctor.

After the death of Roy Snyder, the Gallatins hired Johnny Cover to be the foreman of their E4 Ranch. For eighteen years, Cover had managed Malcolm Moncreiffe's polo horse–breeding operation. He quit because Moncreiffe had used Cover's team without his permission. It wasn't a matter of Moncreiffe using Cover's horses; it was the fact that Moncreiffe didn't think he needed to ask permission since Cover worked for him. With Johnny Cover, there was right and wrong, never mind who you were.

He had managed the Boer War corrals and had ridden some of the toughest broncs for the inspectors there. As a young man he was one of the top relay riders in the country and had won at the Sheridan Fair several times.

As a polo player, Johnny Cover cut a splendid figure on the field, and it was his calm demeanor teamed with perfect horsemanship that carried Big Horn polo teams to victory over Denver and several army teams.

Cover guided the E4 into being the showcase cattle and horse ranch in the West. He did his job calmly, conscientiously, efficiently, and always honestly. He took on the hardest backbreaking jobs for himself.

A proud cowboy, Cover kept his horse and himself spic-and-span at all times. No matter how early he started, his horse's mane and tail were always combed and his tack was always spotless. Even on the long cattle drives, Johnny wore a clean white shirt, which his wife brought to him every evening.

In a land where all men are equal, Johnny Cover stood head and shoulders above the rest in the eyes of his peers. If a man had a hard day in the saddle over rugged country, Cover would think of something for him to do which, without hurting the man's pride, gave the man a break the following day. His talent for leadership was evident, and no one who worked for him or with him would have dreamt of disrupting his authority. He was a fair and thoughtful foreman, and as a consequence, all his men loved him. Over the next forty years, Johnny Cover became part of the Gallatins' extended family.

Unfortunately, the effort that Edith Gallatin put toward helping others was taking a toll on her. Shortly after the war Edith returned from a long ride one day, and after putting her saddle on its rack, she fainted. Johnny Cover carried her to the house, and then sent for a doctor. In her typical lightheartedness, she laughed at the incident, but the heart that gave so much to her neighbors was beginning to give out.

During the winter of 1919, blizzards killed thousands of cattle as temperatures dropped to fifty below zero. Allen Alderson, a nephew of Nannie, worked for the Three Circle Ranch after returning from the war. One day he reported coming across dead cattle that were frozen stiff, leaning up against trees. Smaller, subsistence ranchers who lived from crop to crop were wiped out. The fall harvest didn't raise enough money with which to buy seed to plant the following spring. Losing a dozen calves and three cows would financially ruin a small rancher.

In the drought the following summer, crops and grasslands were ruined. Homesteaders who had little more than a shack left the country for good. One poetic farmer tacked a farewell note on his front door:

Forty miles to go for water,
fifty miles to wood,
ten miles to hell,
and I've gone for good.

With no market to speak of, the homesteaders' horses were turned loose on the plains to join the wild horse herds. With no army buyers in the area, the price of horses dropped from $150 to less than $5.

While one man's bust is another man's boom, men like Charlie Thex and John Kendrick expanded both their cattle and land holdings by claiming abandoned livestock and homesteads or offering the owners a small percentage of the value. A man who was constantly in the saddle, Charlie Thex had nevertheless raised a large family with Bertha Hagan, a Norwegian woman who had migrated to Otter Creek.

When the war with Pancho Villa shut down the racetrack in Tijuana, Mexico, plans were made for some of the best thoroughbred racers to travel to Sheridan for a two-week race meet. Betting windows were put in and odds set on all the races.

RACERS COMING FROM ALL POINTS OF THE COMPASS

"They're coming!" Those thoroughbred racers that make the blood tingle with excitement . . . Last Sunday a combined carload of horses and equipment arrived from Louisville, Kentucky, and are now stationed at the racetrack . . . On June 4, four carloads of horses, 65 in number, will leave Hot Springs, Arkansas, for this city, and on June 5 two carloads containing about 30 horses will leave California for Sheridan. Three more carloads will leave Louisville, Kentucky, on the first of June, and one carload will leave Baltimore, Maryland, for the city on the same date.

Ranchers who had a full schedule of work during the week made an excuse to go to Sheridan for supplies during the races. Despite the arrival of quality racehorses, locals felt they had the best horses and jockeys in the world in their own backyard. Some of the world's premiere equestrian bloodlines had been grazing the bunch grass from Miles City to Sheridan for forty years. Vess Hardee of Sheridan had raised a horse that ran in the Kentucky Derby, Black Diamond had set the world record in the half-mile in Chicago, and Paget, Moncreiffe, and Wallop had sent world record beaters to the four corners of the globe.

41

Good horses cost no more to raise than plugs.

—U.S. Army Remount manual

THE WORLD'S POPULATION OF HORSES HAD BEEN DECImated in World War I. The U.S. Army cavalrymen were presently mounted on inferior mounts, and the military leaders realized that in the event of another war, few horses would be serviceable for the troops. Breeding and processing stations like Fort Keogh (Miles City) and Fort Mckenzie (Sheridan) were costly and ineffective. Consequently, in 1919 the War Department looked into issuing mostly thoroughbred stallions to civilian ranchers who would raise horses for the army.

One source of those stallions was the racetrack across the United States. Because states banned gambling along with drinking during Prohibition, the army could buy thoroughbred stallions off the racetracks for next to nothing, as the racing industry was suffering. And some of those stallions were the best in the world. Sir Barton, the first Triple Crown winner, was issued to a Douglas, Wyoming, rancher, and Behave Yourself, a Kentucky Derby winner, was issued to a rancher in Cheyenne. The general public could breed a mare to any Remount stallion while it was in the custody of the ranchers for a ten-dollar stud fee.

To qualify to breed a stallion, ranchers had to have a safe pen and shed to keep him in and eight brood mares. Ranchers who didn't have enough mares of their own borrowed them to qualify. It was a no-lose proposition: ranchers initially received $10 for each mare they bred and additional expenses to keep the stallion. Having a stallion guaranteed an army horse buyer would visit your ranch periodically to inspect the stud.

The stallions came with a halter, a set of hobbles, and an instruction manual published by the quartermaster general's office of the U.S. Army. Crib notes at the bottom of each section were supposed to get the attention of ranchers who might not be big readers.

Breed sound horses . . . Eliminate poor mares, get good ones . . . Good horses cost no more to raise than plugs . . . Begin gentling foals early . . .

Keep horses away from barbed wire.

If their horses passed inspection, the ranchers could sell them to the army for $165. At a time when a five-dollar bill was as big as a window shade, and cattle were selling for $2 a head, it gave ranchers a shot at selling horses to the army for $165. The only drawback was that it would take four years before ranchers started to see profits. Most ranchers who signed up for the program already owned saleable horses to start with.

Luther Dunning, his brother Grant, and his cousin Mansfield were issued the first stallions in the area. Luther was already a legend among horsemen and was called on to sell the government some of his thoroughbred stallions that went back to the Paget and Wallop bloodlines. Goelet Gallatin was issued Mentor, a stallion who had sired Wise Councilor, a one-time horse of the year in thoroughbred racing. Al Irions, John Kendrick, the Eaton brothers, the Aldersons, and the Brewsters were some of the more than fifty ranchers in Absaraka who participated in the Remount breeding program.

In the first fourteen years of the program, 7,243 stallions were issued and bred to 178,000 mares that produced 106,080 foals across the United States. Those were the ones reported; thousands of others weren't.

The government stallions were rotated every two or three years to keep ranchers from inbreeding their stock. One year Luther Dunning might get a stallion formerly run by Bill Eaton or the Bones brothers, and they might get a stallion that was run by John Kendrick or Warren Brewster.

Army inspectors soon learned that inspecting horses in Absaraka could be a unique experience. Colonel E. M. Daniels, who had been part of a military expedition on the Mexican border to catch Pancho Villa's army, wrote fondly of his experiences during such inspections:

> *Our inspection of prospects is accomplished somewhat as followed: the horses are first led out from their stalls to a piece of level ground. We see them led off at a walk to and from us. We pass them for type, size, soundness, and suitability. If desirable, they are then ridden under saddle at the walk, trot, and canter and winded. Then, if passed, they are branded. A problem usually occurs in the heating of the irons, especially if no forge is available. A wood fire must in this event suffice. The wind scatters the embers; it cools the irons; the horse shies at the wrong time; the numeral 2 is used in the place of the 5 (and many times upside down in our eagerness to proceed). However, after the use of some strong-arm work aided by the modicum of profanity, we have finally purchased and branded five head of very nice, type 7/8 thoroughbred horses.*
>
> *At four a.m. we are broken out from our sound slumber by the call of our rugged host. Breakfast is eaten by lamplight, and we await dawn to see the horses which are being run in from a pasture of some five thousand acres, just below the house.*
>
> *The breeding on this ranch is all done on the open range. The mares run out year round, the stallion only being brought up, fed, and exercised during the off-season . . .*
>
> *Travel over the open prairie country, encountering countless wire gates, and make for the main road. All roads very well may lead to Rome; only one main road leads to Miles City . . . Then we leave for the Otter Creek country at Ashland, Montana. Here they have decided to take advantage of importations made by wealthy Britishers some forty-five or fifty years ago. Here are hearty people of old stock, anxious and eager for our visit. To them it means the tiding-over of bad financial period—the drought and low prices for cattle. The breeding of horses in this section has been carried on for years, mating thoroughbred sires on*

old English female lines. They run their mares and young stock in a large pasture and during the breeding season ride out on a so-called "teaser" or mounted on a government stallion, to select or bring in the mares in season to be bred and then turned back into the band, later to foal and rear the offspring on the range. The stud meanwhile is kept up, exercised, and cared for as in the "dude" east, or an environment that is in keeping with his "Majesty," as he is affectionately thought of by these people. Through the years they have learned the value of thoroughbred cross on better western mares.

Colonel Daniels began a lifelong friendship with Luther Dunning on these inspections. The colonel recognized in Luther one of those unique horsemen whose passion for horses made him savvy in every aspect of horsemanship, a trait few who spend their entire life around horses achieve.

Up in the Bighorn Valley of Wyoming in a land pregnant with romance, where the best of our Red Men fought relentlessly the advance of the boldest and heartiest of our white men, where high stakes were frequently played for at a card table and half continents and life itself were gambled for on the battlefield—there lies the Circle V Ranch, one of the largest polo pony-breeding establishments in the world . . .

—Major Harry Leonard, *The Sportsman* magazine, 1927

AS THE REMOUNT PROGRAM WAS GETTING UNDER WAY, Milt McCoy, who had raised polo ponies with Malcolm Moncreiffe before the war, partnered with Goelet and Edith Gallatin to build the world's premier polo-breeding facility, called the Circle V Polo Company. It would be the most elaborate horse-breeding facility in the history of Absaraka.

In stark contrast to the Otter Creek ranches, the estates of Gallatin, Moncreiffe, and Wallop in Little Goose Canyon impressed Colonel E. M. Daniels in a different way.

> *Polo fields are in evidence, and the whole section gives the appearance of being a real horse center. The breeding area is all done by hand and the methods are the same as carried on by our larger breeding establishments in the Blue Grass. The mares are prominently thoroughbred and registered. The sires for many years back are of the same breed. Many of the playing ponies on Long Island are reared and trained in this section, and some really high-class racehorses on the tracks today know the "Bighorns" as home.*

At the Circle V, a massive hundred-stall barn with an eighth-of-a-mile shed row was built to accommodate the mares and foals. A polo field was built on which to train the young stallions. Three separate indoor riding barns were built in which the walls slanted out; this would guarantee that when young animals were put through their paces, neither the riders' nor the horses' knees would be harmed.

The Gallatins collected retired polo mares from the best polo players in the world. Dev Milburn and Tommy Hitchcock, the two boys who had studied Johnny Cover's back shots and were now the premier polo players in the world, sent out their best mares, Irish Rose and Barbaretta, to Wyoming. F. Ambrose Clarke sent Turco and Kitty, each having been named an International Champion Pony of 1914 and 1921, respectively. Harry Payne Whitney, whose father had partnered with Sydney Paget, sent his ponies: Yaqui, IXL, and Bar None.

In the Circle V Polo Company's first year, more than sixty foals roamed the ground. By the early 1920s, the Gallatins had one-hundred-plus mares in their breeding program, and it was attracting international fame. The head stallion of the Circle V was Kemano, a chestnut imported from England that had won top honors in stallion classes both in England and at Madison Square Garden. His offspring were already some of the top horses on American and English polo fields. Following Kemano was the stallion Black Rascal, whose father, Black Tony, had sired two Kentucky Derby winners. William Ziegler's Phantom Prince was also bred, and the Gallatins' own Mentor had a nice crop of colts on the ground.

The Gallatins hired the best horsemen available to work the horses. Curley Witzel, Bobby Connelly, Lee Moore, and Dave Whyte rode the rough string; Ray May, Slim Holloway, Red Guy, and Milt McCoy trained on the polo field. Billy Mann, an Englishman who followed Walsh and Wallop from Miles City, rode for Gallatin as well as for Moncreiffe. The former steeplechase jockey would amaze the cowboys by riding bad buckers in a flat saddle.

Horsemen from all walks of life made pilgrimages to Little Goose Canyon to see the Circle V, for it had became the crown jewel of polo operations during the golden age of polo. The games between the United States and England were covered with as much fevered enthusiasm as the World Series. Thousands crowded the polo games in Meadowbrook, New York; newspapers from

Boston to Miles City featured pictures of sports heroes Tommy Hitchcock and Dev Milburn, who had become sports heroes as they led America's team against the Argentine and English polo teams.

While the Gallatins' operation focused on polo, Ridgely Nicholas, now a major in the U.S. Army, focused his breeding operation on jumping and racehorses. Nicholas's D-D Ranch bred for size; four of his five thoroughbred stallions were better than sixteen hands tall.

Major Nick's jumpers were broken in the fall of their third year and jumped indoors in the winter without a rider until they could clear three-and-a-half feet. The following spring they were jumped outside over a variety of obstacles and were then shipped east as hunter prospects. The horses that were raised for racing were shipped to New Orleans.

Major Nick devised an ingenious system of accelerating the growth of his foals so they might compete as two-year-olds with eastern horses, which usually foaled earlier than western horses. He foaled his mares in the barn in January. The foals were tied in the barn at night and turned loose during the day, regardless of weather. After the first three months, his foals were fed a mixed diet of bran and crushed oats until they were weaned at five months. Their bran and oat mix was raised to twelve pounds a day during those two months, supplemented by alfalfa hay occasionally mixed with timothy or native grass hay until spring, when they were turned out on alfalfa fields. There the colts remained until the first frost.

With this method, thoroughbred yearlings grew to equal their Kentucky cousins and could race on equal terms as two-year-olds, with one exception. Having been raised in a higher altitude, these horses had lungs superior to their Kentucky counterparts.

Major Nick used thoroughbred mares from eastern tracks and the best of the bloodlines already in the area. One mare was a daughter of Blitzen, a stallion imported by Noll Wallop. Blitzen's sire, Robert Emmet, was the winner of thirty-four steeplechases in England. Like Goelet Gallatin, Nicholas entered into the Remount program and was issued Majority, one of the top stallions of the day.

Eva Nicholas financed the ranch. She was the major's eccentric, often bizarre wife, who was prone to fits of temper. One famous incident involved Eva throwing all her husband's racing and horse-show trophies into the pond next to their house. Another incident concerned a ranch worker who got too close to the house with a manure spreader, so far as Eva was concerned. Fresh from a bath, she stormed outside buck-naked and cursed the man to within an inch of his life.

One day after a deer hunt, Edith and Goelet Gallatin were invited into the Nicholas home for some refreshments. Edith was carrying a rifle that Major Nicholas asked to inspect. "Goelet tells me you're the best shot this side of Annie Oakley," he said. Then he got an idea. The front door of the house was an elaborate stained glass window with the figure of an elk in the middle.

"$10 if Edith can shoot the eye out of the elk from the living room. One shot, and she has to fire while sitting on the couch," Major Nick challenged.

"You're on," Goelet and his wife agreed.

Eva Nicholas, somewhat illuminated with brandy, joined in.

"Use the shotgun. I hate that ugly monstrosity of a door," she yelled.

Goelet went outside to make sure that no one rang the doorbell at the wrong time. After Edith fired, it appeared she missed the door. Major Nick ran his finger over the glass and found a hole the size of a pea was missing where the eye of the elk had been. For the next year visitors strained their eyes to find the hole in the glass until Eva, in one of her fits, threw a chair through the door.

The Circle V Polo Company built a winter facility in Aiken, South Carolina, to work the horses there. A barn with twenty-three stalls was erected next to a polo field and racetrack. In the fall, Milt McCoy, Ray May, and a crew of workers boarded trains in Sheridan with the Circle V four-year-olds to play and sell in the south. More than a thousand polo horses shipped in each year to Aiken, which was the winter polo capital of the East Coast.

The Gallatins rented a house in Aiken for the winter. The small resort town was full of other affluent New York families who foxhunted, played polo, and trained racehorses that season. For Edith and Goelet Gallatin, it was a reunion of their old friends the Hitchcocks, Milburns, Von Stades, and Posts.

Edith Gallatin was at her barn when Milt McCoy notified her that Bea had been involved in an accident. Bea had rented a horse to jump through Hitchcock woods, but each time she pointed him at a jump, he grabbed the bit and charged at a high speed despite her efforts to hold the animal back. Over one jump, the horse stumbled and flipped over, throwing Bea into a tree. After the loose horse was spotted running through the woods, riders combed the area until the girl was found unconscious. Although Bea regained consciousness in the hospital and was uninjured, her confidence was shaken. She refused to ride despite her parents' reassurances she would not have to ride that horse again.

The Hitchcocks were at the head of the horse world in Aiken. Thomas Hitchcock had been one of the best polo players in the world, and Louise Hitchcock taught children and women riding and polo and was master of the Aiken hounds. Before Bea was given a chance to protest, she was put on one of Louise Hitchcock's large jumpers. He was a beautifully trained animal, but Bea remained pensive.

"Alright, Bea, put your hands down, put your heels down and go!" Louise said. Two hours later the three returned; Bea had cleared dozens of jumps. The following winter Louise put Bea on the Aiken ladies' polo team, which defeated a team from New York.

Back in Wyoming the following summer, Bea, encouraged by the cowboys, was game for trying anything on horseback. With her friend from the Fermata school in Aiken, Josepha Hoffman, Bea hitched two pairs of horses together, and the young women attempted to Roman-ride across the ranch hayfields. With one foot on one horse and one on the other, they started slowly at a walk, then accelerated to a trot. Before long Bea and Josepha were cantering across the fields and jumping irrigation ditches, but not before they had taken a few minor spills.

In the following summer, Edith and Bea Gallatin were guests of Willis Spear at his ranch on the Crow reservation, deep within the Bighorn Mountains. Spear was one of the biggest ranchers in America, running close to three hundred thousand cattle. He was also a state legislator and local historian who had heard both Indian and cowboy myths about a strain of palomino stallions whose bloodline had passed down through the generations.

Spear invited dozens of riders to his ranch to help corner a wild stallion and his band of mares. This was partly a social gathering but mainly a chance for Spear to be rid of a stallion that had been stealing his horses, pushing his cattle out in bogs, and running through his fences. The riders spent the night at the Spear Ranch, and a dinner and dance were planned for after the roundup.

The plan was to ride out before dawn to position themselves for the trap. Close to a hundred riders hauled into the range the yellow stallion frequented. While that number seemed like a lot, in the broken, open country east of the Little Bighorn, a hundred riders were hardly sufficient to corner a stallion known for his wits.

From a high windblown flat overlooking Rotten Grass Creek, the yellow stallion watched the far-off specks of riders approach. He had smelled the riders long before he saw them. Despite the several wild bands of horses that separated his band from the riders, he decided to take his mares away to the northeast.

For Bea Gallatin the roundup was one of the most exciting experiences of her life. She was accompanied by her mother, Johnny Cover, and several of the cowboys who worked for her parents. While on top of a ridge, Johnny Cover stopped their group.

"They've got a band turned back toward us," Johnny said.

After sending members of the party galloping off to various hilltops, Cover led Edith and Bea on a long gallop to a far hill, where he stopped and looked through his binoculars. "Looks like they've got him turned; let's go," he shouted, and with that, Johnny signaled the distant riders to gallop in and tighten the trap.

After an hour Bea caught a glimpse of the wild horses. They appeared drawn and skinny, but on closer inspection she saw they were muscled. Yearlings, foals, mares, and a rangy-looking brown stallion were circling in confusion, herded by Spear Ranch cowboys. Willis Spear's daughter Elsa had her camera set up and managed to snap a picture of a few of the horses coming over a ridge.

Bea watched as a Crow rider, one of the Holds the Enemy family, rode over to Johnny. "He ain't in here; I could have told them that. A hundred riders aren't going to do it. Ol' Willis, he'll need a thousand cowboys if he wants the yellow stud."

Ten miles distant the yellow stallion let up on the mares. When he found a high spot and looked back, he saw no riders. He lifted his head to smell the air. He would remain free as his father and grandfather had before him. Though many of the stallion's bloodline had been captured and used for buffalo runners, cowponies, and army horses, no one as far back as the Crow had ever managed to capture one of the head stallions.

43

The word "dude" . . . was a friendly nickname for an easterner while he was a paying guest at a western ranch.

—Edmund Randolf

WORLD WAR I HAD CAUSED NOT ONLY A BONANZA IN horse sales in Absaraka, but also a boom in the dude ranch industry. Wealthy families turned to the American West and horseback riding for their family vacations instead of the war-torn landscape of Europe. Close to ten thousand horses were spread over ninety dude ranches in Montana and Wyoming.

For the majority of the ranches, the dude business seemed the easiest way to boost the rancher's income. Almost all ranchers needed something other than cattle to make the ranching business work. Often it took no more than putting up tents in the backyard for the summer.

Charlie Thex had bought the Bank of Ashland, but he had sold it after he became disillusioned with administrative duties. It was rumored that Charlie shot a man who had refused to make his loan payments. Another rumor circulated that Thex had purchased the bank a month after the Northern Pacific Railroad was robbed by a lone gunman. Thex laughed at the rumors, but he had to admit that having this sort of a reputation tended to minimize the number of people who did not pay their bills.

For the dudes it was a bargain; a man might put his entire family up on a cattle ranch for the summer for a fraction of the cost of what a summer on the French Riviera might cost. For between $20 and $40 a week, each member of his family could be fed hearty ranch meals, have their own cabin with maid service, and experience unlimited horseback riding over some of the most scenic areas of the world. By the summer of 1925, more than five thousand dudes were spread over thirty ranches around Sheridan alone. Entire trainloads of dudes would arrive at the Sheridan depot, where they were met by a cowboy swing band that played on the platform. When the dudes stepped off the train, they were in the middle of a square dance. The dudes would then be met by representatives from their respective ranches and whisked away to the mountains. Eaton's ranch would treat their dudes to a fifteen-mile stagecoach ride to the ranch.

Some of the easterners were heavy drinkers who were sent west by their families hoping to dry them out. It was a misguided assumption; the town of Sheridan, and pretty much all the dude ranches, had access to bootleggers, so there were some wild parties on the ranches and extended visits to Sheridan's booming speakeasies. Some of the more creative, fun-loving people from the East partied their summers away in Absaraka and returned home proclaiming to have been "cured" by the mountain air and long horseback rides in the mountains.

Most dude ranches staged rodeos each week for the visitors' entertainment. Eaton's, Teepee Ranch, Bones Brothers, and the HF Bar Ranch were loaded with "dude wranglers," such as Curley Witzel, Ewin Neely, George Gentry, and a slew of others who were competent at roping and bronc riding. Some of the top young cowboys in the country took jobs at dude ranches for a variety of reasons. First and foremost, lots of pretty women worked at the ranches. Second, dude ranchers like Bill Eaton and Frank Horton rodeoed themselves, and they let the cowboys practice on their stock. Finally, unlike most ranch jobs, which entailed digging postholes, putting up hay, and irrigating, dude wranglers spent the majority of their days in the saddle.

Nannie Alderson had moved to Eaton's ranch and become somewhat of a celebrity among the dudes because she was a genuine product of the open range, Miles City, and all the characters who had gone with it. Famed opera singer Richard Crooks became such good friends with Nannie while vacationing at Eaton's that when he performed on radio shows, he would dedicate songs to her on the air.

Two of Nannie's nephews, Allen and Irving Alderson, were working at Eaton's as dude wranglers. Their father, Lew Alderson, had come up the Texas trail with Nannie's husband, Walt. Allen and Irving and their elder brother, Floyd, grew up working as horse wranglers for the Three Circle Ranch on Tongue River.

Floyd got the nickname "Skin and Bones," or "Bones" for short, from the ranch cowboys when he was a skinny fourteen-year-old. His younger brother, Allen, was a husky youngster and thus earned the name "Big Bones." Irving, the youngest, was given the name "Little Bones." From then on, the three Alderson brothers became known as the Bones brothers.

After a few years at Eaton's, the Bones brothers returned to their cattle ranch in Birney, Montana, which they fixed up to accommodate dudes. The ranch, located on a tributary of the Tongue River called Hanging Woman Creek, became known as the Bones Brothers Ranch. The young men liked people and were known to kick their heels up with the dudes when the occasion arose.

Some of the wealthy easterners made dude ranches their summer homes, and a few even stayed all winter.

"How do you like the dude business?" a cattleman once asked Big Bones.

"Fine," he replied. "If I lose a cow, I'm out $200, but if I lose a dude, I'm only out a 17¢ telegram."

44

TRAVELING RODEOS WERE THE NEW RAGE OF THE COUNtry in the 1920s. Skills that were part of cowboy life in Absaraka were now captivating audiences the world over. Each year New York's Madison Square Garden featured fifty-six performances and Boston featured thirty. In the early days of rodeo, men in Absaraka might wrestle a steer, ride a bronc, enter a horse race, or even get in the wild horse race or the wild cow-milking just for fun. Men like Walt and Lew Alderson, George Brewster, and the Eaton brothers had pioneered the rodeo as ranchers, but it was their sons who would define rodeos as a sport.

Paddy Ryan and Curley Witzel were two former Gallatin bronc fighters who became rodeo stars. They had a toughness that had filtered down from the original cowboys who had come up the Texas cattle trail. Part of what made them great bronc riders was the horses they learned to ride on. The bloodlines that Paget, Wallop, Tom McAllister, Al Irions, and others brought into the area, combined with the strong feed indigenous to the area, produced buckers like nowhere on earth.

Paddy Ryan's family had homesteaded near Miles City, where Paddy had found work as a cowboy and soon became skilled riding broncs. He first rode in the Miles City roundup of 1916, and by 1922, he tied for the championship in the bronc riding at San Francisco.

In 1925, when Paddy won at both the Cheyenne Frontier Days and the Pendleton roundup, he was awarded the World Championship Roosevelt trophy. Rodeo, like golf, had major circuit events, the three biggest of which were Pendleton, Calgary, and Cheyenne.

The press had blown up the five-foot, six-inch 165-pound Irish cowboy into legendary status, and Ryan did not let them down. He was personable with the public and as tough and skilled as the rodeo men came. Paddy rode in a smooth, effortless manner on some of the meanest broncs known to man.

His style was set to the way rodeos were evolving at the time. Men had begun to ride broncs to a whistle instead of to a standstill. There was no set time; if it looked like the cowboy was riding his bronc, he might get a quick whistle. If it looked like he was going to buck off, judges might extend the ride to see what would happen. By 1918, bucking chutes began to appear at rodeos, although it would be a good twenty years before the old technique of roping the bronc and dragging him out to an open area would be totally replaced.

Much of Ryan's success resulted from his having befriended and partnered with Bob Askins, another world champion from the Miles City area. Though Ryan and Askins hailed from the same small community of Ismay, Montana, early on they were rivals on the circuit and did not speak. Things came to a head when, full of liquor, they passed each other in a hallway of the Queens Hotel in Miles City. They exchanged insults, and the fight was on. They destroyed a hotel room in a fistfight, in which neither could gain an advantage, and then they decided to fight a duel with pistols outside.

They staggered to the street, but each was too drunk to hit the other—or too sober to really want to shoot the other—so after firing a few wild shots, they decided to go to a bar to have another drink. From that evening on Ryan and Askins were friends for life.

On any given day they were the best in the world and could count as their friends the Prince of Wales, Teddy Roosevelt, and numerous celebrities. Despite that status as rodeo heroes, however, neither forgot where he came from, and they both knew how much their presence meant to the area and its people.

In 1918, Curley Witzel had ridden to Sheridan from Billings, where he hired on as a cowboy at the PK. From there he worked at the Gallatins and the Eatons, where he won his share of local rodeos. He was a personable man with a quick wit, and he got along great with people, which made him a natural with the dudes. Like Paddy Ryan, Curley was not a large man, but he was as tough as any man in the country. Both men embodied the friendly, wide-open personalities that cowboys were famous for at the time, but when it came to playing pranks, they took on a sinister glow.

When Paddy and Curley arrived in New York for the Madison Square Garden rodeo, Bob Askins was there to meet them. Curley was bucked off the first night, and Ryan and Askins were scheduled to ride the next night. After the show the three headed to a local speakeasy.

Across the circular bar from them sat a midget, whom they recognized as a clown act in the rodeo. The spectators would gasp as a huge bull would charge the midget until, at the last minute, he would dive and disappear into a barrel. The trick set up the crowd for the finale, in which the midget let the bull beat him to the barrel. The terrified crowd held its breath as the clown ran for the arena wall, which was too tall for him to climb as the bull charged right behind. At the last moment, the clown would disappear through a trapdoor, after which he ran back into the arena to take a bow before the applauding crowd.

With a few drinks in him, the clown's humor turned sour. "I thought Montana cowboys could ride, but I guess that one got bucked off. Har-dee-har, cowboy," he pointed at Witzel.

"Get that man a drink; he knows talent when he sees it," Paddy said and slapped Curley on the back.

"I got five bucks says the other two get bucked off tomorrow night," the midget yelled across the bar. The three cowboys smiled incredulously at one another.

"He's kind of a nasty little bastard," Curley said under his breath. The clown continued his banter.

"Maybe you boys ought to get another occupation. I hear the circus is looking for monkey handlers," he said, which got a laugh out of all three, Curley laughing the hardest.

"They'll have to get some real Texas cowboys to show you Montana boys how to ride. Har-dee-har," he said.

The next night both Askins and Ryan rode their broncs, but they finished out of the money. The cowboys had been invited to a party at the home of the Astors, who were rodeo fans, and were eager to go clean up, but to their surprise, Curley insisted on staying and watching the midget do his act.

"Let's go," Bob called to Curley.

"Yeah, Curley, let's git," Ryan called.

"Watch this," Witzel said as the midget was finishing his act, the bull right on his heels. Just as the clown hit his trapdoor, the three cowboys heard a thump and saw the midget flung eight feet into the air by the bull as outriders galloped in to attempt to save him.

"Har-dee-har, looks like his door didn't open," Witzel yelled, watching the bull grind the clown into the Garden arena. Paddy went over and saw Curley had nailed the trapdoor shut.

"Damn it, Curley," Paddy said. A couple pickup men had hazed the bull away, and a few cowboys stood over the cursing midget, who was rolling around in the arena dirt.

After Curley Witzel went to work at Eaton's ranch, he and Bill Eaton became close friends. Witzel was invaluable for Eaton as a top cowboy and a man who loved people. The problem was, Witzel lay awake at night thinking of pranks to pull on Eaton. This wasn't the best idea, as Eaton was six inches taller than Curley and outweighed him by sixty-five pounds.

Curley was shopping with some dudes in Sheridan when they stopped in Ernst's Saddle Shop. Curley went in the back to look at the saddles and noticed a new one with Bill Eaton's name on it with a cushioned seat. Curley reached into his bag of vet supplies and injected the seat with horse liniment from his bag of vet supplies.

Two weeks later Curley spied the same saddle in Eaton's barn; the cushioned seat had been cut out. When Curley inquired about it, Bill told him he had sat upon the saddle on an all-day ride and it blistered his butt so bad he had had to lie on his stomach for two days. Bill knew Witzel was behind it somehow, but he couldn't figure out how he did it.

Three weeks later, when Bill and Patty Eaton were in Denver for the stock show, the two stood in the lobby of the Shirley Savoy Hotel visiting with some other Sheridan couples. When Bill noticed Curley Witzel in the lobby, he got an idea.

"Hey, Curley, do me a favor. I left my wallet in my room; would you run up and get it for me?" Eaton asked. The moment Curley disappeared in the elevator, Bill Eaton went to a phone and called the hotel detective and said he thought there was a prowler in his room. The detective caught Curley with Eaton's wallet and brought him to Eaton.

"Bill, tell this guy who I am. He thinks I stole your wallet," Witzel said. Bill walked over to the detective, who handed him his wallet and gave Witzel a dirty look.

"That's my wallet, but I've never seen this guy before in my life," Bill said and then left for the stadium. Curley spent the night in jail until Eaton picked him up the next morning on his way back to Sheridan.

While Curley Witzel pulled pranks, Paddy Ryan started riots. On a rodeo trip to Chicago, Ryan and his buddies traveled in one railroad car, while their horses rode in another.

Ryan carried a pistol loaded with blanks as he made the tour of Chicago speakeasies. With two of his cowboy friends at a dark nightclub, Ryan fired three shots in the air as the terrified crowd dove under tables and ran for the door. Paddy ran out and hailed the police at the door.

"Hurry up, there's a gang war. I think they're still in there," he said and beat it for his hotel room with his friends.

It was at Idaho Falls that Paddy's luck went bad. He was enjoying the nightlife after the show when he ran into a bootlegger from Miles City with whom he had had a previous run-in. In a matter of minutes the fight was on. Soon the bootlegger had the thoroughly drunk Paddy down and was pounding him. Turk Greenough, a burly young bronc rider traveling with Ryan, pulled the bootlegger off, and with some help from other cowboys, he got Ryan to their hotel room and to bed.

The bootlegger had followed the cowboys to their hotel with reinforcements, and he sent word for Paddy to meet them outside. One of the cowboys woke Paddy, who ran out on the sidewalk to meet the challenge but was blindsided by the bootlegger, who wore brass knuckles. Ryan was out cold, yet the man continued to pound Ryan unmercifully. A friend of the bootleggers was covering the other cowboys with a pistol so they couldn't help their friend, who was dangerously close to being beaten to death. Howard Teigland, a champion bronc rider, ran inside and found Ryan's pistol, not knowing it was loaded only with blanks. He ran out and pointed his gun at the bootleggers; fortunately, the bluff worked and Paddy was taken off in an ambulance.

Paddy had a fractured skull and severe nerve damage to his face, and one eye was stuck open and looking off to the right. His friends had to hold his arms and legs while his face and eye were being stitched in the hospital. His head injuries were so severe that the doctor kept him in intensive care. When his friends left him to travel to Jackson Hole to the rodeo the next weekend, Paddy hailed them from his bed. "Enter me up in Jackson."

The next day it was with disbelief that Turk Greenough watched Paddy walk up to the bucking shoots in Jackson Hole. His stitched face was swollen to double its normal size, and his eye was still stuck open and looking off in the wrong direction.

Despite his friends' efforts to talk him out of it, Paddy entered the bronc riding and drew a nasty little bronc named Corkscrew. Corkscrew bucked out into the middle arena and threw Paddy off the back end. To everyone's horror, Corkscrew managed to kick Paddy square in the head on his way down. Everyone fell silent as the thud was heard across the arena. Paddy lay motionless with his face in the dirt. Greenough ran out to help, but Paddy pushed him away. The pride that made Paddy a world champion also showed the arena a display of cowboy tough.

"I can get up on my own," he yelled and struggled to his feet. Much to Greenough's chagrin, Ryan appeared to be laughing.

"My eye!" Paddy screamed.

"My damn eye is fixed!" He yelled. Turk looked over and saw it was true. His eye that was stuck off in space was now straightened.

"That was a million-dollar kick!" he yelled.

Legendary outlaws named Skyrocket, Steamboat, Flashlight, Midnight, Five Minutes to Midnight, and scores of others made their rounds through the country and flung all but a few of the most acrobatic men to the dirt. Al Irions on Powder River was producing such a line of bucking horses that people would travel to the corrals on his ranch every Sunday during the summer just to see the shows. Big and Little Bones Alderson rode broncs and also began to raise some of the best bucking horses in rodeo. Along with Bill Eaton, the Bones brothers became instrumental in promoting Sheridan's rodeos into epic events.

Rodeos were becoming a combination of western skill and eastern imagination. Some events were staged for the pure thrill of it; these ranged from Roman races and trick-riding exhibitions to the drunken race, in which contestants raced the length of the grandstand while standing on their saddle. The teepee contest featured Crow and Cheyenne women racing each other—and the three-minute world record—to pitch a teepee.

While bronc riding, roping, and some of the bizarre events like wild cow-milking captivated audiences, nothing matched the thrill of a horse race. Since the early horse fairs held by the Indian tribes in the 1700s, horse racing had been a passion for horsemen of the area.

The most popular of the races were the men's and ladies' relay races. The riders raced three horses around the half-mile track until they approached the grandstand, where they brought their horses in for a stop, yanked their saddle off, ran to the next horse, threw the saddle on, swung up, and left at a gallop. The ladies' relay was the same, with one exception: each horse was saddled in advance to eliminate the saddle switch.

From the turn of the century, the Crow had dominated the races in local fairs, riding such legendary horses as Colonel T, who was known from Billings to Sheridan. Names like Holds the Enemy, Takes the Gun, Yellowtail, Medicine Crow, Small, and Laforge became legends on local tracks. Jim Carpenter and Jim Cooper, two early Crow bronc riders, had long been two of the top rodeo men in the area. George Defender, a Lakota, won at Miles City in 1914 and competed from Calgary to Madison Square Garden. In 1915, Sampson Bird-in-Ground became the first Indian to ride a buffalo at the Miles City Roundup. By the 1920s some of the best cowboys on the professional rodeo circuit were Indians. Jackson Sundown, a Nez Percé, was one of the all-time greatest bronc riders.

Local Indian jockeys—Holds the Enemy, Medicine Crow, and Yellowtail among them—were some of the best racers in the area. Sheridan hosted the second stop of a world championship relay race series that began at the Calgary Stampede and ended with Cheyenne Frontier Days.

One of the biggest staged events of the century came after a Billings, Montana, rodeo in the early twenties. A rivalry between the cowboys south of the Yellowstone River and those to the north culminated in a matched bronc ride. A Crow bronc rider named Jim Carpenter, who had won a steer-roping contest in Sheridan twenty years earlier, was nominated by the cowboys south of the river. Carpenter was one of the old-time cowboys who could do it all. A black gelding named Midnight was chosen for him to ride. It was decided both men would have to ride their horses to a standstill. Cowboys, both Indian and white, bet their money, boots, shirts, and hats on their man.

When Carpenter mounted Midnight, the horse exploded with a high, twisting motion and then, in a flash, bucked both Carpenter and his saddle to the ground. As the cowboys from north of the Yellowstone headed for their pile of loot, it was discovered that Carpenter's latigo strap had been cut and had broken during the ride. The cowboys agreed he should have a second ride on Midnight the next day.

A huge party and dance was held that night. Carpenter's friends, some of whom had literally bet their shirt, were worried he might get too drunk, which would affect his riding the next day. The bettors decided they did not want to risk the chance of Carpenter riding poorly the next day because of drinking too much that night, so they lured him into a shed that locked from the outside and left him there throughout the night so he would be fresh for the rodeo the next day.

The next day Jim stuck the spurs to Midnight and brought home the "loot" for the cowboys south of the Yellowstone in an event that was as colorful as it was athletic for both men and horses.

While Paddy Ryan's protégé, Turk Greenough, was on the road to becoming a four-time world champion, Turk's sisters Marge and Alice were about to join a group of the toughest women in the country as rodeo stars.

Ben Greenough and his wife raised eight children on their Red Lodge, Montana, ranch. Three of their sons, Bill, Turk, and Frank, had grown to be top bronc riders; Bill, like Turk, ended up a world champion. The Greenoughs' daughters proved as ranch hands to be as good as any man in the country, breaking horses, running a pack string into the Bear Tooth Mountains, plowing, and doing general ranch work. Growing up, they rode relay races and broncs in exhibitions around the area. Starting at age fourteen, Alice had ridden a mail route from Red Lodge to Billings for three years in forty-below winters and ninety-degree summers.

When they were in their midtwenties, Alice and Marge Greenough answered an ad in *Billboard* for bronc and trick riders in Jack King's Wild West Show. King telegraphed the two girls and asked them to join him in Ohio.

Ben Greenough choked down the hurt as his girls stood in front of him to ask his blessing. "I guess that's all right. You two always had more guts than good sense anyhow. Just make sure you write your old Mom and Dad while you're gone and don't forget to take old Willy with you." It was Ben's word for willpower: something he had instilled in each of his children.

Though they sometimes achieved worldwide fame and adulation, the sport of rodeo paid its contestants enough to live little better than hobos. In the off-season these men and women had to find another source of income. Fortunately the performers were one big family and quick to help one another out; it was an unwritten law of the road that if you won, it was your duty to determine if any of the other performers needed financial help.

The girls traveled all over and became local celebrities. Young girls idolized them, and people like the Chryslers and Vanderbilts entertained the girls in their New York homes.

In an El Paso rodeo, Alice's foot hung up in the stirrup on a bucking horse. She was kicked, stepped on, and dragged across the arena. Her foot was almost twisted off, and after Alice had spent nine months in a hospital bed, the local doctors decided to amputate. Luckily, just before surgery, a German doctor heard of the rodeo star's condition and offered his expertise. Using ivory pegs, he wedged the bones in Alice's ankle back together. Not only did Alice recover, in a matter of months she was back in the rodeo, riding broncs and bulls through the aid of a special boot. Old "Willy" had pulled her through.

At Fort Worth, Alice met a Spanish promoter who hired her to ride fighting bulls in Mexico and Spain. She trick-rode and bucked bulls before they fought the matadors in the ring. The crowds loved it. Alice and Marge traveled to the south of France, England, Australia, and every state in America except three, cheered by spectators everywhere they went. Alice was also commissioned to write articles for several women's publications.

> *You don't see dull-eyed, hysterical women in the saddle. Cowgirls learn early that the wants of the soul and body are first controlled by the mind... The daily routine is both mental and physical training... She learns to take care of a horse, and as some girls learn to love dolls the small westerner learns to love an animal and thus appreciate natural beauty.*
>
> *A cow woman takes no coddling, gets no martyr complex just because she is going to have a baby. She rides in the show up until two months before she is going to have a child—and she is back in the saddle bronc-riding in contests no longer than six weeks afterward.*

The women who competed in the trick-riding competitions of the early thirties may have been the toughest female athletes ever to compete. Trick-riding was judged on speed, danger, and how few handholds the competitor had tied on her saddle. Maneuvers such as the Russian or "suicide" drag killed three cowgirls before the competitions were changed to exhibitions. At the Pendleton Roundup in 1929, bronc rider Bonnie McCarroll was killed, which caused some promoters to limit that event thereafter to men only.

45

IN 1900, SEVENTEEN-YEAR-OLD RED TATE STEPPED OFF the train in Sheridan with his life savings in his pockets. He had met Willis Spear at a St. Joseph, Missouri, horse sale and decided to follow him to Wyoming. As a boy, Red shined shoes, delivered newspapers, and worked in sale barns with one goal in mind: to become a cowboy. He had worked hard to get west, and no one was to enjoy it more.

The day Red arrived in Sheridan, he grabbed his saddle from the train landing and checked into the Sheridan Inn. Pulling on a pair of cotton gloves, he sat down at the piano in the parlor. His hat cocked back on his head, Red played and belted out *Old Mrs. Kelly with a Pimple on Her Belly* to the amusement of the patrons of the inn. For three days he played the piano, ate steaks, bought drinks, and visited with ranchers until he had spent his last dime.

Red soon landed a job as bronc rider at the Malcolm Moncreiffe Ranch during the Boer War inspections. Johnny Cover befriended Red and helped him obtain shoeing and riding jobs. Within the week he was working three jobs. Tate spent his evenings breaking Wallop horses and nights shoeing under lantern light. Eventually Red's brother, Sam, followed him from Missouri and took a job in Big Horn.

After a few months, Red left Moncreiffe for a job riding young horses at Beckton Stock Farm. Waldo and Cameron Forbes, who had settled in the area from Boston, owned the stock farm. The irrigator who worked for the Forbes brothers intimidated the younger cowboys into doing his irrigating and fencing duties for him. The man took offense that the young cowboys were getting out of irrigating and fencing duties just to ride horses. It bothered him to watch the young cowboys ride out every morning, wearing clean shirts and whistling away.

Red had been warned about the man, so when the irrigator demanded that Red clean ditches after he had finished his day of riding, Red smiled and said he would if the irrigator would slip over to Big Horn and shoe the five horses he had waiting for him there after work.

"Be careful," one of the cowboys warned. The irrigator was rumored to have beaten a young cowboy for crossing him.

When Red Tate returned to Beckton that evening from working some cows, the irrigator was waiting for him. As Red rode into the barn, the irrigator walked up behind him and hit him with his shovel. Red hit the ground with a thud.

"There, you loafing son of a bitch. You'll learn you're going to work like the rest of us," the irrigator said.

Half-unconscious, Red heard a man's voice as he rolled over on the ground and tried to regain his senses. While not very big, Red had a temper, and as he struggled to his feet, he reached over and grabbed his shoeing knife. In a crazed fit of anger, he threw himself into the irrigator with a fury. In an instant the man lay motionless on the ground.

"There yourself; I didn't hire on to irrigate, and I'll be damned if I ever work for you!" As his head cleared and anger subsided, Red looked down and noticed the man was neither moving nor breathing. The irrigator didn't seem to be cut, but on inspection he couldn't revive the man either.

Red caught up his own horse from the corral and rode the five miles to Big Horn to get Sam. With one brother driving their wagon and the other brother driving their horses, they rode east toward Devils Tower country in Hulett, Wyoming. They hired on as cowboys for the Three Vs Ranch and took up a homestead where Red shod horses and Sam made moonshine in a house they built.

While working for the Three Vs Ranch, Red served as a representative in 1905 for one of the last big roundups on Powder River. He kept a small covey of horses and sold some coach horses to Buffalo Bill Cody. Red participated in a bronc-riding exhibition that Cody witnessed, and as a result Cody offered a position in his Wild West Show, but Red declined. He had his blacksmith business and was making good money selling moonshine with his brother.

In 1857, Jeremiah Bush was in a wagon train on the Oregon Trail that was attacked by Indians. He was shot in the shoulder, his sister was scalped, and his niece was killed. The men responsible proved to be bandits posing as Indians. Jeremiah survived to mine gold in California, and his sister survived, minus her scalp. After accumulating a small fortune, Jeremiah returned to Missouri and then moved to Hulett, Wyoming, where he raised a family. His daughter Erma met Red Tate at a Fourth of July picnic at Devils Tower and was immediately enamored with the antics of the wild young cowboy.

Erma Bush was a cross between frontier competence and feminine refinement. Her parents had sent her off to Spearfish, South Dakota, to a convent for a proper education, part of which was to witness a public hanging. Despite the fact that she could harvest, plow, rope, and ride as well as her brothers, her mother insisted Erma wear a dress. Erma often followed her brothers hunting, butchering and packing the meat as penance for tagging along.

Red Tate was honest and hardworking, but he was not the kind of man you would want your daughter to fall in love with. He rode broncs, made moonshine, got drunk on occasion, and with the tribe of wild brothers who had followed him from Missouri, put on lively concerts at picnics, parties, and weddings in the area.

Despite Jeremiah's watchfulness, Erma Bush used to sneak out an upstairs window and shimmy down the porch pole to ride to the dances with Red and her brother Walter. In an effort to break up the love affair, Isabella Bush took Erma and her sister to California for a summer, where they bought a second house for the family.

After Erma Bush returned from California, she got a job teaching school in Ridge, Montana. It wasn't long before she and Red eloped to Bell Fourche,

South Dakota. After the wedding, the two returned to Hulett and lived on a homestead that Red filed on and began breaking horses. Red rode them until they quit bucking, and Erma would ride them from there.

During the winter they started a business hauling freight to Moorcroft in two wagons: Red would drive the eight-horse jerk-line team and a trail wagon, and Erma had a six-horse team and a trail wagon. They hauled everything from wool to groceries to apples. As Erma later described their life at that time, "It was rather nice when the weather was good, but we had some rather rough times when it was snowing and cold. Sometimes my feet and hands would be so cold they felt like boards. One blessing was that we had good horses and we really needed the extra income."

Red also branched out as a doctor's assistant. He kept a team ready for his friend Doctor Bostwick and would occasionally make the rounds with him. Red also made friends with the county sheriff, who would often stop at Red and Erma's after busting up a still or confiscating liquor. Red and the sheriff would usually check the "shine" to see if it was fit for human consumption. Ironically, Sam Tate's own still was in a building marked with a sign on the door warning of scarlet fever.

Before long Red and Erma Tate were raising three children, breaking horses, driving a team, and at times doctoring the neighbors.

When the Remount came around, Red was quick to sign up for the program. The army officer who inspected the Tate horses had a cane with a brass tip on the bottom of it that he used in measuring the height of the horses. On the afternoon before the inspection day, Red took the army officer to a Moorcroft bar and got the man fairly loaded on drinks. Red convinced a Chinaman who worked in the back to slip out to the parking lot, find the measuring stick, take off the brass tip, saw off the end of the cane by an inch and a half, and put the tip of the cane back into place. The next day Red mixed some of his horses in with the ones the officer had come to inspect. Because of the new length on the cane, both horses passed inspection, making Red $320 richer.

By 1925, Red and Erma's children Naomi, Jerry Belle, and Bob were performing riding stunts at the Fourth of July picnics at Devils Tower. Red and his brothers performed and sang. Later that summer, Red was outside a saloon in Moorcroft, Wyoming, when the bartender hailed him from inside. "Hey, Red, there's a guy from Sheridan in here drinking. I'll introduce you."

Red stuck his head in the door and was shocked to see the irrigator he thought he had killed almost twenty years before. "That's okay, I already know him," Red told the bartender. Realizing he was cleared of manslaughter, Red decided to move back where he could sell polo horses and work teams.

With family in tow, Red drove to the 1925 Sheridan Fair and race meet, where his brother Albert was racing his horse Tom Aimes in the Sheridan Derby. The horse had won the half-mile race the day before on a muddy track, but the Sheridan Derby was a mile race against two of the top racers in the Northwest. Grover Gilbert from Montana brought a string of fifteen racehorses to the fair, and Thomas La Forge, a Crow Indian who had won races all over the state, also brought a string.

The Indians of Absaraka, although impoverished, never let their standing hinder their love of a good horse. In one trade during this time, John Stands In Timber, a Cheyenne, traded a top racehorse to some Crow at Lodge Grass, Montana, for a team of horses, a harness, and a practically new wagon.

At the fair, Erma Tate sat in the grandstand with her two daughters and Bernice Carrels while Red made the rounds and caught up with old friends. Bernice's husband, Jack, had owned the Mint Bar in Sheridan, but after Prohibition forced the bars to close, he had opened up two bootleg speakeasies.

Erma pointed out a woman jockey to her daughters. "Look, there's Danny Gilbert." The diminutive wife of Grover Gilbert was scheduled to ride against the men in the derby.

Big Bill Eaton swung a rope off to the side with the other ropers, and the Bones brothers were riding back and forth organizing the arena. The newly appointed racing association board of Noll Wallop, Harold Hilman, Goelet Gallatin, Bill Eaton, Malcolm Moncreiffe, Bob Walsh, Ridgely Nicholas, Bradford Brinton, and Milt McCoy oversaw the racing portion of the fair.

The fair showcased the unpredictable excitement that the cowboys of Absaraka were famous for. Curley Witzel was shot skyward by the Bones brothers' bucking horse W. O. Gray. Another of the brothers' buckers, Duck Soup, tossed H. D. Staley at the entrance of the bucking chutes and then proceeded to knock some railbirds off the arena fence.

Burton Brewster, the son of Tongue River pioneer rancher George Brewster, won the bronc-riding contest. In a trick-roping exhibit, Bill Eaton threw a huge loop over seven men on horses galloping in front of the grandstand.

Curley Witzel and George Gentry won the wild cow-milking, an event during which one contestant caught fire. A cow's horn had hooked his shirt pocket, which was full of matches.

During the roping, a dog kept running into the arena and harassing the ropers until Big Bones Alderson rode out and fired the starter's pistol at the yapping intruder, who tucked tail and left, to the cheers of the crowd.

Red Tate's eight-year-old son Bob was into everything: talking to contestants, walking through the barns, investigating the Indian village, and scurrying under the grandstands. Young Tate never met a stranger and talked constantly to anyone. For his age, he was keenly perceptive and had a passion for horses. Being the youngest and only son, he had become a strong rider just trying to keep up with his two sisters, twelve-year-old Jerry Belle and fourteen-year-old Naomi.

Just before the Sheridan Derby, Bob Tate finagled his way to the rail in front of the grandstand, where eight thousand spectators were packed in to watch. Red's old friend Johnny Cover rode out with Little Bones Alderson to align the racers for the start of the race.

When the gun fired, White Lightning jumped into the lead, with La Forge challenging. On their first trip by the grandstand, Albert Tate's horse, Tom Aimes, moved into second place with La Forge and Danny Gilbert pressing. On the final stretch, Tom Aimes's jockey, Jimmy D. Bray, went to the whip and swept past Grover Gilbert's horse for the win in front of the cheering fans.

"We won! We won!" Bob Tate pushed through the crowd and ran alongside Tom Aimes as he was led to the winner's circle, where a horseshoe of flowers was placed around the winner's neck.

After the 1925 Sheridan rodeo, a young Crow girl took Edith Galletin by the hand and led her from the grandstands to the Indian camp set up next to the racetrack. In an informal ceremony the Crow presented Edith with a pair of antelope skin moccasins decorated with elaborate beadwork.

This display of honor was a result of Edith's own reaching out with love and hospitality to the Crow, Cheyenne, and Lakota. On her ranch and at the local rodeos, she always welcomed the Indians back into a community from which they had been ostracized. In a town named after the general who once said, "The only good Indian is a dead Indian," she took a personal role in preserving and showcasing their native culture.

When she had first traveled to the reservation fifteen years prior, Edith saw how the children were living, and in her typical fashion, went to the agency and asked how she could help. She then anonymously donated food, money, and books. In her role as state chairman of the public welfare committee of the Wyoming State Federation of Women's Clubs, Edith Gallatin dedicated her activity to the care of crippled children and Indian welfare. For her efforts she was the only white woman who could claim to have been made a member of the Crow, Cheyenne, and Sioux tribes.

Each year she invited chiefs of the tribes to her ranch as guests. Having hired an interpreter and a court reporter, Edith made sure to record some of their fast-fading history. It was on one of these trips that the Crow discovered that the Gallatins were in possession of their sacred medicine pipe that they had lost in a raid to the Cheyenne years before. Goelet Gallatin had bought the pipe from a member of the Cheyenne tribe, along with a number of other artifacts. There was much consternation among the Crow elders when they saw the pipe. The Gallatins offered to return it, but after much deliberation, the chiefs decided the family should keep it, since the tribe had lost it once and could lose it again. However, the elders believed Edith Gallatin should be educated in the pipe's power, and in an elaborate three-day ceremony, she was made a medicine woman of the Crow tribe.

After the rodeo, Red Tate drove his family into the city park on Big Goose Creek, where he stopped to repack the car before the trip back to Hulett. A group of Indians were standing next to a wagon while a few loose saddle horses grazed nearby. Erma walked over with Naomi and Jerry Belle to listen to an old Crow who was speaking in his native tongue while a young Crow was interpreting for the crowd gathered around them. The old man was a survivor of the Battle of the Rosebud, and he had fought next to General Crook against Crazy Horse forty-nine years earlier.

"The Crow warriors were painted for war, dressed in their best war clothes to help the soldiers fight the Sioux," the interpreter explained as the old man motioned across the flats where Sheridan's Main Street ran.

"We galloped down here, in front of the soldiers who sat on their horses grouped together by color. Bays here, sorrels there, and black horses over there. We were given a great feast and danced all night. The Shoshone came too. With the Shoshone and our Crow warriors fighting next to the soldiers, we thought we could whip all the Sioux on earth.

"The next day the walking soldiers were put on mules that were not used to being ridden. The soldiers that tried to ride them could not ride much either. There was bucking everywhere. One soldier, I remember, was holding on to the mule's neck, and they ran right over there." The old Indian pointed to a spot up Big Goose.

"The mule turned quick, and that soldier went flying and landed in the water." The old Crow's wrinkled bronze face lit up in a smile. He laughed and began to cough, losing his breath. The old warrior paused and gasped out something.

"Too much smoking," the interpreter said to the assembled crowd as the old man continued.

"The next day we were off to fight the Sioux with General Crook. The Sioux scouts were all around us as we rode north and camped. The day after, we had a great battle. I charged in with a soldier chief when the Sioux attacked."

The old man had been talking louder, and now he began to sing. The interpreter remained silent, letting the old man sing his war song.

"I suppose that man has seen a lot," Red said as he and young Bob walked over and joined Erma and the girls.

"I wonder what they think of cars," Jerry Belle asked, looking at the Crow's wagon and horses. Suddenly, she noticed her brother was over leading one of the Crow's horses around. The horse still had on war paint and a feather braided in its forelock and tail from the fair.

"Bob!" she yelled at her brother.

"I ain't stealing it. I'm just looking at it," he said.

Young Bob Tate had not been this close to an Indian horse before. It looked the same as his father's horses, only it was painted and extremely quiet. Jerry Belle took the Crow horse from her brother, and the two began to argue before a hard look from Erma and a motion from Red let them know it was time to get back to Hulett.

It was evident to the Tate family after their visit to the fair that Sheridan was the place for them. Johnny Cover had convinced Red he could succeed in raising polo horses there. The deciding factor for Erma was the construction of a new high school in the town. In November the Tates loaded their belongings into two wagons and two cars and headed for Sheridan. Young Bob Tate took the reins of the four-horse team that pulled the wagon. Red drove another team while Jerry Belle and Erma drove the family's two cars. Naomi rode along with the hired man, herding thirty loose horses along the road.

It was a cold, miserable two-week trip. Because of the mud, the cars had to be abandoned on the road until it dried out. When they finally arrived in Sheridan, Red rented a barn on Works Street with a stable in back and rented a pasture on Prairie Dog Creek for the rest of his horses.

Red began trading horses out of his barn and took a side job shoeing horses at the HF Bar Dude Ranch. To train these horses for sale, Red would give his three children mallets, and the four of them would ride up the hill from their house to a small polo field belonging to Bob Walsh above the park. On weekends, Naomi, Jerry Belle, and Bob would ride and lead the horses twelve miles to Big Horn, where Red played polo on Malcolm Moncreiffe's field.

In addition to shoeing and selling horses, Red Tate resumed operations as a bootlegger in Sheridan. Red soon became partners with Jack Carrels, a heavyset, jovial man who was quick to loan money to any cowboys down on their luck or back them in the cattle or horse business. He also ran gambling and a had a unique roulette wheel: he would spin a box in which he'd placed a mouse, and the patrons would bet which numbered hole the rodent would crawl out of.

Liquor was smuggled in from Canada and the stills outside town. Burlap bags, full of flat bottles from Canada and round bottles with local moonshine, were put in hayracks in Red's barn—the designated drop-off point for the smuggled liquor. The trick was to get the liquor from Red's barn to the speakeasies in Sheridan undetected as federal agents patrolled Sheridan, watching for suspicious establishments. Red and Jack knew the law wouldn't do much to a kid who got caught, so they decided to use their kids to deliver the liquor.

Jerry Belle Tate and Marge Carrels, both teenagers, delivered bottles to stores in Sheridan by hiding the contraband in baby carriages. For the larger deliveries, Bob drove his pony cart.

Bob Tate had taken to horses like ducks to water. Being the youngest and the only boy, he was spoiled by his parents. When he had first shown an interest in riding, Red Tate immediately swapped two saddle horses for forty-eight mainly unbroken ponies for Bob to herd—even though his sisters were both accomplished horsewomen.

Red also bought Bob a small four-horse buggy and a two-horse sleigh and proceeded to break some of the ponies to drive as teams. He would send Bob around town with his buggy and team, giving kids rides. Soon all the other kids were pining for a pony like the Tate boy had. Red contacted the mothers, letting them know he might just have another pony available for sale.

On delivery days, Red hid the burlap bags full of liquor bottles in the floorboard of Bob's pony cart. Bob drove boldly down the street, waving to people as he made deliveries to a speakeasy behind the Elks Club. The speakeasy owners got a kick out of the brash cowboy and sometimes paid him as much as a dollar a delivery. For a nine-year-old, Bob Tate was developing a keen eye for business and dealing with people. He was let into the speakeasies for no other reason than he was usually sent in to get Red.

Federal agents had raided the Elks Club twice during the previous year. During the first raid, all the liquor had been poured down the drain before the agents' arrival, but they unscrewed the curved pipe underneath the sink and found enough liquor to get Jack Carrels arrested. The next raid was foiled by the bartenders, who placed two large vats of creosote on either side of the bar. At the first sign of trouble, the liquor was dumped in with the creosote, which made the hooch impossible to detect.

46

BY THE MID-1920s THE EASTERN FACE OF THE BIGHORN Mountains was filling up with Ivy League horsemen. At dude ranches like Eaton's, HF Bar, Teepee, Spear O', and TAT, easterners were riding over the Bighorns across the rivers, and over grasslands with wide horizons and broad vistas. Many families were buying their own ranches for a summer home. John Morgan, an Amherst College graduate from Cleveland, met his future wife, Mary, at Eaton's ranch, and soon after they were married and bought the PK Ranch in Beckton. The Rudolphs, also from Cleveland, built a home outside Big Horn.

In Big Horn, Bradford Brinton, a Harvard graduate and farm implement dealer from Chicago, had bought the William Moncreiffe Ranch. Brinton kept a stable of racehorses both in New Orleans and in Chicago. He took long rides around his Wyoming ranch and bought the stagecoach that was parked in front of the Sheridan Inn to drive at rodeos and other functions. William Moncreiffe moved to France with his wife, but before he left, in his typical generous fashion, he gave land to several of his employees.

Edward S. Moore, a Yale man who was one of the top racehorse men in the country, bought land in Big Horn. The son of a railroad magnate, Moore had horses running in New York, Kentucky, and California. He bought the Sheridan newspaper and the majority of the shares in the First National Bank from Malcolm Moncreiffe.

Another Harvard man, Alan Fordyce, whose father had bought Teepee Lodge from Mike Evans, was playing polo in the area. Young Oliver Wallop was attending Yale and was poised to take over his father's ranch.

The one thing the Ivy League ranchers had in common with the cowboys, Indian jockeys, and horse traders of the area was a knowledge of and appreciation for good horses. The mutual respect for horses and a fun-loving spirit were basis enough for many lifelong friendships. The wealthy ranchers stood elbow to elbow with illiterate cowboys who had scratched out a living, trading, raising, or riding horses.

Figuratively riding "Lord" over the entire group was Noll Wallop, who had been one of the largest and most innovative original horse ranchers up on Otter Creek, Montana. He had weathered the frontier but at the same time was educated and extremely good-natured. In the middle were savvy dude ranchers like Bill Eaton and Frank Horton. Horton became a U.S. senator, and Willis Spear, who owned a dude ranch deep in the Bighorn Mountains, became a state legislator.

Polo was now in its thirtieth year in the community, and Malcolm Moncreiffe was still playing with a mix of old-timers and newcomers. A group of three teams played for the benefit of the Sheridan pool. Each team had at least one player who came to the area as a dude and bought a ranch. The first team consisted of Fred Skinner, a merchant; Johnny Cover, a cow foreman; Malcolm Moncreiffe, a Scottish nobleman; and Tip Wilson, an Ivy League rancher.

The second team was made up of Red Tate, a horse trader; Harold Hilman, an early settler and dude rancher; Milt McCoy, a horse rancher; and Alan Fordyce, a Harvard graduate whose father owned a dude ranch.

The third team consisted of Bill Leech, an owner of a Story dude ranch; Oliver Wallop; Ray May, a cowboy; and Bob Walsh, now a bank president. His past sometimes caught up with him during his tenure as bank president, however, as when one of his ex-wives from Miles City appeared in the First National Bank with a loaded gun. Hell has no fury like a woman scorned, and a chase ensued, with Walsh exiting out the back door of the bank, circling back on Main Street, and reentering the bank. He finally locked himself in an office until the storm passed.

With local know-how, imported finances, and enough color to shame a rainbow, some of the great equestrian events of their day were about to be staged.

47

That bear-faced statement the fraternity of the horse world will mingle in convention. There will be nervous thoroughbreds, trim polo ponies, stolid mares with shy colts by their sides, prancing hunters and jumpers, shifty cowponies, spotted pintos, lank Indian horses, raring stallions, and red-eyed outlaws that do not know how to act when out in public society.

—*Sheridan Post Enterprise,* August 22, 1926

THE GREATEST HORSE FESTIVAL EVER THROWN IN THE history of horse shows was about to take place on the Gallatins' ranch. With the area filling up with a variety of horsemen, it was only a matter of time before eastern imagination caught up with western know-how to create an all-inclusive festival of the horse. With their generosity and integrity and the emphasis they put on having fun with horses, it seem to make sense that the Gallatins would plan the festival and make it happen. With the Gallatins' generosity and integrity, the emphasis was put on having fun with your horses while inviting the best of the best to participate.

After Bea Gallatin finished school in 1925, she made her debut in New York and then was escorted with her parents on a world cruise. On the trip, Goelet and Edith Gallatin planned an all-inclusive two-day celebration of the horse at the Circle V. Goelet wanted an event to showcase and promote the Remount along with polo; Edith, with her vivacious energy, wanted to include the Indians, cowboys, children, and dudes. In the end the couple compromised, planning an event for the spring of 1926 that included jumping, polo, equitation, roping, a series of fifteen flat races, a rodeo, and a steeplechase.

While the Gallatins were away on their cruise, their neighbor Ridgley Nicholas laid out the plans to build a five-eighths-of-a-mile racetrack, complete with rails, a judge's tower, and a grandstand on the Gallatins' hayfield. Johnny Cover contracted Red Tate, who already had the Gallatins' shoeing account, to level the track using teams of horses and a skid. Red hauled in sand and leveled the track with footing as good as any in the East.

The top horsemen from each discipline were called on to coordinate the event: Bill Eaton and the Aldersons planned the rodeo; Major Harry Leonard and Bob Walsh planned the horse show; Milt McCoy and Malcolm Moncreiffe planned the polo matches; Ridgley Nicholas planned the racing events; and Billy Mann, from the old Miles City days, planned the steeplechase. Edith Gallatin was in charge of communicating with the Cheyenne and Crow tribes, who were scheduled both to race and, in the evening, to dance. The elder chiefs, including survivors of the Little Bighorn battle, were scheduled to run in the war bonnet race. Cheyenne and Crow horsemen would bring their own racehorses. Horsemen from Fort Mckenzie were coming too, as were the Otter Creek gang of Charlie Thex, Luther Dunning, and the Brewsters. The old British horse breeders, Noll Wallop, Bob Walsh, and James H. Price, were also there.

It was a celebration of the horse in all its many forms. It was no more in the planning stages than local newspapers and national sports publications picked up on the buzz.

Track Being Put in Shape for Races to Be Held in August
Mounts are working out for Big Horn Show
Indians Taking Part in Racing Meet

Ridgely Nicholas, secretary of the Big Horn Racing Association, announced that many entries had been received by the Indians off the Crow reservation. Mortimer Plenty Hawks and Francis La Forge will be among the riders.

Troop B, 15th Wyoming Cavalry, will camp near the racetrack during the two days of the meet. The enlisted men will give a mounted drill and also participate in a military race.

Big Horn Racing Association, Big Horn, Wyoming
Will Hold a Two-Day Race Meet and Horse Show
August 27th and 28th, 1926
At the 5/8-mile track on the Gallatin Ranch near Big Horn

Horse Show Events

Class 1: Broodmares with foal at side. Best type to produce Cavalry remounts $40

Class 2: Yearlings by U.S. government stallion. Best type for Cavalry remount $40

Class 3: Two-and three-year-olds by U.S. government stallions $50

Class 4: Geldings and mares any age by any sire, 15 to 16 hands, to be ridden and judged for confirmation, manners, and performance at walk, trot, and canter $50

Class 5: Polo ponies to be ridden and judged for manners, handiness, and confirmation $50

Class 6: Jumpers to be ridden on each afternoon over eight jumps (brush and post and rail), not higher than three feet, six inches $50

Races First Day

1. *3/8-mile open, minimum weight 135 lb $100*
2. *The Remount Special ½ mile, for three-year-olds sired by U.S. government stallions, minimum weight 120 lb $300*
3. *The Clouds Peak 5/8 mile. Open. $200*
4. *¼ mile for saddle horses; thoroughbreds not eligible $50*
5. *The Little Goose 1/8 mile for ponies 13 hands and under, to be ridden by children not 12 years of age $25*
6. *The Big Goose 1/8 mile for ponies over 13 hands but not exceeding 14.2, to be ridden by children not over 14 years of age $25*
7. *¼ mile for dudes. Horses must be the property of a dude or belong to a dude ranch $25*
8. *5/8-mile relay race. Three horses $150*

There was no entry fee, and the Gallatins donated all the purse money for the classes. The event was staged the week before the Sheridan County Fair so that the racers might get two weeks of racing in on their horses without having to travel. The five-eighths-of-a-mile racetrack lay on the edge of the hayfield, and the judge's tower rose from the infield. A jumping course was also set up on the infield of the track, and a steeplechase course surrounded the track. The polo field was not a quarter-mile off. Grooms, jockeys, spectators, horses, and children all mixed together on the flat near the Gallatins' racetrack. The Crow tribespeople pitched twenty teepees along the banks of Little Goose and performed dances nightly for the spectators.

The horse show took place in the morning, followed in the afternoon by the polo games, bronc riding, calf roping, and the races. In addition to the more serious horse races were contests like the keg races, in which mounted cowboys roped a beer keg to see who could drag it the farthest.

The *Sheridan Post* plastered news of the Gallatin meet across the front page: "Fast Horses Thrill Big Horn Crowd."

In this area that prided itself on its horses, the event took top billing over the following headline at the bottom of the page.

AMERICAN TROOPS ARE LANDED NEAR THREATENED TOWN

FINEST PONIES IN THE WORLD HERE, SAYS LEONARD

Fame of Ranches Is Spreading Through Country
A vision of the Bighorn ranch region as the center of the Remount horse industry of the United States was painted by Major Harry Leonard, noted horseman of Colorado Springs, in commenting upon the first annual race meet and horse show of the Big Horn Racing Association Saturday.

"The polo ponies of the McCoy-Gallatin stables are the best in the nation," he declared.

A foothill racetrack banked by the sharp peaks of the Bighorns became the "Saratoga of the west" Saturday.

The track was lined with cars with license plates from twenty-eight states. By the end of the two days, better than five thousand spectators would be guests of the Gallatins and the Circle V and E4 ranches.

Eight-year-old Wilson Moreland, leading three polo ponies toward the Gallatin racetrack, was lost in the throng of people and horses that moved in all directions at once. The boy had ridden the twelve miles from Sheridan, leading Bob Walsh's polo horses. Wilson tied the horses up in some trees and walked into the crowd, looking for his brother John or someone who could tell him where the polo field was. After wandering through the crowd of several thousand people, looking through their legs, the boy regretted getting off his horse. There were soldiers in uniform, Indians, cowboys, and horses being led and ridden.

As if being lost in the crowd were not enough, Wilson got yelled at by an attendant. "Hey, boy, keep away from that food, that ain't for you!" he yelled. Wilson froze where he stood and looked back at the man.

"I wasn't looking for food, I'm looking for the polo field," he stammered, but before he could finish, Edith Gallatin appeared in a flowing dress and large-brimmed hat.

"Ray, this is my friend Mr. Moreland. Could you make sure he and his friends get some lunch? The main reason this race meet is taking place is for the children," she said pleasantly. Young Wilson was dumbfounded. He had never met Mrs. Gallatin, nor the man, whose demeanor improved considerably once she got there. Wilson was surprised Mrs. Gallatin knew who he was. He had seen her once in town talking to his father about horses.

"Will you be racing today, Mr. Moreland?" Edith asked. Wilson pulled his hat off as he spoke to the lady.

"No, ma'am, my brother John is in the pony race. I was just trying to get to where Bob Walsh's horses are supposed to go. We got them tied in those trees back there."

"The polo field is beside the track," she replied, "and please tell all the grooms that we are expecting them for lunch after polo. They can come right to that table over there," she said, pointing to the refreshments area.

"Thank you, ma'am," Wilson said, making his way through the crowd.

"And Wilson, we're glad you came. Please wish your brother luck for me," Edith called after him.

Later in the day Little Bones Alderson rode over to Bob Tate while some Crow were parading through the arena. "See that old Indian, Bob?" Little Bones said, pointing the chief out. "That's White Man Runs Him. He was with Custer at the Little Bighorn." Little Bones reached in his pocket and produced a nickel and handed it to the boy. "That's him on the nickel," he said, giving the boy the coin.

Bob rode over and looked at the Crow chief and then back at the nickel. The chief was going to compete in the eighth-mile war bonnet race.

At the 50th anniversary of the Custer battle, the seventh cavalry was sent up from Texas for the occasion. Luther got to looking through the horses, and he spotted several that he had sold to Uncle Sam. Luther was quite a roper and used to enter the steer roping in Sheridan. Steer roping was a good one-man event then, and a cowboy had to have a good horse and know how to handle a rope.
—H. J. McCullough

Luther Dunning, now fifty, was already somewhat of a celebrity among horsemen, even in military circles. From the Cheyenne and the Otter Creek ranchers to the rodeo crowd around Sheridan and Miles City, he was considered in the upper echelon of a fraternity of horsemen both red and white. It was at the Gallatins' race meet, however, that he showed what he was truly capable of as a rider.

The atmosphere between cavalrymen and cowboys being what it was, everyone took great interest when Luther Dunning entered the stake race against Colonel Milt McCoy.

Colonel Milt McCoy was one of the better polo players in the United States and had already won the polo pony classes at the Gallatin meet and the county fair. Backed with the Gallatins' money and the stable they had built in South Carolina, he enjoyed an elevated status among the polo elite.

Luther Dunning had never played polo, nor had he ridden in a polo pony class, but he could ride a course like that in his sleep. Since the days when Sir Sydney Paget had tutored him thirty-five years earlier, he had put thousands of thoroughbred horses through their paces.

The race called for a series of maneuvers that tested the quickness and temperament of the horse and rider. The rider would first gallop a horse to a point and then stop him, pivot, and leave in another direction.

Noll Wallop, Charlie Thex, Bill Eaton, the Bones brothers, Burton Brewster, Buster Brown, and a slew of others lined the horse show area to watch. Some of the Cheyenne who were Dunning's neighbors were already at the rail. After McCoy finished on two horses and a couple of other riders finished their rounds, it was Dunning's turn.

"Let's go watch Luther ride," Johnny Cover said to Bea Gallatin, who was warming up one of her show horses. Bob Tate rode over to Cover on a pony. "I just betcha Luther beats him, alright, army or no army."

As Luther rode in on a bay gelding, the crowd got quiet, and even young Bob Tate stopped talking.

"I think Milt might get his feelings hurt," Edith Gallatin said to her husband, watching Luther Dunning enter the infield of the racetrack.

Luther rode out on the superbly trained thoroughbred, which slid to a stop, rolled back on his hocks, and stood perfectly still, ears pricked toward the judge after a flawless performance. An uncharacteristically loud cheer rose from the spectators. There were plenty of top horsemen present, but Luther Dunning was already a legend.

Major Harry Leonard, who was judging the contest, chuckled. He realized he had just witnessed the best rider he had ever seen, never mind the performance. Though Milt McCoy was a colonel and manager of the Circle V, Leonard was no man's patsy. He had lost an arm in the Great War, and despite the injury, he always saddled his own horse and mounted by himself. Leonard walked out and pinned Dunning first in the class, and Colonel McCoy rode over and shook Luther's hand.

"Bravo, Mr. Dunning." Edith Gallatin congratulated Luther. As she ran a hand down the bay gelding's neck, she asked, "Would you ever part with such a wonderful animal?"

"Yes, ma'am, he's for sale," Luther said, and with that, Edith Gallatin made arrangements to purchase the horse. McCoy rode over to Edith Gallatin to protest.

"I don't think we need to be buying more horses, Edith. We don't have enough riders as it is, and we may be running short on grass."

Johnny Cover, seeing what was transpiring, rode over to throw some gas on the fire. "If you don't buy that horse, Mrs. Gallatin, I will. I could use another horse to ride the cattle on, and I suspect he'd be a good polo pony, too," Cover said.

"Luther, please come to the party tonight at Brinton's. We have room for you and Leota in the cottage down on Trabing Creek."

"We've got our horses back in Sheridan, so we'll have to tend to them," Luther said.

"Well, come back when you're through and bring your son."

"We'll try, Mrs. Gallatin," he replied and thanked her.

"Luther, I've known you for too long; please call me Edith," she said. "We'll come by to look at your horses in the morning if that's okay by you. And please make sure your people get something to eat," she said, motioning to the large buffet that was attended by servers.

Edith excused herself just in time to see her daughter win first place in an equestrian class on Watch Charm. Earlier that morning Bea had won an equitation class on Lucy Glitters.

Oliver Wallop took third place in the jumping contest and had won the saddle race the day before on one of his uncle Malcolm Moncreiffe's horses. He was now a member of the Yale polo team.

As young Wallop left the ring, Luther Dunning rode over and stopped the young man. Luther saw in the youngest Wallop son an indifference toward his father. Luther had seen the boy roll his eyes at his father earlier that day and ride off when old Noll was speaking to him. It was obvious that Oliver was somewhat embarrassed by his father's stutter and his tendency to babble on at times about subjects that had no rhyme or reason. Luther doubted that anyone had ever taken the time to tell Oliver what kind of man Noll had been when he first came to the country.

"That's a nice horse your uncle gave you to race yesterday," Luther said casually.

"Thank you, Mr. Dunning. You sure showed Colonel McCoy up. That's a nice horse you have," Oliver said.

"He's a grandson of Columbus, a stallion that your father brought over from England."

"My father's not much of a rider," Oliver said, causing Luther to shake his head.

"Your father can look at a horse and tell more about him than anyone I ever met. He taught me more about horses as anyone. He's also about one of the toughest men I know." Luther paused. His statements had taken Oliver by surprise. The younger Wallop assumed that everyone looked at his father as some kind of bumbling eccentric. No one had ever spoken to him this way about his father before.

"I've seen your father flat-broke, and I've seen him when he had lots of money," Luther continued, "and it never changed the way he did business. Your father's an honest man, and he's helped a lot of people in his time. There's no man more respected on Otter Creek than your father."

"You sure showed Colonel McCoy," Oliver repeated.

Luther smiled and picked up the reins on the bay. "I suppose Johnny Cover would have done the same."

"Johnny's a better polo player, too." Luther winked and loped his horse off.

That night, Bradford Brinton threw an extravagant barn party for the contestants after the Gallatins' race meet. The barn party was a rollicking affair of dancing and music. Charlie Thex pulled out his fiddle, and together with Otter Creek rancher Kidd Anderson on banjo, he played "Leather Britches Full of Stitches." Red Tate, fueled with the liquor he'd brought in from town, sat at the piano and began to belt out tunes from "That's My Baby" to "The Yellow Rose of Texas."

On the second day of the Gallatins' race meet, Jerry Belle and Bob Tate entered the races. Bob won the pony race, but Jerry Belle, who had been breezing some racehorses for Major Ridgley Nicholas, was given the opportunity of a lifetime: he asked her to ride Cabin Maid in the featured Cloud Peak Open. Having been broken by professional trainers in Mexico, Cabin Maid, the mare, was teaching Jerry Belle, the horsewoman. This would be the younger Tate daughter's first big race against the best jockeys and horses in the country.

The Cloud Peak Open entailed circling twice around the five-eighths-of-a-mile track. Grover Gilbert's White Lightning was the odds-on favorite and had so far been the best miler in the country.

Major Nicholas offered his young jockey some last-minute advice before the start of the game. "You've got the best horse, remember that. Don't worry about the crowd. Stay with Gilbert's horse and then make your move on the back side of the last lap."

Just before the race began, clouds settled over Little Goose Canyon and rain began to pound the track. Red Tate, riding his saddle horse, led Cabin Maid and Jerry Belle past the line of bettors lined up at the rail. His horse was decked out with a silver concho breastplate and bridle. He wore a small brimmed hat with a tie, as most of the cowboys did at the function. "You're as good a jockey as they are, Jerry Belle. They've just run more races," Red told her.

Danny Gilbert, riding White Lightning, came up alongside Jerry and Red. "Good luck, Jerry Belle," she said, smiling. Danny Gilbert was a hero to her; she had raced in Seattle, Calgary, and all over the West as a professional jockey.

Jerry Belle tried a small smile, but she was so nervous she could barely feel Cabin Maid underneath her. Soon the lead ropes were unsnapped from the lead ponies and the jockeys were instructed to follow Johnny Cover, who led the racers to the back side of the track on a large thoroughbred gelding.

"Try to relax and don't forget to breathe during the race," Cover instructed and gave Jerry Belle a wink. He could see the sixteen-year-old girl was tight as a drum.

Cover rode in front of the nervous racers and reined his horse over to the side.

"Everybody about ready?" he asked, raising his red flag and looking over to the judge's tower across the track. When the judge waved a flag back, the cowboy yelled, "Go!" and the pack was off.

In the infield, young Bob Tate galloped his pony, Duke, alongside the track as the racers passed the grandstand. White Lightning was in the lead, but Cabin Maid was right on her hip. On the back stretch, both horsewomen let their horses out. For a full quarter-mile around the final turn, they were neck and neck as five thousand voices ascended with the approach of the field.

Jerry Belle could feel Cabin Maid stretch out under her. She hung on and let the mare run. Around the last turn White Lightning and Cabin Maid ran for home side by side. At the wire it was Cabin Maid by a nose. The rest of the pack finished three lengths back.

"She won! Jerry Belle won! That's my sister!" Bob Tate shouted over and over again. Red galloped alongside Cabin Maid and finally picked her up on the far side of the track, clipping his lead rope onto the mare's bit.

"Oh, my God, what a horse!" Jerry Belle yelled between gasps of breath.

"Thank you," she tried to blurt out to Major Nicholas, who trotted out and congratulated his jockey. Jerry Belle was presented with a bouquet of flowers and a silver trophy. The upset victory made front-page news in Sheridan: "Cabin Maid Captures Feature from White Lightning Here" (*Sheridan Post*, 1927).

Ray May, a Gallatin cowboy, walked over to Edith Gallatin just before the race.

"It's a big day for Bea," he said.

"She's entered, but she hasn't a chance. She's riding against professional jockeys," Edith said.

"She might surprise you; she's got a lot of her mother in her, Mrs. Gallatin," the cowboy said.

For over a month Bea had been up every morning at the crack of dawn galloping Let's Go, a ranch horse she was training for the half-mile ladies' race. Only four women had entered the race, including Jerry Belle Tate and Danny Gilbert. Johnny Cover coached Bea much as he did Jerry Belle in the previous race. "Stay with the leaders until you reach the end of the back stretch, then let her run for home. It's a sprint, so don't be afraid to open her up when the time comes."

> *Miss Beatrice Gallatin Rides Neck and Neck with "Pros" Before Huge Crowd at Big Horn Track*

Although she was opposed by two professional jockeys, Miss Beatrice Gallatin, daughter of Mr. and Mrs. Goelet Gallatin, rode Let's Go, one of her jumping horses, to a very close second in the half-mile ladies' race.

Ray May, a cowboy on the E4 Ranch, saw the disappointment on Bea's face after she had lost by just an inch. After Bea hot-walked Let's Go, she passed him and another man who had just walked up.

"Well, I suppose she's got it made. I wish my parents owned all this."

"Don't fool yourself; she worked hard for that," Ray said. "Watch this," he said to the man. "Hey, Bea, I bet you $5 you can't ride that horse around the steeplechase course with no bridle," he challenged.

Bea mounted Let's Go, now cool and dry, and walked over to the men. She reached forward and pulled the bridle off, handing it to Ray. Using her hands to guide Let's Go, she galloped around the track taking each jump until she was back in front of Ray, who handed the bridle back to her.

"I'll be darned, that girl can ride," the man next to Ray said and smiled.

48

THE GALLATINS' RACE MEET HAD BENEFITED A VARIETY of people on several fronts. After the event, the Cheyenne and Crow chiefs were welcomed into the community they had formerly been ostracized from. Edith Gallatin had made the entire community feel welcome, and she was especially attentive to everyone's children. Bob Tate had won his first horse race and was now convinced he was a professional jockey. He idolized all the racers and jockeys and was convinced that racing, roping, and riding were his future. The following week, during the Sheridan County Fair, he won the Big Goose pony race on his pony, Duke. He had procured a racing hood for his pony and wore the racing silks his mother had made for him.

Bob Tate had also become the mascot of the cowboys. At the fair Curley Witzel tied one end of a rope to the boy's saddle horn and the other around the neck of a calf that was inside the shoot. The object was to open the gate, whereupon the young Tate was to get off, wrestle, and then tie the calf: "The crowd was given several laughs toward the end of the program when Robert Tate, ten-year-old son of R. T. Tate, dashed out on his 260 lb pony to rope a calf. After the calf had won the wrestling match, Bob attempted to ride one, but again he came out second best."

The boy's botched exhibition was just the start of the things that went wrong during the rodeo. During the relay race, Emmit Marsh had a commanding lead until he switched to his last horse. Frankie Takes the Gun, a Crow racer racing the Francis La Forge string, had a lightning switch to his last horse, but he collided with Marsh, which caused Marsh's elastic cinch to come unhooked. As Marsh was passing another racer, that man saw the loose cinch swinging. He reached out and gave Marsh a shove, and Marsh landed in a heap—still sitting in his saddle—in front of the grandstand, a foot from the finish line. Within moments, an eight-man fistfight broke out on the track in front of the grandstand.

After order was restored, thirteen-year-old Doris Ranger attempted to jump her horse over a whippet roadster, but the horse jumped short, resulting in an ugly pileup in front of the grandstand. The crowd held its breath until the girl was brought back to wave to them. The crowd rose to give her a standing ovation, whereupon she fainted away.

During the wild horse race, a horse broke through the infield fence and got away. Lee Moore, a Gallatin cowboy, was temporarily knocked out from being kicked in the head when he was thrown from his horse. Bronc rider Archie Campbell was thrown and trampled, which badly injured his leg. If that weren't excitement enough for one rodeo, there was a second donnybrook on the racetrack that was reported in the Sheridan paper:

> *A spirited fight between Fay Harper and Mose Ranger made the quarter-mile for roping horses true to cowboy style. The men were in front of the judge's stand when they became engaged in an argument concerning entries in the race. Harper is said to have struck Ranger with his whip. Both men leaped from their horses to the ground in order to "mix." A swing of Ranger's whip butt cut open Harper's cheek, just below an eye, as he went sprawling flat in the dust. A crowd quickly gathered, and the irate men were parted.*
>
> *A loose saddle, a runaway horse, tumbling Indians, and fallen horses played an exciting role in the one-half-mile Indian relay race Friday afternoon.*

If the twenties had been a decade for the wild cowboys, it was no less a platform for wild horses. In the saddle bronc riding, Rompers threw such a fit in bucking his cowboy off that he was judged to be "unrideable." The next night, Paddy Ryan was matched against Rompers, who tried for five full minutes to unload the acrobatic Irishman. If the phrase "there never was a horse that can't be rode" proved true, Ryan's last evening proved that "there never was a cowboy that can't be throwed." Ryan drew the Bones brothers' W. O. Brown, who bucked Paddy over the fence and out of the arena.

After attending the Gallatins' annual race meet two years in a row, John and Mary Morgan hosted a rodeo on their own ranch near Beckton. If the Gallatins' race meet was huge, the Morgans' PK rodeo was epic. Like the Gallatins, the Morgans had the funds to put up a jackpot to draw the top cowboys from all over the country. Only the top riders and ropers from the world of rodeo were invited to compete in steer roping, bronc riding, and calf roping. While the Gallatins' race meet was an all-encompassing festival of horses, the PK rodeo stuck strictly to rodeo events. In addition to the prize money, the Morgans ordered a brand-new 1929 Grand Page sports roadster direct from the factory for the winner in the All-Around event.

The rodeo was held at a natural amphitheater at the PK Ranch. It was the biggest event between the Cheyenne Frontier Days and the Calgary Stampede, as rodeo fans traveled from across the United States to Sheridan to watch. Dudes from nearby ranches rode in on horseback, but the majority of the twenty thousand spectators drove, and parked their cars along the steep side hills above the rodeo grounds.

For the merchants in Sheridan, it was Christmas in July, as hotels, restaurants, and shops were crowded with rodeo fans three days before and after the performances.

Because of the Sheridan rodeo, the county fair, the Gallatin race meet, and the PK rodeo—supported by wealthy easterners and produced by eastern horsemen and western cowboys—Absaraka had become the world's showplace for equestrian extravaganzas. Not since Buffalo Bill Cody's Wild West Show had such a variety of horsemanship been seen in any one area.

As Red Tate had the shoeing account of both the Gallatins and Major Nicholas, and Jerry Belle was exercising horses for Major Nicholas, Bob Tate had the run of Little Goose Canyon. When Jerry Belle went to ride horses on Major Nicholas's ranch, Bob would tag along with his pony. Ray May, a Gallatin cowboy, was sweet on Jerry Belle Tate and taught Bob how to hold a polo mallet and hit the ball off his pony. Ray gave the boy a polo trophy he had won in Aiken, and the boy was hooked. He tried to stow away with the Gallatins' crew when they left for Aiken with the horses for the winter, but he was discovered and sent home.

When Colonel McCoy was showing the Milburns from New York some of the Circle V stallions, Bob Tate was there, listening to every word. The stallions were exercised in a circle on a long lunge line. They bucked and played while they were exercised. McCoy looked down at Bob and then to the buyers. "You have to see this kid," McCoy announced to the visitors. "Come here, Bob," the colonel ordered.

Young Tate walked over, and McCoy picked him up by his belt and placed him on top of Black Rascal with no bridle or saddle. The stallion had had his mane shaved, so Bob had to lean forward and hold on to either side of the stallion's neck as best he could.

"Watch this," McCoy said to the amusement of the onlookers and cracked a long lunge whip, whereby the black stallion began to jump and kick up in a circle. With Bob clinging to Black Rascal, McCoy let the stud out to the end of the thirty-foot lead rope.

"Whoa!" Bob yelled as Black Rascal jumped. It was not enough to buck him off, but enough to give the boy a wild ride. Bob was half-terrified and half-exhilarated to be putting on a show. Pulling the stallion to a stop, McCoy grabbed the boy and sent him to the barn.

"I got one more stud I want you to see," the colonel announced. "Bob, bring Duke out." Bob was off like a shot, and a moment later he led out a small Shetland pony. Bob looked at the Milburns, cocked his hat back like McCoy, and imitated the colonel's walk and talk in promoting his pony. He walked to one side so the men might inspect the diminutive shaggy beast, and he pointed out the attributes of the pony while he lunged it around like McCoy had done with Black Rascal. It was a comical scene, but the Milburns were careful to just chuckle, lest they make sport of the boy.

"Son, you wouldn't sell that pony, would you?" Mr. Milburn asked.

"Yes, sir, I would, but he won't be cheap. He's the head of my breeding program."

"You've got a breeding program?" the man asked, amused.

"I've got forty-eight head of ponies in Sheridan," Bob said, his shoulders thrown back. He stopped the pony, making it stand, and backed away and cocked his hat back.

"I can make you a deal on eight Shetland mares; in five years you'll get your money back, and after that it's all profit," he said.

"Where did you find this one?" Milburn asked.

"You think he's something, just wait till you meet his father," McCoy said and smiled.

On the weekends and after school, Red Tate would send Bob to herd his forty-eight ponies as they grazed on vacant lots around Sheridan. "Take those ponies back up the hill, and don't let them in the park or on Mr. Kendrick's lawn," Red instructed. John Kendrick had by now built his wife a mansion on the heights overlooking Sheridan. Other than the park, the Kendrick estate had one of the few large irrigated lawns in town. Red knew the green grass of both lawns would be tempting to a herd of ponies if left unattended.

Bob and his friend Dick Woods trailed his pony herd up the hill to graze, pretending they were on a cattle drive in charge of the covey. Red even hauled an old wagon up on the hillside for the boys to sleep under. They lit a campfire, told stories under the stars, and inevitably fell asleep. In the morning, the ponies were gone and there was a mad scramble to find them. To Bob's horror, he found his ponies on the lush front lawn of the Kendrick mansion. The terrified boy flew into the ponies.

"Get off the dang lawn!" Bob said, trying to keep quiet while at the same time spooking the ponies off the grass. He waved his arms at the ponies, but they were gorging themselves and shifted merely a few steps out of Bob's way and resumed their grazing, drifting farther onto the lawn. As Bob tried frantically to move his herd, he looked up and saw the form of none other than John Kendrick himself, home from Washington.

John Kendrick had been a trail cowboy, governor of Wyoming, and now a U.S. senator. He had married the daughter of a wealthy cattle baron, but despite his social obligations and increased time in Washington, D.C., he was still the man he had been when he arrived in the country. At a ball thrown at the Kendrick mansion, Bea Gallatin once remarked that when John Kendrick made an appearance at a function, "you knew there was a man in the room." It was this man that young Bob Tate found walking toward him.

"I'm sorry, sir, my ponies . . . they run off last night," Bob stammered. The sight of the scrambling young cowboy and the herd of horses on his lawn had touched the old cowboy, reminding him of the difficult times he had experienced coming up the Texas trail.

"Hold on there, son, don't be in a hurry. I want to take a look at them," Kendrick said to the young horseman.

"I'm awful sorry, Mr., 'er, I mean, Senator Kendrick. They got away from me up near the fairground," Bob apologized once more.

"Not to worry, they look like nice ponies," Kendrick said. He barely had time to visit his ranch up in Montana, and now this young boy had brought a piece of his past to his front yard.

Young Bob looked at the man; he was one of the real old-time cowboys. *Wait till I tell Dick Woods that John B. Kendrick has been admiring my ponies,* he thought.

Realizing he wasn't in trouble, Bob walked over to Senator Kendrick and cocked his hat back on his head. "You know that little black one is the best one, he's for sale . . .," Bob started.

"I can't *believe* you tried to sell John Kendrick a pony!" Erma Tate scolded her son.

"But Mom, he was nice, he said he wanted to look at them," Bob protested, still excited over meeting a famous man like Kendrick.

"You better hope Dad doesn't find out about those ponies getting on Mr. Kendrick's lawn," Jerry Belle said.

Bob Tate was beginning to find other ways to get into trouble too. He rode his ponies into the Sheridan pool, and he had one pony fall through a footbridge on Big Goose Creek near his father's barn. The pony hung there, suspended, with its legs dangling through the bridge, while Bob tried to find someone to help him who wouldn't tell on him. His plan was foiled, however, when pedestrians became alarmed at the sight of the suspended pony and called Red. With the help of his hired man, Red lifted the pony off the bridge and began a search for his son.

"Dad, it was the Moreland boys . . . I was just . . .," Bob stammered as Red snatched him up by the arm and took him to the barn.

"He's finally going to get it now!" Jerry Belle said to her mother, watching from the kitchen window.

Inside the barn Red pulled his belt off. "Don't you blame the Moreland boys, and don't try to tell me you don't know how it happened," Red said.

"You could have snapped that pony's leg off crossing that footbridge, and I'd be shooting him now, all because you wanted to see if you could get it across. I'll sell every pony we got if you're going to play games with animals." Red could see the boy's bottom lip start to quiver, and soon Bob's quiet tears began to hit the hardpacked ground. Bob stood head down, and his slumping shoulders began to heave. The brash young horseman had now been reduced to a scared, embarrassed ten-year-old.

"Having animals means being responsible; it's our job to look out for them and make sure they don't get kicked or hurt. Do you think that pony would have tried to cross that bridge by himself?" he asked.

"No, sir," the boy said.

"That pony would have never crossed that bridge on his own; he would have gone down to the crossing, which is where you should have taken him. If that pony had broken his leg crossing that bridge, it would have been your fault, and no amount of me whipping you would have helped him. Do you understand that?" Red said.

"Yes, sir," Bob said, trying to compose himself.

"What do you think someone like Johnny Cover or Luther Dunning would say if they heard about that?" Red said, knowing the boy fairly worshipped the men.

In the house Jerry Belle looked out the window as Erma made lunch. "I hope Dad gives it to him. I'd like to whip him myself," she said.

"Jerry!" Erma said.

"It's true, Mom, he gets away with murder, If Dad knew half the stuff that little imp did, he'd whip him into next week." Jerry Belle's older sister Naomi was in the house helping her mother and looked at her younger sister.

"I bet Dad might be whipping more than Bob if he knew half of what you and Marge Carrels did at the Brinton dance," Naomi said to her younger sister, who swung around and gave Naomi a scowl.

Erma Tate had to laugh. Bob was pretty spoiled, but he did love horses. She felt the same way about Red sometimes. She had been a large reason that Red had succeeded as a working horse trader. When Red was off at the HF Bar or Gallatins shoeing, it was Erma who fed and rode the horses in Sheridan with the girls. She had the foresight to see that the future in the horse business was the Remount, which required that horses be registered. This meant filling out paperwork on foals born. Erma took charge of filling out the paperwork for Red, and within a short time, Erma knew more about the bloodlines of their horses than Red did.

Red Tate had more irons in the fire than just the ponies; he had polo horses for sale, was busy with a steady shoeing job, and much to Erma's dismay, had traveled to Kansas City with Jack Carrels, the bootlegger, to buy an expensive pair of Shire work stallions for $200 each. Although workhorses were still used in some areas, trucks and cars were replacing them to the extent that the market was all but shot.

ONE OF BOB TATE'S BIGGEST THRILLS WAS TO ACCOMPany old Lew Alderson, the Bones brothers' father, to the Lotus movie house in Sheridan to watch Lew's son Floyd star in the western movie *Tearin' Loose.* Floyd had just signed a contract with Action Pictures. The producer had changed his name to Wally Wales because he thought Alderson resembled a cross between Wallace Reid and the Prince of Wales. The name stuck. Using the stage names of Wally Wales and Hal Taliferro, Floyd worked as an actor for almost forty years. The former horse wrangler for the Three Circle Ranch made the transition from silent movies to talking movies while some stars such as Tom Mix, who was born with somewhat of a high-pitched voice, was phased out to some extent.

Westerns, because of the world's fascination with the Wild West, cowboys, and the wide-open spaces, enjoyed a fifty-year run. Hollywood produced hundreds of westerns that promoted the area for dudes that flocked there by the thousands. In addition to bringing in dudes, Hollywood drew on the cowboys of Absaraka for its stuntmen and leading men.

Dave Whyte, a Gallatin cowboy and world-champion bronc rider, had landed work as a stuntman and bit actor in silent films. After a stint in Hollywood, Whyte showed up in the Big Horn church one Sunday with his mother, wanting to make a grand entry as a movie star and world champion. His mother, a pioneer woman, was less than impressed.

Bea Gallatin, an impressionable teenager, was sitting in a back pew when Whyte and his mother entered the church. He was dressed in the style of a Hollywood western star: tall boots, a loud western shirt, and a bright scarf.

"Who's gonna show me where to sit?" Dave said. Bea looked on with adoring eyes until Whyte's mother spat a small stream of tobacco juice into a nearby pew.

"You'll sit right thar," she ordered. Bea giggled until her mother placed a hand on her leg to steady her. Despite whatever pedigrees, accolades, or education one might have, the locals still took people for how they handled themselves, be they rodeo star, movie star, or not.

Walter Sibley, an Otter Creek horse breeder and trainer for Luther Dunning, moved to Hollywood and got a job managing horses for the dozens of westerns produced during that era. Turk Greenough followed, doing stunt work for John Wayne and other actors. Both Paddy Ryan and Bob Askins went to work in the movie industry as stock handlers.

No one was to make a bigger ruckus in Tinseltown than Curley Witzel, however. While a Hollywood producer was a guest at William Eaton's ranch, he offered Curley a job in the film *Whirlwind Driver.* Witzel's character had to fistfight with another man on the top of a runaway stagecoach. During the filming, the stagecoach hit a bump, causing the man to stagger forward into one of Curley's punches, which knocked the man to the ground ten feet below. When the stagecoach was brought to a halt, the producer ran up to Curley and said he would give both men ten extra dollars for the stunt. Curley had one eye on the man he had accidentally knocked off as he stomped up the road headed for Curley. "Better give my share to him," Curley told the producer as the man neared the stage.

Over the years Curley enjoyed starring roles in such films as *La Bonita Rides Again.* While he could be wilder than most men, Curley honored the old chivalrous code of cowboys when it came to women. His demise in show business came when an actress came to him in tears over the producer's sexual harassments and rough treatment.

Curley marched up to the producer's office and let the man know in no uncertain terms that if he ever bothered the girl again, he would answer to him. "Why, you ungrateful little runt. If I hadn't given you this job, you would be nobody," the producer yelled. "That's better than you will be if you ever touch that girl again," Curley said. After a heated argument the man reached across his desk and slapped Curley.

If there was an actor in Hollywood that a producer did *not* want to slap, it was Curley Witzel. He picked up a chair and broke it over the producer's head and, with a hard right, broke his jaw. He bailed into the goons with the spare parts.

When the smoke cleared, Curley, realizing he was probably looking at jail time, went to his actor friend Hoot Gibson for help. The producer had stirred up the law enough that there was an all-points bulletin out for the arrest of Witzel. Gibson smuggled a police uniform for Curley out of the costume department of one of the studios. In the meantime Curley's landlord hid him in her apartment when the police showed up. Gibson smuggled Curley in his police outfit to the train station, which was swimming with police who were looking for him. Gibson pulled all the money he had on him at the time and hurriedly slapped it on the ticket counter.

"I want a one-way ticket, for as far as this will get," he said. Curley got to Butte, Montana, with only the clothes on his back and dead-broke. He had only to find his rodeo pals to be taken in until Gibson forwarded his saddle and the rest of his clothes a week later.

50

IN THE EARLY 1920S, LOCAL CATTLE RANCHERS HAD BEGUN leasing grass on the Crow reservation for their cattle for 10¢ an acre. These ranchers soon complained to the secretary of the Department of the Interior that wild horse herds were depleting the grass, pushing their cattle out into bogs, and tearing down fences. With several large ranchers controlling political interests in the area, it was decided to destroy the wild herds. The contract to exterminate the horses went to Matt Tschirgi, who hired a group of gunmen. The Crow leaders were told they had seven months to bring their horses in from the range on the reservation before the rest were killed.

Reportedly more than forty thousand horses were breeding in the wild on the Crow reservation, part of which encompassed the Antler Ranch. The unmanaged herd contained inbred wild horses, some of which turned out to be common-headed, cow-hocked, or bad-footed horses. The whites called these inferior horses "cayuses." Cayuse was the name of a western Indian tribe that bred good horses to trade to other tribes. The name evolved into a description for all Indian horses, and then by the 1920s was used to describe the culls of the wild herds that were descendants of the Indian herds, cavalry horses, thoroughbreds, and abandoned homesteaders' horses.

Initially, the lure of quick money resulted in dozens of local men signing up to hunt the horses. A bounty of $4 was paid to any man who turned in a pair of horse ears. Along with local white cowboys, a few Crow cowboys also signed up for the hunt. When the Crow leaders heard of this, they summoned the Crow cowboys to a tribal council before the shooting started. The tribal elders explained that killing horses for money was bad medicine, like shooting your brother, they warned. The three Crow cowboys ignored the elders and joined the hunt.

It was gruesome work. With cowboys shooting into the herds, animals with broken legs and bullet wounds tried to drag themselves away from the shooters. Herds disappeared down draws along the broken country, taking their wounded with them. Foals dragging back legs and mares with their bottom jaw shot off eventually died, and their ears were cut off. Once the hunt started, the entire area around Lodge Grass smelled of dead horses. Within weeks most of the hunters quit, unable to continue participating in the gruesome job. Texas gunmen were brought up to finish the job, which quickly got out of control. On one occasion, an elderly Crow woman found her old pet horse dead in her backyard with its ears cut off.

After a while the three Crow hunters also quit. Ironically, all three later died in some type of horse-related accident: one died riding a bronc at a rodeo, one was killed in a Billings horse race, and one was kicked in the head at a Crow fair while shoeing a horse.

In the end, between forty and sixty thousand Crow horses were killed.

The government did not limit the extermination to the Crow herds. The Cheyenne tribe would fare no better. The agent for the Cheyenne tribe had declared that he was going to put the impoverished Indians back on their feet again. He made good his promise by taking their horses, leaving the tribe standing on the ground.

In 1912, the northern Cheyenne reservation ran fifteen thousand horses on the open grasslands of their reservation. Seeing a chance to save money, the government issued one hundred horses per month from the Cheyenne's horses to supplement the beef rations of the starving people living on the reservation between the Rosebud and Tongue rivers. The Cheyenne were given $6.50 per horsehide for the slaughtered horses. The better horses were shipped off to buyers, with no compensation to the owners. By 1929, twelve thousand horses had been butchered or stolen.

During the slaughter of the Crow horses, a few old horsemen took an interest in the status of the palomino stallion, whose bloodline went back before their grandfathers' time. Crow and Cheyenne elders retold the stories of the endurance of the yellow stallion's warhorses and buffalo runners. Stories of the yellow stallion's captured offspring circulated from the Cheyenne to army buyers. Noll Wallop claimed he had a mare by the stallion that produced some of his finest horses. To date, no yellow stallion in charge of a herd of mares had ever been caught.

Some of the Texas gunmen had pooled their money, saying that it would go to whoever bagged the yellow stallion, yet after several years no one had succeeded. Like a white buffalo or a royal elk, the yellow stallion became a prize the hunters sought after intensely.

Once the killing started, most of the local horsemen found themselves rooting for the stallion to escape. He was part of the heritage of Absaraka, a heritage of warriors, cowboys, and horses. Whenever the old-timers inspected a string of ears, they were relieved when no yellow ones were attached to the wires they were strung on. Despite the efforts to capture him over the years, the stallion and his band of mares still ran free.

The stallion had moved his mares to the shelter of the Wolf Mountains, between the Little Bighorn and the Rosebud rivers. During the early stages of the wild horse hunt, two mares from the stallion's band had been shot from a long distance, but like his great-grandfather before him and every generation since, the yellow stallion—through his tenacity and vigilance—kept his band at bay.

51

FEW MEN SINCE CRAZY HORSE KNEW ABSARAKA BETTER than Noll Wallop. He had ridden over the grasslands and mountains for forty-five years as a hunter, horse rancher, and deputy sheriff. A veteran of the frontier years, he had eaten dog with the Cheyenne, lived among the Crow, and shot a hole in the ceiling of the Sheridan Inn with Buffalo Bill. With his love for the people, the horses, and the land, he could count among his friends Crow chiefs, trail cowboys, hotel proprietors, and politicians.

He bore a long scar on his nose, acquired when he was teaching one of his dogs to bear-hunt. Noll had draped a bearskin over himself, and the dog had bitten through the skin and into Wallop's nose, leaving Noll with a conversation piece forever after.

For those who didn't know him, Wallop's eccentricities hid his genius. Many who were unfamiliar with him called him a fool, but the old-timers knew better. They knew what he had built and the style with which he built it. They knew he had lost and regained two fortunes in an honest, though sometimes unconventional, manner. They knew that as a Wyoming legislator, he had pioneered laws that protected the area's game from extinction, something that had befallen the local elk herd before they were reintroduced during his tenure as the state's congressman.

The decision that faced him now tortured him far beyond any obstacle he had experienced in his life. His older brother, the seventh Earl of Portsmouth, had passed away in England. The title was supposed to fall to Noll's son, Gerard, but unfortunately the Labor Party in England was trying to block Gerard's succession to the title, saying that if Noll did not assume the lordship, the family would lose the title.

The only way to resolve the matter was for Noll, now in poor health, to serve as Earl of Portsmouth for at least four years. He realized that if he resided in England's damp climate for that length of time, he might not see Wyoming again.

Now in his midsixties, Noll was riding into his beloved Bighorn Mountains to say good-bye. He guided the thoroughbred gelding along the steep switchbacks of an old Indian trail that tribes had used to cross the mountains fifty years prior. After only a quarter-mile, he had climbed a thousand feet, bringing the distant Wolf Mountains into view beyond the town of Sheridan sixteen miles away. As he crested out on top of Little Goose Canyon, he paused to let his horse rest and to watch the sun rise beyond Moncreiffe Ridge in front of Red Cloud's lookout. He skirted Teepee Lodge because he wanted to be alone to think. He wound his way past the abandoned mines of his old friends the Stockwells and stopped at Devil's Lake.

Picketing his horse in the tall grass, he untied his fly rod from behind the saddle, assembled the pieces, and began to fish. To his delight, he caught three trout in less than twenty minutes.

He pulled a small pan from his saddlebag, along with an envelope of a spiced cornmeal and flour mix. He took his knife and slit the fish from gill to tail and scooped out the guts, which he flung into the tall grass. He reached down, rinsed the fish in the lake, took his knife, and carefully cut the meat from the bones, leaving small fillets to roll in the spiced cornmeal and flour. He placed the fillets on the greased pan and produced a small side of bacon, which he sliced and dropped into the pan, which he held over a fire he had built.

When the trout turned golden brown alongside the sizzling bacon, he retrieved a loaf of bred from the saddlebags and cut a slit down the center, where he placed the bubbling hot fish and bacon fillets. It made a fine meal.

He rinsed the pan in the lake and took a pan full of water and threw it on the fire. He put the pan back into the saddlebag and took out a small curry comb and gave his horse a good currying until he realized how much the long ride had taken out of him. Walking stiffly over to the saddle lying in the grass, he laid his head back on the seat and was soon in a deep sleep in the warm afternoon sun.

In an hour, he awoke to the sound of tearing grass next to his head, for his horse had grazed over to him. As he lay and watched the horse eat, he thought of his old original stallions, Sailor and Columbus, and daydreamed about grizzly bear and buffalo hunts, old Milestown, and his early neighbors, Paget, Howes, Charlie Thex, and Brewster.

What he had accomplished on the last American frontier meant little to his family in England. To them he was the affable, stuttering, absentminded family member who had gone off to play in America. Noll had never felt equal to his father, nor any of his brothers, who had each made a name for himself in England's political circles. Now he had buried both parents and two older brothers.

A western jay flew in and began to squawk and eye the remains of the fish in the grass nearby. Noll watched the bird dip down, grab a beak full of guts, and fly off. Slowly and surely his heart began to fill with resolution for what he knew lay ahead of him. He had a ranch, a son in politics in England, another in college at Yale, and a woman he loved as much now as the day he had met her in Chicago, thirty-four years earlier. Marguerite had told Noll about when she visited his family estate in England as a young girl and dreamed of one day being Lady Portsmouth. The thought of him making Marguerite's dream of one day being Lady Portsmouth a reality cheered him somewhat, but it hurt him terribly to leave these mountains. He had mined gold and hunted the length and breadth of their most remote regions dozens of times. He had built his dream house in a Wyoming canyon that was cherished by men as far back as the Crow.

As he rode back through the flower-covered meadows, Noll began to recite poetry to the Bighorns. The sun was dropping by the time Noll reached the top of Little Goose Canyon. From this vantage point he could see the entire area below: Moncreiffe's polo ranch, the Gallatins' ranch, and his own canyon ranch. He looked off to the haze of the north past Sheridan, where his old Otter Creek homestead lay in Montana.

What would they think of him for leaving? he thought.

"Good-bye, old friends, I hope we meet again." He took one last look down Moncreiffe Ridge to Red Cloud's lookout, gave the gelding his head, and descended into the canyon one last time. From Miles City to London, Noll Wallop's picture was already plastered across the front pages of the newspapers. It made good copy; a Wyoming cowboy was leaving to serve as an English lord. He would be ninety-ninth in the line of succession to become the king of England.

Earldom Descends to Oliver Wallop

Oliver Henry Wallop, pioneer of Bighorn, became a member of the English peerage Tuesday night when his elder brother, John Fellows Wallop, the seventh Earl of Portsmouth, died in London.

Boston Herald
December 3, 1926

Oliver Henry Wallop, who for more than forty years has managed his 3,000-acre ranch near Sheridan, Wyoming, has decided to take his seat in the British House of Lords as Earl of Portsmouth. The title became his on the death of his elder brother, the seventh earl, in September 1925, and at that time he hoped he might remain "a man of two countries." That could not be. He was already a citizen of but one country, having on his naturalization here renounced allegiance to the British sovereign. The hereditary title, a family possession since 1743, he could not renounce. Through neither merit nor fault of his own, he was the eighth Earl of Portsmouth. Yet he could not take his seat among the peers without taking the oath of allegiance to the king. One can understand how he felt as he said: "I never shall forsake my mountain home in Wyoming; I have made my home here, and I have my friends here." But must the home he made be sacrificed to the earldom he inherited? Not necessarily. By a way of compromise, both may be retained, though not without the very reluctant laying down of American citizenship.

For the sake of his family—perhaps especially for the sake of his eldest son, who had been an officer in the British Army during the World War—Lord Portsmouth finally felt it his duty to relinquish his citizen-

ship here in order to fill his place in the British peerage. He wishes now to get through with the formalities quickly, not waiting five years for British naturalization, because, as he says, being 65, he is not exactly a spring chicken and it would be rather trying to wait so long. The passing of a private bill by Parliament would permit his early entrance. Lord Portsmouth has gone to London to see about this, after a six months' visit to the ranch, and this he intends to repeat annually, though his nominally permanent domicile will be the old family mansion, Barton House, Devonshire. Whether on this side of the Atlantic or the other, he may be as good an American as ever, or at any rate a peculiarly fitting link between the two peoples.

His stories of folly were many, but to his old friends, no man was more fit to be a lord than Oliver Henry Wallop. He was the dean of Absaraka's horsemen, who were now famous around the world. On his Otter Creek ranch, Charlie Thex smiled when he heard the news. He doubted the English knew what kind of man was about to serve them as lord. Noll Wallop had shared the area's bounty with his neighbors but had also suffered the area's droughts, blizzards, and long days in the saddle. Charlie Thex doubted there was a member in the House of Lords that was as tough as old Noll. From his Otter Creek ranch, Charlie Thex wrote a letter when he heard the news.

Old friend Noll,

All of the Otter Creek gang wishes you the best in your new endeavor as "Lord." England is getting a good man.

Your friend,
Charlie Thex

In their typical caring spirit, Goelet and Edith Gallatin insisted on escorting the Wallops back to New York and hosting them at their New York home at 444 Madison Avenue. Because of Noll's age and penchant to forget, the Gallatins saw the Wallops off at the dock. Noll was chattering on, telling stories right up to the time the last horn blew, calling the passengers to board.

"Ticket, please," the ship's steward said. He grew impatient at Wallop, who was conversing as cheerfully as ever while searching his pockets. A foghorn blared again. "Mister, this ship is leaving with or without you." It soon became obvious that Noll had forgotten the tickets.

Edith Gallatin looked to Goelet. "I'll stay here with Noll and Marguerite; you go back to our apartment and find the tickets." Goelet jumped in his car and ran every red light in his race home. He found the tickets there in the trash can!

Back at the docks, Edith was doing her best to delay the ticket-taker. Just as the porter signaled for the ramp to be pulled up, Goelet trotted up, tickets in hand. Thus began Noll Wallop's journey to become the eighth Earl of Portsmouth. Over in England, the country was amused by the ascension of a Wyoming cowboy to the House of Lords. Before Noll and Marguerite's ship arrived in England, the *London Times* had already run a cartoon depicting Noll as a lord in the House of Commons.

As the ship moved away from the dock, Noll and Marguerite waved goodbye to the Gallatins on the docks below.

"Well, Lady Portsmouth, are you happy now?" Noll asked and smiled. It was with some satisfaction that he could give his wife such a position. Long after Marguerite retired to their quarters below, Noll stood on deck, looking west to America's shoreline and beyond. His heart was heavy with the fact that he might never see his beloved Absaraka again. He would forever remain a son of a frontier.

52

ON A DARK OCTOBER DAY IN 1929, THE LIFEBLOOD WAS swept from the great horse fairs of Absaraka forever. The stock market crash had begun what was to be a nationwide economic depression. Goelet and Edith Gallatin, who were invested heavily in the stock market, were hurt terribly. The same went for the Morgans and most of the other wealthy families around Sheridan.

Goelet was aware that if he went under, he would take a dozen cowboys and their families with him. He rolled up his sleeves and did what he could to save the Big Horn ranch. The family's home on Madison Avenue and their barn in Aiken, South Carolina, were put up for sale. The Circle V Polo Company would be phased out in a series of dispersal sales. The Gallatin race meet folded after its four-year run, and the PK after two.

For Edith Gallatin, selling the Circle V horses was like selling her grandchildren. She stood stoically with Bea and watched as fifty-six of their horses were auctioned off. Descendants of Kemano, Black Rascal, and Phantom Prince and some of the great mares from the world of polo were sold for next to nothing.

Young Oliver Wallop topped sales with the purchase of Sprite III for $250. Having recently won the collegiate polo national championship playing for Yale, Oliver also bought the crème of the polo ponies from his neighbors. He paid a little over $100 per head for six horses and thus built one of the best strings of polo ponies ever assembled. Major Ridgley Nicholas made plans for a massive clearance sale of his show-horse and racehorse breeding operation.

HUNTERS AND JUMPERS
6 Half-breed heavyweight prospects
16 to 16.2 hands . . . Can be shown over jumps at any time.

POLO PONY PROSPECTS
10 horses, 2-and 3-year-olds, by the U.S. Remount stallion Majority . . . halter broken and thoroughly gentled but have not been ridden.

BROODMARES
Being short of feed, I also offer 10 broodmares with foals by Majority or Sir Luke.
Personal inspection invited.
Ridgely Nicholas
Big Horn, Wyoming

Few buyers responded, so the major was forced to sell his horses to the U.S. Army's Remount program. Colonel E. M. Daniels drove out to look at Major Nicholas's horses and shook his head. It seemed a crime for horses of this quality and breeding to go into the army.

"My God," he said to Red Tate after he had viewed half a dozen thoroughbreds, "you don't see this class of horse being offered to the government." Daniels bought the entire bunch. "This is the best load of horses I have ever bought in one place," he said.

Eva Nicholas, while eccentric, loved her horses and knew what desperation it was to sell to the government. When Colonel Daniels and an army veterinarian drove up in the yard to look at the horses, she accosted them. "Horse thieves, government horse thieves, and sons of bitches!" Her caustic voice resounded from the house to the stable. Major Nicholas, embarrassed for his wife, began to backpedal.

"I would invite you men to lunch, but it seems my wife is in a foul mood," he said.

It was a hard fact that $165 was a lot of money in some circles, but considering horses of this quality, to buy them at such a price was stealing. Red Tate bought twenty-four head of brood mares from Major Nicholas for next to nothing. His son trailed the mares to Sheridan with a hired man because buying gas for the trip was out of the question.

If the Depression had hit the wealthy horsemen along the Bighorns hard, it all but destroyed the small ranchers out in the country. Were it not for the Remount program and dude ranches, some would have lost their ranch. And the horsemen were not the only outfits to suffer: the price of cattle went so low that the government bought the hides for $2 just to give the ranchers some financial assistance.

Once again, the dude ranches were a bright light in a dark time. While some of the wealthy in the East could no longer afford summer vacations in Europe, they could for a fraction of the cost ride horses through the wide-open spaces of Wyoming. Prices were still just $18 to $30 a week for ranch meals, unlimited riding, and a private furnished cabin. Of all the ranches to survive during that period, none did it with more style than the Bones brothers' ranch in Birney, Montana.

While Floyd Alderson was off in Hollywood making movies, his two younger brothers, Big Bones and Little Bones, made a go at entertaining rich easterners and raising cattle, Remount horses, and bucking stock for rodeos. The brothers' southern upbringing, mixed with western wildness, was a combination people fell in love with. Unlike at William Eaton's ranch or HF Bar, Birney had no snowcapped mountains for the dudes to enjoy, but they had the foothills of the Wolf Mountains. The road to the ranch even led through Battle Butte, where Crazy Horse had fought his last battle against General Miles less than sixty years prior.

The Bones brothers' dude ranch was a working cattle ranch where dudes could pitch in and help with the work or just take long rides in the country. Dudes often participated in the rodeos and horse races, and in some instances they became competent help around the ranch. For the pent-up easterners, it became a way of life. With bootlegging and speakeasies in full throttle, trips to Sheridan, though long, became wild events.

While the Bones brothers were weathering the Depression somewhat comfortably, some of their neighbors were bordering on starvation. Little Bones Alderson called Colonel Daniels on behalf of one impoverished family that had one horse they hoped might be fit for the Remount. Fortunately, Colonel Daniels had a deep affection for the people and the area, and he agreed to take a look.

When Little Bones and Colonel Daniels arrived, the enthused rancher led the two men to a rickety set of corrals next to a shack that must have been the family's home. Inside the first corral a small, homely horse that wouldn't possibly meet army specifications looked at them through the split rails. As the rancher went inside to put a halter on the horse, the colonel looked at Bones.

"Bones, why did you bring me out here? This man doesn't have anything that will suit the army."

The rancher was going on about his horse's attributes when something caught the colonel's attention at the far side of the corral. When he glanced over, he caught the large eyes of two shy, barefoot children watching him from between the poles. They neither spoke nor came out in the open. In fact, from a distance they appeared to be wild.

Colonel Daniels had fought in World War I and had chased Pancho Villa on the Mexican border, but what he saw beyond the corral poles hit him hard. The eyes of those children bore a hole into his heart. He looked at Little Bones, who kept his eyes on the horse. It became obvious why Bones had brought him here: $165 might be the difference between the family eating that winter or starving to death, and this rancher was not one who would accept handouts.

"Bones, we'll load that one. That horse is exactly what I need for the Colonel Rand's daughter," Colonel Daniels said.

"Would you two join us for lunch?" the rancher asked.

"We just ate, thank you," the colonel said.

As Little Bones and the colonel drove out for Birney with the horse loaded on their trailer, there was not much said after the sobering sight of poverty to such good people.

"We'll find a place for that horse somewhere," Daniels said to Bones, who knew he had brought the right man to inspect the horse.

Not all army horse buyers got along so well with the locals as did Colonel Daniels. On the Irionses' Powder River ranch, a very different army horse buyer showed up on a snowy day. He was cold and was looking to get back to Sheridan, where he could get warm and get a drink. Tim Irions led out some fit thoroughbred prospects he had been chasing coyotes on. The army buyer thought the horses were too thin, and he told Irions so. Then he commented on the state of the stud barn, which had not been cleaned but was dry. After observing the cocklebурs in the horses' manes and tails he refused to look at any more. Irions, who had been raising some of the finest thoroughbreds since Paget and Wallop settled the area, was thoroughly insulted. As the army buyer was walking away, the cowboy blew up.

"You government men don't know squat about a horse! You don't know if a horse roosts in a tree or sleeps on the ground!"

The next day Little Bones Alderson called Irions and had him haul his horses to the Bones brothers' ranch, where they pulled the burs out of the tails and knocked the mud off them. A week later the same army buyer, unaware that he was looking at the same horses, bought them all.

Some of the inspections led to colorful stories in their own right. One former stakes-winning stallion that had been issued by the army to a Blackfoot Indian in Browning, Montana, for breeding turned up missing with the rancher. After a prolonged search of the area, the stallion and rancher were found on an obscure Canadian racetrack, where the Remount stallion was running in a race.

Two Sheridan cowboys, Deacon and Jack Reisch, crossed their fingers when they watched their horse being ridden for inspection. Their brown gelding had bucked them both off more times than they could count, so they finally turned to Curly Kelly, a local bronc rider, to ride the gelding past the government inspector. Kelly rode the horse down to exhaustion for a week before the government buyer arrived. The Reisch brothers held their breath when Curly rode the outlaw at a trot and then a gallop in front of the army buyers; they needed the money. At the end of the ride, Curly quietly dismounted, and the inspector checked the gelding's eyes, listened to his breathing, and measured his height.

"Turn him in the corral," the officer said as he wrote the Reisch brothers a voucher for $165.

As soon as they were out of earshot, Curly Kelly looked at Deacon and Jack. "Those soldier boys will get a suntan on their moccasins when they try and ride that one," he said.

Bob Tate had saved every dime he got during the summer and bought a horse at the Sheridan sale barn for $17. He rode the horse every day, doing his best to train it to show to the army buyers. The problem was, the horse was just a shade under the height required for army regulations. When Colonel Daniels returned to Sheridan for an inspection, Red told him that that his son wanted to show him a horse. Bob led his gelding out for Daniels to inspect. Major Wilkins was there as inspecting veterinarian.

"You better lead him up on that manure pile or he might not measure out big enough," Major Wilkins said. The horse just barely passed the height test and Bob was given a voucher for $165. This was by far better money than a dollar-a-day ranch wages given for backbreaking work.

The young man tilted the hat back on his head. "Thanks, Colonel Daniels, I'll be sure to have some more for you when you come back," he said.

"I may have just created a horse trader," Daniels said to Red, and both men laughed.

When the PK rodeo had to be canceled, merchants in Sheridan, spoiled by the Christmas-in-July rush, teamed with interested rodeo supporters to bring the spectators back. A lawyer named R. E. McNally organized a group of locals to promote a professional rodeo in the middle of July called the Sheridan Wyo Rodeo. Bill Eaton was brought in to direct the arena, and the Bones brothers supplied the rodeo with bucking horses. Edith Gallatin was in charge of bringing the Indians. (She would be so influential that at the second Wyo Rodeo, she would convince the Crow and Cheyenne, former enemies, to smoke the peace pipe together.)

Despite the fact that her ability to help the underprivileged was now limited financially, Edith Gallatin could still offer her compassion in the area. On a trip to the Pine Ridge reservation with an interpreter and a court reporter, Edith made an effort to further preserve a fading history by recording Native American stories. Whenever she inquired about old Lakota traditions or history, the answers usually pointed her toward one man.

"You should ask He Dog, he will probably know that," the agency Indians would say. Sixty years before, He Dog had lived off the land as one of the last of the free-roaming horsemen. He had hunted and fought on horses across the length and breadth of Absaraka. He had stolen horses from the Shoshone and Crow and had fought Fetterman, Crook, Custer, and Miles in some of Absaraka's great cavalry battles. At the Little Bighorn, he had led a group of warriors that slaughtered Custer's E troop in a ravine on the battlefield.

After his surrender, He Dog remained active in tribal politics as a judge, although the white agents had usurped all power that the former chiefs had held. Now in his nineties, he knew of Edith Gallatin before she arrived. He was informed of the woman's benevolence toward Indians, how she had brought medicine and food to the children. He knew the canyon where she lived. He had hunted there and fought the Crow in a running battle where he understood her ranch to be. The ridge that ran east had served as a lookout point for soldiers and wagons. He Dog also heard this woman raised many horses, always of interest to him.

Edith Gallatin had heard something of He Dog also. He had been a Lakota warrior and chief and had been a lifelong friend of Crazy Horse. Before any palaver began, she had a smoke in silence with the man. After a few minutes He Dog spoke. "What do you do with your horses?" he asked. Edith smiled and began to explain that they were thoroughbreds out of racing stock that were trained to play a game called polo, which she slowly explained to the old chief. "I would like to see this game," he said, whereupon Edith invited him to her ranch as her guest.

Edith also mentioned that she had been on a roundup trying to corner a yellow stallion near Rotten Grass Creek on the Crow reservation. When the interpreter relayed the story to He Dog, his eyes lit up. The interpreter listened and looked back at Edith. "He says there was a yellow stallion on Otter Creek when he was a boy. Crazy Horse rode a son of his in a battle with the Crow. He had gone to trade with Crazy Horse for a bay mare that was maybe a granddaughter of this horse."

He Dog sat in silence for a long time as the mention of the stallion brought back a flood of memories that filled him with emotion. He could picture Lone Bear and Crazy Horse as boys, the great council on Horse Creek, the battles with the Shoshone, Crow, and Pawnee, and finally the battles with the whites. He began to think of the bad times, when children were starving in the snow, the winter before he and Crazy Horse had come to the agency.

He Dog rose on stiff legs to see Edith Gallatin off. He liked her; he felt her heart was good. She was a horsewoman, and she helped children.

Edith saw him brighten at the prospect of coming to Little Goose Canyon, but they would never meet again. He Dog was growing old and blind, and Edith Gallatin's own health was failing. The woman with the benevolent heart was now experiencing fainting spells that none of the doctors in Wyoming or New York understood.

Despite the financial pinch that the Gallatins experienced, 1931 rang in happy for the family with Bea's elaborate wedding ceremony on New Year's Day at their E4 Ranch. Members of the Crow and Cheyenne tribes danced, and hundreds attended, including ranch cowboys, Willis Spear, Senator John Kendrick, the Eatons, the Forbes, and all their neighbors.

Carlo Beuf, Bea's husband, was a flamboyant Italian count who was a published author and artist, an accomplished alpine mountain climber, and a fencer. He had served the Allied forces in World War I as a machine gunner and was decorated with the Knight Officer of the Crown of Italy for gallantry in action.

Carlo was not a professional rider, but as a game adventurer, he learned to ride while playing polo at the ranch. His fearless enthusiasm provided some comic relief to the local horse community around Big Horn. In one of his initial matches, for example, Bea gave him a boost onto his horse only to have him land in a heap on the other side. Carlo took to jumping the same way; one day while watching a horse show, he decided to try it by pointing a horse named Cricket at a three-and-a-half-foot jump. Cricket had been a top calf-roping horse that, if touched on the neck, jammed on the brakes with his front feet. Cricket was making a run at the jump when Carlo leaned forward and grabbed a handful of mane. Needless to say, he was sent flying over Cricket's head.

"Hit him over the head with the seat of your pants, Carlo!" yelled one of the cowboys, watching Carlo sail through the air. In a fraction of the time it took most people, Carlo was working cattle and playing polo at Moncreiffe field.

Soon after Carlo and Bea married, he landed a job in Hollywood subtitling films for MGM, and the couple left the ranch. Bea sold her favorite mare, Sprite, to pay for a new car for the trip. Before she left, she said good-bye to the horses.

53

NOTHING COULD HAVE BEEN IN SHARPER CONTRAST TO the Great Gatsby–esque equestrian estates in Big Horn than the Chapel Brothers Corporation—or CBC—out of Miles City. It specialized in rounding up the stray horses that had been turned loose and multiplied on abandoned state land all the way from the Canadian border south to Colorado.

The better-built horses were broken and ridden as five-or six-year-olds, but the majority were trailed to railheads and sold for meat. In addition to owning packing houses, CBC bought thousands of acres on both sides of the Yellowstone River for $17 an acre, which entitled them to all the range horses that grazed there.

CBC turned out draft stallions with range horses to produce more meat on the hoof. At one point one thousand stallions were trailed into the range from Texas and scattered from Laramie, Wyoming, to Wolf Point, Montana. At the height of the operation, CBC had seventy-five to one hundred thousand horses running wild over 100,000 square miles from the Canadian border down to Laramie, Wyoming. From the early 1920s to 1938, CBC—or "Corned Beef and Cabbage" or "Cowboy Be Careful," as the locals called it—was a renaissance of the roundups of the 1880s. Thoroughbreds, draft horses, and range mustangs ran together in the wild and multiplied, reverting to the wild state of their ancestors. These herds contained rogues that were hard to catch even by the most well-mounted, wily cowboy. Stud fights for those who witnessed them were horrid, bloody affairs.

The roundup wagons operated with crews of twenty to thirty cowboys. Crews slept out on the range and ate from a chuck wagon, working as the trail herders had done fifty years before. The big difference, however, was that these crews were chasing wild horses over expansive, rough country where a horse at full speed might step in a hole or stumble over a hidden cut bank, resulting sometimes in bone-breaking wrecks. Wild horses were roped and wrestled to be branded, doctored, or castrated. Some men had taken to wearing a baseball catcher's chest pad to protect themselves. Few cowboys had not been severely kicked at least once during this procedure. Cowboys set the broken bones themselves, and many chose to work in spite of injuries just to avoid bumping along in the cook wagon.

CBC cowboys started with a string of ten to thirteen horses and were expected to break wild horses and use them on certain parts of the roundup. They spent all day in the saddle and rode "broke" horses or "rim rockers" only when it was absolutely necessary. Crews adapted to the work and soon became hardened professionals at their jobs. They were predominantly young men, with tough, seasoned cowboys sprinkled among them. Because of the danger factor, younger cowboys were asked to sign releases, and the turnover rate among some crews was high.

Work was hard to come by during the Depression, and the average wage for ranch hands had fallen to $30 a month. CBC was able to hire crews of top-notch cowboys for $40 to $60 a month. The cowboys were masters at breaking and roping wild horses. The men rode two horses per day, switching at noon. Sometimes the horses were too tired to carry the rider back in the evenings, however, and a fresh horse had to be brought out from the roundup wagon.

Small herds of around 150 wild horses were gathered and held on cut banks, where they were roped. Men on the ground tied the legs, and the male horses were branded and castrated. Between eight and nine thousand colts were branded each year. The larger ones were left as stallions, while the less fit ones were gelded.

Horse sales in Miles City, Montana, and Laramie, Wyoming, became huge events. During the three days of buying and selling in Laramie, for instance, a sea of horses could be seen in four directions from the water tower. The separate herds were kept a half-mile apart to keep the stallions from fighting. Once each herd was brought into the yards, they were separated by color: bays, grays, sorrels, blacks, buckskins, and roans. The best and worst of the horses were then culled and auctioned off by the sale pens. The best were broken and sold as saddle or military horses; the culls were shipped east, saving many horses from starvation, and turned a profit for the company.

The danger and physical exertion of the work instilled a spark of both camaraderie and self-assuredness that was unique to the American cowboy. CBC's cowboys were the wildest bunch of men to ride over the area since the Crow, Shoshone, Sioux, and Cheyenne horsemen before them.

54

RUSTY WELLS TOPPED A HIGH RIDGE OVERLOOKING THE Powder River and drew rein on the black gelding. The horse pawed at the dry ground beneath his hoofs, causing small waves of grasshoppers to rise off the drought-stricken land. The year was 1932. The Great Depression that had swept the land had had little effect on either the horse or his fifteen-year-old boy. Rusty had never felt more alive than he did at this moment. All his dreams of the past five years had come true. He was on the open Montana range; he was working for the biggest horse outfit in the world; he was riding a magnificent thoroughbred that was as attractive as he was athletic. Rusty wasn't playing cowboy, he was living it.

The young cowboy paused and admired the majesty of the scene below, giving silent thanks to God for putting him there. Reaching forward, Rusty stroked the gelding on the neck, letting his hand run through the coarse black mane and savoring the smell of horse and leather. Rusty then felt the scab over his left eye, a reminder of the beating he had taken back at camp a week before at the hands of a crew cowboy four years his senior. Neither the cut nor the thought of the cruelty mattered at all now. The biggest country he had ever seen lay before him in all its glory. His ride with Tom McAllister was interrupted only by flashes of white from retreating antelope or the silhouettes of the gray mule deer trotting over the horizon in front or on either side of them. He was in wild, uncivilized country, and he loved it.

The sun reflected bright on the famous muddy river that wound through the dry, hilly country. Along its banks, more than a thousand horses grazed or watered. The current moved over some shallow gravel, giving it the appearance of sparkling lights. The air was the clearest Rusty had ever seen and carried the smell of sage, cedar, and sweetgrass. He watched a flock of pintail rise in unison off a far bend of the river and disappear over a high butte to the south.

The horses drifted along, always remaining loosely grouped. The herd seemed to have a life of its own. The late afternoon sun reflected off the tails of the horses as they swatted flies. A dozen horses stood in the water on a shallow gravel bar. Rusty smiled as a mouse-colored mare pawed the water, splashing a fifteen-foot area around her and waking others who were dozing, soaking sore feet. Rusty spotted a 77 brand on a gelding. Though he did not know the horseman personally, he knew the brand belonged to Al Irions. The boy was pleased with himself, feeling like he was becoming acclimated with his job.

With ears pricked forward and an impatience to travel, the black gelding had detected the presence of the horse herd a mile before the boy had seen them. After eight hours of riding, the gelding showed few signs of fatigue. He was powerful and at the same time sensitive to the bit: Rusty only needed to move the reins for the horse to stop, slow, or turn. He put his feet down exactly right every time, never stepping on a rock or stumbling. What impressed Rusty most was the way the horse seemed to float when he moved. Sitting in the saddle on this horse felt so smooth that it "made your ass laugh," as Sid Vollen, CBC's wagon boss out of Miles City, said about such horses.

The gelding had been put in Rusty's string three days prior. Rusty had shod him and topped him off after supper while the other cowboys played cards and relaxed around the chuck wagon. He rode him for just twenty minutes to see if he'd buck, and then Rusty had spent twice that time brushing the dust out of his black coat until it resembled velvet. Tom McAllister, the near-seventy-year-old cowboy Rusty was riding with, seemed to know about every horse they saw. Rusty heard Tom say to Vollen that this horse's bloodline could be traced to a bloodline Lord Wallop had brought from

England in the 1880s, when he was building his massive herd of horses on Otter Creek south of Miles City.

For Rusty Wells, CBC had been an opportunity to get out of the stockyards in Kansas City and into the country he had dreamed about since he could remember. After their father was killed in World War I and their mother died in the influenza outbreak of 1918, Rusty and his sister, Mattie, were placed in an orphanage. Rusty developed a passion for horses at age ten when he worked as a chore boy in the afternoons at the Fred T. Platt horse barns next to the orphanage on Genesee Street.

He cleaned stalls and fed the livestock there and at the stock exchange nearby. He followed horseshoers and veterinarians around the yards like a shadow, watching with fascination and absorbing everything he saw. Eventually, Rusty graduated to riding rough stock through the sale ring. He learned to listen to horses and to understand their movements and their dispositions. At a horse sale in Kansas City, Rusty caught the attention of Tom McAllister, who was there buying stallions.

Tom McAllister was a legend among horsemen of the West; he had raised thousands of horses in northern and eastern Montana at the turn of the century. Sid Vollen, who ran the CBC out of Miles City, had asked Tom to keep an eye out for riders. Tom noticed the boy worked hard, had a lot of horse sense, and was quiet with horses.

McAllister's only reservations about Rusty were his age and his quiet temperment. The cowboys who worked for CBC were a tough breed. He knew Rusty would work, but Tom worried he might be taken advantage of. If that were the case, McAllister would take the boy with him to check stock.

McAllister had no children of his own, but he had raised several ranch kids, buying their clothes and paying for their school. One of the kids was Sid Vollen himself, who years before as an adolescent had shown up at Tom's ranch wanting to become a cowboy. Tom was now approaching seventy, and doctoring a cut horse on the range was more of a job than it used to be.

Fred Platt was fond of Rusty, but he knew his desire to go west. And since the Depression had hit, he wasn't sure he could afford to keep the boy on. Plus, Rusty could earn $35 to $40 a month working as a cowboy in Montana.

"He's got good hands, and he won't talk your ear off," Platt told McAllister. That suited Tom fine. He could not tolerate these young, insolent cowboys wanting to ask about the "old" days, when all they really wanted was the chance to run on about how they heard it had been.

After two months under McAllister's direction, Rusty became skilled enough with a rope to catch a horse in a rope corral. He had learned the technique of holding a horse's head back while it was on the ground being castrated and branded. As a hand on a horse, he was as good as any on the crew. Unfortunately for Rusty, his thirst for knowledge, shy manner, and assignments with Tom McAllister won him no points with the other young cowboys.

Rusty Wells had taken a beating from Mitchell Kaycell, a cowboy out of Texas, after he had taken a four-day trip with Tom McAllister to Glendive. When he got back, the cowboy, jealous of what he considered preferential treatment bestowed on Rusty, began to badger the boy incessantly, until he caught Rusty alone brushing his horse in the remuda corral. Rusty never had a chance; Mitchell Kaycell was almost two hundred pounds, and Rusty was barely one hundred thirty. The nineteen-year-old knocked the boy down, cut his lip, and bloodied his nose. It didn't bother Rusty as it might, because now, the following week, Rusty Wells was riding over the prettiest country he had ever seen, riding the best horse he had ever sat on and working for the greatest horseman he had ever known.

They were south of Miles City, riding up the Powder River, when McAllister rode off from Rusty and trotted over and down a side drainage. Nothing was said, and barely a look was given, but Rusty had learned to continue on his course while Tom roamed some other hillside. Rusty had also learned when to follow and when to stay put. In big, wide-open country, you could easily get lost. If Rusty stayed on his course, McAllister would find him. Rusty had followed Fred Platt's advice to pay attention and keep his mouth shut. It was the code of the West.

After riding alone for a few miles, Rusty began to recognize landmarks. He had ridden to this area on Powder River, around eighty miles southeast of Miles City, once before. A mile away, Rusty saw the form of Tom McAllister topping out on a ridge. Like a ghost he would appear and disappear down draws, out of sight, only to appear again on a faraway ridge like a silhouette. He never seemed to get out of a walk or a slow trot. That a man could appear in two distant places in such a short time without running his horse flat-out seemed impossible to Rusty.

From the ridge, he looked down and saw the herd from under his broad-brimmed hat, and immediately Rusty searched for the blooded, better-built horses. Though he was only fifteen, Rusty had developed a keen sense of judging horseflesh. From a quarter-mile he immediately picked out the stallions of the separate groups and noted the horses that were obviously physically superior to the rest of the range horses CBC ran.

Rusty gave the black gelding his head and let him pick his way down the bluff to the river. On uneven rocky ground the horse descended the quarter-mile effortlessly, all the while with his ears pricked toward the massive herd grazing on the green flats next to the Powder River. High brown and gray bluffs punctuated the sun-parched land that rolled on for miles. Rusty gave the herd a respectable distance and unhooked his rope from his saddle and hung it over his saddle horn just to be safe. The knot end of a rope can sometimes turn a stallion on the fight. On two occasions he had seen cowboys carelessly wander into horse herds and be taken by aggressive stallions.

Rusty rode over next to Tom McAllister, who was reading brands and examining the animals. The boy did not speak but sat on his horse patiently. He stroked the black gelding's neck with his hand and smiled sheepishly at the cowboy, whose old, wrinkled face lifted slightly into a small, brief smile. The two paused, dwarfed by the immense country, the herd of horses, and the famous Powder River, whose name symbolized part of the history of the American West.

Tom McAllister rolled a Bull Durham and looked at the boy. Rusty was a good hand with the horses, had no bravado, never ran his horse unnecessarily, and paid attention. He figured things out and did what he was told. He was good company on trips, never asking stupid questions or constantly talking as many cowboys did. In fact, Rusty rarely spoke at all unless spoken to. Tom had given him the black gelding to ride because he liked the way he rode. A rough cowboy on a hot thoroughbred did not mix. He could see by Rusty's expression when he rode up that he appreciated and respected the horse.

"How'd you get the name Rusty?" the old cowboy asked.

The question almost knocked the boy off his horse. He had never, in more than five hundred miles of riding on different trips, been asked anything by Tom McAllister, much less a personal question. Instructions had been given or directions given out, but never a direct question. The boy had been sitting at peace with the world, watching the beauty of a wild horse herd, and now he sat shaken and tongue-tied. He reached in his tattered vest pocket and produced an old leather billfold, which he handed to McAllister. The word "Rusty" was embroidered in fancy lettering on the front.

"My dad sent it . . . from France . . . when I was a baby," Rusty stammered. His eyes were as large as hens' eggs at the prospect of having to hold his own in a conversation with a man he considered a legend. His face was so flushed that even his ears turned red. McAllister looked at the billfold and the picture displayed inside.

"That's a fancy wallet. Is that a picture of your girl?" he asked, handing the wallet back to Rusty.

"No, sir, that's my sister. She's the one that writes me all the time." Rusty paused, feeling he had said too much. He panicked in his thoughts; Mr. McAllister had not asked him about his sister or about the letters. Now he would probably think Rusty was rude or, worse, a blabbermouth. He heard men complain that some cowboys could talk the ears off a wooden Indian, and now he had blabbed. He wanted to apologize, but he opted to sit and be quiet, so embarrassed and self-conscious that he wanted to shrink into his saddle.

"Watch it!" Tom yelled at the same instant the black gelding spun and jumped a good six feet out from under Rusty, which left the boy dangling off the horse's right side. The gelding was racing back the way he had come. The only part of Rusty left on top of the saddle was his left calf and his hand, which clawed at the saddle horn; the rest of him hung off the side of the runaway horse. His face was a foot off the ground, which was going by in a blur.

"Hold on!" he heard Tom yell. The cowboy's voice inspired Rusty to hang on. With all his might, he pulled with his left spur, which was hooked over the back of the saddle. He felt the panic in his horse and heard hoofbeats beside him. With a combined effort of stomach, arm, leg, hand, and back muscles, Rusty pulled with a twisting, strained motion and righted himself on the stampeding horse. He reached for the one rein that had not dropped, just in time to feel a sharp blow just above his knee.

At once he saw the wild look of a charging stud, his teeth bared, just inches away. In one swift motion the stallion grabbed Rusty by the chest with his teeth and pulled him a foot out of the saddle. Rusty's expression went from alarm to pain to fight in less than a second. His right arm was useless, as it was under the horse's head, but he brought his left around and slapped the stud with the end of the bridle rein, to no effect. Rusty was now in a runaway, and had lost his rope, hat, one rein, and been bitten twice in a matter of seconds. He yelled at the attacking animal, which suddenly fell with a crash to the ground in a cloud of dust. Still atop the stampeding gelding, Rusty pulled to the left with the one rein he had left and circled the horse to a stop. He reached down to retrieve the other rein and looked back to see what happened. Tom McAllister sat on his horse, facing the downed stud and holding a dally to his saddle. He had roped the stud by the front feet while he was in the middle of charging Rusty. McAllister's rope ran from his saddle horn to the stud's front feet, and every time the stud struggled, McAllister's saddle horse would back up and work the rope, pulling the enraged animal back to the ground.

"You okay?" Tom yelled to Rusty.

"Yes, sir," the boy responded, sheepishly riding over.

"We'll let him soak awhile, and maybe he'll let us alone when we let him up. That was a nice ride; I thought you was gone," he said calmly, knowing the boy's confidence was shaken. When Rusty turned the gelding, Tom noticed the blood on the boy's shirt and pants and a small wave of anger came over him. He backed up his saddle horse, causing the stud to thrash against the ground as the rope pulled on him.

"You'd better start treating humans better or you'll end up on some Russian's plate," the old man threatened the stud, before releasing the pressure on the rope and enabling the horse to rise and step out of the loop. The stud jumped up, looked at the riders, and ran back to the herd. Rusty was completely overtaken with awe at the calmness and speed with which the old cowboy had handled the situation.

"You saved my life," Rusty said, forgetting his shyness.

"The hell! You had him pretty much beat back by the time I got there," Tom said, noticing the spreading blood spots on Rusty's leg and chest as he coiled his rope. The older man cursed himself for not seeing the stallion charge earlier. He had been looking at the boy's wallet, and now the boy was hurt. "Better get off and let me have a look at those bites," he said.

The boy, embarrassed, protested politely, but the old cowboy took him over to a spot where the river flowed clean over a gravel bar and inspected his wounds. It was worse than he thought: part of the boy's chest muscle had been torn away, and there was a deep gash almost to the bone above his knee. The old cowboy bandaged Rusty's wounds as best he could with what he had. He sprinkled lime that he carried in his saddlebag for doctoring cuts on horses. The leg wound bothered him most, as it had taken quite a lot of pressure from tying Rusty's neck scarf around his lower thigh to slow the bleeding.

"We'll ride over to the Leitners' and get a car to Dunning's place. Can you ride?" Tom asked.

"Yes, sir, I'm fine. It was my fault. I'll be okay," he replied, mounting the black gelding after having inspected him for bites or kicks. He was self-conscious of having caused a change of plan. Tom McAllister made Rusty put on his coat, knowing the youth could go into shock soon. It was about an eight-mile ride to Leitner's ranch.

"Cross your leg over the saddle horn to stop the bleeding. Don't worry about old Black, he won't buck you off," Tom said. Rusty smiled and stroked the gelding's neck. He was becoming light-headed. He looked to the old man who was riding alongside him.

"I'll tell you about some of these big horse outfits," the old cowboy said. He was both worried for the boy and agitated at himself for not seeing the stud charge sooner. If he were a young man, he would have taken out his rifle and shot the stallion, but as judgment is tempered with age, he realized that the stud was merely doing his duty to his herd. McAllister told him of the Indian horses, Sydney Paget, Oliver Wallop, and the thousands of well-bred horses that had roamed the country. He described Indian battles, horse thieves, sheep wars, hangings, horse races, and anything else he could think of to keep Rusty's mind off his injuries.

As some horses will do, the black gelding sensed the boy was hurt and rode along as gently and smoothly as if Rusty was riding an old horse.

"Hang in there, we ain't got far to go," Tom said. The boy had lost so much blood that he was in a dreamlike state. The fact that Tom McAllister was riding alongside him, telling him stories, made Rusty feel safe and that his injuries were nothing more than a scrape. He felt the need to doze, but every time he did, Tom would raise his voice slightly to get the boy's attention.

As the two cowboys rode off, the brown stallion raised his head, snorted, and herded some mares away with a bite to the back or an aggressive hazing with ears pinned back. After his show of dominance, the stallion had rejoined the grazing herd.

Rusty did not remember much about how he got to Luther Dunning's ranch on Otter Creek. He thought he remembered Tom pointing to a formation of rocks laid in a circle in the short prairie grass and telling him they were Cheyenne teepee rings. Rusty had dreamlike memories of riding in a truck with a rancher he did not know. The idea that Tom would ride for miles and do nothing but talk now confused him. He lay in bed, thinking it must have been a dream since the horseman had hardly spoken to him at all before that.

When Rusty arrived at Dunning's ranch, he was given some "strong" soup and had slept almost an entire day. When he awoke, he was mortified at being bedridden and doctored by a woman. They would not let him out of bed for two days, until the swelling in his leg subsided. The doctor had come and placed a splint on the leg to immobilize it, and he had given Leota Dunning supplies and instructions on how to care for Rusty.

Leota, or Aunt "Lodi," told Rusty how she had come up the Yellowstone River on a steamer when old Milestown was a haven for buffalo hunters, cowboys, Indians, prostitutes, cattle barons, and English remittance men. And how as a young girl she had received buffalo-fur hats and leggings from the soldiers at Fort Keogh to shield her from the brutal Montana winters. Her kindness and riveting stories made Rusty's convalescence relatively painless. During his stay at the Dunnings, the two became fast friends.

Rusty looked around his surroundings and noted the simple, clean ranch house. What mattered to the boy most was the fact he was at Luther Dunning's ranch. This man was famous for horses clear back in Kansas City. He was the most famous horse breeder in the entire U. S. Army Remount breeding program.

On the fourth day of Rusty's convalescence, Dunning rode up with Tom McAllister and Walter Sibley. Rusty was both weak and faint, but when he heard Aunt Lodi say that Luther was riding in, he immediately got out of bed, dressed, and headed toward the door, where he was stopped.

"Tom told me you'd be hard to keep in bed. You stay right here, Rusty, and I'll make you some tea," she ordered, noticing the pale look on his face as the blood left his head. She quickly pulled a chair across the kitchen for Rusty to sit on, which he did, as his chest and leg had begun to pound. Leota smiled. She liked the boy; he was quiet, polite, and had plenty of try.

"Luther will have you in a card game as soon as he gets in," Leota laughed. Both Leota and Luther were known for their western hospitality.

Rusty tried to rise again, but he became dizzy.

"Here, Rusty, sit down and eat this cookie. I'm liable to miss you with this chair if you keep getting up." Leota once again slid the chair under the wobbling boy, who resigned and sat.

Of all the luck, he thought. He desperately wanted to go out and be with the cowboys and look at the horses. He sat perplexed, holding the cookie. He was soon to be in the company of the two greatest horsemen in the West, maybe even the world, and he could hardly get out of his seat.

Minutes passed like hours, until finally, Tom McAllister, Walter Sibley, and Luther Dunning walked through the door.

"This must be the stud fighter," Luther said, shaking Rusty's hand.

"He's been trying to get up since he heard you fellows come in," Leota said. Rusty looked at the three older men as they sat at the kitchen table. They were the picture of what cowboys should look like.

"Pull your chair over, Pistol," McAllister said.

"Luther will coach you. It'll be like he knows what cards you have," Tom said, glancing at the tilted mirror high on the wall behind Rusty. To those who knew about Luther's mirror, it was all comical, because Luther Dunning was far and wide the most honest man that anyone in the country knew. On occasion he invited some Cheyenne over to play cards. It was rare that Luther ever came out ahead. It was his way to settle the price in a horse deal they were haggling over. He was the only man in the entire Remount program who could send the army a boxcar-load of horses without being inspected. It was a compliment to Luther's competency and honesty as a horse dealer.

"Say there, Pistol. If a fellow had a pair that matched, I might throw the rest away and try for three of a kind," Luther advised. Rusty indeed had a pair of tens and incredulously drew another. The men at the table tried not to laugh too hard at the boy's gleeful expression when he drew the third ten.

"Try not to frown too much if you draw a bad hand, or smile too much when you draw a winner."

Walter Sibley was privy to the sparring about who had more horses that went on between Dunning and McAllister.

"Walter, have you seen that bunch of mares and the dun team that runs with them? There must be over sixteen hundred head in that bunch," Luther said with a smile. Tom McAllister studied his cards.

"Luther, was you with us when we trailed that bunch of four thousand to Dakota? No, I guess that was Tom Reed," Tom said. Luther laid two cards on the table.

Rusty looked incredulously at the old cowboy. Did he really move that many horses? McAllister noted the boy's stare and gave him a wink as if to say, "You bet I did."

It was a month or more before Rusty was well enough to travel. In that time, he had learned the difference between being a cowboy and being a horseman. All three of the men he had watched and listened to during his recovery were or had been some of the best bronc riders of their day, and they were scholars in breeding, training, and raising horses on the free range. They knew army colonels, polo players, racehorse trainers, hunter-jumper buyers, and ranchers. Rusty listened as the men talked of Noll Wallop, who was now an English lord, and the Gallatins' breeding operation in Little Goose Canyon.

When Rusty was up and around, Luther introduced him to "His Majesty," as he and Leota referred to their government Remount stud. Luther had already been in the thoroughbred breeding business for thirty years before the army started its program. Luther's government stallion was kept in a separate barn with his own small corral. His name was Spearpoint, and he was the most beautiful animal Rusty had ever seen. He was perfectly built, his muscles rippling under his coat. Even though he was deep chestnut in color, he was referred to as a sorrel, as were all light brown horses with matching manes in the West. The stallion had a brother that had won the English Derby.

Spearpoint was also playful. Every morning when Rusty would hobble out with his cane to feed him, Spearpoint would take the brush from Rusty and hold it in his mouth. He whinnied at Rusty as soon as the boy set foot out of the house.

Rusty's black gelding was also becoming a pet. After a few days of meeting him in the field with feed, Rusty had only to make his presence known in the yard and the gelding would meet the rider at the gate. After Spearpoint and the gelding ate, Rusty would brush their coats until they shone.

During the time Rusty was at the Dunnings, a fear began to build in him. His wounds had healed, but he was unable to walk straight. He waited anxiously for Tom McAllister's return from a long trip. To the old cowboy's surprise, the soft-spoken boy limped over as the cowboy rode in, and spoke right up.

"Am I going to have to go back to Kansas City if my leg don't heal?"

The question amused Tom, until he saw the look of pure fear on Rusty's face. "No son, you work for me. I just loan you out to CBC on occasion," Tom said and smiled. He noticed the expression on the boy's face change to one of extreme gratitude.

"Better throw a saddle on your gelding tonight and let him soak awhile. You don't need to get bucked off on your first day back." Tom never gave a thought whether the boy could ride, so Rusty, who was all-trusting in the horseman, figured he could.

The next day they were off to Miles City. Rusty was riding the black gelding, and McAllister was riding a small sorrel and leading a packhorse. Aunt Lodi came out and saw them off. She reached up and took Rusty's hand in hers. It was a mothering hand to a boy who had never been mothered. "You write me when you get to Miles City and let me know how that leg is doing," she said and smiled at Rusty.

"Yes, ma'am," he said and felt a strong wave of emotion come over him. He had to lift his hand silently to say the words that were caught in his throat. He ducked his head to hide his face under the greasy felt hat so as not to show his emotions and neck-reined the black gelding toward the gate.

"Hey, Rusty," Leota called cheerfully. The boy turned.

"What do you call your horse?"

The boy was at a loss. It wasn't his place to name horses, so he looked to Tom McAllister and shrugged.

"Call him Colstrip," she called.

Rusty looked at the horse and then at Tom, who nodded his head. The two started off again, but Rusty stopped and overcame his shyness long enough to turn the gelding back and face Leota.

"Thank you," he called to her, then turned to follow Tom. Leota waved and smiled, but she turned away as tears began to well up in her eyes. She knew what could happen in a hard country, and she had a bad feeling that she could not explain.

After twenty yards or so, Rusty reached for the lead rope to the packhorse. "I can take him," the boy said softly. It was as the older man thought; riding didn't bother the boy at all. As they approached the entrance to Dunning's ranch, Rusty rode past Tom, swung down off his horse while holding the reins of the black gelding and the lead rope to the packhorse, and limped over to open the wire gate for them. Tom knew the boy had to prove something, and besides, that was the last fence they would hit on the eighty-mile trip to Miles City.

They passed two riders as they crossed the road to Ashland. Both had dark skin, beat-up saddles, and poor horses. Tom greeted them with a nod when they passed. "Cheyenne," Tom said to Rusty, who twisted around and watched them as they faded away over a hill.

"They had horses as good as anyone's until the government stole them because they ate too much grass," Tom said, pausing and then looking back. "I ain't talking about the Indian wars; I'm talking about ten years ago. It wasn't fair. Luther and I tried to help them out, but it wasn't any use . . ." Tom trailed off. "We all bred to Indian mares in the early days: myself, Wallop, and Paget."

Rusty didn't respond. McAllister, in an uncharacteristic move, pulled his reins up and loped off for a couple hundred yards. Rusty gave the man his space and then eventually caught up to him. He reached in his vest pocket and produced a button, which he silently handed to Tom.

"Well, I'll be. Where did you come up with this?" he asked, turning the button over in his wrinkled hand and noticing the eagle stamped on the front of the tarnished metal.

"I found it back at the river," Rusty said.

"The Powder?" he asked.

"Yes, sir."

"You've got yourself a cavalry button. Might have come off one of General Crook's men or even earlier, from some soldier during the Powder River fight. Them boys lost a lot of horses to the Indians in that one. There's a pile of horse bones over near Powderville yet called Dead Horse Camp, where hundreds died in one night during that march. The soldiers had to walk out.

There's a cannon barrel sunk in the Powder up there, too." He handed the button back to Rusty.

"Crazy Horse never did get beat in this country. The Sioux and Cheyenne ruled from the Platte to the Yellowstone and whipped any Indians or soldiers that stood against them."

The vibrations of thundering hooves on plank boards rattled the building, jarring everyone in the Range Riders Saloon in Miles City. A moment later Red Tate burst in, riding a bay gelding.

"A round for the house and a beer for my horse!" he yelled above those inside who shouted his name. Red's horse was outfitted in a silver-trimmed breast collar and bridle. A silver spade bit hung from its mouth, and Red wore a small-brimmed hat and a fancy western shirt. The bartender shook his head and smiled along with everyone else in the bar—even Tom McAllister smiled.

Rusty was too concerned for the horse to pay attention to Red Tate. It looked like the gelding was none too gentle, and there was white showing in his crazed eye. Red seemed unfazed that his horse was getting madder by the second.

"Hello, Tom!" Red yelled, as he leaned over to accept a glass of whiskey from the bartender. The horse began to dance in place just as Red took the glass. In one smooth motion Red downed the whiskey and tossed the glass back to the bartender, who caught it on the fly. The horse began to run sideways toward some tables, whereupon Red touched a spur to its outside ribs and at the same time brought the bridle reins down with a crack on the horse's shoulder. The horse stopped its rush and stood trembling for a moment before he calmed at the touch of Red's hand stroking his neck.

The colt now stood perfectly still under the relaxed cowboy, who resumed his conversation. That the horse relaxed at all amazed Rusty, who was sure there was going to be a wreck. Without pausing, Red dismounted and took a chair at Tom's table and left the horse ground-tied, standing in front of the bar. Rusty's eyes were wide open from the scene that had just unfolded.

"Now you stay right there!" Red yelled at the horse, which turned an eye toward the cowboy but stayed where he was standing. The reins hung from the fancy silver bit to a coiled pile on the floor. A couple of men in business suits walked through the door and stood still, stunned at the sight of a horse standing at the bar.

"Well, if you're not gonna drink, back away from the bar and give somebody else a chance," Red announced to the horse, who was well aware of being spoken to.

"Back," Red instructed from his chair, with a firm yet soft tone.

"Back, back!" he repeated louder. The horse took one step back, then another, dragging the reins on the floor in front of him.

"Hey, Red, you gonna back him down to the livery stable?" someone yelled from across the bar.

"No, I'm backing him down to the train station to pick up my brother." Red looked at his pocket watch, to the laughter of the small crowd.

"Whoa!" he yelled, whereupon the horse stopped in the middle of the room. "The train ain't due for ten minutes," Red commented. The bartender set a fresh drink on the table.

"Hello, Red. What brings you to Miles City?" Tom asked.

"Horses. I'm meeting Colonel Daniels here and taking him up to Jordan to look at some of Harry Ross's stock."

Rusty studied Red Tate with fascination. The man had more color than anyone he had ever seen, and he had only known him a few minutes. He was equally amazed at the horse, which showed no inclination to move from the middle of the saloon, though he wasn't exactly what you would call relaxed. Rusty got up and stood a respectable distance next to Red before the cheerful man turned to acknowledge him.

"Son, where did you get that hat?" Red asked, looking at the limp, greasy felt on the boy's head. It resembled a rag more than a hat.

"Uh, excuse me, sir, but would you like me to put your horse in a pen next to ours?" Rusty had been so intent on being bold enough to ask Tom McAllister's friend if he could take care of his horse that he totally forgot the question about his hat.

"That'd be just right. Throw him some hay, too. Then get yourself over to White's Saddlery and buy yourself a new hat." Red handed the boy $3, which the boy declined.

"Alright, then, buy me a hat just like yours, only brand-new, and I'll wear yours till you get back." At that, Red took the boy's hat and put it on himself, after sailing his own over the bar till it spun onto a deer rack that hung over the mirror. Rusty looked back at the man and then to his horse.

"What's his name?" Rusty asked, looking at Red's horse. He wasn't surprised to learn it was Blue. At once Red and Tom took note of the way the boy approached the horse. Though Blue was trained, he was not particularly gentle, a fact that Rusty recognized, and in a nonaggressive smooth motion, he walked up to the horse and let him smell his arm. He stood to the side of Blue's head and slowly placed a hand along his shoulder, and then below the horse's ear, stroking his neck at the throatlatch and all the while speaking softly to him. Rusty picked up the reins from the floor and, without pulling the horse, moved slowly toward the door, giving Blue time to figure out which direction he wanted to go by moving the reins. The boy walked out, and Blue followed.

Red noted the torn boots and the mended back pockets as the boy walked out. Even the poorest cowboys were particular about their dress, and this boy's spurs didn't even match.

"Has CBC quit paying their cowboys?" he asked Tom.

"The boy has his check sent to his sister back in Kansas City. The two are orphans. He's been with us about three months. He's a good hand with the horses," Tom replied.

Red smiled. He himself had come west from Missouri thirty-five years earlier.

"The artist's touch!" he announced to the bar and sat down at the piano in the corner of the room. Red pulled on a pair of cotton gloves before launching into his song.

"I got the same size head as you," he sang, banging out a chord on the piano and singing to the boy.

"Buy me a hat, and when you're through, put up my horse, whose name is Blue." With that, Red broke into a lively rendition of *Camptown Races,* and the people in the bar began to shout and stomp their feet.

The following summer, Leota Dunning's uneasy intuition about the fate of Rusty Wells would prove true. Rusty had ridden north to Wolf Point, Montana, to pick up two horses for Tom McAllister. While there, he lent a hand to the northern CBC crew, who were trailing a herd of horses across the Milk River. When a cowboy who could not swim lost his hold on a skittish horse in the water, Rusty jumped his black gelding into the river and pulled the cowboy out. He then swam his horse back across toward the other bank to retrieve the cowboy's horse. Rusty tried to lead the horse across the river, but it wouldn't lead, so he switched to the scared horse and tried to ride it across.

The horse panicked even more when its feet first left the river bottom. Instead of swimming, it tried to leap up and out of the water. Rusty fought to keep the horse pointed toward the opposite bank, but he eventually had to release his hold and fall back into the water. As Rusty slid off the rear of the horse, his spur caught in the back cinch. Before he could free himself, the horse twisted and fell over on top of him, pinning Rusty to the bottom. Cowboys jumped their horses into the river to save the boy, but by the time the horse was roped and pulled to the shore, Rusty was dead.

It had broken Tom McAllister's heart. Rusty was buried on the bank of the Milk. Tom took the boy's effects and mailed them to his sister in Kansas City and rode off alone. The boy was now part of the country he had worked so hard to get to. After living the life he had always wanted to live, he had died as a horseman.

Bea Gallatin Beuf sat in a Beverly Hills restaurant and daydreamed of her horses. Carlo was speaking about filmmaking to a captive audience around the table. He was a brilliant man whom she loved very much, but her heart was being pulled by her love of the Gallatin family ranch in Wyoming. Hollywood had lost its luster, and she longed for the beauty of Little Goose Canyon. Most of all she missed the horses. Although Goelet Gallatin had scaled back his horse operation, more than one hundred head still lived at the ranch.

From her table, Bea gazed out the window at a Japanese tree trimmed into an elaborate shape. The tree made her think of the tree just south of the house that William Moncreiffe had told her an Indian had been buried in. She then thought of how the Bighorn Mountains rose out of the back pastures of the ranch, and how a person could ride a short distance behind the house and see a hundred miles to the north on a clear day. Two creeks, Little Goose and Trabing, full of trout, wound their way down through the ranch, running clear, cold water from snow-covered peaks.

Bea thought of the ranch foreman, Johnny Cover. A cowboy's cowboy, he was honest, hardworking, and loyal. Horse trainers, Hollywood stuntmen, rodeo stars, and almost every good cowboy in the country had worked at the E4 Ranch at one time or another, and Bea had worked alongside them on the roundups and in the hayfields.

"Hey, Carlo, does Bea become an Italian countess now that you two are married?" an MGM executive at the table asked, snapping Bea from her thoughts. Carlo looked at his wife and smiled.

"Of course she does," he replied, giving his wife's hand an affectionate squeeze. Bea looked around the table. They were all nice-enough people, but she longed for the honest simplicity of those whom she had been raised around.

"Bea, wasn't your great-grandfather Thomas Jefferson?" One of Carlos's clients addressed Bea in an attempt at conversation.

"No, he was Albert Gallatin, the secretary of treasury under presidents Jefferson and Madison," she replied. She did not elaborate; it would be lost on these people. There were signers of the Declaration of Independence on both sides of her family. To some, that meant entitling one to a certain status of breeding. To Bea, it meant that two of her relatives had put their name on a public document expressing their convictions against an oppressive government, the very act of which would very likely cost them their lives. The man looked at the couple and raised his glass. "To the 'Cowgirl Countess,'" he said, to the applause of the table. Bea smiled politely and lifted her glass.

"Are there still Indians out west?" someone asked. It was a ridiculous question. Little Nest, a Crow, was a friend of the family, as were several old Cheyenne and Lakota chiefs who had befriended her mother. As conversation continued, Bea let her thoughts drift back to the horses that grazed across the high meadows at the foot of the Bighorns. Her father's ranch was calling her to come home. She made a silent vow that somehow she would take Carlo back to the ranch for good.

When Noll Wallop fulfilled his tenure as an English lord, his son Gerard was allowed to succeed him as the ninth Earl of Portsmouth. Noll was eager to get back to Little Goose Canyon. However, Marguerite enjoyed her life as Lady Portsmouth. So, to keep domestic harmony, Noll kept their residence in England for the winter.

After graduating from Yale, Oliver had taken over running the ranch. When Noll returned, Oliver had little patience for his father's ideas. Few around Big Horn, including his son Oliver, really appreciated or understood the unique pioneer.

Wallop's first stop in Wyoming was Otter Creek, where he visited his old friend Charlie Thex and the Brewster and the Brown families. At the latter's Three Circle Ranch on Tongue River, Wallop joined the family for dinner. Captain Brown had schooled his children on how to address Noll as "Lord" Wallop and not Mr. Wallop. One of the younger Brown kids, trying to get Noll's attention, was confused with the new title of Lord Wallop.

"God, please pass the potatoes," he blurted out.

At the Sheridan Inn, Wallop was approached by Miss Kate, a hostess who had known him for almost thirty years. "Do you want me to call you Lord Wallop or Mr. Wallop now?" she asked.

"Please c-call me Noll, Kate," he said.

55

RED TATE HAD BOUGHT LAND OUTSIDE RANCHESTER, Wyoming, at the height of the Depression and was working at the laborious task of building corrals and a ranch house. Logs were cut on Black Mountain and placed on a large wagon pulled by four horses. The way up was easy, but the way down was dangerous. Logs were dragged on the ground behind full loads to serve as a brake and to reduce the chance of the wagon breaking free. All the way down the mountain, Red worked the brake with all his strength, Bob Tate pushed against the load, and the four horses braced themselves until they had reached flat ground. It was backbreaking work, something Red's seventeen-year-old son had tried to avoid for most of his teenage years.

What Bob wanted was to be on the back of a horse. He had already quit school to become a horse trainer, but as he saw it, his father was holding him back by making him work at the ranch. He could be stick-and-balling the horses, getting them used to polo, or putting racehorses through their paces.

Toward the end of the summer, Bob got a break from logging when Erma informed Red that thirty-five head of horses were missing from one of their pastures.

"Are you sure they're not in some draw?" Bob asked.

"They're gone," Erma said.

"You wanted to ride; now's your chance," Red said to Bob.

"Where am I supposed to look?" Bob asked.

"Well, I doubt they ran into the mountains or swam the Yellowstone, so I'd suggest you head north till you hit the Yellowstone and then turn east," Red said.

"Take that six-year-old bay and pack the sorrel we got from Major Nick," Erma suggested.

"Hell, why can't we just take the car?" Bob asked.

"We don't have money for gas. If you don't want to find the horses, I'll send the hired man and you can haul logs," Red said.

"Don't come back till you find them," he added.

It had been a bad summer. During one twenty-day stretch, the wind blew across the dried-up country with such a fury that the dust cut visibility to merely a few feet. To ride in such weather was impossible. Ranchers called and warned each other of hordes of crickets and grasshoppers moving across the country. The insects moved onto ranches and ate the clothes women left out on the lines. If windows were left open, they ate the curtains. Gardens, pastures, trees, and shrubs were ruined. The insects were so thick on the railroad tracks that on one occasion the coal train spun out on the greasy rails on Parkman Hill outside Ranchester. Railroad crews had to cover the rails with sand for the train to make the grade. Nose flies drove the horses mad, and the animals stomped their feet and tried to strike at their heads to scare off the insects.

When the phone rang at Red Tate's during a winter storm, he got the news he had feared. "Red, it's Bud Alderson." The temperature had sunk to around thirty below and was steadily dropping. Storms had already piled up snow and frozen a layer of ice on top, preventing horses from reaching the grass.

Moving the horses might be more stressful on the animals than leaving them, but if the cold spell didn't break, the entire herd might be lost. Red arranged for hay to be brought to a place near Decker, Montana, which was a day's ride south from Alderson's pasture.

Bud Alderson, his son Billy, and Red and Bob Tate eased the weak horses through the drifts as best as they could. They trailed the horses over the Wolf Mountains headed for Decker as the temperature dropped to fifty-two below zero. Two horses froze to death the first night before they could get them to the hay. The horsemen led the surviving horses to the large stacks of hay, and the foals were given grain Erma had brought.

Red was shoeing at the HF Bar Dude Ranch the following summer when he met Robert King, the president of Pennzoil, who was vacationing there with his family. King's wild twenty-three-year-old son had been the boxing champion at Yale. After one summer in the west, young Bob King dropped out of Yale and disappeared. Since Red Tate was familiar with the boy and his friends out west, Robert King hired him to find his son.

After some detective work, Red found the boy in Cimarron, New Mexico. The young man who had previously had an $800-a-month allowance was now herding sheep at $30 a month. Red brought him north and sold his father some horses and helped him get started in a ranching business on a ranch King bought in Colstrip, Montana.

Like Bob King, Bob Tate had also quit school early. The two young men hit it off immediately, and within the year, young Tate had Bob King in the polo-pony business in Big Horn. Bob got King to buy some of Gallatin's horses at a dispersal sale. In all, he bought eleven head of mares and polo prospects for just over $80 a head.

Bob King bought a house and barn in Big Horn to be close to the polo field, but the young man spent most of his time in the Mint Bar in Sheridan, twelve miles away. King was a hard-drinking ladies' man. He might be scheduled to play polo on Sunday at Moncreiffe's field and take off on a three-day horse-buying trip with Bill Eaton and Curley Witzel on Saturday, leaving Bob Tate to fill in for the feature games on Sunday. This didn't sit well with some of the Big Horn crowd.

Tate was somewhat wild on the polo field. While he was careful not to run into old Malcolm Moncreiffe, everyone else was fair game. He knocked Bill Leech, a wealthy dude ranch owner, off his horse when the man crossed in front of him, and Bob accidentally broke Carlo Beuf's jaw when the Italian count rode into one of Tate's backshots.

In 1931, polo took on a resurgence in Absaraka. Cameron Forbes took the Gallatin stallion Black Rascal and began his own polo-breeding program called Neponset Stud Farm in Beckton, Wyoming. When Forbes became governor of the Philippines, at the suggestion of presidents Theodore Roosevelt and William Taft, he introduced polo to that country and wrote the definitive book on polo, called *As to Polo.*

Forbes had recently been named ambassador to Japan and had traveled to Haiti to defuse a revolution there. When his health began to deteriorate, he retired to his ranch in Wyoming in the summer and raised polo ponies.

When Cameron's brother, Waldo, died prematurely, the bachelor adopted Waldo's children, Amelia and Waldo. Now in his seventies, Cameron started Neponset Stud for Amelia to enjoy. A polo field was built at the ranch, complete with scoreboard and tie lines for the horses. Seventeen polo mares and a stallion named Art Nouveau were imported from Argentina, and soon the Forbes were on their way to rival the Circle V as the premier polo operation in the world. After Black Rascal died, Forbes traded five young polo horses for a Hawaiian thoroughbred stallion named Aloha Moon. Just as the Gallatins had done in Aiken, South Carolina, Forbes would ship his better young polo horses to Boston to sell.

By the mid-1930s, Neponset Stud Farm began to host polo teams from all over during the summer. The Big Horn area now had four polo fields within ten miles of each other, and the area players made a circuit among the Gallatin, Moncreiffe, and Forbes fields. Teams from all over the United States were hauling their horses out to play on the famous Moncreiffe field. Burnt Mills, New Jersey, sent out a team for a series of games.

In Big Horn, spectators came out to Moncreiffe's field in flocks on Sundays to watch the games. A ten-day polo tournament on the Moncreiffe field, featuring six visiting and two local teams, culminated with Fort Riley defeating the Colorado Springs team in the final match. Young Oliver Wallop took his horses to Santa Barbara in the winter and played at his uncle Malcolm's field in the summer.

In 1935, *Horse and Horseman* magazine featured the area's five prominent polo-pony breeders: Gallatin, Forbes, Oliver Wallop, the Bones brothers, and Alan Fordyce. Malcolm Moncreiffe and Johnny Cover were in their thirtieth year of playing in Big Horn. Tommy Hitchcock, who had studied Cover's booming backshot fifteen years before, was still the best player in the world, and a national hero. His picture was often plastered on the sports pages across the country.

56

THERE WAS NO BETTER TIME TO BE A COWBOY. AMERICA and the world were in love with the romantic image of a cowboy on a horse. It only stood to reason that the daughters of the Ivy League ranchers, while spending their summers in the west, would get caught up in the frenzy. Eastern dude girls didn't mind that these men earned less than $1 a day. Despite the fact that some of these men earned little more than a janitor back in the East, they sat tall on their horses and were stars in the local rodeos.

As a group, cowboys were poor, and as a class, there was little room for advancement. There was no graduation to a better life, only deterioration of reflexes that kept them alive while bronc fighting or rodeoing.

Once the eastern women had a taste of these knights of the plains, they were putty in their hands; throw alcohol in the mix with an active local social scene, and the Depression took on a sunny disposition. The cowboys, though wild, had a respect for women, which ran back to the original cowboys of the 1880s.

By the 1930s, dozens of cowboys in the area had married into ranches financed by eastern in-laws. Curley Witzel married Annie Laurie Jacques from New York, and Paddy Ryan married Elisabeth Rudolf, whose Cleveland family had set up roots in Big Horn. Wales Wolf married Margaret Ennis from Chicago. Oliver Wallop married Edward S. Moore's daughter, Jeanne. Moore was now one of the largest ranchers in the area and one of the biggest names in the world of horse racing.

The most well-known cowboy and eastern girl to marry were four-time world-champion bronc rider Turk Greenough and internationally known pop star Sally Rand. Turk had also become a stunt double for silver-screen heroes like John Wayne, and Sally drew huge crowds dancing naked with only a feathered boa, fans, or beachballs to conceal her from the crowd.

After the Rand-Greenough wedding, the couple invested in a ranch in Absaraka on the Little Bighorn River. Sally, a shrewd businesswoman, was alarmed to find that although Turk was raised a cowboy, he was inept at ranching. Turk had no idea of the gestation period of a horse, a cow, a sheep, or a pig. Within a few years Sally had sold the ranch and divorced Turk, who went back to his first wife.

Despite the fact that some eastern women became disillusioned with the West and the life of being married to a cowboy, there were eastern women like Francis Alderson of Birney, Montana, and Big Horn's Edith Gallatin who endeared themselves to the community and its way of life.

On the other side of the coin, some of the cowboys, now familiar with the dudes, began to make pilgrimages back east. Howard Eaton used to visit East Coast cities frequently, and the Bones brothers were making pilgrimages to places like Southern Pines, North Carolina, to foxhunt with James Boyd and make connections with and promote their dude business among easterners.

In the small community of Birney, Montana, the Brewsters at the Quarter Circle U Ranch had cleared off a sagebrush flat next to the river and challenged the Bones brothers to a game of polo. Neither side considered a polo game a success if someone didn't get knocked off their horse. Warren and Burton Brewster had Eddie and Paul Roberts, two polo players from Philadelphia, visiting at their ranch as dudes. With these two secret weapons, the Brewsters figured they could easily handle the Bones brothers. What the Brewsters did not know was that the Aldersons had two ringers from New York visiting their ranch. In a game where the whiskey flowed freely before and after the game, with dudes from both ranches serving as spectators, the Bones brothers won in a close contest. To the surprise of everyone, the Brewsters and Bones turned out to be better polo players than the dudes from the East. Later on the Bones Brothers brought a ranch team to Big Horn and defeated the Teepee Ranch team captained by the ranch owner Alan Fordyce.

Horseracing had become both the national and the local pastime. Warren Brewster, Bill Eaton, Dave Carnahan, Alan Fordyce, and the Bones brothers were part of a racing association that replaced the pioneer racing board of Noll Wallop, Malcolm Moncreiffe, Ridgley Nicholas, Harold Hilman, Goelet Gallatin, and Johnny Cover. Cover and Gallatin were asked to umpire the polo games to retain their integrity. Likewise, Gallatin, Bob Walsh, and Malcolm Moncreiffe were asked to serve as racing stewards.

Sheridan lit up with an aura of festivity at racing time. People vied for invitations to the racing parties. Futurity parties were thrown at the Sheridan Inn, where the foals were led down a red carpet and paraded in front of the admiring partygoers. Formal black-tie balls were also held at the Sheridan Inn and at the Kendrick mansion that were a throwback to Miles City frontier days.

Newcomers to the community who had little or no experience with horses were encouraged to own racehorses and to become part of the local racing scene sponsored by the Sheridan Racing Association. On the other end of the spectrum were seasoned veterans. A series of race meets scattered across the summer became the focal point of the social scene around Sheridan. Odds were set, and two betting windows were installed at the fairgrounds.

The racing season began each year with a race meet in Birney, Montana, hosted by the Bones brothers. It was followed by three other race meets: one at the Wyo Rodeo, one at the County Fair, and one in the fall put on at Dave Carnahan's Island Ranch in Big Horn.

Unlike the races at the fairgrounds, the Carnahan race meet was a more social event. There was no roping or bronc riding, but there was a mile steeplechase for three- and four-year-olds, a mile-and-a-half steeplechase for four-year-olds and up, a mile flat race, and a three-mile steeplechase for five-year-old horses.

Most races paid winners between $50 and $400, but the Futurity paid $1,000. The 1939 list of future race nominations ran like a Who's Who of area horsemen: Aldersons (Bones), Eatons, Mary Irion, Brewsters, Forbes, Skinner,

Luther Dunning, Dick Glenn, R. T. Helvey, Teepee Lodge, Mrs. Annie Laurie Witzel, and Brown Cattle Company, among others.

Alan Fordyce enjoyed entering horses in both steeplechasing and flat racing. His jockey, Wales Wolf, both trained and rode Fordyce's horses. Fordyce had bought part of Edward S. Moore's ranch with money from the sale of half the cattle that came with it in a dispersal sale. Later, Fordyce created a buying fervor for a curious type of Hereford cow he was promoting. Expounding the value of an animal that carried the largest percentage of beef on the hoof, Fordyce's Compact Herefords were all the rage in the country, and he made a healthy profit selling them.

57

Man shot at in argument over horses

—Buffalo Bulletin

ROBERT KING, TRYING TO FIGURE OUT WHAT TO DO WITH his wild son, bought the 3Ts Ranch in Kaycee, Wyoming, hoping his son, Bob, might take an interest in ranching. The first thing the son did was hire Bob Tate.

The Prohibition Act had been repealed, and people were once again free to drink in public. Bob King sent Bob Tate to the Invasion Bar in Kaycee to buy all their liquor. He wanted to throw a party for the whole town. "It'll be the best way to meet my new neighbors," King told Tate.

Bob did exactly what he was asked. "I want to buy all the liquor and beer you got," he told the owner of the Invasian Bar.

"Where you gonna get money to buy all my liquor?" the proprietor asked.

"The new owner of the 3Ts Ranch is gonna buy it."

"I can't just sell you all my liquor; I won't have any for my customers," the man said.

"He ain't gonna take it anywhere. King's gonna buy it from you and give it away. He wants to throw a party for the whole town in your bar. He thought it would be a good way to meet his new neighbors."

An old cowboy at the end of the bar looked up. "The way to Kaycee's heart is through her liver," he said.

With King's money behind him, Bob Tate's next mission was to buy horses. At a Gillette, Wyoming, rodeo, he noticed that a quarterhorse stallion named Bitter Creek, ridden by Lloyd Cain, was stealing the show. Over the weekend, Bitter Creek won the quarter-mile race, the eighth-mile race, and ran anchor on the winning relay-race team. Cain then bulldogged a steer off Bitter Creek and won $50 on a bet that he could rope five calves off Bitter Creek without a bridle. Tate arranged to buy the horse for $200. Cain's eight-year-old daughter, Doris, rode the stallion to school every day and considered it her pet. It was a teary farewell for her and Bitter Creek when King and Tate showed up to pick up the horse.

Bitter Creek turned out to be a natural at polo. After a polo match at Moncreiffe field, the players were having drinks on the sidelines when Bob Tate challenged Oliver Wallop in a race the length of the polo field.

"King's got a horse right here that will beat any horse you got for the length of the field," Tate said.

"I think you've been challenged, Oliver," Alan Fordyce said and smiled. Fordyce, a Harvard man, decided to have some fun with Wallop and King, who had both attended Yale. "A Harvard man might just be colorful enough to stage a race for this crowd," Fordyce said.

"I got $20 says Bitter Creek will whip any horse you got, and I ain't been past tenth grade," Tate broadcast to the crowd.

"Let's make it $50," Wallop countered, knowing Tate wouldn't have that kind of money.

"Let's make it $100," Bob King said, walking through the crowd with a drink in his hand. At the time, $100 was three months' wages to the average working man. Within moments the horses were led out from the tie lines. A flurry of side bets changed hands.

When the horses crossed the end line, Bitter Creek was ahead by a full length. Oliver Wallop rode his horse back to his barn without returning.

"I don't think he's coming back. I'll buy a drink for everybody," Bob King said, and he proceeded to get gloriously drunk. Bob Tate took the stallion back and rubbed him down. With the Wyo Rodeo and County Fair coming up, it became clear as a bell to young Tate what he wanted to do: he was going to be a racehorse trainer.

The 3Ts Ranch was a hundred-thousand-acre cattle ranch that had two hundred head of horses and six thousand acres of irrigated fields. Red Tate made arrangements with Robert King to graze his horses at the 3Ts. Bob helped Red trail seventy head of Tate horses the ninety miles from Ranchester to the 3Ts.

The 3Ts Ranch foreman, George Johnson, was aggravated that King had given young Tate a position as horse foreman and was equally perturbed that Red Tate was running his horses on the ranch.

Bob Tate had got King assigned a Remount stallion, and the two young men were starting a horse-breeding operation on the ranch. The ranch foreman was livid at the young man's brashness and was looking for an excuse to throw him off the ranch. The trouble was, the young man and Bob King were friends.

The matter came to a head during the bad winter storms of 1936. Bob Tate had been working on cleaning out an old barn to build stalls for Bitter Creek and the Remount stallions. Johnson appeared at Tate's stud barn one day and yelled, "You need to get these horses out of here. I'm putting sick calves in this barn."

Bob looked at the empty equipment shed across the yard. "There's a barn over there you can clean out like I did this one. Why don't you use it?" Johnson blew up; he'd be damned if a twenty-year-old kid was going to tell him anything. "I'll tell you what, you little son of a bitch. Either you get these horses out of this barn, or I'll turn them out myself," he screamed. Almost thirty years before, Red had found himself in the same situation at Beckton. Bob was not a big man, but he stood his ground.

"You stick your head in this barn again and I'll run a pitchfork in you," Tate challenged the foreman. Johnson left, furious. When Bob went to dinner that night, the ranch cook took him aside. "You'd better watch out. Johnson said he was going to shoot you. I think he means it." Tate was living in the bunkhouse the Johnson County invaders had spent the night in forty years earlier. When he went to the outhouse that night, he carried a gun with him in case Johnson was waiting for him. When Tate returned, someone had left a dead calf next to his bed. The next morning the cook again warned Tate. "You better go get King. I think Johnson might make a move today; he's acting crazy."

Bob King was off on a bender with a girlfriend in Casper an hour away. Bob left to find him. Later that morning Red Tate drove onto the ranch to check on his horses. Three bullets slammed into his truck. One passed through the driver's side door and lodged in the passenger door. The foreman had mistaken Red for Bob. Red realized he was under fire, spun out, and headed to town to get the law. Johnson was arrested, and Judge James Burgess ordered the man out of Wyoming.

One of the last great horse thefts occurred at around the same time. Gus Rockaman, the owner of the Palace Barn in Sheridan, hosted a horse sale that drew a varied crowd of horse buyers, ranchers, and interested spectators. The night before the horse sale, Rockaman and Oll McKinley had an argument, which threatened to escalate into a fight.

At one o'clock in the morning, McKinley slipped out into the Sheridan sale yards, opened the gates to the pens, and let out all the horses. Riding a saddle horse, he trailed geldings, mares, foals, old horses, and everything in between onto Main Street Sheridan and north into the night, as the sound of the parties blared overhead. During horse sales, the bars always did a booming business, as did the Rex Hotel, which not only continued with gambling, but also had an assortment of sporting women.

Crossing the Montana state line, McKinley moved past the coal mines at Decker and headed toward Kirby near the Cheyenne reservation. A trail of foals and older horses that couldn't keep up followed the main herd. McKinley was past the Rosebud battlefield when he was caught by none other than Curley Witzel, who had gotten a job as a stock detective for various ranches in the area.

"Where you going with those horses, Oll?" Witzel asked, looking over the horses.

"Just as far as I can get," Oll grumbled.

Edith Gallatin watched the unmistakable form of Noll Wallop riding a horse up the mountain from Little Goose Canyon. She was riding through Wallop's land to look at a few horses that were pastured on the old McCoy place.

Edith rode her mare and had paused to look down on the grasslands of the ranch and the rolling hills that fell away from the Bighorns to the north and east. She followed the dark line of trees that lined Little Goose Creek as it wound its way north to Sheridan, where it intersected with Big Goose Creek. From there it continued north and emptied into the Tongue, which flowed north to Miles City two hundred miles away, where it then entered the Yellowstone.

Noll Wallop had brought Marguerite back to Wyoming with him, but she was not happy there after her reign as Lady Portsmouth. She wanted to return to England. Noll was now seventy-six years old and had outlived most of his family, but his own health, after so many ups and downs, was once again failing. In his own adventurous way, he decided to ride over the Bighorns to Thermopolis, Wyoming, and soak in the natural hot springs for a few days. The ride was over one hundred miles one-way.

When Edith saw Noll, she decided to ride over and say hello. His tack was in shambles; both reins had been spliced, and he had a makeshift pack on the back of his saddle. Edith dismounted and opened a gate into Wallops. When she fastened the gate back, she became light-headed and paused to get her bearings before re-mounting. She rode to a high flat and waited for Noll to ascend the hill.

"Edith, what a p-pleasant surprise. I'm heading to Thermopolis for a soak. It looks like good weather for a few days. I'll spend the n-night at the Dome Lake Club, then it's on to Hyattville."

Edith pulled a small box of matches from her saddlebag and handed it to Noll. "Be careful, it's a long way." Ever since Roy Snyder had perished in the snowstorm, Edith had insisted on all of the cowboys carrying matches.

"I'm sure I've p-packed matches, well, I think I have. In any case, I'll take these as a precaution. Many thanks."

"Would you like me to send a truck over in a few days to haul you back? It's a long way."

"To t-tell you the truth, I'll probably board the Burlington Northern in Worland to Thermopolis and then return on the train to Billings and Sheridan. L-look up some old friends. This m-might be the last time I'll see them. There's nothing like riding over the mountains."

"Would I impose if I rode along for a while?" Edith asked. For the next hour and a half, Edith not only listened to Noll's endless banter, she enjoyed it. Before she began her return home, they both paused and looked over the rolling pine forests of the mountain topped by rocky snowcapped peaks. "*Amor patriae*" (love of country), Noll said and smiled. Before he could turn his horse away, Edith called back. "*Natura beatis omnibus esse dedit*" (nature has granted all to be happy).

Oliver H. Wallop Gives Interview in Lincoln Barber Shop

The following story, concerning Oliver Henry Wallop, Earl of Portsmouth, who is well known in Wyoming, having lived on his ranches at Big Horn for thirty-five years prior to his removal to England in 1925, when he assumed his title, was taken from a Lincoln, Nebraska, newspaper.

The Earl of Portsmouth, "Old Man Wallop," according to his own statement, "While in America," was found in the barber chair at the Lincoln Friday getting his chin scraped and his mustache trimmed before continuing on to England by train with his wife, the countess.

"You've heard the word 'Wallop' many times," he said, "and it was one of my ancestors who was responsible for starting its usage. He whipped the French 15 times straight in battle, which led to future beatings being termed wallopings."

Speaking of fighting, he is of the opinion that Germany and France will always try to sink their teeth into each other's necks.

The earl bought horses for the British government during the war and had a son in the fighting. "I spent a great deal of time in France and never heard more than a rumble of guns. However, my wife, dear lady, crossed the North Sea about seven times and was bombed by the Germans every time.

"I like America, especially the West," he says. "Everyone is so hospitable and willing to be friendly. It's really the land of opportunity, too. I've gone stone-broke here and got it back in two years."

"We seldom get to London anymore," he stated, "because all my Oxford and Eaton friends have either died or moved away. I'll have to wait awhile to compare notes with them."

Marguerite Walker Wallop, Countess of Portsmouth, Dies.

Word was received late Monday of the death of Marguerite Walker Wallop, countess of Portsmouth, at her home, Morchard Bishop, Devonshire, England. During the World War, Lady Portsmouth saw service with the Red Cross close to the front in France for about a year.

Throughout the years of her life in Sheridan County, Lady Portsmouth was widely known and most highly regarded throughout this section, and the delightful hospitality offered their many friends by her and Lord Portsmouth in their lovely ranch home will long be remembered.

To an unusual degree she was able to bring and adapt to a pioneer ranch country many of the graces of an older society and to combine them with the energetic and cheerful solution of the problems presented by life in a new country. Her many old friends will continue to remember her with gratitude and affection.

In England, Gerard Wallop, the ninth Earl of Portsmouth, stood next to his father at the funeral service. Old Noll had lost not only the sole woman he had ever loved but also the only person who had ever really understood him. He had courted her incessantly as a young cowboy almost fifty years before and had never stopped. The seventy-seven-year-old decided to return full-time to the land he loved in Absaraka.

In the evenings Noll sat alone and wrote Marguerite about the weather, the cattle, the horses, politics, books, and the future. When he finished writing, he would neatly fold the paper and place it in the flames of the fireplace and watch the smoke ascend.

His loneliness was accentuated by the fact that he was steadily becoming more of an outcast. While men such as Johnny Cover had nothing but respect for the man, some of the new dudes in the area considered him an old fool.

Bob Tate was off to California. After the hard winter at the 3Ts, he took a job taking care of Oliver Wallop's polo horses in Santa Barbara. Bob brought $800—his life's savings—and set out to claim a racehorse at Santa Anita. The whole idea was preposterous, but those who knew Tate felt he might somehow pull it off.

Within a few weeks, Tate had locked horns with young Wallop over how he was tacking a horse up. Oliver insisted on putting a ducking bar on the mare, and Tate felt it was too much hardware. When the dust cleared, Tate quit and got an apartment next to Santa Anita racetrack, where he ran into Wallop's father-in-law, Edward S. Moore. One of the top racehorse owners of the day, Moore got a kick out of Tate and gave him a season pass to Santa Anita and two tickets to the Rose Bowl, which Tate sold for extra money. Tate used the pass to get back to the stables and talk to the big trainers and jockeys and see how the pros operated.

It wasn't long before Tate ran out of money and returned to Sheridan, where he was offered a job accompanying a train car full of polo horses his father had sold to buyers in New York. Bob felt he might have an opportunity back east to become a polo player. He had heard some of the great polo players in the world—including Cecil Smith, George Oliver, and Tommy Hitchcock—played in New York at the time.

In Big Horn, where Bob had played polo since he was twelve, people like the Gallatins, Forbes, and Kings were kind to him and treated him as though they all stood on even ground. In New York, Tate wasn't even allowed to pick up a polo mallet. His happy-go-lucky way that got him by in Wyoming did him no good with the bluebloods in the East. With the exception of F. S. von Stade, who was extremely kind to Bob, Tate was a victim of the class prejudice that ran throughout the area.

Nevertheless, in New York, Tate met the Gallatins' cousin, Billy Post, who was three years younger and who had already become one of the best polo players in the world. Billy's father, Fred, had been to Big Horn and Miles City buying horses on several occasions.

Wiley Jones, an old cowboy from Oklahoma, bought horses for Fred Post from as far away as Argentina and England. He also bought thoroughbreds from the Great Plains, and it was there, in Sheridan, that he had met young Bob Tate. Upon remeeting him in New York, Jones took the young cowboy under his wing. After two weeks in New York, Tate approached Jones to say good-bye.

"I'm going home. I came here to be a polo player, not a groom," he said.

Wiley Jones liked the boy and sympathized with his plight. "Don't be in such a hurry. I'll give you a job in Oklahoma riding for me," he said. Bob accepted and took the train to El Reno, Oklahoma, where he was paid $50 a month to ride twenty horses a day. It was good money, but it was wild, dangerous work. Most of the horses were barely broken in. Tate poured himself into bed at night and dragged himself out in the morning.

Tate noticed that although Jones rarely rode, he made a good living from buying and selling horses. Bob was taking note of both Jones's expertise with horses and his salesmanship. In Jones, Tate was beginning to find a mentor. Bob was impressed with how the cowboy owned so many horses and traveled all around the world. Also, the man was his own boss, something that Tate aspired to be.

Exhausted but inspired, Tate began to look toward home again. "I'm going back to Sheridan and trade horses like you," he said.

"That's good, but where are you going to get the money? It takes money to buy horses," Jones replied.

"I'm gonna rob a bank," Tate joked. The way Bob saw it, there were plenty of rich people in Sheridan. All he needed to do was find one to back him financially.

Back in Sheridan, Bob Tate approached Lew Fixen, who had just bought the X-X Ranch near Parkman, Wyoming. Bob approached Fixen with an offer to buy horses for $80 each and sell them to the army for $165.

"We can sell them to the army buyers, or if you want to get into racing, we can train them at the fairgrounds," Bob said. For the better part of the afternoon, Bob told Lew Fixen stories about the rodeo, the Remount program, the Gallatin race meet, and playing polo in Big Horn at Moncreiffe field. Fixen looked at the young man curiously. For his age Tate had not only a lifetime of stories but also an enthusiasm for the horse business that was contagious. Bob was invited to stay and have supper at the ranch. At dinner, Fixen's daughter, Barbara, was intrigued with the young man's brash manner.

". . . they had a big Indian battle on Gallatins', right by where the Moncreiffes' polo field is. Johnny Cover showed me. Mom's father was shot by Indians. I know old man Wallop. Dad said he had the best horses ever in this country—better than three thousand head. Dad's got two Remount studs right now." The young man was all over the place, but he had excited Fixen enough that he went down to a Ranchester bank and co-signed a note for Bob to buy twelve horses to sell to the Remount.

Feb. 1, 1938

My dear Mrs. Mosher,
I recently had a letter from Lewis to the effect that he had gotten nine lovely mares from Mr. Berry of Recluse, and also the news that he had retained the services of young Bob Tate. In this I congratulate him, as young Bob is a fine boy, and a real good horseman, and as far as my observation is concerned, is honest and loyal and a hard worker.
. . . With very best regards, and hoping to see you then, I remain
Very sincerely yours,
John Irving
Major (Cavalry), QMC,
Officer in charge

With enough money to buy a load of horses, Bob showed up at his parents' home fairly proud of himself. "Where's Mom?" Bob asked, looking for Erma. Red had cooled from his last fight with his son, and he seemed neither angry nor cheerful, just exhausted.

"Your mother's in the barn. Spearpoint, one of the studs we were issued last year, is dying of the sleeping sickness," Red said.

Bob walked out to the barn and found his mother struggling with the sick stallion, which was lying in the stall gasping in pain. Her face looked like hell: she had been crying and had not slept in two days. When Spearpoint first stopped eating his oats, Erma had taken his temperature and found he had a high fever. In less than a day, he was down, but Erma kept a constant vigil getting the stallion to his feet. When that finally proved futile, she had begun packing his head in ice.

"Mom, why don't you go lie down? I'll stay here with the stud." Bob put a hand on Erma's shoulder. Then he reached down and felt the animal's neck. "He's burning up."

"Robert, go get me some more ice, please," she said in a weak, almost indistinguishable voice.

"Sure, Mom, but let me watch him. You go inside," Bob repeated, but his mother just shook her head as tears began to roll.

"Hurry, Robert, be quick," she said.

Bob went to the icehouse and broke an ice block into chunks, which he placed in burlap bags and took to the barn. Bob and his mother packed the ice around the fevered animal's head.

"The government vet is coming tonight," Erma said. After more coaxing from her son, she finally relented and went into the house to lie down.

Before long, Red came in, and Bob immediately got on the defensive. "I'm not working for you, I got my own job," Bob said.

"I heard you got an order for some horses from Lew," Red said.

"So?"

"If you go up to Miles City, Binny Binion will know where you can find some horses to buy. You'll most likely find him at the 600 Club," Red said.

Spearpoint began to kick in pain, and Bob knelt down and tried to keep him still.

"How long's he been sick?" Bob asked.

"Four days," Red answered.

Bob began to soften, realizing his parents had been struggling hard to keep the horse alive. The sight of the animal in pain brought him out of his fight with his father. Red's horse operation was almost totally geared to raising horses for the Remount, and losing a stud meant losing all future profits they would have made from its offspring.

Erma Tate had the real knowledge of the Tates' horse operation. With the government Remount, strict records of breeding had to be kept; foals had to be registered when born, and records of the stallions had to be recorded. Often Red would be questioned about the breeding of a certain horse in his herd and Erma would whisper something in Red's ear and Red would answer. Like many of the ranch breeders that raised horses for the government, wives like Erma Tate and Leota Dunning kept the operation running.

After five hours of sleep, Erma bathed, and then returned to Spearpoint. Marge Carrels had driven out from town to deliver food to the family and more ice for Spearpoint.

"We have to get him up now," Erma said. There was urgency in her voice and everyone knew it meant that if the horse didn't stand on his feet soon, he would be as good as dead. Bob, Red, and Erma all put their shoulders against Spearpoint, and with a combined pushing and pulling and propping Spearpoint's legs underneath him brought the stud to his feet. The weak stallion struggled and fell twice, knocking Red and Bob down with him.

"Come on, we have to get him up!" Erma yelled. The stallion wobbled over and Erma began to shout at Spearpoint, as did Bob and Red. Finally the horse propped his legs under him. Spearpoint and the three Tates leaned against one another exhausted, but he was up.

Erma did not leave Spearpoint's side until that afternoon, when the army veterinarian showed up. He was a young officer, new to his profession, and he carried an experimental vaccine with him for sleeping sickness. Within minutes of giving Spearpoint the injection, the stallion collapsed and died.

It was too much for Erma. She had spent days nursing the horse and getting him on his feet, and now the vet had killed Spearpoint in five minutes. "I had him up! Why would you give him something if you didn't know if it would work?" She was furious, exhausted, and heartbroken.

In Sheridan County six hundred horses had been stricken during July and August alone, among them Bob King's beloved Bitter Creek. It was the start of an epidemic that killed hundreds of thousands of horses in the country. Within a year, the army would develop a vaccine that would save thousands of animals, but for Spearpoint, Bitter Creek, and thousands of others, it came too late.

With Lew Fixen's money in his pocket, Bob Tate was off to Miles City. He walked into the 600 Club, where a card game was in progress. Bob worked his way over to the card table. "I'm looking to buy a load of horses. Anybody know where I might get some?"

Binny Binion, who owned a casino in both Miles City and Las Vegas, looked up from his cards. Red Tate had already clued him in that the boy was coming. He was Red Tate's boy, which was good enough for any of the men there.

"As soon as we finish this game, we'll take you to see some horses," Binion said. Within the hour Binion, Tate, and Ed Vaughn were on their way north to the ranch of Harry Ross at Jordan, Montana. Ross had the last of the CBC horse range, where he had seventy geldings between three and four years old that were broken in enough to ride.

Ross had just had a fight with a U. S. Army Remount buyer who had turned down the first three horses Ross led out to show him. Ross lost his temper and threw the man off his property, arguing that his four hundred mares were at least half-thoroughbred. The next day Bob and Ross proceeded to ride seventy head of horses in two days. Bob offered Ross $70 a head for twenty-two horses but Ross wanted $85.

The two couldn't agree on the price, so Tate began the eighty-mile ride back to Miles City. On the way, Ed Vaughn passed Tate on the road with the word that Harry Ross would accept the deal for $70 per horse, but he would only deliver them as far as Miles City. Tate agreed, and a week later he returned and trailed the twenty-two horses the 150 miles to Sheridan.

When he arrived at Lew Fixen's ranch, Barbara Fixen was just coming in from a ride. The sight of the young horseman trailing behind the horses stirred something in her. She spent the rest of the afternoon looking over the horses with Tate as they grazed in a pasture next to the barn. When Lew Fixen returned, he was impressed with both Tate and the horses. To make it all the better, in less than two weeks the army had bought all of the horses for $165 each. Tate's cut was $10 a head, $220. With cash in pocket, Bob Tate was on his way.

58

Sheridan, in Heart of Cow Country, Begins Annual Reign as Queen of West. Her streets are decked in gay colored banners, her citizens dolled up in bright shirts, cowboy boots, and ten-gallon hats, and the pioneer spirit brightly aflame in her heart Sheridan is ready today to begin her annual reign as Queen of the West.

—*Sheridan Post*

IN JULY 1939 MORE THAN TWENTY THOUSAND PEOPLE crowded the fairgrounds in Sheridan, and five thousand attended the Miles City Roundup for its silver anniversary. The rodeos had grown, pushing away the local flavor. Although locals participated in both rodeos, competitors from Texas, Oregon, California, and Arizona were competing and winning. Horse racing was the one event that was controlled and limited to competitors from surrounding counties. The Wyo Rodeo featured a two-mile steeplechase over fourteen jumps around the outside of the arena. The crowds ate it up and flocked in droves to watch.

Right in the middle of the racing fever was Bob Tate, who was now training racehorses for Bob King, Dick Glenn, Neponset Stud Farm, and Lew Fixen, and a few of his own. With the knowledge he had picked up hanging around the tracks in California, Tate won the half-mile at the Sheridan Wyo Rodeo riding Tip Top, Bob King's horse that was sired by the Gallatins' Remount horse Majority.

Bob had visited the Crow Fair races in August and saw a mare that his father had sold to a Crow trainer named Red Wolf. The mare, named Betty Co-ed, had won the Crow Fair mile race, which was for Indian horses only. Bob borrowed Betty Co-ed and won the Sheridan mile race, and then matched the Bones brothers in a mile race against Congo, a horse Bones had bought from the Gallatins.

The big excitement came when a four-horse-match race was staged between Oliver Wallop riding Countess Bye, Bob Tate riding Lew Fixen's Reed's Choice, the Bones brothers riding Congo, and Bob Woods riding Hay Top in a three-quarter-mile race at the fairgrounds. Each owner put up $100 each, and the fairgrounds added $100 for the purse. At the start Tate pulled Reed's Choice past Congo, and the two ran nose and nose for the finish until Oliver Wallop made a late run on Countess Bye to win by a head at the wire.

Down on the racetracks, it was far removed from the cocktail belt. Jockey's fought and did what they had to do to win races.

> *Eugene Basch, a colored youth, was crossing the Sheridan track at the south gate as the two thoroughbreds thundered around the turn.*
>
> *The brown horse, with Danetta Gilbert up, struck Basch, bowling him off his feet. The horse piled up on top of Mrs. Gilbert. The colored youth was rushed to the Sheridan Memorial Hospital, seriously injured. Although it was reported freely that he died on Friday afternoon, the boy has excellent chances of recovery.*
>
> *Chic Hallam, during the afternoon, had been struck over the head by a "two-by-four" by Old Man Marsh, owner of the Marsh stables, because he had lost the relay race the last day. Cy Gray, top relay rider, interfered and then yelled to the cowboys to "come quick" as a man was being "killed." Marsh's two sons and the rest of the stable employees swarmed around Gray and Hallam, and for a moment it looked like something nasty was going to happen. Someone yelled that they had better get Marsh across the Montana state line before he was killed or arrested.*
>
> *Hallam was out of his head for fifteen minutes from the blow; most of the time he spent begging for his gun.*
>
> *Another race at the fairgrounds Friday evening ended in a fellow being struck over the head, but no details of the trouble could be learned.*
> —Sheridan Post

Before the start of one race, Warren Brewster, a racing association board member and race starter, got word anonymously that a racer was using an electric buzzer—a small handheld device that emits a shock to the horse during the race to get it to run faster. Brewster approached the starting line of six jockeys all mounted and ready to go.

"I know someone here's got a buzzer. I'm going to turn my back and let you drop it before we start. If I don't see a buzzer lying in the dirt after I start you, I'm going to ban the jockey, trainer, and owner for life. Don't think you're going to get around the track and drop it, because we have people watching all the way around the track. Drop it now, and not another word will be said."

It was a bluff; Brewster had no idea who had the buzzer, but after he turned his back and started the racers, he walked over and found six buzzers lying in the dirt. Mike's Electric was, predictably, a race sponsor.

Bill Eaton and Patty Alderson's daughter, Nancy, was crowned rodeo queen in the arena, but before the night was out, Eaton's horse blew up and bucked him off in the dust. Eaton was fine, but it was an ominous sign to an end of an era.

59

I got caught in a whirlpool swimming a horse across the Bighorn River.

—Bob Tate

BY NOW COLONEL E. M. DANIELS WAS THE HEAD OF THE entire Remount Program in the United States. He had made close friends in Absaraka with the Aldersons, Dunnings, and Tates. With their neighbors the Browns and Brocks, there were more than two hundred thoroughbred brood mares producing foals for the Remount between Tongue River and Otter Creek. When Colonel Daniels arrived at Red Tate's to look at some horses, he asked about Bob. Red just shook his head. "He's gone to Arizona to be a racehorse trainer."

"Does he have a job?" Daniels asked.

"He figures he's gonna get rich racing his own horse and then take all his savings and claim a good horse," Red said. The colonel looked at Erma.

"He's got Miss Princess and the old horse trailer he made," she said. Miss Princess was a three-year-old filly bred by a Remount stallion to a Major Nicholas mare.

Bob's first stop was Phoenix, Arizona, where the Phoenix racetrack had just been built. In the inaugural mile race for three-year-old fillies, Miss Princess won. Tate and Miss Princess traveled to the racetracks at Albuquerque,

Tucson, and Tucumcari before going broke. Bob sold his car and hitched a ride with two Sheridan jockeys, Rex Hanft and Mervin Duran, who agreed to pull Bob's homemade trailer and Miss Princess to Las Vegas.

Dallas Disbrow, a wealthy rancher from Sheridan who Hanft trained for, met the men in Las Vegas. After a night in a Vegas hotel, Disbrow and Hanft left Tate and Duran stranded, broke, and without a car.

"Son of a bitch left us," Tate said to Duran, looking around the room and noticing that it was cleaned out.

"Disbrow left his coat," Duran said, pointing to a fancy beaver-skin coat on the bed.

"Hell, I got an idea," Tate said, grabbing up the coat. He took the coat to a pawnshop and got $18, which he and Duran bet on two horses they had a tip on at both the Cali-Anti and Bay Meadows tracks. They parlayed the bets and came away with $186, which they split evenly. Tate left Miss Princess with Duran and caught a ride back to Sheridan with Bert Thomas, a Hardin, Montana, horse rancher.

On the trip home Thomas told Tate he had a pasture full of horses up on the Bighorn River for sale. "I'll give you $10 commission for every horse you sell for me," Thomas said. When Bob got home, he immediately went to Lew Fixen to buy another load of horses. Fixen told Bob he would give him $10 for every horse he found that was worth buying. Thomas sold Tate twelve horses for $65 a piece.

When Tate picked the horses up, he had to swim the horses across the Bighorn River. This was not much of a problem, except that Bob couldn't swim. With a Crow Indian boy riding a mare with a foal following, Bob sat nervously bareback on a horse and hung on, following the boy across. Sensing Bob's nervousness, the Crow, who was riding in front, looked back at Bob. "Take your feet out of the stirrups and hang on to the mane, not the reins." Halfway across, Bob and his horse got caught in a whirlpool and his horse began to turn in the water. The Crow called back for Bob to turn the horse's head toward the bank, and the animal swam the two out. Bob collected the $120 from Fixen for the horses.

Bob borrowed Red's truck to drive back to Las Vegas and get Miss Princess. On his parents' ranch, Bob bred Miss Princess to a government stud called Chief Wick. In the meantime he had found another load of horses to sell to Lew Fixen. The problem was, they were down Powder River in Montana. Having no money for gas or a trailer big enough to haul all the horses, Bob trailed the horses himself but soon became disoriented trying to cut across some rough breaks. He decided to stick close to the Powder until he hit a road. Before he had gone much farther, he found himself on top of an old pile of horse bones.

He pulled his horse up and took a look around. *It must have been an old Indian battle site,* he thought, looking at bones scattered as far as he could see. Maybe it was the result of a bad winter, but horses usually never piled up and died like cattle. The young horseman didn't know he was looking at the remnants of Colonel Nelson Cole's death march down the Powder seventy-four years earlier. Bob hurried the horses along at a high trot; the place gave him the creeps.

Bob Tate was lost in his thoughts riding through the country. His mind was locked in how he was going to compete against the racers from Big Horn. The old stallion trotted down a draw and then up a knoll to watch the rider and horses pass. Satisfied the man posed no threat to his band, the stallion turned and trotted back to his band of mares and foals.

He would have liked to investigate and steal some horses away from Tate's band, but after being hunted by gunmen and riders attempting to corral meat horses, the palomino stallion had become wary of any rider. Though he had been run off his range three times, he had still managed to steal horses from other wild bands and some outlying ranches.

Later that autumn on Mizpah Creek, the stallion found himself facing a lone rider who had somehow snuck right up on him. The stallion was grazing a short distance away from the mares when he smelled burning tobacco. He turned to gather the mares and found the way blocked by the solitary old cowboy sitting on his horse. The man seemed to have materialized out of the ground and had somehow gotten between him and his mares.

"Hello to the great yellow stallion," the man said. He had a rifle across his lap and a rolled Bull Durham between his lips. The stallion was caught completely off guard and sprinted backwards, then turned to challenge the man who sat watching him.

"I suppose I knew your grandfather. I saw him on Otter Creek when I was a young man," the old cowboy said and smiled. Tom McAllister was one of the few riders next to a few Crow and Cheyenne horsemen left in Absaraka who could move among the wild horses. He knew he was looking at something few men could appreciate. He was one of few men in recent history to get a close look at the yellow stallion and intended to bask in the moment. He noted the strong bone and confirmation that was legendary among his bloodline.

"I suppose you've stolen your share of horses from me," he said.

The stallion broke to the east and in a flash was around the rider and hazing the mares away. Tom McAllister put the rifle back in the scabbard and watched the horses disappear.

Lew Fixen decided to have Bob train one of the Powder River mares to race. Tate tried to talk Fixen out of it because Bob could see the latest band of horses were not the running type. Tate finally gave in and took the mare to the fairgrounds. After a couple of breezes around the track, it became evident that the mare had no speed.

Cliff Roberts, a trainer from Chicago and an old friend of Bob's, was also training horses at the Sheridan Fairgrounds. Tate went over to say hello, but his attention was really fixed on one of Roberts's black mares.

"Hey, Cliff, I got a dead ringer for this mare. She belongs to Lew Fixen. Come look at her," Tate said.

"If it wasn't for the white in your mare's face, you couldn't tell them apart," Roberts said.

"Can she run?" Tate asked.

"Like the wind," Roberts answered.

"Can yours?" he asked.

"Not worth a damn. I got her entered in a three-quarter mile for maiden fillies," Tate said.

"What are the odds?"

"4-1 is the best you can do at Sheridan."

"We'll put a racing hood on my mare to cover the white on her forehead and nobody will know the difference." Roberts said, and the fix was on.

The day of the race, Lew Fixen's mare was shut up in a stall with both doors shut. She had two blankets on, as Tate gave his groom strict instructions to run her around to get a sweat up on her.

Meanwhile, Tate rode to the starting line on Roberts's mare. At four-to-one odds, Tate and Roberts each bet $50. Tate led right from the start, and as he rounded the first turn he was so far out front that he had to pull her up lest the win look too obvious. After the race, Tate rode up the track to the barns. His groom had the door to the stall open, and Tate jumped off and led the mare in, switched the hood to Fixen's horse, and led her out before anyone saw what happened.

That night, Lew Fixen took Bob to dinner at the Sheridan Inn to celebrate with his wife and daughter. "Lew, I know that mare ran a good race, but if I were you, I would retire her to breed," Tate advised. Lew agreed, and Tate and Roberts were each $150 richer.

60

Bob Tate Hero

—Sheridan Post

THE SUMMER OF 1941 WOULD CLIMAX AN ERA OF FUN-loving easterners who appreciated the West and its people. The wealthy eastern horsemen and the cowboys who married and squired their daughters had created a wonderful spectacle of rodeo racing and polo around Sheridan. The second generation that followed eastern and foreign pioneers like the Gallatins, William Moncreiffe, and Noll Wallop excelled in parties and sporting events revolving around horses. For all the wild times manufactured between the cowboys and the eastern debutantes, a series of youth-oriented horse shows and racing events for children, which were started by Edith Gallatin, were continued by the Carnahans and Alan Fordyce and Neponset Stud Farm.

The main difference between the two age groups was that none of the younger generation had ridden the marathon rides or spent long hours in the field with the cowboys like Noll Wallop or Edith Gallatin. The war in Europe was about to break up this new set of horsemen forever, but for one glorious summer, the atmosphere around the races and polo games resembled something out of an F. Scott Fitzgerald novel.

The town of Sheridan operated six betting windows at the Sheridan County Fairgrounds, where the season climaxed with the fifth running of the Sheridan Futurity. The races were limited to participation by horses and owners from six surrounding counties. One race might be for horses owned by residents of the county, and others were limited to horses that were raised in the counties.

The blending of dudes and cowboys created a social fervor in Sheridan that was unequaled anywhere on earth. Right in the middle of it all was Bob Tate, who at twenty-six was already an old-timer. He had ridden in the Gallatin race meets as a boy and had smuggled liquor to speakeasies out of his pony cart in Sheridan. He had visited with surviving warriors from the Indian wars, played polo with Malcolm Moncreiffe, and sat at Luther Dunning's table on Otter Creek and listened to stories about the old days in Milestown. He had traveled to Omaha, New York, Cincinnati, Santa Barbara, Phoenix, Albuquerque, and Las Vegas, all from his involvement with horses.

Bob had been mentored by Paddy Ryan in rodeo, Billy Post in polo, Wiley Jones in horse trading, and Edward S. Moore in racing. He had worked alongside some of the great Crow trainers of the day in La Forge, Yellowtail, Holds the Enemy, and Real Bird. He had a close relationship with the U.S. Army Remount buyers Colonel Daniels and Colonel Rand. More than anything, he worked nonstop at not being under anyone's thumb. With a keen mind and a lot of luck, things just came to him.

Bob Tate instilled a passion for horses in people. His stories and genuine excitement about racing, polo, and breeding lit a fire in many buyers who had had no desire to own a horse before they met him.

Bob entered two horses in the Futurity: one for Neponset Stud Farm, named Beacon, and one of his own he bought from Bob King, named Prairie Fire. Tate was training racehorses for over a half-dozen owners.

Tate had Beacon, a son of Neponset Stud's Aloha Moon, in training for Bill Gardiner, Forbes's foreman. At the Wyo Rodeo the month before, Tate had run Beacon to a second-place finish in the Absaraka half-mile race; he came in ahead of all his challengers for the upcoming three-quarter mile Futurity. Tate hired Wales Wolf to ride Prairie Fire in the race because Tate himself wanted to ride Beacon for Neponset. Two weeks before the Futurity was run, Neponset sold Beacon to Bob Helvey, the president of the racing association, for good money. Gardiner asked Tate if he would accept half the upcoming pot for training the horse thus far. Tate happily agreed, as $500 was a lot of money.

Helvey asked Gardiner's advice about what to do about racing Beacon. "Keep him with Tate. He knows the horse and he's been riding him," Gardiner said. "He's already got a horse of his own in the race. How do I know he won't try to win with that one?" Helvey asked.

"He won't do that. He needs the money." Gardiner said. Helvey then asked Tate what he would charge to ride Beacon in the Futurity in two weeks.

"I'll take half the winnings," Tate said.

"You already got half the purse from Gardiner!" Helvey protested.

"That was with Gardiner. This is a whole other deal," Tate said.

"I'll get somebody else to ride and train him," Helvey said.

"That's fine. I've got a horse of my own running in the race," Tate said.

Helvey approached Gardiner about the horse in a tirade.

"Tate wants half the purse for two-weeks' training. He's got a horse of his own in the race; how do I know he won't throw the race?" Helvey asked.

"Tate knows your horse. Besides, he doesn't have any money; he's got to make deals like that just to make it," Gardiner explained. It was true; most of the trainers and owners had money of their own, but Tate was in the business by the seat of his pants. Helvey conceded to keep the horse with Tate. Wales Wolf would ride Tate's horse, while Bob would ride Beacon.

If Helvey was smarting before the race because of Tate, Edward S. Moore would soon be fuming. Not only had Moore put together one of the most impressive ranches in northern Wyoming, he had also bought the *Sheridan Press*, which was the largest newspaper in the north part of the state. His horse Big Pebble, a five-year-old Kentucky bred that was racing in Chicago, had already won $157,675 for the year.

Moore was bringing in two of his racing mares, Blue Hydrangea and Esbit, to race in Sheridan. Bob Tate was somewhat disgruntled at Moore's bringing in two $10,000 mares while everyone else was predominantly running $200 horses. While Tate was training his horses at the Sheridan Fairgrounds, Moore sent *Press* reporter Patty Kelly and photographer Walter Harris up to the fairgrounds to photograph Blue Hydrangea for a front-page photograph in the *Sheridan Press*. Unfortunately for Harris and Kelly, he was the only person at the stables at noon.

"We're here to take a picture of Mr. Moore's Blue Hydrangea. Can you tell us where to find him?" Patty Kelly asked Tate. Knowing the racehorse was a *her*, not a *him,* Tate realized that neither the photographer nor the reporter was familiar with horses. An amusing idea popped into Tate's mind.

"I know the mare. I'll get her for you," Tate said. With a straight face, Bob led an ugly, jug-headed lead pony gelding out to photograph.

"Here's Blue Hydrangea," Tate said. When Harris lined his camera up, Tate stepped behind the horse to hide his face. When the picture made copy the next day, Moore hit the ceiling, and his trainer Dave Carnahan was furious. It would be just the beginning.

As far as the races went, Bob had an angle of his own. The legacy of the Indian horsemen lived on in the Miles City, Billings, Sheridan, and Forsyth race meets. Names like La Forge, Small, Holds the Enemy, Yellowtail, Red Wolf, Crooked Arm, Medicine Crow, and Not Afraid raced their horses on local tracks and continued the horsemanship of their fathers. The Crow tribe had some of the best racehorses of the day, like Colonel T and Homework. Bob had a Crow friend named Spotted Wolf who brought his attention to a sorrel gelding, Frankie K, that was owned by an Crow named Holds the Enemy. Frankie K had just run away with the Indian half-mile and ran a blazing anchor leg in the Indian relay race at the Wyo Rodeo.

Tate offered to partner with Holds the Enemy on Frankie K's participation at the fall race meet during the county fair. Frankie K was exhausted after the Wyo Rodeo race, so Tate kept him laid up with stall rest and gradually began to take him out for long walks and jogs.

Bob inquired about blowing out Frankie K before the big race, but Spotted Wolf, who was taking care of Bob's race string at the fairgrounds, told him no.

"He doesn't need breezing; enter him twice in the same day," the Crow said. Despite his experience, Tate was smart enough to know that Spotted Wolf knew more than he did about training racehorses.

Tate kept exercising Frankie K lightly and entered him in the half-mile and the three-quarter-mile race in the same day. First, however, Tate had to run Beacon in the biggest race of the year: the Sheridan Futurity.

HELVEY HORSE TRIUMPHS OVER FIELD OF EIGHT

Beacon, Youngster in Race Game, Wins Coveted Title.

With Bob Tate up, Beacon broke well back from his starting position as sixth and did not take over the lead until he reached the backstretch, but from then on the race was all his and swept home five lengths out in front.

Bob Tate, Hero

But the hero of the afternoon was really Bob Tate.

Of the six races on the program, he rode the winning horse in four and placed third in another—the sixth race he did not enter.

It was merely a repeat of his performance in the rodeo, however, for then he also brought in a lion's share of the winners.

Wins Half-Mile

Riding his own horse, Frankie K, the 10-year-old chestnut gelding . . . Tate won first in the half-mile race for horses trained and owned in Association counties and also the three-quarter-mile race for horses owned and trained in Association counties.

The first of these he almost lost when, with a big lead, he eased off the pressure in the home stretch and was nearly beaten to the finish by Cliff Roberts . . . Tate's fourth victory was in the final race of the afternoon, the one-and-a-half-mile relay, in which he rode the Rapid Creek ranch string. La Forge, riding Tate's string, was third.

Bob Tate and Frankie K had beaten the best horses of the Big Horn cocktail circuit, including both of Edward S. Moore's mares. Moore had gotten over the picture in the paper and had even had a chuckle over Tate's good fortune at the race meet. Bob Woods, a client for whom Tate was training a relay string, was not as amused. Before the relay race, Woods, the owner of the Rapid Creek dude ranch and racing association board member, got into an argument with Tate. Tate loaned Woods two horses for a relay string but wanted to ride his own string and let Thomas La Forge ride the string belonging to Woods. Tate was told that unless he rode his horses in the relay, Woods would scratch the entire race.

"You work for me and will do as you're told," Woods said. Tate conceded, but during the race he took his time switching saddles and rode his horses out in the middle of the track to let Woods know who was really boss. He still won the race, but the damage was done; Bob Woods complained to the racing association, and its members decided to relieve themselves of the young trainer.

Although Little Bones Alderson came to Tate's defense then, Tate was about to lose Alderson as an ally at Carnahan's Island Ranch Race Meet. Like drinking from the silver tea servings in the old Milestown steeplechases fifty years prior, the Carnahan's race meets were a requirement if one was to be accepted into local society, and Bob Tate was not invited to race.

The Island Ranch Race Meet featured a mile race called the Circle M Cup, sponsored by Edward S. Moore. Little Bones Alderson had two entries in the race: the first was Playboy, the Futurity winner the year before, and the other was Congo, a speedster by the Gallatins' Black Rascal. Congo was a three-time winner of the Circle M Cup, along with a slew of half-mile and three-quarter-mile races at both the Wyo Rodeo and the County Fair, but was now showing signs of age.

When Alderson's jockey didn't show up to ride Congo, Little Bones asked Bob Tate, who was there as a spectator, to ride Congo for the Bones brothers.

The Carnahans' racetrack had no rails or borders. The infield was marked with large haystacks, and the outfield was marked with an irrigation ditch. There was a small elevated platform at the finish line. Tate had played polo on Congo and knew his speed and ability to push another horse aside if asked.

Johnny Cover started the race, and Tate took an early lead, but he was challenged to the inside by one of Carnahan's horses. When the horses were side by side, Tate used his leg to push Carnahan's horse and jockey to the inside. Forced to either run into a haystack or run off course, the Carnahan jockey pulled inside and was disqualified. Now it became a race between Congo and the Bones brothers' Playboy, ridden by Frank Blaney. As Playboy made a run to the outside around Congo on the third turn, Tate forced Playboy wide toward the irrigation ditch.

"Bob, pull up or I'll have to jump the ditch," Blaney yelled.

"Brace yourself, Frankie!" Tate said, and with that, Blaney and Playboy sailed over the ditch but still managed to jump back and make a race of it for the wire. When Congo crossed under the wire first, Bones, Carnahan, and the two jockeys were seeing red.

"Bones, that's one hell of a horse," Tate said, referring to Congo, which was of little consolation. Tate stood by on the winner's podium as Little Bones Alderson accepted the trophy from Mrs. Amy Moncreiffe.

"You're in hot water," someone said to Tate, who was somewhat dumbfounded.

"Hell, I won the race for them. I don't know why they're mad at me," he said.

He had not only beaten Playboy, but in the course of the summer he had also beaten Edward S. Moore's Blue Hydrangea and Esbit and Bob Woods's Social Lass and Hay Top. Red and Erma shook their head; even they would have bet against it, but their son had gone off on his own and beaten the best of the racers in the country.

61

SHERIDAN BRONC RIDER WILSON MORELAND TOOK A JOB at Fort Robinson, Nebraska, riding horses, because it paid double what he would make doing ranch work. On the same ground where Crazy Horse was killed and where the Cheyenne made their famous breakout, Wilson was taken to a long barn where soldiers were riding horses. Moreland had not been there more than a minute before a soldier was bucked off at the opposite end of the barn. The loose horse galloped toward Moreland, who walked over to catch the horse, but when he reached for the reins, the horse struck him twice in the face with its front feet, smashing his nose. Moreland was taken to the infirmary, which was full of soldiers injured with broken arms, legs, and backs.

After being patched up, Wilson rode outside in the country around Fort Robinson each day with twenty other riders. The men would ride out together, riding ten horses each day. In this way two hundred horses were ridden each day.

The old pioneers from Miles City and Otter Creek stood together at the Sheridan graveside. Yellow Foot drove down from the Crow agency; Charlie Thex and all his children, Tom McAllister, the Howes, the Brewsters, and Nannie Alderson watched as Luther Dunning and the other pallbearers lowered Noll Wallop's casket into the ground. The respiratory problems that had plagued him his entire life had finally done him in. He had died in a Colorado Springs nursing home, far away from his beloved Little Goose Canyon.

> *Sorrow has cast its shadow over the foothills over the Bighorn Mountains near the mouth of Little Goose Canyon and the people who live there . . .*
>
> *Oliver Henry Wallop is dead.*
>
> *He was educated at Eton and Oxford. In 1883, immediately upon graduation, he came to America. Later that same year he came to Miles City, and from there to Otter Creek, where he was the first breeder of purebred horses in this region. In the late eighties he drove some horses into the foothills country of the Bighorn Mountains . . . .*
>
> *Mr. Wallop became a naturalized citizen of the United States at Sheridan . . . upon his succession to earldom in 1925 occupied the unique dual status of being a titled English nobleman and at the same time retaining his American citizenship.*
>
> *He was an ardent sportsman and especially loved to hunt and ride around the ranch and in the mountains with a gun, a rod, and a dog.*
>
> *It can make little difference to those who knew Mr. Wallop here. The English Crown itself could not carry the tribute, which is granted by Wyoming men and women to those who are pioneers of this new western empire. He was one of the first to dare the rigorous life of the early days; more than that, he has been one of the few who survived the early days whose optimism has had a great part in its progress.*
>
> *If friends can give a sincere tribute to Mr. Wallop today, he has offered one in return. "I have spent the best part of my life in the Bighorns," he has said. "My friends are here, and here I intend to make my home."*
>
> *A neighbor and friend Mr. Wallop has been; there is no better loved figure in all Wyoming.*

Today Mr. Wallop's neighbors and friends in the Big Horn and Sheridan communities who have known and loved him for so many years extend to his two sons and their families their expressions of true sympathy and sorrow.
—Sheridan Post, *1943*

Probably no man since Crazy Horse had ridden over the area as extensively as Wallop. He was the dean of the horsemen in the area, in the frontier years, having owned more than three thousand thoroughbreds that ran from Otter Creek to the Bighorn Mountains. At the time he was the largest breeder in an area where everyone was a horseman to some extent. Noll was the figurehead of Absaraka's horsemen who followed the Plains Indians. He had put money in hundreds of men's pockets during the Boer War. He passed his knowledge of business along to help cowboys from Luther Dunning to Charlie Thex to Johnny Cover. More than anything, he had enriched everyone's life he had come in contact with.

Luther Dunning, now sixty-seven, stood over the grave and thought of the old times. Noll Wallop, like Sydney Paget, had been like a father to him. Luther had never learned to read, but Wallop, often excited over some new book, might ride over and read to him for hours to see what Luther's opinion might be.

After the funeral there was an impromptu meeting of old-timers at the Sheridan Inn.

"See those two holes?" said Dunning, pointing to the ceiling above the bar. The crowd of old horsemen and merchants looked up. "Old Noll and Buffalo Bill shot those there when they were drunk."

Edith Gallatin, now crippled and suffering from a bad heart, drove with Johnny Cover to the cemetery. It troubled Edith that Noll's beloved Marguerite was buried three thousand miles away in England. With two ranch hands they oversaw the planting of four pine trees along a small rise where Noll lay. While the young Gallatin cowboys dug the holes for the trees, Edith pulled on a pair of gloves, got down on her knees, and began to dig. Johnny Cover tried to help, but Edith waved him off. She had always enjoyed working the earth, with strawberries, flowers, and vegetables. Cover knew that she should not exert herself, but after almost thirty years of having worked for the woman, he knew she would not be deterred. She dug with her small spade and let her fingers and hands sink into the rich Wyoming soil. She placed the flowering plants in an arc around the freshly turned grave.

"There," she said, smiling, and noticed the grim look on Johnny's face. Johnny had worked for old Noll as a boy in Big Horn. He had laughed at his eccentrics, listened to his dissertations, and benefited from his kindness. The cowboy had been the corral boss for both the Boer War and the First World War, where cowboys rode thousands of horses for the British and American buyers on Malcolm Moncreiffe's polo field. Old Noll had been the most competent and honest of dozens of buyers. Cover turned away, not wanting to catch the eye of Mrs. Gallatin.

"These flowers will remind him of her," she said.

Cover extended a hand to Edith as she struggled to rise. He turned his face away to compose himself. Noll Wallop, the biggest-hearted man he had ever known, had just died, and Edith Gallatin, the kindest woman he had ever known, was dying.

Mrs. Gallatin feebly rose and looked across at the Bighorn Mountains and then read Noll's headstone aloud. "*I will lift up mine eyes unto these hills, from whence cometh my help.*"

Freda Woinoski faced a dilemma. Tonight was the night of the Gallatins' big dinner party that she was to cook for, but she had no one to watch her two-year-old son, Stan. She phoned Mrs. Gallatin to let her know that she had found a replacement for the event, but Edith Gallatin would hear none of it.

"Bring Stan over, and we'll watch him, Freda. We'd love to have him. I so miss having young ones around," she said. That evening Freda was mortified that Stan would cause some trouble for the Gallatins. When the opportunity finally arose, Freda left the kitchen to check on her son. When she found him, Edith and Goelet had the boy stripped and painted like an Indian warrior and carrying a hundred-year-old coup stick.

"It's fine, Freda; we're having a wonderful time. What a brave and fierce warrior you have here."

At that moment Edith began to reel, and Freda helped her to a chair.

"Mrs. Gallatin, are you all right?" she asked. Goelet rose quickly and went to the bathroom to get Edith's heart medicine.

"I'm just fine, Freda. I just stood up too quickly. Come here, Stan. Let your mother hear your war cry." With that, the boy, delighted with himself, let out a war hoop, and Edith clapped her hands in delight. The hard fact was that the heart that had given to so many was giving out.

If Noll Wallop had been the soul of the area's horsemen, Edith Gallatin had been their heart. In less than a year, she died from a heart attack.

> *The citizens of Sheridan and the surrounding communities who have enjoyed the warm friendship and loveable character of Mrs. Gallatin, and the thousands of visitors who have had the pleasure of her unusual hospitality at their ranch home down through the years, will never forget her charm, her enthusiasm, and her devotion to community interests.*

A delegation of Crow and Cheyenne came for the funeral service. Old cowboys, homesteaders, and the entire horse crowd from Otter Creek to Buffalo also came. The town of Big Horn shut down for the funeral. Edith Gallatin was appropriately laid to rest next to the grave of Noll Wallop, and the site was marked with a modest brass plaque. Her son-in-law, Carlo Beuf, wrote the inscription: *Of all this world the loveliest and the best has smiled and said good night and gone to rest.*

It was the end of an era. People like William Moncreiffe and Edith Gallatin had bridged the gap between eastern money and the western frontiersmen. War was once again casting its shadow over Absaraka, from which the horsemen would never recover.

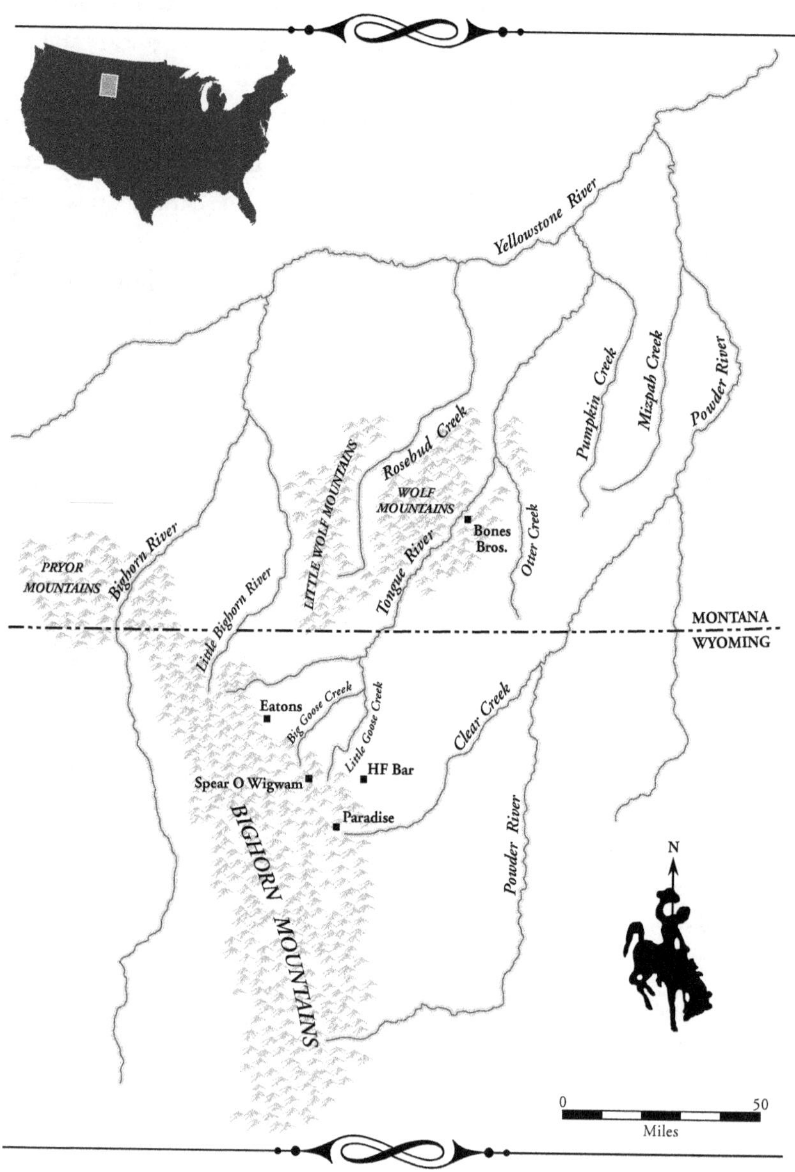

Yellowstone River
Pumpkin Creek
Mizpah Creek
Powder River
Rosebud Creek
WOLF MOUNTAINS
LITTLE WOLF MOUNTAINS
Bones Bros.
Otter Creek
Tongue River
PRYOR MOUNTAINS
Bighorn River
Little Bighorn River
MONTANA
WYOMING
Eatons
Big Goose Creek
Little Goose Creek
Clear Creek
HF Bar
Spear O Wigwam
Paradise
BIGHORN MOUNTAINS
Powder River
N
0
50
Miles

IV

A Horse Trader

62

I hung out with colonels, never privates.

—Bob Tate

THE GERMAN ARMY EMPLOYED MORE THAN SEVEN thousand horses in its march through Czechoslovakia and Poland, which drew France and England into the conflict. With war raging in Europe, the Remount was in full swing, as the U.S. Army had fewer than fifty thousand of the needed two hundred thousand horses it planned on procuring for entering the war. Horse buyers were scanning the country, inspecting Remount horses. Colonel Daniels had one order for twenty thousand horses.

With the mechanization of the army, there had been a debate as to the usefulness of horses in the military. In 1930, General Douglas MacArthur had even gone so far as to order the extermination of excess cavalry mounts. The decision was met with predictable results. U.S. cavalrymen were trained to obey orders, but above all, they were trained to care for their horses. When the order came down at Fort Hutchinson, Arizona, to kill some of the post's horses, a lieutenant and four old cavalrymen deserted and herded the horses north into Canada to spare them from being shot.

The proponents of using horses in the army argued that a mounted force scouting over rough terrain would be effective where vehicles could not traverse.

After a horse-buying spree in 1941, processing centers like Fort Reno, Oklahoma, and Fort Robinson, Nebraska, were overflowing with animals. They were also staffed by some of the best horsemen and veterinarians in the world.

Remount processing centers like Fort Robinson, Nebraska; Fort Reno, Oklahoma; and Fort Keogh, in Miles City, were crowded with horses and getting them ready for service. For example, at Fort Keogh, one hundred civilian cowboys were hired to put the horses through their paces. Some of the best and worst horses were indiscriminately led out for the cowboys to ride.

Men like Red Tate, George Brock, and Luther Dunning were almost entirely dependent on army buyers. Together, they had well over six hundred horses. By 1941, the market for a cow was $30, while the army was paying $165 for a Remount horse.

In the middle of the army's horse-buying spree, Red and Erma Tate bought a ranch on Lyon Creek, a tributary of Otter Creek. The Tates' ranch was located on part of Noll Wallop's old horse pasture. Tate paid $2 per acre for three thousand acres and obtained a lease to graze another thirty-five-hundred acres nearby. Red hired Luther Dunning's grandson, Lee, to ride his horses. The grasslands along Otter Creek had fed the great horse herds of Sir Sydney Paget and Noll Wallop fifty years prior and were bordered by high ridges and pine forests along the Custer National Forest.

The ever-industrious Red Tate decided to create a new market for his horses with the racing fervor that was sweeping the country at the time. When most purses for local races were only $100, he put up a $200 purse at a Glendive, Montana, race meet for horses bred by Red Tate. Over a three-year period, Red sold more than a dozen horses to owners looking to win the race.

Bob Tate had taken part-time work riding horses for Neponset Stud Farm. One day while he was practicing polo shots on a young horse, Bob was bucked off and broke his hip. Lying in bed on December 7, 1941, he heard the news on the radio that the Japanese had attacked Pearl Harbor. He was hurt, unemployed, and his girlfriend, Barbara Fixen, had been shipped east, as her father felt she was getting too close to the cowboy.

Once Bob Tate's hip healed, he was drafted and shipped out to Camp Roberts, California, by train. Once again, all of Sheridan gathered to see its young men off to war. Jack Carrels, the former bootlegger and owner of the Mint Bar, shook hands with every young man as he boarded and handed him a free pint of whiskey. The Sheridan brewery put a case of beer under every row of seats on the train.

At Camp Roberts, Bob was assigned as a forward observer to the Signal Corps of the field artillery. If the war, the loss of Barbara Fixen, and breaking his hip had not been enough, Bob received a letter from the Sheridan Racing Association banning him for life from their sanctioned events. Tate shrugged the entire incident off. Banning a person for life from their hometown racetrack might discourage the average person from pursuing a career with horses, but it wasn't going to slow Bob down.

After a few months at Camp Roberts, Bob was promoted to private first class, but he got into trouble calling in the wrong coordinates on an artillery drill. His job was to repeat the coordinates the officer called over the phone to the artillerist. Instead of calling left 52, Bob called right 52. After an abandoned equipment shed in the wrong direction blew up, Bob was busted down to buck private and made to sleep in the latrine for two days.

After receiving a few sad-sack letters from Bob, Erma Tate wrote Colonel Fudge and Colonel Daniels to see if they might get Bob involved in the Remount. Within a few weeks, Bob was summoned by his first sergeant.

"Tate, this beats everything. Here I can't figure out what to do with you, and now I get two letters from the two highest-ranking officers in the Remount specifically requesting you!"

In mid-1942 Bob Tate was transferred to Fort Reno, Oklahoma, where twenty-six thousand horses and eleven thousand mules were being processed for duty in the army. Five hundred horses came through every day to be issued, and a human assembly line of twenty riders, forty-eight shoers, and a team of vets prepared the horses for service. The animals were run down a chute, and then one man would trim their feet while another would clip their mane off. Each day the riders would gallop twenty-five horses two laps around the arena. If the horses bucked, they went to the right; if they didn't, they went to the left. The buckers were assigned to a group of bronc riders, and the next day they were run into an assembly line, where one man was hired just to tie their feet up so the wilder horses could be managed.

At Fort Reno, Bob ran into an old acquaintance from Wyoming. Charlie Leonard had been a dude at the HF Bar and had remembered Bob's performances in the race meets. Charlie and Bob were both polo players, and they soon struck up a friendship. Bob, with his usual cowboy charm, convinced the first sergeant in charge of the stables that they should play polo on the base. The men met with Major Fudge, a friend of Red Tate's and Luther Dunning's, about organizing polo on Sunday. Fudge thought it was a good idea because the army had previously used polo as a means to teach the cavalrymen to ride.

Once again Bob had landed in tall cotton. While other horsemen ended up working in the pig barn, Bob had talked his way into promoting horse shows for the officers and their children and playing polo.

Dear Kinney,
I had a letter from Dad, and he said the filly would be in anytime you came after her. Not doing much here now, I'm getting ready for the horse show and have a couple of runners, been playing a lot of polo . . . I hope to get home this fall to see the race.
As ever,
Bob

Bob returned to Sheridan on furlough just before the County Fair and race meet. Though he was banned from racing, he entered the calf roping and won the event on a prayer of a loop that the calf jumped through and was caught by the hind leg. The feat made news in the *Sheridan Press*.

In the calf-roping contest, Bob Tate, a Sheridan boy now in the army, provided the thrill of the afternoon.

Tate got his rope on the calf, but the rope slipped off. The calf tripped, however, and slid on its neck for several feet. Tate jumped from his horse and used commando tactics, tackling without its being roped. He got his rope and tied up the calf in 31 and one-fifth seconds.

"That boy has the luck of the devil," said a cowboy who was watching the event. What Bob failed to tell anyone was that by staying home for the race meet, he was now AWOL by ten days. When he arrived at Fort Reno, he was busted back down to buck private and put to work digging a ditch six feet long, six feet wide, and six feet deep every day for punishment. Like everything else in his life, even this worked out for Bob. He had previously been assigned to give the post commander's daughter riding lessons, so when Bob was digging his nightly hole, the girl came out and fed him sandwiches and soft drinks and kept him company.

Dear Kinney,
I was ten days late by the time I got here. They didn't say much; they wouldn't let me leave the base for a week, but I didn't want to go anyway. We are playing polo now three times a week, and I work my ponies the rest of the time, so I didn't want to go anyplace anyway.

They sold my runner while I was gone, but left me my good brown pony. I liked him much the best. They are having a horse show and a few races here next month. I have a couple of runners, so I don't mind so much. . . Tell your family hello, and tell Marilyn to keep her weight down so she can gallop our runners for us.
Bob

It wasn't long before Bob got in more hot water with the army brass. One evening while he was on duty as night guard for Fort Reno, a group of workers asked his assistance in getting a building that was loaded on a truck under some power lines at the gate. Tate crawled up on the roof and lifted the wires with a stick while the men drove the large truck out. The next day the officer of the day approached Tate. "Private, where's the building that was over there?" he asked, pointing to a vacant lot.

"The men who were working on it yesterday took it," he said.

"Tate! You let someone steal a house when you were on guard duty?" the officer yelled. Fortunately for Tate, he had endeared himself to the higher-ups during races and polo games.

He was several thousand miles from home. Bob's passion for his horses motivated him to send a constant stream of letters home in an effort to manage his horses. He had left his friend Switzer some horses to train and was trying to monitor them long distance and keep up with the racing scene.

Dear Switzer,

I hope the saddles got there all right; they're not too good, but I think they will do.

If you can, I would sure try to take the filly to the racetrack so she will know how to run around the turns. She will need more work than your little horse did because he had been run the year before and knew how.

You could start galloping her a mile every day, and start working her 1/8 of a mile, slow at first, then a quarter, then by the middle of July 3/4 slow the first time or two, and don't work her just once or twice a week and by the first of August work her half, then ten days before you run her. Work 5/8 good with something else so she won't be horse-shy. Keep all the weight off her while you're training her.

On Red and Erma's Lyon Creek ranch, Bob's mare, Miss Princess, had a foal named Flick-a-Wick that had grown into a gangly three-year-old. Erma wrote her son explaining that Flick-a-Wick had been wire-cut and could no longer be raced, but she would breed her if he liked. Bob wrote Erma to breed Flick-a-Wick to Luther Dunning's large bay stallion named Friar Dolan. Erma wrote back that they would haul the mare up to Dunning's ranch if they could get the gas. Times were hard, and gas was rationed across the country because of the war. When Erma hauled Flick-a-Wick up to Dunning's ranch, a smaller Remount stallion called Bright Bud caught her eye, so she bred Flick-a-Wick to Bright Bud.

Erma Tate may have been as savvy a horseman as anyone in the country. On their ranch, Erma was in her element. She was right at home canning antelope meat or vegetables she grew outside her home. Red was known to travel up on the flats behind Dunning's and poach a fat antelope off the alfalfa fields in the summer. Syd Dunning posted a sign on the road for Red's benefit that said *No Hunting, Syd Dunning*. After seeing the sign, Red got out his paintbrush and wrote underneath *Too Late, Red Tate.*

Erma fed horse buyers with a western hospitality that might include canned antelope meat with homemade scratch biscuits and gravy. With three children out of the house, she was free to give her attention to the horses.

Though now in their sixties, Erma and Red Tate were still riding and breaking horses. They had no choice; all the young men had been shipped off to war. Red and Erma teamed up on bad buckers; Erma rode a gentle saddlehorse, leading the bronc that she kept snubbed up to her saddle horn while Red climbed aboard. Using teamwork and patience, they got the outlaws gentled down enough to ride.

The Otter Creek country was once again enjoying a resurgence of horsemen because of the Remount. Men like George Brock, Red Tate, and even Luther Dunning were raising horses exclusively for the army. Unfortunately they were about to suffer a devastating blow as horse breeders. In the middle of the war, the government decided to dissolve the Remount program. With the advent of the Jeep in the middle of the war, horses suddenly became obsolete to the army. They came back by the thousands to dispersal centers. At Fort Reno, Oklahoma, Bob Tate worked in the first sale, where the army sold five thousand horses one at a time in two days and a night. At Fort Robinson seventy-five thousand were returned.

Syd Dunning, Red Tate, and George Brock were all well past their prime, but all three men retained a spark from their cowboy roots. Each man had a son in the war that was now raging across Europe and the Pacific. As a diversion, the three men decided to trail seventy-five head of their horses from Otter Creek to a sale in the Black Hills. It was a week of hard riding, hard drinking, and storytelling around the campfires at night by three men clinging to the old cowboy ways. The trip culminated at the horse sale at Spearfish, South Dakota, where the men had sold their horses. Brock, Tate, and Dunning, with heads full of alcohol, decided to win some money on a bet. They were challenged to all three get on an unbroken nine-year-old in the chute and ride her in the ring. The three ended up in a pile of sawdust in the middle of the sale ring, howling in a fit of laughter. Horse buyers held up cash to get the men to repeat the stunt, but the three horsemen, as drunk as they were, knew enough not to tempt fate. Their laughter was a brief respite from their fear for their soldier sons.

Red's son-in-law, Bud Thompson, was killed serving in General Patton's Third Army. Syd Dunning's son, Lee, had been stationed at Fort Robinson but had recently been shipped off to Burma, from whence the Japanese were trying to invade India. Judge James Burgess's son, Henry, was assigned to the Pacific theater, as was Dave Carnahan.

In the small community of Birney, Montana, a group of schoolkids, with the help of some parents and an artist named Jim Ryan, started a newspaper to send to homesick GIs. The *Birney Mirror* was illustrated with wonderful scenes of ranch life in town and along Tongue River. Big Bones Alderson's wife, Dorothy, led the children in the project, and with donations from dudes at Bones Brothers Ranch, the small newspaper made its rounds to Cheyenne and white soldiers in England, France, India, the South Pacific, and all points in between. The newspaper raised money for the war effort, lifted the spirits of homesick GIs worldwide, and let dudes who had returned east for the winter know how life was going back at the ranch.

Twenty-five thousand Native Americans volunteered for duty in World War II. Joe Medicine Crow, a nephew of the Crow agent Bob Yellowtail, was in Europe as part of the "Cactus" Division. While Medicine Crow's K Company was crossing into Germany from France, they were pinned down in foxholes from German small arms and mortar fire. Medicine Crow led a detail through enemy fire and up a hill to procure dynamite.

Later, on a push through a German village, Joe ran into a German in battle and wrestled the man until help came. The final war deed happened when his unit was trailing some German SS officers who were on horseback. The Germans stopped at a farmhouse and turned the horses in to a corral while they rested. When the Americans stopped outside the house, Medicine Crow volunteered to sneak in and run their horses off before they attacked.

He snuck in the mud and tied a string around the jaw of a large sorrel horse with a white blaze. Once mounted, his partner opened the gate, and Joe lay across the horse's back while he ran the horses out under a crossfire between the Germans and the Americans that opened fire on the house. He trailed the horses at a gallop to the safety of some woods nearby and found he had forty head of horses. When he returned home, he realized he had met all the old Crow military requirements to become a chief.

For seventy-two days Bob Tate was aboard a troop ship that passed Australia en route to Calcutta, but because of German submarines in the area, the ship was diverted to Bombay. Men slept four deep in the belly of the hot ship. Bob traded a week's wages for a bunk next to the air conditioner. After landing, Bob wrote his friend in racing, telling him of his experiences.

Dear Switzer,
I was so glad to get off the boat, I didn't give a damn where it was . . . We came across India on a train. You can't believe how people live here till you see for yourself. If England has been running the show here all of these years, they sure have done a poor job of it.

I sure hated to hear about your losing the Futurity because your saddle slipped back; you sure want to use a breast collar even if you don't need it and leave it loose; I thought your colt would be close if you had a good rider . . .

Have you gotten our filly yet? That colt of Woods, Buccaneer, has got a lot of speed if he can run that far, and he is big enough to pack the weight and has a lot of experience. I would rather see anybody but Woods win the Futurity.

General Joe Stillwell was coordinating with Chinese General Chiang Kai-shek to beat back the Japanese, who were moving west to take over the Burma Road into India. General Merrill and his men walked six hundred miles through jungles, over mountains, and across rivers and swamps to capture the airport at Myitkyina, Burma. The goal was to open the road from Ledo to China—called the Stillwell Trail—which ran over the Himalayas and was infiltrated with Japanese. It was jungle fighting at its worst.

To supply Merrill's troops, the Quarter Masters Department sent mules for Merrill to transport supplies. Mules stood up to the heavy packing and the heat and disease better than horses.

Unfortunately many of these animals also became victims of government experiments, one of which was parachuting the animals out of planes. Another Army experiment was to fly mules into the jungle on large gliders. Of the six hundred mules that Merrill ordered, only 360 survived their trip to Burma. The lost mules were replaced with Australian horses.

Bob was assigned the duty of driving and leading the mules in the hot, dirty surroundings to General Merrill over the Ledo trail to Myitkyina. Bob rode one mule and led four, two on each side.

Moving behind Merrill's troops to Bommell, the dead bodies of Japanese soldiers were laid out alongside the trail waiting to be buried. The remains of the mules stuck up in trees were grim reminders of the parachute fiasco. Bloated bodies floated in pink water amid stagnant green scum. Dogs and pigs rooted among the decaying corpses in the streets, and crows pecked out dead eyes. The stench was appalling.

On Christmas Day 1943, Tate, stationed in Ledo, Burma, was homesick, scared, and sick of losing mules in the jungle. Out of the blue, a soldier told Bob he thought there was someone at the mess tent from Wyoming. Three Absaraka horsemen, Al Smith from Buffalo, Wyoming, Lee Dunning from Otter Creek, and Jiggs Yellowtail from Crow agency, were sitting together listening to someone outside singing *I don't want to set the world on fire, I just want to go home.* The trio was somewhat surprised to see that the singer was none other than Bob Tate. It was a cause for celebration. Tate kept them all entertained as he recalled races the four of them had entered and some of the characters from Sheridan.

"I heard Curley Witzel is training pilots for the navy," Dunning said.

"Mom said Curley wrote the Sheridan newspaper and said that he was breaking horses for the navy." The four had a laugh out of that.

"How about a drink, Bob?"

"Where'd you guys get whiskey?"

"It's more like gin," Dunning chuckled, and soon they were walking down a path into the jungle where a plume of smoke rose. Dunning was in charge of the stable and had an unlimited supply of grain, and Al Smith was in charge of the kitchen, so he had unlimited access to sugar.

"It's a little green, but it makes this place a little more tolerable," Dunning said, and the men raised their tin cups in unison.

Dunning and Tate spent most of their time chasing the mules that got loose. The mules trailed fine, but the Mongolian ponies that were also being used to transport goods would duck off the trail and lead the mules into the jungle.

"Merrill's Marauders" prevailed in defeating the Japanese on the Ledo road, but that victory was costly. Of the 2,900 American soldiers who followed Merrill over the Himalayas to open the Ledo road, only 1,310 survived. All the Australian packhorses died, as did many of the mules.

Near the war-torn town of Bommell, Tate sat on the bank of a flooded dirty river one afternoon, fighting the heat, when Colonel Rand showed up and recognized the cowboy from Wyoming. Bob had played polo with Rand at Fort Reno.

"What do you make of all this, Bob?" Rand asked the young cowboy.

"I'd hate to say, Colonel."

"Go ahead, son, you can speak frankly," he said.

"Well, Colonel, I think it's one big screw-up," he replied.

Rand suppressed a smile at Tate's candor, but for as long as he had known Bob and his father, there was no telling what would come out of their mouths. Whatever the subject, their opinions were likely to be entertaining.

"Charlie Leonard said you might like to come and work for me at headquarters," Rand said. Within the week Bob was in Calcutta, serving as Colonel Rand's driver and dressed in Levi's and a cowboy hat that Erma sent him for most of the war.

In Calcutta, a foal arrived that had been born to an Australian mare on a transport ship. The order came down to kill the foal, but Tate, with some fellow soldiers, rescued the animal and smuggled the colt on base. The men bottle-fed it, and soon the colt, named Ike, became the camp pet. It would wander into the barracks or the mess hall and follow the men around the base like a dog. For the horsemen stationed at Calcutta, it reminded them of home. When the army pulled out of Calcutta, there were no plans for the colt.

"If we leave it here, they'll just kill it," Tate told Colonel Rand.

"Go down and make arrangements to ship it to New Delhi," Rand said. Tate knew better than to tell the officer in charge of the trains that the horse was an officer's mount.

"You tell your colonel there's a war on. I don't have a car for any officer's mount," he yelled at Tate.

Bob called Colonel Rand, who told Tate to get packed and get the colt and be ready to go. Within the hour Tate received a call that a royal palace racehorse car had arrived for his officer's mount. With a duffel bag in one hand and a lead rope in the other, Tate hurried Ike into the luxurious car built for the viceroy of India's racehorses. The car had a sleeping compartment for the groom and a stove for cooking, in addition to a spacious stall with a supply of fresh hay, oats, and water. The stationmaster was furious when he saw that all the commotion that had been for a colt, but soon Tate and Ike were enjoying the scenery along the six-hundred-mile trip to New Delhi.

Once there, Tate, still a buck private, was treated to living in officers' quarters. He was also reunited with his friend Charlie Leonard. Despite the war, thoroughbred racing continued in New Delhi, so Bob and Charlie went to the horse races each week, and Leonard even bought a racehorse that he hired an Englishman to train. Colonel Rand and Leonard rode the officers' horses for polo matches, which they played with the viceroy himself.

Dear Switzer,

I haven't heard from you for so long I thought the army might have you; I don't think the damn thing can last much longer.

I really have a good job now in New Delhi with Army hqtrs. The only horses here are officers' mounts, and we have one Indian for each horse. No work.

We just moved into new quarters, only four of us, and we have three rooms, a big sleeping area, bathroom, and kitchen. Tell Marilyn we have a cook and Indian house boy, so I could have breakfast in bed if I wanted, but I don't believe I'll ever get that bad.

They race every Saturday. I won four hundred dollars the last two Saturdays betting. We got a racehorse, going to run her next Saturday.

This is the best thing I ever had since I been in the army. I was glad to get out of Burma, it was rough up there. We were taking mules right up to the front to the Chinese. Are they going to race in Sheridan, or is everything closed down?

By 1945, a series of seventeen races were run in Sheridan. Army jockeys from Fort Robinson, Nebraska, traveled in to ride in the fall race meet. The Futurity was won by Prairie Lark, and Playboy, owned by the Bones brothers, took a half-mile race in the Bot Sots Stampede. Quarterhorses were starting to make their appearance in the area, as cutting contests and one-month-mile races were added to rodeo events.

While serving as Colonel Rand's driver in New Delhi, Bob Tate began a romance with the colonel's young Indian secretary, Sharon. In the evenings after driving the colonel home, Tate would take drives with Sharon. The two went for rides in the countryside around Calcutta and attended functions around the city accompanying the colonel. Sharon was an excellent rider who had been educated in England and had foxhunted there and in India. After Berlin fell and the bomb dropped on Japan, the war began to wind down.

Absaraka had produced some of the best soldiers in the war. Four officers from Wyoming's 115th Cavalry Regiment, known as the Powder River Gang, had distinguished themselves in the Pacific. George Pierson, Nat Ewing, Henry Burgess, and Dave Carnahan were among 19 out of 101 surviving officers who had landed in New Guinea in 1944. Burgess had led a rescue mission at Los Banos liberating American prisoners, resulting in Burgess being promoted the youngest full colonel in the U.S. Army.

Though the war was over, Tate got into trouble one more time. In a bar in New Delhi, a sergeant got his nose out of joint over the freedom that Tate had been enjoying. "If it ain't the colonel's suckup; why don't you drop down on the floor and give me some push-ups, Tate?" The sergeant grabbed Tate's shoulder. Tate knocked the man's hand away. Tate was all of 135 lb and about 5'9".

"Get your hand off me, you square-headed son of a bitch," Tate said, and before the large man could land a punch, Tate broke a beer bottle over the man's head. The two rolled across the floor until the military police hauled them off to jail. Tate was arrested and fished out of the guard house by Colonel Rand.

"I'm sending you home early before you get into any more trouble, but I want you to buy a train car of polo horses when you get home and send them to a friend of mine in Connecticut. His name is Frank Butterworth and he coaches the Yale polo team," Rand said.

Tate shipped out across the Red Sea and the Suez Canal and arrived in New York on Armistice Day. With an order for 11 horses, he had his first break as a horse trader.

63

TATE'S FIRST STOP WAS THE GALLATINS' RANCH IN BIG Horn. When Tate showed up to look at their horses, Bea and Carlo brought out three playing horses. Bea did not particularly trust Bob, because he always seemed to have an agenda. She asked $200 apiece for the horses. Bob countered with $150.

"Nothing doing," Bea said, but Bob was undaunted.

"I'll tell you what; I'll flip you for the difference," he offered. Bea looked at Carlo, who seemed to get a kick out of the young man. Bea and Carlo went into the house and got Mr. Gallatin.

When the three came back out, Gallatin walked over to Tate. "We'll do it, but we'll use my coin. Bea will throw it, and Carlo will call it."

"Well, throw it high," Bob said. Bob lost the toss and paid Mr. Gallatin the extra $150 for the three horses.

Bob next bought four horses from the Gallatins' foreman, Johnny Cover. Bob didn't even ask to try Cover's horses; he had seen Cover ride, and Tate knew if you got a horse from Cover that you were *mounted*.

When Frank Butterworth got his horses at Yale, he was thrilled and immediately ordered another train carload to be shipped. In another example of blind luck, Bob Tate stumbled onto an affordable supply of trained horses in Miles City. His first stop was the experimental station at Miles City, which was formerly Fort Keogh.

Between twenty and thirty horses were in use by the eight cowboys that rode more than four thousand cattle. The thoroughbred cross horses were branded XS for experimental station.

Bob drove into the fort and found Major Quesenberry. "What are you going to do now that the government has stopped buying all your horses?" Tate asked.

"I'm going to sell them to you," he said and smiled. Tate could not believe his luck.

"Say that again," Tate said.

"I'm going to sell them to you," Quesenberry said.

"I don't have a lot of money, so I can't pay a lot for them," Tate said.

"I'm not going to give them to you for what the army paid, but I'll let you have your pick for $200. You should still be able to resell them if you have buyers," Quesenberry said.

"You wouldn't shake on that, would you?" Bob asked and held out his hand. The government had been buying cavalry mounts for $165 each. Tate could resell these easily for $400, especially since he now had an order for twelve horses.

Major Quesenberry shook the young man's hand. Tate rode twenty horses and took the top twelve. He shipped them east on a boxcar to Colonel Rand's friend Frank Butterworth, who was so pleased with the horses that he immediately ordered another load.

When Bob first arrived at his parents' ranch after the war, he was greeted by a foal that was the granddaughter of Miss Princess. Bob looked at the fair-colored foal and back at his mother. "How can a dark brown mare and a dark brown stud throw a chestnut colt?"

"I saw a stud at Luther's I liked better, so I bred your mare to her," Erma confessed. Bob had to admit, he was a good-looking colt.

"What'd you name him?" Bob asked.

"Pill Box," Erma said.

Luther and Leota Dunning invited the Tate family to Thanksgiving dinner at Sydney Paget's old ranch, which Luther had bought. Bob sat mesmerized by Luther's stories about the open range days, the sheep killings, the Cheyenne rodeos, and Sydney Paget. The holiday spirit did not hide the fact that the end of the Remount would be the end of the line for the Dunnings and Red Tate as horse breeders. After fifty-five years in the business, Luther had seen the market rise and fall, but now it seemed to be gone for good. There was no market for an average horse anymore, except for the depressed meat market, and anyone who thought they could raise only top horses was a fool. Luther left what horses he and Leota had to their grandson, Lee, and Red gave half-interest of his horses to Bob.

Tractors made work teams obsolete, yet Red Tate still clung to working with his team of horses. Jerry Belle and her husband, Howard Allen, moved to Red and Erma's place on Otter Creek. Howard had bought a new Ford tractor, which Red scoffed at. Red prided himself on the speed with which his team could mow.

"I got $50 that says I can make it around this field faster than that tractor and do a better job to boot," Red announced. Harry took the bet, and with Jerry Belle, Erma, and a few friends watching, Red lined up opposite the tractor.

The race was over before it started. By the time Red made it around once with his team of horses and mower, his son-in-law had lapped him twice. Red headed for the gate, unhooked his team, and put his horse-drawn mower away forever.

Bob Tate, however, was on a roll. He got a call from Colonel Rand's mother-in-law, Mrs. Franklin, in Philadelphia. The woman said she wanted tall, unbroke horses for jumping. She felt that cowboys taught horses bad habits. She felt by buying untrained horses, she could ship them back east and have her equestrian trainers train them properly. What she didn't realize was that the Otter Creek grass grew horses that could be first-rate outlaws if left unbroken.

In the end, Mrs. Franklin bought twelve of the horses, which were to be shipped back to Philadelphia by train.

"Mrs. Franklin, I wish you would let me hire a cowboy to ride these horses before I ship them to you," he said.

"Nonsense. I have some of the best horse trainers on the East Coast working at my stable in Pennsylvania. They're more than qualified to give them a good start," she said.

"Yes, ma'am, but at least let me send a cowboy back east with them to ride them the first few times." Mrs. Franklin stuck to her guns, and when the horses arrived at her farm exhausted after a long week's ride on the train, she telegraphed Bob.

The horses arrived in good condition. STOP. Better than expected.
M. Franklin.

After two weeks of rest and feed, the horses from Absaraka turned into the wild animals they were, which was too much for the eastern trainers.

A second telegram followed:

Please send cowboys to ride these horses. STOP.

64

He seemed to have stepped out of a western story book one hundred years ago.

—Colonel John Rand

ON OTTER CREEK, A YOUNG NIECE OF CHARLIE THEX WAS at Luther Dunning's, giving Luther and Leota vaccinations for ticks, when Bob Tate stopped by looking for horses. Aileen Hagen was from an old Norwegian family from Otter Creek. She had gone to school in Miles City and had boarded at the home of Bill and Gert Hawkins. Bill had been one of the original sheriffs of Miles City and told Aileen stories of his times with Calamity Jane and Wild Bill Hickok.

Bob Tate immediately used his charm on Aileen and whisked her off to the races with him on the leaky roof circuit. Within a year the two were married and went to the races in Great Falls with Ken Schiffer, a Yale polo player who served at Fort Robinson during the war. After hearing Colonel Daniels expound on the horse activity around Sheridan, Schiffer visited the area while on furlough and decided he would buy a ranch there when the war ended. Schiffer was soon playing polo at Neponset Stud Farm in Beckton and entering races with Bob Tate from Miles City to Great Falls to Helena and Billings.

In addition to traditional flat racing, a new interest in endurance races swept through Absaraka. Miles City hosted three or four endurance races each summer from different locations. The biggest of these was the 153 miles one-way from Billings to Miles City. In 1946, fifty-three riders from six states competed in the race down the Yellowstone River. The riders left at four o'clock p.m. and had two-hour layovers at Hysham and Forsyth. A carrier pigeon was released in Billings and flew to Miles City to announce that the race had started. Like the early rodeo events, which entertained horse buyers, a Billings-to-Miles-City race was scheduled to finish during the old-timers cowboy reunion called the Range Riders. Tim Irions, the son of the early Powder River horse rancher Al Irions, had the winner with Drifter, ridden by Bill Stewart.

During the time the Remount stallions were retired, Ken Schiffer imported a world-class yet dangerous stallion to his ranch. Schiffer decided to take a chance on it to breed in Wyoming. New World had beaten Whirlaway, the horse of the year, by ten lengths and set track records doing it.

Aileen Tate soon gave birth to a son in Miles City. Doctor Randal, the same doctor who had delivered Aileen, delivered Tommy Tate. Within three years, the couple had four children: Tommy, Mimi, and twin boys, Hardy and Dick. It was hard living for Aileen while Bob was off buying horses, but with the help of neighbors, she got by.

Schiffer was about to relive polo history. Along with teammates Mike Long, Merril Finks from Billings, and Neponset Stud Farm's foreman Bill Gardiner, the "cowboy team" traveled to the Broadmoor Hotel in Colorado Springs for the Pacific Northwest Polo Championship. The match took place on the same field where Malcolm Moncreiffe, Johnny Cover, Lee Bullington, and Bob Walsh had defeated Denver forty years earlier. The Absaraka horsemen brought home the trophy over teams from Massachusetts, Texas, Colorado, Spokane, and Chicago in a year that marked the passing of Malcolm Moncreiffe.

With polo celebrating its fifty-fifth year in the area, teams from Spokane, Pierre, Jackson, Denver, and some eastern cities traveled to Neponset and Moncreiffe fields to play in summer tournaments. Noll Wallop's grandchildren were now playing. A friendly rivalry would start between the Neponset and Moncreiffe fields. At the heart of the matter was Oliver Wallop of the Moncreiffe field and Bill Gardiner, foreman of Neponset Stud Farm.

The wild horse crow of the thirties now had children. The Schiffers and Gardiners and Carnahans combined to produce horse shows at Neponset

Stud Farm in Beckton and the Island Ranch in Big Horn. Jeanne and Carolyn Wallop were competing in horse shows with their brothers John and Malcolm. Kay Brewster and the Alderson grandchildren were now competing in the races and horse shows.

At one of the Neponset horse shows, Bob Tate entered his two-year-old chestnut filly, Pill Box. In the halter class, Pill Box won first place over a well-bred two-year-old stallion imported by Neponset.

Bob Tate was expanding his domain as a horse buyer at this time. Bob and Ken Schiffer went to a Fort Robinson dispersal sale after the war. Miles City also had a large postwar horse sale; five thousand horses were sold in six days and six nights. The majority of them went for meat.

In 1950, Miles City advertised a Bucking Horse Sale. Area ranchers brought their worst outlaws in the hopes of getting better than meat prices for their horses. The rodeo paid local cowboys $5 to $10 for every bronc they rode. It was a unique event that sometimes featured inexperienced riders riding inexperienced buckers. The results were pure western entertainment.

Leota Dunning smiled at Luther when she showed him the letter. "It's from Colonel Rank. He wrote an article in *Western Horseman* magazine about you. It says, 'To Luther Dunning, one of the best of friends, Colonel William A. Rank, Co. US. Ret'd.' The article is called 'Thoroughbred Tradition in the Northwest.'" Leota sat down next to Luther and read him the letter. Luther, now seventy, and Leota had moved into Sheridan when they found out Luther had cancer.

> *Miles City, Mont., was the largest range-horse market in the world, and Montana had more range horses than any other state . . . In the premises of the Range Riders Bar, Miles City is an appropriate starting place for a story of thoroughbred blood. One evening in 1944 a dude cowboy was building up his impressions of western life while wetting his whistle at the Range Riders Bar. Suddenly the street door swung open, and old Red Tate from Otter Creek rode in on his gray roping pony of thoroughbred breeding. Red reined the gray pony up to the bar, ordered drinks for two,*

and rolled out of his saddle in the direction of the piano. While the pony was licking the foam from a schooner of beer, Red pulled on an old pair of cotton work gloves for the artist's soft touch and began tapping the ivories in search of a melody—"Take Me Back to My Boots and Saddle."

On the occasion of the writer's first visit to the Range Riders Bar, a tall, thin old rider was attracting attention of newcomers merely by reason of his ancient appearance. He was not feeble, quite the contrary, but so wrinkled, leathery, durable, and dignified that he seemed to have stepped out of a western storybook of a hundred years ago . . . this was 91-year-old Tom McAllister, one of the largest operators in the Montana range-horse industry of 50 years ago, who still was riding the range straight up in his saddle on lively mounts of thoroughbred breeding . . . Tom used to buy registered thoroughbred stallions by the carload at eastern racetracks, ship them to some point on his Montana range, and kick them out to rough it on their own or, in Tom's way of thinking, do or die, depending on how much real horse was under a well-groomed hide.

It was in the Range Riders Bar that the writer first heard the story of Indian Runner. Indian Runner was a Montana range-raised horse of unknown breeding and marvelous speed that beat all registered thoroughbreds on the big racetracks until the Jockey Club, in furious embarrassment, established the rule that only registered horses were eligible to race on tracks under the jurisdiction of the Jockey Club.

Now let us journey out of Miles City about 80 miles up the Tongue River, thence up Otter Creek to the mouth of Paget Creek . . . in ultra-primitive surroundings, a hundred miles from the outer fringe of civilization, Sir Sydney Paget, an English horseman, established a registered thoroughbred stud enterprise with the best foundation of breeding stock that could be obtained and imported from England.

On a beautiful little meadow in a bend of Otter Creek, one may see the faint outline of the old Paget racetrack and visualize the former log stables, corrals, and bunkhouse nearby. Here in the long shadows of the Custer National Forest and under the curious eyes of the still half-wild fighting Cheyenne Indians, a thin, wiry, freckle-faced and blue-eyed boy daily galloped the thoroughbreds on the racetrack under the expert guidance of Sir Sydney, a master horseman. Sir Sydney raised horses under range conditions, the natural and most suitable environment for a horse.

The blue-eyed, freckle-faced boy in the article was Luther Dunning, of course. This was a tribute from one horseman to another whose time had already been forgotten.

After the war, range horses were hunted, run off their home range, and driven into corrals. Men sometimes tied pieces of scrap metal to the captured horses' forelocks to prevent them from running while being trailed to market. Horses that were too wily to catch were run to death by airplanes. It was between Tongue River and Rosebud Creek that two riders approached the carcass of one such horse. "I guess that's him," one of the riders said. "They ran out of gas trying to run him down. They said he got away through here. He must have run himself to death."

He looked at the stallion with regret. Since his boyhood he had heard of a yellow stallion that ran mares and stole saddlehorses in the area. It would be a blessing to be rid of horses that ran through the fences and pushed cattle into bogs, but if this was the last of the bloodline of the yellow stallions, he felt a deep regret.

When the young cowboy dismounted and took out his pocketknife to cut off an ear, the old cowboy stopped him. "Leave him!" It wasn't just the tone that stopped the boy, but a realization that what he was doing was somehow wrong. He looked at the older cowboy, folded his knife, and got back on his horse.

Alan Fordyce's daughter and son, Helen and Ike, were saddling their horses to get ready to ride with Johnny Cover. The Gallatins' foreman, though now old, was an icon to the children, and they wanted to be on time to make a good impression. Cover had been suffering from ill health, but it had not stopped him from riding. The horseman was brushing out the mane on his favorite mare that morning before he rode. Cover always groomed his horse to perfection, even if he were only riding out to check an irrigation ditch. Cover's wife called to him, and when there was no answer, she went to the barn and found him dead of a heart attack, lying next to his mare.

When Bob Tate returned home from a horse-buying trip, Aileen met him at the door.

"Luther Dunning died," she said and turned and went back into the kitchen. The news hit Bob hard.

"Does Dad know?" Bob yelled after his wife.

"He's getting drunk at the Elks with all the old gang," she called back.

Erma and Red Tate had moved back into Sheridan more than a year before. When Erma got a call to pick Red up from the Mint Bar, Erma sent Bob, who pulled up to the alley where Red was standing.

"Get in, Dad!" Bob said. He was angry at his father for being drunk. Jack Carrels walked out to help.

"Dad, get in!" he said. Red stood with his hat cocked back like it was an effort to hold it on top of his head.

"He can't," Carrels yelled to Bob.

"Why can't he?" Bob asked.

"He's got his pants around his ankles," Carrel explained.

Red Tate's grandchildren last saw him in the Wyo Rodeo parade, riding his horse down Main Street and dressed as an Indian princess.

"Look, there's granddad!" Hardy Tate said to his twin brother, Dick.

"Hey, Granddad!" The two boys waved, and Red Tate smiled and waved back. Within the week, he was killed crossing Main Street from the Elks Club to the Mint Bar. The local citizenry wanted the driver prosecuted for manslaughter.

Shortly thereafter, Goelet Gallatin passed away on his ranch, leaving the E4 for Bea and Carlo to run.

Cameron Forbes died, which would wind down the reign of Neponset Stud Farm as a breeding operation.

The era of the range horsemen in Absaraka that had begun with the Crow, Lakota, Sioux, and Cheyenne was all but over. No more armies would come to buy their horses; polo wasn't being played for the first time since the 1890s; and even the race meets were scaled back to almost nothing.

65

BOB TATE CONTINUED HIS LIFE ON THE ROAD BUYING horses, and often Little Bones Alderson made the rounds with him to the horse sales. They regularly would stop in a bar and shoot a game of pool or throw silver dollars at boots to decide who got first pick on the horses they bought.

When Aileen's father died, Bob and Aileen inherited his ranch on Otter Creek. Tommy was now old enough to accompany Bob to the horse sales in South Dakota, Montana, and Wyoming. Watching the young boy follow Bob around brought out the compassion in even the hardest of horse buyers, and Tommy had usually filled both pockets with candy by the end of the sales.

Charlie Leonard often came to the Tate Ranch for visits, and he brought with him on occasion a variety of eastern horse buyers. Bob organized polo games for them, got them drunk at the Elks Club, and generally showed them a genuinely good time. Often he would take them to Fort Keogh and let them pick out which horses they wanted. Bob bought the horses for $200 and resold them for $400. By now, Bob's list of polo buyers read like a literal Who's Who in polo: Paul Butler from Chicago, Cecil Smith from Texas, George Oliver from Florida, and Frank Butterworth from Connecticut.

Bob Tate's horses were also beginning to make a name in the equestrian world. He had sold Pill Box to an Olympic rider, Wilson Dennehy, and soon the horse won the Pan Am Games as a jumper. Cecil Smith, the top American polo player in the game, played five out of his six Tate horses in the U.S. Open. High Tension, a horse co-owned by Tate and Alderson, had made it to Madison Square Garden as a bucker.

The last of Tom McAllister's range horses, however, was the one Bob was proudest of. The mare was being raced by Dick Glenn, a local cowboy who had married a dude girl.

"That looks like Tom McAllister's brand," Tate said. The mare was homely, with lop ears.

"As far as I know, she's the last of the McAllister horses," Glenn said. Her registered name was Zizela Moore, and she had McAllister's Lazy Six brand on her shoulder.

Tate bred her twice to a son of the Gallatins' Black Rascal and once to Ken Schiffer's New World. These three foals went on to be international champions. The colt by New World ended up on the Canadian Olympic team. The other two colts were named after Bob's twins, Dick and Hardy Tate. Bob sold Dick Tate to Mrs. Blackwood, who renamed him Little Sailor. He went on to win Grand Champion Working Hunter at Madison Square Garden. Hardy Tate was raced by Bud Irions and ended up on the Mexican Olympic team.

66

JIMMY McHUGH WAS ONE OF THE BIGGEST NAMES AMONG horse owners in America. He had built a polo club in Brandywine, Pennsylvania, and hired two of America's top polo professionals, Ray Harrington and Billy Mayer, to play on his polo team. McHugh had 140 of the best racehorses and polo ponies in the world. He had recently hosted the Mexican polo team at the Meadowbrook Club in New York for an exhibition match.

Charlie Leonard brought McHugh to Sheridan to meet Bob Tate and McHugh fell in love with the area. McHugh had a fondness for drink, women, and people in general. He was quick to buy a drink or loan money to someone who was down on his luck. Soon Bob Tate had McHugh and Leonard on a cattle drive up on Otter Creek, which ended up in more drinking than riding. While in Sheridan, Jimmy made his headquarters the Elks Club and the Mint Bar.

McHugh, Charlie Leonard, and Frank Butterworth decided to go in together and buy a horse-breeding operation in Sheridan and let Bob Tate run it. Jimmy was drinking at the Elks when Bob picked him up to look at Wymont Ranch near Beckton. Wymont was one of the most pristine ranches in the country, with twelve hundred acres, corrals, a barn, and an irrigated hay field that rolled out to the large, white two-story ranch house.

When the four men were discussing the ranch over drinks at the Elks Club, Bob interjected, "If I'm gonna run the son of a bitch I want 1 percent of the whole deal!" The three men laughed, but they agreed to his terms. The partnership never materialized and McHugh ended up as sole owner with Tate retaining his 1 percent.

No sooner had McHugh bought the ranch than he insisted that Bob move Aileen and their four children into the big house on Wymont. When Jimmy visited, he slept on a cot in back until he built another house next door for himself.

Back on the East Coast, McHugh's steeplechase horse Game had won horse of the year, being the first horse to win $100,000 over fences. McHugh's polo team was in Chicago about to start the 1956 U.S. Open Championship, but unfortunately, their owner was on a drinking binge in Wyoming. His team played the preliminary game with the groom taking McHugh's place on the team. McHugh's team went on to win without him.

In Wyoming, Tate showed McHugh one of the last big horse ranches in the country. North of Forsyth, Montana, Bud Cramer owned more than five thousand horses. Twenty miles before the men even reached the ranch they began to notice bunches of Cramer horses in the fields. When they arrived, they were invited in for lunch. Afterward, Cramer sent six cowboys out to gather some of his horses and bring them to the corrals for viewing. The corrals were as big as a city block with a quarter-mile wing running off to turn the horses.

"How big is the pasture?" Tate asked.

"Oh it's just a wrangle pasture," Cramer said.

"Well how big is it?" Bob asked.

"Eighteen sections." Bob tried to do the math in his head, knowing there were 640 acres to the section.

Tate looked at McHugh. "Whatever you do, don't get pulled in to buying a horse just because his wife rides it, she's a hell of a bronc rider," Bob warned.

The trip was not so much a trip to buy horses as it was a trip back in time.

In Miles City, Paddy Ryan was eating in a diner and conversing with a waitress when three drunken twenty-year-olds staggered in. They began to cuss and bully another waitress until Paddy, now middle-aged, intervened. "You boys need to settle down and watch your language," he warned them.

The largest boy, who was at least two hundred pounds, walked over and put his hand on Paddy's shoulder. "Don't get tough old man," he said.

"I was tough when I walked in here." Paddy replied, and hit the boy in the jaw so fast that neither of the other two boys had time to react. He hit the second twice sending the third backpeddling before he had even been hit. "Get your friend and get out of here, and don't come back till you learn some manners," Paddy ordered them.

Paddy laughed as the three stumbled out the door. The boys had no idea what a fighter this man had been or that he had entered several bare-knuckle fights in various eastern cities while he had ridden his way to a world championship in bronc riding.

Curley Witzel had started a charter flight service in Sheridan. On one flight into Denver, the control tower put him in a holding pattern. Tired of waiting to land, an impatient Witzel radioed the tower.

"This is Curley Witzel. I've got an emergency. I'm coming in on only one engine!"

"Do you have any emergency equipment?" the tower asked.

"Yeah, I got a pencil and a pair of sunglasses," was Curley's wise-guy reply, but he was cleared to land immediately.

Fire trucks and emergency crews were scrambled to clear all runways for an emergency landing of what they assumed was a jumbo jet full of passengers. What they saw, however, was a small one-engine plane landing in the middle of the runway. Witzel was summoned into the office of the airport's director forthwith!

Curley Witzel had moved to Eaton's ranch after his wife, Annie Laurie, left him. Curley had a daughter by another woman who had died shortly after giving birth to a girl, who he named Betty. While playing poker at Eaton's, Curley made a habit to set aside silver dollars every time he had a winning hand. Betty was in boarding school in Arizona, and he had promised her a new car when she graduated.

On graduation day, Curley showed up with a wired-together station wagon that he had driven south from Sheridan. One door was missing, blue smoke poured out of the back, and a loose belt made a screaming sound as the engine ran.

"Wanna drive your new car?" Curley asked. Betty was somewhat embarrassed until Curley pulled into a car dealership and began to haggle with the manager, hoping to whittle the man down to $1,200 for a brand new car. Betty was beside herself, but it was typical Curley. When it came time to pay, Curley dragged a sack of twelve hundred silver dollars out of the back of the old station wagon and over to the manager.

"You want me to count these?" he asked. "There might be some extras in there."

Bob Tate grabbed a taxi from the New York airport. He was in the city to visit Charlie Leonard. "I'm headed for the Racquet Club," Tate told the driver.

"I got news for ya pal, they only let blue bloods in the Racquet Club," the driver said. When the cab pulled up the entrance, he waited after Tate paid him.

To the cabbie's surprise, the doorman gave Tate a warm welcome.

"I would have bet against it," the cabbie said.

Tate paused and returned to the cab and shook the man's hand.

"Thanks pal," Tate said. "If you ever get to Sheridan, Wyoming, look us up."

Bob and Aileen's daughter Mimi was now old enough to accompany her father to horse sales.

In Billings, a Crow horseman named Jesse always entertained the crowd that gathered for the event.

"He's a good one, boys!" Jesse would yell up to the rafters as he rode through the ring. "He's got all the good in him, 'cause we 'ain't got no good out of him," he announced to the crowd.

He was known to ride a horse through the sale ring barefoot. During these rides he would yell out, "Hey boys, buy this horse cause I need some shoes."

Bob would sometimes buy horses from the Real Bird family outside of Crow Agency, Montana. While looking at one racehorse, the owner led it up to Bob and said, "This is the best-bred horse in Montana; he's a stepbrother to Northern Dancer."

Horses had been the one constant to bridge the relationships of white and Indians in the area. Bob Tate had raced with and profited by the horse knowledge he had learned from Indians like Spotted Wolf and Red Wolf. He had won races on Indian horses like Betty Co-ed and Frankie K.

While Bob Tate had a connection with Indian racers, his son Tommy and his nephew Harry were about to uncover a part of an Indian horse culture long past. While the two boys were riding the rough country near Otter Creek they stopped on a hill topped with large rocks. The spot had been a former battleground between Crow and Blackfeet Indians.

"Help me push this rock Tommy," Harry said getting off his horse. Tommy dismounted, and the two rolled the large rock off the steep hill and watched it roll fifty yards downhill, taking out a section of barbed wire fence in the process.

"Look here, Tommy," Harry said. Underneath where the rock had been was a perfectly preserved stone pipe.

67

AT FORT ROBINSON, NEBRASKA, A SIGN READS *THROUGH These Halls, the World's Great Horsemen Pass.* The same could be said for the front gates at Wymont Ranch. Bob Tate and Jimmy McHugh created a breeding establishment somewhat reminiscent of the Gallatins' Circle V Polo Company of the 1920s. Horsemen from all over the world began to make pilgrimages to Wymont. George Oliver, Paul Butler, Frank Butterworth, Cecil Smith, and Pat Connor topped the list. They were greeted by Aileen Tate, whose western hospitality and kindness endeared her to people from every facet of society. By 1960, Bob Tate was selling close to a hundred horses every year.

Tucked back in Absaraka remnants of the old cowboy horsemen culture remained. Bob would pick the horses up at a sale and drop them off at a cowboy's ranch to be ridden for thirty days. When Bob got his horses back from men like Alan Bard, Junior Johnstone, or Jack Carrel from Birney, they were ready to be shown to a buyer.

In addition to polo ponies, Bob was selling show horses for $7,000 to $8,000 per champion. He was also keeping an eye on the successful bloodlines in the area, buying up horses from Alan Fordyce and Bob Helvey, who had each bought from the Gallatin and Forbes bloodlines.

Dick Tate had worked his way up as a racehorse trainer and won the Hollywood Turf Express with a horse named Summer Sale.

In the meantime, Mimi Tate was showing a horse named Sky Chief and won three classes in Denver in the American Horse Show Association medal class, Jr. Equitation to qualify to show at Madison Square Garden. She didn't go to compete, but she did go to New York to watch the show. Ken Schiffer's wife, Babe, who had helped Aileen Tate while she was raising four young children when the family lived on Otter Creek, called her sister in New York to take Mimi around the show. On the first day, Mimi recognized the horse named Chili Pot that won the Jr. Hunter class. Chili Pot was a descendent of Core De Lion, which was a stallion her father had raised. Core De Lion was a granddaughter of the great Man O' War.

Over time it became harder to find broke horses. Bob and Mimi traveled as far as Minnesota, eastern Nebraska, and Oregon to find horses. It probably never dawned on Bob that he was retracing the steps of Noll Wallop in his search for horses to ship to South Africa a century before.

During one trip to Aiken, South Carolina, Bob Tate traded Pete Bostwick Superflash, a horse he had raised at Wymont, for thirty-five yearlings. Bostwick sold Superflash for $50,000; and six weeks later the horse sold for $120,000. Superflash lived up to his name, becoming the Hunter Champion of Madison Square Garden for three consecutive years. Another horse raised by Tate was Slide Step, which he sold to Patty Huegeroth. Slide Step won Green Confirmation Champion at Madison Square Garden. Tate now had two champions raised at Wymont in the biggest horse show in the country.

In 1963, Pill Box was retired in a special ceremony at the Denver Stock Show. Bob and Aileen Tate were invited and watched from the stands as a blanket of flowers was placed around Pill Box's neck and the announcer read off the horse's accomplishments as a jumper.

Something about the chestnut mare as she ran through the sale ring in Miles City caught Bob Tate's attention. The girl she belonged to had been barrel racing on the horse, and the more Bob looked at the mare, the more she seemed familiar. He bought the mare, along with several others, and took her home to Wymont. The next week Pat Connors, a horse buyer from Chicago, was in town looking for a horse that he could ride while playing indoor polo. He asked about the chestnut mare.

Suddenly it hit Bob. “I think that’s the mare I bought out of Miles City twelve years ago,” he said. When the men went in the house for lunch, Bob got the sale papers and looked at the brands. “I’ll be damned, that’s her. I sold that mare to Charlie Leonard, and he sold her to Ray Harrington. She went to Florida and then New York. Somehow she ended up back at the sale ring in Miles City,” Bob said.

Connors bought the mare for $600 and took her to Chicago, where she played indoor polo.

68

IN THE MID-1970s, JIMMY McHUGH WAS KILLED IN A CAR accident in Palm Desert, California, while driving to a barn. He had run into trouble with the federal government over taxes and was in jeopardy of losing the Wymont Ranch. Bob Tate's classmate and friend, Henry Burgess, had become a lawyer. He was able to leverage a deal for Bob and his family so they could keep Wymont free and clear.

On a trip to Florida, Bob Tate met Summerfield "Skey" Johnston from Tennessee. Skey's grandfather, James Johnston, had been an adventurer who traveled from Tennessee to Pocatello, Idaho, during the gold rush. While there, he was named a board member of the bank in Pocatello. When the standing president was shot and killed, Johnston was appointed president solely because he was the only member of the board who could read and write. The bank prospered in the booming mining town. Eventually, however, Johnston took his earnings back to Chattanooga, to invest in a bottling scheme. He had heard about a fountain drink named Coca-Cola, and Johnston soon became the world's largest independent bottler of the product.

In Tennessee, the Johnstons raised horses and cattle, played polo, and were avid hunters and fishermen. After James Johnston passed away, the business fell to his son, Summerfield, who continued as a horseman and became involved with raising horses and mules for the Remount. His son, Skey, grew up working with the horses, playing polo, and foxhunting. He worked his way up to become chairman of the Coca-Cola Enterprise Company and chairman of the United States Polo Association.

During Johnston's visit at Wymont Ranch, Tate sold him a nine-year-old horse that had never worn a shoe or eaten oats. The horse ended up being one of Johnston's best-playing polo ponies. Through his love of both horses and hunting, Skey was drawn to Absaraka. Bob Tate got Johnston to buy the X-X Ranch that had once been owned by his old partner Lew Fixen. Bob loaned a stallion to Johnston that he had sold to Henry Burgess for Johnston to use as the foundation for his breeding operation. The stallion, Prairie Admiral, was the grandson of the great War Admiral.

Before long, Bob had Johnston driving hundreds of miles to look at horses as he had done with Little Bones Alderson and Jimmy McHugh.

With Bob Tate's urging, Johnston bought part of the old Gallatin and Moncreiffe ranches in Little Goose Canyon, which he named the Flying H Ranch. Within twenty years, the ranch was stocked with more than two hundred mostly thoroughbred horses. Like the Gallatins, Skey Johnston was an avid collector of Western art and, more importantly to the area, a dedicated horseman. In 1996, Skey Johnston inducted Bob Tate into the National Stockman's Hall of Fame in Houston, Texas.

Bob Tate had begun selling horses to a second generation of horsemen, one of whom was Memo Gracida Jr., who was growing into one of the world's great polo players. With his father, Memo Gracida Sr., and his father-in-law, George Oliver, Memo had bought dozens of horses from Bob.

Memo reached the pinnacle of his polo career winning the Argentine Open in 1983. Bob had sold a horse named Sunday, or *Domingo* in Spanish, to Memo that his old friend Alan Bard on Dutch Creek had raised. Gracida played Sunday three periods in that victorious match. During the next twenty years, Memo Gracida Jr. became the polo player with the most worldwide wins.

On one trip to Wyoming a tall, rangy gelding in Tate's corral caught Gracida's attention. It soon became Gracida's most-celebrated horse and would go on to win the U.S. Open's Best Playing Pony twice and be inducted into the National Polo Hall of Fame in Florida.

In 1997, Bea Gallatin Beuf, at ninety years old, walked to the corral for her morning ride on what was left of the old Gallatin Ranch. The ranch hand had not shown up, so Bea saddled her own horse and left at a lope. She ascended the gradual slope of the hay meadow behind the house. After a quarter mile, she stopped and let the mare catch her breath. She turned and looked back on the ranch, down the valley into Sheridan and beyond to the Wolf Mountains. A group of three young buck deer paused at the tree line at the base of the mountains, studying the rider. With the grass burnt off, she could see the outlines of teepee rings on the flat over on William Moncreiffe's old ranch from more than a half dozen tribes who made pilgrimages to the area in the times of the Plains Indians, where they fought, hunted, courted, and cut teepee poles.

Bea thought of all that she had experienced in her lifetime. It was like a dream to her, the horses, the cowboys, the Crow and Cheyenne who used to come to camp on her parents' ranch. She was with her mother the day Chief Packs-the-Hat described the battle between the Crow and Cheyenne that had been fought across the Gallatins' hay field. As a girl Bea had followed Buffalo Bill Cody into the Sheridan Inn and seventy years later, she had christened a U.S. Navy destroyer as the oldest-living relative to Captain James Nicholson. As a teenager she had gone on a ride with dozens of other cowboys on the Spear Ranch to capture the yellow stallion in Montana.

Bea's great-grandfather had served as governor of the Dakotas, long before Wyoming was a territory. One of his paintings hung in her living room alongside coup sticks, lances, daggers, shields, and paintings by Ed Borein and her late husband Carlo.

She thought of her beloved horses: the cantankerous Crow pony Birdy, her beloved Billy, Sweetheart, Let's Go, and Sprite. Now she was sitting on a retired polo mare from the Evanses' ranch in Texas. She walked the mare around the pasture cautiously. A few months prior, she was dumped when a pheasant rose out of the tall grass and spooked her horse.

Now she rode back to the barn past the dead tree that once had held the body of an Indian when Bear Davis first settled the area. She had ordered the ranch crew not to cut down the tree. It was a reminder of the great horsemen of Absaraka long since vanished.

Crazy Horse, Noll Wallop, Edith Gallatin, and Bob Tate defined their eras as horsemen. The great rodeos and horse fairs of eastern imagination and western color were gone forever. Individuals and venues would however show spark, spurred on by the legacy of what had come before.

In 1986, a racing association was formed to hold a series of steeplechase races around the newly built polo field outside Big Horn. The series lasted ten years, and at its height featured four summer races that each culminated in a three-mile race over nine fences. Tommy Alderson, the great grandson of Walt and Nannie Alderson, won the inaugural steeplechase race, and Mike Lohof, a great grandson of pioneer George Brewster, both raced and roped steers.

In 1989, Otter Creek rancher Dave Bliss and a group of horsemen started an event at the Big Horn Equestrian Center to honor Don King, a former jockey, saddle maker, cowboy, and rodeo supporter. Don King Days featured polo, steer roping, matched bronc riding, wild cow-milking, steeple chasing, and Indian relay races. In 1992, seventy-five-year-old Wilson Moreland won an eighteen-mile endurance race in Wyoming from Big Horn to Dayton riding a thoroughbred named Chance. Twenty-two horses had entered, and one died on the way. Moreland trotted his horse almost the entire way and won by a length. More than fifty years earlier he had ridden horses for the Remount at Fort Robinson, and he had also won prizes riding broncs at Madison Square Garden.

In the mid-1980s Paddy Ryan and Bob Askins were inducted into the Cowboy Rodeo Hall of Fame. Only Ryan was there to accept the honor, and he was in a wheelchair. "I wish Bob were here," Paddy told his daughter Toni. True to form, Ryan rose to the occasion that evening—despite his respiratory problems—and waltzed across the room with his daughter well into the night.

The names Harry Brennan, Turk and Alice Greenough, and Bill Linderman, join Ryan and Askins in Cowboy Rodeo Hall of Fame.

Today, J. R. Olson from Sheridan, one of the top steer ropers in the world, draws cheers from the local crowd. If he goes on to win a world championship he will join a long list of the area elite, including world champions Dave Whyte, Dolf Aber, Bill Linderman, Ralf Buel, Deb Greenough, Ronnie Rossen, Dan Mortenson, and Chris LeDoux.

Bryce Miller and Mo Forbes are two Kaycee, Wyoming, bronc riders who are currently working their way into pro ranks.

Between 1951 and 1963, Clinton Small, a Cheyenne, won the Sheridan Wyo Rodeo bronc riding eight times, the All-Around Cowboy three times, the calf roping once, and the team roping once. His father and several of his bothers also had a string of rodeo wins among them. The Fishers, another Cheyenne family, also had a string of local wins.

The Not Afraids and Real Birds led the Crow cowboys in rodeo, and far off to the east, long removed from the area descendants of the Lakota tribe like the Walns, the Whipples, Colombes, Sierras, and Twisses do their tribe proud as rodeo stars.

In 2004, a Crow relay team won the world championship Indian relays at the Sheridan Wyo Rodeo, establishing them once again as the great horsemen of the north. At the event's height, nine tribes, among them the Sioux, Shoshone, and Blackfoot, participated in the Indian relay races. The excitement of these races brought new life to the Wyo Rodeo. The riders displayed feats of horsemanship reminiscent of the warriors who rode over the grasslands 130 years prior. Merchants, ranchers, and tourists stood shoulder to shoulder and soaked up the action.

By 1995, the Big Horn Polo Club had become one of the three largest summer clubs in the nation, due in a large part to Skey Johnston's Flying H Ranch polo operation. As many as eight players at one time from the Flying H participated in Big Horn. Ten years later, Johnston formed the Flying H Polo Club, which offered high-goal polo for the first time since polo began in the area in 1893. Like Malcolm Moncreiffe, Oliver Wallop, and Cameron Forbes before him,

Johnston was passionate about the sport and was responsible once again for putting the area on the map as a renowned center for polo.

Over the years, visiting players at the Big Horn Polo club read like a Who's Who in the sport, from Tommy Hitchcock in 1915, to Adam Snow eighty years later.

In 2002 and 2003, two polo teams from Absaraka won the most prestigious tournament in America. Skey Johnston's daughter Gillian, playing some Wyoming-bred horses, won the U.S. Open Championship in Florida for the Diet Coke team, and the following year, Tommy Boyle, a Parkman rancher, won with his C Spear team.

Epilogue

AILEEN TATE HOSTED COWBOYS, JOCKEYS, POLO PLAYERS, businessmen, and people from all walks of life in her home. She said horses were the great leveler that put people on an even plain. The last time I saw Aileen, she was walking up the stairs of her ranch. She was trying to say goodbye, but Bob was busy telling me about horses. She and I just waved to each other. She was born in Miles City and had ridden a horse to school as a girl, She had lived out in the wild country on Otter Creek and raised four young children. She died just after Christmas in 2002.

Less than a year after her mother's death, Mimi Tate called me in Florida from Sheridan Memorial Hospital. "Sam," she said, "if you got any of your book done, you better send it on. Dad's not doing so well." Bob Tate was in intensive care and struggling, but Mimi put her father on the phone.

"How you doing Bob?" I asked.

"I'm a goner," he said. I had a brief conversation and promised to send him a prologue I had written about Tom McAllister and his father.

About a week later I got another call from Mimi. "Sam, I read what you sent to Dad."

"I hope he liked it; it's pretty rough," I said.

"Dad wants to talk to you."

Ten years before, I had sat at the War Bonnet Inn in Billings, Montana, with Bob, Wilson Moreland, and Don King. We were there for the horse races. As the three horsemen told stories about the Remount, racing, and rodeos, patrons of the restaurant sat mesmerized at Bob Tate's voice, which carried through the room and into the lobby.

Now, over the phone, his voice was barely audible.

"Sam, I wanted you to know I got the last of the Tom McAllister horses. I raised three good foals out of her. One was hunter champion at the Garden, one was the Canadian Olympic champion, and the other was on the Mexican Olympic team," he said.

"How you getting along, Bob?" I asked. He ignored my question. He had had just enough in him to tell me what he wanted to and that was it.

"One was called Dick Tate one was Hardy Tate and one was called Gray Blanket . . . Mimi knows."

It was important to Bob that I know the details. He had a passion not only for horses but also about the area's history of horses. He had already told me the story once. Repeating himself was something he rarely did.

"Dick Tate, Hardy Tate, and Gray Blanket . . ." he repeated. He tried to get on one of his story-telling rolls but he couldn't. Mimi got back on the phone and politely said how much her father liked the manuscript. I wasn't so sure. It had been a lot of ground to cover and I wasn't near finished. I had over twenty-four hours of Bob's stories on tape and rarely were any repeated.

In the last few years, Bob had made a habit of dropping in Skey Johnston's Flying H Ranch to look at the horses. Tri Robinson, the horse trainer at the Flying H, was used to the visits. Tate usually showed up on Mondays in the winter.

"I used to exercise polo horses for the Gallatins right here. Major Nicholas raised some of the best racehorses and jumpers right out of this barn. "When I was a kid, I saw Mrs. Nicholas break out every window in this barn with rocks. She was crazy as hell." Colonel Daniels told me the best load of horses he ever bought was from right here. You can ask Skey."

In the winter of 2003 Bob Tate died. The following summer, horsemen from all over Absaraka and the United States gathered for a memorial in his honor at the old Sheridan Inn.

The land has changed little since the horse was first introduced to the area. For the most part, it is still used for grazing. Farming is limited to the flats along the rivers or to irrigated meadows. The Rosebud Creek battlefield sits in the vast open ranchland just over the Wyoming line in Montana. The Little Bighorn battlefield sits on a hill overlooking Interstate 90. A casino, a hospital, fairgrounds, and trinket shops stand next to the vast grassland where a United States colonel was killed by mounted Stone Age warriors.

Among the warriors, that day was one of the great cavalrymen defeats of all time. Crazy Horse, along with an assemblage of mounted leaders, had defeated U.S. Army contingents under Cole, Connor, Fetterman, Crook, Custer, and Miles. His war shirt was decorated with scalps from Shoshone, Pawnee, Crow, and white enemies. A monument, four times the size of Mount Rushmore, is slowly being erected two hundred miles away from where Crazy Horse lived and fought for most of his life.

The Connor battlefield is now a campground on the bend of the Tongue River in the town of Ranchester. The battles of Cole and Walker and the Dead Horse Camp on Powder River are left unmarked.

Fort Phil Kearny and the Fetterman massacre site are haunted grounds, as is the long ridge whose point is called Red Cloud's lookout. The Wagon Box, Hay Field, Crazy Woman, and various other fights occurred on ground that is predominantly unchanged from the time of the events.

The old Moncreiffe polo field, where thousands of polo games were played for almost a century, has been covered with a shed. The historic site, recognizable only by an old line of cottonwoods that shaded spectators, had played host to army horse buyers from four countries. More than a hundred thousand horses were ridden, bucked out, and inspected on that patch of ground. One of the largest cutting horse competitions in the nation was held on the grounds in the 1990s.

William Moncreiffe's old home, now called the Bradford Brinton Memorial Museum, represents the wealthy estates that once sat in the hollow of Little Goose Canyon. Next door, Noll Wallop's canyon ranch hosted such guests as Buffalo Bill, Teddy Roosevelt, and the Queen of England.

The Gallatin house is gone, but a large rock wall with an oval entrance marks the site to Edith Gallatin's moon garden. In the tall grass in early June, bright orange poppies grow wild along the fence line where Mrs. Gallatin planted them ninety years ago.

Over on Big Goose Creek, the remains of a scoreboard rise from the end of an abandoned polo field at the former site of the Neponset Stud Farm. Just outside of the Forbes Ranch is a hill where hay cutters from Fort Phil Kearny made a stand against several hundred Sioux warriors.

On Otter Creek, the faint outlines of Sir Sydney Paget's racetrack can be seen where Luther Dunning's great-grandson, Dee, operates the Elk Creek ranch. Fort Howes still stands on a knoll as a monument to clashing cultures. Over the divide in Birney, Montana, Irv Alderson, the son of Little Bones Alderson, runs the Bones Brothers Ranch. His cousin Tom Alderson manages a grazing association east of Sheridan. The Bards, Hilmans, and Brewsters still ranch in the area—horsemen all.

In the 1960s, Little Bones Alderson's sons Irv and Allen made their mark in the rodeo world. Irv won the Pendleton Roundup as a steer roper and Allen won at Sheridan in 1963.

Dee Dunning won the All Around and Bull Riding at the Sheridan Wyo Rodeo in 1973.

In 1983 Queen Elizabeth II traveled to Wyoming to visit the Wallops' ranch in Little Goose Canyon. Noll Wallop's granddaughter Jean had married Lord Porchester, who managed the queen's horses.

Jeanie Alderson Punt, a great-granddaughter of both Noll Wallop and Lew Alderson, works on the Cheyenne reservation as a teacher and lives with her family on the Bones Brothers Ranch in Birney. Jeanie and her husband, Terry Punt, are active in preserving the area from proposed railroad development, which would destroy the battlefield where Crazy Horse won his last fight over General Miles.

The Carnahan steeplechase course in Big Horn is subdivided, and like much of the area, it serves as a suburb for the affluent professionals who work in Sheridan.

There may be no other town on earth with such a history of horses as Miles City. The rollicking old town now sits quietly at the fork of the Tongue and Yellowstone rivers like an old ghost. It leads the area in preserving its history.

The Bucking Horse Sale is held every May in Miles City and the Billings rodeo is an indoor event in the fall. The Wyo Rodeo in Sheridan has taken on a new life since reintroducing the Indian Relay Races. The Crow Fair and Cheyenne Pow Wow breathe life into a depressed people by connecting them with their history as horsemen.

Sheridan still enjoys the influx of dudes. Eaton's, HF Bar, Paradise, Rafter Y, and Spear O' dude ranches are still a viable economic industry and draw horse lovers from all aspects of society. It is still the best family vacation a horse lover can spend with their family. Bill Eaton's grandson Bill Ferguson served as arena director for the Sheridan County Rodeo for years.

The families still live on the same ground as their forefathers, but the bloodlines of the horses have been all but forgotten. Sydney Paget, Noll Wallop, Luther Dunning, Malcolm Moncreiffe, Edith and Goelet Gallatin, Ridgley Nicholas, and Cameron Forbes had brought in the best of the best from around the world.

The bloodlines of Sailor, Empire Regent, Columbus, Black Diamond, Colonel T, Black Rascal, Kemano, and Aloha Moon have blended into obscurity, as have whatever offspring the yellow stallion produced. Like the warriors, pioneers, soldiers, CBC cowboys, and the Great Gatsby bunch in Big Horn, the thoroughbred bloodlines have faded.

The two hundred head of wild horses that now run in the Pryor Mountains are supposed to retain DNA from Spanish Barbs that were trailed into the country by the Crow. It matters not, for if what the old ranchers say is true—that the old wild stallions were prolific horse thieves—then there could be traces of some of the world's great thoroughbred bloodlines running through the herd.

The modern horses of Absaraka have made an impact in various venues. More than two thousand horses support the dude ranch industry of Absaraka. Two thousand more horses barrel race and team rope, and another thousand support the polo matches in Big Horn.

The horse sales in Billings, the largest in the nation, total close to ten thousand each year. Sheridan, Miles City, and Buffalo also support horse sales.

History is gradually acknowledging the contribution of horses in the area. One of the newest monuments at the Little Bighorn battlefield is a head stone commemorating the U.S. Army horses that died in the battle. Thousands of army horses served and died during campaigns in the Indian wars. Fights on the Powder, Tongue, and Little Bighorn rivers; on Rosebud Creek; and on Lodge Trail Ridge left thousands of dead horses in their wakes. The bones of Indian warhorses and cavalry horses lay sun bleached until they became part of the rich grassland.

The numbers pale in comparison to the stolen horses that were driven across the landscape in forgotten raids among Crow, Shoshone, Arapaho, Sioux, and Cheyenne. Tens of thousands changed hands and lived off the grass that also fed buffalo, elk, deer, and antelope.

Today's image of a man riding a bucking horse on Wyoming license plates originated with an army officer riding a Crow horse named Red Wing. It is an appropriate tribute as armies from all over the world came here to buy horses and it was the Crow who brought the horses into the area. The Crow and Cheyenne taught the cowboys and English horsemen how to keep their herds alive in all types of weather conditions. Stallions imported from all over the world were taken from their box stalls and turned loose on Absaraka's grassland. Their offspring multiplied from the Powder River to the Bighorn River and were shipped to the four corners of the world. Red Wing ended up in a French riding school. Thousands more went to England, South Africa, the Philippines, Cuba, and Germany.

They won polo matches, horse shows, and horse races. They fox hunted, pulled cannons, and carried cavalrymen in Cuba to South Africa, Burma, and France.

When Noll Wallop moved to Little Goose canyon outside Big Horn, Wyoming, other wealthy horsemen followed and built large estates. Through a mutual passion for horses, wealthy Ivy Leaguers and cowboys united to produce all-inclusive equestrian events unequalled anywhere in the world. Champion polo, roping, bucking, racing, and jumper horses competed across the former buffalo range. Ranchers survived the depression breeding horses for the U.S. Army until the end of World War II.

A young son of a cowboy horseman would scrape and hustle to find the best horses in Absaraka to continue the tradition of providing the world with top horses. Through his wits and perseverance, Bob Tate put the area on the map for horsemen from every equestrian disciple in the country.

In Absaraka, where the rivers run north from the Bighorn Mountains, the history, families, and bloodlines have continued to produce some of the strongest horses in the world. Just east of the Powder River, Hank Franzen raises some of the world's best bucking stock. In 1993, polo horses from five Sheridan ranches competed in the World Cup, played at Palm Beach Polo. Most of the ranches started their breeding programs with horses bought from Bob Tate.

It takes an active imagination to fathom what horses meant to Absaraka in the past. Dozens of ranches were paid for and stocked from the horse boom brought in by Noll Wallop and William Moncreiffe during the Boer War and World War I. Hundreds of ranchers, merchants, and rodeo riders today have descended from a union of eastern dude girls and local cowboys.

In King's Museum in Sheridan, an old horse jawbone with a bullet embedded in it is a remnant of General George Crook's retreat up Clear Creek from Crazy Horse and his warriors. In another part of the museum, an old oyster can full of cut up mule shoes sits in a display case from the 1874 miner's invasion of Indian land. The makeshift cannon ammunition had saved the miners lives against Lakota and Cheyenne warriors.

The pictures on the walls of the Mint Bar in Sheridan or the Last Chance Bar in Big Horn document the area's history.

And it's a patchy history at best. What does a Crow Indian have in common with an Ivy League rancher or a cowboy with a dude from the East? I suppose it is the human spirit that is elevated through horses. The romance of a man on a horse is undeniable. The Plains Indians of Absaraka have come to represent all Indians in popular culture, and the appeal of cowboys to this day is a culture unto itself. A wealthy industrialist is easily connected with an impoverished Cheyenne if the common thread is in a shared passion for a horse. Cowboys, Ivy Leaguers, and millionaire businessmen have shared friendship through a lively string of equestrian events for more than one hundred years.

Much of the spark and passion for fun is gone, replaced by horsemen trying to make a business out of it, but there are a few sparks left over from the old days. You can see it in the eyes of the old who drag their folding chairs onto the curb of Main Street in Miles City or Sheridan for the rodeo parades. It is a passion, a devotion that is fading fast in the area.

In Ten Sleep, Wyoming, seventy-three-year-old Jr. Johnstone saddles a young horse he raised and then rides out to check his cattle. The act in itself is now a rarity among cattle ranchers, who more often than not jump on a $5,000 four-wheeler to run errands. "I don't know how they get their horses made," he said. The answer is they don't.

In Miles City, just across the road from the Bucking Horse Sale, fiddle music spilled out into the night as old dancers, the last descendants of area pioneers, circled the room under portraits of the Range Riders. Photographs of Tom McAllister, Luther Dunning, and hundreds of other range riders with their brands loomed above the visitors. Curator Bob Barthelmess is the grandson of Lieutenant Christian Barthelmess, whose early photographs at Fort Keogh defined life around General Miles's camp. As a boy, Bob helped Tom McAllister, then in very old age, trail a group of horses by their ranch.

Sheridan has benefited from numerous acts of generosity from wealthy horsemen. John Kendrick left a park to the city of Sheridan on the forks of Goose Creek, where the swimming pool carries Edward S. Moore's name. The Women's Club, the blacksmith shop, the church, and Town Park in Big Horn, as well as the trees that stand in the cemetery in Sheridan are gifts from the Gallatins.

The public library, one of the best in the nation, carries the name of Harry Fulmer. A picture of Fulmer's father sitting on Black Diamond hangs next to the door of the Wyoming Room. The horse, raised on Big Goose Creek, set the world record in the half mile in Chicago, won races in England, and ended up in Miles City. The Bank of the West in Sheridan carries portraits of area horsemen from John Kendrick to Bradford Brinton. Today, the hospital carries the names of several area horsemen who are benefactors. Three area horsemen—Paul Denison, Kelly Howie, and Lee Taylor—financed one of the biggest children's riding programs in the country.

One time in Sheridan, Bob Tate spotted me walking down the street, and after parking his car as well as can be expected by an eighty-five-year-old, he got out and walked up waving two hundred dollar bills. "Here, I've been meaning to give you this for kid's polo." Just like that. Never mind his car was blocking traffic. In a minute he was off. It was a throwback to the old cowboy generosity of men like William Moncreiffe, Luther Dunning, and Little Bones Alderson.

Tom McAllister raised several orphans, and Edith Gallatin gave money, kindness, and care to hundreds. The Gallatins, Noll Wallop, and Moncreiffe's lie in Sheridan cemetery, not far from Red and Erma Tate, the Dunnings, and Charlie Thex. The cemetery sits on a high knoll overlooking the Bighorn

Mountains to the west and just below where Big Goose Creek runs into Little Goose and where the Shoshone and Crow joined General Crook to fight the Sioux. From here Goose Creek runs into the Tongue River, which runs north through the Wolf Mountains where Crazy Horse had his last victory against General Miles. At the site of the old Fort Keogh and the frontier town Miles City, the Tongue empties into the Yellowstone. Here, Tom McAllister, the largest range horseman of them all, lies in the city cemetery. A single horseshoe atop the brass plaque is the only clue to an almost forgotten history.

On several sites along the Powder River and Rosebud Creek, rock drawings foretell of hunts, fights, visions, soldiers falling, little people, great mammoths that once roamed the land, and, more importantly, horses. For in this area where the rivers run north, the great horsemen of the world made their mark in battle and in competition for more than two hundred years.

Bea Gallatin Beuf, now one hundred years old, is down to only one bred mare, but she has not lost any of her passion as a horsewoman. She is surrounded by history, art, and artifacts, but it is all incidental to her as she waits patiently for a foal to be born.

> *A horseman is someone who achieves total empathy with their horse.*
> *—Bea Gallatin Beuf*

> *A horseman?... I don't think anyone can answer that. There's all kinds of horsemen. There's good polo players who don't ride well. There's guys that are good horse breakers, which is an important part of it. I don't know... that's a tough question. There's good rodeo riders that can't ride a lick but they can ride a bronc... I think a horseman is somebody who knows what a horse can do and what a horse is capable of...*
> *—Bob Tate*

My horse fights with me and fasts with me because if he is to carry me in battle he must know my heart and I must know his or we shall never become brothers. I have been told that the white man who is almost a god and yet a great fool, does not believe the horse has a spirit. This cannot be true. I have many times seen my horse's soul in his eyes.[1]
—Plenty Coups

In the Red Desert of Wyoming, Frank "Wild Horse" Robbins captured a palomino stallion. Like many other range horsemen, Robbins knew of the palomino bloodline that had run wild herds across Absaraka and beyond. Robbins tried to break the stubborn stallion he had named Desert Dust. The stallion would have killed himself had Robbins continued his quest. The horseman knew the days of the free-roaming stallions would soon be over. After capturing thousands from wild herd, Robbins dedicated the rest of his life to protecting them. He turned Desert Dust loose to run with the wild horses in the Red Desert.

In memory of Betty Nimick, Eva Deischler, Deacon Reisch, Bob and Aileen Tate, Lee Dunning, Sally Springer, Kelly Howie, and Paul Denison, whose generous contribution to this book and encouragement brought the stories to life.

Notes

Chapter 1

1. Peter Nabokov, ed., *Native American Testimony* (Penguin Books, 1992), 44.

Chapter 2

1. John J. Killoren, S. J., *"Come, Blackrobe": De Smet and the Indian Tragedy* (University of Oklahoma Press, 1994), 149.

Chapter 4

1. Wolf Mountains.
2. Present site of Sheridan, Wyoming.

Chapter 7

1. Present site of Casper, Wyoming.

Chapter 8

1. Present site of Ranchester, Wyoming.

Chapter 9

1. Official report of Henry B. Carrington, submitted January 3, 1867.
2. Present site near Story, Wyoming.

Chapter 12

1. Cholera.
2. Present site of Dayton, Wyoming.

Chapter 17

1. John Neihardt, *Black Elk Speaks* (University of Nebraska Press), 109.

Chapter 18

1. Wild horse, mustang.
2. Present site of Alzada, Montana.

Chapter 20

1. Theodore Roosevelt, *A Biography,* 1973.
2. Beech, *Faded Hoofprints*, 154.

Chapter 23

1. Alderson and Smith, *A Bride Goes West,* (Bison Books, 1969) 109.

Chapter 24

1. Brown, *Before Barbed Wire.*

Chapter 25

1. *Stock Growers Journal,* May 9, 1891.

Chapter 27

1. Present site of Arvada, Wyoming.

Chapter 28

1. Alderson, *A Bride Goes West,* 109.
2. *Stock Growers Journal,* September 2, 1893.
3. *Stock Growers Journal,* July 4, 1891.

Epilogue

1. Frank Linderman, *Plenty-Coups: Chief of the Crows* (University of Nebraska Press), 55.

CPSIA information can be obtained
at www.ICGtesting.com
Printed in the USA
FSHW020957080419
57059FS